The Max Porter Paranormal Mysteries

Volume 1

Stuart Jaffe

THE MAX PORTER PARANORMAL MYSTERIES: VOLUME 1

All rights reserved.

Copyright © 2018 by Stuart Jaffe
      Cover art by Duncan Long

      ISBN 13: 978-1717432018
      ISBN 10: 1717432018

      First Edition: May, 2018

      This compilation includes the following three novels:

SOUTHERN BOUND
All rights reserved.
Copyright © 2012 by Stuart Jaffe
Cover art by Duncan Long

SOUTHERN CHARM
All rights reserved.
Copyright © 2012 by Stuart Jaffe
Cover art by Duncan Long

SOUTHERN BELLE
All rights reserved.
Copyright © 2013 by Stuart Jaffe
Cover art by Duncan Long

Also by Stuart Jaffe

Max Porter Paranormal Mysteries
Southern Bound   Southern Curses
Southern Charm   Southern Rites
Southern Belle   Southern Craft
Southern Gothic   Southern Spirit
Southern Haunts   Southern Flames

Nathan K Thrillers   *Parallel Society*
Immortal Killers   The Infinity Caverns
Killing Machine   Book on the Isle
The Cardinal
Yukon Massacre
The First Battle
Immortal Darkness

The Malja Chronicles
The Way of the Black Beast
The Way of the Sword and Gun
The Way of the Brother Gods
The Way of the Blade
The Way of the Power
The Way of the Soul

Stand Alone Novels   *Gillian Boone Novels*
After The Crash   A Glimpse of Her Soul
Real Magic   Pathway to Spirit
Founders

Short Story Collection
10 Bits of My Brain   10 More Bits of My Brain
The Bluesman

Non-Fiction
How to Write Magical Words: A Writer's Companion

Introduction

Many years ago, my wife and I moved from Pennsylvania down to Winston-Salem, North Carolina so she could get her Master's degree from Wake Forest University. One day, I was looking to start a new series, something different than anything else I had written to date. So, I found myself at Wake's library (I think I was waiting for my wife for something) and I simply started looking around. I didn't know much about Winston-Salem, so I poked about the historical sections. And it was in doing this, that I stumbled across a piece of information regarding World War II that I won't divulge here because it became the spark that created *Southern Bound*.

The idea of taking real history and mixing it with my love of the fantastic excited me, and as the series has progressed, it has clearly excited many of you, too. For me, one of the best parts of each novel is discovering the strange and bizarre bits of history North Carolina has to offer. Luckily for us both, it has a lot! Doing the research is always a blast. I drive all over the area in search of these places, and I've had the opportunities to meet many of the real people involved. I've had the immeasurable help of librarians and the great resources of their libraries. Google is a wonderful tool, but it doesn't yet beat a library.

But more than fun research or cool history, the thing that really attracted me to write these stories was, and continues to be, the characters. Max, Sandra, and Drummond have been some of the most fun I've ever had writing. I never tire of the playful, biting, caring, and frustrating ways they interact. More than any other characters I've created, these three have come to feel quite real to me.

I'll forever be grateful that they have become quite real to many of you, too.

- North Carolina, 2018

Southern Bound

Chapter 1

MAX PORTER STOOD AT THE DOOR of his new office — old wood with a frosted-glass window; the 319 painted in gold and outlined in black. The keys jingled in his trembling right hand. His left held Sandra's hand tight. He wanted this job to go well for them. It had to.

Seven months without work had cleaned out the savings account Sandra's father started on their wedding day. They had nothing left. The endless job search during a recession had been gut-wrenching. So when an opportunity came along, even one that meant moving to the South, even one as weird as this one, Max grabbed it. Seeing Sandra's huge smile as he handed her the key made the decision feel right.

"You're sure it's okay for me to come in?" she asked.

"The note didn't say anything about you."

"I know, but it was so specific about a lot of things. Maybe we should check it again."

Max laughed. "Go inside. I've got the job."

With a girlish shrug, she kissed him quick and unlocked the door. The office dated back to the 1940s, and much of the original work remained — hardwood floors, two built-in bookcases with ornate but not obnoxious molding, a small bathroom on the opposite side, and three large windows giving view to the old Winston-Salem YMCA across the street (the word BOYS carved into the stone above one entrance, the word MEN above the other). Faux-lemon cleaners coated the air, and Max noticed the lack of dust anywhere.

He stepped closer to the bookshelves. His footsteps echoed around the high ceiling. He saw rows of reference materials — two German-English dictionaries, a full set of encyclopedias, a ten-volume local history, basic biology, geology, and physics textbooks, a few bits of fiction, and even some on divination.

"Strange," Max whispered, letting out a long breath he didn't know he had been holding.

"Got another note," Sandra said standing in front of an imposing oak desk with a heavy, leather desk chair and two less impressive guest chairs. He followed her gaze to the desk blotter where he saw a manila envelope with his name written in a fancy script bordering on calligraphy. Beneath his name, in bold block letters read — OPEN IN PRIVATE.

Sandra hugged Max long and tight. "Told you he didn't want me here."

"What makes you think my boss is a *he?*"

"Much too dictatorial for a woman."

Max thumbed the envelope's corner. His failure to deal with a dictatorial boss had led to his firing. *It was more than that*, he thought but buried those memories as fast as they threatened to emerge.

"You have your own job to get to, you know."

"Danishes and bread can wait."

"Honey, oh my, gee whiz, you should've told me you became the owner of a bakery. I can quit right now."

"Don't you dare," she laughed. "And don't worry. I'm going," she said with a wink. "Unless you want to play on the desk."

Chuckling, Max pointed to the door. "You're only offering that 'cause you know I can't accept."

"You'll have to wait until tonight to find out."

A man standing in the doorway cleared his throat. He wore a tailored H. Huntsman suit and smelled clean like he had just stepped from a shower. Not a whisker stood on his face nor did a hair dare to stray from its assigned location. "You're early," he said.

Max recognized the voice right away. The same voice that had called to interview him for a job for which he had not applied. The same voice that had hired him and helped negotiate the move to North Carolina. The same voice that had set him up with a used car, a decent apartment, and a signing bonus to get them started. Mr. Modesto.

"We are early," Sandra said, extending her hand. "We were too excited to wait."

Mr. Modesto looked upon Sandra like an insect. "You were not to bring guests this morning."

"I was just leaving," she said, mouthing *Told you so* to Max and adding, "Have a great first day. Love you."

Sandra patted the door as she exited. He watched her move down the hall to the stairs on the end — her dark hair dancing on her shoulders, her not-too-thin *I'm a real woman* physique moving with enthusiasm. She made waking each morning worthwhile.

A hall door opened and an old lady with a coffee mug picked up her morning paper. She scowled at him. Modesto closed the door and said in his deep voice, "This building consists of apartments, some offices, and on the first floor, a small art gallery. Please keep in mind you have neighbors." With a disapproving glare, he added, "You've not opened the envelope?"

"It says 'Open In Private'."

"Then I'll wait in the hall," Modesto said and stepped out.

A little part of Max, a childish, naïve part, wanted to sprint down the hall, out the building, and head straight back to Michigan. He understood Michigan — Lansing, Alpena, Kalamazoo, it didn't matter what part of the state — cold, hard, practical with a side of cutting loose. This envelope had none of those qualities. It was a bizarre way to handle business.

A book clattered to the floor, and Max jumped in his seat, letting out a girlish screech. Then he laughed at himself — hard. Modesto probably thought him mad.

Careful, Max, the South just might make you nutty.

Max recomposed himself and opened the envelope. It read:

MR. PORTER —

WELCOME TO WINSTON-SALEM AND YOUR NEW OFFICE. IF YOU REQUIRE ANYTHING, DO NOT HESITATE TO CONTACT MR. MODESTO. YOUR FIRST TASK IS TO RESEARCH UNITAS FRATRUM. THE BOOKS PROVIDED HERE SHOULD SUFFICE BUT IF YOU REQUIRE ANY OTHERS, DO NOT HESITATE TO CONTACT MR. MODESTO. AT THE END OF EACH DAY, REPLACE EACH BOOK IN THE EXACT PLACE YOU FOUND IT. MAKE NO MARKS IN THE BOOKS. WITH THE EXCEPTION OF BASIC USAGE OF YOUR CHAIR, DO NOT MOVE ANY FURNITURE IN THIS OFFICE. DO NOT ADD OR REMOVE ANY FURNITURE IN THIS OFFICE. IF ANY LIGHT BULBS NEED TO BE REPLACED OR ANY OTHER SUPPLIES ARE REQUIRED, DO

NOT HANDLE IT YOURSELF. PLEASE CONTACT
MR. MODESTO INSTEAD.

No signature. No explanations.

He pulled open the top-right drawer and found a small ledge with three pens — nice pens, Monte Blanc. He picked one and then tried the drawer beneath. As he leaned down, he noticed some metal screwed into the underside of the desk. He had seen this type of thing before but only in old black-and-white movies. It was a gun tray meant for holding a small caliber weapon that would be pointed towards the door.

"Wild," he said.

In the bottom drawer, he found one plain, spiral notebook — the kind he preferred to work with. *Well, the boss does his homework,* he thought, smirking at his own use of the male pronoun. Sandra could turn him around on many things with just a few words.

Mr. Modesto returned with his eyes surveying the office (*checking that I haven't moved anything,* Max thought), and said, "I trust everything is clear and to your satisfaction."

As much as Mr. Modesto already pushed Max's desire to spew out sarcasm, he had to focus on keeping the job. Strange orders and a pompous manager should be the last of his concerns. "Um, just one thing," he said, hating the contrition in his voice.

"Oh?"

Gesturing to the empty desk, Max said, "No computer. I've got my own laptop. I can—"

"Our employer wishes for this room not to be altered. A technology such as that would severely alter the room."

"Perhaps our employer did not explain to you that you're to help me out. It says so in this letter."

Mr. Modesto's face tightened. "The contents of that letter are marked 'private' and you should not be divulging them to me. As for my duties, I am well aware of what I am to do."

"Our employer wants some in-depth research done, and I'm assuming he wants it done in a timely manner. Without a computer, this task will be—"

"It is a short drive to the Wake Forest campus. You will find an excellent library there which will supplement any research requirements this room does not fulfill. Including a computer."

Max held his tongue for a moment and forced a pleasant face. "My apologies. I'm sure the University will be more than enough."

"I'll be checking in this office a few times each week. If you require anything for your research that does not violate my other orders, I'll be more than willing to help you. Also ..." Mr. Modesto's eyes narrowed on the floor as he walked toward the bookshelves. In one graceful motion, he swiped the book off the floor, snapped it shut and returned it to its rightful place. Without looking at Max, Mr. Modesto said, "Keep your focus on your research. These other matters are none of your concern. Good day." He walked out of the office, never once glancing back.

Max rubbed his forehead with his sleeve. A little sweat had broken out — he had to be careful. Mr. Modesto had been working for their boss a lot longer — Max had no leverage.

He could hear Sandra warning him to keep his cool, and she was right. In this economy, he had been more than lucky to land a good-paying job. Especially considering that right before the market crumbled, Sandra had just started out as a real estate agent in Michigan. She had a few contacts in the Southern real estate world, but upon moving, they all told her the same thing — find a different job. She did, at a bakery, but that didn't bring in enough on its own. Max needed to keep his job.

With a stretch, Max stood and checked out the bookshelves. He wasn't trying to be difficult. He simply couldn't stand when people purposefully did the wrong thing because they had the power to do so. Like Mr. Modesto and this job — they wanted him to do research. No problem. Let him do the research. Don't make up all these stupid rules to control him. No computer? Don't move the furniture? Come on.

To prove his point, Max lifted the edge of the desk and set it down an inch forward. He waited. "Nope," he said to the room. "Not struck by lightning."

From the corner of his eye, he saw something. Max jumped back and scanned the office. Empty.

With cautious motions, he turned his head toward the floor. There, curving under his desk, Max saw the edges of colored lines. Something had been drawn on the floor.

His hand tapped the edge of the desk, wanting to shift it just a tiny bit more, but his heart pounded a warning. "Aw, hell. In for a penny," he said, grabbed the desk and yanked it to the side.

A large circle had been painted in red and blue. Zodiac symbols marked compass points on the circle's inside edge. Two concentric circles were inside the largest one, and each also had symbols on the inside lines, but Max did not recognize them. Painted blood red, a jagged-toothed mouth occupied the center — one of four serpent heads attached to the same body.

Cocking his head to the side, he read the words *cruor* and *teneo*. They meant nothing to him but sent shivers straight through to his hands.

He slid the desk back in place, covering the circle, and glanced at it from several angles. It appeared to be in the same spot. He checked from his desk chair — only with a flashlight would he have ever found the circle.

Research, he thought with relief. Get out of the office. Get fresh air. Do what he had been hired to do. Forget about this other nonsense.

Max gathered his things and headed out. As he walked by the bookshelf, his eyes caught the book that kept falling out. Its cracked spine read — WITCHCRAFT IN WINSTON-SALEM, VOL 7, 1935-1950.

"Holy crap," he whispered and hurried his steps.

Chapter 2

MAX LOVED THE WAY the Z. Smith Reynolds Library at Wake Forest University really was two separate structures — the former alleyway had been enclosed long ago to form an exquisite reading space full of light and air. Like any good library, Wake's was a labyrinth of floors and nooks and dusty corners each promising to hold great discoveries for anybody bold enough to explore. For Max, if he wanted to be honest with himself, he would admit that he loved doing research, and he loved being in this quiet, solitary sanctuary. Teaching had its joys, but the students always made him feel unfulfilled.

After several minutes on the library computers, Max had a few call numbers to check out. Later, he could use what he learned to validate the accuracy of any websites claiming to have information. This approach took more effort than just using Google, but since he was being paid for quality work, he figured it was worth it. Which meant that for now, books were the place to start.

He climbed a narrow staircase to the seventh floor. Most of the lights were off and each row of stacks had a separate switch. In the quiet, he worked his way through until he matched the call numbers, popped on the light, and started searching through the old titles.

Research was a treasure hunt, and as the familiar sensations of discovery flooded into him, he began talking to the texts — a habit that Sandra found amusing, annoying, and sometimes cute. "You look promising," he muttered to a reddish-brown book.

Hours passed with Max sitting in a cubicle, his head stuck between book covers. His hand ached from taking notes (he made a mental note to bring his laptop next time), but a picture of Winston-Salem's early years had formed, one that struck him as both daring and desperate.

In the 15th Century, in Moravia, a Czech named Jan Hus preached about a church based on moral purity and conduct rather than doctrine and consistency. His disciples, the Brethren, called the new church

Unitas Fratrum, and by 1467, they seceded from the Church of Rome.

Max predicted the backlash would not be pretty. Nobody seceded from the Church without repercussions — often violent repercussions. For the Brethren, he read on, persecution and dispersal rained upon them for hundreds of years.

"Told ya," Max said.

A door squeaked open. Max glanced around, heard a few footsteps, and settled back to his book.

In the 17th Century, the Brethren hanging on in Germany found a safe haven in Count Nicholas Ludwig von Zinzendorf. He provided them his Saxony estate, an arrangement that lasted many years. In 1722, the Moravians (as they were becoming known) created the Renewed Unitas Fratrum ("Such originality," Max said) with Zinzendorf as their leader. Shortly after, they began missionary work.

Max jotted down these key dates. He imagined Zinzendorf angered a lot of Brethren. Many would have accused him of purchasing his leadership role. Others, well, religious politics always had been as bloody as the secular variety.

Max heard a single beep and whispering. He swore he heard his name. He glanced around, but the stacks and the darkened floor hid just about everything. Again, he heard the whispering followed by the beep.

"Now," he said, trying to bury the nervousness growing inside, "America has to come into the picture."

Seeking religious freedom, word of America worked its way to the Moravians. In 1741, after a failed attempt to settle in Georgia, they founded the town of Bethlehem in Pennsylvania. A decade later, they bought land in North Carolina and settled Bethabara. Later growth led to Bethania, and in 1765, construction of Salem began.

Another beep.

"Hello?" Max said, his voice sounding unnaturally loud in the library's quiet.

Several stacks down, a figure darted into the main aisle. Max jumped from his chair to peek down the aisle just in time to see the fire door closing. His skin prickled.

He shook off the feeling, unwilling to give it much credence. After all, if he voiced the idea that somebody had been watching him, perhaps following him, perhaps checking up on him — he didn't want to consider what that implied.

By noon, Max was finished with his initial survey. He met Sandra at a little diner and was surprised at her excitement.

She bit into her cheeseburger with a strong appetite. "This has been a great day," she said. Max gnawed on a fry and quivered out a grin. "Everybody's been so nice."

"Nice?" Max said. *The word* creepy *described things far better.*

"I mean it. We have this reputation in the North of being harsh and cold and full of bite. I never felt it I guess because I lived there my whole life. But now, meeting these people down here — it's weird. Every single person here is nice."

"Real nice," Max said, thinking of the stranger in the library. In Michigan, he didn't have these kinds of problems. And they said the economy was picking up back there. Something would have come his way. Or he'd have done something online. Lots of people telecommute nowadays. This whole job smelled illegal anyway — but he had known that from the start.

Sandra continued, "I called to set up DSL today and when the lady found out we'd just moved in, she gave me the warmest welcome. Up North it's all, 'What do you want?' as if you're imposing on their time to sit on their asses and do nothing. Here, I don't know, I guess I expected banjo-pickers at the gas station ready to string us up if we looked at them wrong."

"It's definitely not like back home."

"And did you notice all the Japanese restaurants? There's also some Indian places and even Greek. We never had that. They're more cultured than we've ever been."

Max looked at Sandra's beaming face and his stomach dropped. First day of work, less than a week living here, and she already had fallen for the place. And the money — they would never get back on their feet without real money coming in like this.

She must have picked up something in his body language, she could always read him well, because she stopped talking, clasped his hands, and said, "Did something go wrong at work?"

Max sniffled and shook his head. "Mr. Modesto. I don't care for him."

"Well, no job is perfect, honey."

"I know."

"And we need this money. We still owe the credit card company—"

"I know," he said with more force than he intended.

They grew silent, and Max thought about the tension their silences had acquired. There was a time when he would bring her a single rose every day. She would see it, smile, and say nothing — those were the silences he craved. He leaned closer and said, "Hey, hon, guess what? I know my boss is a man."

"I told you that," she said with less bite and more play.

"When I was talking with Modesto, I referred to the boss as 'he' and the guy didn't say a word. Didn't even flinch."

"You're quite the detective."

"I try," Max said, a genuine smile opening up.

Sandra took his hands again. "I want you to help me make this work. This is our best opportunity."

"I will."

"And we can't afford not to take it."

"I know."

"So please, honey, deal with whatever nastiness this Modesto ass sends your way. Please."

He looked at those brown eyes and his heart lurched. "Okay," he said. "I'll try."

"Promise?"

"I promise."

"Then you are definitely getting lucky tonight."

Max burst into laughter and that sent Sandra into her own fit of giggles.

When he returned to his office, he received a surprise. Behind his desk, admiring the woodwork, sat a well-groomed man in his thirties, dressed in an old-style suit. He did not appear embarrassed at being caught messing with the desk nor did he even acknowledge Max's entrance.

Max cleared his throat. The man startled at the noise, then looked at Max with a different sense of surprise as if amazed Max could produce such a sound. Finally, he stood (a rather tall, strong body) and said, "You the boss here?"

"Max Porter. Pleased to meet you," he said offering his hand.

The man ignored Max's hand but said, "Name's Drummond. Marshall Drummond."

"Well, what can I do for you?" Max said as he sat in his chair, forcing Drummond toward the guest side of the desk.

"Other way around, friend. I'm going to help you."

"You are?"

"Maybe. After you do something for me."

"Make up your mind," Max said, writing a mental note to ask Modesto for some kind of security.

"What I mean is ..." Drummond said, his focus drifting to the bookshelf.

"Mr. Drummond?"

"The world is much stranger than I ever thought."

Max shifted in his chair. "If I can help you with something, please tell me. Otherwise, I've got a lot to do and I'm going to have to ask you to leave."

Drummond's eyes snapped onto Max with a fierceness that dried Max's throat. "Are you?"

"Yes."

"I'm waiting."

"Excuse me."

"You said you'd have to ask me to leave. Go ahead. Ask."

"Um ... will you please leave?"

"No."

Drummond sat in the left guest chair, leaned back, and rested his feet on the desk. Max sighed as he rose to his feet. "Look, I'm not interested in stupid power games. Leave or I'll call the police."

"You need to listen up. I know a heck of a lot more about things around here than you. And I'm willing to help you out because right now, our interests are pretty much the same. After all, don't you want to know who's pulling your strings? So, sit." Drummond waited. Max held still a moment, his brain tumbling to catch up on how fast the tone of this meeting had altered. He sat. "Good."

"What do you know about my boss?"

Drummond chuckled. "Stan Bowman."

"That's his name?"

"No. That's the name I want you to find out about. I want to know what happened to that bastard. You find that out, and I'll tell you all about this office, that book that keeps falling out, and the witch's spell under your desk."

Max's stomach churned hard. "Witch's spell?"

"Stan Bowman. Research him and I'll tell you."

With a shaking hand, Max pulled out a pencil and wrote down the name *Stan Bowman*. "O-Okay," he said, "What else?"

"Don't do this from here. Got it?"

"Yes."

"I'll meet you tomorrow."

"Okay."

"And don't say a word to Modesto about me, Bowman, or this meeting. You so much as hint about it, you'll find out how bad things can get."

Chapter 3

MAX TRIED TO KEEP SILENT around his wife that night. He told himself that he wanted to find out all about Stan Bowman, find out about Drummond, find out anything, any concrete answer, before he spoke with Sandra. Otherwise, she would be full of questions and he would be full of idiotic silence. She would worry and regret relocating. She would find some way to blame herself.

But as he searched and googled and combed through the quieter corners of the internet, as he learned more about Stan Bowman and what became of the man, Max knew he had to release the mounting pressure within. He had to tell her so he could blot out the pictures in his mind. He had to tell her so he could sleep. Not all of it — he couldn't be so cruel, but some ... yeah, he had to tell her about that sick monster.

Around nine, they settled in for a late meal of fried rice, lo mein, and some wine, and he started. "I met this man, Drummond," he said, keeping his eyes on his food. "He had me look into this horrible story about Stan Bowman."

"What?" Sandra said, her voice snapping hard as her face twisted into a *you've-got-to-be-joking* smile.

"It's just a little side trip, that's all. And he said he could give me information about —"

"Stop it. Right now. I mean it. You can't go screw this up for us."

"Honey, I'm not going to —"

"You have a job. One that pays you well. And you know if they find out you're working for somebody else on their dollar, they'll fire you." All the harshness fled Sandra as she crossed her arms and fought her tears. "We can't afford that. We'll lose everything."

"I'm not getting fired."

"You said that in Michigan," Sandra said, her mouth a tight line.

Max downed his glass of wine and then breathed deep. "I thought that was all behind us. You said you forgave me. We're supposed to be building a new life down here. Now I'm trying my best. You like it here, right? The people are nice and all, right?"

Sandra nodded.

"Okay. Then allow me a little room to find where I fit in. I won't lose my job. I'm doing this research at home on my own time. I never signed anything, never agreed to anything that says I can't do this thing at home. Besides, if they try to fire me for the way I use my personal time, we'll sue them for millions, and then all our money troubles will be gone."

Sandra let out a relieved shudder. "I'm not happy about it."

"I see that."

"But okay."

Max kissed her hand. "I love you."

"You piss me off lots, but I love you, too."

Refilling their glasses, Max said, "So, do you want to hear about Stan Bowman?"

"No, but you'll tell me anyway."

They both laughed a bit too hard — the wine contributing as much as the tension. "Okay," Max said, and as he summoned the images and story in his head, his face hardened. Sandra must have seen the change in his demeanor because her laughter died and her concern returned.

"During World War II," Max began, "Winston-Salem gave three-hundred-and-one men to the fight. Stan Bowman lucked out, though. He only got shot in the leg. Before he left, he was a decent enough man, I guess. Helped out with the scouts and stuff like that. I don't know for sure, of course. Online info isn't that trustworthy. Plus, there's only so much you can get from newspapers and police statements."

"Police? That doesn't sound good."

"It isn't. He had a girlfriend, but she left while he was in Africa. By the time he returned to the States, she had married and had a kid. But he met a new gal and married her — Annabelle Grier. She told the police that Stan suffered terrible nightmares, waking up drenched in cold sweat, that kind of thing."

"Sounds like Post Traumatic Stress."

Max nodded. "Everything probably would've just settled into your typical nuclear-family, fake-happiness thing, been just fine — except the POWs arrived."

"POWs?"

"R. J. Reynolds just about owned all of Winston-Salem. His tobacco company employed a huge percentage of the city. Heck, he built Wake Forest University."

"Well, his money did."

"You know what I mean. Anyway, at the time, he was providing the cigarettes for the soldiers. Demand was huge, and he started having trouble keeping up production. So, he managed to get a deal with the government to ship over German POWs and put them to work in his factories."

"Are you serious?"

"It's all true. Two hundred and fifty soldiers came, all of them from Rommel's Afrika Korps."

"And Stan served in Africa."

"Right."

"Oh, that can't be good," Sandra said, and Max saw that she had become intrigued. He had to admit it — despite his fears, he was intrigued, too. He sipped his wine, making her wait a moment before he continued.

"About a month after the Germans arrived, Stan goes missing. Annabelle contacts the police, says she hasn't seen Stan in two days, but apparently, they don't give her much credence. Stan had been known as a heavy drinker, so the police figured he'd gone on a binge and would turn up sooner or later. Of course, Stan wasn't drinking."

"Of course."

"One by one in turn, seven POWs go missing. Each one abducted from the factory floor," Max said, pausing to let his words sink deep inside.

"Wait," Sandra said a moment later. "How's that possible? I mean, these are POWs. There had to be guards all around. I know our government can do some stupid things, but they wouldn't let a bunch of German soldiers loose in America. Would they?"

"No, honey, there were plenty of guards. Best anybody figured out was that the abductions took place during bathroom breaks. But here's where it gets interesting. In each case, the prisoner was found several days later, gibbering like a madman, completely nuts. Only one thing they said made any sense — each one mentions the name Stan Bowman. The police go on a manhunt, but nobody ever finds Stan. A private detective, however, does locate this little apartment-type room in an old warehouse. The place must have reeked of tobacco. Inside, they find Stan's workplace. He'd been torturing these men, but not just physically. He messed with their heads. Hours and hours of slow, mind-boggling torture."

Sandra stood to clear the table. "And they never found him?"

"He disappeared."

She placed a hand on her hip. "You can't possibly be serious about following this."

"Why not? It's fascinating."

"Hon, you're talking about crazy people doing crazy things over seventy years ago. Nothing good could ever come from digging this up."

"Come with me," Max said, getting up. "I want to show you one of the crime photos. Relax, it's not bloody. I just want you to see something that'll make it clearer to you."

With a reluctant stretch, Sandra followed. The bedroom of their apartment doubled as an office for Max, so she settled on the bed while he scooted into the small desk chair in the corner. He pulled up the photo on his laptop and angled it for her to see.

The black-and-white photo depicted a stool in the middle of an unfinished room. Two buckets had been placed next to the stool, one clearly filled with a dark substance. Gruesome pictures of women and children being shot or tortured had been nailed to some of the wall studs. Straight in front of the stool, Stan had mounted a film screen. Two detectives were shown in the photo — both looked queasy.

"Stan forced his victims to stay awake the whole time, or I suppose, as long as Stan could handle it himself. Nobody ever found what film he showed them but based on the wall pictures, I'm guessing it ain't a Disney classic."

"Okay, now I'm thinking this Stan guy is super nuts. Why is this going to convince me you should get involved?"

"Because," Max said pointing to the detective standing near the stool, "this man here is the spitting image of Drummond. Very strong family resemblance."

"It's still a bunch of crazy people."

"You're missing the point, honey. Drummond is interested in this because of a family matter. This detective had to have been some close relation. The Stan Bowman crazy part of all this is secondary. This guy is just looking for a lost relative."

Sandra frowned. "You really believe that?"

"If that's all it is, then I might be able to help him out, help him find his family. I do that, and I'm sure he'll pay well. We need all we can get." Before Sandra could speak, Max put out his hand. "If it's something more, I'll let it go. Don't worry. I'm not getting fired."

Sandra crossed her arms but didn't protest further. Max smiled.

The next day, Max bolted down his breakfast and rushed to the office. To his pleasure, he found Drummond waiting for him.

"I take it you found some things," Drummond said.

Max circled his desk, pulled out a hard copy of the photo, and tossed it down. "I'd say I'm getting somewhere."

Drummond looked at the photo and grimaced. "Boy, I haven't seen this in a long time."

"So, what's the relation?"

"I can still smell the place."

"Your grandfather?"

"What?"

"Huh?"

Max sat on the edge of his chair, his knee bumping the gun tray screwed into the desk's underside. "You've been to this place?" he asked.

"You think this is my grandfather? You did look closely at this picture, right? I'm right there."

"Mr. Drummond, that picture is seventy years old."

"I know. Last one of me ever taken. Two days later I wound up dead. Shot right here in my office."

"Your office?"

"Are you pretending to be this lost?"

"No," Max said, his face locked in total confusion.

"Let me lay it down for you. In the 1940s, I was a private investigator. The police called in for my help on the Bowman case, and then I was murdered. Pretty clear now?"

"So ... you're ... dead?"

"Yup, I'm dead."

Chapter 4

MAX LET OUT A NERVOUS LAUGH as he stood and worked his way from the desk. His chest tightened and his face heated up. Now he understood why rich people had panic rooms or emergency buttons installed.

"You don't believe me," Drummond said.

"Take it easy. Just stay calm."

"I'm completely calm. You're the one whose voice is rising. I'm sorry to rattle you, but this is the way it is."

Max wanted to break for the door, but he would have to pass right by Drummond. He glanced out the window. Three stories high — too far for any kind of escape.

"Look," Drummond said, straightening his blazer as he stood. "Let me prove to you that I'm dead. Then, if you can't handle it, I'll just go away. Okay? That sound fair?"

Max nodded, his mind otherwise blank.

"Good," Drummond said and stepped forward until he stood in the middle of the desk, the top slicing right through his body.

Max let out a tight-lipped screech. With his eyes locked on the bizarre sight, blood drained from his head, paling his skin and making him light-headed.

"Don't pass out on me," Drummond said. "I hated it when women did that, I'm really going to be angry if you do it. Just take some deep breaths and sit down."

Following instructions, Max breathed deep and eased down to the floor. The room swirled around him as sweat beaded on his forehead. For a second, he thought he was nine and visiting the Fun House for the first time. He motioned for Drummond to step away, and Drummond complied.

With a smile from one side of his mouth, Drummond said, "You're going to be fine, kiddo. I see color coming back to your face. Have a drink. That'll do the trick."

"I-I don't have anything."

"Lucky for you this is Marshall Drummond's old office. Fourth book from the right, bottom shelf — my gift to you."

Despite his shaking hands, Max crawled to the bookshelf and found a copy of *Beyond This Horizon* by Anson MacDonald. Inside the hollowed out book, he found a silver flask. He glanced at Drummond, received a knowing nod, and grabbed the flask. The whiskey it contained slipped down Max's throat, warming his body, and calming his nerves.

Without waiting for Max to settle back, Drummond said, "Good. Now that that's done, let's talk about Stan Bowman."

"B-But you're a ghost."

Like a weary school teacher, Drummond said, "We've covered this already. I'm a ghost and you're in my office. You're going to help me and I will help you."

"But you're *a ghost.*"

"Are we going to have a problem?"

Max's gut dropped a bit, but he managed to shake his head. "You need to answer some questions first."

"My, aren't we bold with well-aged whiskey?"

Perhaps a little whiskey had helped. It certainly relaxed him enough to see that this thing — this ghost — before him could not be denied. It was real. Ghosts were real. Marshall Drummond, dead since the forties, stood in Max's office.

And he hadn't tried to kill Max. Or even scare him. Drummond was asking for his help. With his brain wrapping around this idea, Max felt much better.

With a slight grunt, Max got to his feet and paced the room. The movement got his circulation running again, and he could feel his thinking process kicking in. "For starters, why did you wait until now to show yourself? I've been here for awhile."

"I couldn't. All I could do was drop that book."

"That was you?"

"You know any other dead people?"

"Okay," Max said, his pacing getting faster. "Why couldn't you show yourself?"

Drummond nodded towards the floor. "That symbol is a curse that was put on me."

"A curse?"

"A witchcraft sort of thing. I'd been investigating the Stan Bowman case when it happened. They attacked me with four guys, and the next thing I know, I'm spread on the floor, bleeding slowly all over, and they've drawn this whole mess here. When I finally died, I was stuck."

"Stuck?"

"I can't leave. Not with that thing here. The curse ties me to this office. And as long as everything in here is in the exact place it was when they finished the curse, I can't even show myself. If I move something, like the books, it doesn't matter. I've tried. It only works if a living person does it, and whatever was moved has to stay moved for quite awhile. Otherwise, I'm locked away."

"But I see you now."

"That's right. You moved the desk."

"I put it back," Max said, his eyes darting to the desk's feet. Looking far closer than ever before, he saw a sliver of a circle marking where the desk had been for many years. "Modesto," he said.

"Yeah, I'm pretty sure he noticed," Drummond said.

"Wait a second. Modesto knows about the desk, and I was even given orders not to move the desk. Are you telling me my employer did this to you?"

"What do you know — you're not so slow after all."

Max rubbed his face. "I think I need another drink."

"We got a lot of work ahead, so take all the liquid courage you need."

"No, no, no. I'm not getting into this any worse. No. I'll quit the job. Sandra and I, we'll go back to Michigan. The heck with this."

"Sorry, pal. Maybe last week you could've gotten away with it. I doubt it, but you could've tried. Now that you've seen me, now that Modesto knows you moved the desk, Hull's not going to let you go."

"Hull?" Max asked. "Is that my employer's name?"

Drummond pulled back. "You went to work for somebody you never met, and you don't even know his name? Are you insane?"

"I'm not the one ended up a cursed-ghost, so you better hold off on all the judging."

"Whatever."

"You speak like somebody from today? I thought you died in the forties."

"Back to doubting me, huh? I did die in the forties, kiddo, and I've been stuck here ever since. I've seen generations come through these doors and I've *listened* to them. I remember in the sixties, this couple squatted here for awhile. Used to screw on my desk everyday when they weren't too stoned to do it. I got so sick of the word *groovy* I wanted to die — if I wasn't already dead."

Despite all the fear and trepidation surging through Max, he chuckled. "Okay, so who's Hull?"

"William Hull, and I don't know much about him other than what everybody knows — very rich, very powerful, very private family. I was just turning my focus onto him when this happened to me."

"You think he did this to you?"

"I'm sure of it. This is his building."

"So, he finds out you're interested in him in connection with Stan Bowman and he kills you?"

"Strikes hard and fast. He's a dangerous man, that much should be obvious, and that means you are in a dangerous situation."

Max grabbed the flask and swung back a little more whiskey. "What was the connection to Bowman?"

"I don't know," Drummond said. "His company owned the warehouse where Stan took the POWs. That was it. I wanted to talk to him as a matter of routine but his people stonewalled me. That got me heated up. I started looking into court records, newspapers, anything I could find his name on. It all turned up empty, but I must've been getting close to something because here I am."

"Here you are," Max said, his brain finally putting pieces together. "Why, though? Why do this whole curse thing to you? Why not just kill you and get rid of the body?"

"You figure that one out, and we'll both be a lot happier."

Max grew quiet for a moment as he let all the things he had seen and heard settle inside him. In a calm tone that frightened him more than his anger ever had, he said, "He's going to come after me, isn't he?"

"Hull? Maybe. He might play this one a little different. In my case, he was trying to shut me up. For you, though, he hired you. He wants you looking into some things, right?"

"History of the area. That's all."

"As long as he doesn't know that we've talked, you should be able to stay alive long enough."

"For what?"

"To solve the Stan Bowman case."

"No way. No. Not going to happen."

"You don't have a choice, unless you want Sandra to be a widow. Or worse, they might go after her. Threaten you through her. I've seen much less men do much worse things."

Max blotted away the image of Modesto beating Sandra and focused on Drummond. For the moment, at least, Drummond made sense. What other choice did Max have? Of course, Drummond could be lying, but Max would have to figure that part out later. Whatever the truth, Max knew he stood at the foot of a mountain range of old pain, deceit, and treachery. He just prayed he'd find a way to climb to safety.

"Okay," he said, clearing away all the nagging words his conscience wanted to weigh on him, "where do we start?"

Chapter 5

BEFORE DRUMMOND COULD ANSWER, the office door opened and Mr. Modesto walked in. He nodded at Max, clearly unable to see Drummond, and sat in a guest chair.

"You and I are to have lunch," he said, disdain dripping from every word.

Max tried to look at the desk, to keep his eyes off Drummond, but he caught sight of the ghost disappearing into the bookcase. "It's a bit early for lunch," he managed to say while staring at the books.

Modesto stood, straightening his suit, and stepped between Max and where Drummond had been. "There is no need for rudeness. You and I are to have lunch this afternoon."

"I've got a lot of work to do. Instead, can we —"

"What makes you think our employer is any less specific with me in his instructions? Now, please acknowledge that you understand what I've said, so I know you will meet me."

"Okay, sure."

"Twelve-thirty."

"I'll be working on —"

"I don't really care."

When Modesto left, Max slumped into the desk chair and let out a long sigh. This was how he had lost his job in Michigan — an early morning request to join the boss's assistant to lunch. False accusations came with that lunch. Before the entrees hit the table, his job had disappeared.

He should call Sandra. She would ease his mind. She knew what to say. But if he called her, she would also know that something else had happened, and he wasn't ready to explain about ghosts. Besides, there was no reason to think he had lost this job. He had moved the table, true. But could they really know that?

"Not unless they're bugging the office," Max chuckled. His eyes darted to the dark corners of the room. No, he refused to let paranoia attack. He had no control over this lunch, so best to just go to the library and get some work done. Whatever happens after that would happen regardless.

At 12:30 exactly, Mr. Modesto arrived and brought Max to the Village Tavern — a small restaurant adjacent to the university campus. Max loved the place the instant he stepped inside. It reminded him of visits to New York City — the dark, cramped restaurant that utilized every last inch of space, the jostle of people all grumpy with hunger, the clatter from the busy kitchen underscoring the delightful aromas drifting throughout. When they had money again, Max wanted to bring Sandra here to celebrate.

After they were seated, Mr. Modesto folded his hands on the table and said, "Tell me everything you've learned."

Max frowned. "I'm confused. I assumed I would be writing a report for our employer," he said, fully conscious that he had just used the phrase Modesto always applied to their boss.

"You will write a report, too. However, our employer desires a faster reply at the moment. So, tell me what you will eventually write down."

"Okay," Max said, holding back a sarcastic — *you asked for it.*

Halfway through their filet mignons, Max entered into the work he had explored in the last few days — the Moravian congregational government. "It's fascinating stuff," he said. "They divided their government into three branches just like America would do shortly afterward, but these branches acted very differently." Modesto appeared to pay attention in a polite manner but showed no surprise as Max explained the system. "The first branch was the Elders Conference. They dealt with the spiritual affairs of the congregation and ensured that all the various officials worked well together. The Congregation Council handled broader issues that affected the long-term — like an overseer. And last was the Aufesher Collegium which dealt with secular matters such as town administration."

"And this system worked?" Modesto asked, but something in his voice told Max he could care less. Max didn't mind, though. He'd babble for a week if it kept his mind off of ghosts.

"Well, it worked for them. They used their three-branch

government to regulate all aspects of life so nobody would profit at somebody else's expense. They sought harmony for everybody."

"But it didn't always work that way, did it?"

"Of course not."

"And do you have any examples of this not working?"

Max took a bite of his steak to force a pause. Even as he discussed Winston-Salem's history with more enthusiasm than he realized he had for the subject, he found Modesto's attitude disturbing. Perhaps that's what the man wanted — he clearly did not like Max. Yet something else gnawed at Max.

"Surely you've come across at least one example?" Modesto said. "Our employer would be unhappy if your research was so superficial."

"I have examples."

Modesto ordered a cup of coffee and said, "I'm waiting. Just one example, please."

Like a bull let out of the shoot, Max barreled into a verbal assault. "In 1829, there's a man with the ironic name of Thomas Christman who decides to become a Baptist. He takes his son with him in this move away from the Moravian beliefs. Christman is ordered to leave town, but he refuses. This is considered a spiritual problem, so the Elders Council is called. They decide not to evict the man — they don't want to go through the North Carolina legal system. Instead, they buy the house from under Christman. He can still live there, but he owns nothing and has nothing for his son to inherit. They've effectively removed him from their world, though he still occupies its space."

"I see."

"You don't. It's not how strict, vengeful, or even creative these people can be, but rather how patient. They wanted a man who had betrayed their beliefs to be driven from their town, and they were willing to wait a lifetime in order for it to occur. Compare that to the Christians or the Muslims — two groups of many that are prone to act now in order to achieve their goals as soon as possible. The kind of patience displayed here is an amazing quality of the Moravians."

Modesto let out a sly grin. "You seem to be very excited about our little city in the South."

Not sure how to take the comment, Max sat back and spread his hands. "If I can't get interested, I wouldn't do a very good job at the research, would I?"

"That is beyond my expertise. Excuse me a moment," Modesto said as he stood. He placed his briefcase on his chair and inched by a waiter as he walked toward the restrooms.

Max looked at the briefcase and wondered at the point of this display. Was Modesto testing Max's trustworthiness? Was this an order from the boss or just a game from a jealous employee? And Modesto was jealous, Max had no doubt. The condescension oozing from Modesto's words could not be mistaken. Somehow he felt threatened by Max's presence. In fact, this entire lunch may not have been ordered by the boss.

Peeking over his shoulder, Max checked to see that Modesto was not heading back. Could this be some sort of probe into his work by Modesto? Max envisioned the arrogant prick groveling at the boss's feet, presenting Max's information as if it were his own.

As he considered this possibility, Max noticed the tip of a paper poking from the front sleeve of the briefcase like a teasing leg-shot on the cover of an old girlie mag. Checking once more that Modesto was not on his way back, Max leaned closer and made out a logo — the letter H in a blockish style, colored blue, with a white rectangle on the right leg as if it were a door or window.

When Modesto returned, he said, "I just spoke with our employer. He's pleased with your work."

"Good," Max said, and then part of what bothered him finally discovered its form. "Everything I've told you today was not difficult information to find. Rather basic, actually. Why would our employer want —"

"Our employer recognizes that you need a little time to catch up on the foundation before you can do the more serious studies. After all, you're still talking about the Moravians. You haven't even begun to look into the Reynolds family which made this city noteworthy. So, your immediate job is to catch up. Our employer does not want to waste more than another week, if even that. I've hired an assistant for you to help you along. We particularly don't want you bogged down with the busy work of the reports."

"An assistant?"

"Yes," Modesto said as he readied to leave. "Once you're ready, the real work can begin. We'll be researching various land deals. I must go now. I'll be in touch next week."

As Modesto walked away, Max was surprised his thoughts were not of land deals, the blue H, or even Modesto. Instead, Max thought only of two names — Marshall Drummond and Stan Bowman.

Chapter 6

"I MUST BE CRAZY," Max said to his empty car as he drove toward the campus. "No, no. They say if you can think that might be the case, then it's not. Crazy people think they're perfectly normal. Then again, I'm talking to myself in a car, so what does that say for me?"

When his cell phone rang, Max answered it without looking at the name. His mother's voice screeched in his ear. "Max, I've been so worried about you. I've been trying to get you for days."

"Hi, Mom."

"You eating all right?"

"I'm fine, Mom. The move went fine, Sandra's fine, and we're just busy getting settled in."

"Oh, that's wonderful. Listen, I sent you a housewarming gift. Did you get it?"

"Yes, thank you," Max said, trying to blot out any memory of the ugliest ashtray ever made in the seventies — something she had lying around her attic.

"I'm glad it arrived. You never know with the mail. And since I didn't get a thank you note, I wasn't sure."

"Like I said, it's been busy."

He could hear his mother working herself into a nitpicking froth. "Well, I have to say that it doesn't take that long to write a thank you note, and it's very important. I know I taught you better than that. Now, I'm not joking. People will look down upon you in your life if you fail at the little things. It's that important, and it's a mark of a civilized person. For me, it's okay, it doesn't matter, you understand. You forget me, I don't mind. You're my son. I know you love me. But other people, they need to be properly thanked."

"Yes, Mom. I'm very sorry. I'll try to be better," Max said, not paying attention to his words as he took the Wake exit. By the time he found a parking spot (and hoped he'd avoid a ticket for using the student lot), his mother had wound down and said her good-byes. As annoying as she could be, though, Max wanted to thank her this time. By distracting him from all that had occurred that morning, she had managed to untangle his thoughts enough for him to function.

He still shuddered at the idea that a real ghost haunted his office, but he no longer feared the thing — especially since Drummond needed his help. His own situation bothered him far greater, yet even that no longer rattled him like earlier. Now, he started to see that Stan, Annabelle, Hull, and Drummond all were just the dots he had to connect. If he could do that, then perhaps he had nothing to worry about. Besides, as odd as his employer had been, it was only Drummond saying that Max was in danger.

A ghost might say anything to be freed from a curse. And what, exactly, did he do to deserve a curse?

By the time Max entered the now-familiar library lobby, his curiosity had risen above the tide line of his fear. No matter what else, Max agreed with one thing Drummond had said — he needed to find Annabelle Bowman.

After an hour had passed, Max admitted that all his research that day on Moravian history did nothing to help him find Annabelle Bowman. It did, however, help Max avoid thinking about ghosts and dangerous bosses. *Don't slow down. Keep pushing ahead.* As long as he kept moving forward, logic and common sense would prevail. He hoped.

Leafing through a pictorial history of Winston-Salem as he climbed a stairwell, Max jolted at the sound of his cell phone ringing. A glance at the phone's face — Sandra. Max sat on the stairs (cell phone reception only happened in the library's stairwells) with the book on his lap and answered.

Sandra's day had not fared any better than Max's. She launched into a detailed account of being rear-ended by "some jerk in a jaguar who insisted on pulling over and getting an official police report even though all I got was a scratch on the bumper." She ended up late to work and had to deal with a lecture from Mrs. McCarthy, the owner, that ended with a reminder, "There's lots of good people looking for work right now. People who know how to be on time."

Max listened and did not interrupt. The more she spoke, the less he wanted to say. What could he tell her? That a ghost hired him on the side and promised him that his new employer, the one that would save them financially, was somehow associated with the spawn of evil, Stan

Bowman? But he didn't want to lie to her either.

When she finished, still huffing at unspoken thoughts, the dreaded question came out. "So, what happened with Drummond?"

Turning the page in his book, Max saw a picture of a large building on fire in the middle of a field while numerous, well-dressed people stood at a distance and watched. The caption explained that on November 24, 1892 the Zinzendorf Hotel (named after the beloved former leader) tragically burned to the ground in about two hours. Max looked at the billowing smoke and wondered if he had started his own tragic fire.

"Honey?" Sandra said.

"I'm here. Things have gotten a little bit more complicated, but don't worry."

"Just tell Drummond —"

"Don't do that."

"Do what?"

"Try to solve my problems and tell me what to do. I've got it all being taken care of. And I can decide for my own career if I want to do a little work for Drummond or not. I promise you I won't be fired from my job. Okay?"

"I guess I'm just a little worried that —"

"We're not in Michigan anymore."

"I know," Sandra said. With forced levity, she changed the subject, and as she chattered on, Max flipped through a few more pages.

"It can't be," he said, staring at a picture from the 1980s. He read the caption twice.

"What did you say?"

"She might still be here."

"Who?"

"Annabelle. I've got to go. I'll see you tonight," Max said, cutting the connection without any further good-bye.

He went to his cubicle, gathered his things, and rushed to the microtext room. With the aid of a librarian, he found several spools containing all issues of the local paper, The Winston-Salem Journal, for the year 1989. In a short time, he found the story he had sought, and the photos of several Winston-Salem residents, including an older lady attempting to hide behind harsh-looking men — but her spry eyes gave her away. Annabelle Bowman. A quick search online gave him the address.

As he drove to the South Side home, Max considered calling

Drummond. Two thoughts stopped him. First, he saw no reason he should feel obligated to make reports. Second, and far more important, Drummond was dead. How would a ghost answer the phone?

The house appeared to be nothing special. A beaten Chevy with a layer of dust resided in the driveway and leaves dotted the walk. Fall would arrive soon, but for the moment, the warm air felt just right. As Max waited on the brick porch for the doorbell to be answered, the distinct odor of stale flowers and unwashed blankets drifted from a rocking chair at his side.

"Yes?" a weak voice asked from behind the door.

"Annabelle Bowman?"

"What do you want?"

"My name's Max Porter. I was hoping I could talk to you for a few minutes. I have a few questions for an article I'm researching."

The door opened a crack. "Article?"

Max flashed his warmest smile as he peeked in at the elderly woman. "Yes, I'm writing an article for, um, I don't know yet. It's kind of a freelance thing."

"Freelance?"

"It means that I don't have —"

"I know what it means, you idiot. Sure, what the hell, I ain't had anything interesting happen in months," she said, nudging the door open and shuffling toward her living room. "Besides, I don't think I've got to worry about you raping me, and there ain't anything here worth stealing."

Max stepped inside to find a home cramped with books, statuettes, and trinkets of all kinds. Next to a mirror, a framed cross-stitching hung on the wall declaring "Home is life." Two overstuffed sofas dominated the living room. A coffee table covered with photos of young children, sat between them.

"My nieces and nephews," she said.

"They look lovely."

"The one in the green shirt is. The other two are a pain but they'll outgrow it. And this picture is my sister, Emily. I haven't heard from her in awhile. Her husband thinks I'm a bit of a bitch, I suppose. Excuse my language. I used to be more refined but at my age, you start to realize all that politeness doesn't get you very far. Better to be honest and direct, even if it does piss off a few people along the way."

Max chuckled as he sat. "I won't take up too much of your time," he said.

"I'm not going anywhere. Would you like some sweet tea?"

"No, thank you," he said. Sweet tea was everywhere in North Carolina, but for Max's northern tastes it was much too sweet, not enough tea.

"What do you want to talk about?" Annabelle asked.

"Well, I saw a picture of you in a story about Millionaire's Row."

Annabelle snorted a laugh which fast turned into a rasping cough. "What in Heaven do you care about all that?"

"I just found it interesting. It's not every day that a bunch of people wake up instant millionaires — sort of like winning the lottery."

"Loyalty gets rewarded sometimes," she said, pulling a knitted blanket over her lap. "Even if the reward comes from a bastard."

"Would that be F. Ross Johnson?"

"Those families had all worked for Reynolds Tobacco for most of their lives. They were loyal to the company. They bought stock in it. Reynolds made this town, y'know? Then suddenly the company becomes RJR Nabisco, and that wasn't so bad at first, but Johnson screwed us all — sent the headquarters off to Atlanta. I swear, if lynching had been legal, I don't think Johnson would've lasted the week."

Max nodded. "And then he let the whole thing be taken over in a leveraged buyout."

"That's right. Forced us to sell our shares. We all made a lot of money, sure, but it never was about money. You listen to me. Money's always been an illusion," she said, her eyes glancing at her hands with a mournful hesitancy. She cracked a smile and said, "You know, when the reporters all showed up, they thought they'd get pictures of us hicks spending lavishly on new cars and new houses and diamond rings and such. Instead, they got us. We all still live in the same homes — those of us still alive, that is — and we all go on the same way. We just plunked the money into savings and that was that. So, there's not much of a story here for you."

"Actually," Max said as a nervous throbbing built in his chest, "I did have one little item I hoped you could clear up for me."

"Oh?" she said, her smile turning into a sharp, controlled line.

"It's about your stock. See, according to the newspapers, all the others had bought their stock in small bits over the years of their employment. You, however, never worked for Reynolds. I was just wondering why you would have followed the same pattern as they did."

"My late husband worked for them."

"That would be Stan Bowman?"

"I think you should leave now," Annabelle said, heading for the front door.

The chill that blew into the room struck Max hard. He never had been in this type of situation, and he found himself wishing Drummond could have come along. The aid of a real detective appeared quite attractive at the moment.

"Please, I didn't mean to upset you. I'm just trying to find out —"

"I know what you want. Now, I'm very busy today, so please leave or I'll have to call the police."

"Do you know the name Hull?"

Annabelle stopped. She turned her eyes onto Max with such authority that he half-expected her to demand his hand for a ruler beating. "Whatever you're doing looking into all of this, you better stop it. This city was built on the backs of old families like Hull, Hanes, and Reynolds. You've got to understand that. R. J. Reynolds Tobacco — it's not just a company or a stock, it's a religion. And you don't go messing with somebody's religion."

Chapter 7

DRUMMOND BOUNCED AROUND THE OFFICE, clapped his hands together, and nodded. "Damn, I wish I could've been there," he said, rubbing his mouth. "And I wish I could have a cigarette."

"Sorry, I don't smoke," Max said, slumping in his chair. Sweat still dampened his armpits and his fingers still trembled from all the adrenaline pumping through him. He could hear the menace behind the old lady's voice echoing in his head.

"I'm dead, remember? I don't have lungs to smoke with. She really said all that, huh? It's a religion?"

"Yeah, she said that."

"And you just left?"

"She obviously wanted me to go."

"Of course she did. She knows something. She wanted you out as fast as possible. And that's important because it means somewhere inside her, she knows that she can be pushed into blabbing her secrets."

"It does?"

"Always. Somebody with nothing to hide or somebody who knows he'll never crack, people like that will let you hang out and talk for hours. They don't care. They want to spin you in circles. But the ones that throw you out, those are the gold mines."

Max glanced at the book with the hidden flask but shook his head. "Look, this is all getting nutty. I mean, I took the job with Hull because I needed the money. I'm supposed to be looking up land deals and old history. Now I don't know what you've brought me into."

Drummond halted and stared hard into Max. "You don't get to back out of things like this. You better start understanding that. It doesn't matter what your intentions were or how you ended up here, the fact is that you *are* here. You do know things now that companies like Hull are not going to be happy about. So shut up and start thinking."

"About what?"

"Our next step, of course. You really have no clue what you're doing, do you?"

"Fine," Max said, crossing his arms and spinning his chair so he could pout toward the window. "Tell me, then, what is our next great step?"

"Well, we could follow Annabelle. You could, I mean. Whenever you shake up somebody like this, really throw them for a loop, they usually start acting on whatever it is they're hiding. You follow her and you might learn something."

"No."

"What?"

"I'm not a detective. I do research and I teach. I don't go following people around, taking their pictures, and seeing what they're up to."

Drummond passed through the desk and settled in front of Max. "You must be a great lover or hung like an elephant or something because I can't see what your wife sees in you."

"Thanks," Max said, plastering a sarcastic grin on his face. "You really know how to speak to my heart."

Drummond stared at Max for awhile without saying a word. Max stared back, wondering if this had become a game of chicken or if Drummond actually had started thinking about the case again. With another clap of his hands, Drummond broke the silence and said, "Okay. You say you're the research man, then let's do some research."

"What now?"

"Stocks. You said Annabelle made a fortune in Reynolds stock, right?"

"That's right."

"But she never worked for the company, and after what had occurred with her husband, you'd think she would never want anything from them. Not to mention that unless she had some rich uncle or something, she and Stan did not have much in the way of money."

Max spun back to his desk. "So where did the stock come from?"

"Exactly."

"She could've bought it in small amounts over the years like the others. Maybe figured RJR owed her something."

"True, but she threw you out of her house."

With a drum roll on the table, Max said, "I'll see what I can find out."

"Good," Drummond said. "But before you do all that, you ought to be ready for Modesto."

"What about him?"

"I just saw him walk into the building."

"Great," Max said, took a deep breath, and opened a notebook. "You stay quiet," he said and attempted to look busy. Drummond exaggerated locking his mouth as he floated toward the ceiling. Max chilled at the display but said nothing. He had to start getting comfortable with ghostly ways.

A moment later, Modesto opened the door and took a seat without a word. Max lifted a halting finger, pretended to take a few final notes, and then raised his head with a smile. "Mr. Modesto, it's always good to see you." Modesto glared at Max but showed no sign of talking. "Something you want? I didn't think I had to give a report for a few more days. I suppose if you need something now —"

"I'm not here for a report."

Drummond drifted against the bookshelf and squinted as he scrutinized Modesto. "Be careful, Max. He knows something."

"I can see that," Max said, trying to keep his eyes on Modesto, though he kept catching Drummond in his peripheral vision. "Perhaps you could save us some time and tell me why you're here?"

"Why were you talking to Annabelle Bowman?" Modesto asked, crossing his legs with calm power.

"Don't tell him anything," Drummond said.

"I know how to do my job," Max said.

Modesto gestured toward the desk corner. "You don't appear to understand how to follow instructions."

Using every ounce of self-control he could muster, Max refused to look at the desk corner. "What do you mean?" he asked, knowing that he sounded guiltier than ever.

"You were asked to research the early foundations of this town in order to help us acquire important historical pieces of land. Annabelle Bowman has nothing to do with that."

Drummond stepped in between the men and faced Modesto. He squatted down and said, "You better come up with something quick, Max, and it better be good. I don't think he'll buy much malarkey."

Max reached into his pocket and pushed the vibrate button on his cell phone. Acting startled, he pulled the phone out, checked the face, and said, "Excuse me, one moment."

"Of course," Modesto said.

Max flipped open the phone and said, "Hi, how are you?"

Drummond looked back at Max. "Is there really a call?"

"No, no."

"I see, buying time, huh?"

"Not quite."

"Then what?"

"Look, I'm in an important meeting right now, and I'm not trying to be rude or anything but you're interrupting," Max said. He covered the phone and said to Modesto, "Just a minute longer. Sorry about this."

"I can wait," Modesto said.

Drummond pulled up and stomped off to the corner, stepping through Modesto in the process. Modesto shivered. "I'm just trying to help," Drummond said.

"I know," Max said. "I do. It's just a bit difficult to carry on more than one conversation at a time. I'll call you after my meeting, okay?"

"Not okay. You need me. You screwed up with Annabelle, and you'll screw up here."

"I've really got to go."

"Fine," Drummond said and turned around showing only his back to Max.

Max put the cell phone away and said to Modesto, "Sorry about that. Now, you were asking about Annabelle Bowman. I suppose I understand your confusion in the matter. You're not an expert at research. And, well, I admit I acted a bit too enthusiastically. You had mentioned land deals being our ultimate objective, so I jumped ahead. See, history books will only help us out so much. If I'm to find quality pieces of real estate for our employer then I need to talk to the people who might own such pieces."

"And you think Ms. Bowman is such a person?"

"Well, she did become very wealthy, very quickly. Usually people who win the lottery or inherit a ton of money will buy up some local properties as a place to plunk down all this wealth they don't know what to do with. That's why I spoke to her."

"Why didn't you talk to any of the other stockholders who made it big off of Reynolds?"

"I intend to. Ms. Bowman was merely my first stop. I'm afraid it didn't go too well, she's very cranky, so I decided to rethink my approach before I tackled another."

Drummond spun around. "I can't take this. Ask him the crucial question, already!"

Max continued, "I do have a question for you, though."

"Oh? And what is that?"

Nobody said anything for a moment. Modesto looked at Max expectantly, and then said, "Mr. Porter? Do you have a question or not?"

"Gee," Drummond said, striding back to the desk. "I guess you might need my help after all, huh?"

"Yes," Max said.

Modesto opened his arms. "I can't wait all day."

Drummond shook his head. "Ask him how he knew you saw Annabelle Bowman today."

Sitting straighter, his heart jumping as the question sunk in, Max said, "I'm curious about something. How is that you know I saw Ms. Bowman today? I never told anybody I was going there. I never even indicated in my reports that I would be taking this approach. How is it that you know where I've been? Are you having me followed?"

For the first time, Max saw Mr. Modesto's cool exterior falter. It did not last long, but it scared Max. With a patience that added to Max's growing dread, Modesto stood and leaned on the table. "Yes, I've had you followed. The library trips, lunches with your wife, visits to old rich ladies. I've had people watching you since before you moved here. And I will continue to have you followed until I am convinced that you do not pose a threat to our employer's interests. That is what I am an expert at."

Max struggled to make his throat open enough for speaking. At length, he said, "I-I'm not trying to pick a fight with you. I just didn't like the idea. Listen, you have nothing to worry over with me."

Drummond walked right through the desk, waving his hands, and said, "Shut up. Don't say another word."

"I came down here because our employer offered me a lot of money," Max said. Now that he got himself talking, he found it harder to stop. "I don't have any interest in what he wants with the information I find. I just want my money and that'll be it. I don't care about him or anything like that. I won't go to the police, not that there's anything to go to the police with anyway."

Drummond covered his eyes. "Oh, please, shut up. Please."

The calculating expression on Modesto's face finally got Max quiet. Max tried to speak again but his lips only quivered. Modesto pulled back, donned his coat, and said, "Do your job, Mr. Porter." He slapped a manila envelope on the desk. "Research these properties, take your money, and move away from here. Anything else would be inadvisable."

"Yes, sir," Max managed as Modesto strolled away.

Once the stairwell door clanged shut, Drummond faced Max and said, "What the hell is the matter with you? I told you to ask him one simple question, not divulge every little nuance of your thought process, and certainly not to piss all over the man, and most definitely, most certainly, I did not tell you to mention the police."

"I didn't. I said I wouldn't involve the police."

"You mentioned them. That's enough. It shows that you think there's something illegal, something worth telling the police about."

"I didn't know."

"How could you not know? I've been a ghost for decades now, and even I've heard enough about modern cinema to know that every bum in this country should be aware of basic procedures in this kind of thing."

Max's shaking hands tightened into fists as his anger grew. "Well, things are a heck of a lot different when you're actually in the situation."

"You've got that much right," Drummond said as he sat down and lifted his legs onto the desk. "You know, I think I'd love a cigarette more right now than life itself."

Maybe it was the sudden shift in attitudes or maybe Max had begun to like the gruff detective, he didn't know. Either way, Max could not resist pointing to Drummond's feet. "How do you do that? Put your feet on the desk or clap your hands or anything like that?"

Drummond shrugged. "I just do. When I want to go through something, I do it. When I want to be more substantial, I can do that too."

"So, now I guess we look into that stock information?"

"It's not too late to stakeout Ms. Annabelle."

Max's cell phone buzzed — Sandra. "Hi, honey," Max said while scowling at Drummond. "I'm fine ... well, today's been interesting ... I've still got some research to do ... sure, honey, if it's important, I'll be there ... oh, I see."

"Well?" Drummond said to Max's stunned face.

"My wife has informed me that we have a date tonight."

"A date? With your wife? You're married to her but you're still dating? Oh, hell, the 1940s made a lot more sense."

Chapter 8

MAX DISLIKED LOW-PRICED RESTAURANTS because all the families with obnoxious kids ate at such places. With their finances strapped, however, he and Sandra had little choice in the matter if they wanted to eat out. So, as Max bit into the dry turkey and over-ripe tomato of his club sandwich, he listened to a four-year-old scream "Mine! Mine! Mine!" while the sweet darling's adoring parents smacked him across the head.

Sandra cracked a grin and shrugged. "It could be worse."

"Really?" Max said, thinking about the day he had endured and how little of it he dared to share with his wife.

"Sure. That kid could be ours."

This elicited a slight chuckle. A moment later, they settled into silence and ate. Max wanted to relax, to pay attention, to be a good date, but he could not stop thinking about Drummond, Bowman, Modesto, and Hull. Even if he had the courage to divulge a tiny portion of what had happened, Sandra could not possibly believe him — a detective ghost and office witchcraft and a forgotten madman.

"Come on," Sandra said, her voice soft yet firm. "Please try to have a good time."

"What? Oh, no, I'm fine. Just a bit preoccupied."

"Honey, I know you don't like your job, but you've got to deal with it."

"I am," Max said, snapping harder than he had intended. He drank some soda through a straw and continued, "I've just had a stressful day, that's all."

"Okay, okay. I'm sorry."

The brat screaming "Mine! Mine! Mine!" hit the high-point of his meltdown. He sprawled on the floor and wailed. Two haggard parents scooped him up, dodging his flailing arms, and lugged him outside.

Sandra could not hold back her laughter.

"It's not funny," Max said. "Those are horrible parents and they have no consideration for anybody else."

Sandra whooped a short laugh and regained her composure. "You could really use a hard drink, couldn't you?"

Max sipped his straw again, making a silly face that sent Sandra into more hysterics. "So let me ask you something," Max said, deciding at that very moment upon a way to lightly dance atop the explosives that had become his life. "Do you believe in ghosts?"

Wiping her eyes, Sandra said, "Ghosts?"

"Spirits of the dead. Y'know, ghosts."

Sandra took a long drink, giving Max the impression that she was stalling. "Yes, I suppose I do. Why are you even asking?"

Waving away the question, Max said, "Forget it. How was your day?"

"Fine," Sandra said with a touch of relief. "Actually, I'm still having problems with my boss, but it's nothing to worry about."

"We both have boss problems, then."

"And we'll both persevere. Now, let's talk no more of work and bosses and anything like that."

"Okay. What do you want to talk about?"

Sandra opened her mouth but said nothing. Then, with a shake of her head, she started to laugh again. They enjoyed the rest of their meal, talking about a television show, Max's mother, and something Sandra heard on the radio. Savoring the weightlessness of the evening, they both relaxed for an hour.

Max would later recall two sounds as they headed toward their car in the brisk night air. First, he heard the crunching of heavy feet in the gravel — a sound that spoke of urgency and threat. The second sound, however, would be forever chiseled into his being — Sandra's terror-filled scream as two men wearing ski-masks shoved her aside and assaulted Max.

They each took one of his arms and threw him against the restaurant's wall. The cold brick scratched into his back as one of the men, the heavier one, punched Max in the gut. The other one pulled out a handgun that shined its metallic blue under the parking lot lights and pointed it at Sandra. Max gasped for enough air to speak, his lungs burning and his stomach stuck in a tight clench, but he only managed to cough up phlegm.

The heavy man grabbed Max's hair and wrenched his head back.

Max could see Sandra shaking, her face looking upon him, terrified she might never see him again. He wanted to reach out to her, to give her some assurance they would be fine, but the gun pointed at her head kept him wondering.

"Stop looking into things that don't matter anymore," the heavy man said, his breath reeking of alcohol. Another punch to the gut and a kick in the side capped off the performance. Then the two men dashed off into the darkness. As Max rolled to his side, Sandra raced over and wrapped her arms around him.

She whispered words he could not decipher, and he knew the words were more for her own comfort than his. After a few minutes, his stomach muscles loosened a little, and he found the strength to stand. Pain shot from his side. He prayed they hadn't broken his ribs — paying for medical care was not a line item in the Porter budget.

Later, in their kitchen, Sandra helped Max ease out of his shirt. He winced and groaned but managed.

"That looks pretty bad," she said, placing an icepack over the purple/black bruise on his side.

"Easy," he said, hissing air as he lowered his arm onto the icepack.

"Don't be a baby."

"I got kicked in the ribs!"

"And I had a gun to my head," Sandra said, slamming a second icepack onto the table. Her hands shook, and her face quivered as tears welled in her eyes. She rubbed them away and returned to checking his wounds.

"We're okay now. We can relax. It's all over."

"No, it's not. You know that. I heard what he said to you. This was just a warning."

"They may not even have had the right guy."

"Bullshit! They targeted you and you know it," Sandra said and the two locked eyes like poker players attempting to cover all sense of meaning in their expressions. Breaking away, Sandra fixed a glass of cola for Max and said, "Doesn't look like you've got any broken bones."

"At least that much is good."

"Sure," she said, the sarcasm dripping heavy and thick, "real good. Just wonderful, in fact. We ought to get attacked more often."

Max sipped his cola and said, "I know it was scary and all, but it's over."

"Stop saying that. I'm not a child and I'm not a fool. This was a warning. To you. This is all because of Drummond, isn't it? It is. I can see it in your face. So, you tell me right now, what's going on?"

Despite her stern mouth, Max saw the fear dancing on her skin. He knew exactly how she felt. He felt it, too. Anger strong enough to tear down walls. Fear powerful enough to keep him frozen.

"I don't know if it's the Drummond thing. I don't. Honest. I mean it probably is, but I don't know one hundred percent for sure. But come on, now, this shouldn't be such a shock."

"What?"

"We both know something's not right about my employer."

"What are you saying?"

Max gestured to the chair opposite him and waited for her to sit. Sandra glanced at the chair; then leaned against the counter. "It's truth time," he said. "Okay? Don't you think? No more pretending. We've both kept quiet about it. We've both ignored all the red flags smacking us in the face because we wanted the money, the security. We wanted to get out of the mess in Michigan."

"You made that mess."

"I'm not trying to dredge up all that. I just —"

Sandra shook her head as she pulled a beer from the refrigerator. "I see how you want this," she said. "It's truth time but only when you've got something to say."

"No, I just didn't want us to rehash an old fight."

"Well, we're here, right now, talking about all of this because of that old fight. Maybe we should consider finishing it this time."

Never before had Max seen his wife carry such a harsh expression. Disgust and hatred filled him at the sight — not for her but towards himself. He had caused her to look that way. If this was "truth time," then he had to start with himself. "Okay," he said. "Michigan was my fault, and I think all of this is my fault, too."

Sandra drank her beer as she settled into her chair. Then, with a tired yet still boiling tone, she said, "They accused you of sleeping with a student, and I believe whole-heartedly you didn't do it. So, let's start with that. I want to know why you let them fire you. And don't tell me how you hated your boss and the legal costs were too high and all those other excuses you've used before. I want to know the truth. Why didn't you fight for that job?"

Max closed his eyes and nodded. "It's funny, I always tell myself it happened because of the boss thing or that my ideas were stolen or a number of other excuses. Truth is, though, I deserved to be fired.

That's why I didn't fight. I knew if we fought back, they'd look into my work, my files, everything. They'd poke into everything, and eventually they'd learn that I *had* done something wrong. Not what they accused me of, I never slept with a student, but something that could've landed me in jail."

"What did you do?" Sandra asked, her voice quiet and frightened like a girl being told her mommy was being arrested.

Max swallowed hard. "I found a loophole in their computer accounting system. I was talking with the principal one day and it was just there on her desk and she was nowhere and I don't know what I was thinking, but I just reached over and made a few checks for CASH."

"You embezzled from a school?"

"We were freezing to death, for crying out loud. I'm sorry I'm not the great provider, but I had to do something. And really, isn't that why we're here? We hated how hard our lives were back there. We hated it. All the time, we complained and griped and it was ripping us to pieces. We barely talked about anything else. Then, this job landed in my lap and we saw the dollar signs and that was it, no questions."

"It wasn't like that."

"No, no. This is truth time. We *both* accepted that there was something odd about this job. We both knew it was not on the up-and-up."

Indignation flashed in Sandra's eyes, only to be replaced by calm acceptance. A single tear escaped her tight control, and with a trembling voice, she asked, "How bad is it this time? Are you going to go to jail?"

"What? No. I've done nothing wrong. I'm just researching old history looking for buildings. That's it. But obviously, there's more to all this than real estate deals."

"Obviously."

Max shifted in his chair and fire swelled from his bruises and seared up his side. "It's all crazy. I've actually been thinking how nice Michigan was."

"Michigan was a crappy mess."

"My point exactly." Max dropped his hands to his lap. "I've just got to get through the job. Just do the research, get my check, and then I'll quit. I'll walk away."

"Honey, you're not thinking. When does somebody ever get to walk away from people like this?"

"But I don't know anything."

"Does that really matter? What you need to do is quit all this Drummond business, do your job, and keep your mouth shut and your ears open. We need to find some way to get out, something to hold over their heads."

"Are you crazy? These people sent two men to beat me up. They had a gun to your head."

"I haven't forgotten," Sandra said, her anger erupting as tears streamed out unchecked. "But we can't just sit back and wait for you to piss them off enough to kill us. You need to do something. You don't like my idea, fine. You tell me, then. What can we do?"

Max sagged in his chair. He knew all along this question was coming, and he knew the answer. "You won't like it," he said and finished his drink, the clinking ice cubes underscoring his soft words.

"I don't like any of this."

"I'm going to help Drummond. I know that seems nuts to you, but there's more to it than you know, and if I can find out what happened to ... what happened, then maybe I'll have that missing something you want me to find. Something to protect us from my employer."

"But all of this started with Drummond. Why help him?"

"I think his case is connected to everything else. At least, I'm pretty sure it is."

"Okay, okay. But, honey, I'm scared."

"Me, too," Max said.

Sandra took a shaking breath and placed her hand on the table. Max reached out, and they held hands in the kitchen without another word.

Chapter 9

THE NEXT MORNING, after overcoming the difficulty of taking a shower and driving to work with half his body throbbing in pain, Max opened his office door to discover a tall, blonde man moving papers on his desk. He was young, perhaps still in college, and had a boyish smooth face. He looked up, adjusted his glasses, stood, and offered his hand.

"Are you Mr. Porter?" the young man asked with a slight drawl. He pushed his thin hair back, but in moments it had swooped down to cover his right eye once again.

Max shook the hand. "I am. And this is my office, though that doesn't seem to matter to anybody around here."

"I'm sorry. I was told to let myself in. My name's Taylor. Mr. Modesto hired me to be your assistant."

Drummond slipped out of the bookcase and started shouting. "Can you believe this? A damn spy. I tried to get this idiot to leave. I've been knocking books to the floor and throwing papers around, but the prick won't go."

Taylor moved around the desk, his hands jittering as he pointed at Drummond. "I think that bookshelf is not flush with the floor. Things keep slipping out of it."

Drummond stomped around the room. "I'm sick of him. He's been here less than an hour and I can't stand him. If only I could deck him. I know, I know, but that's it for me — books are the biggest thing I've been able to move. Kind of stings, too, but for this clown, I'll suffer it."

Max tried to ignore Drummond for the moment. "You said that Mr. Modesto hired you?"

"Yes, sir," Taylor said. "I'm to help you however you need. He said you were doing research."

"Um, there's been a misunderstanding. I don't require an assistant."

Drummond slapped another book to the floor. As Taylor placed it back, he said, "Mr. Modesto said you'd say that. He told me that I had to stay even if you tried to fire me. He said only he could fire me. I'm sorry, sir, but I need this job. It pays really well and college is expensive. And, frankly, there isn't much else out there. So, if you don't put me to work, I'm supposed to just sit here." With that, Taylor took the left guest chair, looking more uncomfortable than before.

"I see," Max said. "I guess I'll work elsewhere today."

"Excuse me, sir?"

"What?" Drummond asked.

Max stepped to the side so that he could face both Taylor and Drummond while speaking to Taylor. "I don't mean to offend you. Mr. Modesto can hire you to do whatever he wants. He cannot, however, force me to accept it. I'll do my work elsewhere. Please leave by five and be sure to lock the door."

Drummond walked right through Taylor in his desperate approach to Max. "Don't do this. It's bad enough being stuck in this room all day, but don't leave him here with me."

Taylor appeared to be working a complex problem in his head when Max opened the office door. "Goodbye," he said and walked out.

The lady living down the hall stepped out for her newspaper. She eyed Max as he said, "Good morning."

As Max reached the end of the hall, Taylor exclaimed, "This is a test, ain't it? Don't worry, sir, I'll be right here to five o'clock. You can count on me."

The lady cocked an eyebrow. Embarrassed, Max said, "New assistant. He's a bit overenthusiastic." With a grunt, the lady closed her door.

Max had two distinct impressions of Taylor. One — he was like any other college kid and would goof around all day unless Max stayed in the office. And two — Drummond was right. Whether the kid knew it or not, he had been hired to spy. That last idea sent nervous tingling through Max's skin, but not because he feared its veracity — rather, Max chilled at how easily he accepted the idea of being spied upon. *I'm starting to know my enemy.*

By the time he reached Wake (and after seven minutes of searching for a parking space), he had formulated his next few steps. First, when he entered the library, he found a private corner and sent an e-mail to Roddy, his pal in Michigan. They had been college roommates, and

Max hoped he could still trust the man. Before moving to Michigan, Roddy had worked on Wall Street, and Max's e-mail asked Roddy to draw on those old days to get any information about Annabelle Bowman's stock acquisitions. With the e-mail sent off, Max started his own research on local land deals.

The work kept Max's mind from wandering which kept him from worrying. Hours passed by in research bliss until he had to admit that all his work had turned up no results. According to all the records he could find, nobody named Hull ever owned any land in Winston-Salem. While certainly odd, it was not unfathomable. The Hull's could have numerous dummy corporations set up to hold the land. Such things were done all the time in order to protect family money from litigation damages.

With a loud gurgle, Max's stomach protested the long day. His watch read 3:30, so he hurried over to Benson University Center to grab a quick bite among the students. No sooner had he left the library than his cell phone chirped — his mother.

"Hi, Mom," Max said as he weaved around students.

"Hi, dear."

"I can't talk long. I've got to get some lunch before I get back to work."

"Oh, that's nice. Your work is going well?"

Max sighed. "Yes. It's fine."

"And how's Sandra?"

"She's doing well. Loves it down here."

"I'm so glad. As long as you two are happy, then the rest of it doesn't matter."

Here it was. Max tried to refrain from taking the bait but he had to ask, "The rest of what?"

"Oh, never mind. I'm just an old woman all by myself waiting for her grandchildren."

Bingo! Grandchildren. "I know. But we can barely afford to keep ourselves going. A child is way too expensive."

"Your father and I did fine with you, didn't we?"

"Yes, Mom."

"Times were harder then. So, enough excuses. You talk with that wife of yours and get some children. Why on Earth get married if you didn't want kids? It's beyond me."

"Okay, I'll do that," Max said as he stepped into Benson University Center. "I have to go now. I have to eat."

"Are you eating well?"

"I'm trying."

"It's important. Lucas Hoffmeyer died last week because he stopped eating well. Of course, he was ninety-two but still, you have to take care of your body. Do you know I used to bring Lucas meals and read to him and things like that?"

Max dumped his things at the nearest available table, resigned to the fact that he would not get to eat until the phone conversation ended, and that would only happen when his mother decided it would happen. "No, Mom, I don't think I knew that."

"Well, I did," she said, her pride boosting every word. "He would call me 'one of his gals' and he'd tell me stories of his youth. Remarkably warm, gracious man. I really enjoyed talking with him. Oh, and his grandfather, you wouldn't believe the stories about his grandfather. Why the man served during the Civil War! Can you imagine that?"

But Max had stopped listening. The Civil War. Something about it clicked, and he found no internal resistance to interrupting his mother. "Mom, I have to go. I'll try to call you later. Bye," he said and closed the cell phone before she could say another word. Without bothering for food, Max rushed back to the library, his excitement held in check only by the odd looks he received from passing students.

The Civil War. The Hull family may have covered their tracks with dummy corporations now but back during the Civil War? He doubted they would have been so thorough back then. They would have tried but deleting files is different from hunting down every scrap of paper with the name Hull written upon it.

In less than an hour, Max had sifted through the entire roster of Civil War participants from the Winston-Salem area. It had been a fascinating experience in itself, but more so because of what he discovered. The name Hull came up several times often accompanied by the phrase "of the prominent family" or "married into the notable family" or even in one case, "proud grandchild of the great family." In each instance, Max wrote down the name and any particulars provided. He then began researching land deals from the Civil War era. As dinnertime neared, his unappeased hunger rebelled against his enthusiastic curiosity, and he had to admit that he had come up empty. All those "prominent" Hulls, yet not a single one owned any property.

After shoving down a burger and offering an apologetic call to Sandra, Max shuffled into his office. His watch beeped the arrival of seven o'clock, and thankfully, his new assistant had followed orders. Max dropped into his chair and said, "So, how was your day?"

Drummond stepped out of the far wall, his shoulders raised and his face scrunched. Through clenched teeth, he said, "You must get rid of that bastard."

Max's body still ached, though not as bad as that morning. But the thought of dealing with a belligerent ghost caused many of his bruises to flare up. "I can't fire him and he won't budge."

"Do you know what he did all day while you were out? He opened that window and he smoked. He smoked! Oh, if that smell isn't the most intoxicating, I swear there's a Devil and it wants to torture me every chance it gets."

"I really am sorry. But I have no way."

"Yes, you do," Drummond said, sliding closer with a boyish twinkle. "I've been waiting for you to broach the subject, to even suggest it, but you've clearly got a lot of other things to worry about. Either that or you're a thoughtless bastard."

"I'm really tired. Whatever you want, can it —"

"I don't have to be stuck here."

"You don't?"

"Not at all," Drummond said, his eagerness beaming.

Max had so many little puzzle pieces refusing to fit together that playing a guessing game with Drummond held no appeal. "Just tell me," he said.

"I'm here because of a curse. You can change that. You can undo the curse and set me free. Then I can help you with the case, be right by your side the whole time."

"Oh, sure. That'd be great," Max said, picturing how impossible his research days would be with Drummond floating around the library making boisterous comments — *I'm bored* — *I want to smoke* — *Look at these co-eds.*

"Okay, okay, so I won't be by your side all day. The point is I can do more out there than I can stuck in here. Besides, if Hull wants me stuck here, shouldn't that say to you that I present more of a threat to them if I'm unstuck?"

Max yawned and said, "Hey, I've got no problem with the idea of setting you free. I do, however, have the problem of not having a clue how to do it, and while I know there's a book on that shelf about witchcraft, I find it highly unlikely that they would give me the curse-breaking spell so easily."

"You're right. That book won't help. In fact, you can't go to a book on witchcraft to help me. You have to go to a witch."

Max started shaking his head before Drummond finished speaking. "No, no, no. A witch? No. I am not going to ... no. I'm sorry but that is just ... no."

"Oh, come on," Drummond snapped. "I'm not asking you to give her your blood or something. Just find out what we need to do. That's it. Besides, she's a beautiful woman."

"What? Are you saying you know a witch? A real witch?"

Drummond gave a sly wink. "I knew her grandmother. Look, I promise it won't be any trouble. Just go to her house, explain who I am, tell her I need her help, and she'll help you out."

"She isn't the offspring of your illegitimate love-child or something?"

"Very funny. Now, come on, help me out."

"I wasn't joking."

Drummond stared at Max's pale face and pointed at him. "You're scared."

"I'm not scared."

"You are."

"I don't care about the witch. You want me to talk to her? Fine, I'll go talk to her. Okay?"

"No, you're scared. Maybe not of the witch, but of something. Me, maybe? You're worried that if you let me loose, I'll start haunting you."

"You already haunt me," Max said, trying to let the sarcasm ease his wounded nerves. "Really, though, I'm not scared. I've just got other things on my mind, that's all."

Drummond clapped his hands. "I see, now. You're scared that I'll just leave. Break the curse and your good pal, Marshall Drummond, the detective, will vanish forever."

"You highly overestimate yourself."

"I think you underestimate how dead-on I can be. Go see the witch, Max. And stop fretting. I'm not going away. Even if I didn't want revenge, I'd stick around. This is just too much fun."

Max tried to look away from Drummond, but the ghost kept floating before him. Drummond's eyes pleaded and smiled and harbored hope. Worse, Drummond was right. Max feared being alone in all of this. *But what right do I have to keep this man imprisoned?*

"Okay," he said.

Drummond put his arms out wide. "If I could, I'd hug you right now. Thank you. I promise I'll stick around. You've got my word as a detective and a ghost."

"Just tell me her name."

"Ashley Connor. You go see her tonight."

"Tonight?"

"Come now, my new partner, you're not going to make me stay stuck like this another whole day, are you?"

Like an old cop faced with yet another petty crime, Max donned his coat and said, "Fine, fine. Just give me the address."

Chapter 10

SITTING IN HIS CAR, staring at the two-story office building amongst many clones in the office park, Max shuddered. Across the street, somber brown signs with white lettering pointed to the dwellings of lawyers and dentists. An auto insurance salesmen used the bottom floor of the tan building Max had parked in front of, and just a few blocks over was Hanes Mall and the endless rows of chain stores built up around the shopping Mecca. In this little, tan building, if Drummond had told the truth, Max would find a witch — not somebody playing at being one with nature or hoping to pull off a few sparkly magic tricks, but an authentic witch. He shuddered again.

His mind kept dragging him back in time to the life of an eleven-year-old stuck in an apartment while the Michigan snows piled ever higher on the ground. School had been closed for two days and though Max's father risked his life to escape to work, his mother had been just as stuck as Max. At first, she attempted to entertain him, but he acted so moody that she left him alone most of the time. They would, however, sit together in front of the television for lunch — sipping soup and munching on grilled-cheese sandwiches. Max loved that tiny half-hour — the only minutes of the day his mother did not flit around the house cleaning, organizing, rearranging like a nervous animal convinced a predator lay in wait should anything be out of place.

The strangeness of the memory crept under his skin, jangling his nerves to a higher degree than his fear already had achieved. For now, that predator was a witch. A witch? How can this really be a witch? He never believed in such things. *Until last week, I never believed in ghosts, either.*

From his wallet, Max produced a picture of Sandra. He gave it a kiss and said, "I wish I could tell you all this, but even if you believed me, and I know you'd believe me, I don't want you getting caught up in it."

He could hear her arguing back, saying that they were supposed to be a team, that the whole purpose of marriage was to form that team, and that he could never protect her from bad things by keeping her ignorant of them. "I know," he said to the picture as he placed it back in his wallet.

Max clapped his hands in a way that reminded him too much of Drummond, and he got out of the car. Everything looked cold — the empty parking spaces, the quiet night air, the pale parking lot lights. Even the simple, brown door carried a weight of threat.

Inside, he found a waiting room — one sofa, two chairs, boring coffee table with assorted magazines, jazz playing quietly from ceiling speakers, a few live plants dotting the corners, and framed photographs of deer and elk hung on the walls. A woman behind a counter like that in a doctor's office smiled at him and said, "Evening. How are ya?"

"I'm sorry. I think I'm at the wrong place."

"This is Dr. Ashley Connor's office," the woman said.

"Doctor?"

The woman kept her smile strong, but Max saw doubt entering her eyes. "Yes," she said, "Dr. Connor is an ophthalmologist."

"Oh, then I'm at the right place, I guess. Sorry for the confusion. I've got a lot of doctor appointments this week. Trying to catch up on the backlog," he said, hoping to sound convincing.

"Are you Mr. Porter?"

"Yes?"

"She's got you down for a nine o'clock appointment."

"She does?"

"Yes, dear. Nine o'clock."

"Isn't it a bit late?"

"Certain appointments are considered of the highest priority."

"I see," he said, knowing he would regret asking the next question. "Except I didn't make an appointment. I was wondering how —"

"Everybody does. Now, if you'll just fill out this paperwork, we'll get you back there as soon as possible. Thank you."

Max took the clipboard the woman offered and sat on the leather sofa feeling like he just stepped out of a boxing ring after being pummeled in the head for ten rounds. How could she have written in an appointment when he hadn't even decided to go ahead with this until he left the car? How did she even know his name? Confusion painted every motion he made, but he pushed on despite his desire to run. He hated to admit it, but the more he thought over the possibilities, the more he agreed with Drummond — he needed the detective's help.

Fifteen minutes later, the receptionist sent him back to Room #4 where he found the traditional mechanical chair — several metal arms poked out of the side, each ending in a different tool. A hefty, attractive woman swept into the room and said with a thick Southern accent, "Good evening, Mr. Porter. I'm Julie."

"Good evening."

"You're new here. Where you from?"

"Michigan."

"Oh, that's much too cold for me," she said, as she turned down the lights and covered one of his eyes. With pleasant, pointless conversation, Julie tested Max's vision and finished by putting dilating drops into his eyes. "Dr. Connor will be in here in just a few minutes once those drops have a chance to work."

"Do you always stay open this late?"

"Only when we have special appointments, but then that happens a lot. Dr. Connor is very much in demand. It's a pleasure meeting you," Julie said and whisked out the door.

Max waited. Time crawled.

This is a stupid idea, he thought. Just taking the smallest step back and examining his recent circumstances, Max would have to admit that everything appeared crazy and dangerous. If he told anybody he was at the eye doctor waiting to talk to a witch about freeing a ghost so he could protect himself and his wife from an obsessive real estate developer — heck, just stating it in his head made him want to be committed.

As the impulse to leave gained enough momentum to raise Max from his chair, the door opened and in walked Dr. Ashley Connor. She was younger than Max, looked to be straight out of school, and her features reminded Max why college had been such a wonderful experience. Often when confronted with a beautiful woman, Max would half-jokingly say to himself, "Remember, you're married." This time, however, he found his mind altering the mantra to "Remember, she's a witch."

"Hello, Mr. Porter," Dr. Connor said as the light scent of rosemary perfume drifted toward Max. She closed the door and turned on the lights. Max winced — his dilated eyes unable to see her well in the brightness. The blurry image took him by the hand and headed toward the backend of the room. "Do I understand correctly that you wish to see me not as a doctor, but in a different capacity?"

"That's right," Max said, shading his eyes with one free hand. "I want to discuss an old friend of your grandmother."

"Just wait, please. We'll get to it all."

Dr. Connor opened a door Max had not noticed earlier and escorted him through a brightly lit passage to a round room covered in items. Max squinted, trying to see what the things hanging on the walls and stacked on the floor might be, but everything was a blurry confusion. Dr. Connor placed him by a stool, asked him to sit, and settled on another stool just far enough away that he only saw the fuzzy outline of her shape.

"This is about Marshall Drummond," she said.

"How did you know that?" Max asked. "And how did you know I was going to be here today?"

Dr. Connor leaned forward and whispered, "Because I'm the real thing, Mr. Porter."

"Then I guess I don't need to bother telling you the problem, and you can just give me whatever I need to help Drummond get free."

Though Max could not make out the doctor's face, he had no doubt she wore a broad smirk. She said, "You don't really think this would be that easy, do you? I'm a witch, after all. I don't just give things away. You have to pay for them."

"Something tells me we're not talking about money."

"Now you're starting to think. I make plenty of money as an eye doctor, and it keeps the IRS off my back. But the witch business — there never seems to be an end to people calling for these talents."

"So, what exactly —"

With a swift stroke, Dr. Connor cut the back of Max's hand. Before he had time to do more than jump a little, she scraped something across the wound and settled back as if nothing had happened. "That will do for a start," she said.

"What did you do to me?"

"Nothing bad. Not yet. Just a little insurance. After all, your kind have a long history of poorly treating my kind. So I now have a small sample of your blood. If you ever attempt to hurt me, there's a lot I can do to you with just a few drops."

"Don't you dare threaten me," Max said as sweat trembled out of his body. He tried to keep a brave outward appearance, tried to think of cool Drummond on a case facing some thugs, and it helped a bit.

Dr. Connor walked behind Max and stroked his hair. She then

plucked out a few strands. "No threats. Just insurance."

"Fine. You've got your insurance. So, how do I get Drummond out of that office?"

"We're not there yet."

Max swallowed back his anger and unclenched his jaw. "I am not going to play games."

"It's all games. You can't even see five feet in front of you. You have no concept of who it is you're fighting against or what they're capable of. Because of your dear wife —"

"You stay away from her."

"— you're in a highly vulnerable position. You have high debt and the only money you're receiving is from a man you don't even know, let alone trust. It may just be my opinion, but I think you'd be best off to do whatever I say."

Though he hated hearing his weaknesses pointed out, he had to admit their validity. Even without the eye drops, he had been traipsing through his days blind and ignorant. He felt like the tail of a kite being whipped around in a heavy wind, unable to know what direction events would lead, just hanging on tight.

But it doesn't have to be this way. Drummond could help him get ahead for a change.

"Fine," he said. "What do we do next?"

"Next, you take off your clothes and make love to me."

"What?"

"Just kidding. Though I should tell you I don't care about marriage as an institution. If you ever feel like a little variety, I'd be interested."

Dr. Connor sat again, this time holding a book in her lap. "Let's see now," she said, and her tone told Max that this was going to go on for awhile longer. A loud buzz interrupted his thoughts and Dr. Connor scowled — at least, Max thought she scowled.

She walked to her wall and pushed a button. "What is it?"

"Mrs. Seaton is here."

"Thank you," she said, took a breath and sauntered back to her seat. "Okay, Mr. Porter, you might be having some luck tonight. Seems I'm a bit crunched for time. Everybody needs the help of a strong witch. Your friend, Drummond, has been put under a fairly simple binding curse. The markings used to keep him in one place have to be locked into a book or a scroll or something similar by copying the image on your floor into whatever item was chosen. To break the curse, you need to get ahold of the item, bring it to your office, and destroy it in the center of the floor marking. Understand?"

"I got it. Except how do we know where this copy is?"

"You just ask me."

"Okay, I'm asking. What do I need and where is it?"

"You go back to work now," Dr. Connor said with odd precision. "Please inform Mr. Drummond that when he is ready to talk with me, then I will gladly share with him the information you require."

"Wait a second."

"Good-bye, now," she said and placed her hand on his head.

When Max opened his eyes, he was alone and in his car. His head throbbed. His muscles tightened as a rage built, but he clamped it down — no use getting angry just yet. He couldn't go back to the office, though. The idea of talking with Drummond ticked him off too much. He'd end up saying something he would no doubt regret. Instead, he drove home.

Chapter 11

"YOU HAD ME WORRIED," Sandra said as she refilled Max's coffee mug. "I can't even think of a time you've been out so late before. Maybe in college. And when you got home, you just crashed."

Max's head pounded as if he had drunk whiskey all night. The coffee perked him up a little, but his dry mouth and aching bones made him want to crawl back to bed.

"You better get out of those clothes," Sandra said.

"Sorry," he mumbled.

"It's okay. It's just that with everything that's happened, I was really worried. I'm just glad you're okay."

"I should've called," Max said as he slipped off his clothes and hunted for something clean to wear. "It all came down real quick. I'm sorry."

"I said it was okay."

"Thanks for the coffee."

"No problem." She stopped at the bedroom door. Before she spoke, Max's heart quickened — it knew what she would ask next, and it feared the question. "What exactly were you doing last night?"

He could hear the tenseness, the worry, the battle between the need to be comforted that all was well in their relationship and the terror that things might be as she suspected. A little assurance was all she sought. However, that required Max to tell her not to worry, that all was well — to lie. He couldn't tell her that he had been to see a witch. Would she even believe him? And offering anything simply to acknowledge that he wasn't having an affair would bring up further questions.

"Just work," he said, hearing his shallow lie.

"Oh," she said, that one utterance carrying far more disturbing depths.

"I have to go," he said, rushing downstairs, ignoring the pain in his body, and wishing he could do something to protect Sandra from her false belief.

By the time he reached his office, his horrible mood soured more. Taylor did his best to make matters worse. He offered an exuberant greeting and a cup of coffee. The coffee smelled delicious but Max had no intention of giving the boy any form of encouragement. He took the coffee, grunted, and plopped down at his desk. Before he could finish the first, sweet sip, Drummond appeared — cranky, as usual.

"Oh, the King finally decides to show up," Drummond said, kicking the furniture and acting as if he were destroying it instead have passing right through. "I cannot believe you care so little that you would keep me stuck here all night and tortured by this bastard kid all morning. I swear I've got it in me not to help you at all. Then where'd you be? Huh? You'd be a dead man. Your wife, too."

Max put the coffee cup down too hard and Taylor glanced up from paper sorting on the floor. "Everything okay, sir?"

"Fine," Max said.

"Not fine," Drummond went on. "Not fine, not one iota. Get me out of here, Max. Send this cretin packing and get me free."

Max crossed his arms and leaned back in his chair. With a shocked gasp, Drummond said, "This a joke? You won't help me? For crying out loud, I'm sorry. Okay? I'm just anxious. Please, pull out your phone, so we can have a conversation."

The slim line of Max's mouth curled just a bit. Listening to Drummond whine had brightened his morning, and despite the pounding in his head, the aches in his muscles, or even the consistent pressure mounting on all sides, Max found the discomfort of a ghost amusing. However, the longer Drummond persisted, the more Max saw the play as cruel rather than simple teasing. "Taylor," he said. "I've got a terrible headache. Do me a favor, please, and get me some ibuprofen or something."

"Sure, sir," Taylor said and stepped into the bathroom. "I don't see nothing here. Where else would you have them?"

Snapping his fingers, Max said, "Oh, that's right, I must be all out. Will you please go downstairs and get me some? There's a convenience store on the street. I'm sure you'll find something in there."

Taylor hesitated. The tug-o-war between this request and the overriding rules set out by their mutual employer battled on his face. Max sensed that Taylor was going to refuse, so he added, "Taylor, this is not a test. You're doing a fine job, okay? It'll only take you a minute, and I promise I won't tell on you. I just really need to get rid of this headache."

"Oh, okay."

When Taylor left the office, Drummond clapped his hands. "Well, done. You're starting to get the knack of some of this job. A few days ago, you'd never have pulled of such an easy lie like that."

"I'm not lying. That witch of yours gave me a horrible headache."

"You saw her, then. Great! What did she say? What do we have to do?"

Max got out his laptop and powered up. "Taylor'll be back pretty fast and we can't have a non-stop phone conversation while he's here."

"That's true. You're not that great a liar, yet."

"But I can type out my answers here," he said, pointing to the laptop.

"Fine, fine. Now before that dimwit gets back, what did the witch say?"

"She said that you're under a binding spell."

"Gee, really? I could have told you that."

"Then why didn't you? From what Connor said, I gather you know a lot about witches and voodoo and all that nonsense. Why not just tell me what you need instead of sending me off into the night like that?"

Drummond stepped closer to Max like a father trying to explain the hard choices of parenting. "I'm sorry about that, but I didn't think you'd believe me otherwise. Even though you've handled this whole ghost business very well, and I'm proud of you about that — heck, most people would've packed up and moved home already — but now we're getting into something a little harder to swallow. Ghosts is one thing. Everybody has a haunting story in their lives — friends, family, or personal experience. There's enough evidence out there to bring in enough doubt that you can accept such a thing when it's in front of your eyes. But witches? Magic spells? That's a whole lot harder to accept."

"I suppose. I'm just sick of being everybody's pawn."

"Help me get free from this binding spell and I promise you, I'll do all I can to get you in a better position."

Taylor walked in carrying a paper bag. His eyes burst out at the sight of the laptop. "You-You-You can't do that in here. Please, Mr. Porter, put that away."

"Just give me the bag," Max said, his headache winding up again at the sight of relief.

As Taylor handed over the bag, he said, "You know you're not allowed to use that laptop in here. Please put it away. I promise I won't tell."

Max popped two capsules in his mouth and swallowed them dry. "No," he said, savoring the moment of defiance. "You can tell Modesto or whoever you want. Go ahead. Tell him I don't care about his stupid rules anymore."

Drummond nodded his approval. "You tell him."

With his face tightening, Taylor said in an odd and unnerving quiet, "Okay. If that's what you want. I'll just be over here." He walked to the wall opposite the bookshelf and sat on the floor.

Drummond laughed. "That's one troubled kid. Forget about him, Max. He'll be fine. Now, tell me what we've got to do. See there are lots of binding spells and I don't know this one at all. If I did, I wouldn't be stuck here still."

Max's attention lingered on Taylor. However, Drummond was right. There were more important things at hand. Max pulled the laptop closer, opened his word processor, and typed: CONNOR SAID THE MARKINGS ON THE FLOOR HAD TO BE COPIED IN A BOOK OR SCROLL OR SOMETHING.

"It was a book. I remember that."

WE HAVE TO FIND THAT BOOK AND DESTROY IT HERE.

"Okay. Does she have any idea where to find it?"

SHE MIGHT.

"But she wouldn't tell you, would she?"

SHE WANTS TO SPEAK WITH YOU.

"Crap."

WHAT HAPPENED? WHAT DID YOU DO TO HER?

"Nothing. Not to her, at least."

WHAT DOES THAT MEAN?

"There's got to be another way."

JUST TELL ME.

"I don't want to go into it. You need to find some other way. There's got to be."

The laptop beeped the arrival of an e-mail. Max opened the program and read the e-mail twice. ARE YOU READING THIS?

"Yeah," Drummond said. "Looks like Annabelle got all her stock as a gift."

LOOK HERE. IT WENT THROUGH FOUR DIFFERENT COMPANY NAMES BEFORE IT REACHES HER.

"We need to find out who owns those companies."

SOMETHING TELLS ME THE NAME HULL MIGHT COME UP.

"Congratulations. You've experienced your first hunch. Now do your book thing you're so good at and let's get some answers."

WHAT ABOUT YOU?

Drummond passed through one of Taylor's paper stacks and watched it fall over. "We'll do the best we can until you figure out another way to break this spell or where that book might be."

Taylor jumped to his feet and said in that same odd tone he had used before, "Gee, sir, I'm so sorry. I forgot to tell you that Mr. Modesto wanted to have breakfast with you at 10:30. I believe he said at Cities. I guess you'll be late."

"That little prick," Drummond said. Max closed his laptop and glared at Taylor. "Keep it cool, Max. We've got a lot of information on our side. Just go meet with Modesto and make him think we don't know anything."

Max nodded, grinned, and with as much control as he could manage, he said, "That's okay, Taylor. Mistakes happen. Please be more mindful of my appointments in the future. You wouldn't want me to be late again. Mr. Modesto might ask for an explanation."

Without a further glance in Taylor's direction, Max grabbed his laptop and left the office.

Chapter 12

WHEN MAX ARRIVED AT CITIES, a restaurant not too far from Dr. Connor's office, Mr. Modesto had ordered for them both and offered a curt nod. He snapped his fingers toward the chair opposite him and waited for Max to sit. Though the gesture (too close to being treated like a dog) boiled in Max's heart, he remained quiet and did as commanded.

"I do not appreciate being kept waiting," Modesto said as he typed out a text message on his phone.

"I'm sorry. My new assistant made a mistake."

"So quick to blame others."

"No blame, just a mistake."

"Of course. In other matters, I trust you are settling in fine since I've not heard otherwise. Our employer wishes you to be as comfortable as possible. Also ..."

Modesto droned on, but Max only half-heard anything the man said. The briefcase stole Max's attention. He noticed it when he had arrived, leaning against the legs of Modesto's chair as if it could feel casual and relaxed. Inside, Max suspected, would be much of the information he wanted. It had to be there. Modesto handled Max for Hull which meant that Modesto would have all the papers pertaining to Max. Even if his hopes were misplaced and the briefcase did not contain crucial information, it still had to have something of use. All Max had to do was wait until the end of the meal when Modesto would to go to the bathroom like always.

"... Moravian government proved quite interesting," Modesto went on. "In fact, you've helped us fill in a few blanks we ..."

Even if Modesto went to the bathroom, could Max do it? He stared at that briefcase, trying to hold down the nerves bucking to get out, trying to keep his mind focused. If he got caught, if Modesto returned early — but no, he couldn't think in those terms. In order to rifle through that briefcase, Max forced himself to ignore all other concerns — one languishing moment of fear would stop him from doing what he now believed to be imperative.

"Excuse me a moment," Modesto said and left for the restrooms.

Just like that, Max's opportunity landed. He made no motions at first, caught unprepared. How long had he sat at that table while Modesto prattled away for them to reach this point in the meal? If not for the clicking of forks on plates, Max would have remained frozen until Modesto returned; however, he did hear that sound and it brought to mind a ticking clock.

Swallowing any guilt, Max slid the briefcase toward his chair (it was heavier than it appeared) and pulled a handful of papers out. The top ones carried the Hull corporation header and had been addressed to Modesto. A cursory glance showed they were daily orders with reference to "reports" made by his assistant. No surprises there.

The next was a letter dated the day before and read:

> Mr. Modesto —
> Your recent account of Max Porter's activities, particularly his unforeseen visit to Dr. Connor, requires an acceleration of our timetable. While it would have been preferable to wait for Mr. Porter to conclude on his own that the location of Old Salem was most profitable to our interests, we can no longer afford such patience. Therefore, we ask that you steer him toward that locale.

Max re-read the letter, all the time feeling as if a hidden psychopath stalked his every move. He wanted to rush home and search for bugs, wire-taps, or whatever high-tech surveillance equipment he could find — not that he had a clue how to look for such things, but he could not idle on the idea that he was being watched. He considered reading the letter a third time but instead he pushed the papers back into the briefcase. Modesto would be returning any second. As Max attempted to get the papers to look untouched, the name *Drummond* flashed from one page, and Max turned his head to read it clearer. Laughter from another table brought him to his senses, yet even as he used his foot to slide the briefcase back into position, he caught the words *Broughton* and *Kirksbride Plan*.

"That's really all we have to discuss today," Modesto said as he stepped toward the table. Max put on his best attitude of nonchalance as Modesto lifted his briefcase onto the table and began looking through it. The paper with Drummond's name on it stuck a little higher than the others, and Max felt sure Modesto had seen it. However, the man did nothing but take out a hundred dollar bill and hand it to the waitress.

"I'll be leaving, now," Modesto said. Then, as if just recalling a little, unimportant thought, he added, "By the way, our employer feels you have proven yourself well. Your historical research was adequate and the initial land deals researched was fine. You have enough background to start seeking out the properties we may wish to acquire."

"Okay, great."

"Articulate as ever, I see. Regardless, you'll find it easiest to begin in the historic areas as they have some of the oldest land which I know to be of high value."

"The historic areas," Max said, hoping the sourness he heard in his voice could not be detected by Modesto. "Any suggestions?"

"If I knew the best way to handle this, your services would not be required, would they? But, if I must hazard my opinion on the matter, then I'd suggest considering Old Salem. It's the closest in the area. There are others as well, but I suppose that's a good place to start."

"Old Salem? I'll be sure to look into it."

"I'll let our employer know. I must go now."

Max sat alone for several minutes, listening to the restaurant bustle around him and waiting for his heart to stop racing. When he reached the point that he felt he could stand without an embarrassing stumble, he left the building and settled in his car. Again, he waited awhile, just letting the world slow down around him.

When he finally headed onto the road, his mind juggled one idea after another, trying to make sense of all the insanity that had occurred since his arrival in North Carolina. None of it added up to his liking (though he did admit that some things were coming together). The thought that hit him at least once each day now blared into his brain — *I should grab Sandra, sell the house, and leave this town.* But he knew he would not do it. First — Sandra loved it here, and he refused to ruin it for her like he had in Michigan. Second, and far more important if he was honest with himself — he wanted to solve these mysteries. A sliver inside him understood what drove men like Drummond, what drove many to read about men like Drummond, and what drove even more to watch television shows about men like Drummond. The puzzles had to have answers, and even though his life careened onward like a drunk driver passed out at the wheel, the puzzles could be solved. That's the allure. Solving the mystery gave him a little control in this world.

As he slowed down to pass a parked police car, he decided to put everything into some order. He had a lot of research to do: Old Salem, Hull, and now Broughton and Kirksbride. That alone could take days. The letter in Modesto's briefcase made it certain that Hull, Drummond, and this missing book to break the curse were all related, so his level of thoroughness would have to be extreme. However, his mind gravitated toward Annabelle Bowman.

Hers was the oddity in all this. What about her and her husband, Stan, connected to Drummond and Hull? Drummond said his investigation into Stan Bowman led to Hull. Maybe so. But how and why? Annabelle received a gift of R. J. Reynolds stock via dummy corporations that lead back to Hull. This stock made her millions. Why? What did Hull seek to buy with this money?

"Okay," Max said out loud. "The truth is I'm sick of the library." Research was one thing. Research trying to save your butt was another — a far more stressful way to work.

When his cell phone chirped, Max jumped. He growled at the car, and with shaking hands, he pulled to the roadside before he answered the phone. "Hello," he said, all civility absent.

"Mr. Porter?" a muffled voice asked, but it had a clear Southern drawl.

Max's nerves tightened even more. "Yes?"

"Please start driving your car."

Any threatening message, any bullying tone, would have angered Max, but he would have managed. This, however, churned his stomach. With as nonchalant a maneuver as he could muster, Max tried to look around the area for a spy.

"Please, Mr. Porter," the voice said. "If you want the truth about Stan Bowman, pull onto the road."

Unsure what to do, Max did as ordered. "Who are you?"

"Take Route 40 East to Durham, then take 85 North."

"Durham? That's almost two hours from here."

"From 85 North, get off on Exit 189 for Butner. You understand?"

"Who is this?"

"Do you understand?"

Max repeated the directions.

"That's correct," the voice said and hung up.

Two hours provided Max with plenty of time to think and to worry. Even as the miles droned on and his conscience told him he was crazy to follow these directions blindly, his desire to get some bit of information overwhelmed all other concerns. He banished the idea that he might be in physical danger. Deep inside, he knew that to be true, but to give voice to such fears would only undermine his determination.

He thought about calling Sandra but decided against it. He didn't want to risk missing a call from his informant. *Informant?* Yes, the word fit. After all, the man had contacted him with a promise of "the truth about Stan Bowman."

When his cell phone rang, Max answered it before it finished its first chirp. "Hello?"

"When you come off the exit ramp, you'll see a red pickup truck. Follow it."

As instructed, Max took the exit for Butner and found a red, Toyota pickup waiting. It pulled onto the road and turned west. Max followed.

They headed into a rural area, taking enough turns that Max felt lost. At length, the pickup headed onto a dirt road, drove another mile, and pulled over. Max parked behind the truck and waited.

The truck's door opened and a gray-haired man stepped out. He wore a simple outfit of slacks, an off-white shirt, and black suspenders. A slight bend and a grisly white beard added to his soft image. Any fears Max harbored vanished.

The old man waved to Max and pointed toward the hill across the road. Then he walked in that direction, shuffling his feet in slow but steady steps. Max got out of his car, stretched, and followed.

"Mr. Porter," the man said, offering his hand and a shining smile. "I apologize for the cloak-and-dagger bit. I can get a little paranoid. Then again, when you're dealing with the Hull family, a little paranoia ain't such a bad thing. Oh, sorry, my name's Phillip King."

"Pleasure to meet you."

King chuckled. "You sound awful wary. That's good. You should be. This is wary business."

"I don't mean to be rude, Mr. King, but this has turned into a long day already. You said you have information about Stan Bowman. For that matter, how'd you even know I was interested? Who are you?"

"Calm down," King said, and Max took a deep breath — he had not been aware of raising his voice and clenching his fists. "Now, let's see. I know about you because you upset Annabelle Bowman, and while

Winston-Salem has become a decent-sized city, many parts of it are still very small town. Word gets around. Especially about old sore spots like Stan. As for me, well I used to work for Reynolds Tobacco. In fact, I worked in the factory where the POWs worked, where Stan Bowman took seven of them and turned them into nutcases."

"You were there?"

"I know all about it."

"Then I'm very interested," Max said, staring at the open grass dotted with sparse trees. "Was it really necessary to come all the way out here?"

"It starts here. This field was where the POW camp was. One of eighteen in North Carolina. There was even one in the Winston-Salem area, but those fellas that Stan went after, they came from here."

"Can I write this down?" Max asked, itching to run back to his car and grab a notebook.

"You just listen. You'll remember enough."

"I wouldn't show anybody. I promise."

"No, Mr. Porter. We're going to do this my way."

"Okay. Your way."

"Now, it's like this: I first met Stan Bowman in 1944. He came back from the War with a bullet in his leg — made the thing near-useless. They gave him a medal, too. I hadn't been able to go because I couldn't pass the physical. I've got a bad hip. So, I'll admit I was jealous of him. I could see the way the ladies gave him an extra few seconds with their eyes, the way they seemed ready to break all their vows just for a night with an acknowledged hero or something like that. Point is, I was jealous, and so I took it upon myself to befriend the man. I suppose I thought that by being close to him, I might get something of what he had, but that's an old man talking. Truth is, at the time, I just did what I did. Didn't give it that much thought.

"Stan took a job driving trucks, so I saw him every week when he hauled tobacco in from the farms for processing. It was hard work for everybody but Reynolds took good care of us. Heck, we'd all have been without jobs if it weren't for him. The entire town of Winston-Salem owes that family their lives.

"Anyway, we'd go out every night with a handful of girls and a lot of beer. Every night. It was exhausting fun," King said, blushing and laughing at the same time. "Went on like that for quite awhile. Maybe even a month, though I'm probably bragging. Still, it seemed that long. Until he met Annabelle and the parties stopped.

"The day comes we get word that a bunch of German POWs were coming. Reynolds had finagled a deal to get free labor from them, and the government hoped if we treated them well, the Germans would treat our boys that were prisoners well, too. There were some awful stories coming back but nothing like what we'd eventually find out. By that time, Stan and Annabelle were full on in love and talking about marriage. I suppose it would have happened all like a fairy tale for them if Hull hadn't shown up."

"You met Hull?"

"Yup, I met him. William Hull. His boy Terrance probably runs the whole thing now. If not, he will someday soon, but back then, William strutted around like he was the greatest man in the world. I don't think Reynolds liked him too much. At least, that was the gossip."

"When did you meet him? What happened?"

"I'm getting there. Just let me tell you. Now, I only met the man once. Reynolds was showing him the factory, answering questions about POWs and all that. I suppose Hull was thinking about making his own deal with the government. Reynolds called me over and introduced me. I ain't nothing special, don't mistake me. Reynolds called me over so Hull could hear what it was like from the common man. Could've been anybody but he called over me.

"Hull was a tall fellow with the sternest face I'd ever seen. I mean this man stared down at me like I was a threat to his family and he was prepared to kill me with his bare hands if it came to it. I'm not exaggerating. He shook my hand and stared at me and I'll tell you, I was a bit scared. Never had that happen before or since — that I got scared just from the look in a man's eyes. It was odd, but not nearly as odd as what happened next."

"Wait a minute," Max said, closing his eyes and painting an image of this moment in his head. He knew he would never remember all the details but hoped that a simple snapshot in his brain might help out more than trying to recall King's every word. With a nod, he said, "Okay, what happened next that was so odd?"

"Reynolds calls up some of the POWs and has them line up in front of Hull. Hull paces up and down the line like he's Patton or something. He looked more like a fool than anything else but I just worked steady and peeked at the goings on from the corner of my eye. Now, here's the odd part.

"On his second pass, he's coming in my direction so I can see his hard face clear as day, and he hesitates for the tiniest moment and I swear his face dropped. I mean, he recognized one of them POWs. I have no doubt in my mind about it. That little pause lasted a long time in my mind and I know what I saw. I'm not saying Hull was in cahoots with the Germans, but he certainly knew something about that one in particular."

King stopped speaking and looked upon the empty field that once housed the enemies of the United States with his eyes sparkling in satisfaction. He stood straighter, and Max recognized a man lifted of his burden. For Max, though, the burdens continued to pile on and many could not be seen. Every one of King's freeing breaths inflated disbelief in Max.

"That's it?" Max said. "You brought me all the way out here to tell me that Hull might have, maybe, possibly, known a Nazi or two?"

With a patronizing pat on the shoulder, King said, "You're not listening too well. Hull, who never before and never after, steps foot into our factory, sees a prisoner who he is, in some way, knowledgeable of, and then just a few days later, Stan Bowman, a man who has plenty of good going for him, a stable man with a beautiful woman at his side — well, he goes crazy and kidnaps seven of these prisoners. That seems like a big coincidence to me. Not enough for you? The reason I brought you here is because all seven of those men — one of which was the man I saw Hull recognize — all seven of them came from this camp here in Butner. All the rest of the prisoners who labored in our factory came from the Winston-Salem camp. But these seven are driven hours out of the way to come work at a place that ultimately leads to their torture and madness. Is that really just a coincidence?"

"There was an investigation," Max said, trying to act more like a detective and not an excited amateur. "Why didn't you bring any of this up back then?"

"You think I was going to go up against a man like Hull? I had a life I was building. I didn't want to throw that away over a bunch of Krauts."

"Then why now? You just old enough that you don't care anymore?"

"A little bit, perhaps. Or perhaps I'm tired of sleepless nights, knowing that I failed to do the right thing. Perhaps I see a young man and his beautiful wife lured down here to become mired way over their heads in an old Southern bog, and I see a chance for a little redemption. Doesn't really matter, though, does it? Not to you. You've got what I know now, and I don't ever want to see you again."

"But why did —"

"No more, Mr. Porter. It's time for you to go," King said and crouched in the grass.

Max did not move at first. Too late, the idea dawned that he should have asked if Hull carried a book. He opened his mouth but said nothing. The old man's determined concentration on the empty hills formed a steel wall against further talk. Max didn't even bother with saying *Thank you.*

Before driving away, he pulled out a pad and pen and jotted down every bit he could recall. Detective work had proven to be more taxing than he had expected. All these threads had to be kept in order so that he remembered the questions at the important times. Already, he could hear Drummond complaining about his missed opportunity regarding the book. At least, he had more on the Bowman case.

With so much time to get through until he reached home, he planned to think about all he had learned. However, his head pounded and he found a soothing jazz station to clear his mind from any thoughts. Miles drifted by without his awareness. As his headache eased away, two loud snaps startled him and the car swerved off the road.

Max wrenched the steering wheel to the left but the car barreled forward. The steering wheel shivered in his hands. Gravel peppered the undercarriage like a snare drum. The backend of the car kept turning, turning, and Max had time to think the car might flip if it turned anymore. He let the wheel roll back in the opposite direction, trying not to fishtail. Braking at the same time as he fought the car, he managed to slow down. At length, he stopped. Sweat stung his eyes and his fingers danced on every surface they touched.

He took several minutes to focus on little more than breathing. Cars passed by with gawking faces peering from inside like caricatures at an amusement park. All of life slowed down until he regained enough sense to move.

He stepped from the car and inspected the front right wheel. Little of it was left. Max did not bother getting the donut from the trunk — he had no doubt in his mind the tiny emergency tire had no air in it. Instead, he called for a tow truck. Before he heard the second ring on the phone, he saw a small hole in the car's frame just above the shredded tire — no rust around the hole, and the metal bent toward the wheel as if something had shoved through from the outside.

"Like a bullet," he whispered, recalling the snaps right before he lost control of the car.

After arranging for the tow truck, and being told to wait inside his car, Max paced around, checking for more bullet holes. Somebody had shot at him, and he didn't know what to feel — it had never happened before. He kicked the car and screamed at the sky and spit on the ground. Huffing and red-faced, he opened the car door and sat facing the road with his head in his hands.

Too late to go back now. Not that he could ever go back to Michigan. The people up there were always good to him, but he knew them well — they would not forget. *Probably true down here, too.* That was the real problem. No matter where he could run, Hull would not leave him alone. Besides, Max agreed with Sandra. The only way beyond this was to go straight through.

"So, where am I?" he said, arching his back and tasting the salty trickles of sweat on his lips. "Okay, the best I can see is that near the end of World War II, R. J. Reynolds makes his POW deal and starts using them in Winston-Salem. For some reason, Hull visits this factory and recognizes seven of them. Why does he want them dead? Does it matter? Anyway, I don't know, but he gets Stan Bowman to do it and then pays off Annabelle with stock to keep her quiet."

Only the whisk of passing cars responded.

It would take another hour-and-a-half before his car had been towed and a new tire installed. A few more hours drive, and Max made it home. The day had ended.

Except for the phone call.

Before Max had removed his coat, the phone rang. He answered it, clamping down on his desire to bark out a few rude remarks, with a simple, "Yes?"

A deep voice said, "Last warning, Porter. Next time we won't be shooting at the tires." The phone went dead.

Max slammed the phone down and tore off his coat. "Fuckers," he spat out. Then he grabbed the phone and punched in a number he knew too well.

"Hello, Mr. Porter," Modesto said.

"What the hell is the matter with you people?" Max said, his voice rising as he stormed around his living room.

"Calm down, please."

"Fuck you. You send your muscle to threaten me and my wife, and now you're shooting at me? I'm doing everything you've asked of me. I'm working as fast as I can."

"Shooting? Somebody shot at you?"

"Don't even start with that crap."

"Mr. Porter, I assure you we are not the cause of this. Now calm down and explain to me what happened."

"You know what happened," Max said, but he doubted himself now. Modesto sounded truly surprised by the call.

"Please, take a moment to think this through. What good could possibly come from our employer attacking you? As you pointed out, you're doing a fine job for us. Why would he spend all this money and effort to bring you down to North Carolina and put you to work, if he simply wanted to kill you? It makes no sense, does it?"

Max flopped onto his couch. "No."

"Now what happened?"

In a few minutes, Max laid out the events of the shooting. He avoided any mention of Phillip King, Butner, Bowman, and World War II POWs. The shooting itself was sensational enough to make omissions easy.

"Thank you," Modesto said. "I think I understand quite clearly now."

"So, what do we do?"

"You just go back to your job. I'll handle this."

"I want to know who did this. I want them to be put behind bars."

"I will find out who is responsible, and you can rest knowing that I will make sure they are taken care of."

Max straightened. "Wait a minute. No, no. I'm not saying I want that. Just get them arrested."

"I don't know what you mean by 'that' but don't worry."

"You know exactly what I mean. Don't kill them," Max said, whispering the last two words.

"Good-bye, Mr. Porter," Modesto said and hung up. Max looked at the phone as if he had no clue how it had managed to get in his hand.

"What was that?" Sandra asked.

Max dropped the phone as he jumped. His eyes darted toward her. "Honey, I didn't mean to wake you up."

Sandra stood in the bedroom doorway, her arms crossed, all sensuousness missing despite her negligee. "Who were you talking to?"

"What? Oh, just Modesto."

"Just? Are you going to tell me that I misunderstood? That you didn't talk to him about killing people? Are you?" Angry as she was, Max could see her desperate hope that he would tell her just that —

she had misunderstood.

"Come here. Sit down."

Tears welled in her eyes. "What's happening here? Please, tell me you didn't ... please."

Max waited for Sandra to sit next to him on the couch. He held her hands, and said, "I was shot at tonight."

"Shot?"

"I'm fine. I was just angry. That's all you heard. And I didn't tell him to kill anybody. I told him *not* to. I just want them caught and put in jail. Honest."

"Honest?"

"You know me. I wouldn't try to kill somebody."

"I know."

"It scares me that you'd think that."

Sandra pulled back. "It scares *you?* What am I supposed to think? You've been acting weird ever since that Drummond stuff started. I know there's a lot of pressure on you, and I know this is a tough situation, but still — you don't even call to say where you are, when you'll be home, or anything. I've barely seen you the last few days. And these people — I mean, your employer is powerful. I think that much is clear. And powerful people can be very persuasive. Power can be very alluring. I worry."

"Honey, look at me. I'm one of the good guys."

As Sandra's tears fell, she wrapped her arms around Max and kissed him. He held her tight, pressing his lips hard against hers, his body acknowledging that they had not made love in far too long. Heat washed between them like water cascading across their limbs. Both struggled for breath but neither let go of the embrace.

Max's kissing moved to Sandra's neck and she let out a soft groan. He pulled back and held her face. "I'm scared," he said. "I want to run away from here but we can't."

"I know," she said, kissing him and unbuttoning his shirt. "I know. I'm scared, too. When you don't call, I worry you might be —"

"I'm here. I'm fine." He pressed his body against hers.

Max kicked off his pants and eased inside Sandra. They both let out moans of pleasure mixed with relief. Then they giggled at their own sounds.

"See," Max said, "we're fine."

Sandra rocked her hips back and forth. "That's because you're the good guy."

"That's right. Very right."

Making love erased the world around them. Max gave in without protest. He felt a bit disoriented when, late in the evening, he sat on the couch flipping through television channels. Sandra's head rested in his lap, her soft snores a gentle reminder of how pleasant life could be when given the opportunity.

Max stopped at Channel 12 local news and listened to tomorrow's forecast (cloudy and sixty-five). The anchor came back on and pictures of four men appeared. Two were tattooed thugs who looked as if a few years in prison would be a vacation. The third man, a crew-cut blonde with a tight face and hateful eyes, looked to be the brains among the four. Either that or he would be playing the girl during his prison stay. The last man, a heavyset man — Max recognized him. Max would never forget him — he could still smell the man's reek as he punched Max in the gut.

Max turned up the volume. "... were arrested today on charges of racketeering following an anonymous tip ..."

He hit the MUTE button and gaped at the television. *An anonymous tip.* Modesto? Could it all be over? And if so, then what does it mean that in a matter of hours, Modesto had managed this? Max felt both filthy and relaxed. He had four men arrested with just a phone call.

"Am I the good guy?" he asked. Sandra's soft snores were his only answer.

Chapter 13

AFTER A BREAKFAST OF EGGS AND TOAST smothered in kisses, cranberry juice with a flash of skin, and a glass of water with dessert upstairs, Max extracted himself from Sandra's arms and drove to his office. Their morning together helped keep him from reviewing the disturbing events of the previous night. As far as he cared to recall, the night was filled with making love. What had led up to it needed no analysis — at least, not for the moment.

"Good morning, Mr. Porter," Taylor said.

Max strode by the young man and powered up his laptop. Drummond poked his head from the bookcase, winked at Max, and floated closer.

"Thought I heard you," he said. "Any developments overnight? Any closer to finding that book?"

Once the laptop was ready, Max typed out a quick detail of his meeting with Phillip King and then being shot at. As Drummond thought, he passed through Taylor several times. Max suspected this to be more malice than accident but grinned nonetheless. Before Drummond could ask again, Max typed I'VE GOT NO INFORMATION ON THE BOOK YET.

"As long as you're trying. I've been stuck here for a long time. What's a few more days?"

ASSUMING I FIND IT.

"You'll find it," Drummond said, his façade of confidence unable to mask his nerves. "Tell me, did you get a name for the POW?"

IT WAS YOUR CASE. DON'T YOU KNOW IT?

"That was over a half-century ago. You expect me to remember every little detail? Check the police report, it should be in there."

Max pulled up the file and skimmed over it.

JOSEPH RICHTER?

"That's one of them. Also Günther something. You need to check on those today."

I WILL. BUT I ALSO NEED YOU TO TELL ME SOMETHING.

"What do you want to know?"

WHY IS YOUR NAME CONNECTED WITH BROUGHTON AND THE KIRKSBRIDE PLAN?

Drummond halted.

I CAN DO THE RESEARCH RIGHT HERE, BUT YOU'LL SAVE ME A LOT OF TIME, Max typed. Drummond said nothing, so Max pulled up his internet browser and searched Broughton. As the listing came up, including the heading WEST CAROLINA INSANE ASYLUM, Drummond said, "Stop that thing. Let me tell you before you get it all twisted up in your head. Just shut it off."

Max closed the browser, and Drummond sighed in relief. "Thank you," Drummond said. "Look, this is nothing like it appears there."

BROUGHTON ISN'T A MENTAL INSTITUTION?

"You know it is. You just saw it. But just hear me out, okay? I'm not crazy. Of all the people I've ever told this to, what I'm going to tell you, I think you might believe me. After all, you're sitting here listening to a ghost."

I'M WAITING.

"Okay, okay. Don't get all snooty with me," Drummond said. After a slight swipe through Taylor's head, he settled in front of Max and said, "Well, at first, I was a cop walking the beat, just getting started. I drank a little but not too much and even back then people said I had a knack for solving tough problems. Everybody thought I'd be a full-fledged detective in no time at all.

"One night, a blistering August night, I was done and on my way home when I heard an odd noise coming from a second-floor window. It had a mournful sound like a kitten crying 'cause its mom had died. I saw right away that it was Ms. Holstein's apartment — nice old lady who spent much of her time knitting by that window. I wasn't on duty anymore that night, but when you're a cop, you're never really off duty — not for a real cop. So, I went up to take a look.

"Before I reached the door, I knew Ms. Holstein was dead. That nasty Death-smell had already begun to seep into the hall. And then that sad sound cried out again. I knocked on the door. Said something stupid like 'Ms. Holstein? Are you okay in there?' but of course, I got no answer. I tried the door and found it unlocked. Now at this point, I should have — I don't know anymore, really. Maybe it all was inevitable."

Max watched Drummond fidgeting and felt the sudden urge to pat the detective's shoulder. He couldn't, of course, but the urge grew anyway. The way Drummond had said *inevitable* struck Max with a sense of recognition — he, too, felt much of what had been happening to him was beyond his control. Perhaps, even though he loathed the idea of destiny, perhaps *inevitable.*

"Well, I went into that apartment," Drummond continued, "and I found Ms. Holstein face down by the window. No blood or signs of struggle. It looked like she just finally died and that was that. Then I heard that crying again. I turned around and standing by the bedroom door was Ms. Holstein — only she was shimmering. I guess I don't have to tell you what I'm talking about, do I?"

"You saw her ghost," Max said.

Taylor startled from his book. "What was that, sir?"

"Nothing. Forget it."

Taylor eyed Max for a moment before returning to his book. Drummond tsked. "That boy really should get another job. Anyway, yeah, I saw her ghost and it scared the hell out of me. I probably looked like an imbecile standing there with my mouth open, but I couldn't move. I just kept thinking that it didn't make any sense. I don't know how long I stood there waiting for something to happen, maybe my own death — I don't really know. Eventually, she vanished but slowly. More like she dissipated. Anyway, she was gone.

"To prove how much of an idiot I was back then, I opened my big mouth and wrote up the whole incident in my report. The week wasn't over before I'd been canned.

"The Depression was on, so losing my job was serious. I was lucky, though — no wife, no kids, nothing but myself to cost me a dime. So I rented out this office and became a private detective. The landlord knew I was using it as an apartment as well, but he was a good man and I paid my rent which was more than many people did, so he let me stay."

Drummond took in the little office with a reminiscent gleam. "Anyway," he said, "I did a few jobs here and there, just enough to keep me afloat, but I couldn't stop thinking about that ghost. So one night after I had a whiskey or two too many, I went back to that old place. Nobody had moved in — or at least, nobody had stayed long. I walked inside being cautious and sure that nothing would happen, but there she was standing by the door as if no time had gone since she last saw me. This time she pointed to the wall. It took me forever to move my body, but in the end, I found what she wanted. Hidden in the wall was a box full of cash and a note that she had saved it for her niece. I delivered the cash, almost two hundred dollars, and before you even ask, the answer is no, I didn't take a nickel. Heck, I didn't dare. And that was it for the ghost. She was gone.

"I'll tell you something. If it had ended there, I would've been happier than if I had been Marilyn Monroe's pillow. But a few weeks later, in walks this gorgeous dame, says she needs some help with a delicate situation. I'm thinking it's adultery but it turns out something else entirely. She says she's a witch and she's ticked off some evil spirits. I wanted to think she'd lost it, but I knew about ghosts now, why not witches? And before you ask, yes, she was Connor's grandmother. After that case, word spread that I was the go-to-guy for the weird and spooky. Four cases later and I started looking for a 'special' kind of vacation. When I found out about the whole Kirksbride thing, I checked myself into the asylum."

WHAT'S KIRKSBRIDE? Max typed.

"Well, you know, asylums weren't the nicest places to be, even back then. It wasn't the dark ages or anything, and it certainly wasn't England, but it was an ugly business. Except this Kirksbride character. He had this idea of making a peaceful, open place where one could rest his mind and deal with his troubles. It wasn't a prison guarded by sadists. They offered real help. And by that point, after all the things I'd seen, I was close to losing my mind. I was desperate for help. And that's that. Now you know why I was there. This is a bizarre world we live in, and I just needed a little help in finding a way to cope with it."

BUT THE ASYLUM DOCTORS DIDN'T BELIEVE YOU, DID THEY?

"Of course not. But that didn't matter. Being there, seeing people who had truly lost their minds, helped put everything in perspective. I mean that's a big part of handling life. You have to maintain perspective. You have to realize that all the decisions you make don't really add up to all that much. You're not going to stop the Earth from moving or the Sun from burning. So just relax."

Drummond made it sound simple, but Max did not subscribe to the notion with ease. For him, echoes of the previous night bounced in his head. How could he "just relax" when people had shot at him, when a move to the South to fix his troubled life had only made it worse, or when his own actions may have sent men to prison? Granted, they belonged in prison, but nothing he could reason made him feel any better because in the end, it didn't matter that the thugs were in jail. They were just hired hands. Whoever wanted to hurt Max was still out there.

The rest of the day, Max buried himself in research. He stole his WiFi access from somebody nearby so he wouldn't have to leave the office. Twice Taylor asked if Max would be going out, and twice Taylor fumbled his reaction when Max said he would be staying in.

The research did not go well. He found out the basics about Old Salem — the historic area that comprised some of Salem's original buildings and had now become an attraction with actors portraying the city's early settlers. Before long, however, he scoured the local newspaper websites for reports on the arrests. Upon locating two articles, he read them several times. Except for one bit of information, the articles had little to say. That one bit, though, made up for a lot: the names of the four men — Wilson McCoy, Edward Moore, Chad Barrows, and Cole Eckerd.

The names settled around Max's head like taunting devils — one on each shoulder, one at each ear. These little pieces of evil did not try to tempt him, however. Instead, they threatened him and Sandra over and over. He could hear them saying he should back away before something bad happened.

By the time Taylor gave a weak good-bye and left with his head hanging and his hands stuffed in his pockets, Max had not thought of anything else but those men for hours. The sun had set. Drummond watched Taylor leave and then clapped his hands. "Okay, now we can get to work," he said, settling in the chair opposite Max.

"And do what? Get my house blown up?"

"Look, fella, I'm not thrilled to hear you're seeing the ugly side of this business but that doesn't change a damn thing. You get shot at sometimes. You learn to live with it."

"I don't want to live with it."

Drummond laced his hands behind his head. "Then go."

Max didn't bother with an answer. He delved into more online research and ignored the impatient ghost mulling about the office. He found an article about the POWs that had one interesting point — several politicians were suspected of taking bribes because of the unnecessary and unwanted seven POWs from Butner. No names, though. No pictures.

About an hour later, a man with white hair ringing a bald head knocked on the door. "Come in," Max said and gestured to the chair.

The man stepped in, his eyes surveying the office, and with an astounded smile, he said, "Nothing's changed."

"Can I help you?"

"I don't know. My name is Samuel Stevenson and I was good friends with Marshall Drummond."

Chapter 14

MAX NARROWED HIS EYES UPON SAMUEL STEVENSON, not out of a desire to intimidate but because Max knew that if he allowed himself one moment to breathe, his eyes would dart to the back corner of the room where Drummond, with his chest puffed in triumph, leaned against the wall. Stevenson gazed at the ceiling, then the bookcase, and finally onto the floor. When he saw the markings, he clicked his tongue.

"I always said Drummond would go out 'cause of something like this."

Drummond laughed. "That's true. All my weird cases gave Sam the willies."

Max gestured to the chair once more. "Mr. Stevenson, please have a seat."

Stevenson walked toward the books and began mouthing the titles. Drummond came closer and said, "Don't take offense. Sam here has had quite a nerve-wracking day."

"What did you do?" Max said before he could stop himself.

Sam faced Max. "For Drummond? Never anything official, but I helped out whenever I could."

"He was a cop," Drummond said.

"I see," Max said. "You were with the police?"

With a hesitant nod, Sam descended to his chair. Max thought the man might just hover an inch above the seat, afraid to commit to the act of sitting, but at length, Sam sat. His eyes jittered around the room.

"I can't believe this place," Sam said.

"It is rather a bit of time traveling. So, Mr. Stevenson, what can I do for you?"

Sam shook his head. "I'm here to help you."

"Me?" Max said, finally casting his gaze toward Drummond.

Drummond returned a proud smile and said, "You didn't think I'd just sit around and do nothing. I spent the last twenty-four hours working at getting my voice through the phone."

Max had to focus all his energy not to jump to his feet yelling about the irresponsible nature and uncaring attitude his ghost-partner exhibited. He frowned and said to Sam, "I don't follow you. How can you help me?"

"I see that look," Sam said. "I understand what you see in front of you."

"You do?"

"Sure. I'm an old man whose lost his marbles and is living in days gone by. Something like that I imagine. But you've got to trust me. I am sane. I think. It's just that I've seen something, that is, I've heard something that ... well, I don't know what to say to you. Good heavens, I sound crazier now than when I walked in here."

As Sam rubbed his face, Max looked at Drummond and asked, "What happened?"

Sam shuddered. "I don't know if I can explain."

"Look, I called the fellow, okay?" Drummond said. "I don't know how much he heard, but clearly something made it through. Now, listen to him because you need his help."

Sam cleared his throat, coughing phlegm into a handkerchief, and took a cleansing breath. "This is not going very well, is it?"

Max chuckled. "Let me help you out a bit. Did something strange happen to you? A voice, perhaps, or you saw something that might have been ghostlike?"

Sam's eyes widened but Max could not tell if this was a reaction of fear or astonishment. Then Sam broke into an old man's cackle. "I should've known," he said. "Marshall always was involved with the weird cases. Why should I be surprised to hear his dead voice? I mean, after all, I've seen some mighty oddball things working with him." For a few seconds, Sam's expression grew cold as his gaze drifted into memories. Then he said, "But how are you involved with Marshall?"

"This *was* his office."

"I guess his weird world stays close to home."

"I suppose. So, how exactly are you going to help me?"

"I don't really know."

Drummond stepped forward. "I figured he might still have access to information you can't get on your own. Ask him to look into the names you found of those morons who shot at you."

Max offered the task, and Sam brightened. "That's perfect. I still have a few old friends that could help us out. And, well, maybe that'll ease Marshall's spirit. Do you think? I mean, I know it's just Marshall — I hope — but having a dead man whisper to you over the phone ... look, at my age, I can't handle that."

"I understand," Max said. "I'm sure he'll leave you alone after this."

Drummond clapped his hands. "Don't bet on it," he said.

With the eagerness of a young man, Sam left the office, still talking. "I'm on this right now. I'll call the moment I have anything helpful. Don't worry about it. You hear that Marshall? I'm helping out your friend."

Max pointed at Drummond and said, "How could you do that to a good friend?"

"Who? Sam? Do you have any idea how many times I saved his job? He'd have been a bum in the streets if it weren't for me. He owes me."

"You could've caused the old guy a heart attack."

"If having him help you gets me out of this curse, then I'll risk his ticker. Now, enough of that. Let's find this book already."

"No," Max said, his cheeks heating up.

"No?"

"Before I do anymore of this for you, I want you to promise you won't pull another thing like that, like what you did to Sam. You promise me that."

"You needed help."

"I need to know that you're not going to go haunting people. If Sam had a heart attack, if he died, then we'd have been responsible."

"So what? I'm already dead."

"I'm not," Max yelled.

Drummond rolled his eyes. "Okay, okay. I promise I won't haunt people to help us out."

With two raps on the door, Sandra walked in. "Knock, knock," she said.

"Honey?" Max rushed over to greet her, his mind racing for an excuse if she heard any of his argument with Drummond.

Sandra looked around the room before placing a wonderful smelling bag on the desk. "I brought dinner."

"How sweet."

"Well, with all you've been dealing with, I haven't seen you much. Besides, last night —"

Max hugged her. "Thanks, hon."

"Hey," Drummond said. "Don't stop her. I want to hear about last night."

Sandra shot a nasty look in Drummond's direction. As Max pulled out the fried chicken dinner, Drummond moved closer and said, "Um, I think she can see me, Max."

Max and Sandra traded stunned eyes and both said, "What? You can see him?"

Chapter 15

OVER THE NEXT FEW HOURS, Max and Drummond listened as Sandra told them of her long history with the dead. It began at the age of thirteen when she saw the ghost of a neighbor shortly after the neighbor's wake. From then on, it never stopped. She spoke with the dead sometimes. Mostly she ignored them.

She glossed over much of her story, and Max did not press her for details. Her unusual shy behavior as she spoke told him to back off. Besides, he had enough imagination to paint in the missing parts — he saw the struggle she endured, the attempt to blot it out through destructive behavior, and finally, the acceptance of her ability. And after awhile, it became a regular part of her life.

She said that the ghosts never asked for her help or bothered her. Once in awhile they interrupted her during private moments in her life (like her honeymoon night), and she had to learn to live with the intrusions. Sometimes she found ghosts surprised she could talk to them, but usually they were too caught up in their own worlds to notice a living being — which was fine by her.

She never told anybody about her ability. Once, when visiting a psychic with her girlfriends, she thought she would be exposed. The psychic clearly sensed something odd about her, but he never gave her away — looking back, Sandra often dismissed the whole thing as a coincidence brought on by a clever actor. "The only time I ever truly considered telling somebody was when you asked me to marry you," she said. "But things were so happy for us and I figured no good could possibly come from it. And I was frightened that you might react badly to the whole thing."

"Well, I'm angry. And hurt. You didn't trust me, and here I am trying to get things back the way they were, but now that's not even what I thought it was."

"I know. I'm sorry."

"Don't be. I'm upset, but that's just a gut, of-the-moment reaction. The fact is I'm just as guilty."

He proceeded to explain all about Drummond and the curse and Hull and everything regarding their predicament he had held back before. The words gushed out and relief followed. Even as he spoke, he thought about what her world must have been like — living a duplicitous life like a covert spy only she never saved the world, she only fought for a normal routine.

When he finished his story, he held her arms and said, "Look at that — we didn't explode. We told the truth and we're still here."

Drummond yawned. "I'm still here, too."

Sandra cracked a grin but stayed focused on Max. "There's hope for us yet."

"You know it," Max said. "From now on, no more secrets between us, okay?"

"Okay."

"Is there anything else I should know?"

Sandra steeled her expression before shaking her head. Then she said, "It looks like you boys could use my help."

Drummond jumped so fast he flew through his chair. "Wait just a minute here, young lady. You two can be lovebirds, but this part isn't a game. And it isn't some club you join. This is serious work."

"Marshall, may I call you Marshall?"

"No."

"Call him Drummond," Max said with a chuckle.

"Well then, Drummond, this isn't 1940 anymore."

"I'm aware of that," Drummond said as he flew about the room. "But the people we're dealing with are dangerous."

"Which is why you need me."

"I appreciate that you're Max's wife and that you can see me. But none of that —"

"Have you found your book yet?"

That stopped Drummond. He cast a suspicious eye towards Max. Max shook his head and said, "Calm down. She's on our side."

Sandra stepped closer to Max. "When I started seeing ghosts, especially during my teen years, I spent some time looking into the occult and witchcraft and all of that. I know a lot about what you're dealing with."

"Then enlighten us," Drummond said.

"If you agree to let me help."

Though a pale ghost, Drummond appeared to redden. Before he said a word, Max intervened. "Of course you can help. Whether Casper here wants to admit it or not, we need you. Now, what do you know about the book?"

"I know that it's not something most people would be comfortable keeping. When you bind a ghost, there's the object bound to and there's the holder. In this case, the object would be the page the spell was written on. The holder is the book, and holders tend to radiate energy." As Sandra delved into the finer points of binding spells, Max watched with an awe he had not experienced since he first fell for her. Little lines on her face filled him with excitement. He wanted to kiss her, to let her know that he loved her, to see her understand that all the ups and downs of the past months were coming to an end. Part of him, however, fought back — he feared the worst had yet to happen. It was a dark sensation reminding him of sitting in that witch's office.

"The witch," he blurted out.

"What?" Sandra asked.

Drummond swooped down. "Yes, yes. The witch."

Max said, "She hates you."

"I don't know if 'hate' is the right word."

Max said to Sandra, "There's a witch here in Winston-Salem. Her grandmother knew Drummond. They had a past. Well, not the best of past experiences together."

"You think she has the book?"

"She certainly didn't want to help him out. She told me only what I already knew and insisted on Drummond's apology."

"It sounds like a good place to start."

Max got to his feet, looked out the window as he thought, and then turned back to the others. "Why did you send me to her? No, no, don't give me that crap you said before. It just hit me now — you knew Connor's grandmother. Why would you send me to see this witch when you knew she would be angry?"

"I wasn't sure whose side she was on. We needed that information and you needed to learn about witches. I figured two birds one stone."

Before Max let loose a torrent of cursing, Sandra said, "It doesn't really matter, does it? You can't undo it."

"Listen to the lady," Drummond said.

"And now you know just how little you can trust this ghost."

"Don't listen to that part."

"We've got to deal with this witch, okay?" she said. Max closed his eyes and nodded.

"Great," Drummond said. "So, she works out of an office. Max knows the place. You two could go in after hours."

"Break in?" Max said.

Sandra nodded. "Good idea. We should go tonight."

"Are you crazy? We can't break in."

"Why not?"

"How about jail for starters."

Drummond slid behind Sandra and shared a devilish grin. "Max," he said, "do we really need to put everything in perspective for you?"

"I know, I know," Max said.

"Well, that went easy. You know, Max, even though she doesn't trust me, I think I like your wife."

Sandra looked over her shoulder. "Thank you."

"If you two can tone it down, I'd like to know a few important details. For example, how are we going to break-in? Unless you're going to tell me you were a thief when you were a teen, honey, neither of us knows how to pick locks."

"I can do it," Drummond said, but when the other two stared at him, he added, "Well, I can."

"You'll have to teach me someday. For now, the break-in is off. We'll just have to think of another way to find that book." Max tried not to sound too relieved.

Drummond frowned. He moved his head from side to side, mouthing a debate that only he could hear. A few seconds later, he let out a loud sigh and said, "You won't have any trouble breaking-in because you won't have to. The doors will be unlocked. There's no security system or anything like that to worry about. Okay?"

"And you didn't want to mention this because?"

Drummond turned away and mumbled something. Sandra said, "He wants to come with us, to be useful, but he keeps having to face the fact that he can't leave here."

"Oh," Max said, searching for something to change the subject with. He brightened as he latched onto the first thing to come to mind. "She knew I was coming before. She'll know we're coming again. She must be able to see the future."

"See the future? What kind of bozo are you?" Drummond said with a scowl. "Look, she doesn't live in a vacuum. I'm sure she has all sorts of sources spying all over to help her manipulate people."

"So, she's not a real witch?"

"Of course, she's real. Look what she did to me. It's just that no matter how much she tries to make people believe it, she can't see into the future. As far as I know."

"You're a bundle of confidence," Max said. A new thought struck, and he snapped his fingers. "Why will the doors be unlocked?"

Drummond turned back but stared at the floor. "Because Dr. Connor is a witch. Nobody would dare try to break into her office. Even those who don't know she's a witch sense she holds a lot of power because in all the years she's been in that little place, she has never once had any kind of trouble."

"Was that supposed to convince me?"

"You have to go, so just do it," Drummond said with a harshness that took Max by surprise. Then, in a softer tone, he said, "Please. I need you to do this."

Max closed his eyes. "Don't worry. If she has information that will help us, then I'll find it. I promise."

"Just go do what needs to be done. The rest is nothing to me. I just want a little freedom."

"Then we'll go to the office. We'll go right now."

Sandra winked at Max. "Guess we're back on," she said.

Twenty minutes later, Max sat in his car with Sandra next to him, waiting for the witch to leave her office. They parked in the lot across the street next to a dentist's office. While rain pelted the car and chilled the night, Max lost himself in the office sign's colors reflecting upon the pavement puddles. Neither Max nor Sandra said much at first. Then, Sandra made a tentative step by asking, "Are you mad at me?"

"Not at all. I mean it. I understand why you kept this secret from me. I do. I'm not mad."

"Then why are you acting so distant?"

"I'm just preoccupied."

"That's what I'm talking about. Right there. You're avoiding an answer by dismissing the whole thing, by being distant. Don't do that. That's the way we've always dealt with things. Avoid them until it blows up into a fight or a passionate night. Let's stop that. Tonight. You said no more secrets. I mean you've got to be wondering about me, right? So let's talk about it."

"I just want to be quiet and think." Throwing a charming smile, he added, "And we can still let this blow up into a passionate night later."

"No," Sandra said as she clutched Max's arm. "If everything is so fine, then I want to know why you're so far away. What are you thinking about?"

Max sighed and the sound reminded him of Drummond. He kept his eyes on the puddle, watching as the rain distorted the image thousands of times over. "For one," Max said, "we're about to commit a criminal act. That's not something I've had much experience with. For another, I only see Drummond. I don't know why I thought this, but I had assumed that was it. Not that Drummond was the only ghost but that he was the only one in the area — that ghosts were somehow few and far between. The idea that there are ghosts all over us — it's unsettling. I mean, are there any here now?"

Sandra glanced around the parking lot. "Do you see an old man leaning by that No Parking sign?"

"Nobody's there."

"Then there's one ghost."

Max shifted his weight and said, "That's just weird. I guess I'm also feeling strange about us. Not because of you or your ability or anything like that."

"Then what?"

"I'm sitting here and thinking about all the years I've known you, and I just wonder what our lives might've been like, how different, if I had known the real you. We've had such a screwy time lately, and maybe none of it had to actually happen. Maybe things could've been better. Maybe we never would have come down here and got all caught up with Hull." *Maybe you'd be quietly smiling over a rose every day.*

Sandra stroked Max's head. "You'll drive yourself crazy playing out all the What Ifs, and really, when you get to the end, none of that matters. This is the way it happened. This is the life we've got. Nothing you can say is going to change the fact that we're sitting here now listening to the rain, getting ready to break into an office," she said, curling the corner of her mouth which forced a warm smile from Max.

"No fair," he said.

"All's fair."

"Don't you do that hair flip thing."

"What? You mean this?" she said as she tossed her hair over one shoulder and leaned her head to the side, exposing her soft neck.

Max kissed her from the shoulder up to her ear. "Honey, I'm in love with you. Understand? You don't have to seduce me all over again."

"Maybe I want to."

"Then let's go home and forget about this place for tonight."

A moment passed in which Max thought she might agree. Then Sandra sat back, the glimmer in her eye turned icy, and she looked toward the office. "We've got to do this. You know —"

"I do, I do. It was just nice there for a minute to feel like a normal person again — one who doesn't have to worry about ghosts and curses and Hull."

"Is that her?"

A figure stepped outside, closed the door, and scurried toward a blue car holding a purse over her head. Because of the rain, Max found it difficult to tell if the figure was Dr. Connor — if not the doctor, she had to be an assistant. Once the blue car pulled away, there were no other cars in the parking lot.

"Guess this is it," he said.

Sandra kissed him. "I won't let anything happen to you."

They dashed across the street and toward the office. In just seconds, Max felt soaked through but he kept moving. And because of the cold and wet, Max did not hesitate when he reached the door but rather opened it with brazen abandon.

Inside the waiting room, they both shook off the rain. Sandra walked around the receptionist's desk, flicked on her flashlight, and started opening drawers. Max pointed his flashlight at her and said, "Forget about that stuff. It won't help us. If she has the book, it'll be back there, in her private ... lair."

"Lair?" Sandra said with a smile.

Max shrugged. "She's a witch, after all."

As they headed to the back room, Max listened for any sounds of people. He only heard the rain being blown against the building, their footsteps on the thin carpet, and his own nervous breathing. The air smelled different — partly a lemon-scented cleaner but mostly something stronger and stranger. It had a slight burned odor and a slight sweet aroma as if Dr. Connor had been lighting cinnamon sticks. Max tried not to think about the twisted spells that left such a smell in the air. He could not stop the chills rolling over his body.

When they reached Dr. Connor's private office, Max pointed to a bookshelf. "You look there. I'll check out the desk."

The desk was an exquisite, hand-crafted rolltop with fierce animal heads carved on the sides — snarling wolves, roaring bears, and gibbering hyenas. The shadows cast by the flashlight animated the carvings, and Max had to remind himself that it was just a desk. Dr. Connor was a witch and Drummond was a cursed ghost, but he didn't believe spells to bring wooden carvings to life were real. That seemed to be stretching reality in a way Max refused to accept.

In the desk, he found three books. Each looked very old and had been covered in thin, tanned hides. Sandra peeked over his shoulder and said, "You don't want to touch that."

"Why?" Max said as he picked one up. The covering felt smooth yet stuck on the book when rubbed.

"That's human skin."

With a gasp, he dropped it to the desk, the smooth feel of the cover still tingling his fingers like the remnants of an electric jolt. "A little warning next time would be appreciated."

"There's nothing on the bookshelf that fits the bill."

"What about these?" he asked, pointing to the rolltop.

"No. Human skin is used for very sacred texts. This is just a binding spell. From what you and Drummond said, this should be rather ordinary like a notebook or a journal or even a diary. Something easy to overlook."

Max glanced at the skin-covered books. Before his flashlight could play with the books shadows, he moved the beam to the floor. "Maybe she has a hiding space," he said. "A wall safe or a loose floorboard."

"I doubt it. Not if she's as powerful a witch as Drummond says. She has no need to hide a book, especially a minor binding book. If anything, she would have hidden those books you were looking at. No, if that book was here, it would have been in plain sight."

"Look here." Max pointed to a red, hardcover book with black lettering. "*Cruor Teneo*. That's on my office floor. Could this be it?"

"It means 'Blood Hold' and it's not what we want. That's more of an instruction book on various binding curses."

"Damn," Max said and slouched against the wall. "Without that book, I can't do anything for Drummond."

"Keep looking then."

"Why? You've made it clear that she doesn't have it here. It would be in plain sight and it's not. And for that matter, when I visited her the other night, she was trying to encourage me to find it. Why would she do that if she knew where it was?"

"If she has it, she obviously doesn't want you to know."

"Then why not dissuade me from even searching? I don't get it. I don't get a lot of what's going on. And you know what else? That book isn't here. So why should we keep looking?"

"Because what else can you do?"

"Leave here, for starters. If we were to get caught —"

The unmistakable sound of the front door opening echoed through the office. Without a word, Max and Sandra started scouring the room with their flashlights, each looking for a good hiding spot. Snapping his fingers at Sandra, Max indicated a door on the far wall. Light danced across the desk, the chairs, and the books, as they rushed to the door making as little noise as possible. With a gentle touch, Max turned the doorknob. The click it produced screamed in Max's ears.

"Kim?" Dr. Connor's voice called from the lobby. "Are you still here?"

"Go," Max whispered, following Sandra down a corridor that turned to the right. At the far end was an emergency door. The closer to the door, the faster they moved until Sandra pushed hard on the press bar, banging the door open. Max halted.

"What is it?" Sandra asked.

Max gazed up at her — his face pale, his eyes wide. "Stay here," he said and closed the door on her, leaving Sandra stuck in the rain.

As he hurried back up the corridor, he hoped he had not imagined the piece of paper. He had caught sight of it as they left the office. Amongst the books and shadows and odd-shaped statues, he had seen a paper with the Hull letterhead.

When he reached the door, he opened it with slow, careful motions. He peeked in after turning his flashlight off.

Nobody.

Flicking on the flashlight, he scanned the floor. As he moved into the office, the door behind him closed making a clear sound. Max heard approaching footsteps and Dr. Connor calling, "Hello?"

The flashlight's beam jittered across the room as the footsteps grew louder. "Whoever is in my office, you've made a big mistake."

Max edged backward toward the door, but still he searched. Had he just imagined it? The next sound came from right behind the inner door — the witch chanting.

Spinning around, ready to race toward Sandra, Max saw the paper near the wall just to the left of the exit door. He grabbed it and another and dashed down the corridor. The chanting grew louder, and though he could never prove it, Max felt the air behind him pulling away — not a breeze or a wind but as if the air had a rope tied around it and was forced in a direction it did not wish to go.

When he burst outside, Sandra let out a yelp. He grabbed her hand and never stopped running. They went straight into the darkness of the night, never looking back, just pumping their legs until they both grew tired and cold in the rain.

Chapter 16

BY THE TIME THEY RETURNED TO THEIR CAR, drove home, and dried off, the clock read quarter-to-three and Max could not think clearly enough to deal with the papers he had stolen. Making sense of the word *stolen* in relation to himself was another matter entirely. Had he really become a thief? *It's just paper,* he thought. However, he dismissed such a weak response as the ramblings of his tired mind. Then he tried to dismiss all responses — clear his cluttered brain so that he might rest. Besides, unless he wanted to be haunted forever and pursued by Hull for-close-to-ever, this appeared to be his best option at the moment.

Sandra slumped on the couch with one paper in hand while Max looked at the other. With a yawn and a groan, Max leaned to read over Sandra's shoulder yet again.

SINGLE
VOGLER
SHULTZ
MIKSH
WINKLER
HORTON
BLUM
ACRE
SISTERS

"Names," Max said.

"Of who, though?"

"None of them stand out to me, but then, we haven't lived here that long. If the name were Reynolds, Hanes, or Hull, I'd know it, but these don't mean much of anything."

"Those marks can't be good."

Of the nine names, the last five had little dots in red ink. "Probably not," Max said. "Then again, maybe it's good to have the mark and bad not to — it could mean anything."

"It's not usually good to have a mark by your name." Sandra placed the paper into a tan file folder. "We should ask Drummond in the morning."

"You've done enough. I'll deal with Drummond."

"I'm not stopping now. I want to be a part of this."

"Really? I mean this is not a typical day for me. My work is rarely as nerve-wracking as this."

"I thought it was exciting."

"Most of my time is spent looking up things in books. Exciting is hardly the word for that."

With a look both amused and defiant, she said, "Honey, I'm involved now, and I'll see this thing through. We're in it together. Okay?"

"Then you should see this," he said, handing her the second paper.

"A letter?"

"Read it."

The paper was old and the penmanship hard to read. Sandra squinted and read aloud, "'My dearest Eve, I know you find yourself at a most difficult juncture. Two men vie for your heart and to your loving eyes, we must both seem worthy. Indeed, but a short fortnight ago I would have agreed with the sentiment, and though it would have left me heartbroken should you have chosen T——, no unbecoming scene would I have made. But the time has passed, and should this letter turn your adoring gaze from me forever, I feel it unforgivable should I let you embark upon marriage with T—- naïve to his true nature. He plans to leave, though you probably know as much, and he claims to seek out a greater church. What you do not know, however, is that he leaves not for love of another theology, not out of outrage toward our own failures, not for any noble or worthy cause, but from a demon's bargain. Hull (there, I have named him) has begun an exploration in the darkest of magics. His soul is most likely lost. Please, fairest Eve, I beg of you, do not lose your way to this power seeker. He will sacrifice your soul and laugh at your foolishness.'"

"There's no date," Max said, "but it sounds old. Maybe William Hull's grandfather. Certainly, the Hull family's been dealing with witches and magic for a long time."

"We have to be more careful than we thought," Sandra said, her eyes wide and frightened.

"We will be."

At six a.m. the telephone rang — a shrill sound that promised nothing good. Max and Sandra had fallen asleep on the couch, and both moved into consciousness with aches and groans. Max considered letting the answering machine take care of it, but Sandra shook her head. They both knew this would not be some early-morning drunk calling the wrong number. With a huff, Max reached across the couch to pick up the phone.

"Hello?"

The unmistakable voice of Mr. Modesto said, "Good morning, Mr. Porter. I'd like to have an update report."

"Okay," Max said, running his tongue over the film covering his teeth. "What time?"

"I'm not available for a meeting with you at the moment. I'd like the report now."

"Now?"

"Is that a problem?"

"No," Max said, sitting taller and waving off Sandra's worried frown. "That'll be fine."

"Well, then, where are we?"

"Um ... I've done some preliminary research into the Old Salem area as you requested, and —"

"Preliminary? I expected you to have some viable properties lined up by now."

"I will soon," Max said, wondering how fast he could push something like this through when he had yet to do the most basic research. "Please understand that historic areas require a great amount of subtlety and patience; otherwise, you'll end up with people picketing outside your doorstep. There's always somebody who passionately wants to save every last old building that still stands."

"That is not your concern. We will handle such things, if they occur. You only need to come up with the best historical properties for our purchase."

"Historical? The papers you gave me stated you wanted high-valued locations. That's why I was looking near Old Salem. Now you specifically want historical buildings?"

"You know exactly what we want. Stop wasting my time. Do your job, or I'll see that our employer ends your association with us. Am I understood?"

"Yes, sir."

Modesto hung up. With her hand resting upon Max's shoulder, Sandra asked what happened. Max leaned back and let out a long breath. "I don't really know," he said before detailing the phone call. "Let's get cleaned up and go into the office. We need to talk with Drummond about that list. See if he knows who any of them are."

"We?" Sandra asked.

"You said it yourself — you're involved. Besides, I don't think I can do this on my own, and until Drummond is free, I am on my own."

As Sandra headed toward the bathroom, she looked over her shoulder and said, "You silly boy. You're never on your own."

An hour later, they arrived at the office. Taylor wasted time cleaning the already clean desk. Drummond walked behind him, knocking over papers and books, and chuckling as the young man bumbled about in an attempt to pick things up.

"Take the day off," Max said.

"You know I can't do that, sir," Taylor said as the book he placed on the desktop unbalanced itself and flipped to the floor. "Mr. Modesto told me —"

"I'll make your choice simple. If you stay here, I'm going to hit you."

"Sir?"

Max shoved Taylor. Sandra said, "Young man, you'd best get out of here. Mr. Porter's had a rough night."

Taylor took one clear look at Max and left the office at a brisk clip. Max tried not to laugh, but when Drummond burst into snorting hysterics hard enough to bring tears to his eyes had he been alive, Max let loose his own cackles. "That was fun," Drummond said.

"Unfortunately, the phone call I had this morning wasn't so fun," Max said, sobering as he explained the events of the previous night that concluded with Mr. Modesto's phone call.

Drummond took a seat and listened. His intense focus broke only the two times he glanced at Sandra. When Max had finished, Drummond drifted into the air and said, "This is all good news. Very good, as a matter of fact."

"But we didn't find the book."

"True. But we've found out enough so that Hull's people are getting worried. They came here this morning, as well."

Sandra perked up. "Really?"

"Modesto and Connor. She stood before me and spit out some vile words. Somebody ought to talk to her mother about that. I'm serious. If my mother caught me saying any of those nasty things, I wouldn't have been able to sit for over a week."

"Well, that lifts any doubt about Connor working for Hull. What did they do?" Max asked, scanning the office for any obvious signs of tampering.

"First, they threatened to put a new binding spell on me."

Sandra said, "I didn't think you could put one on top of the other. At least, not of the kind done to you before."

"That's right, and when I reminded them of that pesky little fact, they threatened to burn down the building which, when you consider that the symbols on the floor would become charred ash, would make it very difficult to release me from the binding. They said if you didn't come up with what they want, they'd destroy us all."

"Man, Drummond, I'm sorry."

"I don't really care about it. I mean, nice place and all, always was a good office, but they haven't got anything I want badly enough to give them what they want."

"They've got the book."

"Not if they're threatening to burn down this building. They acted coy, but come on, now, what else could they be after but the book? They know I'm after it. They fear what I might do if I were to gain my freedom. So, it's pretty clear that they don't have it either."

"Then why me?" Max asked. "I'm sick of this. Why go to the expense of moving me down here, setting me up, giving me all this time-wasting research — I mean, they could've done all this on their own. It doesn't make any sense. I didn't have any connection to them. There's no logical reason to bring in a stranger. It only opens them up to outside scrutiny."

Sandra sat in Max's desk chair and folded her arms. "It seems to me that there are three key things going on here. First, there's the book, and I think we're all crystal clear on that one — we want it to set Drummond free, they want it to keep him in place, and nobody knows where it is. Then there's this old case regarding Stan Bowman. Obviously, this ties in with Drummond since it's the reason he's stuck here. So, perhaps they don't want us learning whatever you were getting close to finding out way back when."

"I'm right with you," Drummond said with a wink.

"Last is Max's employment. The Hull Corporation says it's buying up properties and wants an expert to research the area."

Scoffing, Max said, "I'm no expert. I'm good at research but hardly an expert."

"Well, they can't hire anybody too high profile. So, they hire you. Perhaps they know that the answers to the Bowman case or the book can be found in some land here. Perhaps this is all about attacking the same problem from different angles."

"Possibly," Drummond said. "In fact, that makes quite a bit of sense. After all, Hull is a large company. They can't go searching for this book or this land quietly — not under their own name. That would draw plenty of attention. But if they hired somebody ..."

Max nodded. "Somebody with no ties to the community. Somebody from the North that has no family or friends in the area. A couple with no children. A couple down on their luck that would dive in without too many questions. Okay, I'm sold. Now what?"

Drummond thought for a moment, circling the room in a wide arc. "I think Max should go hit the books again. See if you can find more about Hull."

"I've looked into the Hull family but there's not much. A Civil War reference but that's about it. The name doesn't really kick into use until Reynolds and Hanes become big."

"Amuse me. There's got to be something to find."

"They could just be paranoid. Perhaps they think there's something major hidden in the records, but there really isn't."

"Either way, you're the one to go find out," Drummond said and then pointed to Sandra. "You work at a bakery. What can you do?"

With a patronizing shake of her head, Sandra said, "You boys never talk, do you? Max, tell Drummond what I did before the recession hit."

"You worked in a bar. What's that got to do with —"

"After that, honey. Use your brain."

Max slapped the desk. "I'm such an idiot."

"Yes, you are. I didn't want to step in your way, especially when we weren't really talking, but now I can help."

"Great," Drummond said with a scowl. "Now tell me what the heck you're talking about."

"Back in Michigan, I sold real estate."

"Wait a minute. You sold real estate?"

"Not commercial," Sandra said.

"That's not the point. Hull hired your husband as a researcher when they should've hired a real estate agent."

Max said, "Unless they wanted me to do research on more than just properties."

"Keep that in mind. This is getting weird in a way that reminds me too much of the final days in the Bowman case. Everybody be careful."

"Perhaps Sandra should look into recent real estate activities under the Hull name. Can you do that?"

Sandra nodded. "I still have some contacts."

"Good," Drummond said. "And I'll just float around here and play tricks on Taylor."

As Max and Sandra got up to leave, Max had another idea. "What about other ghosts?"

"What about them?"

Sandra said, "I don't see any others in here."

"That's 'cause I'm all alone. I don't have contact with other ghosts."

Max shook his head. "But you were able to make contact with that old guy, Sam. You got him to come here and see me. If you can do that, maybe you can find another ghost."

"And do what?"

"Maybe get a message through to the ghost community. Maybe somebody out there knows something."

"The ghost community? What the heck are you talking about? We're just dead. We don't have a community."

"How do you know? You've been stuck in here since you died. Maybe there's a thriving world of ghosts out there."

"Sandra, set your husband straight, please."

"I don't know," Sandra said. "I've seen lots of ghosts, and they always seem to be unaware of each other."

"That's right," Drummond said, clapping his hands.

"But then again, communities behave in all sorts of different ways. Max might be right."

Max smiled. "Besides, what else are you going to do all day. Picking on Taylor is going to get boring after a while."

"You'd be surprised," Drummond said. "Okay, I'll try it, but don't expect too much."

"Let's meet back here tonight for dinner. Hopefully, we'll all have good news to contribute."

"Aren't you the optimist?"

Max put his arm around Sandra and left the office. He didn't bother with a response other than to whistle a meandering tune. He wished he felt half as casual as he behaved, but a brave front helped him keep pressing forward. Having Sandra by his side helped more.

Chapter 17

THE MORNING DRAGGED ON FOR MAX as he rummaged through one useless book after another. As lunch approached, he closed the last book in his pile and resigned to the fact that no matter where he looked, he could not find anything helpful on the Hull family.

"I'll have to go talk with that old guy in Butner again," he said to the books. That sparked an idea. A second later he rushed to the nearest computer to search Butner and POWs. Only two books showed in the results but that was two more chances than he had before. Twenty minutes later, he had learned that bringing the POWs caused a bit of controversy and required Reynolds to smooth talk a lot of people.

"Yeah, but was good ol' Hull in the picture?"

Not surprisingly, Max found no references to Hull; however, the entire program smelled of the Hull Corporation. Next, he searched through the newspapers and found several articles about the POWs. One in particular announced the special transfer of seven Germans from Butner to Winston-Salem. All seven names were listed: Dietar Krause, Joseph Richter, Herbert Bauer, Günther Scholz, Stefan König, Fritz Keller, and Walter Huber.

Max jotted down the names. "It's a start," he said.

In the course of packing away his notes, he glanced at his scribblings from the first day — Moravians and Unitas Fratrum and the founding of Bethabara. The foundation for this little research construction project had proven quite unstable. "Wait just a moment," he whispered. Why would Modesto have started him out looking into all this old history if all he had wanted was the binding book?

Even as an idea formed in Max's head, he rushed toward the Special Collections room of the library. He spent a short time plugging in keyword searches until he found one promising entry. After handing in the request, he paced in front of the doorway as if expecting somebody to stop him at any moment. Then, before Max knew it, he sat in a private cubicle with the 1825 diary of Jeremiah Childress.

Bound in leather (throwing Max awful recollections of human skin bound books) and written in steep-angled, cursive lines, many of the entries proved to be mundane accounts of the Childress farm. "I know you've got something in there," Max said, turning a page. He learned that Childress was well-respected and that by 1828, he had been invited to become a member of the Elders Conference. Then Max read:

It is to my great dismay this twenty-first day of our Lord's year eighteen hundred twenty-nine that I must partake in a most unpleasant meeting of the Elders Conference. Our good man Thomas Christman, though perhaps I must restate his standing, has made it known his intentions to leave the warming fold of Unitas Fratrum. His soul has been poisoned by those who call themselves the Baptists. Indeed, Thomas claims he has stepped into the waters with their so-called holy men. I have known Thomas for many years, and though I cannot claim to be surprised by this development, I am, as I stated previously, dismayed. It is never a joyous occasion when we lose one of our own. Making this saddening situation worse is the indecent act dear Thomas has chosen to lay upon us. After receiving the Elders Conference's order to depart from Salem, Thomas shocked us all by refusing, such is his disdain for what he once held sacred. I am troubled by what has transpired since that moment of defiance. It was my fullest expectation that the Elders Conference would evict Mr. Christman from his home and send both he and his child away from Salem so as not to pollute the holiness and well-being of our citizens. That has not happened. In this action's stead, the Elders Conference voted not to evict as that would bring unwanted attention to our actions in the public forums. No, this honorable organization deemed it more appropriate to allow a soul-fouled man to retain ownership of his home until the Elders Conference could purchase the house from under its occupants. I spoke against this course and for my troubles discovered myself much alone.

Max skimmed through the next few days, discovering little of value. When he turned the page, however, he found more than he could have wished for.

Only one is willing to stand beside me and for that I thank the Lord for providing and His kindness and His grace. Tucker Hull is a young man in years but wise enough to despise this hypocrisy. We have shared numerous conversations and I believe he may understand our Lord's will better than any other I have ever conversed with. I consider him a friend. His comprehension of scripture far exceeds my limited fumbling and I do believe wholeheartedly that should he ask me I would willingly follow his leadership in any capacity he wishes. Truthfully spoken, I hold suspicions that he plans to remove himself, and those of us who support his ideas, for there are more than just myself, from the Unitas Fratrum and inaugurate a new Church, one unpolluted by the corruption of power, under his supervision.

Max stared at the name *Tucker Hull* for a full minute. He might have spent another five minutes sitting in shock, if not for the two women who walked by murmuring to the tune of their clicking heels. These sounds roused him, and with quiet, determined motions, Max copied down the diary entries. When he finished, he hurried back to the office.

Sandra and Drummond were waiting. Upon Max's entrance, Sandra gave him a quick hug and kiss. Drummond, however, burst into a rant that clearly had been rolling in his head for hours.

"Nothing," he said. "I tried everything, but they won't talk to me."

As Max took off his coat, he winked at Sandra and said, "You mean other ghosts?"

"What the hell do you think I've been doing all day? There's even one standing outside in front of the Y. I know he can see me. He glanced up here a few times, but he won't come in. He won't even shout something my way. And why? I never did anything to him. I don't even know the guy. Oh, I know the reason he'd give. Same reason I've heard ever since I got stuck here. Connor warned me — actually, she taunted me with this but it's ridiculous."

"You're losing me. What reason?"

"The binding. Pay attention. Connor said that I'd be forever alone because no ghost would ever talk with me or be around me or anything if I'm bound. They fear they'll get caught in the binding, too. But this is important. I understand their worried and all, but if I saw some poor muck who had been cursed and I could help him, I'd be there right away. I can't believe none of these ghosts have any sympathy for me. It's downright immoral."

"I thought you didn't know about any other ghosts or a community or anything."

Drummond whisked over to the window, crossed his arms, and glared toward the street. "I may have misrepresented matters."

Max looked at Sandra. "How did it go for you?"

"Better," she said with a chuckle. "I found out that witchy-poo doesn't own her office and she doesn't lease it. She doesn't pay anything for it at all."

"Do I even need to bother guessing?"

"Oxsten and Son own it and they, according to your stock trace for Annabelle Bowman, are one of many dummy corporations. So, that's right, hon. Hull owns it. Owns most of the buildings on that block."

"Hull lets Connor use the office for free but then he has access to a witch whenever he wants."

"There's more. This arrangement goes back well before Drummond was even born. Assuming all or most of the various companies named are dummies, and from what I can tell that is the case, then the Hulls have had a witch on retainer for over a hundred years."

Drummond said, "Two old family businesses. Figures."

"I also looked into this office building," Sandra said, and Drummond faced her. "It's also had a rather unorthodox history. Starts off fairly normal, changing hands a few times, but then the last owner disappears — I couldn't even find a death notice let alone a certificate. The building, however, keeps operating as if it had an owner. Nobody is named on any paperwork, yet no government action is taken. Then, out of nowhere, Hull assumes control. Their name is also missing from legal ownership, but they're the ones paying taxes, collecting rent —"

"Keeping this a cursed office for their own use," Max said.

"Pretty much."

"Good job, hon."

"Any time, dear."

"Enough," Drummond said. "You two have got to curb the mushy-mushy."

"The what?" Sandra said.

Before Drummond could take the bait, Max spoke up. "You guys won't believe what I found."

In a few minutes, Max explained how he found the diary and then, to Drummond's stunned silence, he read the entries. Sandra spoke first. "The Hull family goes all the way back to the seventeen hundreds."

"They go back to the foundation of this entire area. It's no wonder that by the time Bowman is working at R. J. Reynolds, the Hull family has money and power. They'd been at it for almost two centuries."

"You think this happened then — what this man wrote — that Tucker Hull defected from the Moravians to start his own church?"

"Read this," Max said, showing Eve's letter.

"You think this Hull is Tucker Hull?"

"Don't you?"

Drummond nodded. "So Tucker breaks away from the Moravians to start some evil magic religion."

Sandra nodded. "It's all interesting, but how does it help us?"

Max said, "I think it might help clear up a lot, but that's all details. Right now, we've got to find that binding book."

"What about that list from Connor's office?"

"What list?" Drummond asked.

Max jumped to his feet. "I completely forgot. It's a list of names with some checked off. And I've got names of the Butner POWs. But I don't think they match. I'll start looking into them right away."

Drummond slid behind Max and read the list. "Those aren't people," he said.

"What are they, then?"

"Names of buildings in Old Salem."

"Old Salem," Max said. "There's no putting it off, now."

"Slow down, there, kiddo. It's too late in the evening for that. You'll have to go in the morning."

Max checked the window — night. "Oh. Then let's get some sleep. Tomorrow, honey, see if you can find anything more to help us, and maybe check out the background on some of these buildings. I'll look into them directly in the morning. Drummond —"

"I'll just be floating around."

"Help out Sandra. Tell her whatever you know about this."

"Will do."

Max copied the building names on a yellow legal pad and gave it to Sandra. He surveyed the names once more before putting the paper in his pocket. "I'm wired, so I'm going back to the library 'til they close. I'll see what else I can learn. Don't wait up for me. First thing in the morning, I'll go to Old Salem. We'll meet here tomorrow night."

"Be careful," Sandra said.

"It's just Old Salem. I'm going to a public historical site. There'll be tons of people there, tourists, schools, and locals. What could possibly happen? Relax."

Chapter 18

THE NEXT MORNING, Max arrived at Old Salem. There were tourists, but not the thousands he had expected. In fact, if not for the people dressed in historically accurate garb, Old Salem could have been mistaken for any aging, quiet neighborhood. Of the one hundred buildings (so the lady at the Visitor's Center explained), ninety-seven were original, and for a modest price, he could tour all of them.

Before he even entered the town proper, Max knew this promised to be harder than he had expected. A detailed, covered bridge crossed the road below, linking the Visitor's Center to Old Salem's Main Street. Thick beams and struts crisscrossed to form a charming pattern. The strong, flavorful smell of hickory coated everything. Halfway across the bridge, Max stopped.

It could be here, he thought, *hidden in one of these beams*.

He walked back to the front of the bridge and searched with his eyes, looking at each minute detail. He glanced up and drooped with a sigh. Nailed over the entrance, Max saw an oval plate reading *1998* — too new to have an ancient book.

Main Street inclined a bit as Max walked across the old stone sidewalks. First stop was Vogler's Gun Shop established 1831. The building consisted of two small rooms. The front room had a wide-planked wood floor, a long work table, planks in the ceiling, several hand-crafted, period precise hunting rifles, and tools everywhere. A man with a white beard and small glasses smiled and said, "Welcome to the Gun Shop." He then went into his spiel, explaining all about the process of making weapons, the man who originally owned and operated the business, and how he would answer any questions Max had.

Max peeked into the back room. It was smaller and bore a rich, smoky odor. This was where the metalwork was done. A long wooden arm for pumping the bellows hung overhead. There were several anvils (one mounted on a tree stump), a trough of water, and plenty of ash that left the stone floor gritty.

As Max moved around the shop, he shifted his weight from one stone to the other, one wooden plank to the other, but too many of them creaked or moved — any one of them could be the cover to a hiding place.

Stepping back onto Main Street, he pulled out the paper and looked at the names once more. VOGLER did not have a little red dot next to it. Did that mean the witch had checked it out already and came up with nothing, or were the dotted ones the buildings already checked? He decided to ignore the dots since he couldn't be sure and instead headed up the street to the Shultz Shoe Shop from 1827.

This building was even smaller than the first — just one room no bigger than his office. A cast iron stove warmed the room from the back and a wooden table took most of the middle. To the right, sitting between two windows, were a man and a woman, each busy in the process of making shoes. "Hello," the shoemaker said, "and welcome to the Shultz Shoe Shop." Like the old man before, the shoemaker delivered his presentation from memory (though Max was impressed with how enthusiastic the people were after they gave their required talk). Like the other building, the floors here were made of wide planks and the walls were a solid wide plaster-like substance.

As Max pushed onward, a sensation he had become all too familiar with washed over his body — he was being followed. He tried to brush away the feeling, but the uneasiness refused to leave. He scanned the area — an old couple strolling hand in hand, a haggard father being dragged by an eager kid, a gaggle of ladies laughing and chatting. Nobody appeared to have the remotest interest in him. Nobody appeared out of place.

He entered a large house which the lady in the foyer explained was the Vogler House built in 1819 but presented as it was in 1840 (Max wondered if this was the same Vogler that also made guns but decided it didn't matter). On the left side were two connecting rooms — a parlor and dining room. On the right, Max found Mr. Vogler's workroom where he repaired watches and did other such detail work, and a kitchen. Each room was completely furnished with as many original pieces as the Historical Society could acquire.

In the dining room, a grandfather clock towered over him. It must have been near ten-feet tall. The lady in the room said that a man named Everhardt built and signed the clock, but Max could not recall the name from any of his research. It was such a beautiful piece (despite the crack running down the lower front) that even a novice like Max could appreciate it.

Upstairs, Max discovered four bedrooms — one of them a nursery with a crib and toys. Each bed, each writing desk, each planked floor held the promise of housing the book. However, the more he thought about it, the more he decided none of them could be the answer. These bits of furniture had been handled over the years by various members of the Historical Society. How could the book have remained undiscovered if it had been hidden in the crib or the writing tables?

The exit from the house was in the back, requiring Max to walk around in order to return to Main Street. As he turned the corner, he saw a figure dash into the house. It happened too fast to tell if the person was a man or woman or even if the incident was merely coincidence. However, the constant pressure forming on Max's shoulders and tightening his neck reminded him that sometimes being paranoid was warranted.

As he walked onward, he saw the town square on his right — a lovely, open area of grass and trees with four walkways forming an X. Pines circled the center and several benches lined the walkways. Though attractive and peaceful, Max registered little of the atmosphere around him. He only saw hundreds of places to hide a small item.

At the end of the block, on his left, stood a large building called Single Brothers. Max checked his list. The word SINGLE had no mark next to it.

Inside he found a three story home for single men to learn their trades in preparation for getting married. *My mother would love this,* he thought. To the left of the entrance was a wide room like a mini-church (the attendant informed him the room was called the Sall). A boxy white organ took up the back corner and plain, backless benches had been lined up in the center. Like many of the rooms Max had seen, this one contained what he thought to be an ornate heating stove along the wall. The stove had been painted a rich brown-red color, and like the others, this one could be an excellent place to hide something.

The options got worse as Max checked out the other end of the house. Here were numerous rooms, each devoted to a specific trade — joiners, potters, tailors, shoemakers. Downstairs, he found more — blue dyers, tin and pewter workers, and a carved door that led to a kitchen and small dining hall.

Enough, he thought. He was wasting his time with this and unnerving himself with every step that sounded like somebody following him. *But if I'm being followed, then perhaps I'm close to something worth keeping an eye on. After all, didn't Hull order Modesto to get me researching this area?*

Cold air blew across his forehead. Max looked up to find a small vent cooling the room for guests — most certainly not a historically accurate portrayal of colonial times. And, of course, another possible hiding place.

Max stormed out of the building and stomped his way back to his car. He hoped the others had fared better.

With a few hours left before he had to meet at the office, Max went back to the library. He didn't want to show up empty-handed, and he had the research itch attacking the back of his head.

It was those POWs. Too many questions. But now he had names, and names could be researched.

The amount of information regarding World War II would have been staggering had he not seen it before. Even in the subset of POWs (and just German ones no less), Max's searches turned up thousands of hits. Yet when he plugged in the specific names, things became more manageable.

Krause, Richter, and Bauer had little in their records to suggest anything noteworthy other than all three had visited the States prior to the war. Schulz and König were strong men with families and neither had any contact with the U.S. previously. Fritz Keller was the most educated of the lot and had authored several articles in German newspapers before being called to duty. And Walter Huber proved to be the criminal of the bunch. In less than six months upon returning to Germany, he ended up in prison for armed assault. Nothing singled any of these men out.

"Not that I even know what I'm looking for," Max said to the computer screen.

One odd piece of information did perk up, however. Max found an artist's website that included dramatic collages made from World War II paperwork. The papers were chosen to match a theme — a picture of a gaunt Jewish prisoner had been made from Auschwitz population lists; a tribute to the fallen soldiers of D-Day came from copies of Eisenhower's famous orders; and there was even a German POW made from transfer papers.

Max spent close to an hour magnifying each small section of the collage, looking for any of the names, and to his surprise, he came upon the name Butner. Two sheets from about a week apart. The first showed the release orders for seven POWs to be sent to RJR. The second showed a return order, and though it was difficult to read, Max thought the sheet only showed six POWs returning.

"We got nothing," Drummond said before Max could kiss his wife or even sit at his desk.

"Speak for yourself," Sandra said.

"Doll, you were just saying that you didn't turn up anything else. Now that Max is back here, you going to make up some flimflam so you look good for your lover?"

"I swear, you act like you were a teenager when you died."

Max blotted out their noise as long as he could manage. When he couldn't take anymore, he raised his voice and said, "Do you have something or don't you?"

"Honey, relax."

"See," Drummond said, "You're making Max all tense."

"Be quiet. Now, Max, I found out that the Old Salem area is still active. It's not just public, historical buildings. Many of them are privately owned residences. The owners have a strict set of rules they have to follow to preserve their buildings, but they do live there."

Max nodded. "The lady I got my ticket from mentioned something about people still living there. It just makes matters worse. I went into several of the buildings and walked the streets. That book could be anywhere, and now you're saying it could be in a private residence."

"You're not letting me finish."

"Sorry. Go ahead."

"I found out that two of the buildings have been very quietly put on the market."

Max leaned forward. "How much are they going for?"

"Nobody'll tell me, but I wouldn't doubt for a second that Hull could buy them if he wanted to."

"I think he just might."

Drummond brushed by Max, Max's arm feeling as if it had been dashed with icy water, and said, "Looks like we have a bit of a pickle."

"What now?" Sandra said.

"Easy there, I'm just pointing out the fact that if you intend to find this book before Hull, you've got to do it before he buys those homes. Unless you can purchase them."

Sandra said, "It might not even be in those homes."

"That's right," Max said. "All of the building names on the list are buildings open to the public."

"But if it is in one of these private houses, you lose. If it isn't, Hull has a central location from where he can conduct all the searches he wants. Every night, he can check out each one of those old buildings until, voila, he finds his little treasure."

"Then we've got trouble. I was told there's a good chance Hull will make an offer in the next day or two. Well, actually it's that company Oxsten and Son, but of course, that's Hull."

Max glanced out the window. A chubby fellow with a thick mustache hustled up the sidewalk, a blue coffee mug in his hand. Across the street, a woman with her baby in a stroller walked by the YMCA. Normal life.

"I might be able to stall Hull for an extra day," Max said. "After all, I'm supposed to be researching this kind of thing for him anyway. Perhaps if we give him some misinformation, he'll waste a day or two checking it out."

"Ah," Drummond said with a lascivious smile, "we're finally getting into a little deception here. I like it."

Sandra said, "We still have the problem of the book itself. You said it could be anywhere in there."

"Well, true," said Max. Then he paused. An idea popped in his mind, one he knew would work, but he worried about suggesting it. The idea of using his wife, even if in a harmless manner, did not sit well. He could hear Drummond's reply in his head — *Better to use the wife than end up like me.* "I have a thought," he finally said.

"Congratulations," Drummond said.

"Let me meet with Modesto to try to stall Hull. Then, tomorrow night, Sandra and I could go to Old Salem together and you could —" He looked long at his wife. "— well, I'm sure there's a lot of ghosts around there."

Drummond perked up. "Hey, that's great. You could just ask the locals where this book is. Some of them may have even been there when it was hidden in the first place."

Sandra shook her head. "This is not a good idea."

"I don't think we have a better alternative," Max said as he sat on the desk's edge.

"I know, but I haven't told you everything about ghosts. See, when they're not bound like cheerful here, they're a lot different."

"How?"

"More capable."

Drummond pouted. "Hey. I'm plenty capable."

"What do you mean?" Max asked.

Sandra stared right into Max's eyes. "I mean they might not be so friendly, so willing to help. And they might be able to hurt us."

Chapter 19

WHEN MODESTO ARRIVED AT CITIES RESTAURANT for their regular meeting, he looked haggard — still immaculate to most eyes, but Max knew better. His hair perfect but for a few strands, his clothes sleek but for a subtle wrinkle, Modesto moved toward the table with an urgency that lacked grace. With his face crinkled in worry, he fumbled a greeting. Max tried to put these observations out of his mind. He had one job to do in this meeting — buy some time.

As Modesto slipped into his seat, he said, "What's been your progress in Old Salem?"

"Old Salem?" Max said, tinting his expression with as much innocence as he thought Modesto would swallow.

Modesto frowned. "You do recall who is paying your bills?"

"There's no need to be hostile."

"It seems your extra-curricular activities are clouding your judgment. So, let me ask this way: what exactly do you have for me today?"

"Why did you hire me?"

Modesto shook his head. "Mr. Porter, if you have failed in your duties, then please stop wasting my time and admit you have nothing to offer me. If you have information, then let me have it. I am extremely tired and our employer has not been pleased with you so far."

"I've done an excellent job. You asked for research on the Moravians, and I provided. You wanted research on various land deals, and I provided. I'm good at what I do."

"Then you have your answer, don't you? That is why you were hired."

"Why is he dissatisfied, then?" Max watched Modesto's face contort as the man strived for an answer that would not betray anything.

"I do not claim to understand the ranking system of our employer,"

Modesto finally said. "I am merely reporting his concerns to you."

Max said nothing for a moment, enjoying every second of Modesto's squirming. Even in the way they looked at each other through sideways glances and indirect observations, both men were dancing around the facts. "In that case," Max said, "let our employer know that you've informed me of his displeasure. If he desires to fire me —"

"He does not."

"I'm confused. I thought you said he felt my work was unsatisfactory."

"Just focus on your report."

"No, sir. Not when the quality of my work has been called into question."

Modesto glanced upward as if asking for strength. *Or perhaps,* Max thought, *he's looking at what liquor they have on the wall.*

"I assure you, I have found your work superior to most. I give you my word I shall state my satisfaction in my next report. Beyond that, there is little for us to discuss on the matter because I cannot speak for our employer on the subject. Is that enough for you?"

"A little appreciation is all I ask. Thank you, sir."

"What do you have for me?"

"There's one building in Old Salem up for sale."

"Just one?" Modesto asked, and Max saw in his eyes he not only knew that there were two, but he knew Max had lied.

"You'll find the details and my assessment in the folder," Max said, pushing a blue folder across the table. "Little company called Oxsten and Son is in position to take it. I can't find too much about them, but I will eventually. There might be more homes available soon, though. Including one near the Vogler house." This part was an entire fabrication, but Modesto's eager ears perked up, and Max knew he had bought a few hours while Modesto wasted time trying to find out anything about the fictitious house.

"Near the Vogler house."

"Yes, not on the market yet, but my wife has a friend in real estate who mentioned it in passing, so I'm doing the same. I hope you don't mind me using her for a little information. She doesn't know that I'm giving it to you, so don't worry about that."

"No problem."

"Would you like me to keep looking?"

Modesto stuffed the folder in his briefcase and said, "Yes, that would be fine. I'll review your work and we'll decide then what to do."

"I did uncover some interesting points concerning the area. Just a few things that might be of use to our employer."

"Oh?"

"For example, the Moravians put in the first waterworks system right here in Old Salem. Pipes and plumbing and such to bring running water into the homes."

"Mr. Porter, we are well aware of the basic knowledge available from an Old Salem tour."

"You're missing the point."

"And this would be?"

"Obviously I don't know anything specific about our employer but it seems clear that he is interested in antiquities of all kinds. Why else the search for old history and old land? I figured if he could acquire some of these ancient pieces, they would be worth a lot of money."

"I see."

"Another little tidbit I found was that during World War II, the Reynolds family used German POWs to help make cigarettes and such."

"Also a widely-known fact," Modesto said in a way that sounded more like a threat than a statement.

"My mistake. I just thought there might be old bits of memorabilia and such from the Germans, just something of value for the antiquities trade."

Modesto stood, regaining his composure so fast that Max thought he had pushed too far. With a slight bow of the head, Modesto said, "I don't think you're a very smart man."

"Gee, thanks."

"You don't lie very well and the choices you've made seem to be less than logical. I can't imagine how you manage to survive the rigors of life."

"Perhaps I'm not much of a liar, but I don't need to be one for this kind of work. All I need is for the person I'm talking with to be a liar as well."

"Excuse me?"

For the first time since Modesto had arrived, Max looked straight at him. "When you lie, you make it difficult to expose another's lies and near impossible to reveal the truth. It's a case of mutually assured destruction."

"Good day, Mr. Porter," Modesto said and left the restaurant.

Max waited until his food arrived. As he ate, he kept thinking about the little taunts and jabs he had used against Modesto. He had hoped to get Modesto riled enough to slip up with some information regarding Old Salem. Instead, he got little to help save for one thing — his own words. Max had mentioned the possibility of World War II memorabilia still in existence in the area. Perhaps he was right. Perhaps he should take a visit to Annabelle Bowman.

"What do you want?" Annabelle asked from behind her screen door. Her stern brow and hard glare invited little opening for reconciliation — not that he had expected a warm welcome.

"Please, Ms. Bowman, just a few moments of your time."

"I'm done talking with you."

"It's important."

"Go away. I'll call the police."

"I doubt the Hull family would be too keen on the police poking around why I'm here."

That got her. She glanced behind and when she looked back, her troubled eyes undercut her icy face. "If I let you in," she said a bit softer, "they'll hurt ... I ... I don't want this. Please, just go."

"I don't want you to get hurt. I just need to see a few things of Stan's — stuff he kept during the war, during his time at Reynolds, that kind of thing."

With a bit of the cold returning, she said, "I know what you want, but you can forget all about it. I told them the same thing. I destroyed it all. Hull wanted it gone and it's gone. So, let an old woman alone."

"The longer we argue out here, the more likely it is that somebody is going to see us."

"Shit," she said under her breath, opened the door, and rushed Max inside. "Now, look, I'll give you five minutes and then I want you out of here. Do you understand? You stick around any longer and I will call the police and I'll tell them you tried to rape me or murder me or something, but I assure you whatever I come up with will be ugly enough to divert all attention from Hull and me."

"Fair enough," Max said, hoping just to keep the lady talking. His eyes searched the room he sat in the last time he had visited — something had to be here, something from Stan. "I'm just trying to help out a friend. He was involved with Stan back during the whole affair and, well, I just need to clear up a few details. That's all. I promise."

"And what friend is that?"

"Considering how worried you are, it's best you don't know," he said, more confident about his skills than the last time he interviewed this woman but still knowing Drummond could do far better.

"Why can't you all just let that be buried?"

"I wish I could," Max said, as he read book titles, noted old pictures, and spied a dying fern in the corner. Nothing useful. *This is stupid*, he thought. *I'm fishing and I don't even know how to hold the rod.* Just before he apologized his way outside, he processed the words she said only a moment earlier — that she knew what he had come for and something about others coming for it as well. He pictured how Drummond would handle the matter, wiped away all the rudeness, and attempted a suave smile. "Listen, you're a nice lady and I don't want to cause you any more trouble than I have to."

"Then get out of here and leave me alone."

"I can't leave until you give me what I'm here for."

"I don't have it. I never did. Everybody thinks Hull and I were so close, but I'm telling you I never saw any book. After Stan had his troubles and I cleaned out his old footlocker, I did find ... but none of it matters anymore. So let it all rest."

"Hull came to you for a book of Stan's?"

Wiping her hands on her legs, she nodded. "After Stan died. Mr. Hull visited me several times."

"Is that when he bought you stock in RJR?"

"He felt terrible about everything that had happened to Stan and wanted to help me out. At least, that was what he said to me. But he really wanted Stan's book."

"What's in the book?" Max asked and the second the words left his lips, he knew had made a mistake.

Annabelle's posture stiffened and she tapped her watch. "Time for you to go. And I mean it this time. I will call the police. So, please, go."

"But —"

"And don't ever come back again. You are no longer welcome in my home."

Max sipped a mug of hot chocolate at the kitchen table. Sandra stirred her tea from the opposite side. The little wall clock ticked sharp and clear in the otherwise silent room.

At length, Sandra said, "I'm a little scared."

"Me too."

"I just wish we could pack up and leave."

Max set his mug on the table. "You wouldn't believe how many times I've had that thought. You know what, though? These things never leave you. You can't outrun them. Isn't that why we left Michigan — just running away from our problems? But look where we are now."

"This is different."

"I don't think so anymore. When I saw Annabelle Bowman today, I saw an old lady with a lot of fear and regret. Whether she knows about all the witchcraft and Hull and ghosts, who knows? But it doesn't matter. None of that changes anything. No matter how much she pretends the past is over, she can't outrun this. And in the end, because she won't deal with it, she's still just an old lady with a lot of fear and regret."

"Is that supposed to comfort me?" Sandra asked. They both shared a quiet smile and held hands across the table.

Max leaned his head back and said, "Did I ever tell you about Archie Lee?"

"I don't think so."

"He was a guy I knew back in college. I think he was Korean. Well, Asian, anyway. Isn't that horrible? I should know something like that."

Sandra shook his hand. "You got a point to all this?"

"Just that, I remember sitting with him in this house — it was at a party at somebody's house, and he was telling me all about his life. I must've said something to get him going or maybe he was just so drunk he'd have told anybody but he told me about how he had moved around a lot since he was seven years old. I forget how much but it was as if every other year he had to up and move to a new state or a new country or whatever. And he said that, at the time, he learned to love it because he got to try out new personalities with each new place. I remember him telling me that he knew he was a bit of a nerd, and when he would move, nobody knew anything about him. He could pretend to have been the coolest, most popular kid from his old school. He would wear the cool clothes, get the right haircut, the right book bag, whatever it took. Who could say otherwise?

"But then he got real silent. I thought it was the beer finally getting him down but he grew very serious and shook his head slowly. He said that it never worked. That no matter what he tried, eventually, the new kids would figure out that he was just a nerd."

"You think we're just nerds?" Sandra said.

"The reason Archie Lee was still a nerd was because he had focused only on changing the outside. It didn't matter how many times he moved. Nothing was going to change for him because he kept paying attention to the wrong things."

"Still waiting for the comforting thoughts in all this."

Max drank some more of his hot chocolate. "If we were to pack up and leave, run off to some other job in some other state, we'd end up stuck in it just like this time."

"Nothing is like this time."

"Okay, well, maybe not the exact same thing, but the point is we'd still be the same people making the same choices we always make. But if we stay, if we fight our way through all this, then maybe we can improve ourselves enough to make things different. I don't know, make things better. Besides, aren't you the one who told me we had to push through?"

Sandra said nothing for a few minutes, then she looked upon Max and said, "You know something? I love you."

Part of Max wanted to talk this out further, but he tried to listen to his own words. The old way was talk and talk and talk until every angle and emotion had been explored. In the end, they would make love, but the next morning, nothing much would change. This time, Max decided, would be different. This time, he would take her love and hold onto it, forget about analyzing it to death, and instead, draw on its strength. After all, they were about to go ghost hunting in Old Salem. He needed all the strength he could get.

Chapter 20

THEY PARKED ON SALT STREET, a quiet area dominated by one ancient tree and a wall of younger trees, and in full view of the backyards of the houses lining Main Street. Light drizzle fell, and the midnight moon glossed the wet pavement with a dim, quarter-crescent glow. The sound of water drips hitting fallen leaves peppered the air. Though people lived here, nobody appeared to be up at two in the morning.

"See anything?" Max whispered.

Sandra peered around. "There's a dog sniffing that tree."

"You see dead animals, too?"

"No. There's a real dog sniffing that tree."

Max followed Sandra's eyes and saw a small, black Dachshund puttering around a maple tree. Stifling a nervous giggle, Max said, "Let's just get to this."

Sandra pecked his cheek and headed up the street. "Honey, relax. We're just talking to some ghosts."

"There's a sentence I never thought I'd hear."

"I mean it. You've got nothing to fear."

"You're the one who said they can get all angry and hurt us when they're not bound."

"But you're with me. I won't let them harm you."

"You know some special handshake or something?"

"Let's just get this done," she said and turned onto West Street at a fast clip.

Max hurried to catch up. "Where to first?" he asked.

She gestured toward the town square. "That seems like the best place to start. I'll be able to see a lot of the area from the center."

Together they walked toward the grassy square, a truck passing on a distant street the only sound not of their making. Max listened to their breathing, their footsteps, their nervousness. *More than just fear,* he thought. If a person's imagination could have accidentally altered reality, he knew he would be bringing terrible creatures upon them. The idea of abandoning this pursuit, of rushing back to their car's safety and slipping home, seduced him for a fleeting moment. Then they arrived at the center, ringed by tall evergreens scenting the air with their wet fragrance.

"Okay, ready?" Sandra asked. Max could only nod. Sandra took a cleansing breath and turned in a slow circle. Her eyes darted about. She squinted at one spot, glossed over another, until she returned to the position where she had started. Another breath, another slow circular turn, another return to the start.

Max started to speak but Sandra snapped her head to the side. "What is it?" he asked, peering over her shoulder toward the Salem Academy. "What do you see?"

"I don't know," she said. "Not a ghost. At least, not like the ones I've always seen. This was more like a wisp of smoke, like black smoke that moved of its own will. But I didn't see anything solid."

"This place is hundreds of years old. Most of these buildings are original. It should be teeming with ghosts. Shouldn't it?"

"What are you talking about?" Sandra said, raising her voice enough to sound violent in the still night air. "What do you know about it? You've seen one ghost and you think you understand it? I've been dealing with this my whole life, and I've been doing it on my own — no formal training, no mentor, nothing. So forgive me if I can't make it all work just the way you want it on cue."

Max stepped back. "I didn't mean it that way. I don't feel comfortable here. I want this to be over. That's all." But that wasn't all. He didn't want to tell her that he had caught sight of the black wisp, too, and to him it was not a shadowy spirit at all, but rather a shadow — they were being watched.

"There," Sandra said and pointed in the opposite direction of the shadow.

"What do you see?"

"I don't know yet. Something, though. A faint glimmer of something," she said and headed across the slippery grass.

Max followed, glancing over his shoulder several times but never catching even a glimpse of the shadow he had seen before. Perhaps it was just an overactive imagination playing on his nerves. The idea made sense, but Max just couldn't believe it.

Sandra crossed the street and stepped onto the brick laid sidewalk.

Old trees pushed up the bricks with their roots, making the path a series of miniature mountains and valleys. She knelt down and smiled into empty space. "Hello," she said. Max squatted behind her but he saw nothing. "You're very pretty ... I can't hear you too well," she said. Then she jumped to her feet. "Wait! Come back!" Wiping the damp hair out of her face, she turned to Max. "She disappeared. Damn. I don't think she knew, you know? That she was dead? I must've scared her pretty bad."

"Don't be ridiculous. I'm sure she runs from ghost-seeing people all the time."

Sandra responded with just a hint of a smile — enough to ease them both a little. "This is going to be tricky," she said. "Don't worry, though, we'll get one of them to help us."

Together they stood on the sidewalk, each silent, each searching the empty grounds. Max checked every window, every doorway, every nook he thought might harbor an enemy.

An enemy? The idea that he now had faceless enemies to contend with, had been contending with for some time, eroded any illusion of security he still horded. *Come on, ghosts,* he thought. *Show yourselves already.*

Another five minutes passed before Sandra said, "On the corner." She waved and approached like a tourist seeking a little friendly information — not too far from the truth, in fact. "Excuse me," she said, "I'm looking for a book that was placed around here awhile back ... a book ... no, no, a book." To Max, she said, "I think we're supposed to follow."

"Then let's follow."

Max kept a few steps back from Sandra so as not to crowd her or her invisible companion — plus, it afforded him a better distance to react from in case somebody moved against them. Not that he had an inkling what to do should anything happen, but some chance was better than none at all. Watching the sway of his wife's hips sent a jolt through his body — he would rather be at home in bed with her than traipsing in the drizzle, but then he'd rather never have heard of Hull or any of this in the first place.

"This way," Sandra said, pointing to the long building Max had toured during daylight — Single Brothers House.

"How do we get in?" Max asked as he jiggled the locked door handle.

"I think," Sandra said and they heard a click from behind the door.

"Looks like our ghost is being helpful."

"Let's just keep on his good side."

Sandra frowned. "How did you know that?"

"I assume an angry ghost would not be a good idea."

"No, you said *his*. You said, 'Let's just keep on *his* good side.' How did you know the ghost was male?"

Had it been broad daylight, had they not been talking about ghosts of long dead settlers, he might have had a flippant or sarcastic reply. Instead, under the thin moonlight and steady drizzle, his chest grew heavy. "I don't know," he whispered, afraid to think the question through. "Just a guess." Without waiting for a response, he tried the door handle again and this time it opened with ease.

They stepped into the wide foyer, the hollow sound of their footsteps on old wood echoed throughout the empty building. A musty odor tickled Max's nose, thicker than when he had visited before, and though rather open in design, Max felt the walls tightening around him in the darkness. He fumbled for his flashlight, and when he flicked it on, the narrow, pale beam made the claustrophobic sensation worse as if only the illuminated sections of the building existed.

Sandra drew a quick breath. "Wow," she said.

"Ghosts?"

"Just two others, but they're impressive looking. Their light is so bright."

Max moved the flashlight around but saw only an empty foyer. "Can you see our fellow?"

"It's hard," she said, squinting in the dark.

"Call him. Maybe he can still hear you."

"Shh. Please, let me do this."

Max waited, wondering what the ghosts were doing, where they stood. Did they see him? Did they feel his presence? Perhaps that's why he felt so closed in — perhaps he felt them surrounding him.

Sandra turned right and crept down the trade hall. The joiner's room on the right looked menacing in the flashlight beam — wooden skeletons of unfinished furniture surrounded by tortuous tools of assorted sizes. They proceeded further down the hall. The potter's room on the left with its foot-powered spinning wheel turned into a macabre lair where strange experiments of creation occurred under their nighttime gaze. Then, to Max's dismay, the ghost led them downstairs to the darker, colder basement floor.

Max struggled to recall the pleasant daytime feel of this building but even the scuffling of their feet against the stone floor transformed into a hideous monster lurking just beyond the flashlight beam. He followed Sandra and the ghost down the hall until they stopped at a door on the left. A placard on a podium explained that this room had once been used for training but later came to be a storage room. Sandra stepped over the rope barring the entrance and pointed to a dusty pile of junk filling up the corner.

"I think it's in here," she said and started sifting through the pile.

Max entered the room to help. Broken pottery and old wood scraps lay around, haphazardly discarded in the room. A broom, a mop, bits of paper, and other leftovers filled in the numerous nooks of the small room. When Max pulled out a large, metal hook, Sandra said, "Crap."

"What?"

To the empty space, she said, "Book. I said, 'Book.' With a *B*. Damn."

Letting the hook clatter to the ground, Max said, "Great."

"Don't go," she said, stepping toward the outer-wall. Then her shoulders drooped. "He's gone."

"I'm sorry, honey, this was just a bad idea. These ghosts aren't going to help us."

"That's only the second one. We've got to give it more time. It's not easy. Not all ghosts are as connected with the world like Drummond. Some of them are barely here at all. It's like trying to get directions during a snowstorm in Siberia and you don't speak Russian. Get it?"

"I know. I'm not blaming you. But, really, this could go on all night with no luck."

"Or we might hit it big."

Max heard wood creaking from above. "Shh," he snapped and turned out the flashlight. With slow, quiet movements, he edged toward Sandra. He stepped into the corner of something sharp, pain bursting at his hip, and grunted as he wrangled back the urge to yell. He felt around — the podium with the placard. Inching a few steps at a time, he worked around the podium and reached Sandra, put his mouth to her ear and whispered, "I think somebody's been following us since we got here."

"How do we get out?" she asked, her voice steady despite her rigid body.

"To the left and upstairs there's a door. It leads out back to the gardens. When we go, I'll turn the flashlight on and keep it pointed straight at the ground. At the stairs, I'll turn it off and the rest we have to do in the dark. Move quick but not so fast that you'll get hurt. And ... I don't know. That's the best I can come up with."

"It's plenty good."

"I love you, you know."

"Right back at you," she said, turned her face and pressed her lips against Max with such force that his chest swelled with an overwhelming sensation — love and dread swirling like two wrestlers forever clenched together.

When she pulled back, she exhaled slow and deliberate. "Okay. I'm ready."

"Okay," he said, "I'm turning on the flashlight. Get ready to move. Here we go."

Max pushed the flashlight's button, and it blazed light onto the floor. He saw the podium and the various piles of wood and boxes, and in the doorway, he saw the figure of a man lunging toward him.

Chapter 21

TOGETHER, MAX AND SANDRA let out a startled cry. The man leapt atop Max and the flashlight banged to the floor, shutting off, leaving them in darkness. Max shoved hard but could not budge his attacker. Two strong hands gripped his throat, pushing his head back and slicing his ear against the corner of some plywood. Again, Max attempted to push off the man but the struggle for air weakened him.

"Max? Max?" Sandra called as she fumbled in the dark. He wanted to reach out to her, to hold her hand, and the thought flashed in his mind that, at least, it wasn't her throat being strangled at the moment. He pictured this man straddling her, choking her, and hoped she had the sense to run now while she could get away.

The image in his mind brought to the forefront that he should have done what any sensible woman would have attempted from the beginning. Mustering the last of his strength, Max garbled out a yell and rammed his knee upward into the man's groin. His knee hit something hard and he heard a crack. The man grunted a cry and rolled to the side, curled in a fetal position and whimpering.

Max wheezed and gasped as he crawled forward, one hand massaging his throat, the other seeking the flashlight. The fight had sent ages of dust into the air, drying out Max's mouth with its dead taste. Blood dribbled from his ear. He felt a hand grab his wrist, but before he could utter a painful yelp, he heard the welcome voice of his love.

"It's me, it's me," she said. "I can't find the flashlight."

He pulled her hand towards his chest and breathed in her hair. Together, they stumbled to their feet and groped a path into the hall.

"This way," Max said, every syllable searing his throat. He turned left and moved as fast as he dared in the darkness. When he reached a wide door, slants carved into the wood, he searched for a handle or knob.

The door wouldn't open. *Calm down*, he scolded himself. *Don't panic.* "I think it's locked," he said.

"Be sure," Sandra yelled.

"We're wasting time. That guy's not going to be down for long. He was wearing a cup, for crying out loud. A fucking cup. What kind of person wears a cup?"

"A professional, honey."

"That's what I'm saying. Now, let's go back the way we came. I can get us out of here."

"But the door."

"Sandra, trust me."

He heard the rustling of her clothing as she nodded. Then he heard something that shot adrenaline through his body — silence. Why didn't he hear the groans of their enemy?

"Sandra," he whispered. Her hands fidgeted about his arm until they found his right hand again where they affixed firm. Without another word, he led her back down the hall, his left hand trailing the rough wall.

He heard the grunt a second before he felt the man's fist strike his lower back. Max arched as the man grabbed his head and tossed him into the wall. His left arm blocked much of the impact, but still he saw little blue flashes in the darkness.

He heard Sandra scream. He heard the man yell. He heard a body smack into something hard and drop. As he forced himself to stand (he only just noticed he had fallen to the floor), Max felt hands grab hold of his arm. He yanked back, flailing in the dark.

"It's okay. It's me," Sandra said.

"Where's —"

"I don't know. He grabbed me and I bit his hand. Then I swung my fist and hit him — I think in the head but I'm not sure. I can't see anything. Can you walk?"

"I'm okay," Max said, wrapping his arm around her shoulder and using her as a crutch. His head blazed, and he wanted to vomit but managed to keep setting one foot in front of the other.

They reached the stairs and clambered up to the main floor. Light from the streets pierced the darkness in sharp slivers — enough to move fast. Max took three deep breaths, let go of Sandra, and focused on walking in a straight line. Each step sent stabs up his side but he pushed on. Knowing the danger just one floor below motivated him plenty.

Sandra darted ahead, reached the backdoor and rattled the handle until it opened. He could see her triumphant smile. "I got it," she said.

She put her arm around his waist for support, and together they stepped into the backyard, light rain dancing on their faces and filling the chill night air with its fresh smell. They hurried along the path leading to the garden and the fenced-in crops. Max expected to hear the man slam open the door and chase after them but nothing came. Not yet. Sandra slipped on the wet ground, causing Max to stumble as well, but they managed to stay standing and rushed to the garden's end.

"Can you climb over?" Sandra asked.

The fence was made of wood and only chest high, but Max knew the climb would hurt. The idea of going back and around the fence did not sit well, though, so he nodded. Wincing and grunting, and with the aid of Sandra, he managed the small feat.

"The car's this way," Sandra said, heading left.

"No," Max said. "They might be waiting for us."

"They? There's more than one?"

"I don't know, but we're not risking it. Let's go around, take the long way, and we'll circle back. If there's only one or a whole gang it won't matter. Either they'll have left by that time or we'll be able to see them as we approach. We'll know then and figure it out from there."

"Okay," she said, scanning the area. "We're on Old Salem Road."

"Follow it to the right. I think it curves a few blocks up and connects with Main Street."

As they walked along the glistening street, several cars shot by. Max felt too unsteady for this street. He kept seeing himself weave into the path of an oncoming car. With a nod, he led Sandra back onto Salt Street, heading away from their car and paralleling Old Salem Road.

He checked over his shoulder for any pursuit. Just empty street. White streetlamps dotted the right side of the road, one with a white street sign — the paint chipping off. The left side had a brick sidewalk and homes. The cracked pavement pooled water. A weird sensation formed in Max's chest, worked upward until it reached his face, and emerged with a fit of giggles.

"What are you laughing at?" Sandra asked, smiling at his infectious sound.

Max tried to suppress the noise, clamping his mouth down, but it only served to strengthen the laughter until it burst from his nose. He shook his head as he laughed, wiped his tearing eyes, and said, "I'm just thinking about that guy. He's all acting tough and then Wham! You nailed him." The laughter erupted again.

Sandra joined in. "I wish it hadn't been so dark. Can you picture his face? Duh!" she said and crossed her eyes. Max laughed so hard he stopped making sound and clutched his side in pain yet unable to stop smiling. After a few more feet, they had to sit on the wooden steps of a house until all their tension had been released. With a cleansing breath, Max said, "Oh my. We shouldn't laugh. When we get back we should call the police or somebody. That guy might've gotten hurt."

"So what? You really care what happens to him? He tried to kill you."

"I don't know if he would've gone that far."

"They've already shot at you."

"I just don't want to become like them. We can be better people. You know?"

Sandra squeezed his arm. "Okay. We'll call. But right now, let's keep moving. Whoever they are, they probably don't care about being the better people."

"Good point," Max said. They got back to their feet and headed along the street, their steps not filled with as much dread as before. Up ahead, the road ended. The grass rose steeply for just a short step and off to the right they saw a giant, silver coffee pot, at least ten-feet high, probably more, surrounded by flowers. "What the heck?"

A small plaque explained that the large tin coffee pot had been created in 1858 by the Mickey brothers as an advertisement for their tinsmith business. Max shook his head. "This place is nuts," he said.

"I think it's neat," Sandra said. "It's like a touch of the modern day seeping back into history. Granted, advertising isn't the best aspect of us to have seep back but still it just makes me ..."

"Are you okay?" Max asked. Sandra turned around and stared. Max followed her gaze and saw nothing. "Another ghost?"

She nodded. Then she whispered, "It's coming straight at us. It's beckoning us."

"Tell it to go away. We're done for the night."

"I can barely hear him."

"There's nothing worth hearing."

"Shush already."

Sandra leaned forward and cupped one ear. She looked so ridiculous, appearing to listen to the giant coffee pot, that Max felt another wave of giggles rising. But before he could utter one chuckle,

Sandra stepped back with her face drained of color. A few months ago, Max would have said, "What's the matter? See a ghost?" Of course, now, he knew she had and that something far worse bothered her.

She turned her gaze toward him and said, "He says he's been watching us tonight. He says he knows what book we want. We just have to follow him."

"So, what's the matter?"

"We have to go over there," she said pointing further along the way they had been traveling.

"Why's that scare you? I just see trees and the street. Is there something else?"

"One more street over — that's where we're going."

Without offering more, she walked away. Max hurried to her side and attempted to get her to talk, but she behaved in a weird, zombie-like manner. *Shock,* he thought. But from what?

They passed a white building with tall columns that once may have been a mansion or a public assembly but now served as apartments. Turning up Bank Street, they saw sleek black statuettes lining the outside of the apartment building — a lion, a retriever, and some other dog Max did not know. The statuettes held relaxed poses that filled Max with more dread than if they had been menacing in appearance — as if their calm lay in knowing they had to exert such little effort to capture their prey.

"Where's it taking us?" Max asked, not expecting an answer but needing to hear a voice even if it belonged to him. He tasted blood in his mouth and swallowed it down. Sandra moved on, one hand out as if feeling for the ghost more than seeing the thing.

Bank Street rose steeply, and when they finally reached the next street over, Max huffed as he stared at the gothic structure. *A church,* he thought. Then he understood Sandra's behavior. Before them, stretching off into the distance was a low, brick wall with white fencing completing it. An arched gate led into an enormous field. A sign read:

SALEM MORAVIAN GRAVEYARD
"GOD'S ACRE"
1771
PLEASE BE REVERENT AND
RESPECTFUL OF THIS SPECIAL PLACE.

Chapter 22

WHEN THEY PASSED THROUGH THE ARCHWAY, everything changed. Until that moment, even as they crossed the street and approached the cemetery, Max would have been glad to call it a night. His body ached, his nerves jangled, nothing felt right. But when they entered the stone fields, though his fear compounded, his mind swelled with awe — never had he seen a cemetery like this one.

The graves were all the same — flat, white tablets laid in orderly squares; men and women separated; a few American flags the only vertical aspect to the burials. Enormous, ancient trees protected much of the well-manicured area.

Max figured that in daylight this would be a charming, peaceful place. At night, however, the eerie uniformity and stark whiteness of the tombstones mixed with the thick silence surrounding the cemetery created a stomach-twisting sensation. He felt burdened by the graves as if a giant child had placed them so carefully and now hawked over to make sure he did not disturb a single thing.

"There's too many," Sandra said, squinting in the dark. "I can barely see."

Max saw nothing but imagined well that his wife suffered from the many ghosts of a graveyard. He wanted to push her to find the one they had followed but kept silent. She didn't need him to bug her about the obvious.

"This way, I think," Sandra said, picking up her pace while shielding her eyes with her hand.

As they walked, Max read the name, dates, and epitaphs off several graves. From his research he recognized many of them. Joseph Harris (1821-1883) *The Lord is my Shepard*. William Whitt (1900-1923) *Innocence Taken Early Will Shine In Heaven*. Rebecca Burman (1818-1890) *A Light in Our Days*. Eve Hull (1750-1837) *Tucker Loved Her*.

Max paused to read the marker again. So Eve had chosen Tucker after all. Only something must have happened to bring her home. No way would the Moravians bury her here if she was still married to a magic dabbling sinner.

"Honey? Can you see the ghosts?"

Max looked up at Sandra, surprised to see the concern on her face. "No. Only Drummond. Why? What are they doing?"

"The one we're following — it stopped here."

With a nod to the grave, Max said, "That's why." He let out a long breath. "I suppose I'll be digging quite a lot tonight."

"Max," she said, a sudden tremble in her voice that tightened around Max's neck and shoulders.

"What's wrong?"

Stepping back with her hand gesturing to the air in front of Max, she said, "The ghost. It's reaching toward you."

"Tell it to stop."

"Stop it! Please," she said, her eyes glistening. "It won't listen."

A scraping, shuffling sound rolled in. They both peered back toward the street. A dark figure approached, dragging one foot behind, clearly disoriented but determined.

"It's him," Max said.

"Run. Go. This ghost looks mean. I think it's going to do something bad. I think —"

But Max did not move. He watched the emptiness before him, wondering what it wanted with him. Why bring him all the way out here and show him the grave, if it only had wanted to harm him? Why approach slowly, cautiously, if it only had wanted to attack? "It's okay, honey," he said, knowing he sounded weak and unsure. "I think it wants to help us some more."

"You can't see this thing. Run!"

Max heard the shuffling from behind and felt the air in front of him grow cold. *Don't be an idiot*, he thought. He turned away, reached for Sandra's hand, and pushed off his feet but running away did not occur. Instead, he felt ice break into the back of his skull.

"Max!"

He faced Sandra, and before he could wonder what had caused her ghastly countenance, he saw the ghost. It floated next to him, wore a suit, tie, and derby from the late-1800s. Its face had rotted away leaving behind a skull with bits of stringy skin hanging from its jaws like seaweed from an ancient wreck. And it had its hand thrust into Max's head. The cold spreading throughout Max's brain brought sharp flashes of pain.

"Stop it!" Sandra screamed at the ghost, but it did not budge. "Max! Max! What's it doing to you? Are you okay?"

Max looked back toward the man that had been pursuing them. As he turned his head, he saw the blinding light of thousands of ghosts. "I can see them," he said. "This hurts, but I can see them all."

As his ear began to freeze, Max tried to focus on the book. The ghost had helped them get this far, maybe this 'sight' it had given him was also meant to help. *Hurry,* his cold brain implored.

Awestruck by the multitude of transparent figures floating throughout the graveyard, Max could not stop gawking — even as the cold and throbbing pain reached downward toward his chest, even as the man bent on killing them came closer. Like a grand masked ball, there were people of all ages dressed in all forms of clothing from the eighteenth century to present day. A young couple strolled hand in hand as if on a Sunday afternoon. A bent man hugged another man with a loud welcome. They all moved with grace like swans in morning fog.

"Max!" Sandra said, snapping him back.

The book. He scanned the nearest ghosts, hoping one of them carried it. The hand stuck in his head pushed him to the ground so that he looked upon Eve Hull's grave. He started digging around the edges, the stone cold to the touch — or perhaps his fingers had just gone numb, he couldn't tell.

"Hurry," Sandra said, knelling beside him to help dig.

The ghost that held him tugged and pushed. Max ignored these encouragements — he moved as fast as he could and no amount of pressure from a ghost would change that. He glanced up at the approaching man. "Damnit," Max said, turning toward the ghost, the pain in his head firing high at the movement. "Instead of hurting me, get your friends to stop that guy."

As he turned back, he saw at least ten, maybe twenty, ghosts soar toward the man — arms outstretched. As they prodded the man, slipping their hands into his head, arms, legs, stomach, and chest, the man convulsed with each attack. He fought against this invisible assault, forcing himself several steps forward. More ghosts flew in creating a blinding white light centered on the man. In the end, he turned away and scuttled from the cemetery.

As Max turned back to the grave, the cold spreading over his stomach, he saw a ghostly outline inside the grave next to Eve Hull's. It was a glowing rectangle — like a book. He opened his mouth but no sound came out. He pointed but Sandra did not see his shaking hand.

When he fell to his knees, she looked up. "Enough!" she said. "You're going to kill him. Let him go. We'll find the book. Just let him go."

The ghost turned its hand more and Max groaned. Sandra stood and with a sound colder than Max's body felt, she said, "Let go of my husband." When the ghost did not move, she pulled back a fist and smashed the ghost in the stomach. It fell back and disappeared but not before uttering a shocked cry.

With a gulp of air as if he had been drowning, Max doubled over. Warmth flushed his body and every nerve tingled as if it had fallen asleep. "How ... did you ... do that?" he said through gasps.

Sandra smiled with bewildered excitement. "I figured if they can touch us —"

Max looked around but now only saw darkness. "Is it still here?"

"Yes, but it doesn't seem to be doing much. They're all just standing around waiting. I think I've freaked them out a little."

"Come here. This grave. The book is here. That's what the ghost wanted to show us."

Exhausted, but excited as well, Max and Sandra dug around the edges of the stone. Their fingers dirtied with the muddy ground, but they did not stop. Sweat mingled with drizzle, but they did not stop. They had been through too much that night to stop over such minor matters as discomfort.

When they had dug beneath the stone, Max gripped it with the tips of his fingers and lifted. Straining, he pulled the stone from the sucking ground. Sandra grabbed on from the other side and pulled. The gravestone lifted a little bit, but its weight threatened to bring it right back down. With a low grunt, Max lifted harder, getting one foot underneath him and pushing upward. The ground emitted a loud slurp and the stone broke free, sending a wave of warm air upward. It smelled bad, but bad odors were among their least concerns.

Sitting in the middle of the mud square that marked where the stone had been was a wrapped package. Neither Max nor Sandra moved at first. Stunned by the simple object that had caused so much trouble, Max felt a wave of guilt rush over him like he had when he was a kid and broke the law by stealing a comic book. He looked around the empty cemetery, half-expecting to see the police come zooming in with flashing reds and blues.

"Take it," Sandra said. "Take it and let's get out of here."

Max snatched the package and tucked it under his coat to protect it from the drizzle. Like a child anxious to receive a reward, he hurried his steps, clutching the package close to his stomach, protecting it like a baby. It pressed against his skin with a warm touch and the smell of decay drifted toward his nose as they headed back.

Though both wanted to get to the car and leave Old Salem, they took a long route around to continue avoiding Main Street. A car drove by — the lonely sound of its motor in the quiet night reached them long after it had passed. When they arrived at the small Salt Street lot and saw their car sitting under the large tree where they had left it, Max felt both relief and worry. Sandra gripped his hand.

They stood across the street, watching the car, wondering if the man who had assaulted them watched it, too. With water dribbling off of Max's head, his body cold except for the warmth of a package torn from the grave, his bones aching from the night's exertions, part of him just wanted to walk home. *The hell with this moron.* But the idea of walking for miles, of taking hours before he could safely open what rested against his stomach, was more than he could stand.

"Damn," he said, walking to the car with a firm step and a defiant scowl. Sandra came behind, de-activated the alarm, and unlocked the doors before they reached the car.

Once inside, Sandra drove off, not waiting for either of them to settle in, put on a seatbelt, or even open the package. She let out a long sigh dotted with chuckling. Then she reached above, flicked on the interior light, and said, "Well, go on. Let's see if this was worth it."

With careful motions, Max produced the package and unwrapped it. A journal — a leather-covered journal. The smell of old age and forgotten times wafted over him as he opened it to the first page.

"Oh," he said.

"What?"

"This isn't Hull's journal."

"What? No. That can't be," Sandra said, her eyes welling.

"It's okay. Really. Maybe even better. This journal belongs to Stan Bowman."

Chapter 23

MAX SETTLED INTO HIS DESK CHAIR like an injured dog — slow, cautious, and whimpering. Every bit of skin, muscle, and bone throbbed. Every motion, every glance, every sound pulsed pain through his head far exceeding the worst hangover of his college life. Wrapped in a blanket while his clothes dried over a chair, he sipped a little of the whiskey Drummond had provided, turning his whimpers into less embarrassing grumbles.

"Enough of your whining; what's in the journal?" Drummond asked as he paced the room.

Sandra eased in the other dry chair, also wrapped in a blanket, also sipping Drummond's whiskey. She leaned her head back, closed her eyes, and would have fallen asleep if not for her own intense curiosity over the journal.

Max yawned. It was close to four in the morning, and his body reminded him for the hundredth time that night, he was no longer a young man. All-nighters of any variety were a thing of the past.

"Let's see," he said as he opened the journal. Its distinctive, earthy odor lifted into the air as he turned the pages. "You gotta be joking."

"What's wrong?" Drummond asked.

"No dates," Max said, skimming page after page. "Not a single date is recorded. What kind of nitwit writes a journal without dates?"

Sandra smiled. "The kind that only writes it for himself. I hate it when people date their entries as if expecting that someday when they die, the public will cry out to know about their lives and all that crap. Nobody cares about that stuff. He wrote this for himself. And that's good for us. It means we'll get the unvarnished truth as he saw it."

Drummond pointed to Sandra. "You are a bright, bright lady. I'm telling you, sweetheart, if you weren't married and I wasn't dead —"

"I'll keep that in mind."

"Here," Max said. "Yeah, listen to this one — 'It's been a long time since I've written in this thing. Part of me thought I was done with it. I thought I didn't need this old book anymore. Guess some things never finish. They just hang in the back of your head waiting for a chance to spring alive again. The war was like that. I'm done with it. Served my time, did a good job, and gave up good use of a leg in the process. Damn Krauts took my leg. And I'm thinking I'm finished, it's over for me, nothing more to do with it. But some things just never die. I don't think a single one of us will ever be done with this war. We'll be in our eighties, walking with canes, and we'll still be living the whole nightmare over and over. And to prove this, I merely have to think about today. Mr. William Hull dropped by with RJR himself. They walked in like two noblemen come to look at the serfs. For the first time in my life I thought I might know what a negro feels like. I think some others felt it too. Especially Artie Thompson. After the two kings left, one of the black boys who tries to pick up a few bit helping with trash and such came in. Artie hollered on and on, spit on the boy, and kicked him a few times until the tike ran off. But that's not the thing. The thing was Hull."

"Skip all this," Drummond said. "Somewhere in the back there should be papers or drawings or something like this curse on the floor."

Max skimmed through the final ten pages. Then he went backward until he reached the spot he had read from. With a gentle shake of his head, he closed the book and said, "Sorry. It's not here."

"It has to be."

"This is Stan Bowman's journal. Your curse must be in Hull's or the witch's, if either of them even kept a journal."

"Damnit!" Drummond swiped his hand through the clothes drying on the chair, knocking a few to the floor.

Setting her mug on the desk with a hard thump, Sandra bent over to pick up the fallen clothes. She said, "Read some more. Bowman knew Hull, right? Maybe there's something in there that will help us find Drummond's —"

"That's right. She's right. Read more. Come on."

Max re-opened the journal, snapping the pages as he found his place. Drummond hovered behind, his eagerness wrapping around Max like a python. "A little space, please," Max said. Drummond muttered as he drifted toward the door. "Thank you. Now, here it is. 'The thing was Hull. I'd never met the man before today. I'd heard about him, of course, and like many big names, he did not match his celebrity. He struck me as a priss. To be fair, I didn't think too highly of him before any of today happened. He used his influence to avoid serving. How can you respect a man like that? Anyway, there he was acting as if he were better than the rest of us and he starts looking over the Krauts. And here's where today got real weird. I swear he recognized one of them. He doggone knew one of those Krauts for sure. I have no doubt. And the Kraut knew him. They locked eyes for just a second, but I saw it. So, the real question now is what do I do about it?'"

"Well, well," Drummond said. "I smell blackmail."

"You see the worst in everybody," Max said.

"Occupational hazard."

"'I called on Hull today. That must have given his staff a fit or two, crappy little nothing like me just walking up to his gate. They were all ready to throw me out but I told them they'd lose their jobs if they didn't see that William Hull read my letter. There was just enough conviction in my voice that they weren't sure what to do. So, they did what any fearful staff does — they hedged their bets. One took the letter to Hull while the other glared at me and waited for the merest sliver of a signal to pound me into the dirt. Less than five minutes later, I was sitting in Hull's office. The letter said that I saw the look between him and the Kraut. That was it. Simple and direct. I was nervous going in there. Not everyday you try to blackmail a multi-millionaire.'"

"Told you so."

Drummond's crowing rattled Max's ears, sending another splitting ache through his head. "Great," Max said. "You're gifted at predicting the evils within men's hearts. Can I continue now? 'I know it was a bad thing to do but we're just getting our feet back on the ground, and to give Annabelle more than just getting by money. To be able to buy her a nice coat or even (I can't believe I can even consider writing this down) to buy her jewelry, it's just too much to turn away. Besides, Hull don't need all that money. He can spare a little and still live like a spoiled king.' He goes on for a few pages ranting and cursing about Hull."

Max poured more whiskey in his mug. Drummond said, "Hey, go easy. That's all I have."

"You're dead, remember?"

"It's still mine. I like to have it around."

Turning the page, Max read on, "'Annabelle is asleep and I'm sitting here writing and in my coat pocket is a check for more money than I can even think about and now I'm saying the hell with all of them. I'm going to do what the government paid me to do for the last few years. Not exactly but close enough."'

"Man," Sandra said, "this guy is a piece of work. He can justify anything. Blackmail, torture. What's next?"

With a far-off gaze, Drummond said, "Let's just hope he didn't write in detail about that. I've seen the end result of his handiwork. We can skip those details."

Sitting up in his chair, his drying hair matted against his forehead, Max said, "Listen to this: 'I've done it. The bastard Kraut is sitting here in front of me as I write this. I can't believe it. It was so easy. I rented this place with Hull's money, and nobody is going to bother us.' There's a break and then he writes ..."

"What? What does he write?" Drummond asked.

Max swallowed against his nausea. "Details," he said.

"Skip ahead."

"Please," Sandra added.

While Max tried to avoid various combinations of words like 'inserted the rod into his intestines,' Drummond resumed his pacing. Sandra said, "It's a good thing you're a ghost. We'd have no carpet left."

Drummond ignored her. "When I was on this case, we never were able to trace the money Bowman used to finance his torture chamber. Mostly he paid in cash, but this says he paid for it all with blackmail money, and that Hull gave the initial payment by check."

"So, how come there's no record?"

"And why did Bowman take a check at all? He's not brilliant but he never struck me as a dumb man. Why would he leave any kind of a paper trail?"

Sandra yawned. "Maybe he knew from the start there wouldn't be a paper trail."

"The bank," Drummond said. "I'll bet if we look a little deeper into Bowman's bank we'll find it was owned in some large part by William Hull. He could make the trail disappear with relative ease. Whatever was going on with that look, whatever was worth paying off Bowman to keep secret, Hull must have planned to fix the paper trail as well. And it's got to be far easier fixing it when the paper belongs to your own bank."

"He gets pretty nuts near the end," Max said as he turned another page. "It all becomes jumbled rambling. He thinks Annabelle is cheating on him. 'All the time I catch her looking away from me, wracked with guilt. And she stares at me too. She stares and stares and stares as if I'm going to jump up and yell that yes I am the man! I am the one! The scourge who has kidnapped and tortured five German POWs. Look on me with disgust, disdain, diswhateverthefuckyouwant! I am all you hate! So go off and fuck whoever you've got! But she'll get no satisfaction from me. And I'll find out, don't worry about that, I'll find out who she's seeing.'"

Sandra said, "Sounds pretty out there."

Drummond grunted. "You think she really was cheating on him? That'd be great."

"It would?"

"Well, not for him, but for us. Her lover might still be around. It's a lead."

"But we don't know who he is."

"Not yet."

"Wow," Max said. "Listen here: 'Hull came by tonight. I was chiseling out Günther's incisors and then there's Hull standing behind me. He blows on and on about how what I was doing was wrong. But he wasn't there. He never fought against these bastards. Money kept him from serving a day in the war. I got no money. My leg is worthless. But I got these POWs, so I'm not stopping. It's the only thing that gets me through the day. Hull said I'd go to Hell for all this. Probably. But I'm doing it anyway.' That's it. No more entries."

"He must've disappeared after that," Drummond said.

"Well," Max said, "at least you know what happened. Or most of it, anyway."

Sandra collected their mugs and cleaned them in the bathroom sink. "You know," she said, "I still don't understand why all this cursing business happened. So what if Drummond was closing in on Hull? There was no paper trail. Hull bought off Annabelle with a stock option. He covered his tracks except for this journal. Right? Whatever Hull's big secret was, he had buried it fine. And what does it matter now? I mean why was somebody trying to stop us tonight from finding this thing?"

"Honey," Max said as she stepped back into the office. Taylor leaned in the hall doorway, sopping wet, bruised and bleeding, and holding a handgun. "I think we're about to have an answer."

Chapter 24

Sandra edged towards Max. "You?" she said. "You're the guy that's been after us?"

"That just takes it all, don't it?" Drummond said.

Taylor ran his tongue over a bloody gap in his teeth. "You really think I was just some idiot lackey? You really think I just sat around all day waiting for orders from you? I've been working for Hull this whole time."

"Well, we knew that," said Max. "We just didn't think you'd be — what are you?"

"I'm a hitman," Taylor said, kicking at a chair and spitting out blood.

"More like a wannabe hitman," Drummond said as he floated behind Taylor and made goofy faces. The gun in Taylor's trembling hand persuaded Max not to laugh. Sandra, however, took a less tactful approach.

"So," she said, "you're a hitman? Hull hired you to kill us? I don't think so. I mean if that were true, we would've been dead awhile ago. You've been in this office for a long time. You had plenty of opportunities to do away with us."

"I was ordered to watch you."

"That I believe."

Taylor stepped forward, letting the gun lead him. "Shut up, bitch. I'm going to take care of you two and Mr. Hull will know then just who he can count on."

Max spoke up. "Hull doesn't know you're doing this?"

"I'm going to solve his problem with you."

"On behalf of my wife, I take back everything she said. You are a brave man." Max looked right at Drummond and tilted his head toward Taylor. Drummond contorted his face into another silly expression. "After all, you know better than us just how terrifying Hull can be. You know how powerful he is. And I'm sure you know how specific he is in his orders. Yet in spite of all of that, you're still willing to take this matter on yourself. You're making your own decision regardless of how it may go against Hull's wishes. That's seriously brave."

"He'll promote me, he'll be so happy," Taylor said, but doubt covered his face. Again, Max tried to signal Drummond, and this time Drummond looked in the direction Max nodded, then shrugged.

"If he's happy, you're absolutely right — probably. Of course, if you're wrong, if he had you watching us so that he could learn something important or maybe choose a specific moment to hurt us, then you've screwed things up for him. That's a ballsy decision you've made. I admire your willingness to take the chance."

Spitting more blood, Taylor said, "Stop that. You just shut up. I know what I'm doing. Hull needs good thinkers, good soldiers, and best is those who can do both. That's what I'm going to show him right now."

"You know, ghosts did that to you," Max said, once more trying to get through to Drummond. "In the cemetery, when you felt all those cold stabs of pain, those came from ghosts."

"What the fuck are talking about now? Just shut up."

"I'm merely saying that many people don't realize just how strong ghosts are, just how much they're able to interact with our world. People may think they can only move a piece of paper or a book, but they can cause real pain."

Drummond's eyes widened and a malicious grin rose from his lips. With a wink, he made a fist, pulled back, and punched Taylor hard in the ribs. Then everything went crazy.

Taylor squealed in surprise and dropped the gun. Drummond screamed and flew off clutching his hand. Sandra dove for the gun while Taylor looked upon his empty hand in shock. As Sandra picked up the gun, Taylor gained his senses and kicked her in the side. She rolled over seizing her ribs. At the same time, Max launched from his desk to tackle Taylor. The two men tumbled to the ground, grappling and punching while Drummond crouched in the corner wheezing.

"That hurt," he managed to say, but nobody bothered to listen. Sandra struggled for her own breaths of air while Taylor had managed to roll behind Max and get an arm around his throat. Max tried wedging his hand between his throat and Taylor's arm but the boy's grip was too tight. He tried elbowing Taylor, and though he made contact, the boy did not loosen his arm. Max's lungs burned at the lack of oxygen.

"I'm not such a peon now, am I?" Taylor said. "You think you can defy a great man like Hull? You think you can mess with his people? Well, I'm his people, and this is what you get."

When Max saw the ceiling light go dark, he figured the end had come. Then he heard a high-pitched cry and he could breathe again. Taylor shoved him over, and as he strained for air, he saw Taylor rolling on the ground clutching his groin. The ceiling light had not gone out — Sandra had blocked it when she stood and kicked Taylor.

Her sweet hands rubbed Max's back for a moment. "You okay, honey? Can you talk?"

"I feel like dirt," Max managed.

"Me, too."

"Get the gun."

"I got it. Don't worry. Guess Taylor forgot to put on a new cup."

The way her sentence drifted off scared Max. He looked up. Mr. Modesto stood at the door, taking in the disheveled room.

Despite his pain, Taylor rose to his feet and bowed. "Mr. Modesto. I, well, I'm, um, that is —"

"Please be quiet," Modesto said in his rich tones.

"Yes, sir," Taylor said, looking younger with every second.

Modesto offered a hand to help Max, and with it came the rich scent of cologne. Max ignored the hand and, with Sandra's help, stood. "I think," Max said, "we can agree that Taylor should no longer be here."

"I think we are beyond that." Modesto lifted his right hand, and two men entered to escort Taylor away.

"Wait. What's going to happen to him? Don't hurt him."

"He tried to kill you."

"He tried to impress your boss."

"Your boss as well."

"Not anymore. I don't think that I can continue to work for him," Max said, and he could feel Sandra's tension grow.

"I see. Then I suppose I'll have to inform our employer. He will be disappointed."

"I'm sure."

"Of course, you'll no longer have access to this office."

"I only ask for a few days to pack up."

"That should be acceptable. And naturally, our files will remain with us, as will the journal you acquired this past evening."

"Journal?"

"You don't really believe I'll let you keep it, do you?"

Max considered his options and saw fairly fast that, unless he planned to attack Modesto, he had none at the moment. Attacking Modesto did not strike Max as a wise move — satisfying but not wise. Modesto stepped over to the desk, lifted the journal, and placed it in his briefcase, his movements always graceful, always controlled. Then he left, saying over his shoulder, "Good day, Mr. Porter."

"Why the hell did you do that?" Drummond said once Modesto had exited.

"What could I do? He knew we had the journal."

"Not the journal, you idiot. Why'd you quit working for Hull? Now you've lost this office. And that means I'm stuck here — still."

"Don't get mad at me. You didn't seem to be doing much good either."

"I've got a damn foot-long blade of fire cutting through my hand right now thanks to you."

"What are you talking about?"

"You're the one who told me to attack Taylor. Do you know how painful it is to hit somebody in the corporal world?"

"Like a foot-long blade of fire cutting through your hand?"

"I swear if it didn't mean more pain, I'd punch you in the jaw right now."

Sandra helped Max back into his chair. "Back off," she said. "Max has gone through a lot to help you out."

"Some help."

"He could've left you from day one. You'd be a bodiless spirit in the bookcase. He didn't have to do any of it."

"But he did do it, and now he's got my hopes up and what's going to happen? Nothing. I'm given the short stick again."

"Sorry if I don't cry, but my husband has risked his life for you. Hell, so have I. And by quitting this job, our lives may be in even more danger."

"Exactly," Drummond said as if everything out of Sandra's mouth had supported his view. "Call Modesto and apologize for talking so rashly. Get your job back. Maybe Hull won't try to silence you if he thinks he controls you."

"Not likely," Max said.

"Then why'd you do it? I don't get it."

"Because I'm angry," Max said, pushing away at Sandra's fawning. "All that we went through tonight and the moment that ass walked into this office, I knew he'd be taking the journal. It's not fair. How are we supposed to do anything good in here when everything is stacked against us? It's like they brought us down here just to play with us, and I'm tired of it. I just want to go home, get some sleep, leave this place, and move on."

Drummond let out a defiant laugh. "You're only saying that 'cause Modesto showed up. Before that, when you'd thought you'd won the day, you were all smiles. I saw it. You like this. I know. I've seen that look many times — half of them while looking in the mirror. Let me tell you something, though. You can't win every day. Sometimes you've got to be humbled a little. The important thing is—"

"Will you shut up already," Max said.

"Hey, I don't deserve that from you."

Sandra threw a towel through Drummond. "Just leave him alone, already."

"I'm just saying that —"

To Sandra, Max said, "Please go home ... and start packing."

"Okay," she said, her disappointment obvious.

Max buttoned on his shirt and stormed out of the office. "I'm going for a walk," he said, ignoring the chill brought on by his shirt — still damp from the evening's excursion.

At least an hour passed, Max did not keep track, when he found himself rambling down Fourth Street for the umpteenth time. When he had started his walk, he was fed-up and anxious to go. However, after he had calmed a bit, he remembered the way Sandra had fallen in love with the area when they first arrived. And now he liked it a lot, too. Winston-Salem was more than just Hull, and he had to admit that he would miss some of this place. If only he had enough strength to turn away that carrot from the beginning. Of course, then he would never have come here. He and Sandra would be wandering somewhere in the Mid-West or the Northeast, struggling to build a life.

"Some life," he said — ghosts, witches, graveyards, curses, blackmail, and torture. Yet, the morning air smelled fresher than any he had experienced elsewhere. The people (except for those associated with Hull) were genuinely nice.

No, it's none of that. I'm just tired of disappointing Sandra. This move to the South was meant to be their fresh start — his new job, his chance to make it all right. *And it's all just crap, now.*

As the road inclined, Max noticed the sound of a car just behind him — not passing but following. He quickened his pace and tried to get a glimpse of the vehicle in the store window reflections. He saw a dented van with no specific markings. When he turned around the van slowed, inching forward with trepidation. The driver wore a mask. With a sudden motion, the van gunned forward, screeched to a stop in front of Max, and the side door slid open. Two masked men jumped out, grabbed Max, and pulled him inside.

Just got crappier, Max thought as the van drove off.

Chapter 25

A RICH AROMA — cinnamon and burnt incense. The odor was strong enough to wake Max. With the back of his head throbbing in time with his pulse, he opened his eyes. Wolves, bears, and hyenas glared back at him. Wood-carvings. He knew them, too. They were on a rolltop desk — the one that belonged to Dr. Connor.

He sat in a wooden office chair — his wrists and legs tied to its frame. Every muscle in his body complained, and his eyes threatened to close for a long, relaxing sleep. A man crouched nearby and a woman stood a few feet further away. "Modesto?" Max said, a grim, dry taste in his mouth.

"I apologize for the rather rough way you were handled, but I did not think you would have come here otherwise," Modesto said. He had removed his tailored jacket and his sleeves were rolled up like a harried newspaper editor from the 1940s. His disarray frightened Max more than anything else at that moment.

"I already gave you the journal."

"And I thank you."

Dr. Connor bent closer to him and said, "You were an easy one. We led you a little down the path and you went for the bait. I thought you'd have been tougher to wrangle, but —"

"That's enough," Modesto said. "I apologize for the doctor as well. She's a little excited. We've been searching for this journal for quite some time. I had always suspected it was in the cemetery, but our employer has a lot of strong feelings when it comes to Moravian cemeteries. And then there was no way to find out which grave. Until we had you find it for us."

"What made you think I could do it?"

"We simply hired you to help us out. We figured that your information would aid us in our search. I never really thought you'd be the one to locate the journal. You've never shown yourself to be all that bright. So, this was just a bonus."

"This whole job was a setup to find that journal?" Max said. He was about to point out that it didn't contain Drummond's curse but held back. Instead, he added, "All this just to protect Hull? From what? A little embarrassment. The guy's dead now, anyway."

Modesto brought his face right in front of Max and studied him. Then he backed away and said, "I don't think he knows much more. We should be fine."

"Then..." Dr. Connor said like a girl awaiting a pony ride.

"Yes. You may do with him as you like. Just make sure there's nothing left to find."

With a relieved shudder, she said, "Thank you." She handed Modesto his jacket. "If you need anything else, of course, I'm always here for you."

"We appreciate that."

"And I will take care of everything here. Don't worry."

"I never do," Modesto said and walked away.

Dr. Connor turned towards Max. "Let's see now. I still have a little of your blood and hair. What shall I do with it?" She took the seat Modesto had occupied and with a giddy laugh, she folded her hands in her lap. With exaggerated surprise, she said, "Oh, I know, I'll make a little spell you might be familiar with. It's called a binding spell."

Max stayed silent. He guessed that pleading would gain him nothing, and the idea of spending what little time he had left negotiating with this awful person (let alone begging) did not sit well. Instead, while Dr. Connor mashed various plants in a wooden bowl, Max scanned the room for anything that might help.

She had a number of sharp implements — some obvious like knives, some less so like a hooked item that reminded Max of a dentist's pick. The remnants of rope from what they had used to tie him had been piled on the floor. Three candles burned in an ornate holder sitting on the desk. However, nothing could be considered useful unless he got out of the chair.

"Can I ask you something?" Max said, trying to go with his gut like Drummond.

"You can ask. I don't guarantee I'll answer."

"Your grandmother — why did she bind Drummond? I know what you said last time, but seeing as I won't have time to get Drummond to talk with you, I'm just curious. Was it just a lover's revenge?"

After placing another ingredient in the bowl and stirring it up, she said, "A little revenge, yes. I don't think she was too mad at him, though. She was a wise woman and knew what sleeping with a man like Drummond meant."

"Then it was something else?"

Dr. Connor sniffed the bowl and reeled back. "That's about right. Maybe a little more of your blood just to be safe." She walked behind him, and for a second Max thought she would slit his throat. She laughed at his tensed body. "Not yet. You don't die until the end, when your soul gets bound to this chair. Then I suppose I'll put the chair on the curb. Let whoever wants it, take it. Or perhaps the garbage men will take it away and you can haunt the dump forever. For now, I just need this." With a hunting knife, she made a thin cut in Max's bicep and let his blood drain into the wooden bowl. "That's better."

"So, why bind Drummond when killing him off would have worked better?"

"That was the backup plan."

"Backup? Why would she need a backup plan? Unless, you mean, she didn't know if it would work?"

"My grandmother was a fantastic witch. Just because Hull didn't trust her doesn't mean she would ever have failed. And the proof is haunting your office."

"But if —"

With the back of her hand, Dr. Connor struck Max. "Be quiet now."

Using the blood-soaked mixture from the bowl, she drew a circle around the chair. All the time, she chanted. Max could not understand the language she used. The pungent fumes encircling him and the non-stop chanting flamed the pressures mounting inside him. He hated it, but he could feel tears welling.

Before he could control himself, he blurted out, "Please, don't do this. I don't know anything important. This is just a big mistake. Please—"

With a sadistic grin, Connor gazed up at him. She never stopped chanting. She never stopped drawing her circle.

Drummond went through this, Max thought. He saw it as if it was a live performance before him — Hull's witch performing this same spell, binding Drummond to his office; the incessant chanting; the desperation boiling inside. *No wonder Drummond's so pissed off all the time.*

"Okay, then," Dr. Connor said as she stepped back. Max thought he saw a little sadness, pity perhaps, creep into her eyes as she appreciated her work.

"Dr. Connor?" a voice called from behind.

Dr. Connor scowled as she stepped by Max. He heard a door open. "What is it?"

"Mr. Kenroy's insurance company is on the phone."

"Again?"

"They're disputing last May's charges and they wish to talk with you."

"Tell them I'm busy and that —"

"I'm sorry, Doctor, but they're insisting. They said this is the fifth time they've called, and they threatened if you didn't talk with them—"

"Fine, fine. I'll be right there. Oh, and tell Mrs. Johnson she'll have to wait until tomorrow for those curses. My schedule got a surprise booking today."

Max waited. He could feel her watching him, feel her pondering what to do, and finally, he heard her close and lock the door with a huff.

He struggled against his restraints with no success. The idea of hopping to the exit came and went — she would hear, and besides, it was a stupid thought. What would he do once he got there? Hop to freedom?

He fought to move his legs. His right foot had just a tiny bit of mobility. Looking down, he saw the tip of his foot moving right near the edge of the binding circle.

Perhaps ...

Wiggling his foot back and forth, he inched the chair closer to the circle but still could not reach it. Muffled sounds of Dr. Connor arguing over the phone reached Max's ears. He took a deep breath and pushed again with his foot. This time the tip of his shoe touched the powdery substance. Again, wiggling his toe, he made a small break in the circle then worked his way back to his original position.

It would have to do.

He did not know for sure if breaking the circle would have any effect on the spell, but he now knew magic and spells were real — so why not other things he had heard growing up? Wasn't that the way magic circles worked? Break the circle and the spell failed. He hoped so, because even if he had come up with another idea, it was too late. He heard the phone slam down, and a moment later, the door opened.

As Dr. Connor walked by, she slapped Max in the back of the head.

She knelt down in front of him and the circle, flustered but regaining her composure. Max used every ounce of will power not to look at the break in the circle. Each motion of her head jangled his nerves.

After several deep breaths, she began to chant again. She lit a stick of incense and held it above her head, then made small motions with it over the edge of the circle. "Good-bye," she said, raising her eyes toward Max with a look both seductive and repulsive. Then she dropped the burning incense onto the powdered circle.

In the fraction of a second before the explosion, Max saw confusion, fear, and resigned understanding pass over Dr. Connor's face. Then the blast hit. White light splashed from below and intense heat pushed upward. As Max flew backwards, still tied to the chair, he saw Dr. Connor grasping her face and screaming as the powerful waves shoved her flat.

The chair broke through the thin, office wall and pulled Max with it. When he hit the hard floor of the broom closet, the chair shattered, as did his right wrist. Despite the tumultuous noise of the explosion, he heard his bones breaking. Then a mop clattered on his head.

A few seconds passed before he could stand. Holding his right hand close to his chest, he checked the rest of his body for injuries. Just scratches. A hesitant knocking came from the office door.

"Dr. Connor?" the assistant asked. Her meek voice would have been comical if Max had not come close to losing his life only moments before. "Are you okay?"

Stepping through the wall (an effort of sheer will considering the pain in his legs), Max saw Dr. Connor sprawled on the floor, face down, smoke whirling through her hair. Fine with him. He stumbled toward the back exit (one he thought he had become too familiar with already) and walked into the parking lot. The morning sun blazed in the sky.

He headed toward the chain stores figuring public places would keep anybody from moving on him for awhile. His wrist cried out for the emergency room. With his good hand, he checked his pocket — still had the cell phone.

Flipping it open, intending to call Sandra for help, he froze. *One missed call,* the phone displayed. He tried to convince himself that the trepidation he felt worming through him was only a result of the stresses he had endured in the last two days. The phone call could be from anyone about anything. Yet as he pressed the button to play the voicemail, the feeling intensified.

"Um, Mr. Porter, this here is Sam. I've found the names of those hoods that attacked you. That is, their real names." As Max listened to Sam speak the second name, everything changed.

Chapter 26

LEANING AGAINST HIS CAR across the street from the South Side home he had come to know better than he had ever expected, Max finished wrapping his hand. Although he felt the pressure of time upon every moment, the pain in his hand forced him to stop at the nearest drugstore on his way to this house — that and the insistence of his wife. Now, as he looked upon the dusty Chevy in the driveway and smelled stale flowers in the air, he worried he had made a mistake. The fact that Annabelle Bowman was more involved in all this came as no surprise — Max's alarm grew from not knowing where her loyalties fell.

"Keep the car running," he said to Sandra. "I'm not very welcome here."

"I'll add it to the list."

"Cute, honey."

"Just be careful."

Max approached the house, forcing confidence into his unsure demeanor. As he reached the porch, Annabelle opened the front door. She pointed a crooked finger at him, her red face scrunched in anger.

"I told you not to come back. Now get the hell away," she said, spit flying from her small mouth.

"I'm sorry. I don't want to upset you —"

"Then go."

"— but we have to talk."

"I'm going to call the police."

"Just a few minutes and I'll go."

"You go," she said and turned away. "I'll get Stan's shotgun."

"I know about Stephen."

When Annabelle turned back, her face had fallen and her color drained. Part shock, but Max saw fear, too.

"I just need a few answers. Then I'll go. Please."

For a blistering moment, Max thought she might faint or simply go catatonic. Instead, she walked deeper in her house, pushing the door slightly open as she left. Max took this as an invitation.

As he entered, he heard Annabelle call from the kitchen in a soft, dead voice, "Sit down, please. You know where."

He went to the small living room and settled on the overstuffed couch he had occupied in the past. Annabelle had the heat on, blowing hard from dusty vents. The hot air, thick with perfume, pressed on him. He wished he could open a window, get some of the cool, Fall air blowing inside, but he did not plan to be there too long — he could endure. When Annabelle arrived, she carried a tray with two glasses of scotch. She drained one glass in three gulps, set it down, and nursed the second glass.

"What do you want to know about my grandson?" she asked.

"How long were you having an affair with Hull?"

She choked a little on a sip of scotch. "Affair? I wasn't having an affair. And certainly not with that bastard. I hate Hull and all of his people."

"But Stephen's father was born several months after Stan's disappearance, Stan was convinced you were having an affair, and you received a hefty payoff in stock from Hull."

"Stephens father is Cal, and Cal is Stan's son."

"But why did —"

"Young man, shut up, please, and let me talk. You'll get more of what you want that way. Close the mouth and open the ears — my mother often said that and if nothing else, she was right about that one."

"Yes, ma'am," Max said, shrinking a bit in his seat.

After another sip of her drink, Annabelle said, "When Stan came back from the war, he never was the same. Whatever happened over there haunted him every single day. He never talked about it. Not once. But this tension always simmered right beneath the surface.

"And then came that day at work with Hull. The change in him was instant. He obsessed over those POWs and Hull and though he tried to keep it all away from me, I had figured out he planned to blackmail Hull. Well, things didn't go quite as he expected but I guess you know a lot about that by now. And if you don't, well, it doesn't really matter.

"I had become pregnant with Stan's child. Stan, sadly, had lost all sense of reality. The pressure of what he was doing to those POWs and

Hull and memories of the war, I suppose they would call it Post Traumatic Stress nowadays. Back then, shellshock, if they bothered to diagnose it at all. For me, he was paranoid. And I knew he thought I was cheating on him, so I didn't dare tell him about being pregnant. He probably would have killed me. But I swear I was never unfaithful. I loved that man, and that boy is his."

"So when he went missing, he didn't know?"

"Never. He died not knowing about his son."

"Isn't it possible he's still alive? The police never found him."

Annabelle shot back the rest of her drink, then shook her head. "I watched him die — completely mad. I knew where he was hiding, and I tried to bring him back to me, tried to talk him into reality again, but it was too late. He took a shotgun and killed himself right before my eyes. Another week and I would have been showing enough for him to see. Maybe that would've changed his mind. Who knows? Maybe that would have made him turn that gun on me."

"I'm sorry."

She shrugged. "I cleaned it all up and buried him, and nobody will find him because nobody's really looking anymore."

"You had Stan's journal," Max said, the realization hitting him with surprising force. "That's why Hull bought you off."

"With all the police and media attention, he didn't dare harm me. So, he bought my silence, and I hid the journal. That should have been the end of it. But my son, Cal, grew up to be a defiant child. Even from an early age he fought every rule I lay down. When he hit his rebellious teen years, he went for the jugular — he started working for Hull."

"Shit."

"Don't swear in my house."

"Sorry. What happened?"

The skin below her right eye quivered as she looked into her past. "I tried to stop him, but he was a teenager and very much like his father. When Stan set his mind to something, no matter how insane, he could not be stopped. Cal had more than a touch of that in his blood.

"At the time I was furious, and though I couldn't stop him, I demanded he do one thing for me. I can still hear his impatient 'What?' but I held firm. He was to change his name, make sure Hull could not find out who he really was. I told him frankly that if Hull knew he was Cal Bowman, he would end up dead. That much got through. He changed his name. Later, he married and had Stephen. That's the name I've always known my grandson by. Stephen Bowman."

"And Stephen works for Hull, too?"

"Like many surrounding Hull, Cal died under questionable circumstances. But nobody bothered to look into it. So, Stephen picked up where his father left off."

Half to himself, Max asked, "Why would Hull put his own men in prison? Surely not for me. That makes worse sense than anything I've heard yet."

"Hull put Stephen in prison to keep an eye on him and to punish him for acting on his own accord."

This perked Max's attention. "He wasn't supposed to attack me?"

"No. He did that to protect me and his secret. And it was a stupid thing to do. I can take care of myself. Besides, it sparked Hull's interest. He still doesn't know for sure who my grandson is, but I think he's starting to become concerned."

"So he puts him in jail."

Putting her glass on the table with a loud clack, she said, "You are a noisy fool. Now, for the last time shut up. Okay, then. See, my son, my darling little Cal, he didn't want to worry me with what his real motives were. All this time, I had felt betrayed, and it hurt him so bad but he knew he had to do it that way. If Hull ever found out who he was, Hull would come to me and he would see how angry I was and he would think Cal was truly on his side. But he wasn't. Cal wanted to find Hull's journal. That's what he was after the whole time. He wanted to find out what really happened between Hull and Stan."

Max's muscles tensed as he held his breath. "He found it," he whispered.

"No. That's why his son, my grandson, Stephen took over. And bless his heart, he succeeded."

"They really were looking for that journal."

"Yes. Your finding Stan's journal was a mistake. How did you find it anyway?"

A cold, painful thrust of memory spiked the back of Max's head. "I had some unusual help."

"That's all there is. Now, you know my dirty secret. Please, don't tell Hull. For my grandson."

"I won't, but I need you to do something for me."

Annabelle's face turned cold. "What is it?"

"I need you to call Stephen, arrange for him to meet me. I need to talk with him."

"You don't need me to visit the prison."

"I doubt he would talk with me. He tried to kill me."

"He wouldn't have really killed you. He just tried to scare you away from me."

"Look, I've listened to or read so many sides to this story, and I want the last one. Please."

Annabelle frowned as she looked out the window. "Okay," she said. "I'll do it. But go now."

Max checked the window — a green Ford and a grey Honda had pulled up; the Honda in the driveway and the Ford in front of the house.

"I'm sorry," Annabelle said. "I called Hull before I opened the door. I didn't know you were on my side."

"Is there a back door?"

With a nod, she pointed the way. "I'll call Stephen. He'll be waiting."

As he hurried down the hall, Max wondered how much more abuse his body could take. His hand throbbed non-stop, his muscles complained from the previous night, and his head ached with the feeling of ten hangovers. He moved like an elderly man as he negotiated the stairs to the backyard.

When he slid to the side of the house, he could hear Annabelle at the front door. "It's all okay, gentleman. He's gone now. I'm sorry to have bothered you. I'm just a foolish old lady."

The men said something too soft for Max to hear. Then Annabelle continued, "Come in, please. Have a drink. Oh, well, then have a seat. Let me see, he barged in here, very rude, and forced me to sit over there ..."

While she proceeded to fabricate a tale, Max crouched and duckwalked toward the front. He peeked onto the porch. Nobody. Both men were inside. He looked at both cars. No drivers waiting. Finally, he checked out his car. No Sandra.

Looking up and down the street, he sought her with fear rising in his throat. As his gaze passed over the car again, he saw movement — her hair. She was scrunched down in the driver's seat.

Relief swept Max as he rushed down the sidewalk several houses before crossing the street and then working his way back to the car. When he opened the passenger side door, Sandra jolted and stifled a yelp. She motioned him to stay down but get in, and before he could close the door, she hugged him. Wiping at her eyes, she pulled the car out and drove off in a casual manner though Max could see her pulse pounding on her neck. Pride took over and he kissed her cheek.

"Where to?" she asked.

"The prison. It's just a few blocks north."

Chapter 27

MAX SAT IN THE FUNCTIONAL WAITING ROOM, his elbows on his knees, trying to ignore the sideways glances he received from the other visitors. Fluorescent lights turned everything pale. He knew he looked awful — dirty, smelly, bruised, and broken. At least he had Sandra sitting next to him — that made him look less crazy. *Just a little longer,* he promised himself.

"Samuels," a guard called out, and a young, overweight lady went to see her boyfriend.

Each minute that passed by left more questions for Max to plague his weary brain. *What if Annabelle was still with Hull's men? What if she couldn't get Stephen to agree to see him? What if she had lied and was informing Hull of everything right this moment? What if ...* But Max knew that worrisome thoughts would not help him now. The time for over-cautious analysis had ended long ago. He had tested Drummond's way more than once, but now he had entered Drummond's world in full — a gut-reaction and from-the-hip world.

"Spanitti," the guard called out and waited as a woman assisted an old man into the visitor's room.

"I'm sorry, you know," Sandra said.

"For what?"

"The only reason we came down was because of me."

Despite the pain, Max shook his head. "No, no. Don't start that. We came down here together. I screwed things up back in Michigan, I'm the one who couldn't bend a little for my boss to make it work, I'm the one who stole, and—"

"And I'm the one who found this job."

"What?" A chill covered Max, reaching all the way into his wrapped hand.

With her hands clutching her purse, Sandra said, "I wanted us out of Michigan, out of that mess, and I wanted you to feel better, confident — maybe even a bit arrogant like you were when we first met. So I started checking around on the Internet. I found out about this opportunity with Hull, but they didn't actually take job applications. You simply recommended somebody and they said they would look into it if they had an opening, and so, I recommended you."

Max brushed away the tears dribbling down her face. "I don't know what to say. I don't know whether to be mad or flattered or what."

"You can be all of those. Obviously, the plan didn't work out quite the way I had intended."

"Obviously." Max tried to put this new information in place, but it wouldn't fit. "Why even tell me this? What good is it?"

"I'm trying to be truthful. All the little secrets we keep hidden to protect each other, it only ever hurts us. You said we can't lie anymore, and you're right. I know you're mad. I can see it building up, but just know, I did it all out of love. And I'm sorry."

Sniffling, Sandra lowered her head. Max put his arm around her, and the warmth of her body against him was the first good sensation in quite some time. He squeezed her shoulder and kissed the top of her head.

"Porter," the guard called, but Max didn't want to let go of the moment.

As if reading his thoughts, Sandra said, "Go ahead. It's okay. I'll be right here when you're done."

Max followed the guard to a desk where he filled out some papers. Then he was taken to a large room teeming with inmates in orange jumpers, all seated with their loved ones, all talking in hushed, urgent tones. Near one of the wide, frosted windows, Max saw a man seated alone. The guard pointed and nodded.

Stephen Bowman shared a few of his grandmother's attributes — a similar nose and jaw. The eyes were Annabelle's as well. The rest of him came from Cal and Stan and whoever was his mother — harsh and angular. He had shaved his head, and Max noted the knife tattooed on the back of his hand.

"I'm letting you know right now," he said with a force that spoke of more time in prison than just this most recent stay, "I'm only seeing you because my Grandma asked me to. I got no care what happens to you, so long as it don't come down on me or her."

"Fair enough," Max said, sitting in a plastic, blue chair on the opposite side of a small table.

"So what do you want?"

"Your side of this twisted story, and, depending on what you say, maybe we can help each other out."

"Yeah, sure. My side. Listen, man, there are no sides, just the one truth."

"And what's that?"

"The fact is that Hull screwed over my whole family. He took a good, honorable man, a soldier who fought bravely for this country, and he fucked with his head until the guy couldn't think straight anymore and he did it to protect his own ass. Then when it all went to shit, he bought off my Grandma and walked away as if nothing happened."

"That's not quite the story I've heard."

"Well, you don't have what I have, do you?"

Max tried to stay calm. "You have Hull's journal?"

"You know I do. Why else would you be here talking with me? I'm guessing you figured it out the minute you knew who I was. Well, maybe not that fast. You had to check with my Grandma first. Then, you knew."

"I had a hunch you had something on Hull, but I never thought you had his journal."

"Well, you ain't getting it."

"I didn't think I would. But I do need to know what's in it. It's important to both of us. I mean, if I could find out who you are, then Hull will have no trouble finding it out, too. He just has to decide to look."

"That's the thing, though, he doesn't want to look. He's got no reason to doubt me and start looking."

Max gestured around them. "He put you in prison for attacking me. You don't think that'll get him curious about you? Make him wonder why you'd want to hurt me? Besides which, doesn't he know his journal is missing?"

"Of course, he does. He hired you, didn't he?"

"I don't know which journal he wanted me to find."

"Fact is, I joined up with Hull so I could get his journal. That's it. I mean, I didn't know it at the time. Back then, I just knew I wanted to hurt the bastard who hurt my family, took my father and Grandpa Stan from me. Understand? I figured I'd get in and just keep my eyes and ears open and one day, I'd find my opportunity. That's what I was waiting for. A gold opportunity.

"And it happened. Sitting in a bar, listening to college kids playing trivia games, just minding my business. And then I hear this guy boasting loud right next to me about how he knew the Hull family. Good friends, he says. Made a couple of rude comments about the lady Hulls, got himself some laughs. Right then, I decided I'd beat the guy to a pulp. Get myself some points with Hull. I sat there for two hours listening to this jerk go on and on. I swear he just wouldn't shut up.

"Around one in the morning, he finally leaves and I follow him to his car. Then I start bashing him and kicking him and he starts pleading with me. He's crying right there. I say some cool shit about Hull, and he looks at me hard. Like his whole face changed and he became Mister Cool for just a few seconds. And he says to me, 'You want something to really give you power?' He tells me about the journal. Turns out this fool was one of Hull's little gophers awhile back and he saw the journal. Hull found out and fired his ass.

"I thanked him for the info and then beat him some more," Stephen said with a grin.

Max checked the clock — high on the wall, protected by metal bars. He couldn't recall how long the guard had said he would have but knew time would run out soon enough. "So, you've got the journal now?"

Stephen pushed Max's chair with his foot. "It wasn't easy like that. It took planning, cunning, some real smart work. But yeah, I got it."

"Have you read it?"

"Not much else to do around here."

"And?"

"And Hull was a dick just like I thought," Stephen said, his face reddening as he puffed up his chest. A guard at the door looked over, ready to pounce if Stephen grew any more agitated. Stephen waved at the guard and formed a twisted smile. Then he lowered his voice and said, "When Grandpa Stan went to Hull to blackmail him, do you know what really happened? He refused to pay. He said nobody blackmails a Hull. Then he turned the whole thing around. He offered my dad all the blackmail money plus more if my dad would do a small job."

"The POW," Max said.

"Damn right. He wanted a specific one, Günther Scholz, and he wanted it covered up well, so he used Grandpa Stan's nuttiness against him. He paid to have the POWs captured and tortured. Just three of 'em. The one he wanted and two he didn't even know. But Grandpa Stan still struggled with the war and all, and this whole thing just snapped him. He hurt way more than just three. And, of course, he took his life, too. It's all laid out in that journal."

"Are you sure about that name. Günther Scholz?"

"Yup. That's the name. Strange thing, though. Hull gloats about all of this, except he doesn't say why that one POW made a difference anyway. I mean who was this dude who was so damn important that Hull had to screw Grandpa Stan over, wreck my family's life, and send me on a path that led here?"

"I don't know," Max said, but he kept trying to recall the names he had seen on that transfer slip. He thought Günther was not on it. An idea had formed that he suspected might be right; however, with the remaining time, he had a more urgent line of thought to pursue. "I'm going to try to help us both out here."

"Oh, are you?"

"Listen to me, please. You are not in a safe position just because you have the journal. But you can be. Together we can guarantee our safety."

"Nobody's safe, man. Nobody," Stephen said with an all-knowing smirk on his face. "You find some way to get rid of Hull, there'll be some other bastard taking his place. Fuck, our own government is the worst one of all. At least with Hull, I know who I'm dealing with."

"That's fine, if it's just you. But your Grandma is involved in all this, too."

Stephen's mouth tightened into a thin line. "You stay away from her."

"I'm not trying to bother her, but like you, I've got to protect those I love. And right now, you and her are standing in my way. But we can do it all different. The problem for both of us is Hull. So, if we work together, we can solve our problem."

"I'm listening."

"I need something that's in that journal. Not the journal, itself. I promise I won't take that from you. In fact, it's in both our interest for you to keep hold of that. But I do need a page, a single page."

Chapter 28

THE GREEN FORD IDLED just outside the prison. As Max and Sandra exited, its driver straightened and woke the man next to him. Max, however, did not head for his own car. This time, he walked straight toward the Ford. He thought they might drive away, but the closer he came to them, the more he understood that they were no longer trying to hide their interest in him. The driver's side window rolled down, and Max saw a muscular man who would have looked right at home in the prison Max had just left.

"Mr. Porter," the man said as he exhaled cigarette smoke, "we've been looking for you."

Max peered in the car and saw the other man, this one chubby but strong. "I want you to deliver a message to Modesto," Max said, impressing himself with his sturdiness of voice.

"Tell him yourself. We're here to escort you and your wife to see Mr. Modesto."

"No."

The chubby one unbuckled his seatbelt. "Looks like I get to do something after all."

Max knew he had only a few seconds left before these fools would stuff him in the car. "I have what Modesto wants. You guys try to hurt me or my wife, and he'll never get it. Tell him now. Call him up. You can see I'm not running. Heck, I'm the one who approached you, right? So, call him. Tell him I want to meet with him."

Chubby, his hand on the door, looked to Smoker for guidance. Smoker drummed his fingers on the steering wheel while he strained his gray matter. "Okay. Jack's going to help you wait, though, just in case you change your mind."

With more relish than he should have displayed, Jack, the chubby fellow, opened the car door, walked around the front, and stood behind Max and Sandra with his arms crossed over his chest. Sandra inched closer to Max, and her presence gave Max a slight comfort. He hoped he offered her some peace as well.

Smoker flipped open a cell phone and made the call. Less than a minute later, he said, "Okay, Porter, what do you want?"

"Tell him to come to my office in about two hours. We'll deal then."

Smoker relayed the message. "Done. Mr. Modesto wanted me to assure you that if for any reason you fail to deliver what you say you have or you try to run, the order to bring you in unharmed will be rescinded."

"I kind of figured that."

"And we're still going to be following you."

"I kind of figured that, as well."

"Don't try anything stupid."

"No, I won't. I'm just going to the library to do some last minute research. Then we're going to the office to meet your boss. That's it."

As Max and Sandra walked back to their car, Max kept calm. Sandra, however, had enough agitation for them both. "What are you doing? You don't have anything to give him."

"Honey, trust me. I've got this one covered."

Chapter 29

Upon entering the office, Max discovered a thrilled ghost, bubbling and chatty. It was the most frightening experience Max ever had with Drummond.

"Thank goodness you're okay," Drummond said and he flew around the room with nervous energy. "I mean I knew when you called Sandra that you were okay, but after they took you, well, I just started thinking about all of this and how I really got you involved and all that. I'm sorry. Really. I don't want you getting killed on my account. Oh, crap, look at your hand. They tortured you. I tell you if I wasn't stuck in this room, I'd be right out there helping you out. I mean it. I think you're okay, and I'm telling you, you need to have some backup. You can't go charging into a criminal's home —"

"Drummond," Max said. "Be quiet."

"That's a real nice thing to say. I'm just trying to let you know I was concerned and you're putting me down."

"Modesto's on his way," Max said. To Sandra he added, "Help me move this desk."

"Modesto?" Drummond said. "Why's he coming? The bastard already took the journal."

The desk scraped the floor, making a grating, high-pitched tone, but they managed to get it pushed toward the back wall. The binding curse marking the floor could now be seen in its entirety. In the center of the circle the four-headed snake bared its bloody mouth. The creature looked in all directions, promising to see all things at all times. It was disturbing, and Max tried to put it out of his mind even as he walked over the image.

"What's going on?" Drummond asked.

"We need to clean up as much as possible. I don't want anything that could be used as a weapon sitting around."

As Sandra picked up a few items, the old Drummond tones returned. He stood in front of Max, and said, "What the hell are you doing cleaning up for Modesto? You're not making any sense. What happened to you?"

"I need a lighter," Max said.

Sandra looked around in her purse. "I haven't got one."

"Drummond, is there a lighter in here or matches?"

"You tell me what I want to know, and I'll tell you what you want to know."

With the same strong tone he had used with the men in the green Ford, Max said, "If you want to be stuck in this office for all eternity, then keep standing in my way."

"Fine," Drummond said and with a petulant grimace, he pointed to the bookshelf. "The book next to the one with the whiskey — two cigars and matches."

"Thank you. Now, relax," Max said as he retrieved the matchbox and placed it on the desk. "Everything's going to be fine."

"Then tell me —"

"No. Not you. Not even Sandra. I don't want Modesto even getting a hint of what I've done or what I'm going to do until I tell him."

"Son of a bitch, you've got something on him, don't you? You're going to stick it to him."

"Just be here and be ready."

"I ain't going anywhere, and I'm always ready."

Max let the comment stand as he wiped down the desktop. "Watch the window. Let us know when he arrives."

"Will do," Drummond said, his excitement palpable.

Using every last drop of strength, Max attempted to maintain a positive, confident, and winning attitude, though he knew the coming moments might hold the highest risk of anything he would ever do. If Modesto called his bluff, the whole thing would end with their deaths. He had no doubt. But he also believed the bluff was just powerful enough, with just enough proof to give it merit. They had a truly good chance of making it work out.

"He's here," Drummond said.

"Damn, he's early."

Sandra said nothing as she sped up her cleaning. "You can stop," Max said. "This'll have to do. You just stand back there, lean against the wall, and trust me."

"I do," she said. "If I look worried, it's not because I don't trust you. It's because I can see on your face just how dangerous whatever you're planning is going to be."

"I'm only going to talk. Lay out a few facts, and nothing more. Modesto's a logical man. He can understand basic reasoning."

Before any more words could be exchanged, Max saw Modesto's silhouette grow in the door's frosted glass. The door opened and in walked Modesto. He looked awful. Wrinkles marked his shirt as being at least a day old, his skin glistened with sweat, and the pressure Hull had placed upon him registered in the deep lines on his face. He also looked determined — this meeting would be the end, his eyes said. That stern gaze, more than anything else, gave Max both hope and fear.

Max watched Modesto, ready for any threat. At length, Modesto said, "Are we just going to stand here, or do you plan on telling me what you want for the journal?"

"You found Hull's journal?" Drummond asked.

"I don't want anything for the journal. I'm not giving it to you."

Modesto noticed a spot on his shoe, bent down, and rubbed at it. "You really are an idiot. I always thought you were just being blinded by greed or love for your wife or something normal like that, but to stand here and start playing this kind of game with a man like Mr. Hull — you're a fool."

"You don't think I know him? Let me tell you a few things. See, even after I'd put together most of the pieces of Stan Bowman's unfortunate final years, it wasn't until a little bit ago that I finally got it all."

"And now you think you know everything."

"I know enough. I know all about how Hull was responsible for driving Stan insane, how he pushed Stan to torture those POWs, and how he bought off Annabelle's silence. That's nothing new to you, though. But a few things gnawed at me. Why, for example, did you really hire me? How was I connected to all this? And why did you help me get those boys arrested when you had to have known that one of them was Stephen Bowman?"

Drummond's mouth formed an O, and he said, "Who the hell is Stephen Bowman?"

"I can understand," Max continued, "how Hull might've overlooked Bowman — just another cog in his machine. But the idea that you might? There's no way you would hire anybody for Hull's company without doing a thorough check. You knew that kid was Stephen Bowman. But I'm getting ahead of myself."

"May I sit?" Modesto asked as he noticed Sandra standing in the back.

"No," Max said. "The first question that we have to address is why did Hull want those POWs tortured. It's perhaps the most crucial question because everything else, including me, flows from that. See that's what I missed at first. I was too busy dealing with the details that I forgot the bigger questions. You'll have to forgive me, though. I'm new to this side of things."

Drummond snorted. "Savor this moment, pal. I can tell the way you're talking, you've got something on him. Savor this. It's this very moment that always made my job worthwhile."

Taking a few steps closer, Max went on. "The bigger questions. That's what this is about. And that requires a bigger viewpoint — one that stretches across centuries even. When I saw that, it started making more sense.

"Tucker Hull. The founder of this whole clan. The one who left the Moravians to create his own version of religion — a sort of shadow Unitas Fratrum. Very secretive. You guys have gone to incredible lengths to remove as much mention of you as you could find. Hull never wanted anybody to know anything about him. Especially after he married Eve Hull. Especially after she taught him about witches and magic. Hull never wanted anybody to know that he used evil forces to gain wealth and to destroy those in his way. But, of course, you can't become as wealthy as the Hull family and leave no trace behind. And there were those pesky journals. Stan's was out there somewhere, and you needed to get it into your possession. The Hull journal, however — I'm guessing that every patriarch in this family has continued writing in that one. It's the only real record of your organization and your crimes."

Modesto slouched as his face took on a queasy appearance.

Max continued, "So what about those POWs? Stan said he noticed an odd look of recognition between one of them and Hull. That's why he tried the blackmail route. And he was right. There was recognition. The POW was a German named Günther Scholz. Now the Moravians, the branch that led to Tucker Hull living in North Carolina, well they're the German Moravians. William Hull knew of the Schulz family name and when he learned that Günther was being brought over to help make cigarettes, he used his witch to set up a meeting with Günther. He had seven POWs sent to the Reynolds factory in Winston-Salem and arranged to have a tour of the factory the same day. They shared a look, but it told Hull all he needed to know. He had been noticed as more than just a good businessman. Günther saw the leader of the cult who perverted his religion. Of course, Hull couldn't just kill the man. Too much attention gets wrapped up in a murder. So, he used Stan to eliminate the possibility of being revealed. When Stan lost it, he tried to stop the whole thing, but the kidnappings had drawn too much attention. It was too late. That's why Hull couldn't get rid of Annabelle. If she had met up with an accident, the press would've really started digging. And protecting your little cult is everything. So, instead, he bought her off.

"But that was a long time ago, and I suspect William Hull is dead. The Hull in charge now is trying to get back to the world of anonymity that his family has cultured and enjoyed for so long. And that is what this is all about. Secrecy."

Modesto shook his head in disbelief, but his hard face told Max the strikes were hitting close to the heart. "This is absurd," Modesto said. "If the Hull Group wanted secrecy so badly, why on Earth would they hire you to come look into the Moravians? It makes no sense."

"Because you needed to find that journal, and you wanted to test how secure your secrets were. You figured that if I couldn't find out anything about Hull, then the average person not even looking, or maybe some gung-ho reporter, nobody like that would ever find out. And then even if I never found a single thing about Hull, you were planning on doing away with us. Let the witch practice a few spells, perhaps. Get rid of every thread that led to Hull. Isn't that right? No need to answer. For now, there is one question that still bothers me. Perhaps you'll help."

"To this ridiculous —"

"I just can't figure out why you had Stephen Bowman arrested. On the one hand, you were trying to ease my mind, keep me focused, but that's not enough. You could have killed him, gotten the journal, and made up any story you wanted to satisfy me. Why put him in jail?"

Anger, or perhaps burned pride, swept across Modesto like an unforeseen squall. "Kill you, kill him — you're awfully quick with murder, Mr. Porter. We, however, are not. We are not thugs. We are not miscreants. And we are certainly not criminals. We merely appreciate a deep level of privacy, and for that, we are willing to go to great lengths."

"Is that what the witchcraft is all about? Great lengths?"

"There was never the intention of killing Stephen Bowman,"

Modesto said, his fists clutched white. "I had him put in jail so you would not get hurt and so you would not find him. You just couldn't let it lie, though. You had to keep digging."

"It's my job."

"How smug you are now. I assure you that even if we don't kill people with the casualness you suggest, we do know ways to make you pay dearly for threatening us."

"I have no doubt."

This caused Modesto to pause. "Then why do this? You've been running around the city for over a day. You clearly know the kind of trouble you're in. What do you get out of it?"

"The only thing that ever matters — my freedom."

"Perhaps you don't understand the true depths of what is going on here."

"I do," Max said, taking one step further. "And now, I'm going to tell you exactly what will happen. First off, you and Mr. Hull are going to call off all threats against me, Sandra, and the Bowmans. You'll also stop the surveillance. Basically, you're going to back out of our lives and leave us in peace."

From the back corner, Drummond shouted, "Keep the office."

"This office stays with me," Max said.

"Rent free."

"No rent. Consider it part of my severance package. In exchange for all of this, I will see to it that Hull's journal is returned. Of course, a complete copy of the journal will remain in my possession. Should anything happen to me, Sandra, or the Bowmans, the contents of that journal will be made public, as well as the results of all my research."

Modesto tucked in his shirt, straightened his hair, and looked a shade whiter. "All of that would be acceptable, if I believed you actually had Mr. Hull's journal. However, you don't. Everything you've said has been nothing more than conjecture — well-researched conjecture, I grant you, but conjecture nonetheless."

"You might be mistaken," Max said, holding up a sheet of paper.

"What's that?" Modesto asked, a visible tremor rumbling across him.

"This would be the binding curse written into the back pages of Hull's journal. I'm afraid when I return the journal, this page will be missing."

Drummond zipped across the room. "You got it! I never doubted you, ever. You're the best friend I could ever have."

"Again," Modesto said, "without seeing the actual journal, I find this all rather unconvincing."

"I'm convinced," Drummond laughed. "Destroy it. Please. Set me free."

Max removed a match from the matchbox. "I'm standing in the center of the binding circle. When I light this paper, the ghost of Detective Marshall Drummond will be released. I suspect when he finds out why he was cursed, he'll be quite displeased."

"Now you claim to know that as well?"

"You're damn right. Poor Drummond had stumbled too close, and Hull was ready to have him killed."

"I told you, we don't —"

"Yes, you do. See, I found the little bits of a paper trail you've all missed. I found the transfer orders for the POWs, the ones Hull forced to happen. Funny thing about them, though, seven POWs go but only six return. How can that be? This is before Stan Bowman. And then I saw it — Hull had Günther from the start. He just didn't know what to do with the man. Now, this next part is a lot of conjecture, but I think it'll probably be close to the truth. Hull had been sleeping with a young woman, a witch. She also had bedded Marshall Drummond. And together, she and Hull came up with an idea of what to do with his POW problem. He would have her put a binding curse on the POW, just to make sure his privacy was maintained. However, she never did one before, so they cursed Drummond as a test and a way to get rid of Hull's rival."

"Entirely false."

"You may think so. It doesn't really matter. If I were you, being the sole representative of Hull standing in this room, I wouldn't want to be around that angry ghost when he's released. Of course, since you don't believe this is the actual paper, you have nothing to fear."

When Max lit the match, Modesto inched backward toward the door.

"Let's make this simple," Max said. "I'm going to light this paper. If you remain here, I'll know you've chosen to turn down my demands, and I'll release the journal to the public. If you leave, that will be considered acceptance and we can continue our lives in this lovely city with our strained but healthy peace."

"Look at that bastard sweat. Give him a countdown. They hate that," Drummond said.

"I'll count to three," Max said, dangling the cursed paper just out of reach of the flame. "One ... two ..."

Modesto stormed out, slamming the door behind him.

"Three," Max said and let the paper burn. He set it in the circle and stepped back. In seconds, the fire consumed the sheet and there was an audible pop like an enormous light bulb burning out.

Sandra rushed over to Max. "You did great."

"Great?" Drummond said. "Look at me."

Max and Sandra could not find him. "Where are you?" Max asked.

"Behind you."

Floating outside the window, Drummond waved and did a gleeful spin. "Congratulations," Max said. "And thanks."

Drummond slid back into the office. "No, no. I'm the one thanking you. I can't believe you found the journal, and making a copy was a bright idea."

"I don't have a copy. I lied."

"You're kidding."

"No. When I told Bowman my plan, he refused to help me out. He thought it was too risky giving the journal back."

"But he gave you the cursed paper?"

"I threatened to tell Modesto everything about him. Of course, Modesto already knew but Bowman didn't know that."

Sandra frowned. "But Modesto thinks he's getting the journal. What happens when he doesn't get it?"

"He will get it. I'm going back to the jail tomorrow, and I'll tell Bowman what I did. He's got no choice. Either he copies the journal and returns the original to Hull, or his grandmother is in danger and he'll be dead before the end of the week. My only worry was that Modesto would press the issue before I worked out the details with Bowman."

"A good bluff, you rascal," Drummond said.

"Tomorrow, I won't be bluffing."

"I tell you, if I were a genie instead of a ghost, I'd gladly grant you a thousand wishes."

"Throwing in that bit about this office was enough. Now I've got a place to work that won't cost us anything."

"What work?" Sandra asked.

Max raised an eyebrow before he kissed her with a long, loving embrace.

Chapter 30

FOUR MONTHS HAD PASSED. Sitting behind his desk, Max still found the whole experience hard to believe. That first week had been the strangest.

He enjoyed a final visit with Annabelle Bowman in which, for once, she was pleased to see him. He told her the truth about her husband and how she no longer needed to fear Hull. She offered him a bit of vodka and said, "You're a silly boy. I don't fear Hull. There's nothing he could do to me anymore."

A few weeks later, he filed all the necessary papers to officially start his own business as a research consultant. "What exactly is that?" Sandra asked.

Max shrugged. "Whatever somebody wants me to look into, I guess." They shared a look, one that said she knew what he really wanted to call his new venture but could not do so legally — private investigator.

"Do you think there'll be enough work?" she asked.

"I don't know, but I'm tired of us living under other people's rules. It wasn't just Drummond's freedom we won. It's ours, too."

"Sounds like there's going to be a lot of work."

"Why do you say that?"

"Sounds to me," Sandra said with an impish grin, "you'll be needing a secretary, maybe even an assistant."

"Oh, well, now that you mention it — yup, I just might. Maybe a young, hot, buxom little secretary."

"That's the kind of gal Drummond would hire. You need somebody more sophisticated, more reliable, and more sexy."

"You have somebody in mind?"

Sandra playfully slapped his chest. "If you don't let me work with you, you'll sleep on this office couch for the rest of your life."

"How about we sleep on it together, my new assistant?"

The next day, Max left a single rose on Sandra's desk. For a moment, she stared at it and smiled. The silence was wonderful.

Work trickled in — two cases really. One was finding a lost dog, and the other dealt with an odd fellow who wanted help researching his family tree. Max's mother called every week, each time showing her great enthusiasm for his endeavor.

"I don't understand you. You were a bright kid. You could have been a lawyer or a doctor. Why are you doing this?"

"I'm happy. Isn't that enough?"

"But what do I tell the girls at the bridge club?"

"You could try the truth."

"Don't get smart with me, young man. I'm still your mother. Now, what about kids? How are you going to have kids when you have to struggle to make ends meet? I'm not one to butt in your life — you never really listened to me anyway — but you're ruining your life this way."

After Stephen Bowman delivered the journal, Max had not heard from Modesto. That was fine by him. In fact, he only harbored sadness for Drummond. About an hour after being freed, Drummond became difficult to see — even to Sandra. A little bit later, he had disappeared entirely. But Max hoped that Drummond was in a peaceful place, wherever spirits go.

"Wake up, Max," Drummond barked as he flew through the office walls, looking thicker than ever.

"Drummond? What are you doing here? Why aren't you plucking harps or dancing on clouds or something?"

"It was boring. I can't even begin to tell you how boring. Besides, I kept peeking in here and I could see you needed my help. You've had two cases and you botched them both."

"I solved them."

"Well, yeah, but you could've billed them for far more money and used them to leverage out a few more gigs. You've gotta learn about per diem, kiddo."

"You came all the way back here to tell me that?"

Drummond gazed at the second desk in the office. "Well, well, you've got the missus with you, huh? Dangerous move."

"I thought you said you were watching me. Why didn't you know Sandra was here until now?"

"Hey, I can't be expected to take care of all the details. That's your job. I'm the guy who steers this ship in the right direction which it ain't going in at the moment. That's why I came back. You need me."

"Hold on. Stop. You are not a partner in this."

"Sure I am. This is my office."

"It's mine, now."

"Thanks to me."

"You're dead, for crying out loud. You're not supposed to be here."

Drummond sat in Sandra's seat and spun it around. "I know, I know, but really that's a small detail, and one you don't have to worry anything about. They're not going to miss me up there anyway. I think most of them think it was a mistake in the first place. Besides, I'm valuable to you."

"You are?"

"I'm going to bring you clients."

"You are?"

"Got one lined up already."

"A client?"

"Sure. The guy's name is Barney. He made this will, but his wife — who if you ask me may have poisoned the guy, though she's quite a looker — well, she's using the old will, the one that gives her all of his estate. So, he wants you —"

Max raised a hand. "Barney's dead?"

"Of course. There's a whole slew of ghosts who could use of a guy like you. And they'll pay anything. They don't need money anymore."

Max opened his mouth, ready to send Drummond back from where he came. Yes, the bills were stacking up. Yes, he was glad to see his old friend. And yes, the two cases he had were not very interesting because of their mundane nature. But he pointed a finger at Drummond and said, "Look —"

"Sounds like a great idea," Sandra said from the doorway. "Just promise us we won't be dealing with ex-girlfriend witches again, okay?"

"Done," Drummond said.

Both of them looked to Max who shook his head. He opened his mouth, ready to list the infinite reasons this was a bad idea, but said nothing. He glanced at Sandra, smiled, and saw in her eyes something he always trusted whenever he saw it. He just knew she was right.

Afterword

For those of you wondering about the historical facts, I don't want to add pages and pages of non-fiction here, so I encourage you to do some research of your own. I will say that this story grew out of learning about the very real POW camps we had in North Carolina. That really happened.

Also, for those of you wanting to drive around Winston-Salem to see the various places mentioned, I promise you that you'll never find Max's office. The only thing that sits across the street from the YMCA is a parking lot. Many other locations do exist, though I sometimes took liberties with the details. This is fiction, after all.

Southern Charm

Chapter 1

MAX PORTER STARED AT THE RED NUMBER on his computer screen. It taunted him like a tiny, red devil daring him to quit, daring him to run away. His stomach gurgled in discomfort. "It's not fair," he said.

Sandra, his wife, glanced up from her desk. "What's that?"

The office was small, so he knew she had heard him. Just another example of how things had gone wrong. When they had first moved to North Carolina, she worked in a bakery, and though they struggled, they managed to get by — enjoying each other in the process. Since she had joined in the office, though, tension surrounded him. He could never just go home. Work always followed.

Pointing at the devilish number, he said, "I've been so careful, but we're still losing money. It's crazy. Heck, we don't even have to pay rent on this place, and we're still in the red."

Max could feel his frustration rising and tried to hide it. Sandra had been after him lately not to let every unsettling detail rip into him, but being self-employed came with a lot of unsettling details — the health insurance costs alone could send him to a hospital he couldn't afford. Though she didn't say a word, he could feel her thoughts as if they were jagged rocks pressing into his neck.

He rose from behind his huge oak desk and headed toward the office bookcase — a gorgeous built-in case filled with books on the area, its history, as well as a few on witchcraft and other oddities. A bottle of whiskey had been hidden in one of the books, and Max thought a little numbing might be in order. Before he could locate the book, though, Drummond stuck his head through the wall.

"It's a bit early in the morning for that," he said. The ghost slid further into the office, wearing the suit he had died in during the 1940s. Marshall Drummond was tall, well-built, and handsome, but since the office once had belonged to him, his in-house manners were less desirable.

"Good morning, Marshall," Sandra said.

"Morning, Sugar."

Max detoured from the bookshelf and gazed out the window. Though early fog covered Winston-Salem, he could still make out the old YMCA across the street. The office was only three stories up, yet the people heading to work looked small and humble.

"Sometimes," Max said, sitting back in his leather chair and rubbing his face, "I hate to admit it, but I actually think working for Hull hadn't been so bad."

Sandra glanced at Max with her eyebrow raised. "Sure, it was wonderful. Lots of fun and smiles every day — except for the way they threatened us, beat and kidnapped you, and then had their witch try to curse you."

"Yeah, other than that. Really the money's what I miss."

"Patience, honey. It takes a lot to get a business going, and this isn't the kind you can effectively advertise for. It's all word of mouth for us."

Drummond clapped his hands together making a singular, firm noise, and pointed to Sandra. "You listen to her. That gal of yours knows what she's saying. She's got a good head on her shoulders. Beautiful, charming head at that."

"Not interested," Sandra said as Drummond playfully scowled.

Max wished he could be as light-hearted as they were. None of these troubles seemed to bother them. Drummond was right about one thing though — Sandra looked extra beautiful that morning. Shaking his head to refocus, he said, "The problem is nobody knows what to make of us. We're not a detective agency, we're not a research firm doing polls — we're just researchers."

Sandra frowned. "Don't say it like that. You're gifted at this. You find things nobody else can."

"Everybody can. I'm just willing to put in the work."

"Well, that's why people hire us. They don't want to put in the work. And this kind of in-depth research requires waiting for word to get out about us. And look here —" Sandra said, pointing to the empty client chair.

"I know, I know. Let's get back to work. Fill that chair."

"No, Max, I —"

Max raised a hand, his eyes on the accounting program on his screen, the income/expense graphs, the blazing red number, and let out a long sigh. "It's the ghosts," he said.

Drummond perked up. "You're going to blame me?"

"Not you. The clients."

Sandra tried to shush him with her hands. "I don't think you —"

"I don't care if Drummond gets all ruffled. The fact is that we're the only investigative body that will deal with ghosts. Heck, we're probably the only ones that can even see them, and yet they don't really pay, do they? I mean, gratitude only goes so far."

Drummond slid forward, snatching a peek at the client chair. "It's more interesting than looking up somebody's genealogy."

"At least that pays."

Sandra glared at Drummond. "Honey, stop —"

Max's mouth tightened. "You're going to take his side?"

"I'm not taking his side."

Drummond stepped behind her with a sly wink. "Sure she is. The kid knows when I'm right, and I'm rarely wrong."

"You know what?" Max said. "I don't care. This is my business. These are my bills. My name is on it all. So from now on, no ghosts unless they prove to us they can pay."

Crossing her arms, Sandra said, "You are making —"

"Biggest mistake of my life, I know. But, honey, you're not seeing the numbers. You're not the one fretting over the mortgage on our house. And I do understand that you like the ghosts. I mean, for me, I just see Drummond and that's it — which ain't always a picnic. But you've been seeing them your whole life. You see them everywhere. You have a different perspective and all that. A different relationship with all of it. I do understand. But you've got to understand that I'm not going back to the way things were in Michigan. I won't do it. I don't want us to be that desperate for money ever again. Okay? So that's that. No more ghosts unless the damn things pay."

"Are you finished?" Sandra asked in a calm tone that worried Max.

"Um ... yeah."

"Good. Because I've been trying to tell you that there's another ghost sitting in our client chair."

"Oh." Max pushed out a grin toward the empty chair and tried to ignore Drummond's stifled giggles. "Hi, there."

Drummond walked next to the chair and said, "This is Max Porter. Max, meet Howard Corkille, our new client."

Chapter 2

FROM HIS DESK, Max pulled out a notebook and a pen. Despite the previous outburst, he managed a somewhat responsible pose and said, "I apologize for what you heard."

"He says, 'It's okay.' He understands the pressures you face and wants you to know that he can and will pay for your services," Drummond said, settling on the edge of Max's desk. "Besides, Corkille here has nowhere else to go."

"Perhaps we shouldn't insult the client any more than we already have today."

"All I'm saying is that we ghosts sometimes have limited choices, and Howard here understands that."

Max held back from further comment. Experience had taught him that to say anything would only provoke Drummond further. Instead, he looked straight at the empty chair and said, "Mr. Corkille, I'm afraid I can't see or hear you. Apparently, I'm only tuned in to Mr. Drummond. My wife, however, can see and hear you just fine. She can act as our interpreter, if that's okay with you."

Sandra smiled at Corkille, listened, and then repeated his words for Max. "There are ways for you to see me. I could reach into you and—"

"Experiencing that once was enough for a lifetime," Max said. He'd never forget the icy pain he had endured at the Old Salem cemetery when a ghost reached into his head. "Besides, the pain is so severe that I wouldn't be able to listen clearly to anything you say. Trust us. This is the best way to handle this."

Sandra touched the back of the client chair. "It's okay. You can talk with us."

"Did you forget why you're here?" Drummond said. "You asked me to help you out. I brought you to the guy that'll do it. Now out with your story."

Intending to ease over Drummond's harsh approach, Max pushed back in his chair, but Sandra repeated for Corkille, "'Wait. I'm sorry.

Please, don't get up. I'm just a little nervous.'"

Max played along and pulled closer. "What can we do for you?"

"Slow down, Mr. Corkille," Sandra said. Then after a moment, she continued. "'It's all about my granddaughter. Well, her and a painting. I am ... I was ... an artist. My specialty was in replicating the styles of well-known personages and providing those newer artworks to museums and collectors.'"

Drummond laughed. "He's an art forger."

"'Don't be so dismissive. It takes training, skill, and knowledge to successfully mimic the great artists. In many ways, it's more difficult than what the Masters have accomplished themselves.'"

Max pretended to write in his notebook, a touch he'd picked up over the last year — clients liked to believe that every detail was deemed important. "Go on," he said.

"'Yes, well, you see, back in 1930 things were very difficult for me and my wife. The Depression hit us early on. Others we knew managed to survive for another year or so, but we didn't have much to begin with. Before, I had been doing artwork for advertising and such, you see, but the Crash ruined the company I worked for — the owner had been borrowing money to buy equipment but instead invested it in the stock market. One day, they just closed up. After that, I couldn't get work. I tried, but nobody wanted to hire me. And then my darling wife got pregnant.

"'I panicked. I do that. I don't handle that kind of pressure too well. That is, I didn't. I put out the word that I was an artist for hire. I tried everywhere. Mostly, I just got laughed at. I'm not a big man.' He wants me to tell you what I see."

"Okay."

Sandra pointed to parts of the empty chair as she spoke. "He's thin, probably was a bit lanky when he was alive. He's got a mustache ... what? ... he says that he only grew the mustache a few months before he died. Thick glasses, bony fingers." She chuckled. "I'm sorry, Mr. Corkille, I'm just doing what you asked."

Max bristled but wrote down the description. "If you're done flirting with my wife, can we continue?"

A comforting gaze from Sandra relaxed Max a bit. Then she said, "He apologizes. He says, 'The point is that I could never do any of the hard labor that was left to most men. Even if I could've done the work, the brutal fights just to get the jobs — I had heard enough to know that was not the route for me.

"'I was ready to give up. You see, I even stole a steak and traded it for a small handgun. I planned to kill myself and let what little money I had help Clara, that's my wife, but that was not meant to be the way of things.

"'The day I chose to do it — I can see it so clearly — I went out into the tobacco fields and had my gun and I had drunk a bottle of cheap wine to prepare myself. But then a man I had never seen before grabbed the gun from my hand.

"'I asked him what he thought he was doing. I really yelled at him, and I remember thinking how drunk I must be to speak so boldly.

"'He introduced himself — I don't see that his name is important to this, so I'll just call him Mr. Smith.'"

Max put his pen down, making sure the action created a sharp snap. "It's best if you let us decide which details are important and which are not."

"'Oh, I understand that, I do. But you see, in this case, the man has been dead longer than me, so you cannot possibly —'"

"I can't force you, but just know that any details you omit will only make our job harder."

"'Well, Mr. Smith,'" Sandra said, and Max imagined Corkille straightening his back and jutting out his chin, "'asked me if I was the artist looking for work. I was astonished, of course, and I told him so. He said that he'd been looking for me for some time, checking out as much as he could on me, because he had a sensitive job he needed my skills for.

"'I had done some forgeries before but mostly for my own amusement and study. It never occurred to me to try to make serious money off of it. I feared jail too much. But my wife was expecting, we had no money, and by this time my resolve toward suicide had gone away. Mr. Smith wanted me to forge a specific painting, make an exact replica, for which he would pay me five hundred dollars. That was an enormous sum back then. I just couldn't turn that kind of opportunity away. I had to take it.'"

"I understand completely," Max said.

"'I suppose you do. So, I did the painting. It wasn't a famous work. It wasn't a famous artist. Just a landscape, really, with a slight nod toward Monet. He called it "Morning in Red" except it had little red in it. When I was done, Mr. Smith paid me and asked me to hold on to the painting for a few days while he made certain arrangements.'"

Drummond rested his hands on his knees and said, "Never saw the guy again, did you?"

"'No, but I read in the papers he was killed in an accident.'"

"What did you do with the painting?"

"'I held on to it. A few years later, I died. Slipped in front of an oncoming train. Didn't even know I was dead for quite some time. Never got to see my son grow up, let alone the birth of my granddaughter.'"

Max said, "It's an intriguing tale. What exactly do you want to hire us for?"

"'You see, my granddaughter — I've never seen her.'"

"So you want us to find her?"

"'Yes.'"

"What's her name?"

"'Melinda. I don't know if she ever married.'"

"And you think she's here in Winston-Salem?"

"'I don't know, but, you see, we've always lived in this area or nearby. I can't imagine she would go too far. Even if she did, we were always here.'"

"Drummond, write down Howard's address when he lived here."

Drummond scowled — it was painful for a ghost to interact so directly with the corporeal world — but Max wanted Sandra focusing on Corkille. As Drummond wrote, Sandra continued, "'Before you find her, though, first, I want you to find the painting. I've met many unique ghosts in the past decades, one of which was an art collector. We've had some great talks. When I told him my story, he said that some collectors specialized in forgeries and would love to have a piece with such a colorful tale associated with it. You see, I believe that painting could be auctioned today for substantial money. So, I want you to find it and then find Melinda. You may split the proceeds evenly between you and her. I believe that should cover your bill whatever it ends up being. But I want her to have some money. I couldn't be there for her father or her, at least I can do this. And, well, I suppose that's my story. Will you help me?'"

Before Max could speak, Drummond blurted out, "Of course, we'll help you. That's what we do. You just let us do our thing and don't worry at all ... you're very welcome. I'll let you know when we've found the painting ... yes, yes, and you're granddaughter. Don't worry."

Sandra looked up from the client chair. "He's gone."

Too tired from arguing over money, Max didn't bother laying into Drummond. Besides, maybe this painting would actually be worth something. "Okay, let's get organized," Max said, and Drummond's shock made his restraint worthwhile. "Sandra, I want you to check out Howard Corkille. If his family has been here as much as he's implied, there should be plenty of records to find. Drummond, you and I are going to visit that address."

"What about the painting?" Drummond asked.

Max shook his head. "All we have is a name, and Corkille said that the painting isn't famous or by anybody well-known. I doubt it was ever exhibited."

"But the client wants that done first, and that painting is the income source for this job. Besides, there's an art gallery just below us. We can start there and then go to the address."

"Fine, but there's no need to go downstairs. We can search for the painting online. That's what search engines are for."

"In case you forgot, I'm dead. I get to see computers, not use them. I still don't quite get it all, but then again, learning the thing's not been a pressing need. Look, I'm not trying to tell you how to research stuff. I'm just an old detective. When we get to the crimes, I'll know what to do."

"There's no crime in this."

"Art forgery's a crime."

"We're just finding an old painting and a granddaughter," Max said, but he didn't doubt Drummond's cold expression — this was going to get complicated.

A few mouse clicks, a few keystrokes, and Max knew he would not be finding "Morning in Red" online. No surprise, though. The painting pre-dated the computer age, and it's obscurity made it doubtful anybody would bother scanning and uploading the image.

Max tried a few other avenues, but nothing turned up. He didn't want to listen to Drummond's gloating, but the case came first. Grabbing his coat, he said, "Come on. We need to see that art gallery downstairs."

"Oh, really," Drummond said, but Max already had reached the stairwell.

Chapter 3

DEACON ARTS OCCUPIED the first floor of the building. The remaining floors were mostly apartments and Max's office, all of which had been built in the 1930s. This first floor space, however, sported a more modern look — and at first glance, more modern amenities as well.

Like most galleries, this one adhered to an open, flowing layout, with well-lit paintings on the walls and curving sculptures in the middle. An antique desk faced out from the back corner, a computer resting on its edge, and behind it sat a heavy-set man, balding with a white goatee. Flashing an elitist smile, he said, "Good morning." His voice flowed with a smooth drawl that Max had become accustomed to hearing after a year in the South.

"Morning," Max said, looking around the room. The paintings varied in style and color — no specific theme tied any of it together. Drummond floated from one work to the next, his face pressing in close to each painting.

"May I help you?"

Max glanced at the desk's nameplate. "Mr. Gold?"

"That is my name."

"I was wondering if you could help me locate a specific painting that I'm trying to find."

Without looking, Drummond said, "Don't be so wordy. Makes you seem untrustworthy."

Mr. Gold gestured to a seat near his desk and posed his fingers over the computer keyboard. "Let's see what we can do. What's the name of the painting and the artist?"

"The painting is 'Morning in Red' and the artist —"

Mr. Gold did not type. For an instant, Max thought the man might be having a heart attack. Then Mr. Gold said with forced casualness, "'Morning in Red' — I've never heard of it."

"It's not a famous work."

"Well, I'll try online but —"

"I've already tried the public search engines. Mostly get hits on the old, 'Red skies at night, sailor's delight. Red skies at morning, sailor take warning.' You, however, should have access to some kind of art gallery database."

"Naturally, I do, but I can't really abuse that privilege on every request, particularly for such an unknown artwork. Besides, searches on that database cost us money. So, you see, I can't just —"

Pulling out his wallet, Max said, "I'd be happy to cover the cost." Not *happy*, really. He only had three dollars.

"It's not that simple," Mr. Gold said, fumbling with two books and piling them on the floor. "I have to get permissions."

Drummond slid behind him and looked at the books. "This guy's lying. You know that, right?"

Max nodded.

"Good," Drummond went on, "because these books he tried to hide are all about art forgery." Sometimes Max loved having a ghost for partner.

Seizing onto an idea, Mr. Gold said, "Let me take down your name and number, and I'll see what I can learn for you. We're just at the beginning of the day. I'm sure I can —"

"The painting is 'Morning in Red.' My name's Max Porter and my office is right upstairs — 319."

"Of course. I thought I'd recognized you. I see you walk in many mornings."

"Let us know when you find something."

"Us?"

"My wife works up there as well."

"Ah, yes, I see. Well, Mr. Porter, I'll do my best, but I wouldn't expect much. A little painting like that, one that has probably never been shown in a gallery or sold in such, that is most likely not in anybody's database."

"You just give it a try."

Though Mr. Gold prattled on with excuses and concerns, Max never looked back as he left the gallery. Drummond circled his partner with excited swoops. "That's the way you should always do this. You're finally learning. Wonderful. That liar wasn't going to help us out anyway. Might as well give him a hard time."

As Max climbed the stairs to his office, he said, "Don't you think it's weird that Gold is lying about the painting? I mean, we just got the case. Nobody could know we were hired, let alone what we were looking for."

"This is the detective racket," Drummond said. "Just because you can't legally call yourself that, doesn't mean you aren't one. And let me tell you something I want you to remember always. By the time somebody's knocking on your door, by the time they've finally admitted they need you, there are already many others involved."

"So somebody else is looking for this painting."

"More than one somebody, most likely."

"Mr. Porter! Mr. Porter!" Mr. Gold shouted from downstairs. With labored breaths and one arm gripping the railings as if he might fall over at any moment, Mr. Gold reached the third floor.

Not hiding his amusement, Drummond passed through Mr. Gold several times, causing the sweating man to shiver. "Seems to be a draft up here."

"Yeah," Max said. "That happens sometimes. What is it?"

"Here," Mr. Gold said, handing over a paper. "I decided to do a public search — I know you said you did one, but it all depends on what keywords you use and how you put them in. I thought I might have better luck since I do this kind of searching all the time. Anyway, I found your painting and that's the address. So, good luck with that and I'll be going now."

Moving faster than he had arrived, Mr. Gold scurried down the stairs. Drummond watched with disdain. "Well, that wasn't the least bit suspicious."

Max snickered. "Yeah."

Mrs. Amos shuffled out of her apartment to pick up the morning paper at her door, squinted at Max talking to himself, scowled, and closed the door. The old woman never had much more for Max. The most he had ever gotten from her was a "Go to Hell" when he called her by name (a tidbit he acquired from her mailbox). The shock on her face still made him smile.

"You know," Drummond said as he passed through the closed office door, "I like that old gal."

When Max entered the office, Sandra kissed him and asked, "How'd it go?"

"We got an address," Max said, reading the paper for the first time. "Some place west in Clemmons. Probably nothing useful, though."

"I did better than that," she said like a schoolyard tease.

"I'm listening."

"Me, too," Drummond said from his usual perch in the bookcase.

Sandra held out a piece of paper like a winning lottery ticket. "That is the address of one Melinda Corkille. I started checking out the family name when it occurred to me to 4-1-1 her name first. She lives just south of here in Davidson County."

Max frowned.

"What's wrong?" she asked.

"This address. It's the same one Corkille gave us. The one in which he last lived."

Drummond perked up. "Really? Why would he not know where she was living then?"

"That's what I'm wondering."

"Especially after our art gallery visit. You know, I hate to say it, but this whole thing smells real bad."

"Thanks for the input. Why don't you go find your ghost friend and get us some real information? Sandra, find out what you can on Corkille, this house, and anything on that painting. I'm going to visit Melinda Corkille."

Chapter 4

AS HE DROVE DOWN Peters Creek Parkway toward Davidson County, Max tried to blot out any guilt he felt toward Sandra. He knew she would be mad at him later, but for now he had to focus. Except why should he be feeling this way at all? He could tell by how her body drooped when he gave out their assignments that she had expected to accompany him to Melinda Corkille's house — but angry? Why should she be angry?

"Don't act so innocent," Max said to the empty car. He knew from the start that she would want to come along. If for no other reason, it beat the heck out of sitting in the office working on a computer. But he couldn't bring her. He needed some space.

"That's really it, isn't it?" The past year had been hard on them in a way like never before. Always in the office together, always at home together, in the car together — he loved her, deep to his bones love, but she smothered him with her constant presence.

He wanted her to go back to the bakery. She would bring in some money for them while he struggled to get his business off the ground. Most important, she would be happy, independent, and not pissed because Max had to be the boss.

"Only one problem, though, Max." One enormous problem. Sandra could see the ghosts. How could he run his business without that special skill? Of course, he could just go the route everybody else did, but Drummond was right about that — he hated researching one boring genealogy after another. Those just paid the bills, and they often didn't do that much. These types of cases — the ones that were otherworldly — these were the things that gave him that investigative rush. And for that to continue, he needed Sandra.

What about Drummond? He laughed at the thought. He liked Drummond — sometimes — and he did respect the man's talents as a private investigator, but he could never trust the man the way he trusted Sandra.

As he neared the county line, the landscape became a typical suburban sprawl — wide, open land being cultivated into megastores, parking lots, housing developments, and twelve-pump gas station/convenience stores. Widening roads and erecting new streetlights added to the hubbub, slowing traffic and littering the pavement with North Carolina's famous red clay. *In a few more years, Winston-Salem will engulf this all.*

Davidson County proved to be more of a traditional suburban landscape and even a bit rural. It all had been farm land once, but the modern world left its mark. Though it did not bear the industrial charms of Winston-Salem, neither did it cleave to a pristine beauty that is often written about in the history books. Max knew from years of reading such things that the history books lied — the old days were never pristine and beautiful. Still, he wondered if, when compared to today's cities, some rolling farmland might not be such a bad thing.

The Corkille home sat in the middle of several well-tended acres. Though a large place, Max did not consider it a mansion — just a big house. It reminded him of a 19th century estate that grew as the family grew. Then, throughout the 20th century, acre after acre was sold off until all that remained was the house itself and enough acreage to remind the family of what once was.

He pulled up the horseshoe driveway, wheels on gravel crunching his arrival, and stopped at the front door. A young woman stepped out wearing an outfit meant to look casual despite a price tag that would have paid Max's heating bill for several years. She cradled a coffee mug and shrugged her blond ponytail off her shoulder. More than anything, however, Max's attention ignited at the sight of her lips — thick, seductive lips that curved into a welcoming smile strong enough to jump up Max's heart rate.

As he got out of his car, he could only think how fortunate that Drummond had not come along. The comments alone would have driven Max nuts.

"Good morning. I'm Max Porter."

"Good morning. Melinda Corkille. What can I do for you?"

Max chuckled. "You're very friendly. Most people would be a lot more cautious when a stranger pulls up to their door. Especially one in a beat up Honda that probably sounds as bad as it looks."

Melinda sipped her coffee and smiled again. "I'm a firm believer that the world is not much worse than it ever was. It's just that we hear about everything the moment it happens."

"That doesn't mean bad things don't happen."

"No, but it does mean that being friendly to you is just as safe as it was ten years ago."

Max put out his hand. "Since that benefits me, I won't argue anymore. I'm Max Porter."

"You said that already."

"Indeed I did," Max said with a goofy bow. "You have a beautiful home, by the way."

Blushing, Melinda said, "Okay, Mr. Porter, you've made some nice small talk and you're complimenting my home. What's this all about?"

"I'm writing a book on art forgery —"

"And the name Howard Corkille came up, did it?"

"Yes, it did."

"And you just thought you could come by here unannounced with a smile and some charm and what? I'd just hand everything over to you?"

"No," Max said, opening his hands in a friendly gesture, "not quite like that. Really, I only found out about him this morning and I came down in my excitement. I'm sorry. I should've called first."

"Yes, you should've. Where are you from, Mr. Porter? You sound Northern."

"Guilty," he said with a chuckle, but Melinda did not smile. "I'm from Michigan most recently, but I've lived in Winston-Salem for over a year now. I love it here. I don't ever want to leave."

"Pity," she said and turned back to her house.

"Wait, please. I don't want to hurt your family or your name or disrespect you in any way. I simply want to look into how and why an art forger does what he does. Maybe find some of his work."

Standing in her doorway, Melinda said, "None of his work is left. It was all destroyed years ago in a fire."

Max frowned. "I didn't know that."

"Now you do."

"A fire. Was it here?"

Pointing with her coffee mug, she said, "Took the entire East wing to the ground. Became big news for a while and made things hard around here. It was pretty ugly, I'm told."

"Still, there must be some of his work around. Work that wasn't in the house."

With a playful push, Melinda said, "Aren't you cute, trying to dance around a question."

"I only meant —"

"I know what you meant. You want to know about the works he passed off onto others. But, now, you said you didn't want to cause us any trouble or embarrassment. Isn't that right?"

"Yes, of course."

"If you pursue these paintings, don't you think you might cause us a little embarrassment and a lot of trouble?"

Using what he hoped played as boyish charm, he gave in and said, "I'm sorry. Sometimes my enthusiasm gets the better of me. I'm not really that interested in all of the paintings, anyway. Just one in particular. Maybe you can tell me if it survived the fire. It's called 'Morning in Red' and —"

Her gorgeous smile dropped to a tight line. "Goodbye, Mr. Porter," she said and closed the door.

Max stood still for a moment, knowing she would be watching him from some vantage point. He slouched, attempting a defeated appearance, and walked back to his car. From the driveway, he turned right onto the main road and another right at the corner. Then he sped around the block until he came toward the house again and could park a few cars back.

Drummond'll like this one. He could hear the ghost in his head say, "You're finally catching on to the detective racket."

Though he had spent time waiting in a car before, nothing equaled the mixture of tension and boredom that came from a stakeout. Every car passing by, every child shouting to her friends, every protest from the driver's seat when Max shifted his weight, magnified in his ears as he anticipated Melinda. Close to an hour had passed when Max's cell phone rang.

"Hello?"

"Hi, Max. Is this a bad time?" His mother.

"Hi, Mom. I'm working right now. Can I call you back?"

"Sure, that's fine. Just make sure you really do call me back because sometimes you say you will and then you forget. Not that I mind. I'm your mother. I understand being forgotten and mothers don't hold it against their young, but I do have something important to share so —"

Melinda's tan Mercedes convertible pulled onto the road. "I'll call you back. I promise," Max said, snapped the phone shut, and followed the car.

They headed back up Peters Creek Parkway toward the city. Max wiped the sweat from his hands on his pants. Melinda drove fast, forcing Max to find an uncomfortable balance between staying close to her with not being obvious by driving as fast as she chose. She weaved around traffic, never using her turn signal, so Max had no clue where she would go next.

He ran a red light, gained the loving honks of annoyed drivers, but kept sight of the tan Mercedes. As they went downhill, she cut left across two lanes in order to get to the on-ramp for highway 40.

"Damn," he said. Traffic had boxed him in, but as he passed by Melinda, he saw her take the westbound lane.

At the next light, he made a U-turn, sped up and ran the yellow to get onto the highway. Considering how fast she drove on regular roads, he guessed she'd push around ninety on the highway. Crossing his fingers against any cops, he pressed on the gas.

At eighty, the car shuddered. At eighty-five, it whined. At ninety, it made noises Max had never heard.

Slapping the steering wheel and spitting out a few curses, Max eased back on the gas. His old car sighed as the strain released. He looked around on the dim hope he might still see her, but no sign of her car could be found.

Max took the next exit for Lewisville-Clemmons road and pulled into a gas station. His damp collar rubbed against his neck and his hands shook. He left his car, stretched, and tried to calm his racing pulse.

It was possible that Melinda Corkille always drove that fast. And it was possible she knew Max was following her, and she successfully escaped.

Max frowned. *The Lewisville-Clemmons exit.* He rushed back to his car and found the paper Mr. Gold had given him — an address where Max supposedly would find the painting; an address in Clemmons. Before he could ask himself the question "Is it just a coincidence that Melinda Corkille headed in the direction of Clemmons?" he heard Drummond in his head — *There are no coincidences.*

Chapter 5

FROM UNDER THE PASSENGER SEAT, Max pulled out his Winston-Salem map. Styer's Ferry Road began a few miles north and wound all around the area. He had no illusions that he would discover the painting, but he also had no idea what he might actually find — and that troubled him the most.

In just a few minutes' drive, Styer's Ferry Road arrived, and within a mile, the world became rural. Sheep farms and horse farms, pine thickets and rotting houses, all littered the landscape. In front of him drove a pickup truck with several Confederate flag bumper stickers pasted to the gate. One said in proud Confederate print:

I ♥ G. R. I. T. S.
Girls Raised In The South

Max pointed from his steering wheel and grinned. He could hear his mother warning him about moving to the South. No matter how much he tried to convince her that people weren't like the stereotypes down here, she always responded, "Stereotypes exist because stereotypes exist." Looking at Mr. Grits in front of him made her point.

When he pulled in the driveway matching the address on the paper, Max considered pulling away. An unkempt yard fronted a dilapidated double-wide trailer. A brown sedan, dented and dirty, idled in the driveway.

Somebody was home.

Max got out, covered his mouth against the rank car fumes sputtering into the air, and headed up the driveway. As he passed the brown sedan, he noticed that numerous packages covered the backseat. Several more were stacked on the passenger seat, and two clipboards with US Postal Service paperwork occupied the driver's seat.

Something felt off about this place. Not just the way in which Mr. Gold had magically appeared with the address but with the place itself.

Max thought of old horror movies and childhood fears — haunted house tales that left him with nightmares for over a week.

Without stopping to think it over, Max opened the car door and turned off the engine. The sudden absence of the noisy engine left only the wind rustling the leaves high above. That near silence increased Max's unsettled tension.

He glanced back at his car. He should just go. Go back to the office, tell Sandra and Drummond everything, and then come back here with them both.

He glanced at the trailer. But it was broad daylight, mid-day in fact. Nothing to be frightened of here. Besides hadn't he dealt with ghosts and witches? This was just a stupid trailer in the middle of a bright day.

It was quiet, though. Why should Mr. Gold send him to an address in which nobody was there? Except somebody had to be there. The brown sedan had been running.

"Come on, get moving," Max said, and with that he strode to the trailer's front step. He opened the screen door and knocked. "Hello?" He knocked again. "Hello?"

No answer.

He decided to do something he had seen in movies many times and always thought *Who would ever actually do that?* He turned the doorknob. To his surprise, it opened. Before he could warn himself, before he could scream inside to turn around, get in his car, and get the hell out of there, he heard a gurgling moan that chilled his heart.

With cautious steps, he entered the kitchen — a filthy, beaten room that smelled of rotten food and urine. The kitchen opened into a living room that fared no better — stained blue carpet matted and torn, thick stink of cigarettes, and in the center, a large man tied to a chair. He had been beaten. Blood trailed lines down his face, neck, and arms. His right eye had swollen and bloody spittle dribbled from his mouth. The gore still glistened on his US Postal Service uniform and covered his name, Curtis, in dark splotches.

At the sound of Max's footsteps, Curtis perked up his head, his body shaking, and said through a damaged mouth, "I swear I don't know anything about anything. I swear. I never wanted any picture. I swear. Just don't hurt me anymore."

"It's okay," Max said. "I'm not one of them."

"Then get me out of here." Curtis's voice broke into a panic. "Get me out of here before they come back. Help me! Please!"

"Calm down. I'm going to get you out."

"It wasn't me. I didn't do anything. It couldn't have been me. I was just making a delivery."

"I know," Max said, kneeling down.

"I-I ... didn't do anything. I swear."

Curtis held his breath a moment as if he couldn't process anymore without stalling other body functions. Then he exhaled and sobbed. Max stayed silent while he worked loose the blood-drenched ropes that had bound the man. What more could he say? Curtis had picked the wrong time to deliver a package. That's all. And what had been meant for Max had been done on this uninvolved man.

But it had been meant for me. The realization struck the depths of his stomach, threatening to reprise his breakfast. He could see the faceless attackers waiting all morning. Mr. Gold had told those blood-thirsty thugs that he had passed on the address to the target — it was only a matter of waiting. Except one of them or all of them couldn't be patient. When Curtis arrived, they decided to act. It wasn't until they started listening to their victim that they understood they had tortured the wrong person. Then they ran.

Or maybe they never figured out they had made a mistake. Whichever the case, Max knew that they had intended for his body to be covered in blood, his bones to be broken, his mouth to be swollen. This was all for him.

Curtis crumpled to the floor, still crying, clutching his ribs, and rocking like a child. Max pictured himself in that position — the one somebody had intended for him. "I'm sorry," he said, but Curtis did not respond.

"Help is coming," Max said. On his cell, he called 9-1-1, left the address and said a man was dying, then ended the call. "Hang on. An ambulance is coming."

He couldn't wait around, though. There would be questions and a trip to the police and if Curtis didn't make it, there would be no one to back up his story. He had to go.

As Max drove away, his heart racing, the salty taste of his sweat on his lips, he kept imagining his own body curled on that disgusting floor. All over a nothing painting. "Not nothing anymore," he said. Turning onto the highway, heading back to the office, he knew there were several avenues to pursue, but one demanded immediate attention — Howard Corkille.

It took Max twenty minutes to get back to the office, and halfway there, his anger boiled up again. Blood-soaked images of Curtis flashed through his mind. He had to do something about that or somebody else might get hurt — maybe even him. By the time he parked his car, Howard Corkille had been pushed to the number two priority.

Max slammed open the door to Deacon Arts. Mr. Gold, fawning over a customer, jumped at the sound, saw Max, and let out a babyish yelp. "Mr. Porter," he said, backing up with his hands out. "I just delivered the message."

"I'm going to fucking kill you."

The customer scurried out fast, and Mr. Gold could not hide his disappointment at losing a sale. When Max moved in, Mr. Gold's disappointment turned to fear. He stumbled over himself as he rushed back to his desk. Max followed right behind, grabbed Mr. Gold's arm, yanked him around, and punched him in the eye.

Mr. Gold cried out and fell into his seat. "Please, don't. I'm sorry. I had to do it. I'm sorry."

"Where's the painting?"

"I don't know."

"Do I have to hit you again?"

"I swear I don't know," Mr. Gold said, tears and snot flowing down his face. "I never heard of the painting. I was just told to give you that address."

"By who?"

With an incredulous frown, Mr. Gold said, "By Mr. Modesto, of course. Who would you expect?"

Breathing hard, his fist poised to strike again, Max stepped back, stunned by the name. Mr. Modesto. The Hull family representative. And if they were involved, this whole case became far more complicated.

Chapter 6

WHEN MAX ENTERED THE OFFICE, Sandra gasped. "What happened to you?" she asked as she rushed to his side. "Are you hurt?"

Max glanced down — blood marred his shirt. "It's not mine," he said, thinking of Curtis the US Postal Service guy and his wrecked body.

Sandra helped Max to his chair. Without a word, she then pulled one of Drummond's fake books from the bookcase, grabbed the flask inside, and poured a glass of whiskey. Max drank fast, coughed, sputtered, and drank again.

"Don't you look all spiffy?" Drummond said, gliding through the front wall. "Can't say I'm surprised."

"You say anything else remotely resembling 'I told you so' and I swear, ghost or not, I'll find a way to make you sorry."

To Sandra, Drummond said, "Little touchy. What happened?"

"I don't know."

Max rubbed his sore knuckles — punching a person hurt. "What'd Corkille have to say?"

Drummond settled in the client chair and put his feet on the desk. "I couldn't find him."

"What do you mean?" Sandra said.

"Sugar, the netherworld of ghosts is larger than you'd imagine, and there's a lot of us. Of all people, I'd expect you to understand that much. So I looked, asked around, but I couldn't find him. If he wasn't already dead, I'd suspect somebody got to him."

"Don't you think it's odd that Corkille would hire us and then not be available?"

"Like I told the amateur pugilist, by the time somebody's desperate enough to come to us, things are a lot more complicated and a lot more people are involved."

Max barked a sharp laugh. "Let me tell you how complicated things are." He shared everything that had happened to him that day —

meeting Melinda Corkille, chasing Melinda Corkille, discovering Curtis the beaten US Postal Service guy, punching Mr. Gold, and hearing the troubling confession of the Hull family's involvement.

Sandra fell into her chair and whispered, "Shit."

"Not a very womanly way to say it," Drummond said, "but I agree with the sentiment."

"There's no way to back out of this, is there?" Max asked.

Drummond shook his head. "You know better. When you get a name like Hull involved, there's no easy way clear."

"What's Hull want with this anyway?" Sandra asked.

"I don't know," Max said. "I just thought I was done with them the last time."

Drummond snickered. "They do own the building. They probably own half the town. You should expect to come in contact with them once in a while."

"Shut up. I'm sick of hearing your little cracks all the time. It's been a tough enough day without having to hear a dead stand-up comic — and not even a good one at that."

"Easy now. I'm just trying to calm things, and maybe help you all get a little perspective."

"How do you think you're doing?" Max yelled, his face tight and red, his breathing heavy.

Drummond rose toward the ceiling with a placating grin. "Okay, now, there's no need to raise your voice. I'll just go see if I can find Corkille. I'll come back tomorrow morning when you've blown off some steam." And then he was gone.

Max looked at Sandra, the shock on her face matching his. "I can't believe he just backed down like that," Max said.

"Maybe he meant what he said. He was just trying to calm you down and since it isn't working, he left."

"Maybe." Max let out a long sigh. "Take the rest of the day off. I'll see you back home for dinner."

"You sure? There's plenty I can do."

"I just want to be alone."

Sandra leaned in to kiss Max but when he didn't turn to face her, she pecked his cheek and said, "I'll see you later. And don't forget, I love you."

"I love you, too," Max whispered as she walked out the door.

After a few minutes, he poured another shot of whiskey, held it to his lips, and inhaled its rich aroma. Then he tossed the fire liquid into the back of his throat, forced it down and let out a loud, "Ahhhh." Though he never grew fond of whiskey's sharp taste, after seeing Curtis, he welcomed the drink's numbing effect.

Max closed his eyes and fell asleep.

An hour later, he awoke, his heart pounding as he adjusted to his surroundings. He hated falling asleep by accident. He found the whole experience disorienting, at best.

"That's the problem with this case," he said to the empty office. And though he received no response other than silence, he knew he was right. The whole case, in the few hours they had worked on it, disoriented him. Not a single aspect of it seemed solid. Nothing but questions. Who are the Corkilles? What's with the painting that nobody knows about but everybody knows about? Why would Howard Corkille disappear? What did Melinda fear? And on and on.

And now the Hull family was involved.

Disorienting.

Max sat at his desk and tried to pick out a single detail he could count as fact. "Curtis wasn't the intended target," he said and wrote it on a piece of paper. A few seconds of thought, and he crossed out the sentence. Though it was probably true, he couldn't say it for a fact.

He crumpled the paper and tossed it across the room. *Tomorrow*, he thought. He closed up the office and headed home.

When Max entered the kitchen and saw their little table decked out with tablecloth, candlelight, wine, wineglasses, and two combo meals from Wendy's, all of the day's pressures erupted into laughter. He flopped into his chair, laughing himself silent, while Sandra looked on from the hall doorway. After a few deep breaths and a few lapses into more laughter, Max wiped his eyes, walked to his wife, and gave her a firm, loving kiss.

"You're wonderful," he said.

"I know. It's not my fault, though. I was just born this way." He kissed her again, and they sat down to dinner.

They ate in comfortable silence for a while. Then Max burped and said, "Tomorrow, I'm quitting the Corkille case."

"Okay."

Max hesitated. "You're not going to try to dissuade me? Tell me I have to stay on for the money or the business or whatever?"

"I think the name Hull changes this enough."

"I'd be lying if I said I didn't agree, but I've stood up to them before."

Sandra sipped her wine with a calm hand, but there was nothing relaxed in her posture. "I was with you through all that. I was a target of theirs, too. And even if I didn't see this man today all bruised and beaten up, I know the type of people we're talking about. Wealthy, powerful people who murder detectives and cast spells on their ghosts. People who have a long, nasty history in this town. So, if you don't want to risk getting any more contact with them, I completely understand."

"Well, good," Max said, confused at why he thought he should be arguing with her. "We do need the money, though."

"Then stay on the case. I'm going to support you either way. I'm just saying that I understand why you wouldn't want to deal with Hull again."

Max wanted to scream. His chest felt constricted; his mouth dry. "I hate this."

"Hull?"

"Everything. I just want to be left alone, do my research, and enjoy our life together. But ever since we moved down here, we keep having stuff like this happen."

"It wasn't any better in Michigan."

"I know. It's just — I don't know. I don't know how to say any of this." He knew what he wanted to say — that she should stop working for him — but he couldn't do it. After she had set up this silly dinner for him, after she had offered her support, after she had done what little work he asked of her, how could he let her go?

Taking his hand, Sandra led him into the living room. She sat him on the couch and nestled under his arm. She smelled wonderful — a natural smell as if the wind had brushed her with the trees' aroma, a smell as warm and secure as a thick blanket.

If he quit the case, the other ghost cases would disappear. He wasn't faring any better with the living. His fledgling business would die. The burning red number on his computer confirmed that.

Sandra stroked his arm and said, "You know the last time we went up against Hull things turned out okay."

"Yeah, and we figured out back then that we can't keep running."

"It's sure an easy habit to fall back into, though, right?"

"You knew before I walked in here, didn't you?"

"Knew what?"

Max kissed the top of her head. "You knew I'd want to quit the job, and you knew that eventually, if I talked about it even a little bit, I'd talk myself right back into doing it. We need the money, we need the work, and we can't run away. You know me that well."

"Maybe," she said with a toying chuckle.

"Then tell me this much. Since I'm staying on in this mess, how am I going to solve it? Every aspect of it is nothing but tangles of questions."

Sandra sat up, leaving her hand on his chest, and looked upon him with incredulous eyes. "You've drunk too much tonight, if you can't figure that part out."

"What'd I say?"

"Honey, tomorrow, you go hit the library. You do what you know best. Research. It doesn't matter which thread of this case you follow. Pick one and start working."

Max nodded. She was right. He should've gone to the library from the first. Maybe it was the financial pressure or maybe the eagerness brought on by a new client, but he had jumped into the fray too fast. He needed to learn the background, research the names, know who these people actually were. Tomorrow, he would start this case over.

"You're a smart gal," he said and planted a strong kiss on her lips.

"I know that, too," she said, returning the kiss.

Despite the long day, the stress, and the alcohol, Max felt his body stirring at Sandra's touch. They spent a few minutes on the couch kissing like teenagers until finally she pulled back and said, "I've missed you."

"Huh?"

"That's the first time you've really kissed me like that in I don't know how long. This business has got you so worked up, you just haven't been, well, you."

"I hadn't realized. Maybe I have been a bit distant. I sometimes feel crowded by Drummond and you always in the office. Not to say —"

"Don't over-think it, hon. Especially right now," she said and started kissing him again. Max didn't need any more motivation. They went to the bedroom, grasping and gasping, feeling young and fresh, each excited by the other — it had been too long since they did more than just be physically satisfied. When they finished that night, they held each other until they fell asleep.

Chapter 7

WAKE FOREST UNIVERSITY'S Z. Smith Reynolds Library — for Max, the place had become a refuge from the world. It's bright, open study areas balanced with the crowded stacks overstuffed with books. It was the greatest knowledge buffet, and Max loved it.

He launched right into his investigation, confidence and hope blending with his sense of purpose. He started with a computer search of the name Howard Corkille. After receiving over two hundred thousand hits, he narrowed it by adding "North Carolina." This returned twenty-seven thousand. He checked out a few links — some lawyer in California writing about a deal with NCU, a baker in Florida born in North Carolina, and a bar mitzvah blog. Adding "Winston-Salem" brought the number down to one hundred twenty-seven.

"That's better," he said, garnering a scowl from a young gal working at a desk surrounded by books and papers.

Following several links to start and using that information for deeper research, Max learned much about the Corkille family over the course of that morning. Edwin Corkille, born and raised in Ireland, fled the country after being accused of murdering a woman he had been promised to for marriage. He insisted on his innocence but could see that nobody wanted to believe him. So he ran.

His family was wealthy, and when he arrived in New York, he used some of his funds to purchase land in North Carolina. "Then things turn murky," Max said as he wrote down the information. Something had occurred within a decade because the next references to Edwin Corkille involved an involuntary dissolution of property. Several banks fought over what few assets he had left. In the end, he was broke.

The American Corkilles had no contact with their Irish family, and as a result, found no help to regain their standing. They became a working class family, struggling to survive, finding life in the military during the Civil War (and finding death as well). Yet no mention of new fortunes could be found.

Max re-read what he had found detailing the last few decades. The Corkille name was little known except for acreage sales from the property Melinda now lived in and a few mentions of Melinda's involvement with the Second Harvest Food Bank — a charity providing food for the impoverished. Of course, if all the Corkille's money came from selling art forgeries, that type of success would not be found written about in old newspaper articles.

Yet something bothered Max. Something didn't feel right about the sudden re-emergence of Corkille wealth. Art forgery might be lucrative, but the kind of money the Corkille estate appeared to be worth could not have been made that fast. "At least, I don't think it can," he said provoking a hiss from the student looking no closer to finishing her paper.

Max wanted to find a specific reference to Howard Corkille but nothing online provided help. With pleasure, he culled a list of books on art forgery and began searching the stacks. While the computer made life easier, it had also taken away many small joys. The tactile experience of researching book after book in the quiet intensity of a library was just one, but it was one that touched Max every day.

Another joy of library research — discovering new parts of the immense building. Max found the books on art forgery (both history and, amazingly, how-to) in a lovely wood-paneled room with large reading chairs and a warm atmosphere. He settled down with his finds and delved in like a giddy child.

"You won't find him there," a distinct voice said.

Max didn't need to look up to know who stood before him — Mr. Modesto, the Hull family representative.

"May I sit?" Modesto asked.

With a huff, Max closed his book and gestured to the empty chair opposite him. Modesto looked much the same as the last time they had spoken — when Max wrested control of his office space from the Hull Family and threatened to expose them if anything should ever happen to him. A well-groomed, well-dressed man, Modesto's features had evolved for maximum intimidation. Max sat straight but inside he cringed.

"What do you want?" he asked.

Modesto pointed to the art forgery books. "John Myatt is considered by many the greatest art forger of the twentieth century. In the '90s, he was convicted for passing off his own creations as lost Renoirs, Picassos, and Modiglianis. He said he never did it for profit but out of some crazed, perfectionist's desire to create near-perfect art. After he served his time, he started painting again — his own work this time. You can buy it today for around fifty to a hundred thousand dollars a painting. Not bad for a former fraud."

Max tossed the book aside. "Gee, thanks. Now I don't have to read that one."

"Elmyr de Hoy was considered the number two art forger of the same time. He died in 1976, otherwise, who knows what may have happened? Orson Welles made a pretentious documentary on the man."

"It's called 'F for Fake,' I read all about it."

"There's a famous tale about Picasso. He is shown several paintings. He dismisses them. 'They are all fakes,' he says. His friend says, 'But Pablo, I saw you paint these.' Picasso smiles a devilish smile and says, 'I can fake a Picasso as well as anybody.'"

Crossing his arms, Max said, "Whatever you want, I don't want a part of it."

"And then there's Han van Meegeren — possibly the most famous art forger of all time. He was Dutch, born around 1889, and well-known for his Vermeers. He made a 'Christ at Emmaus' that sold for six million dollars. Then he sold a Vermeer fake to a German art collector by the name of Hermann Göring. Things didn't go too well for him after that."

"Do you have a point?" Max said, knowing he sounded impetuous and wishing his stomach wasn't flipping in fear.

Modesto leaned in and said, "All those famous forgers, and not one of them ever knew, ever spoke of, ever even heard of Howard Corkille. Do you know why? Because the truly great art forgers are like the truly great criminals. They are never known. They don't get caught. They don't go to jail. They don't get books written about them. They are ghosts."

This caught Max. He wanted to throw some wiseass comment at Modesto just to tick off the proper man, but he couldn't say a word. Embarrassed that he hadn't come to the conclusion himself and stunned that it would come from Modesto, Max piled his books, stood, and walked towards the exit. He moved fast in hopes of getting away before his legs gave out. He really didn't want to know what Modesto was leading up to.

"Wait, please," Modesto said, following Max into the hall. Max pushed the elevator's call button and considered the stairs, but the narrow stairwell on the right echoed the ascent of two talkative students. Modesto blocked Max's way. "I'll follow you all day, if you make me. And I do know where your office is and your home. So, why not listen to me?"

Impatience, anger, fear — it all swirled within Max. But Modesto was right. If the Hulls wanted him to tell Max something, it would be told. So, with a curt nod, Max walked back into the warm room and sat in the first chair he came upon.

"Thank you," Modesto said, but like everything that came out of his mouth, this sounded threatening. "First, Mr. Hull wishes you to know that he is not the one behind what you saw yesterday."

"You mean the man you had beaten up thinking it was me?"

"That was Mr. Gold's doing. In an eager attempt to display his loyalties, Mr. Gold over-enthusiastically interpreted his instructions. You do recall how Mr. Hull insists on his instructions being followed properly?"

"Of course."

"I will see that Mr. Gold understands quite clearly the error he has made. It won't happen again. Mr. Hull wants you to know that he fully abides by our previous agreements."

Now Max understood. Modesto was here to smooth over any bad feelings Max had over the Gold incident. Hull feared Max would be angry and release the old journal he had copies of, the journal of the Hull family that documented centuries of corruption, manipulation, and witchcraft. This was all about protecting themselves.

"Don't worry," Max said like a benevolent king. "I won't harm you over this. Just see that it doesn't happen again."

"You have my word," Modesto said through gritted teeth.

"Then I think we're done." Max stood.

"One more item."

Max thrust an exasperated glare at Modesto, but the man's stern face reminded Max just how dangerous he could be. "What is it?"

"I must deliver this," Modesto said, handing over an ivory-colored envelope. "I've been instructed to tell you that the letter is not to be opened until you are in the presence of your wife and Mr. Drummond." Coming from anyone else, Max would have been shocked by this statement. But since it was a Hull who had cursed Drummond, who had bound his ghost to Max's office, and who had fought to stop Max from releasing him, Modesto's words were natural.

Max grabbed the envelope and pocketed it without ever taking his eyes off of Modesto. Perhaps it was the mentioning of Sandra and Drummond. Perhaps it was Modesto's incessant air of superiority — even when attempting to apologize for nearly killing a man. Perhaps it was simply the fear of dealing in any way with the Hull family once more. Whatever the case, Max's head spun in fury while his stomach threatened to revolt. His emotions churned with conflict as much as his body, and through taut lips, he said, "I don't ever want to see you again."

Modesto rose to his full height and looked down upon Max. "I appreciate your displeasure in having to meet. Rest assured the sentiment is mutual. However, as I am the top representative for Mr. Hull, I can assure you, we will be in contact again. No matter what you threaten, Mr. Hull will not entrust these delicate matters to another person. As you've seen with Mr. Gold, most others cannot be counted upon to execute instructions properly. I hope you understand the nature of this refusal and will not use it against Mr. Hull."

Modesto bent slightly and walked away. Fuming and helpless, Max watched him go. He pulled out the envelope, flipped it over, and set his finger at the edge to tear it open.

But he stopped.

Printed on the back were the words: NOT TO BE OPENED UNTIL IN THE PRESENCE OF MRS. PORTER AND MR. DRUMMOND. As much as Max wanted to raise a middle finger to Hull's instructions, he knew that doing so would be a bad move at this point. The time to fight back was when he held the most advantage. Besides, whatever this was all about, it was important enough to risk public exposure.

He put the envelope away, gathered his things, and headed back to the office. When he arrived, Sandra took one look, sat him down, and said, "Guess it didn't go well."

Max explained about Modesto's visit and placed the envelope on the table. Drummond shrugged. "At least the bastards haven't forgotten me. I ought to go haunt them for a few years. Just clank around their mansion, make sure nobody gets a decent night's sleep."

"I'll buy you a new set of chains," Max said.

Drummond chuckled. "I think the old, rusty ones have a better tone, but thanks for the offer."

"So," Sandra said, "are you going to open it?"

Max slid the envelope toward her. "You do it." She pulled back from the desk, her eyes narrowing on the envelope as if it might rear back and attempt to bite her.

"They want you to open it, though."

"Yes, but the instructions don't say anything specifically about who opens it. So, screw them. They forgot to be that clear, I say the heck with it."

"Okay," she said, snatched the envelope and tore it open. She read in silence, her face giving away nothing as to its contents.

"Hey, Sweets," Drummond said, "you going to share?"

With a devilish grin, she said, "The instructions were to open it in our presence. Doesn't say anything about reading it out loud."

"Oh, if only I were alive."

Max snatched the letter from Sandra. "Ease it back, you two." With a firm snap of the paper, he read:

> *It is with great pleasure that I cordially invite Mr. and Mrs. Maxwell Porter and Mr. Marshall Drummond to supper with me this Wednesday at seven o'clock.*
>
> *Please dress as befits the occasion. Should the day and time be unavailable, please contact Mr. Modesto at your earliest convenience so other arrangements can be determined.*
>
> *I look forward to our first meeting.*
>
> *— Terrance Hull*

Drummond hovered behind Max's shoulder. When he finished reading, he spoke for everyone when he said, "Well, that's not good at all."

Chapter 8

WEDNESDAY MORNING BEGAN with strong coffee and a headache. Max did his best to ignore the dread building within like a hardening concrete block making every step a struggle, but with the Hull dinner only ten hours away, he found it impossible to think about much else. He tried searching the internet for more on Corkille but he couldn't concentrate.

Across his desk, he watched Sandra immersed in Corkille estate papers, criminal record searches, and other routine research. A fleeting sensation of peace passed through him. She glanced up, perhaps sensing his attention, and threw one of her casual but devastating smiles.

Drummond burst in and, with a clap of his hands, said, "So, we got the big dinner tonight. Too bad I can't actually eat anything anymore. Rich people know how to throw a spread. This'll probably be the best meal you've ever eaten, and I'm going to have to watch. You know, I'll bet that's why the bastard wants me there — torture me with things like that."

Grabbing his coat and coffee, Max said, "I'm going to see Melinda Corkille."

"Something I said?"

"I'm not spending the day fretting over Hull."

"Who's fretting? I think it's going to be a great ol' time. Eat the guy's food, insult him a few ways, hear whatever stupid threats he feels like making, and shine him on. Trust me, there's nothing more satisfying than undercutting some snobby ass like his. He's got a whole plan in his head of what he'll say and how we'll react. They hate it when we screw that kind of thing up. It'll be fun."

To Sandra, Max said, "Melinda Corkille's the only direct connection to any of this we still have. I've got to talk with her. Besides," he added toward Drummond, "whatever Hull's going to say, you know it's going to be about this painting. If I can get any information from Melinda, it'll help us tonight."

"Good idea," Drummond said. "And don't worry. I'll find Howard eventually. We'll have more leads soon."

"Let me just finish up, and I'll join you," Sandra said.

"No," Max said. "I think it's best if I go alone. This lady is touchy. I think we'll scare her away if we come with a whole gang."

"Two is not a gang."

"You know what I mean. If this goes well, I'll bring you both next time."

Sandra kissed Max, concern scrunching her features. "Be careful. And don't go chasing cars again."

"I'll be good," he said, but he didn't smile.

The drive down seemed longer than before. Max's mind zipped back and forth between Hull's impending dinner and Sandra's strangling presence. Apprehensive about the former and guilty about the latter, Max saw little room to maneuver. The dinner would come and go, and he knew he'd have to handle whatever happened. But Sandra — that was a problem that time would not fix on its own.

In fact, if he just let it be, it would only compound and possibly form the root that could destroy them. That's how divorces happened. Little things couples tried to ignore, tried to bury through hot nights, festered until they became monumental, until they led to actions neither spouse ever thought the other capable of.

"Like visiting Melinda Corkille by yourself because she's got your blood going? Little things like that, Max?"

The steering wheel had no answer — and neither did Max. He stared at the straight, unchanging road and promised himself that this would be the last time. Not that he had done anything wrong — but he'd had plenty of guilty thoughts. He just didn't want those thoughts to lead to actions. At the next opportunity, he promised himself, he would hash things out with Sandra, fix things, get them back on the right track. And not just a little talk like the previous night. They needed to find the root of this problem and kill it so it never grew back.

Ten minutes later, he pulled into the drive and parked his car, noticing a new rattle from the engine that assured him of a hefty mechanic's bill in the coming weeks. Melinda must have heard the rattle as well because she opened the front door and walked out as Max stepped from the car. She wore old jeans and a low-cut top that left little to be discovered. He fought to keep his eyes on her face.

"You again," she said with a playful half-grin.

"I'm sorry to bother you, but I just need a few minutes of your time."

"There's nothing I can tell you."

"Please. You don't have to give me loads of information or betray any family secrets. I just need a little help from you to point me in the right direction."

"You said you were writing a book on art forgers?"

"That's right."

She snapped her fingers and pointed at him. "See, that's a lie. Why should I help you out when you've begun this whole thing with a lie?"

Opening his arms like a thief claiming innocence, he said, "I admit it. I lied. But you have to admit, too, that you'd never have spoken to me, if I had told you the truth."

"Depends on what the truth is."

"Well, the truth is that I've been hired to find that painting for you."

"For me?"

"I was told to find the painting, find you, and put the two together."

"And who hired you?"

"I can't tell you that."

"That's really too bad. You almost had my interest." She turned away.

"Wait, please. I don't know what's so special about this painting, but you're clearly in it deep, and you'll get buried, if you're not careful."

"Lucky for me, I'm a careful person."

"Melinda, please —"

She placed her hand on the door and said, "Good-bye, Mr. Porter. Do not come here again."

Desperation took hold. Max blurted out, "You don't want to be messing with the Hulls. They're dangerous."

Melinda froze. Her seductive yet light lips became a hard, cold line. "What do you know about them?"

"Let me in. I'll tell you all about it."

Any sense of wild youth vanished from Melinda. She looked meek and even vulnerable. She stepped back into the house, leaving the front door open.

Max walked into the foyer and tried not to betray his awe. He did not often step into such a wealthy home. Dark wood floors led up a small step into the main foyer which was garnered with a baby-grand piano. The walls were old Southern white, a summer breeze color that whispered of a South that had died long ago.

"This way," she said, passing through a wide arch into a lush living room — thick sofas, a brick fireplace, and paintings on every wall — Max lacked the skill to know if they were authentic or not. Everything he saw looked valuable and vibrant. Even the plants.

Max stood next to a deep red sofa, unsure if he should sully it with his common pants. Even as he had these thoughts, another part of him complained in his head — *Since when do you care about rich assholes? Sit down and take command of things.*

Since when? Easy answer — since he saw that red number on his computer screen.

"Please, sit," she said. Max settled on the sofa's edge and noticed a large plant in front of a narrow door — the rich hiding the broom closet. Concern over his pants itched stronger than before. Melinda slid onto the opposite sofa, her legs tucked under in a pose reminiscent of a college girl, and continued, "So, Mr. Porter, enlighten me about the Hulls."

"I worked for Hull a year ago. He was a dangerous man, part of a dangerous family that shrouds itself in secrecy."

"My family likes secrets, too," she said with a wink.

"This is serious. These people can cause a lot of pain."

Melinda chuckled — a soft, bitter sound that she managed to infuse with a salacious undertone. "You're sweet to be so concerned, but you've only lived here for what? A little over a year? My family has been in North Carolina for generations. I think we understand things down here a bit better."

"But —"

"Do you know why I have this house? I mean, do you understand that every inch of this place was paid for by art forgeries? And yet, I still own it."

"I've been told the best art forgers never get caught. I couldn't find a single word about Howard Corkille."

"That's part of it. An important part. The other is attached to being the best. In order to succeed, you must be able to pass off your work for profit."

"And Howard was good at that as well?"

"A genius. But, you see, the two go together — getting collectors and museums to buy your forgeries and keeping all knowledge of you and your involvement a secret. Even now, all these years later, should it come out that many of the prized works hanging in museums throughout the world were Corkille fakes, I'd lose every dime I ever had. I hope this makes it clear why I don't wish to have an in-depth study done on my family's history."

"This painting," Max said, not knowing what to say but wanting to keep her talking, "the 'Morning in Red,' why are you messing with Hull over it?"

"I'm not."

"You practically jumped when I mentioned his name and now you suddenly don't care about him?"

"I didn't say that. I'm just not involved with Hull over that painting." Despite the young girl clothes and poses, her weary voice and judicious gaze aged her before Max's eyes. "We have other issues at work."

"Well, if I'm not being rude, I'd advise you to have no dealings with Hull at any time, of any kind. That family is destructive, at best, and powerfully so. Whatever you think you're doing with them will hurt you in the long run. I learned this the hard way. Please, trust me on this. You'd best stay away from them."

"How cute. You truly want to be chivalrous."

Max knew he should leave. Though Melinda passed with ease between being a naïve doe and a prowling hunter, Max saw danger in either state. She played both with perfect pitch. The subtle and direct looks she threw at him from behind her hair, casually placed in its most seductive position, flooded him with testosterone and made thinking clearly an impossible task. The only thought he could manage — *leave, leave, leave.*

As if the idea had formed that instant, Melinda sauntered toward Max and bent down with the obvious intent of letting him view her breasts. "We have a few choices," she said, moving closer, her lips near his. Hints of perfume mixing with body heat pressed in the air. "We can continue to tell each other partial truths and partial lies, we can go about our separate interests and know that we'll cross paths sometime soon, or we can stop all the games, go upstairs, and you can do whatever you desire." With the tip of her tongue, she touched his lips. Then she pulled back and turned away. "I know which I choose," she said and removed her shirt in one swift motion. Her smooth back lacked a single blemish. Over her bare shoulder, she added, "I'll wait upstairs."

When she left the room, making sure to drop the shirt on the floor, Max did not move. His brain had shut down and struggled to reboot. His heart pounded in a fear only matched by the longing in his groin. He felt guilty for being hard and stupid for even imagining following this crazy girl. Drummond would tell him to sleep with her but never forget that she's only trying to distract him from the case. Maybe.

Or maybe, despite all his big talk, Drummond would race to the car — he cares about Sandra a little bit. Max, however, cared about Sandra infinitely. No amount of marital bickering would change that.

With his body cooling down, his heart slowing, his brain function returning, Max willed himself to stand and walked out of that house. His eyes lingered on Melinda's discarded shirt and he imagined her upstairs, draped across her bed, waiting for him. Never had a woman come on to him like that. He could feel a pulling in his body as if the mere scent of Melinda that dwindled in the air could call him up like a siren's song. He had been wrong to leave Sandra behind. He needed her as a shield against this seductive woman.

He stopped by the baby-grand piano and pictured his lovely wife. *That's who matters. The other thoughts are just hormones.* He stepped outside, got to his car, and let out a long breath. Pushing his foot hard on the gas, he promised he would not make that mistake again.

"I KNOW YOU'RE NERVOUS," Sandra said as they drove to the Hull family estate, "but try to relax. You won't be thinking clearly if you're all stressed out."

"What's that supposed to mean? That I 'won't be thinking clearly'. I can make clear decisions."

Drummond, floating in the backseat, said, "Hey, relax. You know that's not what she meant."

"I didn't ask you."

Tense silence filled the car. They drove out of Winston-Salem, south on Route 77 toward Lake Norman. Max tried to focus on the dinner, on the case, on anything but Sandra, Drummond, or Melinda.

He peeked at Drummond in the rear-view mirror just in time to see Drummond's head stretch backward and to hear him scream. Sandra jumped at the sound, took one glance back, and yelled, "Pull over! Pull over!"

As Max edged to the shoulder and slowed down, he swore he could see through Drummond as if the ghost had become less substantial than usual. Drummond held his elongated head with one hand and strained his muscles but still growled out his pain. With his free hand, he pointed behind them.

"What is this? What's going on?" Max asked.

"I don't know," Sandra said. "I've never seen a ghost do anything like this before."

With a great effort, Drummond pointed and said, "Back!"

Max hit the hazard lights, set the car in reverse, and eased back along the shoulder. In just a few feet, Drummond's head returned to its normal shape, and he seemed to be in less pain. A few more feet and the ghost had become solid in appearance once again.

Max stopped the car and turned around in his seat. "What the heck just happened? You okay?"

Drummond rubbed the back of his head. "Damn, I wish I could

drink. My mouth is begging for a whiskey right now."

"He's alright," Sandra said with a relieved chuckle.

"Look at that. You do care."

"Don't push it."

"Cute, you two," Max said, "but nobody's answered my question. What just happened?"

Repositioning his hat, Drummond said, "It looks like I can't go any further. I've heard talk about this but figured it was just ghost superstitions — hoped it was, at least."

"What *what* was?"

"A ghost exists in two realms. There's the ghostly realm where I found Corkille. It's like a separate plane or world. That world, the ghost world, it's enormous and I can go anywhere in it I need to go.

"Here, however, in the corporeal world, it's different. The rumor is that every ghost is sort of tethered to the place they died. I guess it's true. I can't go too far from the office without a heck of a lot of pain."

"You're okay now, though, right?"

"I think so."

Sandra said, "There's a third world, too, don't forget. You can always *move on* to there."

Drummond looked away like a boy avoiding punishment. "I'm not ready for that."

"Now what you talking about?" Max asked.

"Heaven and Hell," Sandra said. "If you believe in them, that is. Call it the real afterlife. Being a ghost means you're not letting go, but once you do, you move on to that third world realm. You find out what really happens."

"Can we just turn around?" Drummond said, crossing his arms.

Checking his watch, Max clicked his tongue. "That's going to be a problem. We can't go all the way back to the office and then back to Lake Norman and still be on time. For that matter, Hull wanted you there, too, and you know that guy is nutty about his exact orders being followed."

"It'll be fine," Sandra said. "He won't even know Drummond's not there. He can't see ghosts, can he?"

"I don't know."

"No," Drummond said. "I don't think he can. But he knows about ghosts and witches and all of it. And that means he knew I couldn't actually be there tonight. This part of the evening was merely to show me he's still out of my reach. The bastard is just rubbing my death into my face."

"You might be right."

"Don't worry about me. I'll go to the ghost realm and use that to get back to the office. The two worlds don't synch exactly, so I'm sure I'll be back long before you."

"But —" Sandra started to speak, but before she could utter her objection, Drummond had disappeared.

"I guess that's that," Max said, pulling the car back to the highway.

When they arrived Max first noticed that, for a mansion, the place was small. Elegant, yes, but not the sprawling acreage one would expect from a family rich enough to own half the state. As they walked toward the front door, a young, blonde man wearing a flawless black suit stepped out to greet them.

"Mr. and Mrs. Porter," he said, his drawl smooth and refined, "it is a pleasure to meet you. I'm Terrance Hull."

Max had to grip Sandra's hand to avoid tripping. This was Hull? This kid whose face barely grew a whisker was the one he had feared so much?

Hull led them into the house with a mock laugh. "You're not the first to be surprised at my youth," he said. "Or my informalities. I apologize if you expected a butler. I do have help at my main home, but this place is usually used as a miniature vacation spot, and as such, I don't often want staff bothering me."

"It's a lovely home," Sandra said, though Max thought she growled more than spoke.

Hull didn't appear to notice. "Thank you," he said, taking their coats. The inside of the home was immaculate. Every piece of crystal, every gold trim, every framed picture, shined in its cleanliness. Light played against these objects, brightening the house and warming it. If Hull didn't employ the help, he must have at least sent Mr. Modesto ahead to clean up the place. Max couldn't picture Hull working the elbow grease to keep up this level of clean.

As Hull walked down the hall, Max glanced back. The front door had been left open. He went to shut it when he noticed there were no locks on the door. None. Once before he had seen such a thing — the office of a woman who turned out to be a real, spell-casting witch. Drummond told him the witch never needed locks because nobody dared to rob her. Not only did Hull not have locks, he didn't even bother closing the door. Max felt that old fear creeping back into his stomach.

The dining room's beauty surpassed any room Max had ever stepped foot in — hardwood floors reflecting like mirrors, candlelight twinkling like stars, and a simple but elegant meal served on shining silver. With swift grace, Hull pulled out a chair for Sandra, indicated a chair for Max, and then took his own seat at the head of the table. The food — duck with mushrooms in a white wine sauce — filled the room with its gentle aroma.

"It's not often I get the chance to cook for anybody," Hull said, his pleasure warming the room like the candlelight. "Please, enjoy the food."

Max's anger strengthened with every pleasantry. This was the man who had tried to hurt Max and Sandra on several occasions. Did he really think so little of them that he expected Max to bow down before the almighty wealthy despite the past? Sandra rested her hand on Max's knee, patting him to stay silent, *stay calm*. If not for that soft hand, he would've jumped to his feet and let his mouth loose. Instead, he ate the sumptuous meal and tried not to enjoy it.

He lost on that last account. The food was damn good.

"Is Mr. Drummond here?" Hull asked after a few minutes.

"No," Max said. "But you already knew that."

"I was not certain whether the spatial limitations were true or just a myth. Next time I'll be sure to utilize a location closer to Spruce Street."

"Next time?" Sandra perked up.

"I think so," Hull said and rose to his feet. He paced around the dining room as he spoke, his agitation palpable. "I suppose there's no point in being coy. After all, it's not often that I call somebody for dinner, is it?"

"We wouldn't know," Max said, but something ticked in his mind. He suspected Hull *never* had guests for dinner — certainly never in this way. Alone and without even the minimum servants. Not even Mr. Modesto.

"I prefer anonymity. However, in this case, I don't think you would be convinced by a letter. In fact, a letter from me might make the whole idea ludicrous."

"What idea is that?"

"That you come work for me again." Sandra blurted out a shocked laugh while Max stared at the man, too stunned for more. Hull continued, "Before you say a word, let me speak. I fully recall how things stand between us and have full respect for the threat you hold over me. That is another reason why I've been forced to present myself to you this way. As to why I wish to hire you — you're a smart man. You know what this is about."

Max put his fork onto the plate with a hard clank. "The painting. *Morning in Red*. Right?"

"Exactly. Since you're already searching for it, I simply wish to have you locate it for me. Of course, I'll be happy to pay you double your normal fee. And I can assure you, this will in no way impact or alter our previous situation."

Max shook his head, unable to talk for fear of shouting. Sandra, however, did not hold back. She bolted to her feet, pointing at Hull like a stern mother reprimanding an insolent child. "How dare you even think of such a moronic idea. How dare you. You think your money can buy us off? You think we're greedy? Of course you do. Look at this place. You only understand money. Well, your wealth won't help you here. Our answer is no. Emphatically, *No*."

"There's no need to get upset."

"You think you can threaten people's lives and not have them be upset? You're a monster."

"Did I really *ruin* your life? Would you prefer to go back to Michigan, have your husband go on trial for embezzlement, spend another year freezing with little heat in the house and no husband in your bed? It seems that through my former employment, you've made a big step upward in your life."

Max held Sandra's shoulders to keep her from raising a fist at Hull — and possibly using it. Seething, she struggled against him, but he held her still. To Hull, he said, "Thank you for dinner. As to your offer, I think you can figure out our answer."

Hull raised a glass of wine, sipped, and in a quiet, threatening voice, said, "That's a shame because I will have that painting, and if you are not helping me, then you are harming me. Do not get in my way. No matter what guarantees you think you hold against me, there are some things that are worth the risk. I promise you, this is one. Whoever got you into this, I urge you to sever those ties. Leave this whole affair."

Sandra made one last lunge, but Max held her firm. Hull oozed condescension, and for a fleeting moment, Max considered letting his wife take a swipe at the man. He held back, though — partly because it was the right move to make, but partly because something still gnawed at him about the entire evening and the way Hull had behaved, something seemed out-of-place when compared to the Hull he had come to know through Mr. Modesto.

The drive home consisted of Sandra venting her anger for most of the trip until Max began laughing. "What?" she asked. "Why are you laughing?"

"You were the one telling me to stay calm all night."

Sandra began a protest and then filled the car with her own laughter. And though the weight of the evening pressed heavier on Max than at any time throughout that day, he found the release of Sandra's tensions a release for himself as well. He drove the rest of the way with a smile.

The next morning Max and Sandra entered the office holding hands and giggling over nothing in particular. Drummond sat behind the big desk — his face drawn, his arms crossed.

"You couldn't stop by here last night? Let me know what happened? I worked hard for you and you made me wait until this morning? And to top it off, you're all cutesy together."

With a light-hearted grin, Sandra said, "We're sorry. It was a long, late night, and we just needed —"

"I know what you needed. That doesn't change the fact —"

Max motioned Drummond out of his chair. "You're acting like my mother. We couldn't make it back, so just accept it at that. We're sorry if it inconvenienced you. Now, if you want, we'll be glad to tell you about all that happened."

"I'm listening."

Max delved into a recap of the evening. When he finished, Drummond's frown continued but now it was directed at the story and not the storyteller. "When you say Hull was a young man, was he really young or did he just look that way?"

"As far as I could tell, he was young."

"That's right. No more than thirty," Sandra added.

Drummond shook his head. "Then that wasn't Terrance Hull you were dining with. Hull was born sometime in the forties, maybe the fifties at the latest. He's got to be near sixty-years-old by now."

"Maybe this was Terrance Junior."

"Possibly, but I don't recall another Hull being born in the last few decades. If it happened, they've kept it a tight secret. Which isn't to say it didn't happen. These are the Hulls after all. I just find it disturbing that he picks a place for dinner he knows I can't go to when I'm one of the few people who knows what a Hull looks like."

Max said, "It doesn't matter. We turned him down and we're not interested in his games. We'll find this painting before him and then we'll have the leverage."

Drummond clapped his hands. "Well, then, you're going to need what I have for you. I spent all night working my skills, and I have for you this present."

Drummond reached into the bookshelf wall and pulled something back. He shoved it into the client chair, his face glowing with pride. Max looked to Sandra whose expression told him little. "Well?" he finally said in frustration. "What's in the chair?"

Sandra said, "Howard Corkille."

"No," Drummond said. "That's the big news. This ghost, the one who hired us, he is not Howard Corkille."

Chapter 10

MAX WATCHED THE EMPTY CHAIR as if he expected the ghost to spring before him. At that moment, he decided he hated art forgers and everything connected to them. "So, who is he?" he finally asked.

Drummond gestured to the chair. "This is Jasper Sullivan."

"And why are you pretending to be an old art forger?" Sandra asked before Max could clear his mind enough to do so. He bit back on a sharp remark.

As Sandra frowned at the response, Max snapped his fingers. "Well? What the heck is he saying?"

"Sorry," she said. "He says, 'Please, don't be mad. Please. I'm very sorry. It wasn't my intent to deceive you.'"

Max huffed. "You lied about who you are. That seems pretty intent on deception."

"'I know, I know. It's not like that, though. You see, I couldn't tell you the truth, but I'm prepared to tell you everything now.'"

"Because we've caught you."

"'Just listen, please.'"

Max looked to Drummond who signaled agreement. "Okay," Max said. "Let's hear it."

"'Much of what I told you was true,'" Sandra went on translating. "'I did live during the Great Depression. My wife, Clara, and I, we did suffer hard. I lost my job; I couldn't get work. All of that is true. I wasn't an art forger, obviously — just a clerk. Filing papers, keeping records, all sorts of paperwork, that kind of thing.

"'And ... I did buy a gun, and I did plan to kill myself. In fact, if you look up my name, you'll find my records indicate that I did commit suicide. Only I didn't.

"'Back then, you see, back during the Depression, sometimes people were removed from their homes rather quickly. Sometimes there were robberies, and sometimes there were deaths. The point is that sometimes people who shouldn't have certain items, who couldn't dream of affording such things, found them falling into their possession.'"

Impatient, Max gestured to the empty chair. "Is there a reason you find it so difficult to admit you had some stolen property? You're dead. The police can't get you now."

"'I still have my name, my pride. But I see you don't care about those things. Fine. Through connections that don't matter to this case, I came to own a certain painting.'"

"Just a wild guess, but was it called *Morning in Red?*'"

"'No, but I'll get to that painting in a moment. The painting I had come across, well, I didn't know anything about art back then, but I was sure it was worth something. It wasn't by any artist I knew, it wasn't going to make me rich, but it was a beautiful painting and I thought to myself, *there must be some way to make some money from this*. That was a common thought back then — thought it about pretty much everything.

"'I put out word about the painting in the few places I knew. Then along came Howard Corkille.'"

Max didn't need Sullivan's nervous presentation to see where things went to next. After all, Corkille, the real Corkille, was an art forger. He, no doubt, recognized some worth in the painting and offered Jasper Sullivan a unique proposal. Corkille would make an identical painting, and they would sell it. Using Corkille's established connections, they would receive far more than Sullivan could acquire on his own, and splitting the profits even at an unfavorable 70/30 split would net Sullivan handsomely. Plus, Sullivan would retain the original painting.

Thinking about the other interested parties in this case, Max said, "I'm guessing Corkille sold the painting to a member of the Hull family."

"'William Hull.'"

Drummond patted the empty space as if consoling. "He was a dangerous man. You're not the first to be hurt by him nor the last ... that's right, William Hull was responsible for turning me into a ghost, too."

"Wait," Max said. "Hull killed you?"

"You knew that."

"Not you. Sullivan."

Sandra continued to translate. "'Not Hull directly. He had a hired hand take care of it. You see, he found out about the painting. I never learned how Hull knew. Maybe he knew his art that well, maybe

Corkille screwed up doing the forgery, or maybe — probably — Corkille betrayed me. After all, I never saw the painting again. Corkille disappeared, the painting disappeared, and only Hull remained. It doesn't matter now, though. Hull figured it out. I'm sure you can imagine how he reacted.

"'I was frightened, and I wanted to protect Clara and my unborn child and, looking back, I was a bit of a coward. No, I was a lot of a coward. So, I did go to that tobacco field. I got drunk on cheap wine. And I did bring my gun. I planned to kill myself. I figured that would end Hull's interest in me and leave my family out of the matter.

"'But I couldn't do it. I couldn't pull the trigger. I sat in that field feeling the cold metal touching the skin on my head, and I kept picturing my dear Clara — how sad she would be when she found out what I had done. I saw how she would someday have to explain to my son what I had done. All I saw was pain. And I was afraid. I didn't know if there was an afterlife, but I figured if there was, I wouldn't be going anyplace good. And then I felt a hand cover mine. This hand that took hold of the gun, the one I told you saved me — the truth is that the hand belonged to Hull's man. He helped me pull the trigger.'"

Max jotted a few points down. "So, you and Howard Corkille try to pass off a forgery on Hull and it gets you killed. This certainly fills in some gaps, but you said the painting wasn't *Morning in Red*. So why did you hire us to find that one? And why are you coming clean now?"

"'I'm telling you all this because I did some checking of my own in the Other.'"

Drummond said, "He means the ghost world."

"I know what he means," Max said.

"'I came to you because you're the only ghost detective around. Or researcher, if you prefer. But as things started moving, I thought I ought to know more about you folks. So, I asked around about Drummond. When I learned of his being cursed by Hull and all, then I knew I could trust you with the truth.

"'As to the *Morning in Red* painting — I first heard of it about twenty years ago. Corkille caused my murder, and that's not something I can forgive. My wife spiraled into a sadness that claimed her. Once our son had reached fifteen, my Clara killed herself. My son, a boy I never met in life, became a violent and abusive man. Without his father to guide him, he turned to a criminal's life. So, you see, Corkille's damage to me went far beyond the theft of a painting. He destroyed my family. I spent many years looking for him in the Other. I wanted to hurt him, but he's always eluded me. And then a few decades ago, I heard he searched for this particular, odd painting.

"'That's how I learned about it — I heard Corkille wanted it. He's been looking hard — hard enough that I found out about it. So, whatever it is, it's important to him. Enough to get too noisy about it. It must be worth quite a lot and so I want it.'"

"You sent us to Melinda Corkille to get us started on the right track."

"'Yes.'"

Max walked the room with no destination. He just needed to move. He tapped his chin and licked his lips. "I'm confused. What do you want to do with this painting? You can't sell it. Even if I did it for you, it might not be worth all that much. Besides, money is worthless to you."

"'It's enough to deny Corkille what he is desperate to get. I don't know why he wants it, but I want him to have to come to me to get it. It may seem petty, I know, but if your life had turned out like mine, you'd spend hundreds of years plotting such revenge.'"

Drummond said, "Give the guy a break. As revenges go, this one is mild. I've seen enough blood-spattered walls to know that hatred can get real nasty."

Something was wrong. Why was Drummond acting so nice? Max focused on Drummond but couldn't get a sign from him. "Fine," he said. "You have anything else for us?"

"'I don't think so. If I think of anything, I'll let you know. And I'll be available. Don't worry.'"

"We trust you," Drummond said. "You relax. We'll find that painting for you."

Sandra looked up from the chair. "He's gone."

"What's with you?" Max asked Drummond. "You're not really going for all that."

Drummond slid into the client chair, propped his feet on the desk, and opened his arms like a conqueror. "Of course not. But you've got to learn how to be nice sometimes. This guy, if we came in bullying him, he would've seen us like another one of Hull's men. He said it himself — he's a coward. I just played nice while you were being all aggressive."

"Are you saying we just played Good Cop/Bad Cop?"

"You didn't know that's what we were doing?"

Max turned away but he caught the amusement on Sandra's face. He tried not to get angry or have any reaction to his embarrassment. Drummond saved him by clapping his hands together once and jumping into the air. "Okay. I think we need to pay a few visits."

Sandra helped by following along with this get-back-to-work attitude. "What do you have in mind?"

Though Max did not look at Drummond, he heard the hesitation, and it chilled his skin. "Old Jasper there had a few good nuggets to share," Drummond said. "The one that I keep hearing is that all of this is tied to Hull. In particular, to William Hull. Did you notice the way Jasper reacted when we were talking about how Hull had me cursed?"

"What reaction?" Max said turning to Sandra.

She said, "I couldn't tell you with him sitting right here, but he got very tense. If he wasn't already a pale ghost, I'd have said he turned white."

Drummond slid behind Sandra and put both hands on her shoulders — not enough to cause pain but enough to make the contact known. "I think Hull might've done more to Jasper Sullivan than just kill him. He did it to me. Thanks again, by-the-way, to both of you for freeing me from that."

"You can thank me by letting go of my wife," Max said.

Drummond raised his hand up. "Sorry. Just friends."

"Get to the final point or I'll have you re-cursed." Every second in this case filled him with unease as if he walked on fragile crates knowing any wrong step could smash them open, and he had no idea if they contained soft pillows or jagged knives.

"My point is simply that if William Hull cursed Jasper, he would have used a witch — a particular witch whose daughter is continuing in the family tradition."

"No," Max said, picturing jagged knives.

"She's the one with the answers."

"She tried to kill me."

"She failed."

"I am not going to see her and act all nice so I can get some information from her. I won't do it."

Sandra grabbed the car keys. "I'll do it for you. Drummond'll come with me."

Drummond perked up. "Spend the day with a pretty gal like you? No problem. Don't worry, Max. I'll be a gentleman."

The two headed for the office door. Defeated, Max said, "Just hold on. Let me get my coat."

THE DOOR HAD A LOCK NOW. That was the first difference they noticed standing at the office of Dr. Connor, optometrist and witch. The second was the quiet.

Not absolute silence but a muted quiet strange for this area. Westgate Center Drive, with its numerous doctor's offices and outpatient facilities, ran somewhat parallel to Stratford Road — one of the busiest roads since it connected to Hanes Mall. Tons of restaurants and loads of shops, yet despite the steady number of passing cars and the occasional delivery truck, things remained quiet. Even the birds stopped chirping around Connor's office.

Though he had survived their last meeting, Max could not avoid the horrible, gut-churning sensation thoughts of Dr. Connor brought upon him. She was not somebody to mess around with. Whatever information she might have for them, he knew it would come with a price.

"Are you going in or not?" Drummond asked.

Sandra took hold of Max's hand. "It'll be okay."

"You don't know that," Max said, but he opened the door anyway. The darkness inside matched his fear — heavy and pressing. When they stepped inside, however, the mood lightened considerably. He had seen poverty before — desolation, dereliction, destruction, even blood and death. Until this moment, he never felt a sense of relief (and even a tinge of joy) at seeing such things.

The witch's office lay in ruin. Not because some tornado of ruthless vandals had swept through but rather out of neglect. Dust covered the few bits of furniture that remained. The shades were drawn, letting the sun peek in at odd angles. Empty food containers littered the floor as did the blood-markings of a half-completed spell (at least, Max thought it looked half-completed). A picture lay smashed in the corner next to a hole in the wall at about the height of an aggravated kick. An empty bottle of Jack Daniel's leaned against a half-empty bottle.

"Dr. Connor?" Sandra called.

Somebody stirred in the back. Sandra called out again, and this time they heard coughing before a bent lady shuffled toward them. A year ago, Dr. Connor had been a vibrant, frightening woman — young, powerful, and eager to use both to her advantage. Max looked upon her now with pity — she appeared to have aged twenty years or more in just one year.

When she saw her visitors, her face flushed with fierce venom. "You! Demon! You dare come back here. Just because you hurt me once, you think you can finish me off? I'll whip you to the ground," she said, raising her hands as if to hurl herself upon Max. She froze in that awkward position, her eyes searching, her ears perked. Then she let out a sinister smile. "You brought the ghost with you. Good. I'll smite all three of you. Send you to Hell where you belong."

All of the past few days burned through any sense of calm or fear Max had possessed. Before he could think about it, he let loose the fire. "You piece of trash," he said, showing no restraint. "You're the one that deserves Hellfire. You threaten my wife and my friend? You threaten me?"

"You destroyed my office. You broke my spell."

"That would be the spell you tried to kill me with."

"When others saw what you had done, I became a failed witch — tainted. I lost respect. I lost most of my business because of you. Who wants to get magic done by a tainted witch?"

"I doubt that's the whole problem. Look at yourself. You're a drunken slob. You're falling apart."

Raising her torso, breathing deep like an animal preparing to battle, she bared her yellow teeth. "You are a demon sent to me by order of Hell. I know how your kind thinks. I know your plans. And I won't be your pawn in any of it. I defy you demon from the North. I defy you. You want to kill me? Fine. I'll take your bitch with me and make you watch."

Sandra stepped forward and slapped Dr. Connor so hard that the woman fell to the ground. "For a witch, you sure are a fool. You were the killer, not us."

"Don't bother," Drummond said as he poked around the office. "She's out of her mind. Or just plain drunk."

"She has a book," Max said. "At least, she had one when I was last here."

"She's a witch. She has lots of books."

"This one's all about curses."

"I'll check on it." Drummond stepped through a wall deeper into the office.

With a garbled chuckle, the witch raised her head. "You want to know more about curses, eh? You want to know about a specific curse." Her eyes struck upon Max with an intensity unmatched by her slovenly appearance. Her youth returned to her eyes. "And a painting, I think."

Max's fears resumed their play on his nerves. "What do you know about Jasper Sullivan? How was he cursed?"

Still chuckling, Connor's eyes slipped away from Max and fell upon the half-empty Jack Daniel's bottle. She crawled over moldy pizza to the bottle and suckled it with wet, slobbering noises. With a relieved smile, she said, "I know all about that man and that painting. You may have ruined me, but I've still got contacts. I still have opportunities. Witches are like cats. Nine lives. You watch yourselves because I know everything you want to know."

"I'll bet you do. Your mother was the witch in charge back in William Hull's day, right?"

"Oh, yes. She was dangerous."

"And William Hull was angry that he had been duped on that painting. So he wanted her to hurt Jasper Sullivan in revenge."

"You sound like you know it all, but you don't."

Sandra leaned toward Max. "She's nuts. Let's just go."

Max squatted in front of Connor. He looked at her expectant face and knew the time for payment had come. She had acknowledged that she knew something and, by sharing this fact, that she would be willing to tell it — but no witch does anything for free.

"Honey," he said without looking away from the witch. "Go to the ABC store and buy two, make it three, bottles of Jack Daniels." To Dr. Connor, he added, "Will that be enough?"

Connor swung her bottle upward and guzzled the remaining alcohol. "It just might."

She refused to say another word until Sandra returned. Drummond flew in, listened to what had happened, and said to Max, "You keep impressing me. If this were back in my time, we would've made a great team."

"We're barely partners."

"If I were alive, I'd make us a team, but I guess we do okay. I found the book back there. It's in pretty bad condition. Her private office is every bit as messed up as the rest of this place and keeping care of her books doesn't seem to have gotten any priority. Looks like she's been living back there for some time now."

"I'll look at it later. I don't want to leave her alone for any length of time."

Dr. Connor pointed at Max with a curved index finger that wavered in little arcs as she said, "Smart man. I still can do amazing things if I want to. Just takes a little focus and then that's it for you." She gazed in the vicinity of Drummond. "I know you're there, ghost. I feel you. I can still hurt you, too. Don't even think about touching me with your cold hands. I'll bind you back before you know I've even moved."

Drummond yawned. "Your wife better get back quick. I'm already tired of drunken witch-rantings."

Twenty minutes more passed before Sandra arrived with the whiskey. She handed the bottles to Max, gave the witch a vile glare, and stepped back near Drummond. Max handed one bottle over to Dr. Connor who broke open the seal with practiced efficiency and drank.

"Now," Max said, "if you want the rest of them, you'd better start talking. Why was Jasper Sullivan cursed, what kind of curse, and how do we break it?"

"Don't forget the painting," Drummond said.

Max motioned for patience. Connor flashed her best insanity glower, and said, "You've got the whole thing wrong. Jasper Sullivan was never cursed. Executed, yes, but not cursed. After all, William Hull was not a bad man, not an unfair man. He understood why somebody like Sullivan would do what he did. This was the Great Depression. Times were hard and everybody needed money."

"Except Hull," Sandra said under her breath.

"Even the Hull family fell hard," Connor said, turning toward Sandra. "When the market goes bad, it goes bad for anybody with money. Now it's true that the Hulls did not suffer like a Sullivan or a Smith or even the Connor family — but they did have to go without many of the things they had become accustomed to." To Max, she continued, "William Hull would never order Jasper Sullivan to be cursed. But when they decided, in those uncertain times, to spend their money on a painting and then discovered they had lost their money and the painting both, well, Hull's anger could not be matched. Those responsible would have to pay. So, Jasper Sullivan ended up dead. Howard Corkille, however, became another matter entirely."

Max handed over another bottle. "Tell us all about it."

"I wasn't even born, remember. I only know what my mother told me when I took over the family business. It's important to keep track of curses and bindings and such. So she told me all about Howard Corkille in case I should ever have to deal with him or his curse. Very sad tale actually, but I suppose money will make people do sad things.

"In the case of Howard Corkille, he had done well as an art forger for almost a hundred years by the time he met Jasper Sullivan. Didn't know that, did you? It's true, though. Corkille was born in 1841. He was just over ninety when they met. I doubt he had done any forgeries in decades." Dr. Connor pulled more whiskey into her mouth, swished it around, and swallowed. "Whatever possessed him to help out Sullivan also brought back the thrill of screwing people over through his profession. Still, you'd think living around North Carolina for ninety years should've told him enough about the Hulls to dissuade him."

"So your mother bound him?"

With a snorting laugh, Dr. Connor stumbled to her feet and weaved her way down the hall toward her back office. Max and Sandra exchanged confused and curious looks as they followed the drunken witch. Drummond flew ahead through the wall.

The back office looked as if it had not been repaired since Max destroyed it over a year ago. The hole in the wall formed when he had broken her attempt at cursing him, the disheveled books and papers, the burned circle in the floor all flooded memories upon him — memories of the most harrowing time of his life. Max suspected she had brought them back here just for that reaction. The selfish amusement on her face supported this notion.

"You're very narrow-minded," she said, her speech clearing despite the bottle in her hand wetting her lips every few moments. "All three of you. You think that a binding curse is the only kind? You really think somebody who would employ a witch would be so uncreative in their choices of revenge?"

"You admire Hull," Sandra said.

"Of course, I do. The whole family is made of brilliant minds that don't fear the powers of life but accept them just because such things are — and they're willing to make use of it all. The trees, the sky, the water, the earth — all filled with great, untapped powers. Howard Corkille didn't understand any of that. He does now. All this time later, every day, he understands it. I'm sure Mr. Drummond understands it, too."

"Shut up," Drummond yelled as he soared at her. He slashed his hand through her body, and she let out a yelp. She shivered so hard, the bottle dropped from her hand and shattered. Then she began a long, sadistic cackle.

"Guess he doesn't like the truth too much," she said. "Shame I lost the bottle, though."

"Stick to Corkille," Max said, his eagerness for information the only thing keeping his distaste for this woman in check. "What kind of curse did your mother use?"

"She gave him immortality."

Max's eyebrow raised. "You can do that?"

"Do a little math — my mother was the Hull's witch during the Depression but I was born in 1973. She looked to be about thirty-five. If a spell can slow her aging, why not a spell to stop dying?"

"And this is a bad thing?"

"It is when you don't couple it with eternal youth. He's about two-hundred-years old now. I'd imagine every bone in his body aches. Food is tasteless. His eyesight, his hearing, even his sense of smell have all faded. Everyone he has known and cared about has grown old and died. But he is still here. Forever. I think that's quite cruel and imaginative."

Max's initial reaction leaned toward disbelief. But if ghosts, witches, and binding curses all were true, then why not immortality? Why not anything? The rules of the world he had been taught were wrong. Though he knew this to be true, he still struggled with it every day.

"Is this the curse?" Sandra asked. Max had not been paying close attention to her, and now saw her holding a thick, bound book — a book of curses.

Dr. Connor nodded without looking at the page. "There's only one in there that would match what I've said. You'll find it without any trouble."

Sandra flipped through the pages. Max watched her face reacting to the different words and images that passed under her gaze. Drummond, reading over her shoulder, jutted out his hand and said, "There. That's it."

"You're sure?" Max asked.

Sandra turned the book to face Max. Under some text he could not make out from that distance, he saw a clear, hand-drawn picture of a decrepit, old man — one who had to be centuries old. "We're sure," Sandra said.

Turning back to Connor and ignoring the snickers coming from Drummond and Sandra, Max asked, "What does the painting have to do with this curse? Is it like the binding curse — attached to an object?"

"I'm done talking. No more," Connor said.

"You've got —"

"Out! Get out!" Waving her hands, she moved toward Sandra as if shooing cats away. "And take your ghost with you."

Sandra and Drummond backed out of the office. Dr. Connor turned to Max and with surprising speed, rushed close to him, her face so near his that he could smell her mouth washed in whiskey. Whispering in a hoarse voice, she said, "Come back here tonight, midnight, and I'll tell you exactly what you need to know about Hull. He's messing around with very dangerous magic, and we're all going to pay for it."

"Tell me now."

"Tonight. Midnight. The witching hour," she said and backed off with a sloppy, sinister grin.

Chapter 12

"THIS IS A BAD IDEA," Drummond said as they left the office parking lot. "Whatever she wants to tell you is not worth meeting her at midnight."

"She could barely stand up."

"I don't care. A witch is not to be underestimated. If she had drunk herself into a coma, I'd still be worried."

Making a baby face, Max said, "Aw, are you worried about little ol' me?"

"On second thought, go get yourself killed."

"I promise I'll be careful. And the first part of that is being prepared. I think we should go visit with Melinda Corkille again. And this time around, I don't intend to leave without some answers."

"Good idea," Sandra said. "While you're doing that, Drummond can help me find that painting."

With a lecherous purr, Drummond said, "I love how you keep finding excuses for me to be with you."

"I need somebody who can go to the ghost world. You know any other ghosts that can help me, I'd be glad to work with them instead."

"If my heart were still beating, you'd have broken it."

"Wait a second," Max said. "I need you to come with me."

Sandra's odd expression told Max he teetered close to a fight. "You need me there?" she said, and even Drummond quieted down. "Every time you've gone there before, you refused to let me come along."

"Do we have to keep dredging this up? I made a mistake about that before, and I'm trying to do this the right way now. You understand?"

"You really just want to keep digging yourself deeper? No, don't bother saying anything. We are either in this together, husband and wife, or we're not."

"What are you talking about?" Max said, exasperation painting every word.

"I've tried sitting back and letting you be the boss, but that's just not us. We don't rule over each other. So, while I appreciate your consideration, the fact is that I've got a few ideas on how we can find that painting. Going to Corkille's is a good idea. You can use her to locate — what is he? — her great-great-great grandfather? If the curse is real and he's still alive, you can find him. Drummond and I will get the painting, and you'll have all the leverage you need when you see that witch tonight. Now, if you've got a better plan, then I'll be happy to listen, but if you just want to boss me around ..."

"That's not fair," Max said. From the shocked look on Sandra's face and the echo in his ear, he realized too late that he had shouted the words. With a little more control, he went on, "I know I haven't done the best at any of this, I'm learning as I go, but you've got to cut me some slack here."

Shocked or not, Sandra plowed on. "Really? Cut you slack? What about me? I've been busting my ass in every way possible to help get this business going. How about a little appreciation?"

"This was a bad idea from the start." Max wanted to stop talking, wanted to rebuild the wall that crumbled around him, but he couldn't fight the momentum. The words kept spilling out of him. "If it weren't for your ability to see all the damn ghosts, you could be off doing something you really want to do instead of being stuck in my office all the time."

"That's it right there, isn't it? My ability. You want to play this off like it's all about me being around all the time, that I'm crowding you, but the truth is that you resent the fact that you need me. You hate it that without me, you don't have a business."

Drummond coughed and said, "I don't think I should be here now. I'll come back later."

"You stay still," Sandra said and Drummond obeyed.

"I'm trying to do right by us," Max went on, his face flushed and his brain trying to find a way out of this mess of an argument. "I screwed up in Michigan ..."

"You sure did."

"... and I'm trying to make up for it. But having you scrutinize everything I do all day long isn't helping."

"I don't scrutinize."

"It sure feels that way."

Shaking his head more to himself than anyone else, Drummond floated between the couple. "Look, you two, we have a case to solve and a painting to find. That means time is a bit of a problem. So save the fight for when you're at home. We've got work to do."

"Fine with me," Sandra said. "Drummond and I have things to do."

"Fine," Max said. "I'll go see Melinda Corkille."

So, despite his decision never to do so, Max found himself in his car heading toward Melinda Corkille — alone.

The familiar drive performed its usual trick of pumping up Max's nerves. He already was fuming over fighting with his wife. But the closer he got to the Corkille house, the more his mind jumped from Dr. Connor and Terrance Hull to Sandra and Drummond, all the time dancing away from (yet sneaking glances at) memories of Melinda Corkille's naked back as she seductively stepped towards her bedroom. He had to calm down. A spat with the wife coupled with a seductress like Melinda only meant trouble. By the time he pulled into the Corkille's driveway, his hands were sore from tapping out every song the radio played.

She was out. Her car was gone, and a brown, dented Ford sat in its place — *Super-M Maids* printed on the side. Max blotted the back of his sleeve against his sweating forehead.

The front door to the house stood ajar while the sounds of vacuum cleaners and country music drifted outside. Max scanned the surrounding area — nobody watching. He hadn't trespassed since the Stan Bowman case last year, the same case that connected him to Hull and Connor and a whole mess of trouble. Max noted the irony as he stepped from the car and slinked toward the front door.

Though his heart pounded with adrenaline, a sense of relief washed over him. At least he had avoided meeting Melinda again. By comparison, this should be easy.

Standing in the open doorway, Max leaned in and listened. The twanging music came from his left — probably the kitchen. The vacuums whined away upstairs — not a place he wanted to visit. Most important of all, no sounds came from his right.

He took off his shoes and walked across the gleaming, hardwood floors in his socks. When he reached the room with the red sofa, he took a few gulps of air and looked around. Nothing appeared out of the ordinary. Just an average, filthy-rich living room. No desk, no papers, no bank statements.

"Of course not," he whispered. He could hear Drummond in his head — *This was the room she brought you to. Why would she let you spend time in a room with anything important in it?*

"But she's arrogant," he said. He bent over to look closer, going over the same pieces he had seen before — the same pictures, the same furniture, the same paintings, the same plants.

The door.

His head snapped up, and he stared at the narrow door with the plant in front of it. On his prior visit, he had assumed it was a broom closet. But she had him sit opposite the door, as if challenging him to see it, to ask about it.

No. I'm just reading into this. But what if ...

Making sure none of the maids were coming his way, he pulled the heavy plant to the side and opened the door. It led down a tiny hall and opened into an art studio — an art forger's studio.

In one way, the windowless room could have been an artist's studio. Canvases, paints, and brushes all had their special spots. An easel with a cloth-covered painting dominated the middle of the room. Two smocks hung on hooks to the side of the entrance, and several bulbs hung from the ceiling.

However, the room also looked unlike a typical artist's studio. On the wall opposite Max, he saw a utility sink next to a kitchen counter and a small refrigerator. On the counter were bread, a potato, coffee, tea, olive oil, gelatin, and flour. Max opened the fridge to find eggs and milk. A stove book-ended the counter and stacked on it was a pestle and mortar, two ice trays, a scale, some plates, detergent, and various papers and boards.

Max rummaged through the counter drawers. He found quills, numerous old pens, bottles of ancient inks, and sepia. One drawer had been filled with brushes stained in ink, charcoal, chalk, and other dried mediums.

And the key detail, the one Max knew he noticed only from spending time learning from Drummond — no dust. This art forging studio was still being used. It was possible Melinda had followed in Howard's footsteps, but that did not seem likely. Melinda came off as too selfish to apply herself to the years of study required for such a thing. Of course, the alternative had yet to penetrate Max fully. He knew curses and witches were real, but to accept that somewhere in this mansion rested a two-hundred year old criminal, pushed Max's sense of the world further than it had ever gone before.

"Only one way to be sure."

Max slipped his shoes back on and walked into the kitchen. He made sure to use heavy steps, the kind that echoed throughout such a large house. One maid, a blonde girl no more than eighteen, stood on a stepstool and scrubbed at food caked across the inner face of a microwave. When she saw Max, she stepped down and wiped her hands.

"Excuse me," Max said with a disarming smile.

"Who are you?" the girl asked, lacking all the Southern friendliness he had come to know.

"I'm sorry," he said, and put out his hand. "I'm Trevor Denton." He had no clue where that name came from but did not question himself either. "I'm Ms. Corkille's personal assistant."

"What happened to Jenine?"

"She still works for Ms. Corkille, too. I've just been brought in to help out with a few things. It's a busy time right now."

Still cautious but softening a little, the maid said, "Oh. Okay, so what do you want?"

"Ms. Corkille asked for some papers but this is my first time in her house, and well, it's big."

The girl laughed. "Yeah. It took me a few times before I figured the whole thing out."

"I imagine so. But I'm pressed for time. I've got to get the papers to the courthouse today or Ms. Corkille will be very angry."

The girl blanched. Nobody wanted to see Ms. Corkille angry. "I can show you her office."

Up until this point, his bluff had been quite easy. With what little he knew, the maid seemed willing to believe just about any basic idea. The problem was now. Where would Melinda be hiding Howard? "No," he said on instinct. "She said they were in a different room."

"Which room? There are quite a few."

Which one, indeed? Howard Corkille would not be hidden in any common room or any room that the maids were expected to clean. "She wasn't too clear," Max finally said. "It sounded like she was driving when she called me. She told me it was another room but it wasn't one with a name like kitchen or bathroom or anything like that. Is she always like this?"

With a conspiratorial wink, she said, "Not always. Just most of the time."

"Because the last person I was an assistant for drove me nuts with these half-explained requests. I mean, what am I supposed to do? Go through every room in this mansion?"

"What kind of papers are these?"

"I don't know. They're in an envelope. Just get them to the

courthouse. That's all I know."

"I wonder if she meant the Other Room."

"What's that?"

"Just a third guest room but she never wants it cleaned or even opened. We call it the Other Room because sometimes you hear things moving in there. If I believed in ghosts, I'd say that room was haunted. But, of course, that kind of thing is silly."

"Of course," Max said with a knowing smile.

"You better call her before you go in there, though. She's very strict about it."

"Thank you. I'll do that. Where is this room?"

"Upstairs at the end of the hall."

"Thanks again."

The maid offered her first flash of warmth — a slight curve of the lips.

Max found a set of servants' stairs from the kitchen and climbed up. He walked along the wide hall and listened to the upstairs maids working. They were in a bedroom on the left, and Max did not stop when he passed by. They either didn't notice him or didn't care. He was happy enough whichever way it was.

As he neared the end of the hall, his nerves reignited. The Other Room awaited just beyond a dark, wooden door. If he took too long, the maids might wonder about him — What's with the guy standing in front of the Other Room? That might lead to questions and then the whole thing would blow up. No, he had to do this now.

He opened the door and stepped in.

The Other Room was another guest room — enough space to place a twin bed, a bedside table, and a small chest of drawers on the side. One window spread sunlight into the dingy interior. The walls were covered in wallpaper from another era, brown vertical designs that hid dirt better than brighten the room. In the back corner, a Japanese tri-fold screen stood with a delicate painting of two birds on a ghostly limb. At the foot of the bed, a rocking chair faced the window. Max saw a man sitting in the chair.

"Mr. Corkille?" he said, his voice distant and inconsequential. "Howard Corkille?"

The rocking stopped and a single hand emerged from the side to gesture Max closer. When Max obliged, he saw a man hunched over, covered in wrinkles and age spots, destroyed by a lifetime over a century too long. The man peered up and grinned.

"Nice to see a different face," he said. He spoke with a sickening crackle that underscored every word.

Max's muscles refused to move. The man sitting before him frightened him as if he looked upon the living dead — not a rotting zombie from the movies, but rather a warm, fully fleshed but decrepit human being. Max feared to shake the offered hand, feared it might crumble in his grip.

Perhaps reading Max's expression, Corkille said, "Don't worry. You can't hurt me. Nothing can."

"The curse?" Max said, shaking the coarse, dried hand lightly.

"Oh, yes. I didn't believe in magic and curses and such until I tangled with the Hull family. Now, I know. When I was first put under this curse, I tried to prove it wasn't true." Corkille pulled back his sleeve to show long scars stretching from the crook of his arm to his wrist. "The skin would just seal back up. I once bought a shotgun and thought to blow my head off. It jammed. Every time I pointed it at myself, it jammed. Point it at the wall, no problem." Corkille gestured to the scattered holes in the wall. "Point it at myself — click."

"I can't imagine."

"After a while, I stopped trying. Then I just got older and older. My body got weaker. My eyesight's remained. Thank the Lord for that. My hearing sucks. I smell horrible. Bladder control went out ninety years ago. Everything's failing little by little. But my mind won't ever go. Curses work that way, y'see. It won't let me have the pleasure of escaping any of this through dementia. I have to experience it every step. And I'm tired. I just want to die, just close my eyes and sleep forever."

When Corkille closed his eyes, Max thought he might fall asleep. He thought he had to keep Corkille talking, but with his next question, he found that Corkille was eager to talk with anybody. Isolation can have that effect.

"And you need the painting?" Max asked.

Corkille looked at his hands. "Painting was my life. I loved it since I was a boy. I remember an artist traveling through town, stopping wherever to do portraits to make a little money - - that's when it all started for me. He gave me a brush and he taught me a bit. I caught the bug.

"My father was dead and my mother, she supported me. We worked hard to pull together enough money to get me schooled. And I learned to paint.

"I suppose some psychiatrist would blame it on being raised poor, would say that's why I took to forging. Maybe it's a little true. I certainly was attracted to the money and to thumbing my nose at the art world — they can be such asses. I don't know if this is true for all criminals, but for some of us, for me, there was an attraction to breaking laws. Not that I wanted to go hurting people but that I discovered a sense of freedom, a sense of invulnerability, that I've never found at any other time in my life.

"Felt it right up until the moment that witch came along and laid a curse upon me. But then, you know all about this kind of thing."

Through deadening eyes, Corkille stared straight at Max. Max fought the urge to flee. "What do you mean?"

"No need to play games, Mr. Porter."

"You know who I am?"

Corkille cracked a sly grin that could have belonged to Melinda. "Do you think you're the only one who does research? I was cursed by a witch that worked for the Hull family. I pay attention to anything involving those two."

"You've been watching me."

"Not me personally. I'm too old for that. But, yes, since you first moved down here. That whole business with Stan Bowman and the Drummond curse — I followed you through every step. You handled yourself well, and I thought even back then that if I needed your type of services, I wouldn't hesitate to call. And now I need you."

Max shook his head. "Wait. You didn't call me. I found you. You've been hiding out all this time, not trying to contact me."

"True, I did not try to contact you. Not true, that I've just been hiding out here. I've been searching for that painting for many years."

"What's so important about it?"

"This is dangerous. I had hoped to avoid involving you, and I feared doing so would gain the attentions of Hull or the witch, but it seems they already are paying attention. So, now that we're talking, now that I've met you in person, I think you are the perfect man to find that painting."

Max leaned against the window frame with an exasperated sigh. "Really? I'm *the perfect man*? Is this a joke? No one will even tell me why some painting that has no apparent value is so important. And I'm perfect. So, why do you want it?"

"To help break this curse, of course. Surely, by now, you've come to understand that much. Why else would a witch be involved if not for magic? Why else would an occultist like Hull care so much? Listen, I will pay you double your fee, and I promise that when you find me that painting, you'll have plenty more."

The bedroom door burst open. "What the hell are you doing in here?" Melinda Corkille said, her face taut and red.

Max stammered but Howard turned towards her, raised his hands in celebration, and said, "My dear, we've just hired Mr. Porter."

Chapter 13

WHEN MAX WALKED INTO HIS OFFICE, Sandra and Drummond turned, ready to launch into whatever business they wanted to share. One look at his stunned face stopped them. As he explained what happened since they had argued, their faces also dropped into shock.

After Max finished, nobody said a word. The only sound was the droning buzz of a fan Sandra had set on her desk. Drummond was the first to break the silence. "So, we're working for Corkille now?"

"I think so," Max said. "I think his side of this story is the most honest."

"You know he's lying about something, though, right?"

"Don't they always?"

Drummond clapped his hands. "There you go. That's what I like. Healthy skepticism. I can see now that I'm doing a bang-up job. Teaching you perfectly."

"I guess," Sandra said, "it's time for me to earn my keep."

Max shook his head. "Can we not start in on that fight right now?"

"I wasn't being sarcastic. And considering all of this Corkille stuff, I think you'll be very happy with what I have to say."

"Hey," Drummond said. "I was part of this, too."

"I haven't forgotten."

"One of you tell me," Max said.

Sandra puffed up a little. "I think we've found the painting."

Until he heard those words from his wife's lovely lips, Max didn't think his day could get any weirder. So many questions flooded his brain that he shut down, staring stupefied at his wife. The ghost behind her spoke first.

"I'm the one who figured out the name change."

Max snapped to. "What name change?"

Drummond slid into his chair, kicked up his feet, and said, "I've been spending a lot of time with ghosts lately, trying to find out whatever I can about Corkille and Sullivan and everything else. A lot of them, not all ghosts, but a lot of them moan and groan about the lives they had. Just a bunch of pansies. And they cry on about how many people came to their funerals and who said what and so forth. I was trying to have a pleasant conversation with this figure skater who cracked her neck on the ice, poor thing was only twenty-three, beautiful gal who had a promising career. Great mouth, too. Smile that just melted me."

"The point, please."

"Oh, right. Anyway, we were just talking and I was about to lay a good line on her, the kind that would've led to a date without a doubt, when this old lady floats by wailing and wailing about being dead. I lost it. You know, sometimes these things just build up inside you and her little tirade set me off. I yelled at her. And she turned to me with such hatred and self-pity and she said, 'I'm sure you had a wonderful funeral with plenty of people to cry for you, but not me. I was a good person and only three mourners came. Just three.' She yapped on, but I didn't hear any of it. Because it hit me just then — what if the painting was actually called 'Mourning in Red,' as in at a funeral?"

Sandra flitted about with sudden energy like an excited schoolgirl. "When Drummond told me about his idea, I just knew he was right. We did some searches but came up empty. Then we tried some of the art dealer forums, and guess who we found to be looking for the same painting?"

Max looked at the floor. "Gold," he said as if he could shoot the name into the art gallery below.

"Bingo. But it doesn't look like he's had any success."

Drummond said, "Gold's not looking under the right name. He's still just an idiot."

Sandra continued, "The name is a big part of it, but then I realized that we were searching the wrong way. This painting is not a valuable painting. The artist isn't well-known. Nothing we've been told indicates that anybody not involved with this whole curse even knows the painting exists. It's not a famous painting. It's common. So, we should go where we little common folk go."

"First, we checked eBay," Drummond said with a twinkle of pride at using computer lingo, "but nobody had listed it."

"This is my part of the story," Sandra said.

"Sorry."

"Next we went to craigslist, and again we found nothing. And then I decided to post on craigslist myself. I simply named the painting and how much I'd pay for it. Don't worry, not much — but then, it isn't worth that much to most people."

"And we got a hit."

"Drummond!"

"I'm sorry, but I'm just as happy as you are."

Max waved off their little spat. "You got a hit? Where? When? Heck, who?"

Sandra said, "A guy named Chris Thorne, and he lives just north of us in Virginia. We only need to set up a time and place to exchange for the painting."

"Don't you usually send a check and get it in the mail?"

"Do you really want to risk it that way, or do the whole thing in person?"

"I guess we're taking a little trip to Virginia. When do we go?"

"He should e-mail me tonight."

"Great," Max said. "You've both done a great job."

Sandra kissed Max on the cheek. "Since we can't do anything about the painting until we get the e-mail, why don't we do a bit of premature celebration. Care for an early dinner and some alcohol? I think we could both use it."

"Hey," Drummond said. "That's not very fair to me."

Sandra rolled out her bottom lip. "So sorry. But there's not much we can actually do for you, is there?"

"You could quit mocking me. And you don't have to rub it in all the time. I know I'm a ghost."

Max put his arm around Sandra's shoulder. He knew things were not suddenly okay between them, and he knew she was aware of it, too. But one thing he had learned through the course of their marriage — some days it paid more to let the ugly stuff slide away for a while. To Drummond, he said, "We'll be back later to check on that e-mail."

Dinner was a pleasant affair. They went to Fourth Street and enjoyed the Italian wonders of Dioli's Trattoria. Despite the shadow of the witch's impending midnight meeting looming over him, Max managed to push fear away long enough to eat. He drank in the beauty of his wife and the joy of her success, and he felt capable of facing the witch. If all went well, within the next day or two, he would have that painting, this case would be over, he'd get paid, and life would become easier. If.

By the time he wiped cannoli crumbs from his mouth, the fears had resurfaced. Sandra knew, of course — she took one look at his troubled face and he saw her understanding. He shook his head, and she stayed quiet.

They went home, watched some nonsense on television, and when it was time that they normally would get dressed for bed, Max donned his coat. This time, however, Sandra did not stay quiet. "I'm coming with you," she said, and Max knew better than to argue. Besides, if he was honest with himself, he wanted her along.

Twenty minutes later, they sat in their car across the street from the witch's office. "It was about a year ago that we were sitting here like this," Max said.

"Yeah," Sandra said. "This time feels worse."

Max watched the digital clock in his car stereo add another minute. "Yeah," he whispered. With only two minutes until midnight, Max stepped out of the car. The 'door ajar' bell chimed repeatedly, its sharp tone standing out in the quiet night air.

"How long should I wait?" Sandra asked.

"Until I either come out or you hear me screaming."

"That's not funny."

"Wasn't meant to be," he said and walked toward the office.

It never got easier — crossing that small parking lot in the dead of night. He had done this several times, and each instance twisted his nerves into a ball of wriggling worms. He hated the witch's office — hated that he never knew what he would find when he opened the door.

The cool night air prickled his skin, and when he reached the overhang, he wondered if he might be better off turning around and leaving. Yes, the witch promised important information, but she had done terrible things before — cursing him would be the least of her sins. Still, the desperation in her eyes that morning led Max to believe that this was no trap. The question that plagued him, though, was *What exactly is this?*

The door was unlocked. Max touched the knob, his fingers trembling over the rusting metal, and pushed the door in.

The darkness in the waiting room neared pitch black. If not for the lone candle at the far end of the hall, Max would have seen nothing. But she wanted him to see a little bit. That much was clear. She had left a blatant marker, and as Max headed down the hall, as his gut tightened around the remnants of dinner, he considered that the drunken soul he had seen that morning might have been acting.

When he reached the candle, he smelled incense burning from the closed office door. "Come in," Dr. Connor called.

Last chance, he thought, looking back down the hall.

But the office door opened, and Dr. Connor stood before him wearing a black gown and looking more in control of herself. Four clusters of candles lit the room, one cluster at the mid-point of each wall. They cast competing shadows behind her as she stepped back and gestured to one of the two chairs facing each other in the center.

"You seem much better than this morning," Max said as he leaned against the entryway. The warmth of the candles pressing against him matched the pain in his stomach pushing to get out.

"I was not at my best," she said with a fluttering chuckle. "But I want to thank you. You've given me a little ray of hope, and that has made me feel much, much better."

"I did?"

"Only fitting since you were the one who destroyed me."

The ice in her voice struck out at Max, reminding him that no matter what, this woman should only be seen as dangerous. "What do you want?" he asked.

"Information, of course. Isn't that what you trade in?"

"I don't have anything for you."

"You definitely do. And in exchange, as promised, I will tell you what Terrance Hull is doing and why it is vital to you and your interests."

Despite his pounding heart, Max acted as if none of this mattered. "Fine. You go first."

Dr. Connor licked her lips and said, "Please, sit down." With a sweeping motion, she went to her desk and reached underneath. A string quartet piped in from ceiling speakers. Max didn't recognize the piece but it was a somber, slightly dissonant sound that made the witch appear more devious, more of a threat.

Exactly what she wants.

"Come now," she said, stepping toward the chairs. "I promise I won't curse you tonight."

"How comforting."

The idea of heading further into this spider's web did not appeal to Max, but he wanted to hear what she had to say. There were so many loose threads, and if this witch would tie some of it together, even just one or two things, he had to take a few chances. No risk, no reward —

Drummond would be proud.

When Max settled into his chair. Connor sat opposite him. "I'm sure Howard Corkille has told you his pathetic little story. He probably even told you some of the truth. But what you should know is that Terrance Hull is not seeking the painting as some sort of retribution upon Corkille for deceiving his grandfather. He never even liked the old man that much. No, Terrance Hull needs to find the painting for the same reason he needed to get his journal back a year ago. They are two of three key charms to a powerful spell. I was to cast that spell, but because of you, Hull is not as confident in me as he once was. When you help me get this painting back to him," she said, her eyes turned toward the ceiling as if peering into the future, "he will care about me again."

"So, what's this spell?"

"Simply to raise Tucker Hull back from the grave with more power than he ever had when alive, to restore him to his place as the head of the Hull family, but this time, with an enormous fortune to wield."

"Is that all?"

Dr. Connor curled her lip. "For now."

"And you actually think I'll help you do this?"

She placed her middle finger on Max's forehead and slid it down to the tip of his nose. "You will be eager to help me."

Max swore she kept speaking, but he could not hear anything. A weight pressed into his body as if a sandbag had been dumped into his lap. At first, he thought it was fear taking over. As Dr. Connor edged back, concentrating on him and mouthing silent words, he knew the weight was not fear but some kind of spell.

"Stop this." He tried to lift his arms but they wouldn't budge from his side.

"I just need to ensure that you won't do anything rash."

"I'm not going to help you," he said, while a voice deep inside questioned his timing for bravado.

"I wonder what your wife will say about it?"

"What?"

"She must be feeling a bit lonely outside, in that cold car, waiting for you to play your little detective game with me. She must be wishing something more exciting would happen."

Max strained against his invisible bonds. Though he knew she would never hear him, Max screamed Sandra's name, begged her to drive away — even as he pictured Dr. Connor's hired hands ripping open the car door and yanking her out. She would struggle. She would fight back with a kick or a punch, but they would overpower her.

The witch had his wife.

Dr. Connor sauntered to her rolltop desk and opened the half-empty bottle of Jack Daniel's. She tipped back her head and guzzled for a moment. With a satisfied exhalation, she returned to Max. "Now," she said, "you will help me get that painting, so that I may return to Terrance's favor. If you don't, I'm sure the Hulls will always have need for a good blood sacrifice."

With the coldest, most hateful scorn he ever held, Max nodded. He thought to threaten her should anything happen to Sandra, but he could see in her eyes that she knew. And though Drummond was not in the room, Max could hear his strong voice saying, "There's no way this is going to end up good."

Chapter 14

MAX SLAMMED OPEN HIS OFFICE DOOR, cracking the glass right across the gold-painted 319, and headed straight for the bookshelf. He grabbed the first book he could reach, opened it, found only pages, and tossed it aside. Another book. Another. And another.

Drummond entered from the ceiling and said, "Um, Max? You feeling okay?"

"What does it look like?" He tilted three books from the shelf and watched them fall to the floor.

"Take it easy. Those are my books."

"You got a gun here and I want it."

"I don't have a gun."

Max grabbed the well-used book that hid Drummond's whiskey bottle. "You got this. And I don't believe at all that you ever went around without a gun when you were alive. So, where is it?"

"Calm down."

"Get me the fucking gun!"

"I swear I don't have one."

Max scanned the room until his eyes rested on the floor. "Of course," he said, and stomped on the floorboards. "Which one is it? Tell me."

"I don't—"

"Damn it!" Max said, hammering his desk with his fist. "They've got Sandra. You understand that? That witch took her from me. So, you tell me where that gun is. I've got to get her back."

Despite the pain of corporeal contact, Drummond concentrated enough to push a chair closer to Max. "Tell me what happened."

Max stared at the chair, his hands itching to rip up the floor, but finally lowered his head with a sigh. He pulled the whiskey from the book and drank. Then he told everything as best as he could remember. Twice he had to stop for another swig. He hoped Drummond would cut him off and reveal the location of a gun, but the ghost only listened until the telling finished.

"This is bad," Drummond said.

"Now you know. Please, where's the gun?"

"What do you think you're going to do? Go blazing into Hull family headquarters and demand Sandra back or you'll start shooting?"

Sheepish, Max said, "Something like that."

"No." The timbre of Drummond's voice caught Max's attention — filled with sorrow and shock. Drummond closed in on Max, his body lacking the usual grace of a ghost and instead moving like he felt every year since his death attacking each muscle. He was worried. That worried Max more. "I've dealt with things like this before," Drummond said. "And we've both dealt with Hull. You know you can't just go running in there. You'll only get her killed and probably yourself, too."

"I can't just sit here."

"You need to get control of yourself so we can plan. Now, you said they want you to find the painting, right?"

"Yeah."

"Well, we have found it. Let's see if our seller wrote back to Sandra. If we're lucky, we can get that painting fast, and then we'll have something of value to them."

An e-mail awaited them on Sandra's computer (Max felt weird using her property as if he was already stepping toward the acknowledgement that she might no longer need such things) — the seller wanted to do the transaction by mail. Max wrote back that the painting was meant as a gift, so he needed it right away. The seller replied that for a few extra dollars, he'd use overnight shipping.

"We can't do that," Drummond said. Max agreed. It was too easy to see Hull somehow intercepting the package.

Drummond clapped his hands at a new idea. "Tell him that we'll pay an extra fifty percent if he'll meet us tomorrow."

"In case you forgot, we don't have any money."

"It's going on a credit card, isn't it?"

Max kicked the desk. Then he wrote the offer. The seller agreed to meet at the North Carolina Welcome Center off Route 77, but he wanted to meet right away.

"He thinks we're doing something illegal," Drummond said. "Could work to our advantage. Meet him at two a.m. It'll give you time to get ready but it's so early that he'll still feel secretive about it. That's good for us."

Max wrote back and the deal was set.

"Get some rest," Drummond said when Max turned off the computer. "You'll be on the road in a few hours. I'll come as far as I can, but I suspect the border is a bit longer than my leash will allow."

Max threw back a last shot of whiskey, barely feeling the burn in his throat, and propped his feet up on the desk. *Just like an old detective,* he thought, picturing Drummond back in the 1940s. It almost felt good. But with Sandra in such danger, good feelings, like sleep, would not come.

The Welcome Center had always struck Max as more than a glorified rest stop. Situated on the slope of a mountain, Highway 77 barely audible from the distance thanks to copious trees, the place reminded Max of a lovely park. In fact, were it closer to home, he might have considered it a nice place for a picnic, though the terraced land had been designated mostly for parking. At the top of a series of stairways, the open building sat providing bathrooms to weary travelers.

Max stood by his car and watched as the few people on the road this late at night stretched and walked. The lot below rumbled with the sounds of numerous trucks — most set up for the driver to sleep for a few hours. A heavyset man paced at the top of the stairs leading to the bathrooms.

Max waited as two groups of travelers arrived, used the facilities and left. For the moment, the Welcome Center was empty except for Max and the heavyset man who still paced atop the stairs. With a final scan of the area — too dark to make out much at all — Max climbed the stairs.

"You Max?" the man asked.

Max nodded. "Where's the painting?"

"In my truck. Come on."

The man wore a yellow windbreaker that made an odd shushing sound as he walked. He checked out Max a few times, bashful when caught, and wiped his hands on his coat several times. Max glanced around as they walked.

Nothing in this man's behavior signaled a threat. If anything, the guy struck Max as somebody who came upon the painting and now hoped to make a quick buck selling it. The late-night exchange made the guy nervous but not enough to turn down the cash. And since no matter how many times he looked, Max didn't notice any danger, he felt better about the situation.

They approached a rusty Ford pickup, and the man said, "Y'know, we've had this painting for years. Just catching dust in the shed. I would never have found your ad 'til my brother phoned me up. You suppose it's worth something?"

"Not really," Max said. "It's not famous or anything. Just an old family painting that got sold off long ago by accident. In fact, we always thought we had it until my grandfather died and we learned that it was gone. That's why we put out the ad." Drummond would be amazed at how smoothly the story slipped off his tongue.

The man nodded with regret as if to say that things always turned out this way for him. He pulled out a smartphone to run Max's credit card. "Well, I can't say I don't wish it were something worth millions but I'll take what I can get."

"Millions would be nice, wouldn't it?"

The man laughed, a big rosy-faced grin, and then his lips formed a small O. A little red trail leaked from his hairline. Only when the man's eyes rolled up did Max's brain register the sound of a gunshot. The man dropped to the ground dead, and Max dropped, too. His mind raced to catch up with events.

The gunshot had sounded far off. A sniper? And the bullet had struck the man somewhere on the side of the head — which meant Max had no real cover at the moment. As if to illustrate the point, a bullet shot through the side of the truck just above his head.

Max rolled underneath the truck and shimmied behind the dead man's body. Now he had cover — for the moment. He was impressed with himself for not panicking and for acting with some thought. Not too long ago, he probably would have ended up dead. Now, at least, he had a chance. Except waiting to be shot again while congratulating himself wasn't going to save his life. He cleared his mind and focused on the present.

He needed to get out of there, get to his car, get to safety. But he needed that painting, too. Without that, Sandra had no hope.

Max reached forward and patted the man's pants. *Stop being a tentative prick and get the keys.* He shoved his hand down the pockets nearest him. Neither one had a key. With a deep breath, he reached over the body and fumbled for the far pocket.

Another shot popped into the truck above. Max's hands shook but he worked for the pocket as best he could. Trying to keep some cover, his face buried into the lifeless man's stomach. The man smelled of aftershave and alcohol — not a bad scent but a combination Max hoped never to smell again.

He felt a wallet but no keys. Another gunshot popped in the distance, and the dead man took a bullet in the shoulder. Max jumped at the hit, smacking his head against the underside of the truck. He hurried back underneath, rubbing his head. That's when he heard the jingle of keys.

Without exposing himself to the sniper, Max placed his foot on the dead man and gave a soft push. Again, the jingle of keys. Not a pants pocket, then, but a jacket pocket.

He rolled closer to the body and reached into the near-side jacket pocket. With closed eyes and a silent prayer that he wouldn't have to go over the body to the other side pocket, his finger felt around. And he found it. A ring with five keys.

He snatched the keys free, rolled to the passenger side of the truck, and crouched beneath the door. One by one he tried the keys. The first two wouldn't go in. The next three went in but wouldn't turn the door. Before he let despair take over, though, he heard Drummond in the back of his head — "You're nervous. Try again."

The first key failed, but the second key actually slipped in and turned. Max opened the door. In the back of the cab, behind the passenger seat, he found a painting wrapped in brown paper. It wasn't large — all of two feet long and a foot-and-a-half wide. He pulled it from the cab and crouched back down.

His pulse hammered as he clutched the painting. He kept expecting a shot to hit him. But the sniper hadn't done anything for the last few moments. Why? "He's a sniper," Max told himself, his words coming out in shaky breaths. "He's going to reposition."

Max looked down at the brown-wrapped painting. An idea popped into his mind. Without debating himself, he dashed across the parking lot with his body in a low crouch like soldiers did in the movies — and he held the painting like a shield. Whoever hired this gunman to kill him wanted the painting. Anybody willing to kill for a painting wants it undamaged — no excuses. As long as Max didn't provide a clear target, as long as the sniper risked hitting the painting, he would be safe. At least, that's what he hoped for.

When he reached the stairs, the thought that he might survive sparked. He turned toward his car, putting the painting behind him, and scurried to the driver's side. Two shots snapped the asphalt at his feet. Max didn't stop. He couldn't — his body refused to do anything but keep running for the car.

He wrenched the door opened with a screech and jumped in. Tossing the painting to the side, he shoved his keys into the ignition. He kept his head low as he started the car and turned on the brights. The entire Welcome Center lot became washed in the strong car lights. Peeking over the dashboard, he searched for any movement, any sign of his attacker.

Though the restrooms were uphill and covered with trees, Max swore he glimpsed a thin, blond-haired man dashing off. He waited and watched. Nobody came out.

He slipped the car into drive, and with his body hunched over the wheel, he tore off onto the highway. A mile passed by before he would sit up straight. Another mile passed before he slowed down enough to stop the car from shaking.

Now only he was shaking.

Chapter 15

BY THE TIME HE ARRIVED at Melinda Corkille's home, Max's head had entered that late-night fuzziness. His dashboard clock read 2:57 am and he felt every second of sleep deprivation dancing along his skin. When he rang the doorbell and knocked on the wood, the sounds echoed in his ears.

Several minutes later, the porch light winked on and the door opened. Melinda poked her groggy face outside and squinted. "What the hell are you doing here?"

"I've got it," he said and pushed his way in. "Get Howard."

Melinda's mouth tightened into a firm line. "I am not waking up that man in the middle of the night for anything."

"You don't understand."

"Go home, Max. I'll call the police if I have to. And I don't care what Howard said before. He is not getting worked up into all this just to have you ditch him in the end. I've seen it before. Idiots come along intrigued by his story and they want to help him break the curse. Only thing that gets broken is him."

"But I've got the painting. *Mourning in Red* — I've got it."

Melinda stood dumbfounded. As her thoughts finally connected, she stammered a few syllables and finally managed, "I-I'll get Howard."

"Thank you," Max said with a sarcastic bow.

While she left the room, Max hurried back to his car to retrieve the painting. He paused at the door, his eyes searching the darkness, his heart pressing against his chest. Just because he got away doesn't mean the sniper gave up.

"I'm not giving up, either." He pictured Sandra, tried to will his good thoughts toward her, and then set about his work.

When he returned to the house, Melinda was escorting Howard to his art studio. Max hadn't noticed her when he had first arrived — he just wanted to get to Howard — but seeing Melinda in a silk robe and a revealing piece of flimsiness underneath caused his pulse to quicken in a different manner than before. But that was just testosterone doing its thing. He closed his eyes, pictured Sandra once more, and focused on what was important.

Melinda waved him in. Max could see the excitement on Howard's face. With care, he set the painting on one of Howard's easels and stepped back.

"It's still wrapped," Melinda said.

Max nodded. "I didn't want to take anything away from Howard." As much as he felt the clock ticking against him, Max did find the resolve to let Howard have his moment.

Howard lifted a shaking hand to the painting. His bony fingers found a small nick, and with surprising strength, he ripped off the brown-paper wrapping. Melinda helped remove the remaining strips.

All three stared at the sad painting. It portrayed a voluptuous, nude woman posed on a red couch with her left hand covering between her legs. Her right hand pressed against her brow creating a shadow over her closed eyes that only accentuated the deep sadness she clearly felt.

"Is this the right painting? I thought it was supposed to be a landscape."

Howard's unsteady finger traced the bumps of paint, getting stronger as he moved along the canvas. "This is the right one."

"You painted this?" Melinda asked.

Corkille's mouth twisted like a disapproving teacher. He reached for a bottle on his desk, soaked a rag with its contents, and wiped it on the painting. With only three broad strokes, the paint smeared off.

"Stop him!" Max said. Each wipe felt like a strike against Sandra.

Melinda put her hand on Howard's shoulder but he threw it off. "No," he said. "Watch close."

A few more strokes of the rag and they all saw what Howard wanted them to see — underneath the paint was another painting.

"I don't believe it," Max said. "What the hell is that?"

"That," Howard said, working off more paint with a gentle touch, "is what we all are after."

The second painting, the real painting, sent tremors along Max's nerves. It showed a dark figure, a huge man, standing in a doorway. Little wisps of smoke snaked from either side of his head. The doorway overlooked a room without any defined end. Strange symbols, the kind Dr. Connor used, floated around another nude figure — Max couldn't tell the sex because the figure was curled into a ball.

Melinda's face brightened. "Can this do it? Can this really help you break the curse?"

"Of course," Howard said.

Max put a hand on the edge of the painting. "Then break your curse now. I need to take this painting."

Melinda shot to her feet so fast she startled Howard. "Don't you dare."

"This isn't the way I want it, but I don't have a choice."

"Was this the point all along? Just use Howard like everybody always did?"

"They have my wife. Sandra. They have her, and the only leverage I've got is that painting."

"Well you'll have to find something else. This poor man here has suffered long enough. He needs this painting, and that's it."

"We're talking about the witch, Connor," Max said, his voice breaking.

In a grim tone, Howard said, "And that means the Hull family, too."

"I don't know. Probably. I haven't thought it out that far. All I know is Connor and her thugs have my wife. They'll kill her. Or worse."

Melinda sat back with Howard and rested her head on his shoulder, leaving Max standing alone and feeling a thousand miles away from that painting and even further from Sandra. Tears welled in his eyes. His lungs didn't want to breath in. Everything inside his body wanted to shut down.

"Please," he whispered.

Melinda didn't answer him, and Howard continued to run his fingers over the painting. Max could hear what Drummond would say, and a trace of his usual fiery passion simmered deep inside, but he stayed still. His mind conjured images long forgotten.

He remembered the final days of his grandmother. She had outlived all her friends. She had lost her hearing years before and her sight amounted to fuzzy blobs of light and dark. Her bones were brittle and her muscles weak. At ninety-four years old, she had been reduced to spending her days sitting on the balcony of her nursing home and barely noticing the world drift by.

At ninety-four.

Howard had surpassed that age by over a century. Though he was in better health, that wasn't saying a lot. And as he got older, his body would get worse. Eventually, he would be just as broken, just as empty. Then he had eternity to look forward to. As much as Max wanted to snatch that painting and run to Hull, to Sandra, a part of him couldn't deny this ancient man a release from immortality.

"Okay," Max said. "You tell me what needs to be done with this painting to break the curse, and I'll do it. Afterward, whatever is left, give it to me. Let me save Sandra."

Howard looked up as if he had just become aware of the others around him. "No. You must help your wife now."

Melinda sputtered. "W-What? But the curse —"

"I'll get rid of the curse. Don't worry. But I don't need the painting itself. This is not a sacred object. It's really more of a map. And once I decipher it, then I'll know where to go to find what I do need."

"A map? To what?"

Howard grinned and Max's bones chilled. "To one of the most powerful bits of magic I ever heard about."

Melinda rubbed her temples. "Fine. Okay. Then we still need the painting, even if it's the only map."

With his hand shaking again, Howard pointed to the living room. "Get your purse." Melinda complied, and Howard said, "You have a phone that takes pictures, right? Take one of the whole painting. Then form a nine-square grid in your mind like a tic-tac-toe board, and take several pictures of each square — one of each square must be as close to the canvas as you can get, so I can see the textures. When you finish, give Max the painting and I'll get started."

As Melinda took the photos, Max asked, "You're going to forge this painting?"

"That's what I'm best at."

Melinda left the room to download and print out the photos. Max sat next to Howard and stared at the dark painting. "Are you sure you don't need the original?"

Howard patted Max's knee. "Even if I did need it, I've long outlived my selfishness. No way could I let Hull's witch curse or kill your wife. But don't worry. I'm not lying to you and Melinda. As long as I can reproduce this painting — and I can — then I should be able to find what I need."

Max picked up Howard's hand and looked the old man straight in the eyes. "When I get Sandra safe, you have my word. I'll come back here. I'll help you."

With a gritty chuckle, Howard said, "I appreciate your earnestness. But no need for promises. I know you'll be back. You know this isn't so simple, and while I do hope you get your wife back soon, even with her in your arms, the Hull family is involved. They won't let this rest until they have all that they want."

Max nodded. "They don't want the painting either, do they?"

"It's just as much a map to them as it is to me."

"Okay, then. Get working on the painting. I'll get Sandra, and we'll be back to finish this thing."

Melinda returned with the printouts. Using a magnifying glass, Howard inspected the photos. "These are all good," he said and turned toward Max. "Take the painting. Get your Sandra. But be very careful. This is the Hulls."

"I know. All too well."

Chapter 16

WHEN MAX ENTERED HIS OFFICE, he went straight for the bookcase and the whiskey. He would have to watch that or he'd be looking at an alcoholic in the mirror pretty soon.

With a startling clap of the hands, Drummond popped in. "That's the painting? You got it? Good work."

"I also got shot at."

As Max recounted his evening, the ghost detective smiled. "Just like my old days. This is great."

"Great? This is crap, and it's crap that's going to get Sandra killed. Now, come on. Stop being an ass and help me figure out the best way to exchange this thing for Sandra."

"For a start, you can calm down. You won't be any good if you go into this acting crazy." Max took another swig, put the flask back in the book, and slumped in his office chair. Floating in front of the painting, Drummond continued, "Now, you've done a good thing in getting Corkille to recreate this painting. That's an ace in our pocket. Of course, the big ace is the painting itself. So, once you're calm enough to think and speak clearly, you've got to call Connor and arrange a meeting."

"Where? When? You'll have to excuse me, but I've never dealt with a hostage negotiation before."

"Easy does it. I'll help you out."

Rage and tears filled out Max's chest. "I can't lose her. You understand that? She's everything to me."

All the amusement flushed from Drummond's pale face. In his kindest voice, he said, "Trust me, Max. We'll get her back."

Max looked at Sandra's empty desk, took a long breath, and eased back. "Okay," he whispered. "What do we do?"

"We need a location that's close enough so that I can be there. It should be public enough to protect you but secluded enough to not draw unwanted attention. And we need a time that's soon — before the world really starts waking up and getting on with the day. The longer we wait, the worse things have a chance of going. How long will Corkille take on the painting?"

"I've no idea. He's two hundred years old."

"But he's a spry two hundred."

In spite of himself, Max chuckled. Like popping a cork, laughter burst out of him until tears flowed from his eyes. Drummond said nothing. He just floated, waiting for Max to regain control, and Max appreciated it. They both knew this was the release he needed in order to keep functioning.

At length, Max dabbed at his eyes and said, "What about The Grand Theater?"

"The movie house?"

"It's a big eighteen screen theater with a huge parking lot. Nobody'll be there until the first shows — probably around noon. We could meet around the back for plenty of privacy but it's also public enough to satisfy — there are homes bordering one side and a major road with businesses on the other."

Drummond thought it over. "It's also just on the edge of the city. Plenty close for me to get around. Sounds perfect."

The phone call had been strange. Modesto had answered, not Connor. He ignored Max's questions and simply said that he would handle this negotiation. It surprised Max, not because he maintained a steady, in-control voice, but that Modesto didn't sound the least bit concerned. *He expected this all along.* Drummond warned that this whole thing might have been a set up — Modesto may have forced Connor into the kidnapping to make Max get the painting for them. But that much didn't matter to Max. He hated Modesto and Connor equally. Who cared which of them got the idea to use Sandra against him? They were both capable of it, and they both had plenty of sins to be punished for. Still, Modesto's behavior continued to strike Max oddly. Something wasn't quite right with that man.

The Grand Theater always looked like a warehouse club to Max. Large and boxy, the movie theater sat on the top of a high, flattened hill. Like a warehouse club, it mostly was a wide, paved parking lot. Around the side, near a green, dented dumpster, Max and Drummond waited in the car.

Dawn had just peeked over the trees, casting long shadows and orange light. Max sipped on hot, fast food coffee. Not very tasty but full of caffeine. Adrenaline had kept him going in short bouts, fear kept him up the rest of the night, but he felt sluggish after all these hours. He hoped the coffee would, at least, keep him alert until he had Sandra back.

"They're late," he said.

Drummond stared at the entrance to the lot. "They're fine. Don't get all cocked over a few minutes. A slow driver or a flat tire or any number of things can hold them up. Just keep remembering that they want this painting. If Connor is to be believed, they need this painting. So, they'll be here."

"I just wish it were over."

"Stay focused on the moment, and before you know it, it will be over. You remember what you've got to do?"

"What's to remember? Give the painting, get Sandra. It's a straight-forward exchange." Max turned on Drummond so fast, his hot coffee splashed a bit on his hand. Whipping his wet hand out the window, he sprayed the coffee onto the ground. "You're not planning on anything stupid, are you? They've got Sandra. Don't you screw this up."

Drummond rolled his dead eyes. "You have got to learn how this game is played. You really think they'll just walk up and make a fair exchange? That never happens. Never. Even if they do give you Sandra, they'll try something, some way to bring the leverage back onto them."

"Isn't that why Corkille's copying the painting?"

"That's not enough. Chances are they'd kill Corkille, Melinda, and you and Sandra if they found out about that. Heck, they already killed the previous owner and they tried to kill you. This painting is extremely important to them."

"We don't know who shot at me for sure."

"Maybe you can ask them. They're here."

A car more beaten than Max's Honda clunked along the parking lot. Two men were visible inside as the car shuddered to a halt several feet away. Nobody moved for a bit as if the cars themselves were sizing each other up.

With an impatient sigh, Max reached behind, grabbed the painting, and stepped out of the car. Drummond slid through the car door and floated nearby. "Be careful," he said.

Max held back a sarcastic reply. He didn't need these henchmen to see him talking to thin air.

The two men stepped from their car. Max recognized the heavyset man right away — Mr. Gold, owner of the Deacon Art Gallery. With a shiver, Max also recognized the second man — a thin, blond man who was good with a sniper rifle and, apparently, at impersonations.

"Do you have a real name, Blondie, or should I call you Mr. Hull?" Max said. Blondie's lips lifted in a grin that lacked all sense of amusement.

Drummond swooped by them all and peered into the car. "She's in here. Tied up and laying low. She looks okay. Not hurt. Not frightened. Really, she looks more angry than anything else."

Max wanted to laugh. That was his Sandra all right.

"Let's keep this simple," Blondie said. "Mr. Gold will verify the painting, and assuming he gives it an okay, we'll release your wife."

"I don't see my wife," Max said. He had to play his part well, and he figured the further away from their car she was, the safer she would be.

Blondie glared at Max for a brief instant before turning back to the car. He opened the back door and yanked Sandra out. She looked exactly as Drummond had said — unharmed and angry.

"Hi, Sugar," Drummond said and Sandra's eyes flickered in his direction as she tried to take in the situation.

"I believe this is yours," Blondie said, pushing her against the car hood. "Now, let Mr. Gold check out that painting."

"Of course," Max said. He placed the painting on the asphalt and took three steps back.

As Mr. Gold proceeded to examine the painting, Drummond whispered something in Sandra's ear before blocking her from view with his body. Max tried not to watch them too closely or else he'd draw Blondie's suspicions, but he was suspicious himself. Drummond winced in pain but continued whatever he was attempting.

"Well, well," Mr. Gold said, "Max here has been busy. He found the painting underneath *Mourning in Red*. The real painting. Shame you had to remove the top painting in such a brutal manner. I could have lifted it and saved both artworks."

"Neither is really that good," Max said.

"Art can have great value even when it's bad."

Blondie spit off to the side. "Enough with the college debate. Is it what we want or not?"

Flashing a distasteful sneer, Mr. Gold said, "It's what we want."

"Good, then all we need to do now is kill them both."

Drummond's head jutted up for just a second, then he furiously returned to Sandra. Max finally understood — Drummond was undoing her ropes. For a ghost to do such a thing — an act that required dexterity and patience, and an act that would cause a ghost a lot of pain — left Max awestruck.

He would have stared with his mouth agape had not Drummond snapped, "Max, stall him or we're all dead."

This woke him up. Max said, "You can't kill us. We have a copy of the Hull family journal. If we get harmed, that journal will go public. It'll take the family apart. And somehow, I don't think they'll look on you too kindly over that."

Blondie pulled a gun from his jacket pocket — a small, stubby looking thing that, Max had no doubt, could pop a hole right through his skull. "I'm not Hull, and I don't work for him. You want to destroy that family, go right ahead. It'll make life a lot easier on the rest of us."

"You work for Hull's witch. Same thing."

"Not to me."

"But the witch only wants this painting for Hull."

"Lots of people want this thing. If the stories are to be believed, this holds some serious mojo. Me, I don't care at all. I just want to get paid to do my job and I'll be on my way. And right now, my job is to make sure there are no loose ends."

"What about you, Mr. Gold?"

Drummond gave an enthusiastic nod. "That's right. Just keep them talking. Almost got this."

Max took several steps closer to Mr. Gold. "You really okay with murdering my wife and me?"

"I ... I ..."

"See that, Blondie? I don't think he's on board with your plans," Max said. He surprised himself with the firmness of his voice when he knew his insides were jittering as if electrocuted. "I think Mr. Gold is realizing that no matter who you work for that person isn't as powerful as the Hull family. I think he's wondering what kind of lunatic he signed on with."

With a flick of the wrist, Blondie turned the little gun onto Sandra. But Sandra wasn't there. She had stepped to the side and swung her newly-freed fist into his jaw. He lurched to the right and flailed out his hand, sending the little gun into the distance.

Max sprung toward Mr. Gold as Sandra pulled back for another strike on Blondie. The well-trained sniper, however, had other plans. He caught Sandra mid-swing with his forearm and shoved her back against the car.

Mr. Gold held the painting in front of him like a shield. Max felt a stab of pity. Had Corkille not been busily recreating the painting, Mr. Gold's shield would be worth something. As it was, Max had no problem punching through the canvas and into Mr. Gold's gut.

"No," Mr. Gold cried out, scrambling off toward the theater entrance with the damaged painting hooked on one arm, the other cradling his stomach.

Max turned back to see Sandra and Blondie grappling on the ground, rolling toward the little gun. "Drummond! A little help!"

Drummond had been standing near the gun, kicking it out of reach every time Blondie got close. He looked at Max and said, "What more do I have to do? She's putting up a good fight."

"Help her, damn it!"

Sandra wrenched Blondie over, straddled him, and threw a mean jab into his nose. His head snapped back and smacked hard on the pavement. Dazed by the blow, his eyes rolled without focus.

Sandra stood up and massaged her hand. "Get the gun, Max," she said. "And I'm going to need some ice."

Drummond shook his head and laughed. "One hell of a woman."

Chapter 17

MAX DROVE SOUTH ALONG ROUTE 52. They stopped at a gas station for some ice to wrap around Sandra's hand before crossing over to Peters Creek Parkway and down to the Corkille house. Drummond hovered over the back, his arms stretched across the seat like a satisfied king.

"You both did an excellent job back there," he said. "Really top notch. Not only did we get Sandra back safely, but Max, my boy, you ruined that painting. Superb."

Max did not share Drummond's enthusiasm. "I'm just glad Sandra's okay."

"Don't worry about me," she said. "They didn't mistreat me or anything like that. The worst was when they took me. I didn't know what was happening and that was scary. But once they got me to this little apartment, they were very business-like. Dr. Connor came by once to make sure they didn't try anything stupid with me."

Drummond said, "Best to be vigilant right now. Connor's angry at us, and an angry witch is not something to underestimate."

"No risk of that," Sandra said. "She made it all too clear what she would do if Max didn't come through. Believe me, the curses she said she would cast were far worse than living forever or being a bound ghost."

"Hey, I am a bound ghost. It ain't no picnic."

"How about having your genitals dry up and wither away? Max'll be the recipient of that pleasant curse. And for me, she plans to make me barren."

Max couldn't hide the rising pitch in his voice. "W-What? Can she do those things for real?"

"I'm not sure just how powerful witches can actually become. But I know this much — spells against a person require them to be at the casting. She can't do them remotely. So, we're okay, for now. Just don't get caught by her."

Thinking about the time she had tried to curse him before, Max shivered. "I really hate that woman."

Sandra reached out and Max took her hand. As the car sped down the road, their fingers entwined. Max brought her hand to his lips and kissed her fingers.

"I know things have been tough with us, but when I thought I might not get you back — it killed me."

Sandra laid her other hand on top of his, but her eyes remained focused on the road ahead. Max wished he had the right words to say that would let her know just how much he felt for her, but she was a smart woman — smart enough to know that people feel extra passionate after a life and death ordeal. Anything he said, anything he did at this moment would just be dismissed as the results of adrenaline and facing one's mortality.

But she had put her hand on his. She didn't pull away. And from other things she had said and done since this case began, Max gained a little hope. She still loved him. He knew that much. He only needed to break down those protective walls they had both constructed.

The rest of the drive proceeded in silence. Even Drummond had the sense to keep quiet. When they pulled into the Corkille's horseshoe drive, the morning sun was fully in the sky.

Melinda Corkille came out to meet them with a warm smile, but her bloodshot eyes and trembling hands spoke to the long night they had all endured. She watched Sandra get out of the car, and her warm smile fell away. Sandra caught the change, and the two women appraised each other without a word.

Before Max could say anything to diffuse them, Sandra looked at him and said, "Two hundred years old? She doesn't look a day over one-fifty."

"Ouch," Drummond said with an amused click of the tongue. "I think you're going to scorch her with your eyes, Sugar."

Max forced a chuckle. "Honey, let me introduce you to Melinda Corkille. Howard's the immortal one."

"That's right. I forgot."

Melinda refused to take the bait. "Come on, Max. Howard's been working all night. He's almost done."

As they entered the house, Max tried to ignore the frosty glower his wife sent his way. *Deep down,* he reminded himself, *she loves me.* This was just jealousy, and for nothing, because he had done nothing more than been tempted. If men were to be found guilty of infidelity for simply being tempted, there wouldn't be a faithful man alive.

"Melinda!" Howard's voice cracked as he yelled for her.

"Come on," Melinda said with an exasperated huff. "I'm glad I wasn't around when he was in his prime. The man has been insufferable since he got to work on the painting."

They followed Melinda into Howard's studio. The photographs they had taken earlier were pinned on cork boards surrounding the canvas. Most of the painting had been completed and Max had to admire the man's work.

It looked exactly as he recalled the original looked. Not just the obvious details — the dark figure in the doorway, the strong brush strokes, the eerie quality of the painting's mood — but also the smaller details — the thickness of the paint in certain areas, so thick it formed a hill on the canvas; the delicate blending of color; the distressed chipping of poorly made paints dried and abused over years. All of it had been recaptured by Howard Corkille's talented hands.

"Remarkable work," Max said.

Howard beamed. "If for nothing else, I want to thank you for giving me an excuse to break out my paints again. It's felt wonderful to be in front of the canvas once more."

Melinda hugged Howard's shoulders and kissed the top of his head. "Have you found what we need?"

"Sit," Howard said, waving everybody to find a stool or chair. Even Drummond settled on a worktable. Max caught Sandra's eye and grinned. Sandra kept a stoic face.

"I swear, the two of you are hopeless," Drummond said.

Before Sandra or Max could react, Howard cleared his throat and spoke. "You all know that magic is real. One look at me will tell you that much. What you may not know is that magic is quite active and quite common. Those who practice at it use spells and curses all the time. It happened more long ago because more people understood about these kinds of things. One of those people was a man named Edward Teach. Do you know that name?"

"It sounds familiar," Max said. He could picture a page in a history text but nothing more.

"He was born in England sometime around 1680. He became fond of the sea and worked for a while as a seaman in Jamaica. Most of this man's life is shadowed in unconfirmed reports, and his surname of Teach isn't even accurate. It's just a name historians chose to give him because men in his line of work often went by numerous fictitious names. They had to call him something and I suppose they had some source that named him such, so they went with it."

"What line of work was he in?" Sandra asked.

Howard rocked his hands on his knees. "He was a pirate. A very successful one. Took the French ship *Concord* as a prize and converted her into a pirate ship of his own design. He called her *Queen Anne's Revenge* and his name was —"

"Blackbeard," Max said, his eyes wide. He examined the dark figure in the painting again. "That's Blackbeard?"

"Yes. Sort of. See back when Blackbeard was Edward Teach, his success had been more of the failure kind. At one point, it is thought he considered giving the whole notion up. But on a drunken night in Jamaica he met with a voodoo priestess and he struck a deal. Nobody knows, of course, what exactly happened, but Blackbeard was born that night — that much is certain.

"He had always been a big man, but when he left Jamaica, he had become huge. And he had built an image with a great, black beard that he braided into pigtails and tied off with colorful ribbons. He strapped numerous weapons to his clothing, and, most notoriously, he weaved cannon cord into his hair so that he could light it and appear that much more menacing to his adversaries.

"But it was more than that." The group listened to Howard like captivated children around a teacher. "The lighting of his hair was part of the magic spell that had been conjured for him. Without it, he would've just been Edward Teach. Now, two things happened to him that matter to us. The first is that in 1718, King George I sent Captain Rogers to govern New Providence, where Blackbeard had been based. Rogers was the kind of man who would cause Blackbeard trouble, so Blackbeard picked up and moved his entire operation to North Carolina. It's a perfect location — close to the Gulf Stream, excellent places to exploit like Cape Fear, and a ready market in Bath Town for his gains. Not only that but he sold directly at the market and cut out the middle men.

"The second thing of importance to us is that Blackbeard had a soft spot for women. Even fell in love and married quite a few. Several at the same time. But the one true love in his life was the one woman who had any real power over him."

"The voodoo priestess," Max said.

"Exactly. The legend is that when she learned of all his infidelity to her, she traveled to North Carolina and took him to bed. When he awoke, she was gone — and so was his famed burning hair. Not long after this, his career as a pirate and his life came to an end."

Sandra gestured to the painting. "So this is Blackbeard in the doorway watching while his priestess performs a spell on the floor?"

"Sort of," Howard said. "I'll get to the painting in a moment, but it doesn't come into the story just yet."

"Have a little patience," Melinda said. Sandra ignored her.

"Now," Howard went on, "what we are interested in here is those strands of Blackbeard's hair, the ones imbued with magic. You see, there's only one way to really keep a secret. Do you know it?"

Max nodded. "Don't tell anyone."

"Old Blackbeard never was good at secrets. Many people knew of his magic burning hair, and after the priestess reclaimed it, many of these unsavory types sought her out. Because this kind of magic doesn't die until the object is destroyed."

"Like a binding curse," Drummond said.

"Afraid for her life, and rightfully so, the priestess hid the hairs with the thought that she would reclaim its magic once the world stopped trying to find her. She had many lovers and one of them, a young artist living on the beaches, became the recipient of a beautiful new paintbrush with the finest bristles made of the strangest hairs."

"You're joking," Max said. "That's what this is about? A paintbrush?"

"That paintbrush has fallen into many different hands and crossed many oceans over the years but it always manages to get back here. Twice in my life, I've had the opportunity to get hold of it and use its magic to break my curse. Twice it slipped away."

"This painting here, this one depicting the spell's creation, you think it can show us where the brush is?"

"I know it can."

"Then stop telling us stories and show us where."

"I'm well aware of your urgency. I think mine is greater. But without knowing the full background, you'd waste more time with tons of questions that would just have made me tell it all anyway. And so, I have one more thing to explain, and that is this painting."

All eyes took in the painting once more. Knowing what the painting actually depicted did little to ease Max's tensions over the entire case. With only a year under his belt since extricating himself from the horrible situation with the Hull family, he hated the idea that he was tied up with them once more. But this time it appeared that all roads led to them. Even a road that began with Blackbeard the pirate. Just thinking that churned Max's stomach.

And yet — he had to admit that he kind of liked the whole experience. A little. He didn't like being shot at, nobody would like that, but at the same time, he got a sense of why some soldiers can't leave the wars they fight. More than just an adrenaline rush, being shot at, being caught in a dangerous situation, being the target of a powerful family — it all filled Max with a sense of life. As if his heart could only beat under the pressure of these horrible tensions.

He glanced at Drummond and saw it on the old ghost's face. That's why Drummond stuck around. With the binding curse broken, Drummond could easily move on to wherever he truly belonged, but he didn't want to go. He wanted that same high that Max felt. And the fact that a ghost could feel it too proved that it wasn't just adrenaline. After all, a ghost doesn't have adrenaline.

Howard pointed out several brush strokes on the canvas, cleared his throat, and said, "This painting of Blackbeard's cursed deal is unique for many reasons. First off, there are no real pictures of the man. We don't know what he looked like. He loved for his women to be the subject of a portrait but always managed to stay off of the painter's canvas."

"Is that why he's a shadowy figure here? The artist had no idea what he looked like," Sandra said.

"Yes. But these brush strokes tell me a lot more. Earlier I told Max that this painting was a map. Well, the brush strokes are the key. They tell me that the artist who created this was a man named Jules Korner and he lived about thirty minutes north of here in Kernersville. I know these strokes so well because I'm the one who taught Jules how to do it."

Chapter 18

Max HAD TO WILL HIS FOOT to ease off the gas. He didn't want to be pulled over and given a ticket just because his body felt the urgency to get to the Korner home as fast as possible. Sandra sat next to him and placed one hand on his shoulder.

Howard had given them the basic idea. In the 1870s, Jules Korner ran an interior decorating business to augment his painting career. He became most famous for two things — first, he painted the Bull Durham bulls all across the South. These bulls, the symbol for Durham tobacco, were painted on barns and walls all over. Each time, Korner made them anatomically correct, if not exaggerated. He then contacted local papers and, posing as a concerned citizen, complained about the lewd image. Soon enough, everyone knew the Durham bull.

Korner's second claim was his home, dubbed "Korner's Folly." Completed in 1880, the house served both as a showcase and a home. No two doors, no two fireplaces (there were fifteen), no two rooms, were alike. Also, the entire attic had been converted into America's first private little theater. As Max took the on-ramp to Business 40 East, he wondered if the home could live up to its title as "The Strangest House in the World" or if this was just another one of Korner's publicity stunts.

Before they had left, Howard said, "Jules was an eccentric man but he was smart. He was crazy enough to paint this and yet smart enough to cover it up. You'll see when you go to his house. I'm sure that somewhere in there is either that paintbrush or a clue to finding it."

Max didn't know how much faith to put into Howard's idea, but he saw few options at the moment. He did have the sense to send Drummond out searching for Jules Korner's ghost. Perhaps the man would be willing to help.

"It's coming up," Sandra said, pointing to Exit 14 for Kernersville.

Melinda had opted to stay with Howard, and Max felt grateful he didn't have to find some excuse to leave her behind. Though he had managed to avoid Melinda's advances, he knew Sandra sensed something wrong, and a surge of guilt had struck him. It wasn't enough to just be faithful. He had to make sure Sandra knew in her heart how much he loved her.

"When this is over," he said, "you and I are taking a vacation."

Sandra nodded. "We can't afford one, but the thought is nice."

They couldn't miss the house. Its rust-colored, pointy roof cut high into the air. Numerous chimneys poked up from the structure, while the stone- and brick-work drew the eye down to the enormous body of the house. A wide field off to the side with a gravel drive served as the parking area.

"It looks like a haunted house from an old black-and-white fright movie," Max said. "I love it."

They paid for tickets and walked to the front of the house. The porch wrapped around, mostly lined in beautiful brick designs, and the flooring had been done with little mosaic tiles. Near the entrance, Sandra pointed to a small, cauldron-shaped pot nestled underneath a brick shelving. In front of the pot, the tiling read WITCHES CORNER — though the T had been chipped off.

"Not what you're thinking," Max said. "A 'Witches Corner' is an old European tradition. Whenever you were going in or out of the house, you were supposed to put coins in the pot so that any evil spirits nearby would be distracted. That way you could enter or exit in peace. It's not real. Not like Dr. Connor."

"You sure about that?"

Max took a long look at the rusting pot. Then he dug out a quarter and tossed it in. Sandra patted his arm as they walked inside.

The foyer was a small, cluttered space with four doors, all different heights, shapes, and styles. Through a small opening off to the right, Max saw a narrow staircase — connecting to nothing, as far as he could tell. Korner's self-portrait hung to the side of one doorway — an eerie-looking man in a dark suit with the strangest expression on his face as if he could see all these people coming in and counted them all as fools. The ceiling had a painting of two cherubs. It was like walking into the Mad Hatter's home as designed by M. C. Escher.

"Welcome to Korner's Folly," a middle-aged woman said. "May I have your tickets, please?"

As the lady collected the tickets and launched into her introduction speech, Max glanced through the glass on the doorway behind her. He saw a long room with huge, black furniture and a ceiling taller than in the foyer — and on that ceiling, he saw a painting.

"Excuse me," he said and ignored the flustered scowl of the lady. "Are there paintings on every ceiling?"

"Not all. But most. The ceilings are quite interesting, actually. Some of the ceilings are as high as twenty-five feet, and some, like in the children's rooms, are just under six feet. This space was originally used for horses and —"

"And did Jules Korner paint all of them himself?"

The lady forced a smile. "No. He designed them all, but another man painted them. In fact, he designed all the furnishings in this house, and he —"

"I thought Korner was a painter."

"He was," she said, her words clipped. "Most of the paintings you'll find on the walls throughout the house are by Jules Korner. Now, if you'll let me finish, I'll be glad to take any further questions after I'm done."

Max pantomimed zipping up his lips and let the lady complete her job. He tried to listen closely, but his eyes kept trying to snatch a peek of the house beyond. When she finished, she turned her eyes to Max and asked if there were any questions.

With a shake of his head, Max said nothing. Sandra, however, spoke up. "Did you just say this house is haunted?"

Max had not been listening closely and had missed this part. Now he focused intently on the answer. The lady offered an embarrassed smile. "A few years ago, the North Carolina Paranormal Society conducted several tests over a few nights and, according to them, this house is officially haunted. Now, I've been working here for almost ten years, and I've never heard or seen anything."

"Is it supposed to be Jules Korner?"

"I don't know about that. To the best of my knowledge, nothing tragic ever happened here and certainly not to Jules Korner. Don't make a deal out of it. It's just silliness. Now, if there are no further questions ..."

She opened the glass-paned door and ushered them into the rest of the house. The tour was self-guided from that point on. Numbered placards could be found in each room describing the history of the room and noting features. At the bottom of the placard were instructions on where to go next.

Max and Sandra walked through the house like any other touring couple except for where their eyes went. Sandra appeared to be most interested in the dark, open, empty spaces of the house. Max watched her closely at the entrance of each room, hoping to see on her face if she discovered a ghost. Then his eyes examined every painting and mural he could find.

He looked closely for brush strokes similar to the ones in "Mourning in Red." He didn't expect to find some secret clue. Rather he wanted to find proof that Howard Corkille had told them the truth. That this trip to Korner's Folly wasn't really Corkille's folly.

About halfway through the house they climbed an open staircase and entered the children's rooms. Max had to duck because everything in the room, including the ceiling, had been designed for a child's height. It was like being in a giant dollhouse, and despite the ample daylight, Max's skin prickled.

He looked to Sandra. "Anything?" he asked.

Her face had paled and she nodded. "I'm not so sure who it is, though. I can only see a blurry image."

Max frowned. "Has that ever happened before?"

"Not often. It's usually somebody who is both here and there."

"There?"

"The afterlife that most ghosts can't find or are trying to avoid. But sometimes they get stuck. They start to move on and then maybe they can't fully let go or they lose their way or something. Whatever the case, they end up a little bit in both worlds and that makes them blurry."

"Can you talk to them? Can they hear you?"

"I can try," she said but the sounds of footsteps climbing the stairs ushered them on to the next room. A family of five was right behind them showing their impatience as if they were waiting for a turn at mini-golf and Max was holding up the line.

Later, Max and Sandra entered the reception room, a large ball room on the second floor — or maybe it was the third or fourth floor, the house had so many stairs and ups and downs it became difficult to know for sure. In a glass booth, Max saw the most frightening marionettes — one a copy of each member of the family. They had exaggerated features and old, chipped paint.

"Sandra."

When she walked over and saw the marionette family, she let out a gasp. "I'd rather see ghosts," she said.

"They would be a good place to hide a magic brush."

When they reached the attic, Sandra grasped Max's hand with

crushing strength. The entire floor had been converted into a theater with a wooden thrust stage at one end and chairs all around. Off to the right was a large replica of the house with the center cut out and curtained — a puppet theater. The ceiling raised up to a point and on their slanted sides were eight enormous murals.

But Max knew that the impressive sight had not caused Sandra's reaction. "How many do you see?" he whispered.

"I don't know. They're all blurring together." Sandra's skin turned bone white and she leaned in to Max's shoulder. "I don't feel so good."

Without another word, Max escorted her through the house, not worrying about the proper tour path, and garnering a few perturbed glares from other visitors. He led Sandra outside, and the fresh air had an immediate effect on her. Her skin regained some color as she took long, deep breaths.

"You okay?" Max asked.

Sandra nodded. "I don't know what happened. It was just so strange. In my whole life, I've seen maybe three of those blurry ghosts. But up there ... I can't believe how many there were."

"Does that mean the paintbrush ..." Max's voice trailed off as his eyes looked toward the parking lot. He could feel Sandra's quizzical stare falter and felt her shift as she followed his gaze. He heard her breath catch.

Dr. Connor and Mr. Modesto leaned against the old Honda.

"DID YOU ENJOY YOUR TOUR?" Dr. Connor asked. She looked much healthier than at any other time in the past few days. She also looked like somebody savoring her own maliciousness.

"Get off my car," Max said.

Mr. Modesto gazed down to indicate that he did not actually touch the car. The sneer on his face showed that he wouldn't touch the car even if given permission. Dr. Connor, on the other hand, pressed harder against the car door.

"Mr. Porter, let me begin by assuring you that you will not find the object which you are seeking," Mr. Modesto said. He spoke a bit slower than normal, choosing each word with great care and purpose. "However tarnished by you, we still possess the actual painting. We have all the information required and we have a greater desire to acquire this object. So, if you will simply let this go, we can get this object for our employer and no further contact between us will be necessary. Your insurance policy that you so gleefully hold over us will continue to be honored, of course."

"Get off that car, now," Sandra said. Even from his peripheral vision, Max could see that Sandra was about to take a swing at Connor. Perhaps the witch sensed it, too, because she did take one step away — smiling the whole time.

"Furthermore," Mr. Modesto said and threw a distasteful look at Connor, "I believe this woman owes you an apology."

Connor locked eyes with Mr. Modesto just long enough to show that she hated doing this, that he had forced her, and that she didn't mean a single word. She faced Max and Sandra with her mocking grin. "I'm sorry for taking you from your husband, and I'm sorry for causing you so much trouble. The Hull family had no part in it."

"Thank you," Mr. Modesto said. Dr. Connor threw in a patronizing curtsy and stepped back.

Max leaned in towards Mr. Modesto. "Y'know, you keep coming to me with apologies. First, Mr. Gold and now Dr. Connor. The Hull family should look closer at their hiring practices."

"Undoubtedly. They hired you, after all."

Max let out a slight laugh. "And, thankfully, I don't work for them anymore. So, I don't take their orders, either. It's been nice chatting with you. Now, if you'll please move aside, we have to confer with our client."

"Am I to take that to mean you're still going to pursue these matters?"

"Take it any way you want."

"You won't find it. We have the painting. And we know exactly where the object is."

Sandra pushed Connor aside as she stormed to the car door. "It's called a paintbrush. We all know it, so stop with all the 'this object' nonsense. And the answer is no. We are not backing out of this case. Besides, you're a bad liar. You have no clue where this paintbrush is."

Connor came up to the car door and shoved it closed just as Sandra got in, narrowly missing her fingers. "We know exactly where it is. We just have to wait for the right time to get it."

"Dr. Connor," Modesto snapped.

The witch backed away from the car, pulled out a hip flask, and swung back its contents. "I'm watching you," she said and waved a finger at Sandra — naughty, naughty.

As Max started the car, Sandra raised a finger of her own.

They drove straight to the office without a word. Sandra fumed while Max tried to replay the entire conversation in his head. Something didn't sit right. Something felt off in the way Modesto spoke.

When they entered the office, Max felt a surprising twinge of disappointment that Drummond was not to be found. He settled behind his desk, propped up his feet, and got lost in thought. Sandra tapped away at her computer.

"They close at four o'clock," she said.

"Who?"

"Korner's Folly. The house closes at four. I'm assuming you want to go there tonight to see what we can find."

"What about the blurry ghosts?"

Sandra shrugged. "Guess I won't be going into the theater."

"Honey, I don't know if —"

"Don't even start. You know we have to go. Besides, that bitch-witch said they knew where the paintbrush was, they just had to wait for the right time. It's got to be in that house. They wouldn't have come all that way just to mouth off at us."

"No, but if Hull told them to do so, they certainly would come to make sure we had accepted that apology. They don't want those journals released."

"Maybe. But they had to be scoping out the house, too. And it seems they think they know where it is."

Max nodded. "Which means they'll be going after it tonight."

"That's why we have to get there first."

Scratching his chin, Max pictured the house. "We'll all have to wait until dark. Even then, the house is right on a major street. I don't see how we're going to get in without attracting unwanted attention. Not to mention we've got to get in, find the paintbrush, and get out before Hull's people show up. You got any bright ideas?"

Before Sandra could answer, Drummond burst in the office from the bookcase. "I've got an idea," he said as he swooped into a chair.

Startled, Max sat forward, banging his knee on the desk. "I can't believe you. Have you been here the whole time? Just eavesdropping from your bookcase?"

Drummond dismissed the accusation with a shrug. "Seemed like a smart thing to do at the time."

"Don't you trust us?"

"More than most people, but until you're a ghost floating around this office with me, I've got to protect myself now and then. Oh, get over yourself — I wasn't eavesdropping. I only caught the end of what you were saying. Okay, Mr. Uppity-uppity?"

Max crossed his arms and rolled his eyes. "Fine. I've got more important things to worry about. Like have you found Jules Korner yet?"

Drummond leaned back and glanced at Sandra. "He thinks I wouldn't have told him about that already? C'mon."

"Then why are you here and not looking for him?"

"Because sometimes you have to be calm, put out your feelers, and wait. I've spread the word in the right ears, and I need to wait a little to see if Korner shows up. Now, do you want to hear my idea, or do you want to sulk around your office for a few hours?"

Sometimes Max wished Drummond had a more substantial body, so he could smack the ghost hard. "Tell us your idea," he said, slouching back in his chair.

Bringing his hands together with one, sharp clap, Drummond popped into the air and looked at both his partners. "I could go to the house right now. Nobody can see me, so I can search for this paintbrush while the tours are still going on. Then, when evening comes, you guys show up, and I guide you to where it is — or at least, where it isn't, if I haven't found it by then."

Max let Drummond hang in the air with an expectant gaze. He knew the idea was good. It didn't take a genius to see that. But he still felt ruffled by Drummond and wanted the ghost to stew a bit.

Sandra misinterpreted Max's hesitation for doubt, and said, "That's one of the best ideas I've ever heard from you. Go do it, and we'll meet you at Korner's Folly tonight. It's not too far, is it? I mean, you won't get snapped back like you did on our way to Lake Norman?"

"I don't think so," Drummond said, but he didn't seem so confident. "I suspect it's close to the edge of my territory, though, so I might be in a bit of pain. You might have to nurse me a bit when I get back."

Sandra shook her head. "Just get going."

"Sugar, you're a heartbreaker."

Sandra laughed as Drummond flew out of the office. When she turned around, Max had not moved from his desk. His old anger had ignited deep in his gut, and he could see on his wife's face that she knew it, too.

"I don't want to fight," she said, picking at some papers on her desk.

"This is so messed up. You're flirting with a dead guy right in front of me while I'm feeling guilty over Melinda Corkille when nothing happened."

Sandra slammed the papers down. "I knew something was going on with that woman."

"Nothing went on. I mean, she tried, but I wasn't buying."

"But you feel guilty."

"I'm a man. I have thoughts even if I'm strong enough not to act on them. And frankly, things haven't been all that wonderful between us lately, so you shouldn't be surprised that I'm having thoughts."

"Really?" Sandra said in a tone that spewed fire and brimstone. "Is that the way it is for men? The second we have a little marital spat, you just start thinking about screwing other women?"

Max was on his feet now. "Honey, guys think about screwing other women all the time. It has nothing to do with our marriage or love or anything. It's just the way we're wired."

"So what's your problem then? It's okay for you to flirt with Melinda but if I sass Drummond just for fun it's wrong? What kind of fucked up logic goes on in your brain?"

"I'm not mad about that," Max shouted. "I'm not angry at all!"

His thundering voice echoed in the building. Sandra locked eyes with him, both of them seething, and before another word could be yelled, she processed his words and the corner of her mouth trembled upward. The other corner also moved up until she fully smiled.

"This is serious," Max said, but the end of his words were caught in a laugh.

"I know," she said, and stepped back, covering her mouth.

That did it. The two of them burst into hysterics. Sandra collapsed at her desk, clutching her stomach, and letting out laughter with abandon. Max's eyes watered as he followed suit.

So much of their stress poured out with each successive wave that once their bodies got started, stopping seemed impossible. Max's sides ached yet every time they thought it ended, a snort or chuckle would send them off again. And if felt good. More than just a release, the moment brought with it relief.

At length, they managed to speak with only a few giggles breaking through. Max dabbed at his eyes and said, "I swear, honey, you have nothing to worry about. I love you. I always have."

"Then trust me. And I don't mean about jealousy. I know you trust me there, and I know you don't really think anything about Drummond. But in the rest of our life, you've got to trust me."

"I do."

"No, you don't." She stepped near Max and wrapped her arms around his waist. "How long have you been sitting here in this office wishing I'd leave? Hmmm? It's driving you nuts having me here. You said it the other day that you feel smothered. But you're stuck because business is bad and I'm an asset you can't do without right now. I get it. It's tough. But you think it's a picnic being around you all day?"

Max smiled. "Maybe not a picnic, but surely a nice snack."

"Don't flatter yourself." She playfully slapped his chest. "Look, unless you gain the ability to see all the ghosts like I have, you're stuck with me."

"I don't mind having you here."

"Yes, you do. But that's okay. Couples aren't meant to be glued together all the time. We'd kill each other while professing how much we love one another."

"Then what do we do?"

"I don't know." They both let out a short laugh. "But now that we're actually talking again, I do know that we can figure it out. We make a pretty smart team."

Max hugged his wife tight and strong. "You're an incredible woman. Far more than I ever deserved."

"Don't forget it," she said and wiped her eyes on his shoulder. "Now, let's go find that stupid paintbrush."

MAX AND SANDRA HAD TO KILL a few hours before it would be safe to go out to Korner's Folly. They drove to T.J.s Deli, scarfed a few sandwiches — eating too fast from nerves — and they waited. As worrisome as the whole situation had become, a small part of Max enjoyed sitting with Sandra at the deli. It was such a simple, normal thing to do. So unlike their everyday lives that he had to stop just long enough to etch the moment into his brain.

And then it was time to go.

They drove in silence but not a quiet boiling with anger. Nerves, of course, but the tension between them had disappeared. Now, Max could focus entirely on the job at hand.

"I want you to be my getaway man," Max said as they neared the off ramp for Kernersville. "This house is so visible. I need you to stay in the car, keep it running, honk if you see a cop or Modesto or anybody really. If I come running out, open the passenger door and be ready to get us out of there. You okay with that?"

"I can be a getaway gal, if that works for you."

Max smiled. "My apologies. 'Getaway gal' sounds much better."

They pulled in the visitor parking lot and drove onto the grass behind the house. It wasn't completely out of sight, but anybody passing in a car would probably miss them. If someone came by on foot, however, they were in trouble.

Max kissed Sandra on the cheek and headed toward the building. He moved to the side entrance (which was used as the exit from the tour) and tried the doorknob. Locked.

"Drummond," Max hissed as loud as he dared. "Drummond."

No answer. He slid along the wall toward the front of the house, trying to stay behind the various brick walls. From the corner, he saw no easy way to get to the front door. It was probably locked anyway. As he started to turn back, he glimpsed the beaten pot in front of the words WITCHES CORNER.

Why not? He dug out a dime and a nickel and tossed them into the pot. The dull clink seemed loud to his ears, but nobody appeared to notice.

"Drummond," he whispered again as he hurried back to the side door. "Come on. Open up."

The side door lock clicked. Max stared at it as if he had never seen one before. Then he tried the knob and found it opened with ease. He stepped into a long room — the sewing room, if he recalled correctly from the tour — it was hard to tell in the dark. He had a small penlight with him but didn't want to use it unless he had no other choice. With so many windows in the house, he feared somebody might notice the light.

Drummond's ghostly visage seemed to shine pale light all around but didn't illuminate anything. It was a strange sight, one that Max had never noticed before. Drummond looked tired, even for a ghost.

"There's no paintbrush here. I've checked all but one room."

"What? Why didn't you just come back to the office and tell us not to bother?"

"Because it has to be in that room. I just can't go there."

"Out of your range?"

"No," Drummond said, glancing upward with a shiver. "It's not that. The room is at the very top — the attic that's a theater. But it's filled with the ghosts Sandra calls blurs. I can't go in there."

"Why not?"

"It hurts." Drummond turned away and let out an eerie sigh. Max thought, not for the first time, that Drummond could haunt a house to great effect. "I'm going back to the ghost realm. I'll find Jules Korner. He should be looking hard for me now, so it should be easy."

"Okay. I'll check out this theater. Don't worry about it."

"Who's worried?" Drummond said but he looked as if a giant arrow pointed at him.

Once his ghostly partner disappeared, Max headed deeper into the house. He flashed his penlight from time to time but never kept it on for more than a few seconds. The creaking wood floors and odd echoes made him think of a classic haunted house.

Every painting with a face followed his movements. He could feel their eyes upon him. From every ceiling mural, they looked down upon him. From every dark corner, every misshapen doorway, every narrow staircase, Max could feel the growing pressure of being watched.

Maybe he should have had Sandra come with him. The tour lady had said this place was officially haunted. Sandra would be able to see the ghosts, maybe even get them to talk.

As enticing as the idea of getting his wife by his side was, he knew he couldn't go back to get her. If he left this house, he wouldn't want to re-enter. Though not a believer of New Age-type things, he did believe that this place gave off a bad vibe. Something was wrong with this house. At least it felt that way at night, alone and in the dark.

After one wrong turn, he found the main stairwell that led up to the theater. He paused just long enough to feel his legs quiver and taste the dry coating in his mouth. Surely, Drummond could find out from Jules Korner where the paintbrush was hidden. Max didn't need to do this. Except there was no guarantee Drummond would find Korner let alone that the man would talk. And if Mr. Modesto was to be believed, time was not on Max's side. Through force of will, he moved upward, ignoring the strong desire to race back to Sandra, drive off, and never return.

When he reached the top, he found a lone figure standing on the stage — Blondie. The man wore a stylish suit like a true player of the nightclub scene, but his expression was one of impatience and malice. The hot attic air smelled of old wood like an ancient casket which gave Blondie a decidedly murderous aura.

"You sure took long enough," Blondie said. "Frankly, I don't understand why any of these people are worried about you. You can't seem to get any of this right. Although you sure screw things up a lot. No doubt about that."

"For you, I try my best," Max said, pleased that his voice wasn't shaking like his insides.

"Dr. Connor warned me about you. She said you had a smart mouth and a keen talent to get in the way. I figured she was just a little skittish because of your history with her. But it turns out she was right. I've got to know, though, before I kill you — why are you doing this? I mean, what do you gain by messing up things for Dr. Connor and Mr. Modesto? I don't get it."

Max thought about running, the words *before I kill you* often had that effect on him, but instead, he approached the edge of the stage, hoping to keep Blondie talking. He moved on instinct, something he continually tried to listen to more and more. And if his instincts weren't screaming for him to run, his brain must have heard something more important. And then it hit him. *"Messing up things for Dr. Conner and Mr. Modesto? How?"*

"I don't like it when people play coy or dumb, so stop it."

Max squinted in real confusion. "I don't understand. I saw them today. They've got the painting, you know that, they said they were going to beat me to the paintbrush. So, what exactly am I messing up, now?"

Blondie paced on the stage. "You really think this is just about getting some stupid brush? My, my, you are dumb. This, my stupid friend, this is about regaining their lives. Look at what you did to them. You ruined Dr. Connor's reputation and Hull pretty much cut her off from his family."

"Can't say I'm sorry. I don't really care about her. She tried to kill me once and she kidnapped my wife just recently. Seems to me, you were a part of that, too."

"Mr. Modesto didn't try to kill you. In fact, if anything, he's tried to help you navigate all these treacherous waters."

"I don't see it that way."

"Of course not. It's all about you, isn't it? What do you think happened to Mr. Modesto after you got hold of Hull's journal and held copies of it hostage?"

"That's my life insurance."

"I don't care what you call it. It pretty much ruined Mr. Modesto's standing, too. He's lucky they didn't kill him."

Max thought back to the strange dinner on Lake Norman, the one where Blondie pretended to be Terrance Hull. Mr. Modesto had handed Max the invitation. He knew Hull's schedule. He knew when the Lake Norman house would be clear. And that's why there were no servants, no chef, nobody around. That's why they tried to hire him to find the painting. Dr. Connor, Mr. Modesto, even Mr. Gold — they all were trying to get back into the embrace of the Hull family. And that thought brought with it another for the ride.

"Oh, I see," Max said, staring directly into Blondie's eyes. "It's not me that keeps screwing things up, it's you."

"Shut up."

"You failed to impersonate Hull well enough to get me to work for you. You failed to find the painting on your own and had to resort to kidnapping. And now, after all this, you've even failed to find the paintbrush. You just keep failing, don't you?"

Blondie's fingers curled into fists. Max's eyes darted around the room. He didn't see anybody else. Blondie said, "I suppose you found the paintbrush, then. Isn't that what you do? Find stuff nobody else can find?"

"You're pathetic. Not only did you fail at everything, but now you're standing here waiting for me to show up with the paintbrush so you can swipe it from me. No wonder Hull doesn't want to work with any of you. You can't do anything for yourselves."

"You watch that mouth of yours. It's going to get you in trouble."

"Wouldn't be the first time." Max looked over Blondie's waist — no sign of a gun. That was odd. Every time before Blondie had a gun.

Following his eyes, Blondie said, "Not in here. Gunfire would get too much attention, and this place is full of so many little nooks, I might not be able to collect all my bullets should I miss my target. Don't want to leave anything behind for the cops."

"You didn't care about that out at the rest stop."

"Different location, different circumstances."

"Guess we can just add that to your list of failures."

Max had hoped to goad Blondie into making a mistake or revealing something important. He missed just how angry Blondie had become and was taken by surprise when the attack came.

"Bastard!" Blondie said and leaped off the stage. With his arms spread like a professional wrestler hulking in, he slammed onto Max, crashing them both to the floor. The big room echoed their grunts. Momentum took over, sliding them back and spinning them to the side.

Max felt his body roll and helped it along. He popped up on top of Blondie and punched the man's jaw. Blondie's head snapped back. But before Max could pull his fist back for another, Blondie struck hard into Max's sides, thudding against his kidneys.

As Max toppled over, Blondie got to his feet and kicked hard. Max rolled onto his back, every attempt to breathe bringing with it fiery pain below his ribcage. Moving with patience and power, Blondie straddled Max and gripped his throat with both hands.

"Where's the paintbrush?" Blondie said, barely moving his mouth.

"I don't have it," Max said, his voice betraying his fear.

Blondie tightened his grip. "Where is it?" he screamed, his face red, spit flying from his lips.

He's lost his mind, Max thought. He knew that kind of rage, and he knew that Blondie no longer was thinking about the paintbrush or Dr. Connor or Hull. He just wanted to release all his anger and Max was the object in his hands.

"Where is it?" Blondie screamed again and thumped Max's head against the floor.

Max tried to kidney punch Blondie, but he couldn't find the strength. His lungs strained for air. Little pale spots blinked into Max's vision.

He barely saw Blondie, now. His throat ached but even that pain started to lift. He had never asked Drummond what actual death was like, and now he wouldn't have to.

A flicker of a thought hit him. *Death*. He was dying. Those pale spots weren't from lack of air. He was dying — he could see the blurs, the ghosts! They drifted high above as if he were in the bottom of a giant fishbowl and they were the fish.

As Blondie cried out and clenched his throat, Max's eyes shot to the left. A little girl sat on the edge of the stage and watched. She wore a dress straight from the 19th century, and her cold, pale skin seemed to glow against the dress. The blurs hovered around her as she swung her feet. She cocked her head in interest.

Max reached out for her, pleading with his hands, his fingers, his eyes, everything he could — *Please, help me*. Tears dribbled from his eyes. *Please*. Even his lips trembled in an attempt to speak. *Help me*.

The little girl scooted back on the stage, her face startled. She clearly had not expected to be seen by the living. She stood and stared even longer at Max's face.

Watching this dead girl try to decide what to do seemed to last an eternity. He could hear a dim echo of Blondie's voice demanding to know the location of the paintbrush, but it was slow and distant. All he had rested on this ghost, and his mind could not think long on anything else.

As if seeing the full picture for the first time, the girl stepped closer. "Do you not want to die?" she asked.

Max wanted to snap a sarcastic, "What the hell do you think?" but it occurred to him that perhaps not all dead people thought in the same way as Drummond or as the living. Besides, it seemed best to just answer the question. He managed a tiny nod.

"Okay," the girl said.

She glanced upward at the blurs and spoke, but Max could not make out her words. The blurs understood, though. They all stopped their lazy drifting and stretched a bit in the girl's direction.

When the girl looked back at Max, the blurs swooped down, darting straight for Blondie. The first to arrive soared right through him. Blondie jerked to the side as if somebody had dropped an ice cube down his shirt.

Another blur passed through the other side, and Blondie jerked again. He looked around, confused. Then Max saw the change on the man's face — confusion turned to fear. The blurs sensed the change like sharks sensing blood. They shot in on Blondie's head, pushing together and pressing against him.

Blondie fell back, grasping at his face, trying to claw off the unseen threat. But Max could see it. The blurs covered Blondie's head like a plastic bag, and as he suffocated, Max was able to breathe again.

Blondie thrashed on the floor, kicking over chairs, and moaning out a desperate attempt for help. Even if he had wanted to, Max could only muster the strength to breathe. Blondie had seen to that.

And with each breath, the blurs and the girl faded from Max's sight. He was returning to the living. His hammering heart slowed even as Blondie's stopped. By the time Max had enough air to stand, Blondie's blue face stared empty-eyed at the stage.

"Thank you," Max said, his throat scratching the words out. He looked to where the little girl had been and smiled. "I can't see you anymore, but if you're here, please, follow me."

Max crossed to the back of the stage where a narrow staircase led to the dressing rooms below. Leaning against the wall as he stumbled down the stairs, he offered a silent wish of thanks to Jules Korner for building such a strange house — he would have fallen down a normal staircase. When he finally reached the main floor, his skin had stopped tingling.

Outside, Sandra took one look at him and rushed from the car. "Are you okay? What happened?" she said as she scooped him up in her arms and kissed him.

"Throat hurts," he managed and then pointed behind him.

He could see by Sandra's reaction that the little girl had followed him out. He waved Sandra on, nodding that he'd be okay, and let her go talk to the girl. The worried gaze she cast his way filled him with warmth.

Max settled in the front passenger's seat and waited. He tried not to think about anything but the paintbrush and the fact that his wife was about to find out its location. He was fooling himself, though. His mind played out those final moments when he saw the blurs, when he had almost died.

A well of tears rushed up. He tried to hold them back, but doing so constricted his throat, sending sharp pains into his chest. So, he buried his face in the crook of his arm and cried. There wasn't any closer to death he could have gone.

When Sandra returned to the car, she had a triumphant look that fell the second she saw her husband. He wiped at his eyes, but he couldn't hide anything. She came to him and wrapped her arms around his body.

"You're okay," she said. "You're alive."

He let out a shaking breath. "Forgive me. All my stupidness."

"Nothing to forgive."

He smiled and kissed her. "Good thing I married you."

Tears flowed again, only this time they belonged to Sandra. Max brought her in close, held her against his chest, and let her sweet scent fill his lungs. Though his body still shook with adrenaline, he knew he'd be okay. As long as she stayed with him.

"I've got it," Drummond said, appearing just a few feet away. "I found Korner. I know now."

Sandra lifted her head with a cocky grin. "I already know. A little dead girl told me."

"Well, I don't know. What are we talking about?" Max said a bit too hard and winced.

Drummond came in close as Sandra took in the air to speak. Together they said, "I know where the paintbrush is."

Chapter 21

THE OLD HONDA SHIVERED as Sandra pressed the gas pedal further down. Max cringed at the sound of the straining engine, but he didn't say a word. If anything, he wanted Sandra to push the car faster.

Drummond leaned forward from the backseat, his excitement flowing out of him like a faucet opened full. "Jules Korner is one of the nicest ghosts I've ever met. The moment he heard I was looking for him, he started working to find me. Not an easy thing to do when you consider how enormous the Other is and just how many ghosts there are to get through."

Sandra passed an elderly couple in a car that looked a decade older than the Honda. "Well my little girl, Rebecca, she was every bit as nice and helpful. She felt awful about what she saw that bastard do to you, hon."

"Blondie? I'd be dead if she hadn't helped." Max rubbed his throat.

"Don't talk. It'll just make it worse," Sandra said.

Drummond pointed out a speed trap, and Sandra braked until she got to a respectable speed. "I'm glad that little girl helped you, but I got my information from the source. Korner told me that he had had several encounters with Corkille and few of them were pleasant. They weren't the buddies that Corkille suggested. In fact, Korner's pretty sure that Corkille forged a few Durham bulls on a few barns taking money out of Korner's pocket and possibly hurting his reputation."

Sandra scrunched her brow. "So, Corkille never taught Korner?"

"Korner wouldn't admit to it, but he had a funny look about the subject. Besides, he gave Corkille the paintbrush as a gift. In my experience, enemies don't usually give gifts. Best I can figure out, they did some work together long ago and then had a falling out."

Sandra scoffed. "That's putting it mildly."

"Oh?"

"Rebecca died decades before Korner broke ground on that land. Murdered. She's been haunting that area ever since. She told me that

Corkille had become a leach to Korner, and that one evening the Korner's threw a large party in their home. At the party, Corkille told the story of Blackbeard and suggested they call upon the pirate's spirit for fun. Séances and such were quite popular at the time. Korner wasn't happy at all but he didn't want to embarrass his guests with his disapproval, so he went along."

"Corkille tricked him," Max rasped.

"Yes, and stop talking. Corkille was trying to find the paintbrush even back then. So he used a summoning-possession spell, bringing forth a spirit and letting it possess Korner, who then painted the result. They called for Blackbeard, but they only got some poor fool who knew the rumors."

Drummond slapped the back of Max's headrest. "Let me guess — he painted *Mourning in Red*."

"Right. Well, he painted the original piece with the shadowed figure. He painted the woman on top of it later. Anyway, the party ended and Corkille left, but Rebecca told me that things forever changed at Korner's Folly. Some residual piece of that magic stayed with Jules — perhaps the possession had not been a poor fool but actually Blackbeard pretending to be a poor fool. Whatever it was, it drove Jules to find that paintbrush. When he succeeded, he recognized what had become of him and he feared for his soul."

"He also hated Corkille for bringing the spirits into his life."

"Exactly. So, he painted over the original and gave it to Corkille along with all the things associated with the painting — all the paints, the easel, and the brushes."

"Including the paintbrush, right?"

"Right. I think he hoped to break free from whatever magic surrounded him, but also, I think he secretly wanted to put it onto Corkille as well. Either way, Rebecca said he had Corkille arrive at the Folly one day, handed him the painting and the materials, and explained that this ended their relationship. Howard Corkille was no longer welcome."

"And over the years, the painting got lost," Max said. "Corkille never realized he had the brush the whole time."

"Until now," Drummond said. "Korner told me that he had spoken with a witch who summoned him shortly before he learned that I was looking for him."

"Let me guess."

Sandra hit Max's arm lightly. "Stop talking or I'm going to drop you off at home first."

Drummond said, "Dr. Connor knows the whole story, so you can bet Modesto knows too. My guess is that they sent Blondie to the Folly to wait for you, to stall you, while they went to Corkille to get the paintbrush. If Corkille didn't figure it out on his own, he'll know the second they arrive."

"He knows," Sandra said, getting off the highway. "In fact, he's known from the moment we brought that painting back. He looked at it, figured the whole thing out, and then sent us off to Korner's Folly. But he made sure Melinda stayed behind. He was pretty firm about it. Why? Because he needs her help to find the paintbrush and perform the spell. He definitely knows."

"Sweets, you've got great intuition and reasoning skills. Someday, when you die, think about holding on and becoming a ghost. We could have a great time."

Though Max couldn't speak well, he could still scowl. Sandra caught his reaction from the corner of her eye and let out a snicker. "Sorry, Marshall. I'm all for Max." Max's scowl turned upward into a gloat.

As Sandra neared the Corkille house, all the talk ceased. Max wasn't sure what they would find, but he knew enough to be concerned, and clearly so did the rest of his team. *His team.* He liked the sound of that. More than just a nice sounding concept, he knew it to be true.

Each one of the three of them provided indispensable skills they needed. Take out any one of them, and there would be no way to make this business work. Inwardly, Max marveled at the absurd idea that up until this point he had been trying to find a way to get his wife out of the office.

It had been fear. He knew that now. At first, fear of the financial pressures. Then, Melinda and Howard kept them spinning so much, he feared failing the case and losing any possible momentum that would have on their business.

Thinking of the Corkilles did nothing good for Max. He could feel the fires building in his gut. He knew that sensation all too well lately. But everybody in this case, the Corkilles, Jasper Sullivan, Connor and Modesto, every single one of them lied and manipulated Max and his team over this paintbrush. A damn paintbrush!

"Max?" Sandra said, the false calm in her voice easy to catch. "Are you okay?" She must've noticed his rising anger. If anybody could pick up on that, it would be her.

"Let's just get there," he said, and not another word passed in the car. Even Drummond had the sense to stay quiet.

Max had the car door open before Sandra had even stopped. He stomped up to the front door and kicked it in. A bit over-the-top, he'd admit, but it just felt good.

"Max!" Sandra said, and though he heard her calling, his brain shoved any response aside.

He stormed into the foyer. The house was dark, but with so many windows, a full moon, and the Honda's headlights, Max had no trouble finding his way. He cut into the living room (or maybe they called it the receiving room, who knew with folks like this), tore away the plant hiding the studio door, and pushed in.

"Howard?" he called out. No answer came. He flicked on the lights to find the studio unoccupied.

As Drummond slipped in through the wall, Max whirled around to leave. Sandra blocked the doorway. "Look, honey, I can see you're upset, but we need to approach this sensibly."

Drummond said, "Listen to your wife. I've seen too many cops and PIs end up in the hospital because of going into a situation hot-headed. Just calm down and —"

"Out of my way," Max said and barreled past Sandra.

As he worked toward the kitchen, he opened every door he went by. Closets and entrances to a study or a bathroom or a dining room. Stairs to the basement.

Max stared down that dark chasm for a moment. "Howard? Melinda? You down there?" His voice echoed back. He stood still and listened, raising his hand to stop Sandra and Drummond from making noise.

Drummond cleared his throat, and before Max could scold him, he said, "I'm a ghost. I'll just go down and check it out. Be right back." He slid through the floor and was gone no more than ten seconds. "Nope. Empty down there."

Slamming the basement door, Max stomped to the upstairs. He took one look down the long hall and it hit him. The maids didn't go into the one room, the room that Howard Corkille had been living in for more decades than was natural, the Other Room.

Picking up his pace, the grin of a hunter on his face, Max headed straight for the end of the hall. The dark, wooden door had been left ajar. Max burst through, hoping to catch them or surprise whomever might be left, only to find another empty room. Nothing but a bed and that chair facing out the window.

"Damn," he said as Sandra and Drummond came in behind him. "They have to be here. Corkille's too old, too frail, to be moved around. He could barely make it down to his studio."

"We've been gone all day," Sandra said. "Maybe they just took their time moving. Maybe they're far from here."

"No. If they aren't here, then Connor and Modesto got to them. We're too late." Max dropped onto the edge of the bed and rubbed his face. "They've got to be here. I can feel it."

Sandra looked to Drummond. "Go check the rest of the house. See what you can find."

"I'll try," Drummond said with a defeated tone. "Don't expect much, though, and don't think it'll be quick. This place is like Korner's Folly with all its little rooms."

Max lifted his head, more alert suddenly. Something was different. He looked around the room, trying to recall the day he found Howard Corkille. Sandra, bless her, stayed quiet and watched carefully while Drummond left to search the other rooms.

I came in and saw Corkille sitting there, Max thought. He wanted to speak, he thought best when he did so out loud, but his throat wouldn't allow it. Breathing hurt enough, let alone speaking. He didn't look forward to eating anytime soon.

He walked around the room, pointing to different objects until he saw the bedroom's back corner. That was it. A Japanese tri-fold screen had been set-up there before.

Max approached the corner with cautious steps. He pressed his ear against the wall. A muted sound drifted upward like a ghostly moan, both quiet and disturbing.

Stepping back, Max inspected the wall — dirty, brown wall paper above a chair rail and wood panels below. "There," he said despite the pain and pointed at one wood panel. With a gentle touch, he pressed and pulled on the panel trying to figure out how it opened.

Sandra had been watching him this whole time. Crouching next to him, she placed her hand on the panel and slid it to the side. It opened with ease.

She shrugged. "Lucky guess."

Max stuck his head into the wall and looked around. Nothing special. Just wood and wires, dust and dirt. But he could hear that moaning voice more clearly now.

He pulled his head out and thrust his arm in, feeling around. *There's got to be some kind of* — Click. His hand passed over a switch and on the adjacent wall making up the corner, a full-sized door opened.

Max and Sandra looked at each other. "Careful," Max whispered.

"You, too," she said.

Max took one step toward the door when Sandra grabbed his shoulders and kissed him. At first, they pressed hard against each other but then eased back enough to feel lip against lip. It wasn't a sensual kiss. It didn't arouse thoughts of the bedroom. Rather, the kiss filled Max with memories of all the wonderful moments in his life he owed to Sandra. The kiss pulled from him the deep-seated love that made up the core of his being. He could feel his heart bursting for his wife. And just when the thought hit him that should anything bad happen, this could be their last kiss, he understood that she had figured that much out already.

They let go, smiled, and headed through the door. A few feet in, the floor gave way to a narrow staircase. It went down the inside of the house, perhaps riding underneath the original stairwell, perhaps hidden between walls nobody noticed to be too thick. It was a forgery of architecture that traveled below the first floor into a second, separate basement.

As they neared the bottom, the fluttering glow of candlelight lit the way. That awful moaning continued. The closer they came, the more Max could hear that the sound actually came from two different sources. One was a woman's voice, chanting in a long, mournful tone. The other was of a person in pain.

When they reached the basement, both Max and Sandra jumped back in surprise. The room was a large square with a low ceiling. A chalk circle had been drawn on the concrete floor and around the ring were symbols like those found in Dr. Connor's books. Candles lined the cinderblock walls.

Howard Corkille sat in the center of the circle, wearing a white cloth as if he thought himself to be a monk or Gandhi. But one look at the far wall showed his lack of compassion. Dr. Connor and Mr. Modesto stood with their arms chained to the beams above their heads.

Max had just enough time to take this in. Melinda Corkille, dressed in a black cloak, stepped in front of him and raised her hand.

"Always causing trouble," she said and sprayed something in his face. As she waved the spray into Sandra's direction, Max felt the world slip away.

Chapter 22

BEFORE MAX COULD OPEN HIS EYES, he felt pain. His throat stung as if he had a sunburn on the inside; his right hip throbbed as if he had fallen on a concrete sidewalk; his shoulders and arms burned as if two giants played tug-of-war with him as the rope. Everything hurt. He heard Sandra moan nearby and tried to open his eyes.

At first, no luck. Whatever Melinda had sprayed in their faces had left a sticky crust around his eyelids. He tried to wipe it away only to discover that his hands were handcuffed over his head. Thankfully, he wasn't hanging that way other than from being unconscious. Planting his feet on the ground relieved the stress on his shoulders, arms, and wrists though the pain remained.

While trying to stretch his eyebrows high, he managed to crack one eyelid open, then the other. Though he only saw through a crusty residue, he could make out the room and the situation. It wasn't good.

They were still in the secret chamber with the circle, the candles, and the Corkilles. Sandra, Max, Dr. Connor, and Mr. Modesto had been handcuffed to pipes on the ceiling. They were spread out to four points on the circle that, if connected, would form a huge X. Howard still occupied the center (where the X would intersect) and Melinda, dressed in a dark cloak and little else, walked the inner part of the circle while chanting softly to herself.

"Max?" Sandra said, groggy and sore.

Melinda halted her march, tilted her head toward Sandra, and licked her lips. "No, no, foolish girl. Max is of no use to you anymore." She walked the circle again. "None of you can help each other nor yourselves." She stopped at Dr. Connor who looked weak and defeated. "Not even you."

Mr. Modesto held on to a modicum of pride, standing firm and tall despite his chains and bruised face. "You are the foolish girl if you honestly believe that a man like Mr. Hull will let you —"

"Let me? Mr. Hull? You are so naïve it's a bit sad, really. Mr. Hull has had no power in this from the beginning. While you and your witch here spent all your time trying to weasel back into the Hull family's grace, do you really think Terrance Hull had no clue? Let me? No. He *let you* run around like fools. He used you as pawns so he could get to the magic that he sought. And the only reason that he bothered with you at all was so he could get Max to do the work."

"What?" Sandra said as if Melinda's words were smelling salts.

"Good, she's awake." With a triumphant strut, Melinda approached Sandra. "Time to face the hard truth. Your husband would never work for Hull. Hull knows that. So how else could he get Max to put his charming, diligent talents to use? Hull let word slip to his bumbling, idiot cronies that he sought a certain painting, that it was of great power and importance, and that he would reward his people well for finding it.

"Modesto and his witch are not subtle. Hull knows this. He counted on it. He figured that word would get to Max eventually — after all," she said, looking at Max over her shoulder, letting the curve of her breast show just beyond the cloak, "you're the only one around here who really deals with these kinds of investigations."

Max thought of Jasper Sullivan. Hull had put out the word like chum and simply waited for a shark like Sullivan to arrive. Max didn't doubt it to be true. People like Hull and Corkille, people who know about ghosts and magic, they know they are always surrounded by otherworldly things. For another person, the whole plan would be ridiculous, but for Hull — especially considering the vast, spider web of connections the Hull family had created in the area over the centuries — it wasn't hard to believe. Hull knew Corkille had enough enemies over two centuries that someone, alive or dead, would take interest and hire the only man working the magic angle — Max. And if no one had taken the bait, Hull surely had a back-up plan, probably more direct, probably something Max would have hated more.

Looking up at his hands cuffed to a pipe, Max thought, *Hated more than this?*

At the foot of each captive, Melinda had drawn a symbol in chalk. "You people — you're all just pawns. You think you're smart or brave or ahead of everyone else. You're nothing. This fight has always been between the Corkilles and the Hulls, and tonight the Corkilles will finally win. Howard will be released from his dread curse, Blackbeard's magic will be used up in the process, and without that, Hull won't be able to raise his abominable ancestors."

Dr. Connor cringed. "And all that power released — the curse, the voodoo — all of that magic — you won't let it just dissipate into the air, right?"

Melinda arched an eyebrow. "That would be wasteful, and we must strive to be green, mustn't we? No, I think it best if I absorb all of that power. I think this city needs to be rid of the Hulls. And when I have that power, well, a little revenge would taste good, too."

Dr. Connor's face returned to the maniacal drunk Max had encountered on a few days ago. "You're a moronic dolt," she said. "Terrance Hull will destroy you and barely lift his pinkie."

"If you believe that, then you don't understand the great power infused in the brush." Melinda patted the side of her cloak.

"But you don't know Terrance Hull. You think we're surprised that he used us? You think we feel betrayed or even offended? He's supposed to use us. I'm nothing more than a tool for this great man from a great family to use however he sees fit. You should be afraid, little girl. Ask Max. He knows just how hard it is to go against the Hulls."

Melinda whirled to Max, letting her cloak flow back over her shoulders, letting Max see her firm breasts, her flat stomach, her smooth hips. "I can't say I care much at all for what Max Porter thinks. He could've had me. Look at this body. You gave this up?"

Max locked eyes with Sandra. "I love my wife." Sandra's lips trembled a kiss in the air.

Melinda stepped between them. "Aw, isn't that sweet. But so stupid, too. You should've slept with me when I had offered. Then this would've been avoidable. See, Blackbeard's hair may be infused with that voodoo priestess's spell, but it needs a catalyst to get hold of all that power. That catalyst is the life essence. Perhaps Dr. Connor would explain what that is?"

Dr. Connor snarled. "Rot in Hell."

"She's a bit out of sorts," Melinda said, shrugging one shoulder. "Oh well, I've had to do it all myself this long, might as well keep going." She stepped closer to Max, the tips of her breasts brushing his chest. "The life essence is simply any bodily fluid that carries your life. Had you slept with me, I would already have your fluids and you wouldn't be here."

Max looked beyond toward Sandra. "Happy to disappoint."

Melinda's hand moved fast, slapping Max's cheek with surprising force. "Pay attention. Just because you turned away from what would have been the best lay of your life doesn't mean I don't win. You could have had a wonderful afternoon of pleasures your wife can't even begin to imagine. She probably hasn't even heard of half the techniques I know. Instead, you get this. Because there are other life essence fluids in the body. Blood, for example."

Her words died against the low ceiling, leaving the room in cold silence. She stepped back, offering Max one final view of her tone body before pulling the cloak back over. "Let's start proper," she said and faced Mr. Modesto. "No one is more proper than you. At least, no one pretends to be more proper, especially when serving out the most despicable orders."

Despite his bruised cheek and bleeding lip, Modesto raised his chin and managed to exude a small portion of dignity. "It is no wonder that Mr. Porter declined your advances. You're a hideous person."

In a flash, Melinda snatched a simple, wooden bowl and an elaborate dagger from a recess in the wall. She cracked Modesto across his proud chin with the blade's hilt. Max saw Modesto's eyes roll but he came back a moment later. Just in time to watch as Melinda sliced a line open on his chest.

She didn't bother opening his shirt. She let the sharp blade do all the work. Shirt and skin cut open with ease, and a patch of blood spread.

After setting the dagger down, she ripped the cut shirt off. The bowl came next. She placed it against Modesto's chest and pushed on the wound to release more blood. As it collected in the bowl, slowly dribbling like syrup, Melinda whispered foreign words. Max tried to hear her, but he couldn't make sense of it.

He looked everywhere, twisting his wrists around the handcuffs only to find the block wall behind him. Melinda lowered the bowl on the circle's edge, dipped her finger in the blood, and traced the chalk symbols she had drawn earlier. With his foot, Max rubbed an opening in the circle, and while he did disturb the chalk, he uncovered lines that had been painted on the floor. As Melinda rose with the bowl and dagger and headed toward Dr. Connor, Max tried to clear his mind, not to panic, and to find a way out.

"Your usefulness to the Hull family has long since run its course," Melinda said as Dr. Connor glared at her in defiance, "and I can guarantee that I'll have no use for you when the Corkille family takes over. But, if it gives you any comfort, you'll have one final use, and it'll be for this spell."

Snarling, Melinda jabbed the dagger into Dr. Connor's stomach and placed the bowl underneath to catch the blood. The witch grunted and sweat beaded on her forehead, but she managed not to scream.

"Stop this," Modesto said, his voice weakening. "I'm sure we can make a deal."

"Is that right?" Melinda shook her head. "You have some great pull with the Hulls that I don't know about? Even if you did, why would the Hulls deal with me — the woman who will usurp them? Oh, look, I think Dr. Connor is trying to be brave."

To Max's utter shock, Dr. Connor maintained her firm glare on Melinda as if to say, *You'll never beat me*. Melinda jabbed the dagger into the witch once more. Dr. Connor barely reacted. She held her witch's gaze until her eyes lost focus and her head slumped forward.

Modesto let out a whimper while as before, Melinda whispered odd words and then knelt on the circle. She traced the chalk symbols with blood as she continued this strange rite. Max saw Modesto lose control. The once-dignified man kicked and screamed and cried. He tried to free himself but without success.

Each burst of energy lessened in strength from the previous one. It was a strange thing to watch. Max could actually see the moment that Modesto gave up. It held for just a second. One moment, Modesto railed against his bonds and spitted out his hatred for Melinda. Then, for a flashing instant, he froze. Max saw it in his eyes — the acceptance of fate. The next moment, Modesto let his body hang as he wept in silence.

Melinda ignored Modesto as if he were a child acting up for a parent's attention. When she had finished her blood tracings, she rose with the dagger and bowl in hand and turned toward Sandra.

"No," Max said, his body flushing with cold fear.

Melinda watched Max from the corner of her eye as she crossed the room. "It's too bad your sweetheart isn't more awake. I guess I drugged her a bit too much. It would've been fun to listen to her scream. And you, too."

Though tears streamed down his face, Max held his tongue. He looked around the room again, desperate to find anything useful. But he saw nothing that he could reach. Not with his hands cuffed to the pipe above him.

"Still," Melinda continued, "I don't need her to be awake. I simply need to take her blood."

"No!" Max cried out.

"Don't worry. I'll slit her wrists so the blood drains slowly. That way you can watch her death for a long, painful time."

Max yanked against the pipe. With every muscle, every bit of strength he could summon, he let out a garbled cry, his damaged throat scalding pain straight up to his teeth, and he pulled down hard. The pipe didn't appear to budge, but he continued to pull.

"Say goodbye to your love," Melinda said and slashed the dagger across Sandra's wrist.

"Ouch," Sandra said in a distant voice.

Max's eyes widened and he doubled his efforts. Dust sifted off the pipe, drifting onto his face. Melinda raised her bowl to gather the blood and whisper her words.

Furiously, Max yanked down. Over and over. Each time the pipe shook but did not break loose.

When Melinda knelt on the circle and began her tracings, Max screamed out and gave all he could into breaking that pipe. Still, it remained intact.

Melinda stood, gathered her bowl and dagger, and looked upon Max like a lover finally getting her man. Panting, Max looked back with such hatred, Melinda hesitated.

"Oh, now," she said, "don't be that way." She opened her cloak once more and sauntered toward him. Biting her bottom lip, she traced her breast with the tip of the dagger leaving behind a dotted trail of blood. "It's not too late, you know. Mmmm. I think we could have a good time." She placed a hand on his chest and licked his neck. Her hand slid down until it rested between his legs. "Maybe I should coax that other fluid from you while you watch your wife dying across the room."

Max spit on her. "There's a fluid for you."

Rage flashed in Melinda's eyes. Her mouth turned down and she stabbed the dagger at his groin. She looked down. "I missed," she said, pulling the blade from his thigh. "Guess it's your lucky day. You might even get to die before your wife."

While Melinda let Max's blood fill her bowl, she kept her eyes locked on his face. Max felt his blood flow out but he refused to look down. He just watched her and waited. He knew what was about to happen. He waited for it. His only chance.

With the bowl filled, Melinda kissed Max's cheek and turned around to face the circle. This was it. Max pulled himself upward on the pipe and lifted his legs toward her shoulders. He had hoped to wrap his legs around her neck, but he was too weak now to get his legs high enough.

He did manage to kick her in the back, sending her stumbling into the circle.

Melinda let out a screech of surprise as she fell to one knee. All her focus shifted to keeping the blood from spilling out of the bowl. Her body shook as she gently placed the bowl on the floor. Then she let out a huge sigh.

"That's why I like you," she said, turning to Max. "You don't give up, do you? But you failed. Not a drop spilled."

"Come back and I'll try again."

Melinda picked up the bowl and stood straight. "I am coming back, and I'm going to finish this spell. If you try anything again, I'll walk over to your beloved Sandra and slit her neck. You understand? She's dying right now, but she's not dead yet. Who knows? Maybe when I'm done with this, I'll let her live. But if you do anything more to disrupt me, you'll be responsible for her guaranteed death. Am I clear?"

Though Max shook with anger, though his eyes blazed his frustration, though his fingers curled into fists, he nodded.

"Good," Melinda said, approaching as before. This time, as she turned toward the circle, she paused long enough to send Max a warning glance. He refused to meet her eyes. She knelt on the circle and completed tracing the symbols in blood.

"Now," she said, "it's time." She stepped into the circle and knelt right behind Howard Corkille. Like a seasoned caregiver, she eased him back, reclining his body until his head rested in her lap.

"Thank you," Howard said, his words shaky and cracking. "Thank you all for the sacrifice you are making for me. I'm so tired of this world. But to know that my darling Melinda will benefit in such an enormous way makes this parting all that much better."

"Shhh," Melinda said, stroking Howard's head. "It's time for you to finally rest."

"Yes. Rest. That sounds wonderful."

Howard closed his eyes and Melinda lifted her hands upward. She started to moan in low, drawn-out tones like an ancient monk deep in meditation. The only break came when she drew breath.

"Boy-o-boy, that's horrible," Drummond said as he lowered through the ceiling. "I can hear her through the floorboards."

"Where the hell have you been?" Max said despite the hot pain in his throat and the deep relief he felt the moment he saw the old ghost. Modesto looked up, his brow scrunched, but he said nothing.

Drummond raised his hands. "Sorry. I got lost. Y'know, I think old

Jules Korner must've helped design this place. It's a darn maze." After a quick survey of the room, he added, "Doesn't look like things are going all that well for you."

"Shut up and do something," Max said.

"Like what?"

"Like stick your hand into her head and stop all this." Max's face puckered at the pain in his throat.

"Kill her? Doesn't look like things are that bad."

Max's face found enough blood to turn red. "Sandra is dying," he managed. He tasted the bitter copper of blood in his mouth.

Drummond swooped in on Sandra. "Can you hear me?"

Sandra raised an eye. She looked pale and weak.

"Sorry, Max," Drummond said. "I didn't realize it was so serious. I'll take care of everything."

Puffing out his chest, Drummond slid forward, his arms reaching out toward Melinda's head. But when he hit the circle's edge, he screamed out and fell backward. Light tendrils of smoke twined above him.

Melinda paused her moaning chant long enough to laugh. "Sorry. No ghosts allowed."

With one hand rubbing his head, Drummond said, "That hurt."

Melinda watched Max as she rose to her feet. Her eyes widened, her mouth leered, her expression twisted — she was a gargoyle celebrating freedom from its stony prison. "The time has arrived," she said. "I won't be just an obedient little girl anymore. I won't be a caretaker for a fossilized man. Soon, I will have the power to change everything."

She lifted her right hand, and Max saw the paintbrush clenched in her fingers. It was small, pencil thin, the kind of brush used for fine, detailed work. Max marveled at the sight. All this trouble caused over a few hairs on this tiny brush.

"Now," Melinda said turning toward Howard's sleeping body, "you will no longer suffer."

"Drummond," Max whispered softly both to protect his damaged throat and to keep Melinda from hearing. "You have to save Sandra. Nothing else matters to me. Okay?"

For all his sarcasm and foolishness, the core of Marshall Drummond came out when needed the most. The ghost took one look at Max, gave one understanding nod, and whisked across the room. He placed both hands around Sandra's wrist and closed his eyes in concentration.

Her hand turned white as a supernatural cold infiltrated her skin. The blood stopped flowing from her wrist. Sandra's eyes snapped open as the cold shocked her awake. She looked around, confused and desperate to comprehend.

The air inside the circle shimmered and warped around the Corkilles. Max tried to watch Sandra, but the air between them twisted her image as if looking through a glass of water.

"Max," Sandra called out. "Max, I'm okay. Dizzy, but okay."

He wanted to let her know he was fine. He wanted to scream out how much he loved her. But he only had a few more words in him before his throat refused to make any sound until it healed. He thought he should hold on to them.

Melinda held the brush over Howard's body. In a bright flash, the hairs on the brush ignited, burning hotter and higher than should have been possible. Max squinted against the light, but he could still see what happened.

Howard Corkille's arms jerked to the side. Then his legs. Then his entire body spasmed on the floor as if suffering seizures.

"By the blood of those surrounding," Melinda said, "Free this man from that which binds him."

Max couldn't say what he expected to occur, but there was no huge light show, no swirling of spirits, no cracking of the curse. Instead, the air stopped shimmering and the flaming brush lowered to a burning ember. Howard's body settled.

The old man lifted his hand toward Melinda, and his mouth opened into a toothy grin. "I'm free," he said. And his hand flopped to floor. His body empty. Howard Corkille was dead.

Max looked up from the body and saw his wife staring back at him. His eyes glistened as she blew him a kiss. But a frown took over her expression as her eyes focused just above Melinda's head.

"Can you see this?" she asked.

He peered in the same direction, but he saw nothing.

"He can't see it," Drummond said.

"There's an energy above her. It's not like a ghost. It's something strange," Sandra said.

A soft pop of air startled Melinda as the brush ignited once more. The flame no longer hurt to see but it had an odd tinge of purple and blue inside it. It flickered in the air and lit Melinda's face from beneath creating harsh, ugly shadows.

"By the soul of Edward Teach, Blackbeard the Pirate," Melinda said, raising her hands toward the invisible force above her. "By the infinite powers of the great voodoo priestesses of old, I call upon you to take this broken curse, consume its energy, consume its centuries of power, all that it was which now rests in this token of your power —" She shook the brush as if the power would dash from it and sprinkle down.

To the side, Max saw Dr. Connor moving her head. It took a lot of effort but she managed to look right at Max. Her mouth moved but Max couldn't hear her above Melinda's spell casting.

"Dump the bowl!" Sandra said. "Connor says to dump the bowl."

Max nodded and moved his foot toward the bowl of his own blood. Though he stretched as far as his sore limbs would permit, the bowl remained out of reach. Melinda had been careful.

"— take it all from here and release it back unto me. Come into me, spirits of the past, so I may rule as you would once have wanted to rule."

Pointing at Melinda with his free hand, Drummond said, "That woman is nuts."

"Come into me. Come into me," Melinda chanted.

Sandra's face paled, and at first Max thought Drummond had put his ghostly touch on her for too long. Then she said, "Max ... I don't believe it. I think I'm seeing Blackbeard's ghost."

Chapter 23

"COME INTO ME," Melinda said. "I am an open vessel."

Max pulled down on the cuffs, but he knew nothing would come of it. He needed to do something, though. He looked around the room, hoping to find some miracle item that he hadn't noticed before.

He saw Dr. Connor, head hung low, her body devoid of any energy. Modesto watched the circle with an expression equal parts disdain and defeat. Sandra stared at an empty space which, no doubt, contained the apparition of Blackbeard. Drummond, holding Sandra's wrist, also looked upon the pirate ghost.

We're a sorry bunch, Max thought.

"Come," Melinda continued, and waved the smoldering brush in front of her like incense. She reached out with her free hand, and though Max could not see Blackbeard, he pictured the pirate taking her hand like a gentleman asking to dance. But then her body jolted and her twisted face grimaced.

"He's got her," Sandra said. "He's got her."

Whatever pain Melinda had felt, sifted away. Her face softened with a blissful calm. She lifted her eyes toward Max, and looking more sadistic than Max had ever encountered before, she picked up the dagger. "Not enough blood," she said, her voice having dropped an octave. She was no longer Melinda. Blackbeard had control.

She looked down at Howard Corkille and cut open his wrist. Like a vampire, she brought the wrist to her mouth. A little blood pooled but without his heart pumping, there was no flow.

She threw Howard's wrist to the floor and let out an angry grunt. "Need more," she said, and it occurred to Max that the second part of this spell, the part intended to give Melinda such great power, may not have worked entirely. She had said that life fluids were important, but she never said just how important.

Max looked at Howard's corpse. That blood was no good. Howard only provided dead fluids now. So why wasn't Blackbeard/Melinda coming after them, the living, cutting them open?

Max's lips turned up in a devilish grin. Blackbeard may be in Melinda's body, but for now, he was still a ghost. He couldn't get out of the circle any more than Drummond could get in.

Thinking of Drummond and his ghostliness brought another thought to Max like a shining sun bursting through a terrible storm. Knowing his throat would hate him for more talking, Max braced himself for the pain that would come, and said, "Honey, trust me."

Sandra looked right at Max, straight into his heart. "Always."

"Drummond, let go of her wrist and come over here."

Drummond hesitated. "The cold won't last long without me."

"I know," Max said.

"She'll start to bleed again."

Sandra shook her arms. "Trust him, already."

Drummond looked from wife to husband and back. "If you start to get light-headed, you yell for me. I'll run right back."

As Drummond went around the circle to cross the room, Melinda tried to reach out toward Dr. Connor. The circle prevented her from touching the witch. She spotted the blood-traced symbols on the floor, and like a famished wildcat, she dropped on all fours, and licked what hadn't dried yet.

"What now?" Drummond asked as he approached Max.

"Put your hands on the chain between my handcuffs. You freeze it like you did Sandra's wrist, only I want you to put everything into it. I want that chain so cold that it's practically ice itself. Can you do that?" Max said, his voice fading into a whisper at the end.

Drummond nodded. He placed his hand on the chain, closed his eyes, and touched the metal. Max could see the pain this caused. Touching the corporeal world always caused pain. But, if nothing else, Drummond had always been a tough detective. He winced, bared his teeth, and grunted, but he never cried out.

Melinda scrabbled toward the bloody symbols near Modesto. When she finished there, she moved on to Sandra's symbols. Every so often, she reached toward the circle's edge with one hand. Each time, she pulled it back as if stung. Except Max noticed that each time, she kept her hand against the barrier a little longer. Instinct told Max that when she finished all the blood the symbols had, it would be enough to free her from the circle.

He yanked downward. "Colder," he said.

Melinda looked up. Max could tell by her gaze that she now saw

Drummond. A benefit of having Blackbeard inside her, he guessed. Understanding crossed her face, and she sped up her ingestion of the blood.

"Hurry," Max said.

Drummond put both hands on the chain. "Keep trying," he said.

As Max pulled down, Melinda rushed across to the bloody symbols at his feet. She lapped it up, laughing at Max's desperation.

"I'm going to have fun killing you," she said.

He inhaled deeply and put every ounce of strength he had into one crushing pull. His wrists screamed out as the cuffs dug into his skin, but then he tumbled to the ground and little pieces of frozen metal tinkled on the floor. Drummond floated backward, his eyes closed in relief.

"Max!" Sandra screamed.

As he faced her, Melinda stepped out of the circle and backhanded him across the cheek. Not only had Blackbeard giving her the ability to see the dead, but Max learned that she also had gained a lot of his brute strength. The blow to his face sent Max rolling across the floor.

Max stumbled to his feet just as Melinda rushed him. She grabbed his shirt and shoved him against the wall. She punched him in the gut. He doubled over, his lungs giving up all their air, his eyes watering at the pain. Bile raced up, burning the sore tissue as it coated his throat. He struggled to remain standing.

Melinda clasped his chin in her hand and forced his head upward. She gazed down upon him, and Max glimpsed the pirate inside her. He had heard that Blackbeard struck fear in the men he fought against, and Max understood why. The fierce eyes blazing at him lacked compassion, humanity, or even sanity. Had Melinda succeeded, she would have had great power. But with Blackbeard controlling Melinda, her power was vicious.

She pulled back a fist and slammed it across his temple. Max dropped to the ground. The world spun around him.

He thought he heard Sandra screaming his name, but her voice sounded muffled and dazed. He turned his head toward her. The floor rushed up to his face, cold and hard.

He saw a figure stand over him. A dark, shadowed figure. Blackbeard. The pirate raised one, powerful foot.

"Goodbye, Max Porter," a voice said.

But that foot never slammed down. The pain never came. Instead, the shadowed figure arched back and toppled over with a surprised yell.

Max rolled onto his side to see what had happened. The first thing he discerned through his blurred vision was that the fallen figure belonged to Melinda Corkille. That made sense and helped clear his muddled brain. The second thing he saw was Drummond floating above Melinda.

Drummond turned his head toward Max and nodded. He shouldn't have done so. Melinda's hand shot upward and smashed Drummond toward the ceiling.

"Idiot," she said. "I am the great Blackbeard. I can see you, and I can touch you, and I most certainly can destroy you."

Melinda clamored to her feet and swung out with her fists. Drummond moved fast, though, and with the grace of an experienced fighter. He dodged her punches and countered with two strong jabs that popped hard, stumbling her back a few steps. Without Blackbeard coursing through her, Max figured Melinda would've been out cold.

Back and forth Melinda and Drummond traded blows. Max watched from the floor, his body slowly recuperating. He could see one solid image instead of blurred doubles, and he could breathe without hot pokers attacking his lungs. Swallowing still hurt, but then he fully expected to be on an all-liquid diet for the next few weeks.

Drummond dashed to the right, avoiding Melinda's left fist. He grabbed her near the elbow and swung her around. She fell into Modesto who made no effort to kick out — he was unconscious.

Melinda lunged for Drummond, caught him by the leg, and took him down to the floor. She straddled him, pinning his arms down with her knees, and punched him in the face. Over and over, she connected.

Max had been watching the fight fully expecting Drummond to win. But now things had turned ugly. He rolled up onto all fours, held the position a moment until his stomach settled back, and crawled toward the fight. He had no illusions that he could hurt Melinda in his condition, but he did hope to distract her long enough for Drummond to get free.

She spotted him out of the corner of her eye. "Naughty, naughty," she said, but she took the bait. She reached toward him, perhaps planning to shove him away.

Max had enough strength to latch onto her wrist and fall down. His weight yanked her off balance. Like a bird freed from its cage, Drummond shot into the air, curved around, and knocked Melinda to the side. She fought back, but the two were on even ground again.

"Max," Sandra said, calling him from far away. No. Near. His ears could hear her so closely. He inched his head upward and saw that he had moved quite close to his wife.

"The bowl," she said. "Connor said to knock over the bowl."

Like a drunkard, Max lolled to his side. Ahead of him was the bowl Melinda had used to collect their blood. He stared at it, trying to will his body to move. He was so tired, so weakened. He wanted to close his eyes and sleep.

"Hurry!" Drummond yelled as Melinda tossed him against the stairs. He shot back at her but she parried his attacks.

Max crawled his arm in the direction of the bowl. He felt heat radiating from it. Pushing with his feet, he scooted closer until his fingers made contact. The bowl's surface was rougher than he had expected.

"Turn it over," Sandra said. "You've almost got it."

Melinda's head snapped around. "No!" She darted toward Max but Drummond jumped onto her back, wrapped his arm around her throat, and pulled her away. With a lazy smile, Max flipped the bowl closer toward himself.

Nothing happened.

"Sorry," Max whispered. Too tired to go on, Max let his arm flop downward. It hit the bowl, cracking it into three pieces.

Flames, purple and blue like those from the brush, snaked out of the bowl's shards. Drummond shoved Melinda toward the center of the circle. Like a child lost in a store, Melinda looked from face to face, hoping one would be her salvation.

The flames rose higher, weaving in a hypnotic rhythm. If they had eyes, Max would have sworn they were staring at Melinda. Whatever they burned on — chalk, blood, concrete, or the supernatural — the odor rivaled any natural gas leak Max had experienced. He coughed at the horrible smell.

Melinda lifted one hand toward Max, and in a voice that was all her own, that lacked any trace of Blackbeard, she said, "It wasn't supposed to be this way." Then the flames speared her.

As she screamed, Max passed out.

Chapter 24

HOURS LATER, AS THE DAY began beneath his office window, Max settled in his chair and stared at the shot of whiskey on his desk. Sandra had already downed two shots and had prepared a third. Drummond floated by the bookcase, uncharacteristically quiet.

"You going to have that?" Sandra asked.

Max shook his head. He wanted it. He needed it. But he had no doubt that alcohol would light his throat on fire even as it relaxed his frazzled nerves.

His cell phone rang. A glance at the screen told him what he suspected — Mother. Who else would call at the most inappropriate, inconvenient time? He remembered promising her that he would call her back, but if she heard his voice, she'd be on a plane to come nurse him. Probably throw in a few barbs at Sandra while she was at it.

Max pushed the phone across his desk toward Sandra. She looked at the ID and shook her head. "Let it go to voicemail," she said.

When the phone stopped ringing, Drummond said, "You know you can't go to the police."

"Don't we have to?" Sandra asked.

"All that was left of Melinda and Howard were two piles of very fine ash. Everything in that circle turned to ash. You have no bodies, no evidence, no way of proving your story, which — you have to admit — is going to be a tough one for them to swallow as it is. And then there's the tricky aspect that if they believe any of it, they could easily turn the whole thing around to implicate both of you. So, sweetheart, I appreciate you wanting to be honest and forthright, but face it, no cops on this one."

Sandra took Max's shot glass and stared at her wrist wrapped in some yellowed gauze from their inadequate first aid kit. "We should at least go to the hospital."

Max shook his head and pointed to Drummond.

"Honey," Sandra said, "doctors aren't the police."

Drummond slid toward the desk. "I'm afraid Max's right. You can't go to the hospital. They'd take care of him, but they'd also ask a lot of questions. No matter what story you come up with, they're going to notice that the bruises on his neck look like a man being choked to death. Answer the questions, don't answer the questions — either way, the docs are going to notify the police. Then you're back to dealing with the law again."

"We can't do nothing. Max's throat needs serious, professional attention. And my wrist needs stitches, at the least."

"Stitches that'll probably get you locked on a psych ward for a suicide watch."

"Then what do you suggest we do?" Sandra said, her frustration expressing Max's silent anger quite well.

A knock came at the office door which stood open. Mr. Modesto filled the doorway. "Perhaps I can help," he said.

On the surface, Max thought the man looked good. Fresh clothing, a deep shower, and some cologne had wiped away any visible sign of the trauma Modesto had endured. He stepped into the office, his walk formal, his back stiff, his arrogant demeanor all too familiar. Only the moment after he sat near the desk, the moment when his breathing strained and he unconsciously rubbed at his chest, revealed anything improper.

"Perhaps I should be more clear," Modesto said, setting a thin manila envelope on the desk. "I, once again, am in the employ of the Hull family."

Sandra downed the shot of whiskey. "Oh, really? And how are we supposed to believe you this time?"

"Because Mr. Hull is going to take care of everything in a way that is far beyond my meager abilities." Modesto snapped his fingers and a portly, balding man entered. He had a small, black bag at his side, and he headed straight for Max.

"Just these two?" the man asked.

Modesto nodded before continuing. "This man is Dr. Zach Goldman. He is Mr. Hull's personal physician. He will tend to you both right now."

As Modesto spoke, Dr. Goldman treated Max with delicate hands and more care than Max had ever come across in the health care world. He hated to admit it, but the idea of Mr. Hull's doctor working on him gave Max a greater sense of security and confidence than had they gone to the hospital. After all, should the doctor screw up and kill Max,

Hull's secret journals would become public knowledge. *Far better*, Max thought, *than any health insurance coverage.*

"Now," Modesto went on, "Mr. Hull has used his formidable connections to ensure there will be no police investigations into any of the matters that have occurred over the course of this situation. Not the Corkilles, not Jasper Sullivan, not the painting, not Jules Korner, not the Welcome Center shooting, not even the tortured postal worker. As far as the police are concerned, all these incidents no longer exist."

"You've got to be kidding," Sandra said, her mouth agape. "I mean I know that the Hull family is powerful, but—"

"The Hull family has always had more ability in this city than you or your thankfully mute husband ever understood."

Drummond snickered. "Only mute for a little while, pal." Max and Sandra joined in for a chuckle.

Modesto sat straighter, ruffled by the reaction. "Regardless, Mr. Hull has also arranged to purchase the Corkille estate and all of its contents. So you needn't fear the discovery of the forgery studio or" — Modesto shuddered — "that other place we were in."

Sandra opened the book with the bottle of whiskey inside. "You want a drink?"

"No, thank you," Modesto said, but his eyes lingered on the bottle. "Furthermore, Mr. Hull wants you to know that although Ms. Corkille used the brush, not all of it was burned to ash. Mr. Hull has possession of the brush and has his top men working on retrieving a usable hair. For the spell he wishes to cast, all he requires is one. Or so Dr. Connor assures. Yes, she'll be fine. Physically."

Cringing as he leaned forward, Modesto pushed the manila enveloped toward Max. "There is one final matter. While Mr. Hull wishes for you to know that he fully recognizes the security you enjoy because of your possession of a copy of his family journal, he also hopes you now see that he has a new card to play in this game — the police."

"Now, hold on," Sandra said, but Max raised a hand to stop her.

"Please, let me speak," Modesto said as Dr. Goldman finished tending Max, wrote down some instructions so as not to disturb Mr. Modesto, and moved on to Sandra. "Mr. Hull has no intention of involving the police in your lives. He merely wants you to understand that holding the journal hostage will only get you so far, and that should you cross that line, Mr. Hull has tremendous resources at his disposal with which to make your lives uncomfortable. Therefore, Mr.

Hull would like to form a new arrangement with you."

"Oh, crap, this doesn't sound good," Drummond said.

"From this day forward, the Hull family wishes to pay you a handsome fee in return for keeping you on retainer. You will be free to pursue any other cases you wish, and Mr. Hull promises that you will only be called upon for matters regarding your unique talents — those that are supernatural, if you will. All the finer points are detailed in there," Modesto said, nodding to the envelope.

Though Dr. Goldman fidgeted with her wrist, Sandra stood up — her face red, her body swaying slightly, her breath heavy with whiskey. "You're saying that we have to be at Mr. Hull's beck and call whenever he feels the need to deal with a ghost, and if we don't, he's going to drop the police on us? Is that right?"

Modesto stood and put out his hand. "Exactly. Welcome to the Hull family business."

Max buried his head on the desk. Sandra stared at Modesto in shock. And Dr. Goldman made a quick exit.

"Well," Modesto said, dropping his unshaken hand. "I shall assume you'll consent to this arrangement unless I hear otherwise by the close of business today. Good day."

Max saluted with his hand and relished the perturbed huff he received in response. As Modesto exited, Sandra and Drummond closed in on the manila envelope. Max waved them off. He took the envelope and stuffed it in his top drawer. He didn't need to see Hull's specifics. The Hull family excelled at getting their way.

For now, Max thought. He had gotten the upper-hand on Hull once before; he could do it again.

The rest of the day dragged on. Drummond slipped away, and Sandra shuffled papers around in between bouts of alcohol-induced sleep. Max sat at his desk, trying to digest all that had happened.

As the business day neared its close, Sandra stepped in front of Max's desk wearing a stern, determined expression. "We need to talk," she said.

He pointed to his throat.

"Fine, I need to talk. You need to listen."

Max placed his hands behind his head, leaned back in his chair, and propped his feet on his desk. He smiled.

"Don't try to charm me. You listen. If we're going to be on retainer for Hull, and we both know we're going to be, then we've got to work out this whole working together thing for good. You seem to be struggling with the idea that your wife might be good at this."

Max shook his head, but Sandra put out her hand. "You don't get to argue this time. Ever since I started working here, you've acted out of sorts. You've been like another person towards me. I see you with Drummond or others and there's my Max, my honey, but whenever you have to deal with me, you become this other guy. I don't like that guy. Occasionally, you become you again and we have a great night and it seems like everything is okay. But then a day goes by and you're back to the Other Max.

"I don't know what's going on inside your head, but you need to figure it out. You need to remember that before we're business partners, and from now on we are business partners, but before that, we are married. We are husband and wife. And we love each other.

"I tried to work for you. That didn't do so well for either of us. So let's do this my way, instead. Let's just be a married couple. Let's just be in love. And let's let the fact that we work together not get between us. Do you think you can do that? Because I love you, and I don't want to lose you."

Max got to his feet and took Sandra's hands in his own. He closed his eyes as he brought her fingers to his lips. Leaning over the desk, he kissed her with a gentle touch.

"I can't hear you. Is that a yes?" she teased.

Max opened the top drawer of his desk, pulled out the manila envelope, and handed it to Sandra. "Yes," he said despite the pain.

Sandra pulled him close and pressed her lips hard against his. Locked in the embrace, Max never noticed Drummond's arrival until the ghost said, "If you two can stop the smooching, I got news."

Pushing Max back in his seat, Sandra said, "What is it?" She sat at her desk and opened the envelope.

Drummond watched her for a moment, clearly confused by the change in the office dynamic, but shrugged it off. "I thought you might like to know what became of Jasper Sullivan."

Both Max and Sandra perked up.

Drummond went on, "I put out the word that I was looking for him. The word came back to me. Nobody can find him. He's gone into hiding, maybe even found what he needed to move on. I'm not sure, but I can pretty much guarantee that we won't hear from him again."

"Is he that afraid of us?" Sandra asked. "What does he think we'll do to him?"

"You can't do much. But I can. And I would, too. Not only did he stiff us on getting paid, but the whole thing was a set-up for him. And I'll tell you one thing for sure — dead or alive, I do not like being set up."

"So he's running from you."

"I wish," Drummond said, clapping his hands and pointing at Max. "I think ol' Jasper is running more so from what Max did. By destroying the Corkilles, Max released all that energy back into the world, and dead energy released in a living world equals ghosts."

Sandra dug into the envelope as she said, "Jasper is running from the Corkilles."

"Wouldn't you?" Drummond said with a satisfied smile.

Sandra tossed the envelope onto Max's desk. "You ought to look in that."

Puzzled, Max reached in and pulled out their first check from the Hulls. He stared at it. His hands trembled. His stomach complained.

"If you won't deposit it," Sandra said, "I will."

Max looked up and handed her the check. She snatched it from him. Beckoning Drummond to tag along, she promised to be back soon.

Max turned to his computer, brought up the finance program, and entered the new income. It may not be palatable to work with Hull, but he promised himself it would only be temporary. Sandra was right about everything she had said. Together, he knew they could beat the Hulls.

Besides, as he watched that red number turn black, Max felt lighter. He didn't need to think twice about his next action. He hurried out of the office, rushed downstairs, and caught up with Sandra and Drummond on the sidewalk.

"Everything okay?" Sandra asked.

Max hooked his arm around her, kissed her cheek, and strolled toward the bank with a good friend on one side and the woman he loved on the other.

Afterword

Regarding the history in *Southern Charm* - Korner's Folly is a real place and well worth a visit if you are ever near Kernersville, NC. If you don't live nearby, they have a website with photos so you can get a taste for what the place is like. Shortly before I had visited the house, a North Carolina paranormal society had indeed declared the building haunted (which just confirmed for me that it was perfect for this book).

Much of the true history of Blackbeard the Pirate is unknown which, for a writer, is license to create. So, as far as I know, Blackbeard never cavorted with a woman who used voodoo to curse him. It is true that no paintings of him exist and that he ran his operation (and finished his career in dramatic style) off the North Carolina coast, but all of his history with women was the result of my imagination.

As before, while many of the locations and histories are accurate, I do take liberties at times. Never forget - this is fiction.

Southern Belle

Chapter 1

THOUGH NEVER OFFICIALLY TRAINED to be a detective, Max Porter knew that the man in the black suit had been following him. Early that Spring morning, he had seen the man standing near the old YMCA building across from the office. The building had been converted into apartments, yet Black Suit never went in, never buzzed for anyone, never even peeked through the doorway. He only stood there, occasionally sneezing from the heavy pollen that covered the cars and sidewalk with a yellow hue.

Later, when Max left for lunch, he noticed a plain brown sedan trailing him all the way from downtown Winston-Salem, across Business 40, onto 421, off the Jonestown Road exit, and down Country Club Road, past the psychic and the auto repair, until he parked at Little Richard's. The old joint had the reputation of serving some of the best Lexington Barbecue in all of Winston-Salem, but Max thought it too much of a coincidence that Black Suit shared the same craving on the same day at the same time as he did.

A year ago, Max would have been shivering at the prospect of a strange man following him all day, but he had been through enough serious trouble — ghosts, witches, curses, spells — that Black Suit did little more than annoy him. At least, for the moment. Later he might get worried, but no way would he let anyone spoil a trip to Little Richard's.

When Max and his wife (and business partner), Sandra, first moved to North Carolina, they had no appreciation for the artistry of Lexington Barbecue. They had Michigan sensibilities. They understood beef and venison. But after his first taste of Southern-style barbecue, he became a true believer. Pulled pork in a vinegar-based barbecue sauce, piled atop a bun, and covered with coleslaw — the mere thought of it caused his mouth to water. While he had no doubt that the barbecue joints down in Lexington would blow his taste buds away, Little Richard's served the folk of Winston-Salem more than amply.

He had to admit that he was surprised Black Suit followed him into the place. From the outside, Little Richard's looked like a large restaurant — a family-style exterior with a big, neon sign that danced a happy pig across the front. Inside, however, patrons were met with an L-shaped, 50s décor dining room — one side a counter for to-go orders and paying the bill, the other a long, narrow path of tables filled with people. Little Richard's always seemed packed. Not a lot of places for Black Suit to hide.

While he waited to order, he took a seat in the back corner where he could watch everybody who entered — one of many trade secrets he learned from his other partner, Marshall Drummond. Drummond was a strong-willed, smart-mouthed sort of guy with the peculiar characteristic of being dead. He had been a detective in the 1940s when he wound up on the wrong end of a witch's curse. After Max moved in, discovered Drummond, and broke the curse, they'd been together ever since. Watching Black Suit settle into the corner furthest away, Max thought he should thank Drummond for all the advice.

Better not. It'd go to Drummond's head.

A young gal, perky and pleasant took his order — chopped on a big bun. Fans whirred non-stop and the wonderful, tangy smell of barbeque blew through the air. Before Max could identify which Muddy Waters song played through the speakers, the young gal returned with his food. Fast and delicious.

Max lifted the sloppy sandwich to his mouth only to find that he had been focused on the wrong man the whole time. An elderly man — snowy hair, bent body, walking with a rubber-tipped wooden cane — wove his way through the crowd until he reached Max's table. He plopped down, smiled wide enough to revcal a few missing teeth, and took one of Max's fries.

"Hey, that's mine."

"Oh, you can spare one." The old man sounded stronger than Max had expected, but he continually looked around and fiddled with the seams of his pants. A deep scar traced his jawline, and the lobe of his left ear had been cut off long ago.

"Do you want something?"

Pushing his thick glasses up his crooked nose, the man nodded. "I want to hire you."

"This is my lunch. I'll be back in my office in about —"

"I can't go there. I won't."

Max set down his sandwich and picked up a napkin. "You won't go to my office?"

"And we can't talk here. Not in detail. It's too dangerous."

"You're really not enticing me here, Mister, um?"

"Joshua Leed. Sorry. I should have told you my name from the start." He leaned on his elbow but kept his wrinkled face positioned to observe the crowd. "All I ask is that you come out to my house and meet me, hear my case, and that's it. You don't have to help me after that, if you don't want."

"I don't do house calls. It's not really a smart practice in my line of work."

"Of course, of course. Paranormal investigations can be location sensitive, but I assure you —"

"Paranormal? What is it you think —"

"Please, Mr. Porter, no need for that. I sought you out specifically because of your unique talents. After all, not everyone can see ghosts."

"Lower your voice." Max leaned in now, close enough to smell Joshua's heavy scent — some odd combination of herbs and spices as if he were a chef. "I only see ghost — as in singular, as in one."

"That may be, but your wife sees the rest."

"What the hell do you want?"

"Come to my house. That's all I ask. The longer I spend out in the open, the more at risk I am — we all are. Please. My house is in Thomasville — thirty, forty minutes from here. It's the only place that's safe. I'll explain everything else there."

Max shook his head. "Whatever you heard about me is old news. I'm not your man."

"People with gifts like yours don't suddenly lose them. It doesn't work that way. Or were you referring to the stories about how desperate you are for work? That is old news. I suppose all your money troubles have vanished now that you're on the leash of the Hull family."

So much for an enjoyable, peaceful meal. "I think you better leave."

"I'm sorry. I meant no offense. But it's no big secret. There are only three prominent families in this city — Hanes, Reynolds, and Hull. Not much dealing with them can be kept quiet for long. And while underwear and tobacco can be dangerous businesses, they're nothing compared to a family willing to deal with the supernatural. Since that's the same subject I deal with, it shouldn't be so odd that I would learn about you and your unique relationship with the Hull family."

Calling his relationship *unique* was like calling Jeffrey Dahmer's victims *dinner guests*. In fact, if not for a copy of the Hull family journal that would be made public should anything happen to him or Sandra, Max knew the Hulls would have disposed of him long ago. That leverage weakened considerably when the Hulls covered up a series of deaths that surrounded a recent case. Terrance Hull, the supposed family head, made it quite clear that Max, Sandra, and Drummond had no choice but to work for the Hulls. To refuse meant the police would take a sudden interest in those deaths, and Max had no doubt they would find "evidence" that linked him to murders he never committed.

On the positive side, Hull paid Max a hefty sum as a retainer which enabled him to be far more picky about what jobs he agreed to take on. "Mr. Leed, your information is wrong. I'm not interested in going to your house, and I'm not interested in your case."

The old man covered his mouth with his fist. "You've got to," he muttered. "If you don't, she's going to kill me."

"If someone's trying to kill you, you should be talking with the police."

"I doubt the police would take seriously an old man claiming that a ghost was going to kill him."

Rubbing the back of his neck to ward off a headache, Max said, "I'm sorry I can't help you. Perhaps you can —"

"Drummond."

"What?"

"Marshall Drummond was a friend of mine."

"And you didn't think it worth mentioning this before?"

"I don't want him to know about any of this. He can't know we've spoken, he can't visit my house, and if you agree to help me, he cannot, absolutely cannot, know that I've hired you."

Max hated to admit it but mentioning his partner had intrigued him. He knew so little about the ghost he worked with. To find someone who actually knew him, a friend no less and alive, that seemed like too much of an opportunity to turn away.

"Okay, Mr. Leed. I'll meet you at your house."

"Tonight. Meet me tonight, eight o'clock."

"Fine. Give me your address and I'll be there."

"And no Drummond. Whatever you do, do not bring Drummond."

"You have my word."

Leed stared into Max's eyes, searched his face, and finally nodded. "Thank you, Mr. Porter. I promise you won't regret this."

"I'd like to get back to my lunch now."

"Of course." He handed over a business card with a handwritten address on the back. Stealing one more fry, the old man shuffled his creaky body out of the restaurant.

Max watched him leave, and as he passed the far corner, Max caught sight of Black Suit. Of all the people in the packed room, Black Suit's eyes followed Joshua Leed out the door. Once Leed had left, Black Suit tapped away on a smartphone.

Max reached for his sandwich but put it back down. He had lost his appetite. Could this old man truly have known Drummond? The age looked about right. If Leed had been around twenty years old in 1940, then he'd be near his mid-nineties now. He certainly looked spry for ninety-something, but that didn't mean he was lying. Besides, if he were knowledgeable about ghosts and such, then being a youthful ninety wasn't absurd. Max had once met a man in his two hundreds, so he knew magic could be powerful enough to back Leed's story.

He glanced at the card in his hand. It read:

PARANORMAL INVESTIGATIONS
AND REMOVAL
JOSHUA LEED

Max sighed. "I'm going to regret this."

Chapter 2

MAX DIDN'T KNOW WHAT to make of Joshua Leed, but he decided to play along regarding Drummond until he had more information. Experience, however, had taught Max the dangers of going into a situation alone. So he called Sandra and asked her to meet him at his favorite haunt on Wake Forest University's campus — the Z. Smith Reynolds library. Not only did he love the library as a researcher, his true profession, but he loved it because he knew Drummond wouldn't follow Sandra there. That ghost hated libraries and research and books in general.

"Sure I've read some good stories," Drummond had said once. "Zane Gray and the like, but my real life was filled with enough adventure, and frankly, my post-life has had a good share of excitement, too. I don't need a book for thrills. I got memories for that."

When Sandra entered the library's lobby, Max's mind flooded with memories of his own. He remembered a summer afternoon picnic in a park when he first kissed her. He saw them on their first vacation as a couple when they barely left the hotel room. Then he recalled their first vacation as a married couple when they also barely left the hotel room. But mostly, he saw how beautiful Sandra was. They were getting older now, gray hairs had started to sprout, and the beginnings of wrinkles had formed, and yet, Sandra's beauty had grown too. Her dark hair and curvy body still drove him crazy, but that craziness had matured. When he looked at her in the past, he saw a vibrant, sexy young woman. As she walked toward him in the library, he saw a vibrant, sexy angel — a woman who held more than his heart in her hands. She had his very soul.

"You okay?" she asked as she approached.

"Just admiring the view."

She smiled, and he wanted nothing more than to kiss that gorgeous mouth. So he did.

"As much as I like your attention," she said, wrapping her arms around his neck, "I know you didn't ask me to come all the way out here for a kiss."

"Sadly, no. I've got to meet a potential client, and I don't want to go in alone."

Sandra cocked her head to the side. "You don't want Drummond?"

"I was specifically instructed not to bring him along."

Sandra's eyes widened. "That's odd."

"I know. We've got some time before we need to head out, so I thought this would be a good place to fill you in."

"No way Drummond'll come here."

Max laced his fingers between hers, loving the fact that she understood him so well, and he led her to a quiet table. As he told her the story of Joshua Leed and ignored her jibes at him sneaking off to Little Richard's, he never mentioned the man in the black suit. He didn't withhold the information consciously — not at first — but when he noticed the absence of this detail, he decided to trust his instincts and keep quiet about the man. What could he really say? He'd tell Sandra that Black Suit had followed him all morning, and she would bombard him with questions he couldn't answer. He had the same questions — anyone would — so what good would come of worrying her over something so unknown? Better to wait until he had something concrete to say. Besides, it was possible that it had all been coincidence.

With several hours to kill before they could head out, Max and Sandra drove to Hanes Mall and picked up a few things they had been needing for their house. Well, Max didn't think they *needed* any of it, but Sandra insisted that the throw pillows, organizational baskets, and new bedsheets were essential to fixing up their home. Though Max rolled his eyes, he never put up much of a fight. They had spent so many years struggling simply to put food on the table that part of him enjoyed seeing her splurge a little. After a bit more shopping, dodging an early evening rainstorm, and a quick dinner, they drove off for Thomasville.

It turned out there was no direct way to get from Winston-Salem to Thomasville. The major highways, 40 and 85, never reached close enough to be convenient. Looking online at a map, Max saw that with a direct road, the drive should have taken fifteen minutes, but the circuitous route required an additional twenty. Add in being stuck behind an old lady driving an even older Cadillac and the trip took three quarters of an hour.

Thomasville was a true small town. Formerly full of vigor, still clinging to the old glory days. It had only one claim to fame — furniture. Though the town produced far less handcrafted furniture than it had in its lucrative past, it still operated as a main destination for furniture buyers both corporate and individual. Where most towns would garner their main drag with a statue of some important local figure, Thomasville built an enormous chair — something Paul Bunyan would find comfortable.

Further from downtown, Thomasville became a series of large and small farms dotted with the occasional housing development. Joshua Leed lived in a small house on a wide fifteen acres. Other than the half-acre mowed around the farmhouse and a dilapidated barn, the rest of Leed's property grew wild.

A two-story farmhouse, squarish with a wraparound porch, looked rather new — built in the last five years or so — unless it was an old house that had been refurbished on the outside. Max didn't know enough about houses to tell. All he could say was the place looked comfortable, charming even. That was until he saw the inside.

Before they had a chance to turn the car engine off, Joshua Leed flicked on the porch lights and beckoned them in. Max and Sandra hurried, and both of them gasped at the sight. Leed converted what appeared to have been a lovely interior with old-style wallpaper and carefully chosen window treatments into a demented man's sanctuary.

Archaic symbols lined the walls like an insane graffiti artist had been let loose. Pages from equally archaic books outlined the windows. In the corners of each room, thick white candles burned, giving off the unpleasant odor of ripe fish. Salt lined every possible entrance into the house.

"Careful," Leed said so Max would step over the salt and not disturb it.

Max put a hand on his wife's shoulder. "This is my wife —"

"Sandra. Yes, I know. Pleasure to meet you."

Sandra shook Leed's hand as she continued to look around.

Leed followed her gaze. "Do you see any ghosts in here? I've tried my best to keep them out."

"Looks like you've done a good job."

He smiled — but his lips still trembled. "Can I get you anything to drink? Are you hungry?"

"Let's just get right into it," Max said.

"Of course, of course. Please, come in the living room and have a seat. You didn't bring Drummond along, did you?"

"He's not here. Even if he was, I'm guessing he couldn't get inside."

Leed scanned over the wards and spells he had written on the walls before double-checking the lines of salt. "Okay." He led them into the living room, a sparse area with a gray couch and a wooden rocking chair. Lowering into the chair, his joints popped like a string of firecrackers. He closed his eyes. "I can still see Drummond the day I met him."

"When was that?" Sandra asked.

"September 1938. Had I known that in a year Hitler would launch World War II and a few years after that I'd be turning into a human popsicle while fighting off the Bulge, well, I may not have risked so much earlier." He glanced at Max. "We both know that's not true. Risk or no risk, once the veil of the world has been pulled away, you can never truly go back. You sure you don't want a snack?"

"We're sure," Max said. "Please, tell us what's going on."

"Yes, yes. Let's see ... when I was fifteen, my family lived on a farm up in Virginia. I went to school during the day and helped with chores through the mornings and evenings. One day, I came home from school, ready to go milk the cows and whatnot, when I smelled something had died. It's a distinct, foul odor, and once you've experienced it, you'll never forget. Well, I followed the scent into the house and there they were. My mother and father, on the floor, covered in blood."

Sandra placed a hand on Leed's knee. "I'm so sorry."

"It's not something you really ever get over. I was a wreck for a long time. But eventually I began to breathe again, to attempt to live, and when I was around seventeen, I met Dr. Matthew Ernest — a man who changed my life forever. He called himself a witch hunter, and he told me that my parents had been slain as part of a terrible coven ritual. Black magic. That sort of thing. It may sound silly, but for a distraught seventeen-year-old, these words held sway. Dr. Ernest gave me reasons for what had always been meaningless. He made sense to me. And more importantly, he gave me a target for revenge."

Leed's formed a fist with one hand. "I'm not proud that this was my motivation for joining Dr. Ernest, but I can't change things. I became his assistant, traveling, never staying the same place for long, helping him track down any witches we learned about. All the time, though, I kept my eyes and ears wide open, hoping to find a clue that would lead me to the coven that killed my parents.

"And then, one day, without expectations for the day to be different in any way, we found a young lady who wanted to escape her coven — the same coven that I had sought. She needed our help. Dr. Ernest tried to prepare me, tried to see that I would have the proper priorities. Well, you can imagine. It didn't go well. We captured two of the witches, but the rest got away." Leed grew silent, his eyes looking far away, his fingers absently rubbing the nicked part of his earlobe. "Ugly things happened, but I don't believe those details are important to recall for you. Suffice it to say that I had my revenge. Only as in most cases of vengeance, little relief came. I couldn't bring my parents back no matter how much pain I inflicted on those responsible, and I ended up losing part of myself every time I hurt my prisoners."

Max settled deeper into the couch. "I'm guessing the coven witches that escaped found their way down to Winston-Salem."

"Patience. I'll get there."

"Forgive my husband," Sandra said, still patting Leed's knee. "He can get a bit enthusiastic."

"Good. We'll need that kind of passion. But I'm an old man, so I don't move as fast — even in my storytelling. Seems backwards, doesn't it? Seems that with so little time left to live, I should be doing everything faster. Try to get as much crammed in as I can. But that's the way of it."

"Mr. Leed? The coven?"

"Right, right. Now, Dr. Ernest and I spent months tracking the coven. We picked off a few more members during our search but eventually we discovered the majority had slipped into North Carolina. See, we had developed a contact in the warehouse at the Sears & Roebuck Company. He carried a list of supplies that Dr. Ernest devised. It contained the kinds of practical things a coven required but wouldn't want to order in bulk locally in case it aroused suspicion — candles, salt, that kind of thing. If that list was ever ordered together and in large quantities, our man would call and give us the address. I don't think he ever knew why that list was important. And that call eventually happened, leading us to Winston-Salem."

"How did you end up meeting Drummond?" Max asked.

Sandra backhanded his chest. "Let the man speak."

"You have to understand," Leed continued, "Back at that time there weren't many witch hunters around. In fact, most people thought we were nuts. So word spread fast about new people who fought against these evil beasts — at least it spread fast amongst us. It didn't take long to learn of Drummond.

"That day we walked into his office, I knew we had found a man who could really help. So many times, we met crazies who thought cultists were raising Satan in their backyards or scientists who wanted to capture witches for study or overly prepared but intellectually under-qualified warriors. Drummond, on the other hand, stood out as a capable man of action. The kind of man who thought through an immediate problem without causing the mess to fall back on his men. One who understood the necessity of destroying these abominations without falling prey to sympathies because of the enemy's human appearance."

Sandra frowned. "You don't think witches are human?"

"What kind of human would do the things they did to my mother and father? No, I think they gave up that right when they started meddling in magic."

Max saw the strained tendons in Sandra's neck. She teetered on the edge of letting Leed know how wrong he was, but Max's simple touch on her shoulder brought her back. She glanced at Max with an embarrassed grin and settled into the couch, nestling closer to him as they listened to the rest.

"Drummond didn't want anything to do with us. He thought we were the very kind of crackpots we had avoided from the start. But we gave him two names and what information we had, and we left. Before dinner that same day, he contacted us. As we knew he would, he checked out our story and now he believed there was something worth looking into. And boy did he ever.

"I don't know how he pulled it off, but in less than a week, he identified where the witches were staying, what false names they were using, what jobs they held, everything. From there learned the names of the other coveners, and we were set to curse them, to destroy the whole coven in one night."

"Curse them?" Sandra said. "Is that part of your vengeance? I mean, wouldn't it be easier to simply kill them?"

"True witch covens are extremely powerful. They bind and accentuate the energies of all the witches within the coven. Killing one only turns it into a ghost which can continue to feed the coven with its energy. But we knew of a curse that if done properly would break the power of the coven and lock the witches in their dead bodies, preventing them from roaming around as ghosts. It was a difficult spell to cast and required all six key witches in the coven to be killed on the same night.

"In order to protect ourselves and to insure that the coven did not reform or break the curse, we divide the killings amongst the three of us. Each man took two names from a hat. We agreed on the night that the curse would take place and made sure we each understood what was required. Finally, and most important, none of us would know where the others buried their witches. This way, should something go wrong, we were protected from each other. The planned night arrived, and we did what had to be done. And I truly thought it was all over."

"I don't think I'm going to like this next part," Max said.

Leed licked his lips and arched his head back. "It's been quiet all these years, yet something inside me always niggled at the idea that it might not be done. Then yesterday morning I saw this." With his cane, Leed pointed to a newspaper on the coffee table.

Max picked it up and saw a circled article headlined: PROFESSOR OF CULTS MURDERED. "This is Dr. Ernest?"

"Oh, yes. You can take that with you. Read it in detail. For now, believe me when I say that all the signs are there — this murder was an act of rage and revenge and the first step into freeing the full power of the coven. If you look close, read between the lines, you'll see that Dr. Ernest was murdered by a ghost, and the only ghosts in Winston-Salem that would want to harm him belong to the coven."

"But you said the curse prevented —"

"Obviously, somebody found a way to break our curse, didn't they?"

"And with Dr. Ernest's coven ghosts released, you think they murdered him."

"They'll be coming for me soon enough."

"To kill you for revenge?"

"Eventually. But first they'll torture me to find out where I buried their sisters. And if a ghost can kill another ghost, they'll go after Drummond, too."

"Then why all the secrecy from Drummond? If he was the one who helped you down here to begin with, shouldn't we warn him, maybe even elicit his help?"

Leed turned an incredulous eye toward Sandra. "Have you not taught him anything about ghosts?"

"What now?"

Sandra faced her husband. "I think he's referring to the idea that some ghosts can turn."

"Turn?"

With a frustrated huff, Leed said, "Just because Drummond resembles a human being, he's not. He's a ghost. And ghosts have their own set of rules. Supposedly, if you put them in highly stressful situations, ones that make them face their ghostly existence, and keep that pressure on long enough, they can turn into nasty, evil spirits."

"And this could happen to Drummond?"

"It can happen to any ghost. So, we can't trust him."

Max nodded — not because he agreed with Leed but rather because he could tell they had reached the crux of the whole story. "What exactly is it you want us to do?"

Wagging his index finger as if Max were an astute scholar, Leed said, "The witches are in an unusual state at the moment. They are not resting in their graves like dead people nor are they wandering like most ghosts. They've neither moved on nor stayed behind. They are no longer cursed yet they are not free of the curse either. Since at least one of Dr. Ernest's graves has been disturbed, the only thing left for us to do is release the other corpses with a spell that should move them on to the next world while preventing them from rejoining their coven."

"Why didn't you use that spell to begin with?"

"I didn't know it back then. And by the time I learned, I had no way of using it. Dr. Ernest might have been able to be convinced to divulge his burial locations, but Marshall Drummond had been killed. Where he buried his witches is something I still don't know."

"Ah," Max said, getting to his feet. "You want us to find out Drummond's burial locations."

"Exactly. Find the burial locations and perform the spell. Otherwise, we'll have unleashed a powerful coven that will haunt Winston-Salem for centuries to come."

"Mr. Leed, I've done as you've asked. I've heard you out."

"And you'll take this case?"

"I'll look into it. See what I can find to back up your story."

Deflated, Leed put out his hand. "Of course. I shouldn't have expected more." As Max shook his hand, Leed gripped tight and yanked him close. "Just remember — under no circumstances can Drummond know what we're doing. I've dealt with evil spirits before. A ghost like Drummond becoming such a thing, losing all sense of right and wrong, would be catastrophic."

"Don't worry. We won't tell him." Max freed his hand from the old man, grabbed the newspaper, and headed to the door.

Chapter 3

THE FOLLOWING MORNING, when Max thumped downstairs and shambled into the kitchen, a fragrant pot of coffee greeted him. He had slept little that night, his mind replaying the odd meeting with Leed hour after hour, which resulted in becoming intimately familiar with the textural variations along his ceiling. Sandra sat at their table eating over-easy eggs as she read over the newspaper article they had acquired from Leed.

With a piece of toast in her hand, she gestured to the coffee pot. "Not even a half-hour old."

"It could be ice cold, and I'd drink it."

"I didn't think you slept well. Leed get to you?"

Max nodded and poured the coffee into a mug that declared him to be a *#1 Husband!* "The thing that bothers me the most is that I don't doubt him at all. I'll check up on his story, but I have a feeling that Drummond was involved with him and this whole witch coven thing. And it all got me thinking how little we really know about Drummond."

"Don't do that. I know that look."

"What?"

"You're thinking about researching Drummond."

"So?"

"Honey, you do not want to go researching friends. It'll only lead to trouble. You know better. Real friendship is built on trust, and Drummond is a man —"

"Ghost."

"Fine, Drummond is a ghost that you need to trust. Think about the things we've faced with him already. We would never have survived half of it if we couldn't have trusted him."

Max sipped his coffee, wincing as he burned his tongue. "Okay, okay. I'll stick to Joshua Leed. But if I look into him, I'm going to find out things about Drummond by default. He's part of this."

"That's different. That's pursuing a case. Just don't go checking up on a friend."

Bending over the kitchen table, Max kissed his wife's forehead. "My guiding light to what is right. I'll stick to the case."

"Good." She turned her head up and puckered until Max kissed her lips. "How do you want to go about this?"

"I think I'll start with a shower."

"Good idea. You stink."

Max grinned. "Thank you."

"What's a wife for, if not to save you from embarrassing yourself in public?"

"My fragile ego and I are grateful. So, I'm going to clean up and go to the library at Wake. Find out what I can on this witch coven, see if it supports Leed's story. I think it will, but I've got to be sure."

"What can I do?"

Max rubbed Sandra's shoulders and cringed inwardly at what he planned to say. "I need you to spend the day watching Drummond."

"You want me to babysit the ghost?"

"I haven't been in the office since yesterday morning. That in itself shouldn't be too strange, but you know he still gets gut feelings, even if doesn't have a gut anymore. He might grow suspicious. If he breaks habit and risks going to a library to check up on me, I need you to call me, warn me."

"Is that why I'm getting a shoulder massage this morning?"

"I never said I was above bribery."

Sandra stood and faced Max with a devilish twinkle in her eye. "If you want me to spend my whole day with a ghost who loves hitting on me while reminiscing about his glory days, you'll have to do a lot better than that."

"What did you have in mind?"

She kissed Max hard. "Meet me upstairs. And remember, this one's all for me."

"All for you, my dear. All for you."

Not surprisingly, Max had no trouble finding information about witches. Between the Internet and the library, he had more sources than he could possibly consume in a lifetime. But as he narrowed his search, first to North American witches, then to North Carolina witches, then to North Carolina witch covens, he found what he needed.

Like vampires, some form of witch existed in nearly every culture going back well before written history. In the modern world though, witches appeared to break down into two major groups.

The first focused on witchcraft as a religion of nature. Wicca was the major label, and they bore little resemblance to the witches of yore. These were kind, peaceful groups that aligned more with the Native American sensibility of the natural world as a living, breathing godly spirit than they did with spellcasters attempting to manipulate the world around them in some pact with evil.

The second group consisted of those who relished in the tales of old. Those that believed they could control others and tap into mystical powers. They were attracted to the darker elements of the lore and put on a pedestal people like Isobel Gowdie, a Scottish woman who, in 1662, confessed to being a witch and detailed out the practices of witches, first coining the term coven. Gowdie claimed to be able to metamorphose into various animals and gave specific instructions on how she accomplished this. Most modern non-believers considered her confession little more than the ravings of an extreme psychosis, but many practicing witches praised Gowdie as a bold martyr.

While the details of Max's research found much in conflict (one group thought their power derived from the moon, another focused on the healing properties within the Earth, and some groups took a modern bent on the whole thing — such as a motorcycle gang in England replacing witches' brooms with 500cc bikes), there were a few consistent aspects to all witch covens. They held the number thirteen sacred, and many covens limited membership to thirteen people. Members commonly called themselves Coveners and the leader usually took the title High Priestess or High Priest. Most interestingly, all covens produced a book called the Grimoire which detailed that group's specific rules, members, and rituals.

"You're all forgetting one group," Max said to the books he read. This group of witches he knew too well — the real witches. The people who controlled true magical power. They could curse a ghost or raise a spirit. Relieve a pain or cause a heartache. They had tapped into the true powers of the universe and knew how to wield them. He had met one amateur, Melinda Corkille, and one bona-fide witch, Dr. Connor, but that had been enough.

He had no doubt that Dr. Ernest, Joshua Leed, and Drummond

believed the six women they killed and cursed were the remaining members of a powerful witch coven. The question Max had — what kind of witchcraft did they belong to? If they were a true coven, they would have had a Grimoire. And if they were amongst that third, unspoken category, then that Grimoire would be a dangerous book to get hold of. But Dr. Ernest and Leed must have done just that — how else would they have managed to identify and track the six down to North Carolina? Max found the story of knowing a guy at Sears & Roebuck on the lookout for bulk candle orders a bit much to swallow.

He pulled up the browser on his laptop and stared at the keyboard. He wanted to type in the names — Ernest, Leed, and Drummond — but he kept hearing Sandra in the back of his head. He closed the laptop and rubbed his face.

He would find another way. He jotted down a few reminders of things he wanted to ask Leed, particularly about the Grimoire and the names of the witches they had killed. If he could locate an article about a missing girl with the same name from the week after they cursed the coven, that alone would make him feel better about Leed. Yet even as he wrote his notes, he had to shake his head. Whether he had intended to or not, his mind already acted as if he had taken on the case.

"Of course I'm taking this on. Drummond's involved."

As he looked up from his notebook, he caught sight of man sitting at a cubicle in the back corner — his old friend, Black Suit. Too tired to play the cloak and dagger game any longer, Max got up and strode right to the corner. To Black Suit's credit, he didn't attempt to escape. He waited as Max approached, set his jaw and crossed his arms.

"What is it you want?" Max asked in a low, bored tone. He had learned this technique from Drummond — under the right circumstance, affecting a nonchalant manner threatened far more than a dangerous tone. He hoped this was the right circumstance.

"You're a very interesting man, Mr. Porter." Black Suit had a smooth, easy voice — nonchalant even. Max felt a chill across his skin.

"Okay, so you know my name. Do I get yours?"

Black Suit stood and reached into his jacket pocket. For an instant, Max thought he might pull a gun, but before Max could react, Black Suit produced a business card. Max glanced at it:

PETER STEVENSON
SPECIAL AGENT
FEDERAL BUREAU OF INVESTIGATIONS

Max curled his mouth. "I'm supposed to believe this from a business card?"

Stevenson glanced around as he pulled out a black leather ID holder. He flashed his official FBI identity badge. "Good enough?"

Max's gut twisted, and he thanked all things holy that he had declined breakfast that morning. "What does the FBI want with me?"

"Just to talk."

"Then why not come to my office, flash a badge, and talk? Why follow me around?"

"Had to make sure you were the right man to talk to."

"Well, you're still following me, so am I?"

"I think so. But others aren't so sure, and since I don't work in a small group like you, getting decisions made sometimes takes time."

"Am I going to be under arrest or something?" Max asked, the words choking in his throat.

"What for?"

"I don't know. You're the one following me."

Stevenson smirked, and Max wanted both to slap the man and run at the same time. "Relax, Mr. Porter. I told you we only want to talk."

"Fine. Talk."

"Not now. But I'll be in touch soon." Stevenson patted Max's shoulder as he walked away.

Max fell into the nearest chair and said nothing — breathing felt like enough of an accomplishment. He couldn't believe he had managed to say half of what came out of his mouth. It was one thing standing up to the Hulls or taking any of the gambles the world had placed before him, but to talk like he did to the FBI. Yet he did. An odd pride warmed his chest. He had used all he had learned recently in order to maintain his self-control and stand his ground.

"Max, you done okay," he said.

But patting himself on the back only went so far. It didn't change the fact that the FBI had taken an interest in him. He thought over all that had happened since he and Sandra first arrived in Winston-Salem. He had seen magic and ghosts, but unless Fox Mulder was based on a real man, he didn't think the FBI investigated such things. Max had witnessed real criminals and real crimes, though, and those the FBI might be quite interested in. Although his own involvement had been minimal, perhaps the FBI thought they could lean on him hard enough to turn him into a good snitch. Or a patsy. Whatever their interest, he had no doubt it would be bad for him.

His cellphone chirped, jolting him from his chair. His knee slammed into a desk and his heart hammered away in his chest. He glanced at the phone's screen — Sandra.

"Hi, hon."

"You sound funny," Sandra said.

"I just might never walk again thanks to your call."

"As long as it's nothing serious."

"Nah. Walking's overrated. What's up?"

"We just got a strange call that you're not going to like."

Max's stomach churned again. "Tell me."

"Mr. Modesto is on his way to the office. He wants to see you immediately."

Modesto. Terrance Hull's former right-hand man. The one who once handled all the distasteful work that spewed out of that family. Max didn't know Modesto's standing in the family anymore, but based on their last meeting, it had significantly improved. One thing was sure — this wasn't going to be a pleasant, social call.

With a sigh, Max said, "I'm on my way."

Chapter 4

BEFORE MAX HAD STEPPED foot in his office building, Drummond appeared next to him. Wearing the long overcoat and Fedora he had died in, Drummond always looked like a faded picture from the days of World War II. None of the pedestrians on the sidewalk noticed him.

"What in Sam Hill have you been researching all this time that you couldn't come back to the office for a little?" Though Drummond had a tough guy voice, he could whine with the best — spending five cursed decades stuck in one place can do that.

They walked by the empty storefront that once housed Decon Arts — an art gallery that had caused them plenty of trouble in the past. Max peeked in the window and noticed that the back door was ajar. He wondered if they would be having a new tenant soon.

"You see something in there?" Drummond asked, his icy presence freezing Max's shoulder.

I should've met Modesto at a restaurant. While any restaurant convenient to reach would be well within Drummond's range — a ghost could go pretty much anywhere within a wide radius around the point of death — the old ghost avoided certain locations because they reminded him of the things he could no longer indulge in. Drummond loved cigarettes, alcohol, and women. Possibly in that order. Food never ranked high on the indulgence list, but it still made the list. As a result, Max knew Drummond wouldn't bother him at a restaurant unless a dire situation arose. *Too late now.* Modesto might already be waiting.

As they entered the side stairwell that led above the store and to his office, Max said nothing. He didn't need the neighbors seeing him having an argument with empty space. When they reached the third floor, an apartment door opened. No surprise. The crusty old lady living there seemed to camp out right by the door, waiting for any sound of life passing by. She took one look at Max, squinted her eyes at him and scowled.

Drummond snorted — well, he made a snorting sound. Max didn't know if a ghost could truly snort. "I ought to go in there and give that old bat a scare."

Max opened the door to his office and shook his head. "That's all we need. Police investigating a woman dying from fright."

After a kiss from Sandra, Max settled behind the huge oak desk that made up the centerpiece of his office. It had been Drummond's office first and contained all the original furnishing — big desk, built-in bookshelves, small tiled bathroom off to the side. They had put in another desk for Sandra and a small half-fridge for sodas, leftovers, and the occasional bagged lunch, but otherwise, it all remained the same.

"You still haven't told me what's going on. What's been so important that I've been sitting around with your wife all day?" Drummond floated over to Sandra and winked. "Not that I'm complaining. This gal is one of the best women I've ever had the pleasure —"

"You've never had the pleasure," Sandra said with a sly smile. "And you never will."

Max glanced at his watch — 10:30 am. "You called me right after Modesto called?"

"Yup. He should be here any minute."

Drummond perked up even as he shot a frown at Sandra. "You never tell me anything. So, Modesto called? What's he want?"

"That's what I'm here to find out," Max said.

"Oh, I see. If Modesto calls, Max drops everything and comes running."

"He's the face of the Hulls for us, and the Hulls are the ones paying our bills. Would you rather they throw us out of here and curse you again?"

"They wouldn't dare. Not with you holding that journal over them. Anything happens to any of us, and all their dirty secrets will be made public — it'd be the end of that family's power." Drummond poked his head through the outside wall. "Looks like he's here."

"Okay, you two," Max said. "Not a word. Just let Modesto say his piece and leave. I don't want him here any longer than necessary."

"Listen to you," Drummond said as he returned fully into the office. "I think I'm starting to have a positive influence on you."

Before Max could respond, they heard the steady thump of a heavy foot on the stairs. Modesto paused, perhaps considering whether or not to knock, and finally opened the door to enter. As usual, he wore a well-tailored suit and kept his appearance equally well-tailored. He was a tall man who looked rather bookish, but Max knew better. Modesto was the perfect man for his job — the kind of man who would do anything for his boss, no matter how distasteful, because he did the job for more than mere financial gain. He believed in his boss with a religious fervor, and that made him dangerous.

"Mr. Porter," he said in his clipped, exacting manner. "So good of you to be here as requested."

"Of course, I'd be here. I honor my commitments. I've got to say though that I was surprised by your call. Since hiring us on, the Hull family has yet to actually make use of us."

"Yes, well, your vacation comes to an end today. Our employer has a task that requires your unique talents. Or perhaps I should say the unique talents of your wife." Modesto glanced at the empty spaces around the office. "And others."

Drummond took a spin around Modesto's head. "I think he means me. Can I poke him a little? Give him a chill?"

Max could see Sandra biting back her laughter, and a smile crept on the edges of his own mouth. "Look," he said to Modesto, "I know you don't want to be here, so spit it out and let's get out of each other's hair."

"Eloquent as ever, Mr. Porter."

Drummond swiped his hand across Modesto's shoulder. "I hate this prick."

Modesto shivered and snatched a peek over his shoulder. "Our employer wants you to locate an object — a handbell — that is quite important to the Hull family."

"A handbell?" Max looked to Sandra, and she shrugged.

"An old family heirloom which was lost long ago. Mr. Hull has decided —"

"Which Mr. Hull? Is Terrance running the family business now or is it still William? Or didn't old William die?"

Modesto paused, his cheek twitching. "If our employer wants you to know the particulars of his family structure, than our employer will see that you receive such information."

"Must be Terrance, then. If William were still in charge, he'd want everyone to know it. Kind of a virility thing, I guess." Max propped his feet onto the desk.

"Regardless of what you think, Mr. William Hull is still quite active and fully cognizant despite his age."

"In other words, Terrance is in charge."

Drummond brought his hands together in one sharp clap. "O-ho, Max, you got him on the ropes now. He's already saying more than he likes to. Now, keep it up. Get him to reveal something more, anything at all."

"Is it Terrance, then, that wants this object — this handbell?"

"It doesn't matter who sent you this order. You are to fulfill your contractual obligation. The Hulls are spending a considerable amount of effort reclaiming the pieces of their heritage which have been lost over the years. You are on retainer for this very purpose. Find the bell and bring it to me. It's that simple."

"I doubt it's that simple."

"I don't really care what you think. I am only here because I have been ordered to do so. Your success or failure means nothing to me."

Max doubted that, too. Not because Modesto held any regard for Max's well-being, but rather because Modesto would want anything the Hulls attempted to succeed. If dealing with Max was the burden for that success, then Modesto would do it gladly — even if he acted like it might kill him.

"Now that we know where you stand on this," Max said, "how about sharing some pertinent information?"

"What more do you want? I told you what you have to do."

With an exasperated huff, Sandra got to her feet and put both hands on her hips. "I swear, the two of you are children. Max, stop goading him. Just let him do his job. And you, Mr. Modesto, stop being a pain in our ass. You want us to find this bell, then you better start giving us what you know or I'll place a call to Terrance Hull myself and ask him why his errand boy is obstructing our progress."

Drummond turned to Max. "Why can't you be more like her? She's incredible."

Modesto blanched but quickly recomposed his controlled, cold demeanor. He circled the room once, his eyes roving over the furnishings as if he were an appraiser disappointed at what he saw. Finally, he turned on his heel and tapped his chin. "The bell is one of a baker's dozen — handcrafted, brass, and extremely rare. All the bells in the set are identical. The handle is painted white with a red stripe about halfway down. The outer rim of the bell has an ornate, geometric design carved along it and a rather flourished capital H marks the inside rim."

"How old are the bells?" Max asked.

"I don't know the exact age but they've been in the family for generations."

"When were they lost? How long ago?"

"At least a century."

Before Drummond could start yammering in Max's ear, Max sat up. "Why the sudden interest? Or has the family been looking for over a hundred years and still can't find this bell?"

"Honestly, I don't think anybody has bothered before to find it," Modesto said. Max never liked when people began a sentence with the word *Honestly*. It usually meant they were about to lie. "But Terrance Hull wants to restore his family to the great standing it held in the past. And having a complete set of these bells is a symbolic act in that direction. At least, that's how I interpret it. But neither you nor I need to have an opinion on these matters. You now have more than enough information to begin your search. I'll return soon for a full report."

Modesto gave one final look of distaste before turning to the door and walking out in his measured, clipped pace.

Drummond stuck his head outside the wall again. Once Modesto had left the building, he returned to the office. "That guy needs a stiff drink and a fine woman."

Sandra pulled a chair up to Max's desk and sat. "What do you think this is about?"

"Come on, Sugar," Drummond said, floating above the desk. "You heard the man. He let it slip — Terrance Hull has taken over the family, and he wants it to go back to its former glory. You know, the days when they took care of a pesky detective by bumping him off and cursing his ghost."

"You've got the *pesky* right."

Max said, "It's more than that. Remember what the witch Connor said to me the last time I saw her? She said the Hulls were trying to find three sacred objects in order to cast a spell that would resurrect Tucker Hull, their founding father. Tucker's journal, and Blackbeard's hair were the first two. This bell must be the third. That would explain why they want to find it all of the sudden."

"They've never been this close before."

As Drummond peered over the edge of the desk, his attention drawn to something on the floor, he muttered, "And bringing back Tucker would be the ultimate in restoring the family."

To Sandra, Max asked, "Can they really do this? Resurrect Tucker Hull?"

Sandra planted her elbows on the desk and her chin in her hands.

"Beats me. Just because I can see ghosts doesn't mean I know everything about the supernatural."

"Then I need you to find that out. I'll start searching for this bell." Max raised a hand to stop Sandra from protesting. "You know how the Hulls operate. They'll be watching us. If I don't put on a show of at least attempting to find this bell, we'll have a lot more to worry about. Besides, searching for it and finding it are two very different things. And they've been after this for a hundred years or so. I don't think they'll be too shocked if it takes me awhile."

"Okay." Sandra rose and headed for the door. "I'll see what I can learn about resurrection spells."

Max caught her eye and jutted his chin toward Drummond. She shook her head but Max flashed his puppy dog look. She nodded.

"Hey, Drummond," she said. "You want to come with me? It'll be more fun than watching Max read about handbells."

But Drummond did not answer. Max followed the ghost's gaze to the newspaper Joshua Leed had given him. It lay open on the floor next to Max's laptop. The headline of Dr. Ernest's murder seemed to grow bolder every second. Drummond looked from Sandra to Max, his brow locked in confusion.

"What's wrong?" Max asked, hearing the tremor in his own voice.

Drummond pointed Sandra back to her chair. To Max, he gestured toward the bookcase. "You might want a swig."

Max didn't have to ask. He had been thinking the same thing. He walked over to the bookcase and pulled out one of several false books Drummond had always stored. Inside was a silver flask filled with well-aged whiskey.

After Max sat and had poured a shot for Sandra and one for himself, Drummond began to pace the room. He clasped his hands behind his back. He took another glance at the newspaper and said, "We've got to talk."

Chapter 5

MAX AND SANDRA WAITED as Drummond drifted around the room — his version of pacing. Questions stampeded through Max's mind, but he kept quiet. The fact that Drummond caught sight of the newspaper did not incriminate Max directly. After all, Max could have bought the paper that morning, and it just happened to flip open to the page detailing Dr. Ernest's murder. There was no undeniable link between Max and any knowledge of Dr. Ernest. Of course, if Drummond thought about it for more than a second, he'd wonder why Max had a newspaper in the first place when Max had been a digital guy for years.

Then I have to make sure he doesn't think anymore. "Are you going to talk or did you simply want us to watch your ability to float around the room?"

Drummond shot Max a warning frown. "Have a little patience. This goes back a long time. I want to make sure I have the details right."

The details. Drummond had taught Max that when a suspect starts concentrating on the details, chances are that lies will being coming out soon enough. Max exhaled as softly as he could manage. If Drummond picked up on his relief, the old ghost might get suspicious.

"My apologics. Take your time."

To Max's pride, Sandra picked up on the situation as well. "Should we order food? If this is going to run all day into dinner, we'll want to make sure we get something delivered."

"Good idea, dear. You want Chinese or Indian tonight?"

"Okay, okay," Drummond snapped. "I didn't know you were in such a hurry." He gazed at the office door, the frosted glass showing its age with cracks from the corners and stains on the edges, and his face relaxed as if he were sailing back in time, seeing it all happen before his dead eyes.

"That man in the paper, the one that died — his name was Dr. Matthew Ernest. He was a young man when I knew him, and though I only knew him a short time, I've always felt close to him. Sort of like how soldiers become brothers under fire." He pointed to the door. "The day he came through there, I had been working the oddball angle for quite a while. Ghosts, curses, witches — if it had a hint of the unexplained, people found their way to my door."

So far Drummond had stuck to the truth, but Max did not expect it to last. One of the first techniques Drummond taught him — if you have to lie, mix it in with as much truth as you can. It'll make the lie sound real and will be far easier to remember down the line.

Drummond turned back to Max and Sandra. He licked his cold lips and shook his head. "Doc came from up north. Virginia had been his last stop, but he'd been making stops in Pennsylvania, New York, and Ohio. Maybe elsewhere, too. I don't recall. See, Doc was a paranormal investigator. Not that such things officially existed back then — I suppose they barely do now — but back then he had no school behind him."

"So he just called himself Doctor?" Sandra asked.

"I think he had a doctorate in English or History. Something useless like that. Doesn't matter because when it came to the supernatural stuff he was the best. He knew everything. Taught me quite a bit. In fact, had I known he was alive all these years, I would have tried everything I could to contact him, get him to come help me when I was cursed."

"Why didn't he? If he was here all along." Max regretted the question as it left his mouth.

Drummond moved over to the bookcase and studied the titles, but Max caught the pained expression that crossed the detective's face. At length, Drummond rose a foot higher and turned back around. This time, he had complete control over every aspect of his countenance.

"Dr. Matthew Ernest was one of those people, like the two of you, who learned that the world was filled with more than most would even believe. He saw ... well, when he was young, unpleasant things happened right before his eyes. From that point on, he studied all he could, prepared himself for when he was old enough to strike out on his own. When that day came, he waged war on all those creatures and those people who helped such creatures."

Sandra crossed her arms. "I've known those types. Some trauma sets them off, and they decide all things paranormal are cut the same, all things paranormal must be killed. You should be glad he never found out about you. He probably would have destroyed you before he ever considered freeing you from your curse."

"Probably." Drummond's far off gaze returned.

Max had to admit that if Drummond had been weaving lies into this narrative, he did so with extreme skill. Everything sounded authentic so far. But then Max reminded himself that the story had only begun.

"I don't know why I remember this but when Matt walked through the door, I was coming out of the bathroom. I think it's because of the look he gave me. He had this narrow face that somehow managed to widen when he saw the supernatural. I didn't know it at the time, but that was the look he was giving me. I've never been able to figure out if prognostication is real or just another myth that built up over the years, but now I wonder if maybe he knew — maybe he saw what would happen to me.

"Well, he told me he came down to North Carolina because of a possession case. Some nasty ghost had taken over this little boy, and he wanted to do something about it. At first I was going to kick him out of the office. When you're the only paranormal investigator in town, you end up seeing a lot of crackpots. You give it time. Once word gets out about us, we'll have the nutcases lining up. But something in the way he spoke, as if he were embarrassed to say the things he had to say, convinced me there might be something real going on."

"So, you helped him," Max said.

"I did. We got hold of a Catholic priest who didn't care too much for following Church protocol and had him perform an exorcism. That did the trick, boy was saved, and I thought that ended my time with Matt. But he knew of other cases in the South, and soon I was taking overnight trips to the coast, to South Carolina, Tennessee, Georgia, anywhere that I could get to within six hours or so. I don't know how he did it, but I got caught up in his urgency. I believed him when he said how we were doing more than just patching up the dam. That's how I saw myself. I was that kid with his finger in the dam, keeping the supernatural creatures from drowning the city, and here was this guy who said we could do more than plug up the hole. We could climb to the top and push the entire river back a few feet.

"It didn't work out that way. Ernest and I had a falling out, and he went elsewhere to continue his battle. And I continued mine. In my own way."

Max had to admit that he still had little idea what was a lie. Some of it was obvious — Drummond had not mentioned Joshua Leed or a witch coven, but perhaps that had not happened at first. It was conceivable that Dr. Ernest had met with Drummond years before he met Leed. He could have fought ghosts and witches and done exactly as Drummond had suggested. Later, Ernest teams up with Leed and when their coven goes to North Carolina, Ernest already knows the perfect contact to help them out. Of course, it could all be crap. Drummond could have made it all up to bury any information regarding Leed and the witch coven. Yet he seemed so genuinely saddened by the memory of Ernest. The only thing clear to Max — something bad had happened back then.

Sandra asked, "What caused you two to stop being partners?"

"It doesn't matter. The important thing to all of this, the reason I'm telling you anything, is that he was murdered."

"We can read the paper."

"Have you two learned nothing? Every article in the news is about more than the words tell. You have to read beyond the story."

Max glanced at the whiskey flask. So far he had no need for its contents. Something in Drummond's voice told him that was about to change. "Well, my first question then is why was he murdered?"

Sandra picked up the newspaper. "It says he was ninety-three. That's a strange age to be making enemies that want to kill you."

Drummond clapped his hands once and pointed at Sandra. "Unless your enemies are old, too."

"You think some pissed-off ghost killed him?"

Drummond hesitated. "The things that Matt faced, he destroyed. There wouldn't be any left to come after him."

"Then who?" Max asked.

Sandra rattled the pages in her hand. "It's all right here, hon." She winked at Drummond. "The article says that police were called to the scene when neighbors reported of loud screaming and gunfire."

"Ghosts don't use guns."

"Hurts too much," Drummond said.

Though Drummond could interact with the physical world, the longer and more complex the experience, the greater the pain. To load a gun, lift it, aim it, and depress the trigger would be a highly improbable task for a ghost. Besides which, Max reasoned, why go to all that trouble when ghosts had plenty of other means at their disposal. For a ghost willing to endure the sort of pain required to fire a gun, it might as well reach into its victim's chest and freeze his heart.

"So we're dealing with a person?"

"Maybe more than one." Drummond glanced at the newspaper. "Look at the photo. There are two bullet holes in the wall. One near the edge of the photo and one near the top — wild shots. This wasn't a planned murder. This was Matt being in the wrong place, wrong time."

"He was in his home."

"Wrong time then."

"You think this was a robbery gone wrong?"

Sandra shook her head. "Not if this photo is any indication of the rest of his house. He doesn't have much."

Drummond drifted toward the window and gazed outside. "I don't think this was a botched robbery. Not the kind you're talking about. I think this was a robbery for a very specific item."

"Well?" Max flipped his hands outward. "You going to make us guess?"

"Matt's notes. All of his cases, all of the ghosts and witches he fought, everything he ever did would be in a set of well-hidden notebooks. To anybody who sought to know and understand and even attempt to control this other realm, those notes would be invaluable. Somebody, or perhaps a family of somebodies, would certainly find those notebooks worth killing for."

"Wait. You mean the Hulls?"

"You don't find it suspicious that you never hear from them, and then suddenly when this highly valuable notebook comes into play, up pops Modesto with a time-consuming errand to sideline you? Come on. You've been in this game long enough to know that a coincidence like that ain't no coincidence at all. And what's worse, we're just finding out about all this. The Hulls have a few days on us. We've got to get moving."

"At what? We don't have a client. We don't have a real case. We don't even have evidence."

"That's why you and I have to go to the crime scene before it gets turned loose." Before Max or Sandra could object, Drummond swooped in between them. "That notebook is somewhere in Matt's house. They had that much right when they robbed him. I may not have seen Matt in decades, but I guarantee he would keep something that important close by. And since stuck-up Modesto visited with this excuse for research, we can guess that they still don't have the notebooks and need you busy so they can find them. Which means the notebooks are still at Matt's house." Sandra opened her mouth, but Drummond raised his hand and barreled onward. "For the moment, that house is sealed off as a crime scene. That won't last forever. The moment it's turned loose, you can bet anything that Hull will have paid somebody to go squat there until they find the notebooks. Heck, he might even just buy the house and search at his leisure." Max tried to interrupt, but Drummond raised his other hand. "Now the house has been sealed off for a while already. We don't have a lot of time until its turned loose. We need to go tonight. Get in that house while Hull can't easily get in there. If he sends someone to break in like we're going to do, if they get caught, it'll blow back right on the Hulls and that means payoffs and cover-up and all sorts of headaches. Why go to all that trouble when there's really only one guy they have to worry about getting a whiff of this? Why not just send that guy on a senseless research project? This is it. We have to go sneak in there tonight."

Nobody said a word. Drummond stayed quiet, watching for their reaction. Max and Sandra simply waited to make sure he was done.

Sandra broke the silence first. "You can't do this. It's crazy."

"Why?" Drummond asked. "It's not like we haven't broken into places before."

"Those weren't crime scenes. The police already have their eye on this place."

"Lucky for you two, you have a ghost to help out."

Sandra turned her sharp eyes onto her husband. "You just going to sit there?"

Max had not been paying close attention. He tried to place how this notebook and the Hull family and Modesto's research project all fit together. Drummond made a strong case, and while breaking in would be dangerous, it would be far more dangerous to let Hull get his hands on vital supernatural information.

Except Drummond had lied — by omission at the very least. Perhaps there was no notebook. Perhaps this was all a ruse so that Drummond could learn if the witch coven had been involved. If that were the case, then Max should simply tell Drummond about Leed and save themselves the risk of breaking into a crime scene. It would also mean that Modesto's research project was authentic which led to other questions Max didn't want to consider at the moment. Questions of Tucker Hull.

Max glanced up to see Sandra and Drummond staring at him with narrowed, fed-up eyes. Sandra's eyes spoke of Leed and danger and how they needed to figure out fact from fiction before taking any rash actions. Drummond's said that they were partners and that's all that mattered, that he had good reason to lie, that Max needed to trust the ghost that had saved his life in the past.

"I think I'll have that drink," Max said and attacked the whiskey flask. As the fiery liquid warmed his belly, a simple idea popped into his brain. He only hoped he could word it right to satisfy everybody. "If we're going to do this, we need to do it smart. Drummond, I want you to go scout ahead. We've got plenty of time until it'll be dark enough to do this. Go now. Go find out the lay of the house, figure out how I'm getting in, every detail you can think of. We need to get the notebook and get out as fast and safe as possible. Sandra, I need you to stay here and do paperwork."

Sandra's face burned red. "If you think —"

Max raised a hand only to have it swatted away. "Listen to me. This is all about appearances. You do the paperwork while I go to the library to start Modesto's research. You know how Modesto and Hull are — they'll be watching us. If we don't start working as usual, they'll get suspicious."

"Listen to him, doll," Drummond said. "We can't afford to tip them off."

Locking eyes with Sandra, Max hoped she would calm enough to catch what he meant by appearances. It wasn't amazingly subtle, but Drummond seemed to have fallen for the whole thing.

With an ugly glare, she rolled her chair back to her desk and started working, slamming pieces of paper into one pile or another, then typing on her laptop hard enough to make Max cringe. He couldn't tell if she was acting or truly mad. His gut told him to bet on the latter.

Avoiding Sandra's gaze, Drummond shifted his hat down at an angle and headed out the wall. "Looks like I've got scouting to do."

Max exited as quickly if not as smoothly. He fumbled with the door and slipped on the stairs. Once he sat in his car, he texted a simple message to Sandra: *Meet me @ Wake Library*. Hopefully, this would make things clear enough that by the time she reached Wake, any real anger would have dissipated. Once more, his gut contradicted his thoughts.

"Okay," he said to the steering wheel, "let's get to the library and have a little time to relax."

Before he could turn the ignition, Max's cellphone rang. The screen read Unknown but the number looked familiar. He was about to press ignore when it hit him — the card in his pocket. Stevenson the FBI agent.

"Hello?" he said, unwilling to check the business card, holding on to the hope that it might be a wrong number or even a telemarketer.

"Max? It's Stevenson."

Max's heart dropped. "What do you want?"

"Things have changed. We need to talk. There's a ballgame at the Dash Stadium this afternoon. Meet me there when you can get away."

"I don't really follow minor league ball."

"If the game hits the seventh inning stretch and you don't show, I'll come find you, and I won't care who sees us together. You associated with anybody you think might not like seeing you talk with an FBI agent?"

Yeah. I can think of too many. "It's a bit crazy right now. Let's meet tomorrow. I can —"

"Mr. Porter, let me make this quite simple for you. Either you show up at that ballgame, or you'll end up in jail for murder."

Chapter 6

THE SANCTUARY OF THE LIBRARY could not ease Max's nerves. What he had hoped would be a quiet research session followed by an intelligent discussion with Sandra, one in which they found a logical and measured response to Drummond's behavior, had become a mass of confusing, pressure-filled worries. In less than twenty-four hours, his calm, pleasant life had cracked open onto a sizzling frying pan of lies, threats, and secrecy.

He sat at a library computer intending to search for some basic information on handbells, but he couldn't muster the willpower to type in his query. Clouds rolled in, darkening the main floor which took in a lot of light from outside, and soon the heavy hits of a Spring downpour followed. It would only last a few minutes, but it reminded Max of how fast things can change. He had mounting problems to juggle and not a single worthwhile lead, but if he didn't find some angle to follow, the situation would change without any control.

He felt fairly confident Drummond was lying. He suspected Leed was lying. He had no idea what angle Modesto and Hull were taking, or if their work truly had anything to do with this. Then there was FBI Agent Peter Stevenson — the most pressing question in his mind.

What could this man possibly have that would tie Max to a murder? Perhaps it was all a bluff to get Max out to the ballfield. If so, it would work. Max had to know how the FBI fit into this.

"Deep breath," Max said and inhaled. He rested his fingers on the keyboard. Sandra would wait at least fifteen or twenty minutes before heading out to the library — just to make appearances should anybody be watching. It would take at least another twenty minutes for her to drive out to Wake. That meant he had time before she would arrive, time in which he could scramble his senses worrying about things he had no control over, or he could at least attempt to get some research done.

Though his fears continued to nudge the back of his neck, he managed to get his fingers typing and quickly had a list of books and websites to check out. All of this information would be the basics on bells, their construction, their history, that kind of thing. He didn't care about the details, he only wanted to leaf through the books and websites to look at the pictures. He knew from Modesto that the handbell had a white handle with a red stripe, that the outer rim bore a geometric design, and the inner rim had a fancy H. Assuming these things were valuable to collectors, especially since Hull had collected them, Max hoped to find a picture of one used as an example for some aspect of bells.

Ten books and twenty-three websites later, Max had nothing. On a whim, he checked out eBay. While numerous bells were for sale, only two approximated the Hull bell, and neither matched the description close enough to be worth investigating further.

He never expected these avenues to be fruitful, but the basic approaches were always worth trying. Sometimes he got lucky. When it came to the Hull family, though, he knew well the difficulty in uncovering even the remotest reference. William Hull, Terrance's father, had worked hard to erase their mark on the history books.

"Maybe Modesto is telling the truth," Max said. Perhaps Terrance wanted to re-establish his family's presence in the world. Or perhaps he wanted to continue his father's efforts. Either approach would make his desire for the handbell somewhat logical. Unless this was really about Tucker. Best not to think about that — Max had enough troubles to consider.

An idea struck, and he began a new query. Most collector's items, especially ones that had been around for a long time, had some type of pricing authority. Comic books, baseball cards, samurai swords, anything that people wanted to buy and trade, somebody else cataloged it all.

From the handbell musicians association website he began a winding journey that ended with the a cluttered site called A Mostly Complete Handbell Buyer's Guide. Once there, he narrowed the search from a starting point of close to a million. Most handbells were not constructed in a baker's dozen, so that cut the list down into the thousands. Adding in the Winston-Salem, North Carolina area as a criteria brought up seven results. Four of those had been constructed in the last three decades — much too recent for it to be a cherished family heirloom when the Hulls reached back to the foundations of the city. Of the remaining three entries, only one set had been constructed in 1723 — a baker's dozen with white handles, red striped, ornate design on the outer rim, and another design on the inner rim. No mention of the letter H, but Max's gut knew this was his target.

While the listing did not bring him any closer to finding the lost bell, he now had a picture of one as well as confirmation that this wasn't a goose chase to keep him away from other matters. The bell was real, and the price tag of only one — $74,000. The complete set was worth far more than the sum of its parts. According to the buyer's guide, a price of two to three million dollars would be appropriate.

Two to three million dollars.

"I didn't need to know that," Max said, his nerves lighting up once again.

Hands covered his eyes, and Max yelped, jumping in his seat. Sandra's sweet voice giggled. "Sorry, hon. Didn't mean to scare you."

As Max hugged his wife, his heart continued to pound away. "Don't do that to me. Not with all that's going on."

"What is going on? Drummond's worrying me."

"Me, too. All of it is. Even this handbell thing. The timing of it is weird. But Drummond lying, or at least withholding the full truth, that's not like him."

"And this whole notebook thing — I didn't believe his story at first, but now he wants to go break in to that house. There's got to be something worth going in there for."

Max scanned the room to make sure nobody paid extra attention to them. In a low whisper, he said, "I think most of his story was true. I think he had met Dr. Ernest and worked with him well before Joshua Leed came into the picture."

"I agree. But then why not tell the full story? Why stop before getting into the witch coven? Worse, he lied about that. He purposely made it sound like that part of the story never existed."

"That's why I agreed to this break in. We've got to keep playing along with him until we know more of what's going on."

"I don't like it. These late-night things never turn out well for us."

"If you've got a better idea, please tell me."

Sandra stuck out her tongue.

"It's those mature responses that make me love you more." Max kissed her tongue.

"Be careful."

"Of course."

"No, you need to be more careful than usual. Drummond is lying to us and he's lying about something that surrounds a murder. That's stressful and confusing. It means he's got pressure building inside him. I may not be able to help much when it comes to witches and curses, but I know ghosts. Pressure like that — the kind that comes from having to face the secrets of your past — that's the kind of thing that can turn a ghost."

"Turn? That doesn't sound good."

"Not all ghosts are sweet and friendly."

"I'd hardly call Drummond sweet or friendly."

"Good ghosts, kind ghosts, can lose themselves, lose whatever made them decent. They turn. Become evil."

"Like what? Haunted houses, poltergeists?"

"Or worse. A ghost like Drummond, one who knows us well, could cause us both serious harm. He would be like an insane psychotic that still remembers the key details of our lives but has no empathy, no morals, nothing that would stop him from abusing that knowledge."

"I get the picture. What do we do to stop this?"

"I don't know for sure. I've never been in a position to try stopping a ghost from turning before. But I know that the worse this pressure builds upon him, the more likely he is to turn."

"Well, you're full of great news." Max rubbed his face. Now he had to worry about Drummond going crazy. And Agent Stevenson expected him soon. He needed to get going.

Sandra dismissed it all with a wave of her hand, but her eyes didn't believe. "I'm probably being paranoid. Don't worry about it unless Drummond starts showing cracks."

"Cracks?"

"Just an expression, hon. Not literal cracks. At least, I don't think real cracks would form." She trembled out a grin and kissed him.

"I know it's boring but please go back to the office and wait for Drummond. If I haven't returned when he gets there, call me. I've got some more research to do."

"Yes, sir," Sandra said with a mock salute.

Once she left, Max gathered his things together and waited at the entrance. He watched her as long as he could, then waited another three minutes after she left his view. The idea that he hid from his wife wriggled under his skin, but until he knew what the FBI wanted, he wouldn't dare give voice to his concerns. They had enough to contend with. No need to get Sandra fired up with more worry, too.

As he walked to his car, he saw no sign of her. He drove off campus onto Silas Creek Parkway, a stretch of road that made a long arc around the city, until he hit Peters Creek Parkway. A left turn towards downtown brought him straight to the BB&T Ballpark.

He had no trouble finding a parking space — mid-week, afternoon, minor league baseball games never packed the seats. The park had been constructed less than ten years ago and still bore the feel of newness about it. Not really good for a ballpark. The seats were too new, the paint too clean. The place lacked the sense of history which was part of a baseball game experience.

Except I'm not here for a ball game.

Max strolled around toward the left field seating entrance. Partially to stall and partially out of need, he stepped into the men's room. While standing before a urinal he heard the crack of bat and heard muffled cheering. He couldn't go. Though the restroom was empty, he felt a dark presence hanging over his shoulder as if the entire FBI had him under surveillance.

He rinsed his face with cold water, dried off, and made sure not to look at his reflection. Seeing the fear in his own eyes might have been enough to send him running.

"For crying out loud, Max," he said. "You've faced down the Hull family. This is nothing more than an FBI agent with a threat." Hearing it so simply stated raised his confidence. After all, even if he did end up in jail for a crime he never committed, jail could never be as bad as burning alive — and that had nearly happened to him once.

When he finally walked into the seating area, the bright sun warmed his face. Shielding his eyes with one hand, he turned around and searched for Stevenson. It wasn't hard to find him. The FBI agent made no attempt to blend in. Still wearing his G-man black suit and shades, he raised a game program in the air to signal Max over.

Stevenson picked up a plastic cup of beer sitting between his feet on the cement floor. "You had me thinking you wouldn't show."

"Didn't seem as I had much choice." Max watched the game. Winston-Salem versus Wilmington. Fifth inning. 4-2. Two outs, no men on base.

"Sorry about that. I don't like threatening people but I didn't think you'd come otherwise."

"Probably wouldn't have. You don't exactly come off as the real deal." Max sat in the hard wood seat with metal trim. He had never been a big baseball fan, but once in awhile, he did enjoy going to a game, eating a hot dog, and sitting in these seats. It was as much a part of the game as the game itself.

"I am an FBI agent. But I don't handle the traditional cases."

"Does that mean I'm not really going to be charged with murder?"

Stevenson sipped his beer. "That part's real, I'm afraid. There are people I work for who think you are very involved in this thing."

"You want to tell me what this thing is? Who did I supposedly murder?"

"How long have you known Dr. Matthew Ernest?"

Max rolled his head back and looked heavenward. "You've got to be kidding."

"Oh, I don't think you murdered Dr. Ernest. At least, not directly. You didn't pull the trigger is what I'm saying. But the man led a strange life, and he had a way of making even his closest friends turn into vicious enemies."

"I've never even met the guy. Never heard of him until yesterday."

"Was that when you spoke with Joshua Leed at lunch, or was that when you met Leed at his home in Thomasville? How long have you known Mr. Leed?"

Max stared at Stevenson, not sure if he wanted to cry or scream. "I only just met him."

"Yesterday, right?"

"Yes. That's exactly right."

"Seems you just met a lot of people yesterday."

The player at bat cracked off a fly ball to center field for an easy catch, closing out the inning. Max wondered how many outs he played with. How many times would he deal with Hull and avoid losing? Maybe this was his final at bat. "Am I under arrest? Do I need a lawyer?"

Crossing his legs in an incongruously feminine manner, Stevenson said, "Relax. We're far from that sort of thing. Right now, I'm merely investigating Dr. Ernest. Well, and now his murder. Dr. Ernest was wanted for questioning in connection with a slew of murders stretching from here all the way up into Massachusetts, running over the course of the last five decades. Strange cases, too. Not a typical nutcase that wants to cut up pretty girls because Mommy kept him in a diaper too long. No, Dr. Ernest rode the whole magic bent. Killed girls in a ritualistic way. Gruesome stuff. But I don't have to tell you that, huh?"

Even without Drummond there to point it out, Max could hear the agent fishing for information. "I don't know anything about this."

"You ever read *Frankenstein?* I don't mean some bolts-in-the-neck version, but the real book. Mary Shelley."

"No."

"It's a good book. Very different from what you'd expect. Actually, all the classic horror stories are like that — *Dr. Jekyll and Mr. Hyde, Dracula* — and even modern tales like Carrie. People see the movies and think they know the whole story, but they're wrong."

Although the sun burned hot on the open field, Max found the warmth pleasant. He only wished the conversation were equally pleasant. "What does this have to do with —"

"In *Frankenstein,* you've got the monster, of course, and Dr. Frankenstein and his assistant. Since you haven't read the book, did you ever at least hear about the assistant's assistant?"

Max shook his head.

"Of course, you didn't. Nobody's ever heard of that character because the character doesn't exist. The book would've been a failure if there had been a third person in that group. See, when men do evil things they try to keep it from getting known. If they didn't, if they would only come out and proclaim their guilt, well then I'd have an easy job. Dr. Frankenstein, Igor — two people can keep a secret between them if the motivation is strong enough. But three people. That won't work. That always leads to someone being an odd man out. Sort of like you and Dr. Ernest and Joshua Leed. Now I'm not saying you were part of their group or that you encouraged Leed to get rid of Dr. Ernest, but I do know that the three of you are connected, and that whatever secrets you held are now held only by two people. Perhaps you and Leed got tired of taking orders from the good ol' Doctor and thought the time had come to strike out on your own."

"It's not like that at all."

"What is it then? Did Leed convince you that Dr. Ernest led a witch coven into Winston-Salem and you two tried to stop him from turning your beloved city into a haven for the dark arts? Or did he tell you that Dr. Ernest was a witch hunter? It's got to be one or the other."

"Witches? Who are you? Fox Mulder?"

Stevenson chuckled. "As far as I know, the FBI doesn't have a real X-Files division. But we do have people like me, specialists in some of the less traditional areas of investigation. You should be able to understand that. Your little research firm seems quite similar, focusing on lots of cases that are less traditional. Isn't that why you're researching witch covens?"

Max shifted, his seat no longer the familiar, comfortable bit of the game that brought with it pleasant memories. "I didn't kill anybody. And I don't know anything about Dr. Ernest. Leed didn't kill him either. In fact, Leed contacted me because he found out about the murder and he wanted to hire me to look into it. I'm guessing he didn't trust the police to handle it because he knew people like you were looking, too."

Stevenson formed a fist and hammered his chest until he let out a belch. "Why didn't you say so from the start? I could've saved my *Frankenstein* bit for another occasion. Unless, you're not telling me the whole story. Is that it, Max? Are you holding out?"

"Holding out about what?"

"Perhaps Leed wants more from you than you said. After all, he went around the country with Dr. Ernest for years. He's a person of interest as Dr. Ernest's accomplice. Maybe he's thinking of picking up where the doctor left off. Maybe he wants you to join him. Disciples can be like that, you know."

"Why me, then? I told you I've never met either of them before yesterday. It wouldn't make sense for him. Why rest all your illegal plans on somebody you've only met?"

"That's the same problematic thought I've been having." Stevenson patronizing grin scratched under Max's skin. "Unless what you're telling me is bullshit. If, in fact, you did know them, perhaps handled research for them at some point in the past, then it all adds up quite neatly."

"Your math is wrong."

"I hope so. Truly do. You and your wife seem like nice folks, and I'd hate to be the one breaking up a good marriage because I've got to arrest you."

"I didn't do whatever you think I did."

Max stood to go, but Stevenson grabbed his wrist. "You may be innocent of what I'm talking about, but you aren't innocent. So, let me give you this bit of advice — stay away. Everything, everyone connected with Matthew Ernest turns evil. You want to get my people off of you, then remember to stay away. Because pretty soon, I'll have to be interrogating you officially."

"I'll remember." Max yanked his arm free and stormed out of the ballpark. It felt good to stomp up the stairs, shoving out every bit of tension the conversation had created. By the time he reached his car, he was puffing and sweating. He slid into the driver's seat and glanced at his reflection in the rearview mirror. Stevenson told him to stay away and the first thing he'll be doing that night was breaking into Matthew Ernest's home. "Well, I said I'd remember — not that I'd listen."

Chapter 7

AS EVENING APPROACHED, Sandra and Max leaned back in their office chairs and bit into their slices of pizza from The Mellow Mushroom. The restaurant was only a few blocks away, yet Sandra preferred bringing the pizza in. "That place is always jam-packed and noisy."

Breaking the stringy cheese bridge between his mouth and the pizza slice, Max nodded. "That's because the pizza's delicious."

Drummond popped his head through the bookcase. "Are you two done yet? I've got to go over the plan."

"Then stop hiding in the walls and tell us."

Drummond soared out to the middle of the room, chest puffed out, arms crossed. "You know damn well that even though I can't eat any of that food, I can sure smell it. That's cruel. May even qualify as torture."

Max raised his arms. "What do you want from us? We're alive. We need food. I wasn't about to drive all the way home to eat just to turn around and come back here. Plus, we figured it would be worse for you to stretch all the way out to our house. You'd be complaining of a migraine long before we set foot in Ernest's house. This seemed like a fair compromise."

"Fine. Just finish up already." Drummond relaxed his posture and glanced at Sandra. "Sorry I swore. You're too refined a lady to have to put up with that."

Sandra smiled. "The fuck I am."

This tickled Drummond, and he barked out a series of laughs that nearly choked him.

Wiping his fingers clean on a paper napkin, Max wondered how long he could keep his cool. Drummond's lies, the FBI, Leed — it all swirled inside him like a ship caught in a squall. He wished he could tell Sandra, his close confidante. But he had to protect her, too.

He took a sharp breath. He could do this. Stay focused and find the way through. They had survived past calamities that way, and they would survive this one the same.

"Okay, I'm done eating," Max said. "Tell us the plan."

With a longing gaze at the pizza box, Drummond settled in a chair opposite Max. He had no need for chairs, of course, but Max appreciated his effort to seem human. "Matt's home is on Ebert, south off of Silas Creek Parkway." Drummond's enthusiasm for detective work cleared his mood. "It's got crime scene tape around it but no cops anymore. They're probably done with it and waiting for the release order. No need to waste resources watching over it now."

"Then we're too late?"

"We're fine until it's released. After that, somebody will hire a cleaning crew to make it look like nobody ever died in there so whoever owns the house now can sell it. That's why —"

Sandra washed down the last of her dinner. "We know. It has to be tonight."

Pausing to look from Max to Sandra and back, Drummond screwed up his face but eventually shook it off. Fine by Max. He had no desire to explain marital relationships to a ghost.

"The way I figure it," Drummond went on, "I'll go in first and unlock the door. You walk in, get the notebook, and we leave. Should be easy."

Max coughed. "When is this stuff ever easy? Heck, we don't even know where in the house the notebook is."

"I'm pretty sure I know. Most of the house is normal and unimpressive. But there's a room I can't get into. The door has a ward on it. It's a symbol you draw so that —"

"We've seen them." Max recalled the bizarre symbols all over Joshua Leed's house. Then he saw Sandra's shocked face and realized his mistake.

Drummond raised an eyebrow. "When have you ever seen a ward symbol?"

The silent tension around them grew thicker. Max's brain raced for a plausible answer as Drummond stared at him with that detective eye — the look of man who could spot a lie with minimal effort. Max opened his mouth, hoping to sound natural, when it hit him. He had seen a ward before. "Don't you remember the art forgery case?"

Sandra shuddered. Max knew she hated any reminder of being chained in the basement of the Corkille home while that crazy family attempted their awful spells. Still, she understood Max's angle. "That's right," she said. "That Corkille bitch drew all sorts of stuff on the floor, and you couldn't get in to stop her."

Drummond's face turned cold. "Well, we did find a way to stop her. And those symbols were not wards. She used blood to create that barrier."

"The concept's the same, though. Right?" Max asked. "Use some sort of magic to keep a ghost out of a certain area."

"I suppose. Anyway, Matt put a ward on one door in his house. I tried to go through the walls to get around it, but he must have wards on the inner walls of the room because I couldn't get in. Actually, that's not right. I could force my way in, but getting close to an active ward is like touching a hot stove. It burns hot and painful and that's what keeps you away. If I can handle the pain, I could go in."

"No need, though. You open the outside door, I'll go in to the warded room, find the notebook, and we get out of there."

"Like I said. Easy."

Sandra cleared her throat in a melodramatic manner to get their attention. One look at her face, and Max knew he had messed up again. "What's the matter, Hon?"

Sandra looked at the two men and shook her head. "You seem to have forgotten my part in all this."

Like walking through a minefield, Max slowly said, "Okay. What's your part?"

"That's my question to you. You didn't actually think I'd let you go running off tonight alone, did you? We're partners in this outfit. I'm not a secretary. If you think it's important to find this notebook, then I'm going with you."

He couldn't help but smile — her fierce eyes and determined jaw made her even more beautiful than usual. "I'm sorry, but you can't come this time."

"Excuse me?"

Inching back from the desk, Max said, "Honey, I'm going to be committing a burglary on Ebert Road. That's not really an empty road. There's houses all around."

"That's why you need my help."

"If you come with me and we get caught, who's going to bail us out? Our friend, the ghost?"

"You really think breaking into an empty house is somehow more dangerous than the other things we've faced?"

"Of course not." Max felt his pizza lurch in his stomach. "I just —"

"You just nothing. I told you when we decided to keep on working together that it had to be on equal terms. It's been easy to play at equality when nothing much has been challenging us, but this is your real moment of truth. This is the time when you prove you're worth your word. Are we equal or not?"

Max swallowed hard. He looked to Drummond, but the detective stared at Sandra so shocked, he didn't realize he had slipped halfway through his chair.

At length, Max tilted his head in a slight nod. "I said we'd be equal and we will."

Drummond lifted a bit in the air. "Sugar, I've always liked you, but I swear, you make me wish I'd find a way to be alive again."

With a flirting wink, Sandra said, "Now why would you want to do that? I'm a married woman."

"Don't bother me with details. That's the whole point of a fantasy."

"Hey, you two," Max said. "I'm right here."

Sandra giggled and picked up the pizza box. "I'll take this downstairs. Otherwise, the place'll stink by morning."

When she left, Max dropped his head. "Promise me, if something goes wrong, you won't let anything happen to her."

Drummond said, "You know I'll protect her."

"I know. Thank you."

"Don't be so worried. Like the lovely lady said, we've been in scrapes before and we've helped each other out. Frankly, it'll be good to have her along. Trust me here — a woman like that keeps you grounded, keeps you from doing stupid things, keeps you safe."

Max noticed an odd tincture to Drummond's voice. "You knew a woman like that once?"

"You don't want to hear about that."

Bolting upright, Max said, "Of course I do. I'm always happy to hear anything you want to share."

"Oh." Drummond looked genuinely confused as if he never expected such an enthusiastic response. "Um, what do you want to know?"

"Anything. Who was she? How did you meet? Did you love her? Come on."

Squirming in mid-air, Drummond said, "There's nothing to tell. It's boring. And you don't tell me anything either. I don't know much about you and Sandra."

"What do you want to know?"

"Nothing. That's your private business."

For a second, Max thought Drummond might disappear into the Other — a ghost realm that resided in another plane of existence. He stayed, however. He pressed himself into the back corner, but he stayed. Max walked over to him and in a soothing tone, he said, "Maybe this is one of those differences between the era you lived in and the one we're in now."

"Your whole generation wants to share way too much." Though still in the corner, Drummond had regained his sturdy posture.

"It's a good way to build trust. You know as well as I do that we need to trust each other."

"All that we've been through already hasn't proven enough?"

"I trust you. Otherwise, I wouldn't be going out on this job tonight. But you can't have too much trust, and the more we know about each other, the better it'll be for our success in whatever we investigate." Max backed away. "I'll make it easy for you. Let me tell you about one of the first dates I ever had with Sandra."

"Why does that matter?"

"Just listen."

Doing little to hide his perturbed attitude, Drummond gestured for Max to begin.

"Now this wasn't our first date. I think it might've been our third or fourth. We'd both been recently burned — I'd been dumped and she had been cheated on — so we were taking things really slow. I hadn't even kissed her yet."

"Even by 1940s standards, that's ridiculous."

"Point is we were both gun shy. These people we cared about had betrayed us. Maybe you never had that problem, but I'll tell you, it throws you for a loop."

"I'm sure it does." Drummond looked to the bookcase, his eyes lingering on the whiskey book.

"So we go out to dinner, catch a movie, nothing out of the ordinary. A plain old date. I take her to her apartment and at the door, I pick up her hand and kiss it softly. We smiled at each other, and I'll never forget this — she said to me, 'Y'know, I appreciate how you've been with all this.' I knew right away what she meant. I told her that I understood. She said, 'We're never going to get over it unless we deal with it.' I agreed but I didn't know how to deal with it. She said she knew. She grabbed my head and kissed me hard. The next morning, I'm lying in her bed with her beautiful head nestled on my chest and I never had to worry again."

Drummond pointed right at Max's face. "If you think I'm sleeping with you to strengthen our trust, you're out of your mind."

They both laughed harder than necessary.

"You boys ready?" Sandra asked from the doorway.

They took one look at her and burst into genuine, raucous laughter.

Chapter 8

EBERT ROAD RAN NORTH and south starting below the city near Baptist Hospital and heading far down into Davidson County. The properties along this long stretch encompassed quaint starter homes and durable rentals, beat up double-wides and rundown farmhouses, as well as lovely middle-class homes and showy McMansions. Only the destitute and the ultra-wealthy went unrepresented. Dr. Matthew Ernest lived in a single floor, two bedroom starter with a swatch of grass meant to be considered a yard.

Max parked a few houses back and watched the street. Normally, Ebert Road had a steady stream of traffic — a fast way to cut up to Silas Creek Parkway while avoiding the more heavily traveled roads, one of those back routes only the locals knew about. At two in the morning, however, the buzz of an amber streetlight and the clicking of the car's cooling engine were the only activity around.

Clasping Sandra's hand, Max kissed her. "You come in with me, take a look around, tell me if there's anything besides Drummond there. Once we're sure the place is clear, I want you to come back here and start the car. Watch for me and be ready to go fast."

"No problem."

They slipped out of the car and crossed the street. Walking on the grass, they avoided the sound of shoes against concrete. Though the night air had cooled considerably, Max still found it surprising that he smelled burning wood in the air. Who would need a fire going? But he allowed himself a few seconds to indulge in the pleasant aroma before focusing on Dr. Ernest's house.

From the outside, the house appeared to be one of several small properties that received the same lack of care. Tall grass and weeds grew in some yards and a few bore the leftovers of kids at play — plastic bat and balls, rusting bicycle, a baseball cap, a Frisbee, and a discarded t-shirt. The houses across the street were of the same size, yet those owners made a greater effort at upkeep. Max envisioned a

Hatfield/McCoy feud developing between the two sides of the street.

Together, Max and Sandra headed around the back of Dr. Ernest's house. They tried to be quiet but Max kept stepping on hidden dead branches and Sandra tripped in the tangles of Bermuda grass, falling flat in the yard. Each time they froze and listened. If anybody had heard, they didn't take notice.

Max took out a penknife and held it against the first bit of yellow crime scene tape that crisscrossed the door. Most days did not bring him to the point of committing a jail-worthy offense, so he had no experience with what he would feel. His hand did not shake. That was good. But his mind kept flashing images of home, safe and comfortable.

He rapped his knuckles on the rotting wood frame. "Drummond?" he whispered.

The lock clicked, and Max slowly turned the knob. He pushed the door open with care as if handling a newborn. Despite his efforts, the hinges whined in protest.

Drummond popped his head through the door. "Are you two trying to get caught?" They entered a narrow kitchen that led into a wide living room. Once Sandra entered, she closed the door, making less noise than Max, and Drummond gestured toward her silent work. "Next time put her on door duty."

Max flicked on his flashlight and checked out the house. "Holy crap." A raging storm had blown through. Most of the picture frames lay shattered on the floor and those remaining on the wall hung askew. The walls themselves bore jagged cracks from floor to ceiling. Furniture had been toppled over and cut open, foam stuffing strewn about. Hardcover books had been ripped apart. Dishes and glasses covered the kitchen with sharp shards. Even the pillows and blankets littered the floor in strips.

Though Max had seen many bizarre things, this was his first crime scene. He could only wonder at the intense anger required to cause this much damage. On the living room carpet, the dark splotch near the head of a corpse's tape outline reminded Max that the anger went far beyond ransacking a house. This was murder.

"Is the place clear?" he asked Sandra.

Her eyes roamed about the room, her lips trembling. Finally, she nodded. "Drummond's the only ghost here."

"Go back to the car."

Sandra stepped closer to him and brushed her cheek against his.

Before Max could say anything, she pressed her mouth against his ear. "Keep Drummond calm. Don't let him turn."

As she walked back to the door, Max watched her face. She stared at the destruction in the room and shuddered. Max looked over it all again, except this time he imagined a turned ghost, an evil ghost, causing this damage.

Drummond appeared at his side. "Ready?"

Max started, hoped Drummond didn't notice, and stepped further into the house. "So where's the room?"

"First thing's first." Drummond moved about the living room with a thoughtful look on his face. He stopped at one wall, traced the cracks with a finger, and grimaced. Max hadn't noticed it before, but the particular series of cracks Drummond paid most attention to bore a striking resemblance to claw marks.

Drummond then lowered into the floor until he had a close up view of the where Dr. Ernest had died. Max marveled at the sight. He was getting a firsthand view of the way an old detective investigated a crime scene. Not exactly, considering Drummond's current position, but close enough.

"You find anything?" Max asked.

Shooting back up into the room, Drummond said, "Not yet. Come on. Let's get the notebook."

Another lie. Max knew it, could feel the lie as cold as Drummond's skin. That ghost had noticed something about those cracks in the wall.

Off to the side of the living room was a short hallway with three doors at the end. The left went into a compact bathroom. The right entered a bedroom that Dr. Ernest had set up as an office. The door on the end was closed and a series of symbols lined vertically had been carved into the wood.

Drummond floated a few feet away. "That's the one."

"I gathered that." Max rested his hand on the door.

"There isn't a fire on the other side."

"You want to come here and do this?"

"I do, but you know I can't."

"Then shush already."

Max opened the door and poked his flashlight in the room. It looked like a boring bedroom ripped to shreds. Single bed, white sheets, plump pillow, gray blanket, little table with a lamp and a cracked Kindle, chest of drawers and a mirror. Nothing special. Except for the fact that all of it had been struck by the same tornado as the rest of the house.

With trepidation, Max walked into the room. More archaic symbols lined the walls, written in a shaky hand. Of course, at ninety-something, Dr. Ernest's hand might shake from age, but Max suspected fear had more to do with it. Regardless of the reason, the result chilled his skin.

"This wasn't in the paper," Max said.

"What?"

"The newspaper article. It never mentioned this room. Why would they not write up something as sensational as this? It's a bizarre story with this room."

"The photo in the newspaper came from the police. They don't want the public knowing about a possible cult thing in the backyard until they have an idea of who's responsible. That's why they haven't released the crime scene yet. Once they do, the reporters will swarm in and get their sensational story."

As Max searched for the notebook, he thought about Joshua Leed and the angry cursed ghosts of witches, the turned ghosts, that had done this. Sandra was right. They had to make sure this didn't happen to Drummond — or the police would be wrapping yellow tape across their office door, and all that would remain of Max and Sandra would have been shredded into confetti.

"You find it?"

Over his shoulder, Max whispered back, "No. Any idea where I should look?"

"Sheesh, do I have to do everything? Check drawers, check under the mattress, if you need to, pull up the carpet or floorboards."

Since the drawers were already ripped out and strewn across the floor, Max started with the mattress. Underneath, he found plenty of dust bunnies and a forgotten plate. From the floor, it appeared that the drawers had contained mostly clothing, though a few papers, too. Max checked them — correspondences with Wake Forest University and UCLA. Dr. Ernest had begged for funding support, dismissed accusations leveled against him for improperly representing himself, and argued that his research held both valid and valuable purpose. Both universities offered terse replies in the nature of *Don't contact us ever again.*

Max dropped the letters and cruised his flashlight for another turn around the room. About to give up and call for Drummond's advice, he stopped the light in one corner. The carpeting had an odd bulge as if someone had pulled up the edge and failed to put it back completely.

"Max? Anything?"

"Hold on." Max approached the corner, his mouth drying up, and poked at the carpet. He slipped one finger under the edge, felt the coarse weave, and gently pulled it back. The top of a manila envelope peeked out. Max's chest tightened. Ever since moving to the South, he had learned one clear thing — nothing good for him ever came in a manila envelope. "I got something."

"Was it where I said?"

"Nope. It's in a closet." Max had no desire to hear Drummond crow about his great investigative prowess. And even though it was a stupid thing to lie about, Max had to admit he always felt a little satisfaction when he could deny Drummond a chance at bragging.

Snatching up the envelope, Max hurried out of the room. Every second longer in that house meant another second to get caught. He rushed through the living room and out the kitchen, but as he closed the door behind him, he caught a glimpse of Drummond staring at the claw marks in the wall.

Crouching, Max scurried across the yard and up the sidewalk. Sandra had the engine running. She pulled into the street, Max jumped in, and they were off.

"I really hate doing that," Max said, exhaling a long breath. "No more breaking and entering."

As she drove, Sandra pointed to the manila envelope in Max's lap. "Is that it?"

Drummond appeared in the backseat. "Of course. I told you it was there, didn't I? Don't forget, if not for me, you couldn't have done this."

"I *wouldn't* have done this if not for you."

Sandra put them on a main road, and the more distance they traveled away from the house, the better Max felt. "So what's in it?" she asked.

Max slid his finger under the envelope's lip. He pulled out a stack of papers and inspected them. "Damn. Nothing's ever easy."

"What's wrong?"

"It's gibberish."

Drummond tried to grab the papers but his cold hand slipped through. "Let me see those."

"I don't mean it's gibberish like a raving madman, I mean it's just letters and numbers. It's a code."

"That sounds like Matt. He was always a bit more paranoid than necessary."

Sandra peeked at the papers. "Tomorrow I'll get to work on that."

Both Max and Drummond gaped at her. Max said, "Since when did you become a code cracker?"

"Back when we used to get newspapers I always liked the puzzle pages. Crosswords, jumbles, ciphers."

"I know that, but you haven't done that stuff in a long time."

Sandra smirked. "You don't really think I spend all my computer time at work focused on business? I'll have you know that my Daily Sudoku, Daily Cipher Break, Mad Ciphers, and Cipher-Squad skills are also quite adept — in case we get attacked by mutant cipher-bearing zombies. Besides, who else do you know that can help out? Let me take a shot at it."

Max shrugged. "Okay."

"Okay?" Drummond said. "This is serious stuff. Not a fun, little game."

"Like she said, I don't know anybody to turn to for this, and I certainly can't do it. You?"

"No," Drummond mumbled.

"Then it's settled." Max started to stuff the notes back in the envelope when he saw a thicker page inside. He pulled out a torn black and white photograph of a young woman with striking eyes and full lips sitting in a summer dress under a tree with a weird branch like a burnt finger. It looked like a frame taken out of a movie. Mostly open fields around her and the blurry edge of a building in the distance. The setting made him think of the old-time romances with sweeping violins and passionate kisses that faded to black. But her hollow, lost, hopeless face told another story — one of tragedy and horror.

Max heard Drummond's breath catch. Turning around, he saw the ghost's focus locked on the photograph, dread covering his head like the stylish hat he wore.

"You know who this is?" Max asked.

"Looks like some girl." Drummond's tone had lost all emotion. His face colder, deader than normal.

"Who is this? Why does Dr. Ernest have her picture?"

Under his breath, Drummond said, "Son of a bitch." Then he vanished from the car.

MAX SLEPT LITTLE THAT NIGHT. The high of pulling off a successful job, of knowing he had escaped jail, kept him up at first. But then his mind tumbled over black and white images of the woman in the photo. What had happened to her to cause those beautiful eyes to look so haunted? Why did Dr. Ernest include the picture in the coded file? And what about her spooked Drummond?

By the time Sandra woke, Max had already eaten a toasted bagel and granola cereal. She glanced at the cold pot of coffee and grunted.

"Sorry," he said, picking a raisin from his teeth. "The last thing I needed was caffeine. I'm still wide awake."

She shuffled over to the counter and poured the dregs into a mug. "You'll crash this afternoon." Placing the mug into the microwave, she added, "You excited about the case or thinking about that picture?"

"*Excited* is not the right word."

"Confused, then?"

"How about *terrified?*"

The microwave beeped and Sandra sat with her head over the steaming mug of day-old coffee. "That seems a bit much. We've handled stranger cases than this."

"Never one that involved Drummond lying like this or one in which he sees a photo and runs off."

"Maybe we should confront him. Ask him directly."

"How much more direct could I have been last night?"

Sandra placed a hand on her forehead. "Not so loud, hon. Coffee hasn't kicked in yet."

"When it does," he said, softer but no less urgent, "I need you to figure out that code."

"Last night, you guys doubted me completely, and now you think I can just figure it out instantly. Unbelievable."

"I'm not expecting miracles. That's the point. I need you to get started because it's going to take time, and something tells me we don't have a lot of that left."

"You're getting hunches now?"

Max shared a smile with her and kissed the top of her head. "Watch out or pretty soon I'll be a full-fledged detective. Hunches and everything."

"Don't worry. I'll put all my effort into that code."

"You'll do great. Do you want to work at the office, or are you going to stay home?"

She lifted her coffee cup. "No decisions, yet."

"Well, when you're fully caffeinated, let me know. I'm going to take a shower."

Within minutes, hot water cascaded down Max's body, soothing not only his weary muscles but also his weary mind. He knew better than to attempt to solve everything at once. One step at a time and all that. And the first step, after his shower, would be to question Drummond.

"Sorry about taking off last night," Drummond said.

Shouting, Max slipped and crashed to the bottom of the shower. The jolt on his rear sent painful vibrations straight up his spine. "Really? You can't wait until I'm out of the shower and dressed?"

He heard Sandra race up the stairs. "You okay in there?"

"Fine," Max called back. "Drummond surprised me, that's all."

"Drummond's in there?"

"I am, my dear," Drummond said, a hint of amusement in his voice.

After a short pause, Sandra went downstairs without another word. Max grabbed a towel, dried off, and stepped from the shower. He looked at Drummond and shook his head. The ghost hovered above the toilet, hunched over either in thought or with the urgent need to use the facilities.

"You know there's a toilet in the office?"

Drummond raised an eyebrow. "Cute. Now can we focus on the case? Has your better half cracked the code yet?"

"Of course not. She's only waking up, and it's going to take time."

"Can't be that hard."

As Max dressed, he shot Drummond an incredulous smirk. "I dare you to say that to her face." He sat on the edge of the bed. He felt like a mountain climber pausing long enough to see the steep path ahead but knowing that if he stopped for too long, it would be twice as hard to get going again. "Tell me about the woman in the photo. Who is she? Why is she important?"

"She's not. Never was."

"Then you admit to knowing her."

Drummond's face tightened. He loomed over Max, his head brushing the ceiling, and a misty darkness flowed off his shoulders like fog made of shadows. "You listen to me," he said, his voice deepening to the point of vibrating Max's bones. "We're not going to pursue her. She's got nothing to do with this case. Do you understand? Nothing."

"Calm down. Don't get so excited." Sandra's warnings about evil-turning ghosts reverberated in Max's mind. "I understand. I do. Whoever the woman is, she's not important to our investigation."

"That's right." The dark mist drifted into the bathroom looking like more steam from the shower. "Let's stay focused on Dr. Ernest and the Hulls. Forget about the photograph."

"Good idea." Max watched as Drummond returned to his normal, ghostly self.

"Huh?" Drummond blinked fast as he looked around. "Sorry, pal. I think I dozed off. Didn't know I could still do that. I guess you're so boring that my old instincts kicked in. So, what's a good idea?"

It took Max a few seconds before he believed that Drummond had forgotten the last moments, but once he did, he decided to take advantage of that fact. "You, um, had the idea of going into the Other and seeing if you could find Dr. Ernest. After all, he died quite recently. He might be lost and looking for some explanation."

"Yeah. I suppose so."

"It's a good idea. You go to the Other, find him, and tell him all about us. He'll be able to help discover his own murderer."

Drummond smacked his hands together. "That is a good idea. Glad I thought of it. Okay, I'm off for the Other."

"Good luck," Max said. Though he didn't expect Drummond to find anything useful — probably stumble upon some smalltime hood that picked the wrong day to go haunting houses — Max did hope Drummond's excursion would eat up most of his day. In the meantime, he hoped to give Sandra all the quiet she needed to work on the code. He would go back to the office, and —

His phone rang.

As Max picked it up, Drummond waved good-bye and disappeared. "Hello?" Max said.

"Please. Get here quick."

"Who is this?"

"She's coming for me. You've got to help."

"I think you've got the wrong number."

"Mr. Porter, please. This is Joshua Leed. If you don't get here soon, I think I'll be murdered like Dr. Ernest."

Chapter 10

MAX PUT ON HIS COAT and grabbed his keys. He avoided Sandra's glare. Hoping to sound reasonable, he said, "I need you working on that code."

She folded her arms and jutted out her chin. "You cannot go into this situation alone, and Drummond's out of the question for now."

"I won't be alone. Leed is there."

She raised an eyebrow which dismissed that entire argument. They went back and forth for five minutes until Max finally said he couldn't waste more time and rushed to the car. Sandra had a tough, stubborn streak in her, but Max knew she wouldn't jump in the car unclean and in her pajamas — not for this. But he also knew he'd pay for his actions later.

He wished he could have told her the truth. He wanted her to know that the FBI had been pressing on him, that Joshua Leed might be connected with a mess larger than they realized, that Drummond's secrecy might cause them more harm than he wanted to think about — but to tell her would be to bring her closer to the trouble he wanted to avoid. A part of him dug into his conscience, reminding him that they had learned to be open and honest with each other, that they had past experiences which proved hiding things never helped. But they had never dealt with the FBI before, never had to worry about charges and going to federal prison.

The drive to Leed's place did little to ease his mind. Often a drive would be a cleansing experience for his problems, but as he neared Thomasville, his focus shifted away from Sandra and on to Leed. He feared when he arrived that he would only find a body.

When his cell phone rang, he swerved onto the shoulder, the rumble strips shivering the car until he got back in his lane. He glanced at the phone — his mother. He considered letting it go to voicemail, but he had been avoiding her calls too often lately. Another thing Drummond had taught him well — a detective can't put all of his life aside for a case. Do that, and he never has time to live.

"Hi, Mom."

"Maxwell. It's so good to hear your voice. You're a hard man to reach."

"Sorry about that. It's been kind of crazy lately."

"Oh? Is business good, then?"

"We're doing fine. Busy but fine."

"Well, you shouldn't be too busy for your family. That's important. When you forget family, you forget what makes you the person you are, and then where would you be? You listen to me. I may be old, but I'm not an idiot."

"I never said —"

"You kids think I'm a fool but I know what I'm talking about. The ones we love are the most important part of our lives, and you shouldn't take that for granted."

Max thought of Sandra. "I agree."

"You should. So, I want you to come visit me. You're always welcome and I haven't seen you in too long."

"I'll see when Sandra and I can work in a vacation."

"Oh, yes, you can bring Sandra along, too."

Max finished the call, a gentle smile finding its way onto his lips. He could already hear Sandra's reaction to both his mother's lack of including her and the idea of a "vacation" visiting his mother. She would laugh hard before spewing a rapid tirade caused by years of such slights. Then she'd laugh some more.

Before Max could put the cell phone down, it went off again. He glanced at its face and read: *Modesto*. "Damn," he said and answered the call.

Modesto sounded more impatient than usual. "I expected a report by now."

For a moment, Max forgot what he had been assigned to do for the Hulls — Drummond, Leed, and a witch coven seemed more pressing. "Right, the handbell."

"You seem to be very relaxed regarding this research. Do I need to remind you of your current situation? Our employer is not fond of sluggards."

"I've done some preliminary research."

"We had hoped for more by now."

"You haven't given me much to go on."

Modesto could not hide the oozing triumph in his voice. "Why, I assumed a man as brilliant as you would have needed far less to start with. I'll inform our employer that you're the wrong man for our research needs."

Clenching the phone, Max said, "You go ahead and do that. Of course, you better be ready to explain why you failed to give me the necessary information to assist me. I mean, after all, that's part of your job, right? To assist me? And don't think for a second I won't contact Mr. Hull directly and let him know what a swell job you're doing. You do remember what happened the last time you screwed up for Mr. Hull, don't you?"

A long silence ensued. Finally, he heard Modesto's throat clear. "Finish your research soon. I'll expect a full report by —"

"Sounds good. Bye now." Max cut the call. Despite everything, he had to smile. "Sometimes it's the little victories that matter." He only hoped he would reach Leed in time for another victory.

Though he had seen Leed's house before, driving up to it in the daytime made it scarier. Like Norman Bates's home on the hill. Max kept expecting the silhouette of a strange woman to appear in one of the upper-windows.

As he stepped from the car, Joshua Leed opened the front door and waved Max in as if he were a soldier being urged to sprint across an open field. "Hurry!" Leed attempted to crouch low, but with his bad leg, he simply ducked his head and leaned heavier on his cane as he moved to the edge of the porch. "Come on. I can't leave the door open."

Max jogged up to the porch, crouching a bit despite how silly he felt, and entered the house. Leed slammed the door shut, locked the deadbolt, and poured salt across the entranceway. When he faced Max, his sunken eyes and sweating cheeks shivered.

"Thank you for coming," Leed said. "I knew I could trust you. You didn't tell Drummond, did you? Not a word, right?"

"I didn't tell him anything."

"Thank goodness." With trembling hands, Leed limped to the kitchen. He looked thinner than before, frail and unkempt. "I need your help."

Max followed him. "Are you okay? You seem a bit —"

"You'd look the same if you were being hunted down by the dead."

"You mean the witch coven?"

"After I met you and your wife, I set out to destroy the witches I had cursed. I went to each site and I did what I had to. Something went wrong, though. I was never as good as Dr. Ernest at all this stuff. I don't know what I screwed up but things have only gotten worse. One's after me. She won't stop, either. Not until we're all dead."

"You didn't destroy both of them?"

"I did. That's the problem. I did exactly as Dr. Ernest prescribed, but still they come." He tried to pour a cup of coffee but spilled it on the counter.

"When was the last time you slept?"

Leed shook his head. "I won't sleep again. Not until we finish this."

"We?"

"I can't do this alone. I'm too old now. Besides, you and your wife are the only ones around here that know, that understand, what's going on. You've got to find out where Drummond's witches are buried. You've got to do this, but you can't let on that you know anything. Drummond's a ghost and this is personal to him. That's a highly emotional combination — all the ingredients for an evil conversion. But you get that information from him and we'll put a stop to this coven. Then, maybe I'll sleep."

Max sat at a little breakfast nook and scratched his head. "Look, I understand you're scared, and I believe that you and Dr. Ernest and Drummond all dealt with this witch coven way back when. But something doesn't quite fit. Drummond's behavior lately, for one. Something else, though. If you give me a little time to look into this more, then —"

A loud pounding erupted on the walls as if giants threw each other around the house. Max could see the drywall vibrate with each thud and dust sprinkled from the ceiling. A hundred horror movies flashed through his mind.

Leed cowered at the sound, gripping the edge of the sink to keep from falling over. He locked eyes with Max. With each successive thud against the walls, his face shifted to worse levels of terror.

"They killed Dr. Ernest. They're coming for me next. Oh, it's all our fault, all of it. We didn't know, didn't understand. You think you're doing right, fighting evil forces, saving the world around you, but it's never so simple."

Max put out his hand and noticed the tremor in his fingers. "Come. Let's get out of here."

"My soul is damned. I've used the same magic that they used. I did so against them, to save us, but I used it nonetheless. I'm damned."

Glass shattered upstairs and the pounding on the walls intensified. Max's heart pounded in time. He grabbed Leed's wrist but the frightened man found the strength to yank himself free.

"Whatever's doing this," Max said, "it doesn't have to take you. Come with me. We can solve this. Trust me."

Leed straightened and his face shifted from horror to acceptance. He shook his head slowly. "It's over for me. I'm too old, too tired."

The pounding ceased.

Max stood motionless, his skin still jangling with nerves. Leed opened a drawer and pulled out a photograph. He stared at it, and a tear fell down cheek. "I should've known all along that this was more than just a witch coven. Dr. Ernest always held back from telling me the truth. But I was young and foolish. And I wanted the adventure." He held out the photo to Max. "Here. Take this and —"

A screech like an animal being slaughtered erupted around them. An unseen hand flung Leed up against the wall. Pots clattered to the floor. Max winced at the sharp odor of sulfur.

He stepped forward to help but something jerked him backward. He tried to move again and was slammed against the breakfast nook wall. An enormous weight pressed into him as if a huge man leaned back against his chest.

Across the kitchen, he watched as the attack shoved Leed higher up the wall until his head touched the ceiling. Leed tried to speak, but his throat only made a clamped, gurgling sound. His face darkened and his eyes bulged.

Max strained to raise his arm, move his leg, anything, but he had been made immobile by this force. He found enough breath to scream out. "Leave him alone!"

Leed's face opened in surprise. "You did it," he said, staring at the emptiness in front of him. "You killed my parents."

Moaning laughter twisted around the screeching sounds. Max heard a sharp crack, and Leed's head lolled to one side. The weight holding Max lifted, and as he discovered he could move freely, Leed's body dropped to the floor.

Max rushed across the kitchen and checked Leed's body. No pulse. No breath.

Clenched in the man's hand, Max noticed the photograph he had pulled from the drawer. With his sweat soaking his shirt and his mouth bone dry, Max reached for the photograph. Not one to enjoy touching a dead body, especially a freshly dead body, Max tried to pull the photo free without making contact. It slipped out with ease. Maybe fresh dead had its advantages — no rigor mortis, for one.

The photo turned out to be a page torn from a book. The picture was black and white and depicted a large building ablaze, smoke pouring high into the air. A group of onlookers stood by and watched as if it were a grand show.

Max stuffed the picture in his pocket and hurried out of the house. As he drove away, his heart hammering blood into his head, he thought of that picture. What could have been so important about it? He saw Leed's head crack to the side and remembered the feel of the ghostly weight against his chest.

After a few minutes, Max pulled over. He rushed from his car and took a few steps towards the trees lining the road. He threw up.

Max took Exit 103 off Route 85 and parked at Denny's. About thirty minutes later, Sandra arrived, and they shared a booth built for six. Despite the booth's size and the lack of a crowd, Max felt closed in.

When he finished telling Sandra about what had happened, he whipped his head around the room. "She's not here is she?"

Sandra took a quick look. "Not a single ghost here."

"We've been through a lot, but this ... I've never been more scared in my life. I couldn't move. And even though I didn't see anything, I could feel it, smell it — her. Leed said it was one of the witches come to take revenge on him. He said we had to stop it. I think he's right."

"Calm down, honey."

"But she'll come after us. She can't go after Drummond, he's already dead. But if she wants to hurt him, she could come after us. He'd have to watch us die knowing it was his fault."

"This is the reason I should've been there."

Max pulled back. "You're going to give me an 'I told you so'? Really?"

"What I'm saying is that had I been there, I would have seen this ghost. We would know exactly who we're dealing with. I know you want to protect me, but surely we're far beyond that now. You know you need me. So stop holding back and let me be of use."

"Holding back?" Max tried to look surprised but she could always read him.

"I don't know what the big secret is, but you've been as bad as

Drummond."

"It's not like that."

"It's exactly like that." She smiled to show him she wasn't angry, that she worried about him and wanted to help. "You know better than this. If we don't trust each other, then the whole thing falls apart."

Max sighed. He pulled out the photograph of the fire and slid it across the table. Sandra looked it over. "Well?" he said. "Leed died clutching that picture, it's got to mean something."

"There aren't any ghosts around it, if that's what you're looking for. And sometimes an object that gets handled by ghosts a lot will have a glow to it. This has nothing like that. It's just a picture."

Max looked over the picture again — massive mansion-sized house, smoke and fire obscuring most of the building, lots of people sitting far afield watching. They were dressed well. Very proper. Could be any time from the 1940s or before. Max never doubted that the picture held an important clue, but why did it have to be so difficult to find? If Joshua Leed wanted to show him something, why not draw a circle around it? Or write it down? Or for-crying-out-loud, just say it? Why wait until the evil spirit of a witch is killing you? Would it have been so difficult to trust a little before everything went to crap? And Drummond was no better. If he continued to hide the truth, the consequences might be as severe, if not worse, than what happened to Leed.

Sandra reached across the table and rubbed the wrinkled lines on Max's forehead. "You've got a frowny-thing going on there. What are you thinking about?"

"I'm sick of not having answers."

"Then go get some. How many times will I have to remind you that you have a skill beyond seeing a detective's ghost? You're an excellent researcher. Go do some research. Find some answers."

THAT EVENING WHILE SANDRA SLEPT, Max sat at the kitchen table with a notebook, his laptop, and a lot of questions. He decided to focus on Dr. Ernest and Joshua Leed first. By following their path, he hoped to figure out where the other witches had been buried without resorting to a confrontation with Drummond — an unpleasant thing under normal conditions, but now one that might transform the ghost detective into an evil spirit.

Within a short period of time, Max had begun to build a solid picture of this duo. They had done little to cover their tracks (hence the FBI's interest), and Max's research skills had improved over the last few years. One thing became abundantly clear — Leed had lied about a lot.

For starters, Dr. Matthew Ernest never taught at any university. In fact, he never earned anything beyond a Bachelor's Degree. The "Doctor" in his name was a complete fabrication. That he and Joshua Leed became witch hunters appeared to be true. They spent a lot of time in online forums arguing the reality of witches and ghosts, trying to persuade any who would listen that a war existed just beneath the surface of our daily lives. If not for the fact that Max knew they were right — at least about the existence of these things — he would have dismissed their rantings as lunacy.

Unfortunately, the rest of their world view was at best misinformed and at worst, downright deadly. They were convinced that a grand war continually took place between mankind and the supernatural. Max agreed that the two didn't necessarily mix all that well, but a war? No. They thought communing with benevolent ghosts through physical contact would be advantageous. Max had suffered through the intense pain of that experience — not something he would call advantageous. They suggested that all ghosts wanted to move on to a better afterlife, and that their job was to help facilitate the journey. Sounded nice, but Max knew of at least one dead detective that had no interest in moving on anywhere.

By searching old newspaper articles, Max learned that Ernest and Leed spent as much time evading the police as they did hunting witches. Their names popped up in everything from big newspapers, like the Philadelphia Inquirer, to small county newspapers, like The Davidson Reporter. They were sought for questioning in at least a dozen missing person cases and several homicides. Max surmised that most of these interrogations went nowhere since the public police logs lacked arrests following the sessions.

In the 1950s, however, on three occasions, both Ernest and Leed were charged — once with kidnapping, twice with murder. In the case of the murders, whatever evidence the police had went up in flames, destroyed in a bizarre fire. With the kidnapping, the police had the girl in protective custody. She claimed that they lifted her from a grocery store parking lot, told her they knew she was a witch and that they planned to kill her. At some point during her captivity, they decided they had made a mistake and let her go, making her swear to never tell a soul. She swore as instructed, and then headed straight for the police.

"This is where you changed," Max said to the laptop screen.

He could picture them having a difficult conversation. Ernest insisted they use their skills with the dark arts to silence this girl. Leed objected — after all, why did they let her go in the first place if they would only kill her in the end? But Ernest pressed on, pointing out that they had made a mistake, a tragic mistake, that he didn't want to hurt this girl, but that she jeopardized all they had worked for, that if she were allowed to testify, they would go to jail for a long time, and then who would be looking out for mankind? Who would fight the witches?

Max could hear Leed's arguments weaken as well as his resolve. He may have despised the decision, but Leed eventually agreed. They put a curse on the girl, and within a day, she had died from unknown causes.

While a lot of this story was supposition on Max's part, he had done this sort of thing enough to know when his imagination had struck close to the truth. This felt true. The newspaper articles, public police logs, and filed lawsuits that he could find supported his conclusion. And even if he missed the mark a little, it didn't change much.

The facts remained that Ernest and Leed had deluded themselves into attacking women, some of whom were actually witches. No doubt, the ones they tracked down to North Carolina were real. Drummond might have been a bit gullible at the time, but he wouldn't kill random people just on the word of these guys. Since Drummond participated in the curse, Max had to assume the story of a North Carolina coven held merit.

Unfortunately, while Max managed to put together a grim picture of Ernest and Leed — essentially two unintentional serial killers — he found little to link them up with the coven. Their history died when they reached Winston-Salem. Considering Leed's paranoia, Max guessed they purposely hid after dispatching the coven in order to protect themselves from retaliation.

Max thought about different avenues to research — more basics on witch covens, searching for acknowledged witches in Winston-Salem, looking up some of the symbols Ernest and Leed had drawn on their walls. As his bouncing ball screen saver kicked in, he realized none of this would help him much. He already knew most of the witch basics from his previous research and his own unfortunate experiences with Dr. Connor, the Hull's witch on retainer. Finding current witches in Winston-Salem might be interesting, but the coven in question had been destroyed decades ago. The best he could find would be a relative of one of the witches, and he doubted any relative would be very forthcoming in the matter. As for the symbols, he needed to look them up but his mind didn't want to focus on that at the moment. In fact, there was only one thing he kept thinking about — Marshall Drummond.

Max rested his fingers on the keyboard. "Okay, Drummond. You've got more answers than I do, and if you won't tell us, if all you're going to do is lie, then I'm not going to feel guilty about looking into you a little deeper."

He typed Drummond's name into the search field but hesitated. He craned his neck to peek toward the stairs. Listening for any sound of Sandra, he held still.

"Don't feel guilty," he finally said and tapped the Enter key.

After a few hours, he had to admit that much of Drummond's life remained an undigitized mystery. He found several newspaper reports of cases Drummond had worked on as well as records of his private investigator's license and such. Nothing too telling, though. Until he found reference to a book called *The Driving Darkness: One Psychiatrist's Look into the Roots of Mental Illness.*

The book made sure to change all the names of the patients as well as identifying features — sex, weight, hair color, eye color, etc. However, Max noticed that the author, Dr. Paul Clarkson, had worked at the West Carolina Insane Asylum at the time when he wrote the book. A while back, Drummond had confided that he once entered the care of that facility under his own volition.

Drummond had been a beat cop when he encountered a ghost who needed his help getting hidden money to a niece. Talking of the supernatural experience led to his removal from the police force and the start of his career as a private investigator. It also led to a mental breakdown.

An hour into reading the book, Max thought for sure he had found Drummond's case. The book had changed Drummond into a young, pretty girl named Daisy, but only that case matched the tone of Drummond's experience. Max, of course, knew he could be wrong, that he might be finding the outcome he wanted to find, but the other cases in the book either bore no sign of reality or bore signs of too much reality. They were people disturbed by abusive, tortuous childhoods or mystic delusions. Only the case of Daisy spoke of the reality Max had come to know. She had to be Drummond's case.

According to the book, Drummond's therapy session uncovered that the ghost he had encountered was not, in fact, his first touch with the supernatural. His mother, Eunice Drummond, had suffered periodic seizures her entire life. Her parents had taken her to several doctors, but no cause could be determined. When she left home, she stopped seeking out doctors. As she once told her son, "I had no need for them. I've always known what causes my seizures."

She then explained that she believed angels and demons would possess her body while she slept. Even if she nodded off for a quick nap, her soul opened to them. She had no way to prove it. Nothing beyond the seizures happened. But she promised her son that she knew this to be the case — because while in that state, she saw what they saw, she knew what they knew.

She refused to tell little Marshall Drummond the specifics. "If I told you half of it, you'd never sleep again."

Churches became prominent in their lives. She would take Marshall to a new church for weeks on end until she decided whether to move on to another church or to speak with the reverend or priest or whatever title that church used. When she spoke with the man, and it always was a man, he either thought she was evil or crazy. Then Marshall would be taken to a new church as Eunice kept searching for one that believed her.

"But don't think ill of them or their church," she told him on numerous occasions. "A church, the actual building, is like a living being itself. So, you respect those who worship there and you respect the building itself. Otherwise, bad things'll happen."

When Marshall was nine, they joined yet another church but something went wrong. Eunice thought they might have finally found people who understood her, and she excitedly went off late one night to meet the pastor at his home. She came back, bruised and disheveled, spewing hatred towards them and threatening to burn down their church. Marshall tried to remind her that churches were alive, and she struck him across the cheek.

Two months later, at Marshall's tenth birthday party, she suffered a seizure that would not stop. His father and the other adults did all they could, but she died. An autopsy showed that she had a massive tumor in her brain, one that had been growing for years. Marshall then understood that his mother had been imagining the possessions, that she could have been saved if she had seen the right doctor, and that all the stories she had told him concerning the supernatural world were nothing more than the hallucinations of a damaged brain.

But then he saw a ghost.

He learned such things were real.

Guilt plagued him.

The book went on to discuss how these events shaped "Daisy's" life, and as far as Max could tell, Dr. Clarkson was criminally incompetent. After only two months with "Daisy", he concluded that the patient would be served best by a heavy drug regiment and surgery on the brain. Thankfully for Drummond, Dr. Clarkson's consistently draconian prescriptions led to his dismissal from the asylum. Not surprising since Drummond had picked this particular institution for its forward-thinking attitudes towards its patients, an attitude Dr. Clarkson clearly did not share.

Max's cell phone vibrated on the table. He looked at the phone's face to see that somehow it had become seven in the morning and that his unwelcome friend, FBI Agent Stevenson, wanted to talk. "Hello?" he said, his voice scratchy and low.

"Open your front door," Stevenson said.

"Huh?"

"And bring a cup of coffee with you."

Max walked toward the front door. He saw the silhouette of a man standing outside. "For crying out loud," he muttered as he opened the door.

"No coffee?" Stevenson said.

Squinting at the morning light, Max leaned on the door frame. "What do you want?"

"Somebody broke into Matthew Ernest's home."

"Really?"

"Yup. Broke in, walked around, and left. Doesn't look like the person took anything. Guess they only wanted to have a look."

"You came here at seven in the morning to tell me this?"

"Thought you might be interested. Oh, and Joshua Leed was murdered last night." Stevenson paused, and Max could feel the man's eyes probing around, observing Max's reaction, comparing it to the reactions of guilty people. "You don't seem too surprised."

"Leed hired me because Ernest had been killed. He was convinced somebody wanted him dead, too. I've barely started looking into any of this and now he's dead. Looks like he was right."

"That's one possibility. But I don't find that possibility matches my facts too well. Of course, there's the other possibility."

Though Max really didn't want to hear the answer, he had to ask. "What's the other?"

"The other possibility is that you killed Joshua Leed, much like you killed Matthew Ernest."

Max hung his head. "I told you I never met Ernest. And Leed only just hired me."

"But you're the only one who can confirm that story. I'm telling you, Max, it's looking worse and worse. Especially because I don't like being lied to. People do it all the time to me. They lie about their alibis, lie about their involvement in crimes, lie about their guilt and their remorse. It's disheartening after a while. I'm going to tell you something that's not a lie, though. Federal prison — it ain't for you. I've seen plenty of guys go off to do time, and believe me, you won't be able to handle it."

"I won't have to, since I didn't do anything."

"Can I tell you a little secret? Some of us in the FBI, guys like me, we actually prefer the serial killers. Those guys, once their caught, they want to tell you everything. Much more pleasant way to do the job. Guys like you, with all the denials and the lies, it makes my day drag on and on."

"I did not kill anybody."

Stevenson clicked his tongue. "If you say so. I sure hope you're telling me the truth, though. Because when I find out I've been chasing my tail due to your lies, that will piss me off. That's when you'll find out how tough an FBI Agent can be." He lifted his head to see past Max's shoulder and smiled. "Good morning, Mrs. Porter. I hope I didn't wake you. Just having a friendly chat with your husband about federal prison. You have a nice day, now." With that, he walked back to his car and drove off.

Sandra waited until the car had gone. Her face had paled as she put together the bits of information she had. At length, she asked, "Is he serious?"

"The FBI thinks I killed both Dr. Ernest and Leed."

"The FBI? The real FBI?" She closed her eyes and covered her mouth. Unsure what her reaction meant, Max's skin prickled. He warmed when she looked up, determined and strong. "You are not going to jail for a ghost witch's crimes." She gave Max a tight hug. "What do you want to do?"

"I want you to figure out that code."

"I will."

"But first, I hope you know how to stop a ghost from turning because we're done being nice to Drummond."

There were numerous reasons Max loved Sandra. That she knew the perfect balance between when to challenge him and when to support him had to be near the top of that list. As they drove in to the office, she didn't pepper him with questions or doubts. Maybe she wanted to hear Drummond's answers as much as he did. Even so, her strength only propped him up higher.

When Max threw open the office door, he found Drummond waiting near the bookshelf. "You've been lying to us, and it's got to stop right now."

Drummond thrust his hands in his coat and shook his head. "Good morning to you, too."

"Don't even start with the sarcasm. Things are going out of control real fast."

"What are you even talking about?" To Sandra, Drummond said, "Did you guys have a fight or something? Forget to give him his morning coffee?"

"Joshua Leed contacted me and told me all about the coven you guys destroyed way back when. I don't know why you've been lying about it, but the FBI thinks I'm the one who killed Leed and —"

"Leed's dead?"

"That's not the point."

"How? How did he die?" Drummond's eyes flared as he closed in on Max.

"I think it was the same way Dr. Ernest died, and I think you know more about it than I do. So, please, tell me what's going on before this evil ghost comes after me."

"Nothing will come after you. You weren't part of this."

"Didn't feel that way when I was pressed against a wall watching Leed be torn apart."

Drummond turned away and hid his face beneath his hand. "I'm sorry that happened to you. Believe me, I never thought you were in any danger. I never even thought you knew about Leed."

"Obviously."

Drummond rushed over to Sandra. "Have you been hurt in all this?"

"No," she said. "But if anything happens to Max, it'd be worse than if it happened to me. Worse for me, worse for you, and worse for every ghost I can get a hold of."

Drummond recoiled at the venom in her tone. His eye took on an odd, half-lidded look, and Max wondered if he had witnessed a ghost turning evil. But Sandra did not appear concerned, so Max decided to push on. He pulled out the photo of the girl under the tree and slammed it on the table.

"Time to start talking."

Drummond looked at the photograph and bowed his head. He traced the girl with his pale finger and opened his mouth to speak. That's when they heard a knock and the door opened.

Mr. Modesto entered. "I'm here for your report. Make it quick. I dislike spending time around you."

Max looked back to Drummond, but the ghost detective had vanished. "Damn," Max said.

"I take it by your eloquent rebuttal that you have failed in your task and have nothing of significant value to report." Modesto strolled up to the desk and glanced at the photograph. "What does this have to do with the handbell? Anything? Or are you still taking on other cases?"

"You haven't given me —"

"You've been kept on retainer by the Hull family for this very purpose and now you are shirking your responsibilities. Finding this handbell should be your top priority. Any other matter must be delayed or dismissed. Should you fail to find the handbell, your usefulness to this family will be gone. Do you understand? You'll be cut off from our employers support."

"Try not to drool when you say that."

Modesto's nostrils flared as if smelling an unseemly odor. "I admit I would be elated to see your departure from this family, and quite frankly, from this city. If you could manage to screw up enough that you were forced to flee the state or country, that would be ideal. But as it stands, we still need you. Our other researchers have also failed to find the bell."

"Other researchers?"

"Don't be so naive. Do you really think a man like Hull would rest such an important task in just one individual? And *you* for that matter?"

"That's it." The morning alone had been enough to boil Max's tolerance, but adding in the past few days melted away any chance he had at maintain control. Sandra stepped towards him but she saw his red-eyed rage and backed off. "Get the fuck out of my office."

"Excuse me?"

"You want to come in here over and over and threaten me? No. I won't have it. I don't care how much money Hull's throwing at us, and I don't care who he's got on his payroll. The fact is that we still have a copy of the Hull family journal, and while your employer has made it clear that there's a point where he won't care if we make his past public record, I don't think this little handbell comes anywhere close to that point."

Modesto's face turned cold as if a ghost had passed through him. "That would be a serious mistake to make."

"Oh, really? Because I've noticed that you've made a big show of pushing and pushing for this handbell yet you've done little in the way of actually helping us with information. You know how secretive the Hulls are, and yet you expect me to find this handbell on an old legend and nothing else. And now, you want to suggest that you've hired others to do the same. I don't believe any of it. In fact, part of me is wondering if Mr. Hull even knows you're doing this."

"Now you are being belligerent and, to a greater extent, plain stupid."

Max stepped straight at Modesto. "If I'm so wrong, then why are you still here? You've hated me for a long time. Surely I've said enough by now that you could go report this to Hull and have me sent the hell out of here."

Though a trickle of sweat slid down the side of Modesto's cheek, he never flinched. "I assure you, nothing would make me happier. Unfortunately, you have caught me in a bit of a lie."

"I knew it."

"There are no other researchers. That's it. The rest is true, and I have been ordered to tell you to make this the top priority. I suspect the only reason you're still here is because our employer feels no other researcher that could be acquired on short notice will accomplish what we expect of you."

Max did not expect that answer and it worried him. He thought he had pegged Modesto, but this looked to be more serious than he realized. What could be so important about a handbell that they couldn't hire somebody else?

Modesto walked to the door. "I do think I've been a tad unfair with you, however. I could have given you more information but purposely withheld in hopes that you would fail. Your outburst, however unprofessional and distasteful, impressed upon me that by trying to sabotage your efforts, I was inadvertently hurting our employer's efforts."

"I liked you better when Hull had fired you. Since you got re-hired, you talk like a bigger prick than ever."

The corner of Modesto's mouth rose. "The set of handbells were named the Bells of the Damned." With that said, Modesto made a slight bow toward Sandra and exited.

Max looked to Sandra, his mouth agape, his eyes wide. She laughed. "Guess you have some more research to do now."

Chapter 12

MAX STAKED OUT A TABLE at the Z. Smith Reynolds Library that allowed him a good view of those coming and going. The long hall that had an exit at the far end opened to a section with stairs on one side and the checkout desk on the other. All within Max's view. Though he knew he would have his face buried in books and his laptop, he wanted to be able to glance up from time to time and make sure neither the FBI nor a Hull representative watched him. Paranoid, yes, but he knew better than to doubt the value of a little paranoia.

As he set up his workspace, he thought about the best research approach. He already had all the basic information he needed. Normally, if he wanted to find out serious information regarding things that once were part of the Hull family, he would plan to sift through the numerous diaries, legal papers, and letters located in the special collections section. He would still have to do that laborious work, but first, he thought he should try his luck with another Internet search because this time, he had a name.

Searching The Bells of the Damned brought up thousands of hits — bad horror novels, forgotten metal songs, forgotten metal bands, and such. He followed links to several sites that claimed to have pictures or information for the Bells, but they depicted the wrong ones. However, all the sites he visited began their descriptions the same way — *These famously cursed bells* ...

This gave Max a glimmer of hope. A bell with a true curse on it would leave a trail. Of course, most "famously cursed" items were no more than superstitious tales, but considering the source of these bells — the Hull family — Max thought the likelihood that these bells bore a true curse rose significantly.

He checked out a few sites that specialized in hauntings, unexplained occurrences, and strange American legends. Though all of the stories lacked the name Hull, Max pieced together a possibly authentic version by picking out the references to North Carolina, the

Moravians, and other bits of Winston-Salem history he knew. He then spent several hours verifying his guesses with primary source material from the special collections.

As best as he could figure out, the Bells first surfaced long before the merge of Winston and Salem, back when Tucker Hull had broken with the Moravians. His dabbling in magic had caused an irreparable rift that sent him away, but his obstinacy had kept him from leaving the city. Like any predator, Tucker lived on the edges of the herd, watching for any Moravians who felt marginalized, alone, and ignored. He would pick them up in a warm embrace and create servants to his beliefs.

"He started a cult," Max said to his laptop as he typed out his notes.

As numbers in his group increased, his explorations of magic deepened. He would task individuals with learning witchcraft while others spent days in meditation, attempting to open the mind into accepting, and thus seeing, ghosts. No form of the supernatural went untouched. He even had a few members look into some of the ancient Eastern religions, which to his mind seemed to embrace magic.

Living so close to the Moravians guaranteed trouble. The Aufseher Collegium, the section of the Moravian government set up to handle secular matters, forbade any members of their group to associate with Tucker Hull's "new" religion. But they were too late.

Max found a partial letter in the special collections dated 1832 from an unidentified woman to her lover T. It read:

I pray these reports will aid you in all your efforts. They must, otherwise I could not stand being kept apart from you. I cannot stop seeing you everywhere I look. My breath catches thinking of you and even as I write these words, my heart leaps to my breast. My dearest T, how much longer must I continue this charade. Father suspects I have a secret lover but he is too proud to confront me. As much as he is angry, he is too afraid to have it confirmed. And I would, too. If he asked, I would not lie. I would let the Elder's Council throw me out, exile me from all my family and friendships, for then I could be with you always. I want nothing more than to rest by your side, to be yours in every way you desire, to bear your children. My passions for you burn hotter every passing day. How much longer will you make me wait? Let me leave this lie and become yours. Let me study with you. I understand what the others do not. Let me write your Grimoire. Let me be your High Priestess.

Like a twisted Romeo and Juliet, Tucker Hull had seduced a young Moravian woman and kept her amongst the Brotherhood for as long as he could manage. She was his spy.

Max shook his head. "No way could this end well."

Most of the other sources Max uncovered were not so direct, but diaries that on the surface appeared innocuous, actually held enough clues for Max to identify as members of Hulls growing cult. One in particular, the diary of Peter Cottonwall, mentioned a beautiful set of thirteen handbells which his leader, the beloved T, found joy in having his lady play. Apparently Tucker's Juliet played quite well and charmed many the few times she slipped away from the Brotherhood.

Tucker might have been planning to use his spy for many years, but she had other expectations. In another partial letter with the same handwriting, one that the library did not recognize belonged to the same author (but then, most libraries were so poorly funded that they may not have yet gotten to the letter for classification), she wrote:

> *Please do not be cross. To have both you and Father forsake me would be more than I dare consider. If not for Mother, I suspect I would be thrown from the house this very night. As it is, though, I have been given a fortnight and no more to make arrangements for my removal from the house and the Brotherhood.*

Whether this naive girl's father discovered the truth or she outright told him in a fit of defiance, Max could not tell. Regardless, the end result remained the same. She left her home and went to her lover's arms.

Except according to Cottonwall's diary, her arrival brought only trouble. She appeared unexpectedly (as far as Cottonwall knew) during a group meditation session, and Tucker would not embrace her. She had failed him, and he ordered her to leave. The scene that occurred involved plenty of crying, pleading, and begging but in the end, Tucker refused even to look at her. Cottonwall wrote:

> *The strangest sight of it all occurred next. For as I attempted to shut out this annoyance, per T's instructions, I could not but help myself and I snatched a glimpse of this once-prized witch who had now fallen from T's graces. T had his back to her and though she continued to say the words of begging for forgiveness, her eyes told*

a uniquely alternative story. She looked upon T with a fire that bespoke of the demons of old. An ancient, horrifying glare that has caused me no amount of a good night's rest since I laid eyes upon it. I fear what she has planned for T. I fear for all of us.

The next few years progressed without incident, but Max felt confident that during that night of betrayal, this brokenhearted witch cursed the thing that Tucker loved about her most — the handbells. The name, the Bells of the Damned, cropped up later, once the bodies began to fall. And a lot of them fell.

On March 29, 1858, the body of a slave named Eli was discovered in a pond in Bethania, North Carolina. Suspicions fast turned to Eli's wife, Lucy Hine, a freewoman, and a slave named Frank. While searching Lucy's home, authorities discovered the floor still wet from being washed yet traces of blood were visible. Once the floor dried, a blood trail clearly led from the house to the pond. More blood was found on Frank's clothing. The two were convicted of the murder and, by 1859, executed.

But nobody ever could figure out the motive. Lucy and Frank denied being lovers. And Eli was not known for being abusive or in any manner cruel to his wife.

"Why he even bought her a beautiful set of handbells," one woman was quoted in a newspaper article.

In November 1873, according to a report in the *People's Press*, Sarah Tilkey attended her regular music class at Salem Female Academy. The Academy for girls had been founded by the Moravians in 1772, a unique step in the South, and had built a solid reputation for excellence. In fact, girls from all over the country sought a position at the school.

While practicing her music, young Sarah sat close to one of the stoves. It had been a particularly cold winter, so she may have sat closer than normal. That was when an ember popped and landed on her dress.

As she dashed through the school screaming, flames engulfed her body. Physicians rushed to the school, but the burns were too extensive. After a few prayers were read for her, she passed away.

While Max could not learn what instrument she played, he did know that the Bells had been donated to the school two years earlier by the family of Thomas Lash — owner of the murdered slave, Eli.

There were other cases that might have been attributable to the

Bells, but Max could not find the primary sources to confirm. For his own purposes, he considered them valid cases because it let him continue to follow the trail of bodies. This included a few suspicious deaths at the Salem Hotel, a double murder, and a lynching.

Then came the case of Ellen Smith. There was a relatively enormous amount of information available about the case since it made headlines in almost every local and surrounding paper. Even the *Union Republican,* one of the larger presses, wrote numerous articles throughout the years following the case.

In the early 1890s, Ellen Smith had been employed as a maid. She was a poor, portly girl who worked diligently but was considered to be "an idiot" — a term which Max knew back then meant she had some form of mental disability. Most people liked her and thought of her as a good worker. She was fifteen.

Then she met Peter DeGraff, a good-looking ladies' man, slim and fit, smooth tongued, and a bit unpredictable. He met Ellen in January 1890 and began courting her soon after. He was twenty-one.

DeGraff showered Ellen with trips to buy clothes, visits to the local barrooms, and plenty of food. The money, the handsome man, and the attention stole her heart. She became madly in love with him. She also became pregnant.

Unmarried and expecting, she was sent to live and work for a man named Captain Stagg. Max could not find any more about this man, but he did discover another Union Republican article (this one from 1894 looking back at the case) in which the reporter stated that though Ellen Smith delivered her child, it was either stillborn or died within days of birth. Shortly after, Ellen returned to Winston and looked up her lover, Peter. But DeGraff wanted nothing to do with her.

Ellen began stalking DeGraff, and his refusals intensified. On several occasions, people overheard him threatening to kill her. But then suddenly, he behaved nicely to her and sent her a note. The note professed his love for her and asked that she meet him on an upcoming evening by the spring at the new Zinzendorf Hotel.

Built in Winston's West End, the Hotel had been the brainchild of R. J. Reynolds and other community leaders. It was an enormous structure, reminding Max of a Disney castle made of wood. As a gift to the Hotel, an anonymous source donated a beautiful set of thirteen handbells — white with a red stripe and curious markings on the inside lip. They were prominently displayed in the lobby entrance. It was hoped this resort hotel would help make Winston a business and vacation center for the region.

That night in 1892, however, the hopes were in Ellen's heart. She wore a dark calico skirt and a light-colored blouse, and she bought a new, yellow handkerchief, perhaps as a gift. She then headed off to the Hotel.

The following morning, a hotel employee came upon a gruesome scene. As reported in the *Union Republican*: "A white apron was found hanging upon a bush near the body, which was that of Ellen Smith, which was lying face downward, bloody, and the body swollen and disfigured and a prey to flies."

"The old journalists sure could paint a picture," Max said.

What followed went beyond the scope of Max's research but in the end, after much drama and several years, Peter DeGraff was convicted of the murder and hanged. This unfortunate and ghastly murder became one of the biggest stories and trials in all of Winston-Salem history. For Max, however, the most astonishing aspect to the tale came when he learned of the ill-fated hotel.

On Thanksgiving Day 1892, the same year as the Smith murder, a fire broke out in the wooden hotel. It spread fast, and in no time became uncontrollable. Guests and staff rushed to safety in the distance, bringing with them whatever possessions they could manage. A photographer took advantage of the tragedy and made a picture of the event.

Max's heart stopped as he stared at the familiar photo. The massive building awash in flames and smoke while a crowd of onlookers gawked from their chairs and boxes. It was the same photograph Joshua Leed had died trying to give him.

Max picked up the picture and stared at it. There had to be something more to see than just the fact that the hotel had a connection to the Bells of the Damned. Leed could have told him that much. Instead, the man risked and lost his life for the photo.

"What am I supposed to see?"

Using the magnifier on his smartphone, Max searched the image starting in the top left corner and working his way methodically across and down. There were strange images within the thick smoke pouring out of the hotel, but Max thought that might only be his imagination seeing things much like recognizing objects in the shapes of clouds. Whatever Leed wanted him to see had to be more substantial than that.

When he reached the crowds, he found that most of the people had their backs to the camera. A young child stared at the camera, the body blurred a bit but the eyes glowing bright. Was this it? Max couldn't be sure. The figure had a definite supernatural feel to it, but calling it as such made Max feel like he had found Big Foot in a shadow on blurry film.

Then he saw it, and he knew right away Leed had wanted to show him this. He knew it from the way his hands tingled and the way he had to remember to breathe. Sitting behind the blurred figure, clear as the fire itself, Max spotted a young woman, her profile showing enough detail that he knew the face. Without a doubt, he looked upon the same woman as in the photo Dr. Ernest had saved. The same photo Drummond hid from. Strangest of all, the woman in Ernest's photo was no older than the woman at the Zinzendorf Hotel fire — but they were taken almost fifty years apart.

Chapter 13

WHEN MAX ENTERED HIS OFFICE, he found Sandra on her computer working on the code and Drummond floating around the ceiling humming the theme to the '80s television show Mike Hammer. The old ghost had tightened his face like a child throwing a tantrum. When he saw Max, he swooped down.

"It's not that great a life being a ghost, and your wife is making it worse."

Sandra ignored the commotion, so Max headed to his desk.

Drummond grabbed his hat and threw it on the ground, but it vanished and reappeared upon his head. "You know, you ought to be nicer to me. I do nothing but help you."

Max snapped his eyes upon Drummond, silencing the ghost. "Sandra." She didn't answer. Louder, Max called again. "Sandra!"

She jumped and whirled around, her eyes wide with fear. When she saw her husband, she relaxed and pulled her mp3 player's buds out of her ears. Despite his anger at Drummond, Max had to laugh.

"What's going on?" she asked.

Drummond wagged his finger at them both. "Some days, you two are in cahoots against me. It's not fair. I had to spend decades alone here and now that I've got some company, you guys keep trying to shut me out."

This brought Max right back to the problem. "You're the one shutting us out. You've been lying to us ever since you saw that article about Dr. Ernest's murder."

"You better watch it with the accusations."

Max opened his notebook and slapped down the photograph of the Zinzendorf Hotel fire.

"You're getting good at that," Drummond said.

"I'm not in a joking mood."

"Fine, fine. What's the big deal. It's a photo of the big Zinzendorf fire. Pretty famous photo, locally. Not exactly that big of a find."

Max pulled out his smartphone and brought up the snapshot he took of the magnified portion. "Look familiar?"

Drummond's sarcastic expression dropped away. His chin quivered a moment before he locked up his jaw in a tight clench. Narrowing his eyes, he flew to the back corner of the office.

"Come on," Max said. "I'm not an idiot. You've lied to us repeatedly, afraid we would find out about this woman. We've got murders and witch covens and these cursed handbells, and I know you have information for us."

"The handbells are cursed?"

"They're called the Bells of the Damned, and I'm pretty sure they had something to do with this fire as well as quite a lot of deaths for more than a century."

"They're cursed."

"That's right. I want to know how that's connected to your girl here."

With a bewildered gaze, Drummond looked across the room to Max. "And that's really her? Sitting there, watching the fire in 1892?"

"I think so."

"Then I was wrong." Drummond lowered his head and shuddered. Max swore Drummond sounded relieved. A moment later, the ghost returned to the desk, sniffling and dabbing at his eyes. "I'm truly sorry that I caused the two of you trouble and worry and all. I didn't know I was wrong all this time. I thought ..."

Mimicking her husband's usual behavior, Sandra leaned back in her chair and kicked her feet up to the desk. "Care to explain what you're rambling on about?"

Max tried to maintain a serious face, but he knew Sandra had the right idea. Something had changed, had eased, in the room. He sat at his desk. "Please. Tell us what's going on. Maybe we can help."

Drummond looked from Sandra to Max. "If anybody can help now, it'd be you two. Before I say anything, though, I ask one favor. Meet me out at Tanglewood Park. I'd rather not talk of this here where I've spent so many years cursed. I'd rather be where this all began."

"Of course," Sandra said. "It's the least we could do."

Tanglewood Park contained sprawling acres upon acres of wooded trails, a pool, homes from the 1700s, stables, tennis courts, an arboretum, and even an old locomotive engine. Families loved the place as did wedding and event planners. It also sat far west of the city which meant Max and Sandra had plenty of time in the car.

"Of course?" Max said. "Why would you agree to go all the way out here? We don't have time for this. You should be working on that code."

"Honey, sometimes you've got to give a ghost a little slack. Clearly there's something emotional involved with this woman. You could see how choked up he got. Letting him tell it his own way will make it easier on him."

"I don't care if it's easy for him. He lied to us."

"All the more reason to go to the place that is connected to this strong emotion. He'll be so consumed with the memory, he won't realize how much he's telling us."

"Wait, wait. This is going to be a *strong emotion* for him? Isn't that what we're trying to avoid? Y'know, so he doesn't go evil on us."

Sandra shrugged. "I made a tough call."

"Are you crazy?"

"We need to know what he knows. At this point, I think it's worth the risk. What else are we going to do? Sit around and wait to be murdered like Ernest and Leed?"

Max had nothing else to say. She was right, as usual, and he figured he would be better off planning ahead rather than arguing a moot point. Except that his brain had no plan in mind. He drove in a blank daze, trying to make sense of the numerous bits of information he juggled, but made no progress.

When they reached the park and paid the two dollar fee at the gatehouse, they headed slowly along the narrow drive until they passed the stables. A twelve-year-old girl rode her palomino inside a fenced paddock filled with jumps for her to practice on. Two women, Max guessed her mother and a trainer, watched with tense excitement. As they receded in the rearview mirror, Max marveled at how much he had learned to read off of people's body language.

"Over there," Sandra said, pointing to the open field on the left. They parked and walked over to where Drummond floated, staring at a tree.

"I think she knew," Drummond said as they approached. "I don't know how, but she had to have known that the witch hunters were coming and that they would contact me for local help."

"Who was she?" Max asked.

"Her name was Patricia Welling. I was out here for a friend's wedding, but you know me, I don't like that kind of thing. So, I went for a stroll and wound up around here. I looked over and saw this exquisite woman by this tree. She wore a blue gown and we shared a cigarette. I never asked her what she was doing out there. I assumed she was there for the wedding, too, since she dressed so fancy. Well, we talked and laughed and while I'm not one to share this kind of thing, you should know that we kissed, too. In fact, we began to see each other most every night."

Max looked at the tree so he didn't have to meet Drummond's eye. "When you say that you saw each other, do you mean ..."

"Okay, yes. We were like rabbits. You really don't believe in subtlety, do you?"

"Just trying to be clear."

"I know how this sounds, but the truth is that we had fallen in love. Even looking back at it all, knowing that she had arranged the relationship, I know she loved me. She probably had not intended to fall for me, but it happened."

Sandra laced her fingers between Max's. "Is that when Dr. Ernest showed up?"

"We had two incredible weeks together. The kind of time that changes a man, makes him think about packing it in, giving up a dangerous life, settling down, maybe even some kids. I even turned away cases so I could spend more time with her. For those two weeks, I swear I thought nothing could change. Then I walked into my office one morning and there's this professor from up North with his tales of witch covens and special rituals. He came with two names to follow up on. Jane Bitter and Patricia. I sent him and Leed after Bitter. I figured they'd come up with more information from her and I could avoid having to approach Patricia about any of it. Except right then, I don't know if I recognized it at the time but I know it now, that was the moment a darkness began to form inside me."

"You poor thing," Sandra said.

"Turned out Jane was the real deal. A full witch and part of the coven he and Leed had been hunting down. They destroyed her that night but not before getting her to confess a list of six more members. Right away I saw that Patricia was on the list. We each took two names, and since I had supposedly made contact with Patricia already, they let me have her name. We agreed on a night for the job to be done, and I had two days to figure out if she was really a witch or if Jane Bitter had lied."

As Drummond spoke, Max watched him carefully while trying not to be obvious. Sandra appeared to be lost in the romantic nature of the story which worried Max even more. As his resident ghost expert, he needed her to be looking for any sign that Drummond's story might be turning him.

"The evidence Matt had compiled in a file gave me little to help. In fact, the two days passed quickly, and I still had no idea what to believe." Drummond's fingers curled into fists.

Max said, "This is a painful memory. Why don't we take a break, let us process everything you've said, and then we'll come back —"

"No." Drummond barked. "I've got to get this out."

Sandra looked to Max, lines of worry creasing her forehead.

"The night came and I had decided to deal with the other witch first. I guess I wanted to avoid the whole thing as long as possible, as if maybe some savior would come in and make that horrible night disappear. I went to the home of Joanna Lee. She lived in a small house on First Street, and I remember thinking that I'd have to be careful about the neighbors hearing anything."

With a sour chuckle, Drummond moved across the field toward the car. Max wanted to be hopeful that this meant Drummond had calmed down, but the ghosts stern expression left little room for such hopes.

"I walked in there, and she had been waiting. She attacked me with a carving knife. I don't like hurting women, but in this case, I had no choice. She would've sliced me up, if I had let her. So I fought back, and despite her yelling some foul things, her biting and random kicking, I managed to subdue her long enough to tie up her feet and get her hands behind her back. Then I had to do the cursing ritual.

"I drew a circle around her with salt and a pulled out an ivory knife that Matt had given me. With it, I had to carve three symbols into her back, deep enough to hit bone. She screamed as I did this, tears soaking the floor. She wanted to wriggle away but the cuts were so deep that movement only caused her more and more pain. And I suspect that she held on to the hope that whatever curse I inflicted on her did not involve her death. But she was wrong. When I finished the last symbol, I grabbed her hair and pulled back her head, and with that ivory knife, I slit her throat."

They had reached the car, and Max opened the back door for Drummond. "I'm sorry you had to go through that."

"It got worse. She didn't die. She bled and sputtered, but she didn't die. She wrenched her head around to see me, and I've never seen such a tormented face. Blood pouring out of her neck, down her chest, and her eyes blazing at me in pain and hatred. I didn't know why she was still alive, and I had no clue what to do. This was long before cellphones. I had no way to contact anybody quickly. At least, nobody I wanted to contact. With all the noise we had made and that she continued to make, I figured the police would be showing up any second." Drummond glanced at Max. "Close that damn door. I'm not a fragile little thing you need to escort around."

Max closed the door and tried not to show his fear.

"Sorry," Drummond said, but he maintained his intense expression. "Please, let me finish this." He looked back the way they had come. "Blood poured out of her, more than I ever thought a body could hold, but it pooled inside the circle. No matter how saturated the salt became, that curse kept all of her contained. And then I saw it. The middle symbol, the one that cut deepest into her spine, I had missed putting in two lines. I shoved her over and tried to correct the mistake, but she fought back hard. It was all that much harder because I had to make sure not to disturb the salt. I managed to get through it, though, and the second I finished the symbol, she dropped dead. I followed the rest of Matt's instructions, burying the body, covering it with salt, and a page with more symbols that Matt had written for me.

"I spent an hour walking the downtown area — drinking. I'd seen some strange things before that, but nothing so horrifying. I really didn't know if I could do it again, much less to Patricia. After awhile, I ended up at her doorstep. I don't recall what we said, but I think she knew why I had come. She also knew she could change my mind with a kiss. That kiss — that's when I knew without a doubt that she loved me.

"We spent the night together. The most passionate night of my life. Everything we had become together poured out of us, pooled around us, in a desperate, tragic embrace. But then the morning came, and I could only think one thing — the only reason she could possibly have known of the coming tragedy between us was if she had been a witch all along. Otherwise, she would be asking me why I was so intense. What was wrong? Anything like that. But she hadn't. She knew exactly what was wrong because her coven sisters had died that night.

"Knowing that she was a witch didn't make it any easier. But it did strengthen my resolve, because if I didn't finish the job, the otherworldly revenge would be ghastly. See, we weren't just killing them. That's what we should have done. But Matt and Leed convinced me that cursing them would be better. Maybe that's why the universe saw fit to curse me later." Drummond pointed to the car door. "Just because I'm a ghost doesn't mean you can't be polite. Open the door."

Max frowned but a warning look from Sandra kept him quiet. He opened the door for Drummond and then got behind the wheel. "Back to the office?"

"Not yet. I haven't finished the story."

"Then where?"

"Get on 40 East. Back into the city."

As Max drove, Drummond continued his tale. He spoke with such vivid detail, Max had no trouble picturing the scene. Drummond stayed in bed as the morning sun broke through the drab curtains. He listened to Patricia taking a shower as his thoughts tumbled over each other. There had to be a way out of this — some loophole that would both destroy the coven yet somehow let Patricia remain alive and his.

He slid out of bed and into his clothes. The ivory knife weighed heavy in his coat pocket. Magic. Why did people mess with it? In all his time spent dealing with the supernatural, he had yet to find anybody who had benefited from using magic. Then again, there was one way he could stay with Patricia — join her. Leave this world of violence and sadness and join the coven, learn the dark arts, become a husband far beyond anything she could have expected.

"I was seriously tempted," he said before pointing toward an exit. "Take Peters Creek Parkway up into the city. Stay on it for a bit."

Max followed the directions even as Drummond dropped back into the heart of his story. He had been standing in Patricia's bedroom, not moving, just thinking. He wanted nothing more than to throw off his clothes, rush into that shower with her, and forget the world. And why shouldn't he? Because he thought she might have been expecting him? Because she might be this witch? It didn't make sense. He had followed Ernest and Leed blindly and now he contemplated a torturous death for the woman he loved.

He reached up to his shirt and began unbuttoning. She deserved better from him than what he had given. That kiss had said it all.

The bathroom door opened. Patricia stood in the doorway wearing nothing at all, one arm stretched along the frame, the other behind her back.. She smiled at him and his heart skipped. From behind her back, she pulled out the ivory knife and her smile fell.

Drummond's hand reached into his coat pocket – – a flashlight. She had switched them at some point. He looked up at her. "It's true, then?"

"Don't do this to me," she said, her voice soothing and at odds with the tension in her grip. "Whatever you think I am, I'm not."

"Then how do you know what I'm going to do?"

"Because I love you, and when you love someone, you take an interest in what they do. I know the kind of cases you specialize in. A weapon like this — it can't have any good purpose. You've been hiding it since last night. First time you ever refused to let me take your coat."

"You're only protecting yourself, then? Is that it?"

Her throat quivered as she stepped closer to him. Her beautiful body swayed like a snake hypnotizing its prey. He only had to tell her that he didn't care. Give over to her and he could live happily ever after. A fairy tale washed in dark magic.

But as she took her final step, she turned the blade towards him. Drummond reacted to the threat with muscle memory. He deflected her thrust, grabbed the wrist of the knife hand, and redirected the blade into her soft belly.

"A witch after all," he muttered.

She fell over, blood staining the ivory, her breathing the only sound. Though tears blurred his vision, Drummond hurried through the ceremony. His heart broke with each step. He circled her in salt, pulled out the blade, and carved the intricate symbols into her back. Her shock had shut down her reactions. Like an abused wife, she simply took the punishment. It was a small mercy to him, it let him finish the job without pause, but his heart wept with every cut. When he finished the last symbol, he thought he might be able to get through the whole thing. Until he pulled back her head to slit her throat.

Her eyes shot open, and she peered back at him. "Please, don't do this. I'm no witch. I'll forgive you for all of this. Please, don't kill me."

Sandra wiped the tears in her eyes. "What did you do?"

Drummond told Max to pull over. "I killed her. I hated myself for it, but I had to do it. I couldn't be sure what was true, and if I let her go, nothing good could happen. If she was a witch, she would go on and the failed curse would destroy us. If she wasn't, she would go to the police and we'd never have a chance to shut down the coven. Matt and Leed did their best to convince me we had done right. They even stayed around for two months to check up on every lead they could find, to make sure no other witches in the coven could be found. Their assurances plus the fact that no revenge was exacted upon us, led us to the conclusion that we had succeeded.

"But I didn't believe it. I couldn't have been so wrong about her. So, I've spent all these years since wondering, knowing, I had killed an innocent woman. Except when you showed me that picture of her at the fire — only a powerful witch with access to the magic a coven created could have pulled off the kind of spell that'd let you live so long."

Max reached over and patted through Drummond's hand. The act caused an icy chill to cover Max's body, but Drummond clearly appreciated the gesture. Then Max's eyes widened. "Wait a second. Since she really was a witch, we have to destroy her body like Leed said. Otherwise, we'll be attacked, too. Right?"

"About that." Drummond tilted his hat and sat back in the car. "See, after I finished with — after I finished, I had a big problem. Since I had waited until morning to do it, I couldn't easily dispose of her body. Not in broad daylight. So, I wrapped her in the carpet and went back for my car. I stuffed her in the trunk and drove her to the office."

"Are you saying she's in the office?"

"She was. But then some people decided to renovate the Zinzendorf Hotel."

"You mean *rebuild*. Not much left to renovate."

"No, they rebuilt it shortly after the big fire. But in my lifetime, they decided to renovate it, and when the time came, I broke in one night and slipped the body into the walls."

Max clapped his hands once. "Great. Let's go get her."

"Here's our problem."

Max sighed, and Sandra shook her head. "You really thought it would be easy?"

"In 1970, I was a cursed ghost stuck to the office. A squatter had taken up residence — Hal. Real pain in the neck. He had a buddy, Dale, who would stop by to smoke pot from time to time. One day, I'm listening to them talk —"

"You little eavesdropper."

"You try being imprisoned to that office. I took whatever entertainment I could get. Anyway, these fellas are talking and Dale mentions that the Zinzendorf Hotel was going out of business. They were going to raze the whole thing. I had maybe a month before things went sour with the coven's curse. So, I started haunting Hal. He had moved enough furniture around, disrupting the full curse on me, that I could make my presence known. Luckily, Hal had a keen fear of the supernatural. I convinced him I was the ghost of Patricia and that he had to move my body or else I'd plague him forever."

"So where is she now?"

"He found her the night before they tore down her floor. He brought what was left back to the office. I then had him wait until they poured the foundation for the new building and then when the time was right, Hal put her in the mix." Drummond nodded out the window. "That building across the street is where the hotel used to be. She's in the foundation."

Max's hope deflated as he looked across the street. The Federal Building. Well, that's what the locals called it. Really, it was the US District Court — courtrooms and holding cells, bursars and chambers, lawyers and police. "You gotta be kidding me."

Chapter 14

MAX DROVE UP TO Fourth Street and headed for the office. Double parking in front of the building, he faced Sandra. "I need that code finished."

"I will. I'm close, I think. You're not really going to break into the Federal Building, are you?"

"I have no idea what I'm going to do."

She gritted her teeth into a ridiculous smile. "Well, at least you know where you stand."

Max couldn't help himself. He laughed hard as she walked toward the office. "I love you," he shouted after her. In response, she put an extra sway to her hips.

Once Max pulled back into traffic, Drummond slid through the car into the passenger seat. "So what are we going to do?"

"I really don't know overall. Right now, though, you and I are going back to Tanglewood Park. We've got some unfinished business out there."

Drummond tried to pry out a clue as to what Max had in mind, but Max focused on driving. He took it as a good sign when Drummond settled back, tipping his hat over his eyes. Max didn't think ghosts actually slept, but he couldn't be sure.

When they finally reached the park, Max drove out to the open field where Drummond had taken them earlier. He trudged out to the tree and stared at it.

"You came all the way out here to see this tree again?"

Max turned in a circle, his eyes searching all around. "You've taught me a lot about being a detective. I really appreciate that."

"What does that have to do with being here?"

"One thing that's really stuck with me is the importance of having a partner you can trust. Until this whole thing started, I believed I could trust you."

"You know you can trust me."

"Except I'm learning how little I know about you, and then there's the fact that you've been lying to us for quite a while."

"You lied, too. Pretended not to know Leed or Matt."

"I was wrong. That's why we're here. We need to make things right before we go any further. This whole thing is giving me that same feeling I've had before — that we're headed down a dark path. I don't think we can do that and survive, if we don't trust each other."

Drummond thrust his hands in his coat pocket and tucked his chin down. "I got that feeling, too."

"Wrong angle," Max muttered and walked several feet beyond the tree, turned around and nodded with satisfaction. "There."

"What?"

"From this angle, it's clear that this tree is the one in the picture. There's the weird branch and in the distance is the stables."

"What picture?"

"You know what picture. The gal under the tree. It was taken right here. Am I wrong to think that she was Patricia? And that you took the picture?"

Drummond chuckled. "You really are getting good at this."

"What I don't understand is why you buried her in that hotel when it made more sense for you to bring her out here. The way you brought us out, the way you look at that tree, the fact that you took the picture — if you felt so strongly about her, and I believe that you did, then why dump her in some anonymous way?"

"I didn't want to." Drummond stared at the tree as if he could see her still. "My original plan was to bring her here in the middle of the night. But time was against me. It was important for the curse that she die near the same time the others did. At least, I thought it was. I failed that by waiting until morning."

"And if you wanted to bury her by this tree, you'd have to wait until late that next night."

"Exactly. I couldn't wait that long. No way would the curse be effective."

"Okay." Max headed back to the car. "I appreciate your honesty. Now, it's my turn. I have to tell you something, and it may be difficult to hear but you must stay calm."

Drummond floated next to Max. "I'll try. No promises, though."

"Do you know anything about ghosts turning?"

"What does that mean?"

Leaning against the car, Max explained what little he knew on the subject. "That's the main reason we lied to you. We didn't want to upset you."

Drummond pursed his lips. "But I've been upset plenty of times. Heck, every other day with you is upsetting."

"This isn't an everyday kind of case. This involves Patricia." Max gestured toward the tree. "You're already going into this with intense emotions. Add to that the things we've been encountering, that I fear we're going to encounter, and well —"

"You guys thought I'd pop."

"Something like that."

Rubbing his hands together, Drummond said, "Guess I've got to avoid getting too upset. Keep control of my emotions. Right? I can do that. I'm not saying I'll be perfect, but I can do it."

"Good. Because things aren't adding up right."

Drummond rubbed his hands faster. "Now we're talking. You're getting a gut feeling. What about? What's not right?"

"Well, Dr. Ernest and Leed left after that night cursing the witches, right?"

"Yeah."

"At some point, years later, they both come back. Presumably, they didn't bother looking you up because they already knew you were dead. Though, considering their interests, you'd think they would have found out you'd been cursed."

"Maybe they did know. Maybe that's why they came back."

"Then why didn't they ever try to help you? No, they didn't know about you. Which brings me to the question: Why did they come back? It wasn't to retire here. One of them settling down here, maybe I could believe it — retiring but still wanting to keep an eye on the coven that stuck with him. But both of them? No. They came down here with an agenda."

Drummond straightened as his face dropped in astonishment. "Patricia. This is about her."

"How so?"

"They both had pictures of her. The Zinzendorf fire and the one I took. But they already knew she was a witch, so why would the pictures matter?"

An uneasy shiver raced along Max's back. "That's a good question." The silence that settled between them broke only when Max's phone rang. He looked at the caller's name and knew right away what had happened. "Sandra's broken the code."

Chapter 15

"IT WASN'T THAT COMPLICATED, really. Just a substitution code but with a little math thrown in to find the right letter. I should've realized earlier but I started out looking for more difficult methods."

Max kissed Sandra. "I had no idea you were so good at this."

"Well, I had to do some research. It's not like I'm a code-breaking savant. I just like doing puzzles."

"That last part, I knew."

Drummond waved his hand over Dr. Ernest's papers. "Can we dispense with the back-slapping and get on to the actual meaning of all this?"

"Right." Sandra broke from Max's embrace. "Apparently, Dr. Ernest cursed one witch while you and Leed did two. But his was the High Priestess of the coven."

"Why did he lie to us about that?"

"The way he writes, I think he lied about most things. His name wasn't even Matthew Ernest. His real name — Tom Ratzenberg. He seems pretty paranoid in here, so perhaps the lies were an attempt to send witches off on a false trail."

"How do you know any of that's true then?"

"We don't. But he places the High Priestess in a church and that sounds like the kind of place one would bury a cursed witch. Don't you think?"

Max picked up his keys. "Only one way to find out. Thanks for all your hard work, hon. I'll call you the minute we find out anything."

"Ah, no." Sandra put her hands on her hips, and her mouth shrunk into a tight circle.

"What's wrong?"

"You are not leaving me behind. I'm not some fragile little girl you've got to sideline every time you have to go out."

Max attempted a warm smile, but he saw the way she grew angrier, so he cut it out. "I'm not trying to sideline you. I only meant —"

"I know exactly what you meant. And I'm telling you that I'm coming along. Besides, how many times have I been an essential help to you? With you only seeing Drummond, you never know when you'll need my talents."

"That's the problem. I don't like putting the woman I love in danger all the time."

"Well, when you stop playing hero and realize that I'm the one who knows the code and which church to go to, you'll realize that you're stuck with me."

Max paused, his brow crinkling and releasing along with a slew of emotions. Then he wrenched open the door. "Can we go?"

"Of course." Sandra walked out with a perky jaunt to her step.

Drummond followed behind and shared a commiserating look with Max. "All good women can be a pain in the ass sometimes."

"I heard that," Sandra called from the stairs.

In the back of his mind, Max knew Winston-Salem had a lot of churches. All the biggies — Baptist, Protestant, Catholic. Some of the more niche — Korean, Unitarian, Quaker. There was even one synagogue with a fantastic little bagel shop up the block. And, of course, there were the Moravian churches.

These tended to be smaller, less ostentatious affairs. In some of the rural areas surrounding the city, the churches were straight out of horror movie — a one-room building, low ceiling, peeling white paint on the wooden exterior.

"So what's the address?" Max said as he pulled the car into traffic.

Sandra typed away on her laptop. She frowned and typed some more. "It's not showing up on the map. I've tried Google, Bing, Mapquest."

"What's the name of the place?" Drummond asked from the backseat.

"The Moravian Hope Church. You ever hear of it?"

Drummond's casual demeanor dropped. "Oh, yeah. I know that one."

"That doesn't sound good."

"It's not going to be on any map, but I'll get us there. Get on 40 West, like you're going back to Tanglewood, and I'll let you know where to get off."

The day had slipped away from Max, and as he drove, the sun

blinded him. Squinting, he said, "How much longer?"

"Don't be in such a hurry. This isn't the kind of place you want to go to anyway. Even back in my day, this place had been an old wreck. It's off in the woods. People used it in the early 1800s. For all I know, Tucker Hull prayed there. But for whatever reason, they stopped attending it. Maybe they built a bigger place, maybe it went with Hull when he split, or maybe the rumors are true."

"Rumors?"

"It's said to be haunted. Back when I was alive, I didn't give much credence to the idea. The stories about it sounded more like tall tales rather than authentic ghost behavior. Until I met with Ernest and Leed. Then I believed the stories wholesale. But now — I'm not so sure. We best be extra careful."

"What stories?" Sandra asked.

Drummond exhaled slowly. "They said a witch coven would sneak in at night and perform their ceremonies. Of course the stories added sensational details — naked dancing, drinking of blood, baby sacrifices, that kind of thing. That's what made me doubt it all to start. But maybe something was going on back then. Maybe with the same coven we're after."

"With that kind of story, no wonder Ernest buried his witch out here."

Max followed Drummond's directions off the highway and deeper into the countryside. He turned off the paved roads and proceeded along gravel and then dirt until he reached a yellow, metal bar gate. "Guess we walk from here."

"It's not far," Drummond said as he passed through the car door.

Max retrieved two flashlights from the trunk of the car and handed one to Sandra. He then grabbed a shovel and headed out. Though the sun had not quite hit the horizon, under the canopy of trees, blue darkness prevailed. Max shivered. He had grown comfortable at seeing Drummond's pale visage, but watching the ghost float through the woods surrounded by the night and hearing the night's sounds proved eerier than he had expected.

Within five minutes, the church poked out of the darkness like another ghost. Max, Sandra, and Drummond all stood silent before the ruined building's front porch — two steps leading to a warped platform before a double door. Max moved forward, his flashlight drawing freakish shadows upon the building's old white walls.

"Hon." Sandra reached out as if to yank him back. "Maybe we

should check around the area first. In case Dr. Ernest buried the witch out here."

Drummond clapped his hands, the noise echoing around them. "Excellent idea."

Max doubted the body had been buried outside the church, but like his companions, he needed more time to build his courage. "Let's stick together."

As a group, the three worked their way around the perimeter of the church. They saw no signs to indicate any sort of ritual burial nor did they see anything to suggest the ground had been disturbed in recent days. They startled a rat, but Max felt confident the rat had startled them worse.

When they came around to where they had begun, Max knew the time for stalling had ended. He marched straight to the front porch, and not wanting to give Sandra a chance to talk him into turning back, he opened the door. The ancient hinges creaked.

He pointed his flashlight through the door. The open space had little in it anymore but graffiti and layers of dust. On the left side, a closed door had been painted with a crude pentagram. A handful of pews faced the back wall like tombstones. Stepping in, Max's footfalls filled the emptiness with a hollow sound.

While Sandra moved off to the right, Drummond remained in the doorway. "I'm glad I'm already dead."

"Gee, thanks for the confidence booster," Sandra said.

Max tried hard to ignore the feeling of an unseen weight pressing on him from all sides. He had never been the type to get claustrophobic, but he'd rather that be the explanation than anything else. He leaned the shovel against a pew and approached the door with the pentagram. Supernatural possibilities filled his head.

He put his hand against the door as if he might feel a fire burning on the other side. Of course, he only felt wood — rough and cold. Better to keep pushing forward than let his mind play out the endless list of horrific scenarios. He grabbed the knob and opened the door.

An office. Even a small church needed some place for the leaders to work. Pastors needed to write sermons. What little money they received had to be accounted for. Bake sales had to be planned. And then there were the private conversations — the troubled youth, the cheating spouse, the doubting intellectual. They all needed that one-on-one time with their spiritual leader, and this tiny office had to be the cramped quarters for just such conversations.

Max stepped back into the church proper and noticed Drummond hesitating to enter. "Come on. I want you to check the walls, the floors, and the ceiling — all the places we can't get to. See if Dr. Ernest put her anywhere like that."

"That's not a good idea," Drummond said.

Max shined the flashlight on Drummond to get a better look at his face, but the bright light and white walls washed out the ghost's image. "For crying out loud, get in here so we can be done with this. I don't know what's got you spooked, but I'm not eager to hang around here either."

"This is a church," Drummond said, thrusting his hands wide open. "We should have some respect for the place."

"It's not a church anymore. It's an old, rotting building. That's all."

"Buildings like this, ones used for a holy purpose, they hold on to what they were. They don't forget. Aw, heck, I can't expect you to understand. Trust me, okay? I've had experience with this before."

"That's right. Your mother ..."

Drummond's eyes flared as he soared straight at Max. "How do you know anything about my mother?" he asked, putting his cold hand inches from Max's face.

"I ... kind of ... well, you were lying to us and I realized how little we knew about you —"

"You researched me?"

Sandra whirled on Max. "I told you not to do that."

"Thanks, hon." But Sandra turned away, walking toward the front door.

Drummond kicked at the pew and sailed straight through it. "Of all the low, rotten things you could do. You had no right."

"I'm sorry. I am. I was worried about you and afraid and I made a stupid call." Max tried to speak in a soothing voice even as he saw Drummond getting angrier. He knew he should be most concerned with what he had done but he could only think about Drummond losing control and turning. "I know you must be mad, but please, let's focus on why we're here. When we go back to the office you can yell at me all you want. But not here."

Sandra stood in the doorway. "Max?"

Max turned his head toward her but Drummond whisked in to block his view. "What's the matter, Max ol' boy? Afraid I might snap right here, right now? Maybe you should go research that one."

"Max? Do you see headlights coming closer?"

Both Max and Drummond stopped their argument to look at Sandra. Moving to her side, Max said, "It's pitch black out there. I don't see anything."

Sandra swallowed hard. "I was afraid of that." She nodded to the darkness. "Ghosts are coming."

"Ghosts. Wait, what ghosts? Why?"

Drummond moved to the other side of Sandra. "It must be the witches. Those that haven't been destroyed yet. Nobody else would know or care that we're here. They're coming to stop us."

Max stepped backward, his mind racing to keep up with events. "The ghosts of the witches in the coven. If they're coming that means we're in the right place. A witch has to be buried here somewhere." He turned his trembling body toward Drummond. "It also means Patricia Welling will be with them. Listen to me. I'm terribly sorry for what I did. I don't know how to make that up to you, but right now, I need you to put that aside. I need you to stay calm or you risk turning."

"You're the one that needs to relax. I'm fine. And trust me, I'll find some way for you to make things up. And then some."

Sandra gasped. "They're all here. It looks the whole coven. We're surrounded."

Chapter 16

NOBODY MOVED. Sandra squinted as she looked out the doorway, raising a hand to shield her eyes. Max followed her gaze but saw only darkness. He could imagine it, though, plenty clear. Bright, pale women forming a circle around the church, their faces twisted in pain, their necks slit open and bodies baring the brutal scars of the curse Drummond had participated in casting.

Like a summer shower opening up without warning, Max heard a steady rat-a-tat striking the walls. "What's happening out there?"

Keeping her eyes on the witches, Sandra said, "They're throwing rocks at us."

Since any contact with the corporeal world caused ghosts sharp pain, repeatedly picking up and throwing rocks would not be pleasant for them. It might not be excruciating but it certainly signaled to Max that these witches were more than ticked off.

"Wait a second." Max scrunched his face, puzzled. "Why aren't they coming in here?"

"I noticed, too." Sandra walked back to Max and sat on one of the remaining pews. "It's a good thing. It means that one of the lessons I learned growing up was true — that evil and good are natural forces like the opposite sides of a magnet. They repel each other."

"See that," Drummond said. "That means that this isn't just an old building. It still has its church mojo, and that's what is protecting us."

"He's right. Whatever the history of this place, I have no doubt that when it was built, it served an honest, good sort of people."

Max sat next to Sandra. "This means we have time to find that body, right? They can't get in, so we don't really have to worry about them."

"Until we want to leave."

"It's not like that." Sandra hurried back to the doorway. "Most places in the world hold a mixture of the good and evil, so some turned ghosts can manage to get inside. But this church appears to be filled with a lot of good energy. Enough to hold them back for the moment, until they break through the barrier. That's why they're throwing rocks — rocks handled by evil witches. They're looking for weaknesses, some spot that isn't as holy as the rest."

Max planted his head in his hand. "You mean all they have to do is find the one spot where somebody had an illicit kiss or an evil thought or something and they can break through that?"

"Pretty much."

Without lifting his head, Max stretched out his arm and indicated the office door. "You mean like that pentagram over there?"

Before she could respond, Sandra dropped to the ground, covering her ears and wincing. Banging his hip into the pew, Max rushed to her side. Tears leaked from her eyes, and she clasped her ears ever tighter. She groaned and curled into a fetal position.

Max looked to Drummond for help, but he had fallen to the ground, too. "What's going on?"

Through gritted teeth, Drummond said, "The witches — they're screaming."

The wood floorboards rattled and the walls shook. Puffs of dust exploded from every crevice choking the air. Max coughed as he covered Sandra with his body. She twitched and shook as if having a seizure. Wood creaked and snapped. The shovel fell with a clang. One of the last standing pews toppled over.

The wind rose, howling as it whipped around the building's corners. Through the open doorway, rocks and pebbles, twigs and sticks spewed into the room. Max rolled to his side, placing his back between the doorway and Sandra. One pinprick attack amounted to little, but thousands of tiny strikes added up. He felt his blood soaking his shirt.

Bellowing to be heard, Max said, "How do we make it stop?"

Everything ceased. The floor settled. The walls calmed. The wind silenced. Only the final few pebbles rattled as they found places to rest.

Breathing hard and shaking, Sandra attempted to sit up. Damp with sweat, she put out a hand for Max to help steady her and did nothing more than breathe. Max held her hand tight.

"She okay?" Drummond said as he took the air.

"I don't know. What happened?"

"Just because the witches can't get in here, doesn't mean they can't hurt us. The pentagram, the graffiti, whatever else's been done here wasn't big enough, evil enough, for them to gain entry, but they can certainly cause us trouble."

"That was crazy. It was like a —"

"Like a haunting," Sandra said. "That's what evil ghosts do. Haunted houses, all those dark stories — the ones that are true deal with a ghost that turned."

Max brought his flashlight closer and relaxed a hair upon seeing color return to Sandra's face. "You going to be okay?"

She nodded. "They took me by surprise. That's all."

Max doubted that was all, but he let it be. He helped Sandra to her feet. Once he knew she could stand on her own, he stomped toward the back wall, picking up a broken piece of the pew.

"What are you doing?" Drummond rushed over to Max.

"We've got to find that body. Make sure Dr. Ernest destroyed it. Then we can get out of here. Try, at least." Max lifted the heavy wood, preparing to slam it into the wall.

"You do that, you'll kill us all."

"What now?"

From the doorway, Sandra said, "He's right. If you break open those walls, you'll be desecrating holy ground. You'll be opening the entire building to them. Nothing will hold them back."

Dropping the wood, Max said to Drummond, "Then we need you to go into those walls."

Drummond glanced at the wall. "That might be just as bad."

"Because the dead crawling around in the walls would be another form of desecration? Right?"

"Something like that."

"Well we can't wait around for them to attack again."

Rubbing her temples, sounding exhausted, Sandra said, "Will you two be quiet. Please. I'm trying to think."

A hundred sarcastic comments flooded Max's brain, but he said nothing. Sandra was on edge, too. Probably worse since he, at least, didn't have to listen to the intolerable screeching of a witch coven.

Walking toward Max, her steps more assured, she tapped out her points on her fingers. "First, Dr. Ernest cursed the High Priestess, and second, he buried her here. Why here? Because this is sacred, holy ground. A source of good. The coven's ghosts wouldn't be able to get in here."

"Hold on," Max said, his analytical side overcoming his fear. "How could he possibly bury her here? I mean, she's a source of evil, right? So, if her body were put in here, either her ghost couldn't come in, or the very act of burying her in this building would defile the building making the whole point, well, pointless. Right?"

"You got that right, kiddo," Drummond chimed in.

"But the witches," Sandra continued, "They came here, too. They wouldn't bother troubling us here for nothing. Especially when you consider how painful a lot of their actions are to a ghost."

Drummond snapped his fingers and pointed at Sandra. "The lady's got you there."

Max rolled his eyes. "You're a big help."

"Well, have you two geniuses considered this: The witch coven's here because their High Priestess is here, and since you've figured out that she can't be buried on this holy ground, then she must be buried nearby."

"We already checked around the grounds."

"In the dark with a flashlight. Not the best conditions. But let's say you're right. She's not buried right outside. If it were me burying her, and it almost was me, I'd have put her somewhere that the ghosts who wanted to get to her would mistakenly think she was in the church."

"He's right," Sandra said. "She has to be nearby, so close to the building that the ghosts' own fear of this holy ground would confuse them."

Drummond pursed his lips. "The office."

"Of course," Sandra said.

"Huh?" Max played his flashlight's beam on the office door. "You just got through saying she couldn't be buried here at all."

"She can't be buried on the holy ground. The office is physically attached to this church but it's not the holy ground of the church. The official praying, the gathering of people together and all that happened here, not in the office."

"Okay, let's go."

"You can't, yet."

Max threw his arms in the air. "Why the hell not? You want to hang around for those bitches to make your ears bleed?"

"If we destroy the High Priestess now, we won't get out of here alive."

Drummond nodded. "The second we uncover that body, the coven will know what's going on. The office isn't going to hold them off like the church proper. They'll swarm in on us. We won't stand a chance."

Staring at the office door like a prisoner waiting release, Max sighed. "Then what do you suggest we do? I haven't a clue."

Sandra glanced out the doorway then back to Max. He had seen her brave face many times, but the face he looked upon now went far beyond bravery. He saw grim determination in her. It scared the hell out of him.

"Here's what we're going to do." She crouched before Max and waited for Drummond to join the huddle. "You two go into that office and find the body. I'll go outside and make sure the witches are too busy to notice you."

"Wait. What?" Max looked to Drummond for support but he had the same look as Sandra. "No, no, no. You are not going out there. They practically turned you into mush, and they can't even get in here. They were screaming — that's all. You go out there, and they'll kill you."

"I wasn't expecting their attack. But I am now."

"Wonderful. So you can see the killing blow come. I feel so much better now."

Drummond edged over to the office door. "I'll be here when you're ready."

Sandra took Max's face in her hands. "I know how to resist them. I've been doing it my whole life. If I didn't, I'd never have lived long enough to meet you. So, trust me."

"I do trust you." Her hands were cold against his skin — she wasn't as confident as she acted. "But what I saw —"

"Don't think about them. Think about me. I'm the only one you need to believe. I'm telling you, I can handle them."

Max wanted to argue or reason or even bully her — anything to keep her in the church, safe. Her mouth lifted in a sorrowful smile, and he felt tears leaking from his eyes. How many times had he insisted she believe in him? How many times had she been forced to watch him walk off into dangers she knew he had no way to be prepared for? At least in this case, she had some previous experience. But all his debating aside, he knew he would have to let her go ahead with this plan because they had no other.

He reached out and kissed her. Her soft lips trembled against his, and for a fleeting breath, he thought maybe she would reconsider. But an icy finger traced his heart — she trembled because she knew this might be their last kiss.

When she tried to pull away, he clenched her tighter. He pressed in close against her, as if he could pass right through her. He stroked her hair with one hand and brought her closer with the other. At length, she placed her hands on his chest, and gently, firmly pushed back.

"When you finish with the body, run for the car. I'll be right alongside you."

"Don't you die," he said.

"Don't take too long."

As Sandra headed for the doorway, her hand holding on to Max until the last possible second, her eyes closed. Max watched her body straighten, her focus narrow. She turned all her attention to the witches and her plan. Max scurried across the room to the office door. He placed his hand on the knob and waited for Sandra's signal.

Max's heart dropped with every step she took closer toward the outside. In a moment, he would be in the office and unable to protect her. And he had Drummond to worry about, too. The witch attack had hurt his ghost partner. Max would have to keep an eye on him, consider him a mining canary that would tell him if the witches had hit too hard.

Before stepping outside, Sandra's shoulders rose slowly and fell fast — one last deep breath. And then she was gone. Walked straight out until Max could no longer see her.

Drummond endured the pain it took to poke Max in the shoulder. "Time to move."

"Right," Max muttered. Right, indeed. He had to be sharp now, succeed as fast as possible, make sure Sandra spent as little time out there as he could manage.

He opened the door and started knocking on the walls. At the first dull hit, he turned to Drummond. "Why the hell am I doing it this way? Get in there. This isn't holy ground. Check to see where that witch is."

"You got it." Drummond raised his hand in a mock salute and his face locked in anguish.

From out front, Sandra yelled but Max couldn't tell if it was a yell of someone being defeated or raging against her enemy. Drummond cocked his head and held his lips tight. He looked like he fought against vomiting. Then he shook the whole thing off.

"She's okay," he said. "But let's not dawdle."

"I'm waiting for you. Get in there."

Drummond stuck his head into the wall and pulled it back out fast. "She's in there. Looks like Ernest never made it out here."

Max banged on the wall, hoping to break open a hole big enough to grab the body. Again and again he smashed his fist at the wall, but this old building had been made of wood, not drywall, and he only managed to bloody his knuckles.

"You forgetting something?" Drummond said.

"Damn it," Max said and dashed out of the office. In a flash, he returned with the shovel he had carried from the car. All his fisticuffs with the wall had loosened enough dirt and dust that he could see the seam where two boards met. Using the shovel like a crowbar, he shoved the blade in and pushed on the handle.

Sandra screamed out something, but Max deciphered only a few swears. He snatched a glimpse of Drummond. The ghost's face scrunched tight like he suffered a migraine.

Come on, Max, come on. Neither of them can take much more of this.

Max put all his weight behind the handle and pushed. The wood creaked and the rusting nails whined. He shoved the handle harder until a section of the wall leaned out. Sliding the shovel deeper, Max thought of his wife's pain, and he roared, pressing the handle with all the strength he could find.

The wall gave way, wood splintering and snapping. As the shovel lost hold of anything to grip, Max stumbled forward into the wall. The stench of ancient decay poured out of the new opening.

Max stuck his nose in the crook of his arm, yet the polluted air still managed to seep into his nostrils. With his free hand, he tore down those sections of wood still clinging to the wall. He picked up the flashlight and set it on the office desk, the beam focused on the ceiling to cast dim light everywhere — enough to see the body.

Drummond collapsed across the desk. *Crap.* The wind picked up, its howl growing louder. The floorboards rattled. Though Max couldn't hear the horrid shrieks of the witches, his heart quaked at the thought of Sandra stuck outside, suffering, open to attack.

Only way is through. Max looked in the open wall.

The witch's body appeared like the statue of a woman caught in terrible pain. Her mouth open wide in a vicious scream, while her hands appeared to claw at the wall. A line across her neck marked where Dr. Ernest had slit her throat, and on her chest, the dark lines of symbols carved into her pale skin. Dust and grime covered the corpse, along with rat droppings. But no sign of the little animals gnawing at her.

Max raised the shovel. He widened his legs into a firm stance, in case the witch's eyes snapped open or she tried to take the shovel or she had some other magical ability he never knew. Holding the shovel like a poker, he shoved it at the witch's body. As if made of precariously balanced sand, the entire body crumbled into a pile of dirt on the floor. A long hiss of foul air released from her.

The walls, the floors, the howling wind — all ceased.

Wiping the sweat from his eyes, Max rushed out of the office, up the main aisle of the church proper, and straight out the doorway. Sandra lay on the ground, curled in a ball. He hurried to her side, listening for a breath, hoping to see the rise and fall of her chest. She groaned, and Max had never heard a sound so joyous in his life. She had survived.

Drummond weaved towards them like a drunk. "My head's killing me."

"Where are the witches?" Max asked.

Drummond barely lifted his head. "Gone. With their High Priestess destroyed, there's no point to being here."

Max wondered why they didn't retaliate, but for the moment, he turned all his worry to Sandra. "Put your arms around me, hon." He lifted her up and carried her to the car. It hadn't seemed so far away when they first arrived, but Sandra passed out and her slumbering weight had him breathing heavily by the time they reached the car.

Sliding her into the back seat, he called out, "Drummond? Come on."

"I'm right here." He sat in the passenger seat.

On a normal night, Drummond popping into Max's car like that would have caused a jolt of surprise, but exhaustion overwhelmed such simple reactions. Max merely nodded and got behind the wheel. He put the key in and froze.

"What's wrong?" Drummond asked.

"The witches left us."

"We did get rid of the reason they came."

"But they came to stop us, and they failed. So they float away? They don't want to get even or anything? I thought these were evil ghosts. That seems wrong."

"What are you thinking?"

"Those ghosts came here for a reason and now they've left for a similar reason. We're not done. Leed said he took care of his witches, and we've taken care of Ernest's."

"But there's still mine."

Max turned the ignition and revved the engine. "We've got to get to Patricia before they do. We're going to have to get into the Federal Building."

Chapter 17

BY THE TIME MAX reached the office building, Sandra had recovered enough to stand on her own. With some assistance, she negotiated the stairs, and when they entered the office, she dropped to the couch, panting and perspiring. She offered a feeble smile and gulped down the water Max handed her.

"You want to see a doctor?" he asked.

As she drank, she shook her head. She handed the glass back and patted her sweating forehead. "I think I'll rest here for a little. Then I'll be okay."

"You sure? You don't look so good."

"I'll be fine. It's not the first time I've been attacked by a ghost."

Drummond popped his head through the bookcase. "This was a whole coven of ghosts, doll. You ought to be real careful. Take things slow."

Sandra licked the water from her lips. "That's why I need to rest here. I'll be back to my full strength soon enough."

Something seemed off. Max couldn't figure it out, but he had the sense that all these various strands were not coming together the way they should. And now Sandra was one of those strands. But she had gone a few rounds in an unfair fight, so maybe it made sense that she acted a bit different than he would expect.

Drummond snapped his fingers in front of Max's face. "Wake up. Sun's rising and we've got work to do. Federal Building will be opening up in a few hours. We need a plan."

"Unless the Federal government has invented and installed ghost detectors, I figured we'd walk in there and you'd look around. You don't have a problem checking out the walls of a government building, too, do you?"

"Believe me. Those are far from holy ground."

Max started to chuckle at Drummond's comment but hesitated. "If the building isn't holy ground, then the ghosts of the witch coven can get in there every bit as easily as you."

"You're just getting that now?"

Sandra placed her head on the arm of the couch, swung her legs up, and closed her eyes. "You boys have fun with that. I've got to sleep."

Max dabbed her damp brow with the cuff of his shirt and then stepped into the hall. When Drummond followed, Max walked to the head of the stairs and sat. Whispering harshly, Max said, "You've got to go to the Federal building now. I can't get in until they open, but you know those witches are already there."

"Calm down. They don't know where Patricia is. That was part of the whole point of having Ernest, Leed, and I do our cursing separately."

"Then how did they know where we were?"

"Because Ernest and Leed are dead. The coven probably tracked down their ghosts and forced the information out of them."

"Doesn't that mean they'll come after you, too?"

Drummond scratched his cheek even though he no longer grew stubble. "I'll have to be at my ready. In the meantime, you need to go find Patricia's body."

"You're not coming?"

"If I go with you, the coven ghosts will have an easier time finding us. I'm only invisible to living people. The ghosts see me standing out."

"I can't go alone. How would I explain to all of law enforcement that I'm banging on their walls looking for a dead body — oh, and I only know about it because of a ghost! They'd lock me up."

A door opened and the old lady stepped into the hall. She peered up at Max's office, her laborious movements painful to watch. Then she turned her head and part of her body towards Max. She scowled, grabbed her newspaper from her doormat, and returned to her apartment.

Drummond tipped his head back. "I think she's warming up to you."

"Well, I'm not warming up to this idea. I won't have the access I need to find Patricia, and if I do manage to find her, there's no way I can do anything about it with all the police around. So either you go with me or we've got to come up with another plan."

"But the witches —"

"I don't see how we can do anything about that, so we can't worry about it," Max said. Drummond had the look of a conman caught in a lie and straining to find a way out. It hit Max right away. "Are you afraid to see her?'"

"Don't be foolish. I'm not afraid of her. But I do worry about me."

"You think it might cause you to turn?"

"Don't you?"

Max weighed it all out in his head. "I'm sorry, but I don't see another option. We've got to finish this. Ernest and Leed's witches have been destroyed. If we don't do this now, what was the point? Why did they die? Even worse, what kind of power will this coven of ghosts have?"

"Okay, okay. I know. You don't have to be a pest about it."

Max held back his tongue. He could say nothing that would make a difference. At length, he climbed down the stairs, knowing Drummond would follow close behind.

He decided to walk the whole way. It was only a handful of blocks, but the distance ate up some of the time until the building opened, and more importantly, it gave Drummond a chance to prepare. It also meant Max had time to prepare as well. And he needed it.

When they reached the entrance on the corner of 2nd and Main, a line of people waiting for the place to open had already formed. Some held simple forms that needed filing; some held folders packed with paperwork intended to prove their innocence or the guilt of others. Some joked with each other; some pouted, knowing they would be paying a fine no matter what excuses they gave a judge. Max got on the end of the line, leaned against the cool concrete wall, crossed his arms, and watched cars enter and exit the parking structure across the street.

Drummond scanned up and down the street before sidling next to a cocky-looking young man complaining about jury duty to anybody who would listen. Drummond passed his hand through the man and watched the jerk shiver. Max smirked.

"No witches here, by the way. They might be inside but I don't get the feeling they're around."

Max wanted to answer, but the idea of being hauled off for talking to himself like a crazy person didn't sit well. Thankfully, the doors opened and the line began to move. It went slowly though. A few feet inside the entrance was a security check point similar to an airport — guards, scanners, and walk-through detection equipment.

Drummond bounced around the line. "Come on, come on, come on." He zipped to the head of the line, peeking over the heads of those already inside. "This is ridiculous. Look, I'm going in and see if I can find her. When you get inside, call for me and I'll let you know what

I've discovered."

"Wait," Max said, but Drummond slipped through the wall and those in line all stopped to stare at him. "Sorry," he muttered, garnering odd looks.

Security was set up in a white hallway with plenty of windows. Once they checked his ID and he passed through the detector, he walked into another hall. This one made him think of every institutional building he had ever walked through — university administrations, hospital wings, and city councils. Utilitarian and boring.

"Max!" Max glanced down and saw Drummond's head sticking out of the floor. "I found her."

Max walked to a quiet corner and pretended to make a call on his cellphone. "That's good to hear. Where are you?"

Drummond rose through the floor and stood next to Max. "She's down in the basement. Like I said she would be. Near the boiler."

"I don't know how to get there." Max checked around to make sure nobody watched him. "And I don't think it'd be wise to ask anybody."

"Don't bother. She's behind a thick wall of brick. You'll need a sledgehammer to break through."

"Can't you do anything? The last one crumbled from just a touch."

Max glanced up and saw the angry eyes of the ghost. Drummond had used all his inner-strength to face the corpse of Patricia Welling, no way would Max convince him to touch her. Besides, even if he would do so, Max wasn't so sure he wanted Drummond to go back down there. His face had taken on a horrified look — the look of a ghost about to lose control.

"Forget it," Max said. "I shouldn't have asked."

"No, you shouldn't have."

"There's no way we can get to her without being caught." A uniformed policeman strolling by turned his head at the word *caught*. "Let's get out of here," Max said.

Max pocketed his cellphone and headed outside. Drummond followed, swirling around Max like a hawk circling prey. "What the hell are you doing? Leaving? You made me come out here. You made me go find her. And now you want to leave?"

"Calm down," Max whispered through gritted teeth.

"Do you have any clue what I went through? That wasn't easy to do. I had to see her. You understand? I had to see what I did to her. I've spent decades trying to forget about her and you not only make me relive it all, but you forced me to go see her. For what? This isn't right.

Not right at all."

As Max stepped onto the sidewalk and headed back to the office, he said, "I'm sorry. But we had to be sure."

"I was plenty sure before. You just wouldn't believe me."

Max halted. "I'm sorry. Get it? I'm sorry. You need to calm down and think through this rationally."

"I don't feel very rational. Not when I've been spun and hung like this."

More odd looks from pedestrians. Shaking it off, Max stormed away. "Look, I can't change what happened but at least we know she's there and we know the coven hasn't gotten to her yet. All we have to do now is figure out how to clean this up. There's got to be something we can do."

"I got a few suggestions for you, but I don't think you'll like where I put the baseball bat."

Max didn't bother saying more. What was the point when his own anger seemed to fuel Drummond's further? Besides, he had to think. If he couldn't come up with a solution, then Drummond would be right — he would have revisited this horrible event for no reason. Worse, though he did not mention it, he thought the witch coven ghosts would have the Federal building surrounded by the end of the day.

"Tell me more about the actual curse," Max said.

"You're suddenly an expert on curses?"

"I'm trying to get more information. The more I know about all this, the easier it'll be to figure things out. Maybe one of us might catch something in what you say, put some more pieces together."

"What we really need is a witch of our own."

Max nearly tripped. "You're right. That's exactly what we need."

"Don't even think about her. Are you kidding? Have you gone soft in the brain?"

"You know any other witches that might be persuaded to help us?"

Drummond frowned. "You destroyed her practice, turned her into an alcoholic, and caused her downfall with Hull. Why would she even think about helping us?"

"She's not part of their coven, for starters."

"And she tortured you. Did you forget that part?"

"What other choice do we have? Unless you'll go face Patricia's corpse all by yourself."

Though he clearly didn't agree, Drummond nodded. "Okay. Dr. Connor's it is."

Chapter 18

As they neared the office, Max's confidence waned. Bothered by Drummond's acquiescence, he began to second-guess himself. After all, to think Dr. Connor, the Hull's personal witch, would help him out sounded ridiculous. Except that they had helped each other out in the past. Usually through coercion, but help nonetheless. That was the key — he needed some leverage.

Consumed with these thoughts, Max failed to notice Mr. Modesto standing by the stairwell entrance. "Mr. Porter. Once again, it appears that you are failing our employer."

Max put his hands on his hips and sighed. "And how am I doing that?"

Modesto strolled toward Max, his expensive shoes clicking on the sidewalk, arrogance oozing off of his stoic face. "You have shown an appalling lack of regard for our employer and your assignment, but you are mistaken to think you're untouchable."

"I've been trying to find your missing bell, but —"

"Your excuses no longer interest me. I have lost all tolerance for you."

Drummond laughed. "He says that like he ever had any."

"Let me make this clear enough, Mr. Porter. Tomorrow evening, I shall meet you in your office and you will have that handbell. Time has run out. If you fail to show up with that bell, then our employer will be most displeased, and I suggest you and your wife uncover the most rapid exit from Winston-Salem." Modesto's lips part to reveal the tips of his sharp teeth. "Perhaps North Carolina, as well."

Max wanted to act tough, but his face twisted in an effort to hold back a pollen-induced sneeze. Three sneezes later, he said, "How many times are you going to threaten me a year? It's boring."

"These are not threats. These are guarantees. And of all people, you should know full well how much I relish the moment our employer allows me to fulfill those guarantees. That moment is coming. Fail us with the handbell, and I know there won't be any hesitations left."

"I still have Hull's journal."

"If you tire of my threats, I tire more of your attempt to hold that over us. Some things are simply worth the risks. You wouldn't understand. You don't take real risks. You let others do your dirty work. Drummond or your wife."

"Shut up."

"Without them, what are you really? A boy who can research things. Based on your less than impressive skill regarding the handbell, I question even that much of your ability. You are nothing without your wife's gifts and your ghost's connection to the supernatural world. Nothing."

Max couldn't help it. He shoved Modesto's shoulders hard enough to send the man back a few steps. "You've delivered your message, errand boy. You can go now."

Modesto brushed his shoulders and stepped closer to Max. In a low tone, he said, "Tomorrow evening. Bring the bell here or run for your life." He shoved Max in the chest, and Max fell down onto the sidewalk. "Good day."

As Modesto walked away, Max got back to his feet, coughing and sneezing all the way up. Drummond drifted to his side. "Want me give him a brain-freeze he'll never forget?"

"Forget him." Max headed inside. "Hunting down family trinkets doesn't rate too high on my list of pressing issues. Besides, if we don't fix this coven problem, nothing much will matter since we'll probably be cursed or dead."

"You got a good point."

They walked into the office to find Sandra sitting bolt upright. She turned her head toward them — lips pale and cracked, eyes unblinking, sweat-soaked hair plastered to her head. All thoughts of covens and bells and Hulls and Modesto washed away from Max's mind. He lunged to her side and felt waves of cold air coming off her.

Wrapping a blanket around her shoulders, he said, "What's going on? Are you sick?"

"I'm fine," she said in a voice as dead as her eyes.

"We need to get you to a hospital."

"No. I want to stay." She looked to Drummond, an odd smile crossing her face. "Is this the cold you feel? The cold of the dead?"

Drummond put his hands in his pockets and floated back. "Sweetheart, you need to listen to your husband. Something's wrong here. You should see a doctor."

"They've never helped me before." She laughed — a hard, unusual sound that ended in a drunken snort. "I'd be better off at the church."

Drummond paled. "What the hell?"

Max turned to Drummond. "You ever seen anything like this?"

"Have you?" Drummond asked. "If I had to guess, I'd say those witches did something to her before they left. Cursed her, maybe. But I've never seen a curse like this."

"All the more reason to go visit our old friend."

Sandra perked up. "Oh, where are we going?"

"Not you, hon."

"But I want to come along."

"I'm going to see a doctor. You want to see a doctor?"

She pouted. "No."

"Okay, then. Please stay here and we'll be back soon."

"Make sure Drummond comes back. I've got a lot questions about the afterlife for him."

With that said, Sandra returned to the stark position and expression she had been in when they first entered. Max stared at her, waiting for a small glimmer of Sandra to appear. As he watched her with an ache in his chest worsening every second, he held back his tears.

Kissing her cold cheek, he said, "We're going to help you. Hang on for me, hon. You hear me? Hang on, and I'll stop whatever this is. I love you." He kissed her again before storming down the hall and toward the car.

The last time Max stood in Dr. Connor's office, she had become a drunken hag, crawling on the floor for a nip of whiskey. The last time he talked with her, she had sobered up and regained the limited trust of the Hull family. While she certainly had not returned to her glory days, he now saw that she had risen far closer to that goal than ever before.

On the surface, her office looked like any optometrist's office — an uninspired waiting room with a chest-high reception desk and a red-headed woman in a nurse's uniform sitting behind it. An elderly man with thick glasses and an overbite sat on a couch reading an old issue of Sports Illustrated — swimsuit issue, of course. Over the speakers, radio station 98.7 ("We Play Everything") had Styx urging everyone to sail away into outer-space. Underneath, however, Max knew the real business at hand — witchcraft.

Rapping his knuckles on the desk, Max said, "Hi, there. Will you please tell Dr. Connor that Max Porter is here to see her?"

"Do you have an appointment?" the receptionist asked, tapping on her computer keyboard. "I don't see a Porter here. It is P-O-R-T-E-R, yes?"

"I don't have an appointment."

"Then I'm sorry, but Dr. Connor has a full schedule today."

"I'm sure she does. I'm equally sure that she'll drop everything once you mention my name."

The receptionist faltered. Max felt sorry for her since he had put her in a bind. She clearly wanted to turn him away, perhaps even thought that made the most sense, but there existed this slim chance that she should inform Dr. Connor. But if Dr. Connor wanted nothing to do with Max, then the receptionist will have angered a witch for nothing. But if she sent Max away and Dr. Connor did want to see him, she would also anger that same witch. Any decision she made risked pissing off a powerful witch, and Max knew exactly what it felt like to be on the wrong end of that sentence.

Drummond floated behind the elderly man and took a close look at the Sports Illustrated. "Some days I really wish I was alive. Look at these women."

Doing his best to ignore Drummond, Max leaned toward the receptionist. "Listen, I can make this easier for you. If you don't tell her I'm here, she's going to have an entire coven of cursed witch ghosts to contend with." He peeked over his shoulder. The old man ogling Sports Illustrated raised an eyebrow but whether that was because of what Max said or because of the white, wet number some hottie wore on a beach in Brazil, Max couldn't be sure. Drummond certainly liked the magazine. Turning back to the still-hesitant receptionist, Max added, "I'll make it even easier. If you don't go back, I'm going to barrel my way in there and start calling out for her, causing all kinds of commotion. I think that'll tick her off far more than if you interrupt her."

Scowling, the receptionist stood. "Please have a seat, Mr. Porter. I'll be a moment."

"Thank you." Max sat in a chair opposite the old man and snatched up a copy of Southern Living. He snapped the magazine open and coughed.

Drummond looked up. "Did you want me for something?"

Shaking the magazine, Max coughed again.

"Oh, right. You're afraid the old guy here will think you're nuts talking to me. Well? Just cough once for yes, twice for no."

Cough.

"Fine, fine. I was enjoying the swimwear, that's all. I wasn't going to let you go face Connor all alone. And even if I was, what do you care? You've been one-on-one with her before. You've lived."

Barely, Max thought.

"Are you going to sit there acting like a fool, or is there something you want me to do?"

Cough.

"You want me to check on Sandra?"

Cough, cough.

"You want me to get rid of this old guy? Get the magazine for yourself?"

Cough, cough. The old man sneaked a glance at Max. "Sorry," Max said. "Getting over a cold. Don't worry, I'm not contagious." The old man made a face that said how little he thought of Max's assurances. "I do wish I could see what the doc was up to, though, don't you?"

Drummond nodded. "I get it. You want me to check out what's going on back there."

Cough.

"No need to put attitude in your cough. This ain't the easiest way to communicate." Drummond slid through the wall and in seconds, slid right back. "Receptionist is coming."

Before the door to the back opened, Max had tossed the magazine on the coffee table and stood. The receptionist started as she came through, and the old man looked a bit surprised, too. "Mr. Porter, you may see Dr. Connor in her office. Just go down the hall and —"

"I know where it is," he said with more venom than he intended.

As he walked down the hall, Drummond followed. "You know, we really should come up with a system to talk when you can't really talk. That coughing thing won't work."

In a harsh whisper, Max said, "How many times have I had you do recon while I waited somewhere? It should be standard practice by now."

"We never agreed to anything. And I got distracted."

"Looking at hotties in bathing suits isn't why you're here. For crying out loud, you're a ghost. Go peep on somebody in the shower if you've got to, but when we're working, I expect you —"

"Okay, okay. You're going to draw attention."

Max wanted to argue further, but Drummond was right. Also, they had reached Dr. Connor's office door. Max knocked and entered.

The office was small and cluttered. Dr. Connor sat at a desk drowning in papers, some crinkled and faded yellow, some crisp and smelling of inkjet. Old texts had been piled up in the corners and a row of stuffed birds perched on a cabinet behind Dr. Connor's desk. On the wall to her left, Max saw an eye chart with a huge letter E at the top. On the opposite wall, Max saw a celestial map with the moon's phases marked out along with numerous symbols he did not know (though a few he recognized from the walls of Leed and Dr. Ernest).

A few years younger than Max, Dr. Connor had always been a beautiful woman, but the hard times she had suffered through took a toll. Dark hollows had formed around her eyes, and her mouth no longer smiled brightly. Though she wore a white doctor's coat with a spaghetti-strapped summer dress underneath, her once vibrant sexuality had diminished.

Max tried to hide any guilt from his face. He had caused this woman a lot of harm — but often in the course of protecting himself from her vicious attacks.

As Max stepped in, Drummond followed behind only to smack against the opening of the doorway. "What the hell?" Drummond said.

Max turned around, and Dr. Connor cackled. "You don't think I'd be stupid enough to rebuild this office without some protections?"

Drummond pushed on the barrier several more times until he finally leaned his shoulder against it and pursed his lips. "You let her know I can still watch from here. She does anything to you, and I'll find a way in there."

Max took a seat at the desk. "Drummond says you better be careful. He won't let anything happen to me."

"How adorable," she said, her mouth a stoic line. "Shall we get to talking seriously or are you going to waste more of my time?"

Scrunching his brow in thought, Max glanced back at the doorway. "You put up a barrier against ghosts." His eyes widened. "You already know, don't you?"

"Of course, I know. I wouldn't be this town's top witch, if I didn't know what was going on. You really think a witch like me doesn't keep tabs on every witch hunter in the country? You think all the witches around the world don't talk with each other? We can use the Internet, too, you know."

"Then you know why I'm here."

Dr. Connor lifted her head, leveling a sultry yet sadistic look upon Drummond. "Patricia Welling."

Drummond smashed his palm into the invisible barrier. "I hate this woman. Stop playing games with her. Get what we need and let's go."

"That's right," Max said. "We want to stop these ghosts of the witch coven, and judging by your spell at the doorway, you're afraid of them, too. We know where the last one is, but we can't get to it to destroy it. Now, since our interests are aligned for the moment, why don't you help us out? Tell me how to get rid of the last one, and then you won't be needing to lay down a bunch of wards wherever you go."

Dr. Connor wriggled out of her white coat, letting one of her spaghetti-straps fall off her shoulder, and she licked her lips. "Help never goes just one way. You know that."

"If you're trying to tempt me into cheating on my wife, it's not going to happen."

She pouted. "I don't know why you always resist. I'm young, able, and willing to do all those nasty things a proper wife would never dream of doing. We'd have a great time together."

"For one, I love my wife and actually meant my vows when I gave them. For another, you're a witch, and I don't trust you."

"But you want my help."

"I'm offering to help you out, too, don't forget. My problem appears to be yours."

Fixing her strap, Dr. Connor said, "Don't put your faith in appearances."

Drummond laughed. "She shouldn't be talking, looking like she does."

Dr. Connor opened a low drawer in her desk and pulled out a large book. In any other office, Max would have thought he looked upon an atlas from centuries ago. In Dr. Connor's office, he fought the bile roiling in his gut because he knew that the book's lovely brown hide cover was made of human skin. Having touched one of those books before, he had no desire to ever to do so again.

"In this book," she said, caressing the cover with the tips of her fingers, "is the answer you seek."

Max paused. "I have to say I'm surprised but pleased. Thank you for making this so easy. If you'll tell me what page to look —"

"Bless your heart, aren't you the sweetest thing. I'm not giving you this book, and this won't be easy. What kind of businesswoman would I be if I simply gave everything away?"

"Then what do you want?"

Sliding the book back into the drawer with one hand, Dr. Connor raised her other hand. "Not so fast. You've only just gotten here, and there's so much to discuss. I wonder — how much do you really know about Patricia Welling?"

"Max, get out of there." Drummond pounded his fist against the barrier. "Don't play her games. Come on, now. Leave and we'll find some other way to deal with all this."

"I know enough," Max said. "She's the ghost of a witch, and she's killing off those connected with her coven's curse. We know where she's buried, so all we have to do is destroy her body. Beyond that, the details don't really matter much."

Running her index finger across the other, she tutted. "Naughty, naughty. You shouldn't be lying. Especially to yourself. You know very well that details always matter. For instance, wouldn't you agree that it makes a huge difference, perhaps even an insurmountable difference, if your dear Drummond knew all along that Patricia was a witch?"

"She's lying," Drummond yelled. "Don't believe anything she says."

"What if he had been by that tree with the odd branch on purpose all those years ago? What if he had sought out dear Patricia with the intent of seducing her? And if he did that, why? Why seduce a witch?"

Max glowered at Dr. Connor. "If he did that, then I'm sure he planned to kill her all along."

"Except he hadn't met Matthew Ernest or Joshua Leed yet. That happened after he had begun his relationship with Patricia. I wonder what he wanted from her. After all, he hadn't sought out any old witch of that coven. He targeted her, specifically. Of course, I would, too, if I had been him. I mean, if you want to gain control over a witch's power, you might as well go for the High Priestess."

"What?" Max couldn't help himself. He turned toward Drummond.

"It's not true," Drummond said. "She's lying. I mean maybe Patricia was the High Priestess, I don't know. That's my point. I don't know."

Dr. Connor chuckled. "I see your partner neglected to tell you that little fact. Well then, I suppose you two have plenty to discuss. And I should be getting back to my patients."

"Wait," Max put his hand on her desk. He wanted to grab her wrist but didn't dare. "You still haven't told me what the price for your help will be."

"Oh. That."

"A case of whiskey? Information? What do you want?"

The pleasure that filled her eyes could not be mistaken. She thrilled at the words dangling on her tongue. The longer she waited to speak them, the worse Max felt — this was going to be bad. Really bad.

"You want my help in a very serious matter. There isn't enough whiskey in all of North Carolina to buy this kind of help — and that's a lot of whiskey."

"Then what?"

She placed a glass vial on the table. "Blood."

"Excuse me?"

"Specifically, your wife's blood."

"You leave her out of this."

"I can't do that. Either you give me her blood or we have no deal."

Max jumped to his feet. "You can go to Hell."

As he turned to leave, Dr. Connor tapped the glass with her finger. "There isn't another witch in all of North Carolina that can help you. Not when your time is so limited." She tilted her head. "By the way, before you go, tell me, how many times has Mr. Modesto pressured you to find the Hull's handbell?"

Drummond tried to reach Max, to pull him out of the office, but he couldn't get through the barrier. "She's poison, Max. Leave now. We'll go see Sandra, take her to a doctor. Come on."

Max didn't move. He stood rock-still. "What do you know about the handbell?"

"You really aren't too bright," Dr. Connor said. She lifted the glass vial. "Your wife's blood. I'll tell you everything you need to know to stop the coven, and I'll even throw in the handbell for free."

"I thought you didn't give anything away for free."

"Oh, he has a little bit of brains after all. Get me the blood and you'll get what you need. It's that simple. It's a non-negotiable deal. Bring it to me tonight. I'll be here."

Max took a long stride toward her desk and pointed his finger at her face. "You won't win this. Whatever's going on — I've beaten you before. I will again."

"Hallelujah." She lifted her hands toward the ceiling. In one hand, she held out the vial. "Tell yourself whatever you have to, but get me the blood."

Looking at the vial, Max wondered if he could do it. He believed that Sandra would resist. She understood witches and their spells better than he did — no way would she give up her blood. Yet she knew what they faced with the coven. Perhaps she would take the risk and volunteer.

He reached for the vial but pulled back before he touched it. He hated the thought that had entered his brain, but he couldn't deny it — what if he didn't tell her? In her current state, she might not be able to make such a decision. He could simply lie to her, tell her it's for a medical test, and she might not even remember it in the morning. Shaking off such a moral betrayal, Max glanced back at Drummond. Even if Max were so villainous as to attempt such a thing, Drummond would stop him.

Not that I'm seriously considering it anyway. Having the thought was despicable enough. But no matter how desperate he became, he would never stoop so low.

Perhaps the witch could sense the change within him, perhaps she could read his face better than he thought. Whichever the case, she thrust out her hand and said, "Take the vial, go to your pretty wife, and ask her a personal question. I promise you that's all it will take for you to bring me what I want. One intimate, personal question. After that, if I'm wrong, toss the vial and never bother me again. I'm sure you wouldn't object to that."

"Never seeing you again. That would be wonderful."

"One intimate, personal question. That's all."

Snatching the glass vial from her hand, Max whirled around and left the office. To Drummond, he raised his hand. "Don't say a word."

RUNNING THE WINDSHIELD wipers to clean off the layer of pollen, Max grumbled in his mind at the inconvenience of city sprawl. He had spent too much time in the last few days stuck in his car. And now, as he headed back to the office, back to Sandra, he could either stew in his own fears or argue with Drummond. Floating above the passenger seat, his ghost partner made the decision easy.

"You got a problem with this?" Max prodded.

"Don't you?"

"I'd rather swipe a bit of my wife's blood than let her die at the hands of a witch coven of ghosts. You got another way out of this? Oh, wait, there's a simple way, isn't there? You could man up and go take care of Patricia's body yourself."

Picking at his lips, Drummond kept his eyes looking out the window. "For the sake of helping Sandra, I'm not taking your bait. And I know you want to help her, too. I only ask that you think through this some more before you do anything you can't undo."

"Sandra'll understand."

"I'm not worried about her in all this. She loves you. And we've all had to make tough choices when dealing with the Hulls. Of course, she'll understand. But giving her blood to Dr. Connor — that's insane. You can't do that."

Max drove on for two minutes without another word. Finally, he said, "I know."

And he did. Beyond his brain and his gut and his love, he knew it straight through to his soul. It reverberated deep inside him like an adrenaline rush that never died. His heart plummeted at the thought of what would happen if he let Dr. Connor have his wife's blood — they both would be slaves to that witch until they died. Perhaps even beyond that.

But at least they would be alive. If he failed to stop the coven, he and Sandra would be lucky if death was the worst result. More likely, they would learn a slew of ancient curses as each witch carved a new one into their skin.

That's why I took the vial.

"Listen," Drummond said, "I know this is a tough situation, but we need to focus on how to proceed. Forget about the dead ends and find something new."

Max wanted to smack Drummond hard on the back of the head, but the act would hardly satisfy considering his hand would go through Drummond and hit the dashboard instead. Besides, as Sandra had often pointed out — with the Hulls, the best way through was barreling straight on. Before he could do that, however, one last matter needed clearing up.

"Connor said Patricia's the High Priestess."

"I heard her," Drummond said.

"And she said that you knew Patricia was a witch long before —"

"I was there. I heard her."

"Well?"

"Well, nothing. Dr. Connor's a witch. Witches lie to fracture a partnership. You ever heard of divide and conquer? That's all she's up to. Telling you lies to make you doubt me and drive a deeper wedge between us."

"She also mentioned the handbell. Knew all about Modesto bugging us for it."

"You do remember that I was right outside the door? I heard everything."

"My point is that if she's so careful with her words, using them in an attempt to splinter us apart, then what does it mean that she mentioned the handbell?"

Drummond rubbed his chin. "It means we better find that damn handbell."

"It sure is sounding like a lot more than a family heirloom. Maybe they really can pull off this spell. But if that were true, then why would they —"

"Go find it, then. That's a smart move. Stop analyzing and go find it."

Max's face pinched as he bit back his anger. "You've got no idea what you're doing."

"About what?"

"You have any clue what I've got to build myself up to do here? With this vial?"

"I thought we were done with that."

"If I don't give Sandra's blood to that bitch, you know—"

"Okay, okay." Drummond kicked at the dashboard, his leg going straight through and his foot sticking out of the car's hood. "I'll do it. I'll take care of Patricia's corpse."

"You will?"

"I can't let anything happen to that doll of yours. I hoped maybe we'd have some way out of this that I wouldn't have to deal with my past, but the moment Matt Ernest died, I had no choice. I'm sorry. I should've told you from the start. Then there'd be no way for Connor to split us apart."

Max sat up, lighter and excited. "You're right. She wants to split us up, so that's what we'll do. We'll go on separate paths, and if she's watching, her arrogance will make her think she's winning. It'll give us a slight advantage when we see her tonight."

"What? You're still going through with the blood thing? There's no need. I'm going to do the job. We don't need Connor and her blood price anymore."

"I guess not. I just thought —"

"You thought you'd fill it with what? Pig's blood? Chicken? She'd see through it. After casting all the spells she's done in the past, I'm sure she knows her blood."

"I suppose. I want to see Sandra. Make sure she's okay."

"Of course. I'll go do what I have to. You check on your wife."

"After you're done, I want you to search for that handbell. Start at Reynolda House. They had the rest of the set on display a long time ago. Perhaps you can find something to help us. If that's a bust, go to a graveyard or to the Other and talk to the ghosts, or use some of those old detective skills of yours. Do whatever you need to do to find that handbell. When we meet Modesto tomorrow night, I've got to have it in hand."

"You can count on me."

"I know I can. Meet me back at the office by ten tonight. I'll look after Sandra and then do research on my end."

"You got it," Drummond said and disappeared.

As Max entered the city, the glass vial in his pocket grew heavier. He had always considered himself a man who could do what needed to be done, make the hard call, face the sacrifice that would save those he loved. But the gulf between what he considered himself and what he knew to be the truth widened in the face of these supernatural threats.

I'm just glad I don't have to deal with it any further.

He parked the car and headed up to Sandra. When he entered, expecting Sandra to be recovering on the couch, he found her pacing around her desk like a trapped panther. Upon seeing him, she rushed over, wrapped her arms around his waist, and kissed him hard on the lips.

"I'm so glad to see you. My mind's going crazy with worry."

"I'm fine," Max said, pulling back but she held tight.

"I know, I know. I love you so much, and with all that's happened, the thought of you out there, facing those dangerous witches — it just got to me."

Finally freeing himself, Max walked to the bookshelf. He pulled out one of Drummond's special books — the one with a flask of whiskey. "I'm here now. And I'm okay. You look a lot better. How do you feel? Besides paranoid for me."

She watched his movements, her eyes darting toward every creak in the building or chirp from a bird outside. "I feel like I had a thick, heavy chain around my throat attached to a big chunk of concrete, and the whole thing dragged me to the bottom of the ocean. And then suddenly, it broke. I was free. At first, I was disoriented. Sat here awhile waiting for you or Drummond or somebody to tell me what was going on. Then it all came back to me in a rush. That's when I started to worry about you. But you're here now. You're okay, right?"

"Absolutely fine."

Sandra's stomach gurgled loudly. "I guess I'm a bit hungry. Actually, now that I'm thinking about it, I'm starving. Let's get something to eat."

"Sure. Where do you want —"

"Fox and Hound. Let's go there."

Max arched an eyebrow. "Isn't that more for college kids?"

"After what I've been through, I could use a taste of youth around me. Come on. It'll be fun."

Thinking of the glass vial, Max said, "We don't really have time for fun right now. In fact, we need to talk about some serious things. Drummond and I met with Dr. Connor, and —"

"Not yet. I need to eat and it won't hurt anything if we go to a place that's a little fun. I promise I won't tell Drummond that you relaxed before dealing with witches, covens, and ghosts. Okay?"

She lowered her chin to her shoulder and gazed up at him with a coy look that often worked on him. He knew it. He knew she did, too.

This time would be no different.

"Okay. We'll go eat and take a breather. But then we've got to talk."

"Fox and Hound?"

"If that's where my darling wants to go."

"That's where I want to go." She kissed him, pressing in and opening her mouth slightly — a sensuous kiss, the kind that often led them to more physical activities. When she broke the kiss, Max leaned in for more, but she put her finger across his lips. "Nope. I need food."

The Fox and Hound Pub was located on the edge of the city off Knollwood Avenue. It was part of large strip mall filled with restaurants, clothing stores, a bakery, postal service, and the like. The Pub held a large number of people, had televisions blaring away sporting events, and several pool tables set up on one end. Everything was decked out in wood and brass. The back wall encompassed the bar, and the overall atmosphere exuded youth and vibrancy.

Sandra giggled and twirled when they entered as if by being amongst all these young people had rejuvenated her own youth. Max noticed a fresh sparkle in her eye. Perhaps facing down a coven of ghosts and surviving had given her a new appreciation for living. She certainly seemed happier than he had seen her in a long time.

They ordered their meals and a couple beers. Sandra stretched her arms. "I could sure go for a cigarette."

"Since when do you smoke?"

She laughed — a little too long, too forced. "Since never. But, hon, we only get to live once."

"Cigarettes will make that one time around quite a bit shorter. I doubt you're allowed to smoke in here, anyway."

"That's no fun. I want to have fun. Want to play some pool? I'm not very good, but I do know how to handle a stick." When she saw the shocked reaction on Max's face, she laughed. "I'm going to go freshen up. Be back in two shakes."

Max watched her walk off. He swore she added a bit more sway in her lovely hips but not in her usually sassy manner. This time, she wanted him salivating. Had it really been so long since she acted like this? So long that he was shocked at her behavior? They weren't old by any stretch of the term, but they were far from their college years, too.

Those were the wild times. Meeting up on the weekends — starting the weekend on Thursday — and borrowing a barely-running car from her roommate. Driving up the Michigan coast until they reached the little, northern towns that were too small to warrant a dot on a map. They'd go to the local grocer, stock up, go to the nearest liquor store, stock up, grab a room in a motel, and never leave until Sunday night. The entire weekend would be a two-person orgy of alcohol, sex, laughter, and sleep. Once they removed their clothes, they never dressed until the day they left. Sometimes they'd order a pizza and answer the door in the nude. Sometimes they grew serious, held each other close, and talked of their life in the future.

But that was a decade ago. Another life. Before they suffered through poverty and job loss. Long before Max learned of ghosts and witches, covens and curses, Hulls and Modesto.

Maybe Sandra was right to want to cut loose a bit. Even with all that hung over them, taking what little time they had to clear the mind sounded like a smart move. He also had Drummond working to find the handbell, and before leaving the office, Max had left a note telling Drummond where they went. Should the old detective find anything important, he'll be able to tell them right away. The situation was covered. Besides, there was always the possibility that they would end up dead or cursed after all this, so why not find some time for a little living?

As Sandra sashayed back to the table, Max felt his tensions easing. Running her finger along his shoulders, she bit her lip, leaned in and kissed him again. The electricity from lip to toe and everywhere in between brought back more memories than he knew he had held.

She must have felt it, too, because she caught her breath before melting into his side. "Suddenly, I'm not all that hungry."

"At least, not for food."

"At least."

They gazed into each other's eyes with the innocence and desire of hormone-crazed teens. There was nothing innocent, however, in the way Sandra's hand crept up Max's thigh. She nibbled at his neck, and he could smell the perfume she had dabbed on in the bathroom — a sweet, candy smell.

"Let's go for a walk," she whispered in his ear.

Max tossed more than enough cash to the waitress as they headed outside. Sandra led the way, her hand trailing behind to hold his. Max's heart hammered in his chest, and for the first time in ages, the cause was not fear of impending death.

They turned the corner into the back end of the restaurant. A hill of grass led up the left side, and Max heard the steady rush of cars on Highway 421 from the other side. Three cars were parked next to the building and a filthy dumpster after that.

Sandra took Max behind the dumpster, spun back on him, and planted her mouth against his. Fiery lust ignited along every inch of his body. He pressed against her, feeling every soft curve of hers push back. Her candy aroma mixed with the stench of the dumpster, turning the groping into something both erotic and depraved at the same time.

He brought his hand to her breast, but she shoved it away. "Not until I say so." A devilish grin crossed her lips, and she stepped away from him. She leaned against the wall, arching her body to push out her chest like a vintage pin-up girl, and licked her lips. Max stepped closer, but she put up a warning finger. "Not until I say so."

Max had never seen her take command like this. She had often said that she had to be tough all day long in life, so when it came to sex, she wanted to let go of control. Yet seeing her this way, relishing her life in such a forceful way, thrilled him. He never minded the way things were before, but this sudden change had brought with it a wealth of new sensations to his body.

"Okay," she said. "Take me. Take me hard."

Max moved in, shoving her against the wall as her arms and legs wrapped around him. He kissed and suckled every part of her he could reach, and he heard her moan a guttural animal sound — unlike anything he'd ever heard from her before.

He froze.

Nothing about her behavior had been right. Not just the sex, but the way she threw aside their responsibilities, the way she wanted to be around such a young crowd, even the way she spoke. He had chalked it up to post-life-threatening reaffirmation, only now that sounded false to his ear.

Ask her a personal question.

Why would Dr. Connor have said that unless she knew something and wanted to prove it to Max? She had thought that such a question would change his mind about the vial of blood, so what did that mean about Sandra?

One intimate, personal question.

Sandra reached down between his legs. "Come on, baby. Give me this."

He wanted to sound natural, as if he meant every word, but he heard the cold, monotone delivery that his chilled heart could manage.

"You want it like that time in Dallas?"

"Oh, yeah, baby. Just like in Dallas."

The words thundered down upon him, boulders of reality smashing apart the fantasy this woman had built up that he so willingly fell into. He stumbled back a step, afraid to look upon her face, afraid he would lose his will to do what needed doing. And the witch Connor knew all along.

"Honey, don't stop now."

He shook his head slow as the words rose in his throat. "We've never been to Dallas."

Sandra put up her hands in a shrug. "Whoops. Guess you found me out."

"Who are you?"

"This is still your wife's body. You won't be cheating on her."

"Who are you?" he screamed, pulling back his arm and making a fist.

"Sugar, I'm exactly who you think I am."

"Patricia Welling."

She nodded. Max felt as if he had taken a punch. If Patricia possessed Sandra, then what had happened to his wife? Was she still in there or should he be mourning her death? And something bad must have happened to Drummond, otherwise he would have destroyed Patricia's corpse. Had they been set up by Connor?

"Sandra? You in there?"

"She ain't coming out. Now, you come over here and give me a good time. If you don't, I'll go find one of those handsome, young men in the bar. I'm sure they'd love this body."

Max thrust out his left hand, pinning her against the wall. His right hand, still curled in a fist, hung back ready to strike. Looking in her eyes, he didn't see anyone he recognized, but he saw a tinge of concern — what did she have to fear? Drummond?

She laughed. "You going to hit me? Poor little Sandra's face. Are you a wife-beater?"

Something was wrong here — more wrong than the obvious. Max struggled to find Connor's angle, how it might hurt him, but she had wanted him to ask the questions — she had wanted him to learn Sandra had been possessed. Whatever was going on, these witches were not on the same side. And that meant that he needed the blood of Patricia Welling — no, he needed the blood of his wife, possessed by Patricia Welling.

"Last chance, lover. You can enjoy this body in ways you never have or —"

He punched her. One hard crack to the head.

She went down, rolling on the wet, dirty asphalt into the way of any alley traffic. Max rubbed his fist. Punching a person's skull hurt. And he hadn't knocked her out. In the movies, one punch knocked out a bad guy with ease — apparently it wasn't actually that simple.

She raised up to all fours. "Sorry, hon," he said, walked up to her side and punched her on the back of the head. A muffled cry escaped her lungs as she fell forward. Still, she moved. He had to get her unconscious. That's all he could think to do. Get her unconscious, take her blood, make Connor exorcise this ghost from his wife. But she still moved, still tried to get to her feet. He rolled her over, pulled back his fist again, when her eyes shot open.

"Help! Rape!" she screamed.

Two young men the size of linebackers poked their heads around the corner. "Hey!" one of them called out. Before Max could do anything more, they tackled him and a horrible beating ensued.

Chapter 20

MAX OPENED HIS EYES to see Drummond floating above. His body ached, his mouth felt a size too big, and he tasted blood in his mouth. He tried to sit up but his ribs sent sharp pains into his side.

Drummond slid down next to Max. "Easy there, palooka. You got on the wrong end of a lot of fists. You'll live, but I'm glad I ain't you for the next week."

Max spit blood. His tongue ran along his teeth — thankfully, none missing. "She's got Sandra. Your ghost bitch is in my Sandra."

"I figured that much out."

Trying to stand again, Max groaned and flopped back to the ground. "We've got find her. She could be doing anything with my wife. Or anyone."

"We'll find her. Calm down."

"How the fuck am I supposed to calm down? My wife is possessed by a dead witch. How am I supposed to say that sentence calmly?"

"First, you need to listen. Can you do that? Because I promise you, the last thing on Patricia Welling's mind is bedding down with a man."

"That wasn't how she behaved with me."

"She was toying with you. Screwing with your head. Just like Connor. That's what witches do."

Max hesitated. He wanted to believe Drummond, wanted to know that the woman he loved would not have to spend the rest of her life with memories of strangers. He didn't want to think about it either. Drummond's eyes — so sincere, so convincing.

Holding his jaw tight both from frustration and the bruises along the bone, Max finally said, "You promise me. You tell me that she won't defile my wife that way."

"She won't. It isn't easy to possess somebody conscious, somebody who will fight to regain control of her body — and you know Sandra's fighting like a cornered tiger. Patricia's going to be using a lot of energy to maintain that possession. And since she went to all that trouble and fight, there's got to be more on her mind than sex."

"You better be right."

"I am. And I'm sorry. I should've been here instead of wasting time following one dead end after another."

Max glowered at Drummond. "You should have finished the job."

"I did. I demolished that corpse."

"Then it wasn't Patricia Welling in the Fed Building."

"It absolutely was. I don't know why it didn't work, but we did what we set out to do."

"Then why the hell —"

"I don't know. But getting angry won't help us. Let's figure this out, find your wife, fix this mess."

Though he managed to stand, it took more effort than he imagined any simple act would require. Yet with each passing minute, he felt his strength returning. The brutes who had battered him caused plenty of bruises but no broken bones. Even his ribs looked to be in the proper place — purple and black all along his side, but nothing where it didn't belong.

"You okay? Can you walk?"

"Give me a minute," Max snapped. "I got my ass kicked in." He took a few tentative steps. "And my ass hurts, too."

The back door to the bar opened, and a heavyset man stepped out carrying two garbage bags. As he threw out the trash, he gave a few cursory glances Max's way.

Once the man went back inside, Max rubbed his jaw. "Help me think this through. What do we know?"

Drummond made a lazy circle as he spoke. "All the witches we know of have been freed from the curse and destroyed. So is there another one? One we missed?"

"Possibly, but why is Patricia Welling still in Sandra? Why didn't she go poof?"

"Maybe because she has a body now."

Max nodded. "She has Sandra's body, so she doesn't need her old one. She must have taken over Sandra back at the church. I should've seen it. I did see it. Sandra was acting weird from the moment we left that church, but I didn't realize — and now she's fighting for her life."

"Focus, Max. Please. I need your help. Sandra needs your help."

With a deep breath that sent spikes of pain straight along his spine, Max nodded. "I'm sorry. I'll be okay. You're right, I've got to focus."

"That's right. Sandra's counting on you."

Max's eyes narrowed. "Connor knew. She had to."

"That's why she wanted you to get the blood. Not so she would have control over Sandra, but so she could control Patricia."

"But why not take care of it herself? If she's so powerful, why get me involved? She hates me."

"Maybe that's why. Hatred can push people to do some dumb things."

Heading back to his car, Max rolled his shoulder. He couldn't afford for his bruised body to stiffen up at a crucial moment. Despite the pain, he needed to stay limber.

The parking lot had emptied, and his car stood a lone vigil, waiting for a driver. "Connor's not dumb. She used me for a purpose. She's waiting for something to happen, maybe, or she didn't want to be seen doing the job or —"

"Modesto." Drummond clapped his hands, startling Max. "The Hulls must not know what she's up to."

"Which is what?"

"I hate to say it, but it looks like there's only one person who has the answers. At least, one who might be willing to talk."

Max nodded gravely. He opened the car door and its whine sounded much like he felt. "If Sandra wasn't in trouble, I'd never agree to this."

"I know. Can you drive?"

"Unless you can, I don't have a choice."

"I'll go on ahead, make sure it's safe."

"Okay. See you back at good ol' Doc Connor's place."

"Promise me one thing."

"What?"

"Don't kill her."

Max raised an eyebrow, then got in the car. He slammed the door shut and started the engine. Drummond hovered for a moment, but when he saw he would get no further answer, he disappeared.

Chapter 21

THE BLUE DIGITAL CLOCK on his dashboard read three a.m. Though his body complained with every motion, he did not feel tired. Too much adrenaline, stress, and fear.

When this is over, I'm going to sleep for days.

As he stepped from the car, the still air smelled of a coming storm. Hot, humid, sticky — soon it would all break under a torrent of rain. But in the morning, the sun would return and pollen would coat the world. By noon, it would be as if nothing had happened.

Not for me.

Max walked a labored stride toward Connor's office. No matter what happened, he knew he would not be the same. Considering the dark thoughts that drifted through his mind, the horrible things he now thought himself willing to do should Dr. Connor prove uncooperative — he never imagined he could think like that.

I haven't done anything, yet.

The word yet echoed in his head.

"There you are." Drummond zipped out of the office, coming straight through a wall, and darted right at Max. "Hurry. She's dying."

Max managed a slow jog, each footfall sending sharp jolts up his leg. Drummond had unlocked the front door, and Max shuffled down the hall toward the back office. The photos on the wall had been knocked askew. A few lay shattered on the floor. Before he entered the back office, Max saw blood streaked on the baseboard.

Connor's office had been ransacked — papers strewn about, book stacks toppled over, wall charts ripped into shreds. A putrid odor rose from a shattered jar containing a pig fetus. Dr. Connor lay on the floor, her eyes open wide and unblinking, blood pooling beneath her, a wide gash in her forehead. She had strange cuts on her arm like claw marks.

Wrinkling his nose, Max inched forward. "Dr. Connor?"

The witch's eyes rested upon Max. In a weak whisper, she said, "I told you."

"You're alive," he said, pulling out his phone. "I'm calling for help."

"Of course, she's alive," Drummond said. "You think I'd lie about that?"

Connor raised her hand and wagged a finger. "No help. I've reached the end."

Max's thumb hovered over the Send button. He looked to Drummond who answered with a mild shrug. Big help.

Connor lifted her head and coughed blood. "The handbell."

"Where is it? What's it for?"

"Foolish boy. You never listen." She chuckled despite the strain each quiet word cost her. "I warned you what Hull was doing. I warned you."

"You said that they were trying to resurrect Tucker Hull. I listened to you. I did. It's one of the reasons I haven't done any work for the Hulls."

"First, an item from the source — the journal. Second, a powerful charm full of life — Blackbeard's hair. And last, a cursed object that can call upon a soul with all the power of a great witch — the handbell."

"That's really what it's for?"

"Thirteen bells for thirteen witches. And one of them missing."

Drummond drifted in towards Max. "Patricia's bell."

"My mother," Connor went on, "had fallen in love with Hull and knew that if he ever discovered the depth of her feelings, he would destroy her."

"Not a good idea to get emotionally involved with your prime witch," Max said.

"Exactly. She stole the bell to protect herself — she hoped to use its power, if necessary. But she failed and the bell was lost."

"And Hull needs it for his resurrection spell."

Coughing up more blood, Connor nodded.

Drummond bent closer to Max. "Not to be so callous, but if you don't get everything we need from her —"

Max waved the detective off. He knew what needed to be done. "Where's the bell?"

"The bell will draw out Patricia's ghost, leaving your wife an empty vessel for a few seconds. If Modesto can cast the spell at that moment, Tucker Hull can enter your wife's body before her own spirit can reclaim it."

Before she could finish her sentence, Max grabbed her collar and yanked her up. "Then where the hell is the bell?"

Her eyes rolled upward. Max slapped her face hard three times before she focused on him again. "I never found it. That was supposed to be your job."

He dropped her and clutched his head. "We're screwed."

"Don't give up," Drummond said. "Remember, Modesto doesn't know where it is, either. Tucker Hull can't come back without it."

"Great. So, Sandra will just share her body with your old girlfriend forever."

"We'll find the handbell. We'll use it and get Patricia out of there, but we'll do it away from Modesto and his spell. Come on, Max. We're not giving up."

Max glanced down at Connor, her blood pool widening. "You weren't trying to help us. What did you need the blood for? Protection?"

She moved her head up and down slightly, weakly. Inhaling with a wheezing sound, she raised her arm like a marionette on a limp string. She let the breath leave her body and pointed toward her desk. When the last of her breath left her body, her arm flopped to the floor, and she never inhaled again.

"Crap," Max said. Bad enough he failed to get the information he needed from her, but with the way his luck had run, he guessed the FBI would be blaming him for this death, too.

"You okay?" Drummond asked.

"What's it say about me that I'm no longer freaking out over dead bodies?"

"That you're finally starting to understand this world."

Max sighed. "That's dark."

"I'm a ghost. What do you expect?"

Stepping over to Connor's desk, Max said, "She pointed here. Help me look."

Drummond floated around Max as he leafed through her file cabinet. "I see pens, papers, appointment book, some bills."

"I don't need an inventory."

"Well, I can't search like you unless I'm willing to take on the pain of touching things."

"Sandra's life is at stake and you're worried about a little pain?"

"Did you forget what I did in the basement of that crazy art forger? I took on a lot of pain for you both back then. And there was the time—"

"Okay, I'm sorry. We don't need to go into all the times you've suffered for us."

"Then why don't you look at your feet?"

"Huh?"

"On the floor. There's a book at your feet. Must have been knocked off her desk when she was attacked."

Max crouched down and stared at the book. It had that crinkled, leathery covering he hated to see — human skin. With every effort to hide his revulsion, he picked up the book and placed it on Connor's desk. A long feather — maybe an owl, maybe an eagle, probably a vulture — had been used as a bookmark.

Opening the book, Max noticed his fingers shaking. His pulse beat against his neck. As he pushed the cover over, he flinched. He felt like a mouse inspecting cheese on a trap. The bookmark brought him to a page with the words *THE BOOK OF SPELLS* written in a meticulous script.

"I think we've got something," Max said. He snapped the book shut, tucked it under his arm, ignored the involuntary shiver his body made upon contact with the human skin cover, and headed out of the office.

"Where are we going?" Drummond asked.

"My house. We can figure this all out over there."

"But the office is —"

"I'm not sure I want to go back in there just yet."

"Because of Sandra?"

"Why is that a shock? I love my wife and when I last saw her there, she wasn't really my wife. I won't be eating at the Fox and Hound anytime soon either. Besides, if Connor is right, then Hull and Modesto need that bell more than anything. Modesto's been trying to use me to find it, and since I haven't seen him trying to follow me —"

"He's probably staking out the office."

"So we go to my house, take a close look at this book, and see if we can't save Sandra, stop this coven, and prevent Tucker Hull from being resurrected."

"Sounds like a lovely evening."

Chapter 22

As THEY ZIPPED ALONG the highway, the night's lights danced along Max's face. His stern expression cut through the reds, yellows, and whites leaving only the dark. They had been in dire situations before, but this time, he had no idea if he could ever get his wife back. It wasn't a calculated risk. What he had in mind would be a step into a world he wanted less and less to do with.

Stay strong. Stay focused. Only one thing matters — get Sandra back.

When Max neared his house, Drummond leaned forward, squinting as he looked out the windshield. "Keep driving," he said. "Don't slow down."

"What's wrong?"

"Do it."

Max drove by the house and turned at the end of the street. Drummond waved him onward while watching the road behind them.

"Get back on the highway."

"What's going on? Did you see Modesto?"

Drummond settled back. "Worse. The FBI."

Slapping the steering wheel, Max said, "Damn. Now what?"

"You got a lot of people interested in you. I'd say even if you wanted to, the office is definitely out, now. We could go back to Connor's place."

"And get picked up for her murder?"

"Well, there's that, of course."

Max glanced up at the oversized green signs passing by on the highway. One read — LEXINGTON. "I think I know where to go."

"I'm listening."

"You know what's near Lexington? Thomasville."

Drummond shook his head. "Leed's house? The cops'll have that place taped off."

"That hasn't stopped us before. I doubt anybody's going to be out there tonight. Why would they? It's not a pressing murder for the local cops, and the FBI are involved, so the locals may not even have authority to be out there. We know the FBI are out at my house."

"They might be at both locations."

"You really think the FBI is going to put that much manpower onto this little case?"

"I suppose not."

"Something else bothering you then?"

Drummond shifted uncomfortably. "Leed died there ... in a bad way."

"You afraid his ghost might be hanging around?"

"I'm not afraid of him. But I don't necessarily want to see him either. Especially if he's not quite himself."

"You think he turned?"

"From what you said, he had a pretty violent death. I'd think that might push a guy toward the evil side a lot quicker. Don't you?"

"Well, we don't have many options, and I'm not wasting the night searching for a place to sit down while we work this out. Sandra needs us. It's that simple. If Leed is there, you'll either make friends or you'll suck it up and deal."

Drummond tugged at his bottom lip. "I figured you might say that."

The saying goes *Third times the charm*, but Max felt nothing charming about seeing Leed's house again. Cast in the dim moonlight, the old place had died along with Leed. The porch which had seemed quaint, now looked disheveled. The charisma of the warped wood floors and peeling white paint had turned ugly and dilapidated. Instead of the charming old farmhouse on the hill, Leed's place had taken on the air of a haunted house that children hurried by, afraid they might stir something in the shadows. Worst of all, Max thought they might be right.

Drummond floated into the living room, his eyes roving every corner, every hiding place, every darkened nook. "Looks okay."

Max let the witch's book fall to the floor, leaned his back against the wall, and slid down with an exhausted exhalation. He stared at the furniture but couldn't bring himself to sit on anything in the house. Drummond may not have found anything, but somewhere in the house, Leed's ghost had to be hanging around. He had seen that horrible death. No way did Leed peacefully move on to wherever the moving on go.

While rolling his neck and stretching his arms, Max said, "Let's look at the book and figure this all out. I don't want to spend any more time here than I have to."

Drummond's focus turned toward the kitchen — the place Leed had died. "I think something's in there."

"Help me with the book."

"It's like a miniature ghost that's not all there. Like a little bit of ghost but nothing more. I've never seen that before."

"Ignore it."

Drummond entered the kitchen while Max leafed through the spell book. "It can't be bigger than my hand, and — oh. It's Leed. At least, I think it is. But he's not fully formed. Or ..."

"Do I want to hear the rest of that sentence?"

"Probably not. I think Patricia, when she killed Leed, I think she cut apart his soul. There isn't enough left to make a ghost."

"All the more reason to help me out here. Last thing you want is your old girlfriend to shred your soul to pieces."

But Drummond stayed in the kitchen. Max could hear him cooing to Leed like a little girl taking in an injured bunny. If the whole thing weren't so disturbing, Max would have marveled at this unexpected side of Drummond. But things were disturbing. And they wouldn't get any better on their own.

Max turned page after page, the dried pages crinkling as they moved. A rich, pleasant smell rose from the book, but when he remembered what made the book's cover, he shuddered at what might produce that aroma. From then on, he turned the pages by pinching them with the tips of his forefinger and thumb. He knew he looked prissy and foolish, but nobody was looking — and even Hull couldn't pay him enough to dig his hands into a book made of human beings.

"Poor little Leed," Drummond said from the kitchen. "You're really lost. Don't worry. It's confusing, I know. But I won't abandon you."

The next page Max turned brought him to a section marked *Location Spells*. Though the text had been handwritten, Max's experience deciphering the scripts of people writing from centuries ago made reading this relatively easy.

> *All Location spells are easy to cast, entry level magiks which can be used, as the name would imply, to acquire the location of an object, emotion, or soul. Because of its simplicity, any Location magik can divine if the caster has any basic skill or inner-power.*

One who fails at this task will never rise amongst those of our Order.

"We've got something big here," Max called out.

Drummond came back in, his face blank. "Hm? What did you find?"

Max glanced quizzically at the kitchen but decided to let it go. There would be time to ask about Leed later — if they survived. "Well, first, this book isn't a generic spellbook. It's a coven's Grimoire. It's got references to an order and a hierarchy."

"You think it's Patricia's coven?"

"How many covens do you think there are around here? Wait. Don't answer that."

"You're probably right. Why else would Connor point us to this book?"

A disturbing thought struck Max. "Does this mean Connor is part of Patricia's old coven? That it might still be active?"

"Connor and her mother were never the kind of witches to join up with anyone. They worked for hire, and they enjoyed being amongst the most powerful in the area. Covens are formed by witches seeking companions, friendship, access to knowledge, and most of all, they want to strengthen their power through numbers."

"Like a gang."

"And what need does Connor have for joining a gang? My hunch is that she got hold of this Grimoire through one piece of nasty business or another, and the witch ghosts didn't like it too much. That's why they ripped her apart. That's also why she wanted us to take the book."

"So the coven will come after us?"

"They're already after us. But I didn't see any other ghosts at Connor's office. And they obviously didn't find the Grimoire or didn't have time to look or something, because we've got it. Maybe Connor planned to cast some of the spells in it against them. She did want that blood, after all."

"Well, that's the second thing. There's a few location spells in here. I'm thinking we could use one to find the handbell."

Drummond's face dropped. "There's a spell in that book to find the handbell?"

"I think so."

"Then why the hell didn't anybody use it?"

Max read over the spell — its ingredients and procedure. "Maybe it's more dangerous than it looks. Maybe Modesto didn't want Connor knowing what he was up to."

"She already knew. She's been warning you about it for a while now."

"I don't have an answer. And, frankly, I don't care. Not while my wife is in trouble."

Drummond said nothing more. He simply glanced at the list of ingredients and began searching through the house. Max followed suit, checking out each room of the house carefully. They needed four blue candles, a goblet filled with water, and lotus incense.

As they rummaged through the house, Max noticed that Drummond repeatedly patted his left coat pocket and murmured softly to it. Max had a suspicion about that, especially since all mention of the unformed ghost of Leed had disappeared, but things were creepy enough without adding a new dimension to his understanding of the ghost world. If they made it through all this, if Sandra made it through, he would ask. Sandra knew so much more about it all, and she could explain it in a way that wouldn't disturb him, that might actually make the whole thing logical and benign.

In the dining room, Max located a silver goblet with Roman lettering around the lip. Drummond indicated where several packs of incense had been stashed in the bedroom. And finally, in Leed's office, where Drummond could not enter, Max found two plastic tubs filled with candles — red, black, green, white, and a blue nub.

Max picked up a red candle. "Will any one of these do?"

"Spells are very specific. I don't know why the color matters, but it does. Probably has something to do with whatever's inside them to give them the color."

He glanced at the candle, thought for a second about the deep red color, the blood red color. He shot open his hand, letting the candle bang on the floor. "No candles we can use." Wiping his palm against his shirt, Max stepped out of Leed's office. "We've got to find something. There's no way I'm waiting until morning to pick up blue candles at a store. Who knows what your girlfriend will have done with my wife by then."

"She's not my girlfriend. She's not my anything." Drummond cocked his head toward his coat pocket. "Not a bad idea," he whispered.

"What idea?"

Trying to look casual, Drummond said, "We know one place that's filled with the ingredients a witch would need for spells."

"Really?" Max shook his head as he gathered his things. "I hate that place."

But he knew Drummond was right. Despite the late hour, despite the weariness in his muscles and bones, Max trudged back to his car and headed back towards Winston-Salem, towards Dr. Connor's office. The drive would take an hour — a long time to be stuck worrying for Sandra with nothing active to do — but at least Drummond remained quiet throughout the trip. Any talk with that ghost would have led to the thing in his coat pocket, and Max wanted nothing to do with that at the moment. Not that he feared the little thing might be Leed. More that Max feared it might not be — that Drummond's mounting emotions in this case were pushing him towards insanity and turning him into an evil specter.

At length, they turned onto Westgate Center Drive, passed by Home Depot, and drove into the section of doctor's offices, local accounting firms, and small legal practices. Max had traveled this route more times than he had ever wanted. The quiet darkness of a late night visit to the witch had become too familiar. Except this time, the darkness filled up with flashing lights of red and blue.

Three police cars blocked off the parking lot while detectives walked in and out of Connor's office. A WXII News van sat as close to the action as the police would allow, while a reporter taped her story in front of the bright lights provided by the cameraman.

Before Drummond could say anything, Max said, "I know, I know. Keep driving."

They passed by in time to see a covered body wheeled out the front door. Up ahead, Max turned the car back toward Hanes Mall, figuring they could park on the far side away from this action and plan their next step.

Drummond had a different idea. "Go to Matt Ernest's house."

"What?"

"He's got all sorts of magic-related items there. You know it. There's a good chance he'll have the candles. They're fairly common amongst those who dabble in magic. Considering all the candles Leed had, Ernest would probably have more. And besides —"

"Enough. This isn't a court trial. You don't have to lay out all the evidence. If you think we can get the candles there, then that's what we'll do. But if I get caught and sent to jail, you're doing time with me. I don't know how, but I'll make sure you're there."

"You really want me haunting your prison cell?"

Max thought about it and shuddered. "Shut up."

It took about fifteen minutes to reach Ernest's house. Max parked a few doors beyond to be safe. "Stay here," he told Drummond. He expected a protest, but Drummond waved him on, the detective more interested in talking with his coat pocket than arguing with Max.

Max strolled up to the house as casually as he could manage, taking furtive glances around, seeking any sign of trouble. Nobody watched him. Besides, at such a late hour, anybody still awake was probably drunk.

Or an insomniac happy to watch my every move and report me to the police.

He fought off the avenues of thought that wanted to take him and focused on the job. From Drummond he had learned to act with confidence when doing what one shouldn't be doing. Observers would fill in the most plausible explanations if he behaved as if everything was normal. So, Max didn't hesitate when he reached the house. He walked straight to the back door and pulled off the tape he had recently cut.

Had he time to plan for this break-in, he would have brought along a flashlight. Instead, Max had to pop on his cellphone. The bluish hue cast across the crime scene accentuated the claw marks in the walls and disarray of the rooms. The air smelled damp and dead. Every footstep creaked.

Ignoring all the messages his brain screamed at him, all the instincts to run away from this horrible place, Max pressed straight for Ernest's room — the man's last stand. He stood at the closed doorway to Ernest's room, breathing hard though he had done little more than walk into the house. Courage, bravery — these were acts one took despite the fear raging in one's mind. He wished Drummond were here. Or Sandra. Anybody who could tell him if ghosts occupied the house or if he stood alone in an empty hall.

When Patricia Welling attacked his wife at the church, she had not been alone. Yet Drummond had not mentioned any other ghosts since then — except for whatever Leed had become. But surely, the other coven ghosts had followed them.

"No," he said to the house. "They followed their High Priestess." Wherever Patricia had taken Sandra's body, that was where the other ghosts would be found.

Then I'm alone here.

"Okay, then. Go." Max threw open the door, rushed in, and headed for the closet. The symbols on the walls designed to protect Matt

Ernest seemed to slither away in the dim light. He flashed his cellphone around until he saw a stack of boxes. He poured through these as fast as possible, holding his breath most of the time as if to gasp the air in the room would be to inhale evil itself.

On the third box, he struck gold. Well, blue. The candles were square at the base, thin, and as long as his forearm. He grabbed four, stepped away, came back, and took two more — just in case.

Moving fast, he headed down the hall when he heard Ernest's bedroom door slam behind him. Max froze. He tried to sense any change in the air — a drop in temperature, a bright perfume or a foul odor, the general aura of the room. Anything that might hint at a ghost — benign or otherwise. But it was no use. Whatever wiring in his brain allowed him to see and interact with Drummond went no further. He was as blind to other ghosts as any everyday person.

The door banged open and closed again.

Max walked straight toward the back door, not wanting to look behind. As he reached out to open the door, something ice cold tapped across his neck. He whirled around and saw nothing. Fumbling behind him for the doorknob, his eyes darted around the darkness.

Though he could hear the shaking in his breath, he opened his mouth wide and said as firmly as he could manage, "You go tell the High Priestess I'm coming for her. You tell her that if she harms my wife, I'll curse her with the worst things I can find." He swore he could hear confusion and uncertainty in the air. As his hand found the doorknob, he couldn't resist adding a final blow. "Oh, and tell her the spells will come from your own Grimoire."

He opened the door and turned, but before he could exit, the door shut hard enough to crack the panes. An icy touch clamped around his neck. He tried to inhale, but what little air managed to get through chilled his lungs painfully.

Max tried to force the door open. He pulled and kicked at it, but it refused to budge. The darkness in the room grew even darker. Little spots of color danced before him. Max lifted his hand for the doorknob one more time, but his fingers only slapped at it. He couldn't breathe, couldn't feel the air in his lungs, couldn't hear the subtlest wheeze. He fell back, the candles tumbling to the floor, and he had long enough to regret not being able to save Sandra.

"Max?" Drummond's deep voice echoed in the room.

Max saw the detective pop through a wall. Drummond acted fast. Leaping above Max, Drummond engaged in a bizarre fight where his opponent could not be seen — at least by Max.

The grip on his throat loosened, and he coughed and sputtered while Drummond threw punches into the empty air. Drummond ducked, popped back up, and shot a deep uppercut. With his chest puffed, he stared at the corner of the room for a moment before turning to Max.

"You okay?"

Max got back to his feet. "Thanks. Is it a witch?"

"Definitely. Let's get out of here before she wakes up."

Collecting the candles, Max nodded. "Why did you come in, anyway?"

"A car pulled up, parked, but nobody got out. I think the cops are staking out the house. Maybe they found a connection with Connor's murder."

"Or maybe Modesto is playing both sides. The Hulls do have influence with some of the law."

"Doesn't really matter. You've got to sneak out of here without them seeing you. Crouch down, follow me, and do as I say. It'll be easy."

Even as Max crouched before the back door, he rolled his eyes. Drummond passed through the wall and reappeared outside the house. Here we go. Max opened the back door and slipped out. Keeping low to the ground, he duck-walked around the corner. His thighs burned with the effort, turning his quads into sharp rocks that ground into his bones with every waddling step. But pulling a quad seemed a better risk than getting picked up by the police.

Drummond pointed to a telephone pole. "See the shadow from the streetlight?" A thick black line ran from the base of the telephone pole clear up to where Max squatted. "You can stand and walk in that shadow right up to the pole. Our friend is parked across the street. Stay in that shadow and he won't see you."

When Max stood, his legs screamed in both relief and pain. He wanted to move fast along the shadow, but with his muscles protesting every motion, he had to take small, slow steps. Probably saved his hide. Had he raced over to the pole, he would have most likely slipped out of the shadow's narrow confines. Taking a deliberate pace meant he could place each foot carefully.

Once he reached the telephone pole, Drummond pointed down the street to his car. "This is the hard part. When I tell you, you're going to have make a run for your car. Sprint down there, get in, and drive away."

"But —"

"Trust me. Wait for my signal." Drummond slid into the amber pool of the streetlight. "We'll give you as much time as we can."

"We?"

"Be quiet and wait."

Drummond reached into his coat pocket. When he pulled his hand out, he had it shaped as if he held something, but Max saw nothing. Drummond bent over and whispered to the nothing. Leed?

From the look on Drummond's face, Max discerned that Leed had zipped away. A moment of silence passed. As Max wondered what Leed would do, he heard a car alarm go off several houses up — away from his car. Another alarm went off, this one complete with flashing headlights. Max watched Drummond, waiting for a signal. He rubbed his thighs with his free hand, his other clutching the candles against his body — Sandra's life rested in those candles.

A third alarm went off, the kind that changed tones every few seconds. Whatever Drummond had waited for happened. He clapped his hands and waved Max on. "Come on. Go!"

Max shoved off the telephone pole and rushed for his car. He wanted to sprint, pour every ounce of power into his legs, but his thighs buckled. It took all his will to keep upright.

He snatched a peek over his shoulder and saw a man standing next to a car. The man placed his hands on his hips and looked up the street at the increasing number of car alarms. Though Max only had time to see the man in silhouette, he saw enough — Stevenson, FBI.

That got his legs moving. He half-jogged, half-skipped his way to his car, slipped in the driver's seat and turned the engine over. People had come outside to turn off their alarms only to have the alarms start up again. All that noise and confusion masked Max's engine, and as he drove away, he saw Stevenson in the rearview mirror — standing with his hands on his hips, watching the bizarre car alarms.

By the time Max returned to Leed's house, his adrenaline rush had worn off, dropping his tired body a few notches further toward exhaustive collapse. He stumbled into the house and leaned against the living room wall. As his eyes closed and his breathing slowed, he heard Drummond's deep tones arguing with someone.

"They're not going to understand. Hell, I don't get it either."

With his back, Max pushed off the wall and moved closer toward the hall leading further into the house. Drummond stood near the end of the hall, yelling at his hand which cupped nothing at all — which meant probably the ghost of Leed.

"Shut up already. I appreciate what you did but that doesn't give you any right to meddle here. Patricia Welling is my responsibility. You did your part ... What? ... I'm not still in love with her ... You don't know what you're talking about ... If I had known then ... that doesn't prove I knew anything. And besides, raking over the past won't change where we are now ... Don't tell me to calm down."

Drummond's gray face flushed red for a split second. Max cleared his throat loudly and when Drummond spun toward him, Max nearly fell back from the man's glare.

"What do you want?" Drummond said, his brow turned down sharp, his voice graveled as if he had smoked all night. A haze of darkness lifted off his shoulders.

Max tried to keep his face calm. Inside, every synapse fired off red alert warnings. "Drummond? You in there? Calm down. Stay with me."

"You blame me for this, don't you? For what's happened to Sandra. Everyone blames me."

"I don't blame you for something you did long ago and out of love. And I need your help now. Please, don't turn. Stay the man I know. Come on ... Marshall."

Drummond's face relaxed. He lifted his head and looked around as if unsure how he got to the house. "About time you got here." As he moved into the living room, he placed the object in his hand back into his coat pocket. "Best get this spell done before the sun rises. They tend to be stronger when the stars and moon are visible. At least, that's the lore."

Max gawked as the ghost pointed to the empty space by the living room window.

"That should be a good spot," Drummond said. He raised a quizzical eyebrow to Max. "What?"

"Nothing," Max said and gathered the items needed for the spell along with the Grimoire. He ignored Drummond's odd expression, ignored the pressure mounting in the dusty air, ignored all the warnings blazing in his head. If Drummond turned now, Max didn't see anything he could do to stop it. Only way forward was straight through — do the spell, find the handbell, summon Patricia and his wife, hope he figures out what to do after that.

Max opened the Grimoire to the appropriate page and set the book on the seat of a wooden chair. He then sat on the floor in the spot Drummond had indicated. For his part, Drummond went to the book and guided Max.

"First thing you do is put one candle at each of the four compass points."

Max picked up one candle. "Which way is North?"

Without looking up from the book, Drummond pointed toward the kitchen. Max reoriented himself to face the kitchen and placed the candle in front of his crossed legs. Then he set the other three candles to either side and behind him.

"Next thing you do is fill the goblet with water and set it down in front of you."

Max did as instructed. He went to the kitchen to fill the goblet from the sink, and as the water streamed in, he tried to avoid looking at the wall where he had seen Leed murdered. He thought of all the rage and hatred that gave Patricia Welling the physical and mental strength to destroy that man. "She's not going to like it when I get this bell." The thought brought a grim smile to Max's face.

He returned to Drummond, sat as before, and set the filled goblet in front of him. Drummond leaned closer to the book and read. "Light the incense, then the candles." Max did so. "Now you meditate."

"I what? I don't know how to meditate. I've never even tried to do it before."

"Guess you'll be trying it out now."

"Is there another way? I don't want to screw this up."

"You'll do fine. Listen, in the '70s there were plenty of people coming through my office trying all kinds of stuff. Sex, music, drugs. Lots of drugs. I swear they did so much of the stuff that, even dead, I got a contact high. They also experimented with meditation. I think the Beatles had something to do with that."

"Great. So now you're going to be my guru because you were stuck watching a bunch of stoners pretend to meditate?"

"If you have a better idea, tell me. What's the big deal, anyway? If you don't do it right, the spell won't work. No problem."

"Unless not working means the spell kills me ... or worse."

"This is for your wife, remember?" Drummond said sharply, his eyes narrowing as his anger increased.

Max tried to laugh off the tension. "You're right, you're right. Sorry. I'm really tired and worried and I don't know what to do."

"Of course." Drummond's face relaxed. "I understand. You ready now? Good. All you have to do is focus on the object you want to find. Think about it. Picture it. That's all. Take slow, deep breaths and do your best to picture that handbell. Don't let any other thoughts take you away from that image. You think you can do that?"

"For Sandra, definitely." Max closed his eyes and breathed slow and deep. The incense entered his body, and his muscles loosened up. Sleep threatened to take over his weary body; he even felt his head grow heavy. Focus. He had to stay in control of his thoughts. The handbell — that was the only image he needed to worry about. All other thoughts, all other desires, even sleep, had to go away.

Time loosened. Only the sound of his lungs expanding and expelling filled his ears. Only the handbell filled his mind. He saw it from every angle, practically felt it in his hand.

"Something's happening," Drummond said.

Max opened his eyes but still pictured the handbell in his mind. The candle flames flared, and Max felt something tugging on his skin. No. Not tugging on it — tugging from within it — as if thousands of tiny hooks were in his skin and pulled away from him. It hurt and threatened to break his concentration.

"Max? You okay?"

The handbell. Think only of the handbell.

A force grabbed hold of his chest, pressed in and pulled out simultaneously. Max could feel his life draining away as this force exerted control upon his body. He felt as if this power tossed him around the room though he never moved an inch. Blood shot out his nose, and he coughed up an acidic phlegm.

He strained to keep focus but something smashed his head from the inside. Light-headed, his eyes rolled and he flopped forward.

But as his face fell to the floor, he caught a glimpse inside the goblet. Instead of his reflection, he saw a building — *the* building — *his* building — *his office* building — the place where the handbell would be found.

Chapter 23

UPON WAKING UP, the urgency in Max's stomach forced him to roll over and vomit across the living room floor. His head pounded, his thighs ached, and he had a nasty crick in his neck. Golden sunlight peeked through the windows, each beam a blinding spear through his eyes.

"It's about time," Drummond said, soaring into the room.

Sitting up slowly, feeling his stomach curl again, Max scrunched his brow. "That spell hurt. Besides, the sun's just coming up. I was out for what? A half-hour?"

Drummond flicked his hands toward the window. "The sun is setting, not rising. You've been out for almost twelve hours. I screamed at you, I knocked chairs over, I even passed my hand through you. Nothing worked. We've got to go meet Modesto, and we don't have the handbell. In other words, all our leverage is gone." Drummond leaned toward his coat pocket. "And to top it off, you wretched all over the floor."

"Calm down," Max said, gently rising to his feet.

"How am I supposed to be calm? Everything's falling apart."

"This isn't like you. Relax. Keep control of yourself."

Drummond glowered at Max. Bracing himself, Max turned his head to the side. Instead of an attack, Drummond cocked an ear toward his coat pocket, nodded, and eased back. Right there, Max decided not to fret over the little ghost in Drummond's pocket anymore.

In a less agitated voice, Drummond asked, "Did the spell work at least?"

"The bell is somewhere in our office building."

Drummond brightened. "That's great. That's perfect. It's like a homefield advantage. Let's go."

"Hold on a moment. We need to think this through. It's late now. Getting the bell without a plan won't be of any use to us or Sandra. In fact, that'll be playing right into Modesto's hand. There's a lot about this whole thing that doesn't add up."

"We don't really have time."

"Modesto will wait all night if he has to. He wants that bell badly, and if waiting a while longer than he would prefer means getting it from us, then he'll do it. But why is it in the office building? If Connor's mother stole it, why would she put it there?"

"Hiding it anywhere would be smart. Once Hull discovered it missing, he'd have set Modesto loose to find it. Back then, Modesto was young and eager to please the Hulls — more so than now. He'd have been ruthless in his search."

"So, Connor's mother makes sure the evidence isn't on her or near her or in any way connected to her. But why the office building? Why not rent a storage locker? Or hand it to a trusted friend? Or even bury it in the backyard?"

Drummond snapped out his hand as if smacking Max upside the head. "Do you really not understand? This is a cursed bell with a long history of destruction, a cursed bell that became linked to the ghost of a cursed witch. Not any witch, by the way, but the High Priestess of a coven. And most importantly, this was a bell that the Hulls needed if they ever got it in their heads to resurrect their great-great-grandfather — which is exactly what they want to do. If you stole a bell like that, would you really trust it to a friend? Or leave it unprotected in a storage locker or worse still, bury it in the ground where any kid or dog could dig it up?"

"I guess not. But why the office building? Assuming Connor's mother knew how powerful this bell was, wouldn't she want to hide it somewhere that would protect her from its curse? Some place with a lot of magical mojo. Some place ... oh."

"That's right. You think it's a coincidence that they cursed me in my office? That of all the buildings in Winston-Salem, the one Hull owns entirely on his own is that one? There's power in those walls. Always has been. It's a smart place to hide the bell. Hull would never suspect it to be right under his nose, and Connor's mother must have hoped the building's magic would contain any curse the bell truly had. At the least, all that magic would mask the magic radiating off the bell."

"Why would that happen? The building containing the curse, I mean."

"It wouldn't. It didn't. But one witch can't know everything."

Max shuffled to the kitchen and poured a glass of water. He felt no better physically, but his head had cleared. "This is good. We know the bell is in the building, and we're fairly certain the building's magic won't contain the bell's curse. All we have to do now is figure out how to turn that to our advantage."

"Since the sun is about gone now, you think you can do that figuring on the way back to the city?"

"Yeah. Let's go." Max swiped his keys from the counter and reached for the door. Before he touched it, however, three strong knocks banged away.

"Mr. Porter? It's Agent Stevenson. May I have a word with you?"

Max took enough time to send a stern look Drummond's way. "Please be quiet. Let me focus."

"Always," Drummond said.

Max opened the door to find Stevenson standing in the dimming light, a friendly smile on his face that promised he knew all the answers before he asked the first question. "Mind if I come in?"

"Actually, I'm leaving."

"Actually, this isn't your house." Stevenson walked inside, forcing Max to step back or be plowed over. The FBI agent surveyed the kitchen, glanced into the living room, and wrinkled his nose at the vomit on the floor. "You not feeling well?"

Max rested against the kitchen counter and crossed his arms. "I've had better days."

Stevenson turned his trained eye onto Max. "You look like you've gone a few rounds with a heavyweight. You want me to take you to a hospital?"

"No need. It looks worse than it is."

"Kind of like your situation." Stevenson pulled over a chair and sat. "On the surface, it looks like you murdered Dr. Matthew Ernest, then went after his old assistant, Joshua Leed, then broke into Ernest's home to tamper with the crime scene, and on top of all that, there was a bizarre murder at an optometrist's office which, though quite different from these other murders, does seem connected when one considers all the occult paraphernalia found in the victim's office. Looking at all the bruising on your face, you might even be the subject of an assault investigation that occurred last night at the Fox and Hound Pub. Now, that all looks bad for you, and if I were any other agent, I might've hauled you in already."

"But you know I didn't do those things."

"The only thing I know for certain is that you broke into Leed's house because you're here right now. And I'm fairly certain you were at

Ernest's house last night, too. I was there, but whoever broke into that house slipped away."

Drummond perked up, clapped his hands, and opened his mouth. Before he said anything though, he exchanged glances with Max and made a zipper motion across his ghostly lips.

"Am I under arrest?" Max asked, his words sounding more brazen than he felt.

"Not yet." With his index finger, Stevenson tapped a complicated rhythm against his chin and let his eyes rove the kitchen. "It's strange how both this house and Ernest's house had those markings on the walls. Made me think of a cult. Your house, however, doesn't have any markings like that."

"I don't belong to a cult."

"Odd. You don't seem surprised we went through your house." He thought a moment and nodded with a grin. "You came by and saw us, didn't you? That's why you're out here."

Drummond pointed to the wall clock which read 7:30 p.m. Max said, "You seem like a smart guy, probably a good agent, too. But you're not going to figure this all out. I know a lot more of what's going on, and I can't figure it all out."

"Maybe we can help each other. After all, since you know more than I do, and assuming you're innocent of the murders, well then it's only natural you'd want to help the FBI find the real killers and clear your name."

"Do you believe in ghosts?"

"Excuse me?"

"Ghosts. Witches, curses, covens, black magic, and protective wards. Do you believe in any of that?"

"I know that the people involved in all this certainly believed in that kind of thing. But believing in something, no matter how strong the belief, no matter how pure the faith, doesn't make it reality."

"Denying it, even though you can't see it, doesn't make it fantasy."

"You want me to believe in all of this stuff? Believe that the reason Ernest and Leed covered their walls with arcane symbols was because those bits of paint would magically protect them? From what? Ghosts? Except they weren't protected. They ended up dead."

"Leed died outside his protected room. In fact, he died right here in this kitchen."

Stevenson pushed his blazer back enough to reveal his holstered sidearm. "Are you admitting to having killed Joshua Leed?"

"No. Just that I watched him die in here. But I was no closer to him than I am to you."

"Then who killed him? If you're afraid of retribution, the FBI can protect you."

Max knew he should have stopped talking the moment Stevenson had entered, but his mouth had a mind of its own. The pressure and confusion that had been building in him finally released, and if it meant pissing off a federal agent, then so be it. "A ghost killed him."

"A ghost? Really."

"I know you don't believe me, but that's the truth. That's why you can't help me. This whole thing started with a curse cast decades ago, and now it's come back to haunt us."

"Who is *us?*"

"But you won't open your mind to the possibilities, so I don't see how you can help. I doubt you'd even believe that there's a ghost in this room. He's standing near you, and even if you felt his cold hand pass through you, you wouldn't believe."

Drummond waved his hand across Stevenson's neck. The agent bolted to his feet, whirled around, and stared at the empty room. He spun back, eyeing Max while his hand rested on his firearm.

"Enough games, Mr. Porter. If I can't produce results soon, my superiors are going to insist I arrest you, and I now have at least two charges that I can take you in under — tampering with the Leed crime scene and obstruction. I don't want to do that. I think if I do, you'll shut down, and I'll never learn what happened here. But if you give me no alternative, your sweet wife will have to see you behind bars."

"If you keep wasting my time here, my sweet wife won't live long enough to see me ever again."

"What does that mean? If you know of a threat against your wife, tell me. Let me protect her. For fuck's sake, I'm with the FBI. I have access to some serious power."

Max couldn't help himself. He laughed. "You don't know what power is."

Stepping away, Stevenson tapped his chin again. "Maybe I was wrong. You seem crazy enough to do all these things after all."

"Oh, come on." Max instantly regretted opening his mouth. "Don't take the easy way out. I didn't do any of this. You know it."

"I don't know anything."

"Trust your gut. I'm innocent here."

"Because a ghost did it? Did a ghost kill Dr. Ernest, too? Same one,

I suppose?"

"Yes. Exactly."

Stevenson pulled his weapon. "Maxwell Porter, you are under arrest for the murder of —"

"Wait, wait. I didn't do it. Why would I?"

"That's what you're going to tell me when I take you in."

"But think about it. Why would I kill Dr. Ernest when that's what caused ..." Max's brain started connecting information in a fevered rush. "Oh, no."

Stevenson lowered his weapon. "What's going on? What's wrong?"

"The body. It was undisturbed."

"What body? Who are you talking about?"

Drummond shot forward. "The witch in the church?"

"Ernest never got to that body. She hadn't been touched. It bugged me when we saw it, but I didn't know why."

Stevenson said, "What body? Who was with you when you saw it?"

Drummond turned to Stevenson and raised his hand. "Let me put this guy out for a few hours and we can still try to get that bell. If you're right about this, we've got leverage again."

"Wait. Don't hurt him."

"Hurt who?" Stevenson said, his eyes darting about the room. "Is someone else here?"

"Agent Stevenson," Max said, his voice calm and confident now. "I know who killed Dr. Ernest, and I know why. And I need your help."

Chapter 24

AS MAX PARKED THE CAR outside his office building, the blue-green display of the dashboard clock glowed 9:02. He shut off the engine and sat in the silence, mustering the strength for what he suspected would be the end of this case. He simply hoped it wasn't his end as well.

"How do you want to play this?" Drummond asked from the backseat.

While that old ghost could be infuriating, Max appreciated the way he acted when serious business was at hand. It felt strange putting all his trust in a ghost, but Max had grown accustomed to strange. "I don't think the handbell is anywhere in the actual office. If it was, you would have found it long ago."

"You ain't kidding. I know every rat turd, leaking pipe, and dust bunny surrounding our office."

"So, it has to be somewhere else in the building. I want you to do a sweep of the walls, floors, and ceilings. See if it's hidden behind any of the plaster or floorboards or under the boiler or anything. While you do that, I'm going to the office to do my part."

"It shouldn't take me long. I'll let you know what I find." With that, Drummond disappeared.

Max remained in the car for another three minutes, listening to the rain beat against the roof. "You can do this," he told his rearview mirror reflection. "You have to do this. Not just for Sandra, but for yourself. If this doesn't work out, the FBI will have you in jail before the sun comes up. So get your ass out of the car and get moving."

Thrusting open the door, Max exited and walked straight to the stairwell. His chest puffed up slightly, and he had a swagger to his walk. Somebody yelled from down the street, and Max jolted to safety behind a car. Only when he realized the yelling had nothing to do with him could he stand again. With less bravado, he resumed his walk.

Max entered the stairwell. Though he had been in this same stairwell countless times, a cold and inhospitable sensation covered his skin.

Rather than going up to the office, he stepped into the back where a narrow door led to the empty storefront that had once been Deacon Arts. No surprise — the door was still unlocked.

He entered the store, his steps echoing in the wide, empty space. Rain tapped against the large plate-glass window facing the street. A car drove by, its wheels shushing through the growing puddles.

Nothing remained in the former art gallery except for a desk from which Mr. Gold would conduct his crooked business. The desk had been emptied long ago, but Max checked the drawers nonetheless. Not that he expected the handbell to be so easily found, but he had to try. After all, Mr. Gold had worked for the Hulls at one time.

Next, he walked the perimeter of the store, checking for anything unusual, making sure nothing hid in the dark. Nothing turned up. The only real hiding places in the store were in the walls, and Drummond had that covered.

Satisfied, Max left through the back door and headed upstairs to the second floor. On the landing, he stopped to check out the hall before going ahead. There were three doors — two had been boarded over and the third was unmarked. He had never been on this floor before, never had a reason to be, but now he wondered if it had always been like this. He half-expected a serial killer to come busting out the unmarked door, blood dripping from a carving knife.

A loud thud hit the ceiling above — from Max's office. Somebody was up there. Max tore on up the staircase to the third floor, raced down the hall, and stormed through the door.

Sandra/Patricia started at his abrupt arrival, placing her hand on her chest like a proper Southern gal. "My word, you gave me a fright." She chuckled, but her amusement curdled with a malicious tone. "I've been waiting for you all day. That spell you cast really knocked you out. I was beginning to think you might not make it."

Max looked over her — no bruises, no rub burns, nothing to suggest that Patricia had taken his wife's body out for a joyride.

"Relax," she said, sitting on the couch and crossing her legs to show off the fine, unblemished calves. "Do you really think that I would waste my time romping through the young studs of Winston-Salem when there are so many obvious threats to my life right now? That would be stupid. No, I don't screw the town until I know for sure that nobody is going to yank me out of this body."

Now Patricia's earlier words registered with Max. "You knew I cast a spell. You've been following me, watching me, waiting for me to find the bell."

"You *and* Drummond. I'm still in the afterlife. I can see him fine — and he's certainly still a fine looking man."

"So you're here, tearing apart my office, looking for the bell."

"Once I knew where you were headed, I rushed on over here. Frankly, I didn't think I'd get so much of a lead on you."

Max thought of Stevenson bitterly. "We got delayed."

"That's the problem with studious men like you — you're never paying attention to the right things. Always worrying about minor matters while you let the world around you burn."

"Explain that one to me." Max hardly cared what she talked about as long as he kept her talking. Drummond needed enough time to succeed.

Patricia shook her head pitifully. "You really think you're smarter than me. Let me explain to you something far more important. Let me explain why I'm sitting here letting you live. Fairly simple, actually. You are alive right now because you do not possess the handbell."

"Don't be so sure."

"If you had it, you would have used it already. Unless you like seeing your drab wife embodied by a woman who knows what turns a man on." She licked her lips slowly, leaning forward like Marilyn Monroe, and finished the pose of with a tiny bite on her bottom lip.

"Not interested."

"I doubt that."

"There's only one woman I want, and no matter what you look like, you ain't her."

Patricia shot to her feet, scowling and grinding her teeth. She backhanded Max across the face, snapping his head aside and dropping him to the floor. That woman had serious strength. When he could focus again, he saw that his head missed the sharp corner of the desk by mere inches.

She stood over him like a mighty hunter over a lamed lion. "Do you really think your little body can take much more abuse? Come on, now. It's over. You've lost and simply won't admit it. But you and I both know that you're never going to leave this office unless I allow it, and I'm not letting that happen until you tell me where the bell is."

Blood dribbled into his mouth — a bitter, metallic taste. "Why bother asking? You know I don't have it. And if I knew where it was, I'd have gotten it already."

"Unless it's in here. Unless you walked into this room expecting to take it, but then you found me. So, tell me where it is or I'll start hurting you in ways that will pale even the most perverse thoughts you can imagine."

Max wanted to jump up, surprise Patricia by his action, and pummel her into submission. But to do so meant striking his wife, and no matter how brave his words had been, he still saw Sandra's body when he looked at Patricia.

Patricia bent down and raked her nails across his cheek. "I'm so glad you're resisting. I always have fun torturing fools like you, but this will be even better with your wife trapped inside, forced to watch as her own hands rip you to pieces."

She raised her hand again, her fingers splayed in a claw, and Max clenched his fists, wishing he could fight back. But then Drummond's deep voice called out, "Patricia! Stop it."

Turning with a coy, girlish giggle, she said, "Oh, Marshall, please let me have a little fun."

"I can't let you do this," he said, moving back toward the far corner, forcing Patricia to turn her back on Max. "I can't let you harm good people because you hate me."

"Sweetheart, I don't hate you."

"I helped Ernest and Leed destroy your coven."

"You did what you thought was right. And you were hurt because I hid the truth about myself."

Drummond gazed out the window, and Max swore the ghost's eyes glistened as if he tried to hold back tears. "I knew enough to figure it out. I wasn't hurt because you lied. I understood that. I was hurt because you ... you broke my heart. You let me fall for you when you knew damn well what the outcome would be. But you didn't care enough to worry how it would all hurt me."

Taken aback, Patricia's hand covered her mouth. "I'm so sorry. I had no idea."

"You knew exactly how I felt."

"I meant that I had no idea you could feel so strongly. Honestly, my love, I swear I thought I was just a plaything to you. I wanted more. Always. From the day we met by the tree, I wanted more. I knew it couldn't happen, though. I knew the kind of work you did. How could you ever give that up for a witch? And it hurt you bad, I see that now, but don't think I wasn't hurt, too. I was devastated. I knew all along the ending we headed toward, yet I only wanted to enjoy the small time we had until it all came apart."

"You expect me to believe —"

"Only that my heart was true to you. I fell for you every bit as hard. But look at me now. I have a body — one you can touch. With that handbell, I can become whole. And, Marshall, listen to me — I'm more of a witch than you ever knew. I was very powerful back then, and with the added strength of my coven, I can be more. When I'm whole once again, I can even bring you back."

"What?"

"You can have a body of your own. We can actually be together again. In our hearts and our bodies."

Max watched Drummond carefully, but he couldn't read the ghost's face at all.

Drummond pursed his lips. "You're serious? I could be free from this half-dead existence?"

"And we can be together."

"Together."

She leaned towards him, but this time the motion lacked her seductive leer — this time, she clearly wanted to be closer. "Those days we spent meant everything to me. I've never stopped thinking about our tree and our time there. Never. Not even as I watched the decades pass from beneath the city, as I suffered burning pain that would never stop. Only those memories could cool me, help me endure. All I could dream of was returning to our tree. All I wanted was to be in your arms, feel your lips. If I could turn us back, I'd give up all my power and knowledge in witchcraft — if it meant we could be together."

"I want to believe you. I do."

"Then believe. Because it can still be true. This body and that fool on the floor, they will be our vessels. We can return to the mortal world and live out our lives together. And after I bring you back, I'll never cast another spell. I'll put it all behind us. Don't you want that? To be together again. If you can bring yourself to sacrifice these two, we can have everything we always wanted."

"You think it's fun being the ghost lackey for these two? I've got no problem with getting rid of them. But the problem we do have is that we don't know where the bell is. It's in this building, we know that much, but where?"

"If you'll be with me, if you'll love me, then don't worry. We'll find it."

"Do you know where it is?"

"No, but we'll figure it out."

"Well, where do you think it is? Put yourself in that witches shoes. Where would you hide it? The roof? Basement? Perhaps you knew an old crone witch who would take on the challenge of holding it for you."

Max didn't want to believe it, but it seemed that Drummond finally turned. He had expected something more flashy, though. At least something involving all that dark mist he had seen previously.

I'm sorry, my friend. I failed you.

Now Max's last ally had become his enemy. The disappointment filling him made it difficult to think beyond the moment, beyond hearing how Drummond and Patricia planned to kill Sandra and himself. All they needed was the bell. In fact, the only thing keeping Max alive was the fact that they hadn't found it yet. Drummond had even resorted to asking Patricia if she had ...

Wait. That doesn't make sense. Drummond had spent the last several minutes going through the building top to bottom. He already knew that the bell wasn't on the roof or in the basement. Or he knew that it was in one of those places and didn't want her going there. He gazed up at Drummond — *did Drummond just wink at me?* And no dark mist. He hadn't turned yet.

"Patricia," Drummond said, "look in my eyes."

"Yes, darling."

"Let me tell you how I see our future."

Drummond launched into a flowery story that sounded like anything but Drummond. This was it. This was Max's chance to get out.

As quietly as he manage, Max rolled to his stomach and from there, up onto all fours. He knew how absurd he looked, but his pride would have to take a backseat to his survival. Like a cowering dog, he scurried out of the office and into the hall. He could still hear Drummond's tale of weddings and children and a small farm away from all the horrors of the world. How long could he keep up his love-tale before Patricia noticed Max's absence?

He needed to find that bell. He paced the hall, thinking over every word Drummond had said since coming into the office. The answer had to be there or else Drummond would have taken a different tactic. What had he said? He asked Patricia to think about where she would hide the bell — because he wanted Max to think about how Connor's mother would have seen things. But they had already covered that line of thought before. *Wait. What did he say last?* Something about an old witch crone and ... Max lifted his head, his eyes resting on the other door in the hall — the one belonging to the old woman that had always shot him nasty looks when she came out to get her paper.

Though he felt less sure about his conclusions, he also understood that Drummond could only stall so long for him. He had to act or the whole effort had been worthless.

Max crouched in front of the doorknob. Trying to think of what he had in his pockets that he could use to pick the lock, he concluded that even if he had something small enough, he lacked the skill to do it with any speed. He stood and ran his fingers along the top of the molding above the door. No key. He looked around the banister in the hall for a pot or a shoe or anything that one would hide a key in. Nothing.

Except there was a doormat — a coarse, weaved thing, fraying at the edges. Could it really be that easy? Max bent down and lifted the mat. A cockroach scuttled away leaving behind a scuffed, silver key square in the middle.

Max slipped the key into the lock and gently opened the door. Trying to be stealthy, he only opened it wide enough to slide in. He closed the door behind, hoping Patricia had not noticed where he went.

Before his eyes adjusted to the dim interior, he smelled the room — the stale stench of a body unwashed for years. Max tried breathing through his mouth to avoid the odor, but the air tasted awful, too. He could feel it coating his tongue.

Once his eyes adjusted, he noticed that the main living room looked rather bland and unimpressive. An old woman's room, sparsely furnished but each piece held numerous knick-knacks — a coffee table with porcelain figurines, end tables with collector's plates on either side of a long couch, a reading lamp with beaded chains hanging from its neck. The old lady snored peacefully on the couch, one arm draped across her forehead, the other hanging toward the floor and an empty bottle of tequila.

Witches sure loved the hard stuff.

Except this old lady didn't seem like a witch, especially a witch charged with protecting a cursed object. Maybe Drummond had it wrong. But when Max turned to go, his opinion changed. Painted blood-red on the back of the door, Max saw a large pentagram. Beneath it, a series of symbols had been carved into the wood.

Okay. Right place.

A muted screech filtered through the walls. Patricia must have discovered Max's absence. He could hear her yelling as well as Drummond's bass tones thumping a reply. How long would he be able to argue with her before turning? Considering the strong emotions between them, Max didn't think he had much time left.

He figured the old lady wouldn't hide the bell in the front room. Too easy to be spotted by unwanted eyes. The kitchen to his right looked plain and, frankly, untouched. Whatever the old lady ate, it wasn't coming from there. He doubted she ever stepped foot in that room. Which left either the bathroom or her bedroom — both of which were down a dark hall on the left.

The old lady grunted and shifted her body deeper into the couch. With a loud eruption, she passed gas. Other than quelling a juvenile desire to laugh, Max didn't react. Considering the stench in this place, he guessed he would never notice any added odors.

As silently as possible, Max eased down the hall. The closer he came to the bedroom door, the worse the rank odor became. The hall grew darker as if even light wanted nothing to do with this place.

The voices of Drummond and Patricia intensified though Max couldn't make out the actual words. The anger came through clear enough. He hurried to the door, ignoring his internal warnings that urged him to turn around, to get out of that apartment, to run.

"Hold on, Sandra. I'm coming for you," he whispered and opened the door.

He expected to find a room similar to Connor's office or perhaps one filled with protective wards like Dr. Ernest's room. Instead, he discovered a twisted display that belonged in the pages of *Psycho Weekly*. The foul odor that permeated the apartment doubled in the bedroom. Max could barely breathe without throwing up. A bed had been shoved in the corner to his right, the sheets stained with browns, yellows, and reds. Odd-shaped books had been piled next to the bed. Two bookcases leaned against the walls to either side — each one filled with jarred organs, animal fetuses, and various eggs.

Worse — black and white photos covered the walls. A man in hip-waders displaying a half-eaten fish carcass foul with maggots. A girl in her confirmation dress sitting with a book of poetry in her lap and the head of a cat. Children rolling down a hill of corpses. Max couldn't bear to look at any others. He prayed they had been images designed on a computer and not real in any respect.

A wide cabinet sat in the center of the room, out of place and obstructing Max's view of the rest of the room. Slowly, Max entered, walking around the cabinet, trying to prepare for any kind of traps the witch had set, anything that might leap out at him. When he came to the other side, he jumped back, startled by the amazing sight.

The old lady had built a shrine. A circle of salt surrounded the entire thing. Inside, three green candles burned on an altar of wood with a velvet cloth cover, gold pentagrams hanging from the top of the cabinet, and situated on a silk pillow — the thirteenth Bell of the Damned.

Larger than he had imagined, the bell had a small chip in the handle but otherwise matched the photographs exactly. Max inspected around the shrine, attempting to locate any form of security alarm. Then he considered the apartment he was in — witches didn't need security alarms. He reached under the bell and guided the clapper against the side so it would not ring out. Holding it in place with one hand, he lifted the bell with the other. Not a sound. In fact, he had been so quiet, he could still hear the impassioned argument coming from his office.

Max walked around the wide cabinet, took two steps toward the door, and froze. The old lady blocked his way. She stood in the doorway breathing heavy but strong. A growl emitted from her throat, and her head lowered, darkening her eyes, threatening him like a rabid animal.

"I am the protector," she said in a strong but cracked voice, "and you will return the bell or face my wrath."

Had he been a common thief, he might have laughed at the old lady, might even have attempted to bully his way by her, but Max knew witches too well to ignore her threat. Yet as much as he knew he should comply, he could only shrink before her strength and hope that this witch had a heart.

"Please," he said, "I need this bell to save my wife."

"It is cursed, and so will you become if you use it."

"A High Priestess has possessed my wife. The witch, Patricia Welling. I was told that this is the only thing that can save my Sandra. If you know another way, tell me. Otherwise, I must have this."

The old lady thrust out a clawed hand. Max cowered, sure that he would be turned into a toad. When his human form remained, he peeked up at her. She scowled.

"Max Porter, seer of a single ghost, you have been a thorn in the foot of the Hull family since you arrived here. That is the only reason you have remained untouched by me. But should you press forth and remove that bell from this sacred room, I will no longer restrain myself. Put the bell back, and all shall be forgotten. Take one step closer, and you'll learn how powerful an old witch like me can become."

Max clutched the bell closer to his chest. He looked at the hall stretching out behind the old lady. Surely he could barrel her down and make it out through that hall. From there, he'd bust out of the apartment, hurry to his office, ring the bell at Patricia, and pray for the best. Yet even as he considered this plan, the old lady seemed to fill out the doorway even more. It may only have been a trick of his eyes brought on by fear and worry, it may have been an illusion cast by the old witch — either way, he saw his chance to leave diminishing.

He glanced back at the shrine. If he did as she asked, if he returned the bell, would she stay true to her word? Would she let him go and forget his intrusion? And what of Sandra then? A loud crash came from his office. That settled it. If he didn't get in there fast, Drummond would either end up destroyed or turned.

"I'm sorry," he said. "Unless you can help me stop this witch, I don't see any other way."

"Don't think that the bluster you've displayed in the past will aid you today. Turn around. Put the bell back. Forget you ever knew of this place."

Max lowered his body slightly, ready to pounce on the old lady, toss her aside, and race for his office. His heart quickened and sweat broke along his back and neck. He licked his lips and gave one final thought to Sandra.

Before he could launch into action, the old lady's eyes widened. She saw his intentions, and she already had her hand out, prepared to strike with whatever magic she possessed.

"I think you should stop this nonsense," a voice said from the hallway.

Both Max and the old lady peered down the dark hall. Mr. Modesto walked forward. The old lady stepped into the room, allowing him to take the doorway.

"Good evening to you." As always, Modesto wore a smart suit and held his body perfectly straight. "I see, Mr. Porter, that you have acquired the bell after all. Our employer will be pleased."

The old lady squinted an evil gaze at him. "Neither you nor your pathetic employer will ever have this bell. I've pledged my life to protect —"

"Yes, yes. Except, you see, Mr. Porter is the one holding the bell, and quite frankly, you don't have the skill to do anything about it."

"You'll regret those words."

She raised her hands and opened her mouth. A tight, choking came from her throat. Her eyes rolled back and she crumpled to the floor.

Modesto walked in and lifted the bell from Max's stunned hands. Max wanted to fight, but he couldn't imagine how Modesto had defeated this witch with such ease. How could he fight Modesto against that kind of power? It was over. He had failed and now Modesto had the bell. He just couldn't understand what had happened.

As if to answer Max's unspoken questions, Modesto gestured to the hall. A small, thin woman with a deep scar running from her nose to her jaw stood alone. Dressed in a black gown adorned with symbols Max had seen too many times in recent days, the woman lowered her hands and ran a finger along a bone pendant around her neck.

"I'll take care of the others," she said and walked off toward Max's office.

With his free hand, Modesto guided Max back to his feet. "The first rule in fighting with magic," Modesto said, "is to always bring the strongest witch."

MODESTO HAD NO NEED for a gun. As long as he held that bell, Max didn't see any choice but to go along without a struggle. They left the old lady's apartment and walked back to the office.

Breathing clean air once again revitalized Max's dull senses. His mind leaped from one crisis to another — Sandra and Patricia, making sure Drummond didn't turn, stopping Modesto. All these thoughts made the act of entering the office as a failure that much worse.

The office desks had been shoved against the walls, and two chalk circles with symbols had been drawn on the floor. Drummond pressed against the confines of one circle, and Patricia the other. Neither looked particularly happy. Drummond paced the narrow space like a trapped puma, turning every two steps, fuming and grunting. Patricia, on the other hand, settled cross-legged on the floor, her face a cold burn of controlled rage.

Modesto spread his arms as if presenting his vast treasure to a commoner. "This room, Mr. Porter, is going to be the most valuable room in all mankind. Here, we shall return Tucker Hull to the living so that he may continue his important work. And we owe it all to you."

"Pay me back now by releasing my wife and friend."

Chuckling, though he showed no amusement in his face, Modesto said, "Let's begin the evening with proper introductions. This diminutive yet powerful witch is Kalon. Born to a German family with a long history in the dark arts, Kalon will not only bring Tucker Hull back, but she will serve him better than any witch has before. She makes our former witch look like a peasant, don't you think?"

"Dr. Connor looks like a corpse now."

Modesto ignored the comment. To Kalon, he said, "This annoying man is Mr. Maxwell Porter. He is a pest, and I look forward to the day the Hull family allows me to crush him under my sole. Until then, we must put up with his inability to perform his duties properly."

"Hey, don't soft-sell me. I try hard to be a pain in your ass." Max wished he felt half as a brazen as he sounded, but he had to keep pushing. As long as Modesto appeared to be driving this night, he would be looser with his mouth, and Max needed that stuck-up prick to talk as much as possible.

"You often succeed," Modesto said. "Still, despite your innumerable flaws, we do have to thank you for acquiring all the necessary pieces to this complex spell."

The black-draped witch moved like a graceful ballerina as she drew small chalk circles in front of the large ones that contained Drummond and Patricia. Modesto pointed to the first circle. "Here we have the Hull family journal which you stumbled upon for us." Kalon placed the beaten book into the circle.

"Hardly stumbled," Max said, recalling his first case for the Hulls. He had a ghost stick its hand straight into his skull in order to find that book — an agonizing pain he never wanted to experience again.

Kalon placed a small bowl in the second circle. In the bowl, lay a single hair. Modesto said, "This is, of course, one of the last hairs that belonged to Edward Teach, otherwise known as Blackbeard the Pirate. I believe you found this by accident when you were hired to locate a painting by the granddaughter of a dead art forger."

"You're quite good at revisionist history." Max had been hired by the ghost of a man betrayed by the Hull family which led to a cursed art forger, his mad granddaughter, and their twisted plan involving Blackbeard's ghost.

"And last, we have the handbell which you generously provided this evening. All three key elements, all brought to us by you, and all this time you've thought you were working against us, when in fact, we could not be here without you."

Kalon dashed a white, gritty substance into the bowl containing Blackbeard's hair. With a pestle she produced from a black bag, she ground into the bowl, turning the hair and the white grit into a fine powder. As she worked, Modesto's eyes fired up and he said, "It's begun now. Soon the essence of Tucker Hull locked in his journal will be freed, soon he will rise again."

Max looked at Sandra — her body, but where was the rest of her? She had to be inside there. If he could reach her, get her to fight back. Stupid, Max chided himself. Of course she fought back. In fact, Patricia must have had to work three times as hard to keep hold of that body. No way would Sandra take a backseat. Patricia might be barely holding on.

However, Drummond was the one that looked closest to losing control. That dark mist surrounded him like an aura of night. There would be no help from him at the moment. Max was on his own. He only had his original plan, and that sounded awfully weak to his ears.

Still, a weak plan worked better than no plan. Max pushed aside all his concerns for Sandra and Drummond. He had to focus, now. Clear his thoughts because the next few minutes would be a verbal chess game against an agile and sadistic opponent.

"I'm impressed," Max said. "The way you've orchestrated this whole thing shows a high level of skill at the manipulation of powerful people."

Modesto cocked his head, pleased but cautious. "I don't know what you're referring to."

"Of course you do. It takes a good mind to plan several steps ahead, but this ... this takes a special level of creativity and foresight most people can only dream of acquiring. I may not agree with your goals, but I'm always willing to acknowledge the presence of a great thinker."

Though preening and flush with excitement, Modesto said, "Flattery will do nothing to enhance your position. The fact remains that we have already won this battle."

"That's my point. You've been thinking years in advance of where Drummond and Sandra and I traipsed through. The journal, Blackbeard's hair, the handbell — each case, each element, carefully sent our way so that we would take all the risks in finding them for you, that we would have no recourse but to see you take them from us, that we would not even understand their value, even after we had been warned, until it was too late. Until now."

Kalon dug out an eagle's talon from a pocket in her dress. Gnarled and black with pieces of rotten flesh on the end, the talon clinked against the bowl as Kalon dropped it in. Without pause, she began grinding it into the powder she had made.

"This had to be meticulously planned," Max went on. "I can't think of a better person than you to do such a thing. Not only the long term vision, but thinking of this last piece, the way you manipulated us all is amazing."

Modesto could barely contain himself, yet still he said, "I did no such thing."

"Here's what really impressed me: The fact that you murdered Dr. Ernest and staged it to look like the curse. That was brilliant."

"Excuse me?"

"Oh, don't be coy. When we deciphered Dr. Ernest's notes, we found his witch's corpse in an old church. But here's the thing — the corpse was undisturbed. That bothered me but I couldn't figure it out. After all, the whole reason Joshua Leed came to us was that Dr. Ernest had died at the hands of a coven ghost. Except the body was undisturbed. That can only mean that Dr. Ernest had not touched the corpse at all — after all, nobody else knew where it was to begin with. Especially you."

"You have an intriguing hypothesis going, but I doubt you understand the full ramifications."

"I most certainly do. I wouldn't be praising you, if I didn't. Because you have to look at the whole thing in context, don't you? Here you are with the journal and the hair in hand. All you need to finish your spell is something one of these ghost-witches can do for you. But you have a major problem. Back in the '40s, the coven was cursed and their bodies hidden. You had no clue how to find them. But you did know who was responsible. You couldn't go to Drummond. You cursed that poor man. He'd never help you. Joshua Leed's loyalty to Dr. Ernest meant he'd never betray the man. And, in fact, Dr. Ernest was too, well, earnest to be bribed or coerced."

Kalon added what looked like rat pellets to the concoction. Tension seized Max's muscles. How much time did he have left before she would be ready? He had to hurry. But he had to stay calm, too. Act as if he had all the time he could want.

"So what do you do?" Max said, resisting the urge to walk around the room and tap his chin as he laid this out. "You devised a genius plan. You would have the very people responsible for hiding the bodies uncover them for you by killing Dr. Ernest and leaving hints that only someone knowledgeable in witchcraft, covens, and ghosts would notice. The police would treat this as any old murder, but the person with that special knowledge would see something different in the evidence. Of course, that special person was Joshua Leed. When he hired me, the coven was still intact in the original curse that Drummond, Leed, and Dr. Ernest performed. In fact, it wasn't until Leed contacted me and then went off to destroy the witches he had hidden, only then were the corpses actually disturbed. That's why they were able to attack us at the church, why the corpse in the church was untouched, and why you are standing here with Patricia Welling in my wife's body when that witch should be stuck in the walls of the Federal Building downtown. You created a situation on the gamble that it would result in this outcome. Did I miss anything?"

"Well, I hardly think it was gamble," Modesto said. Max fought to hold back a triumphant smile — he had that uptight bastard hooked. Modesto peered over Kalon's shoulder, nodded, and continued. "I've been studying you for years now. I know you better than you know yourself."

"Maybe so, but you couldn't know how Leed would react."

"A simpleton like that? Honestly, he was the easiest to predict. Of course, there were several variables I had to stay atop of, but when you're a thinker, a man who understands tactics and strategy, juggling variables and adjusting outcomes is not terribly strenuous. For example, I could not know with any degree of certainty who the High Priestess would choose to possess. She could have picked a stranger off the street. However, I knew the more I pushed you to find that bell, the more you would resist. That would, in turn, push you deeper into the mess that Dr. Ernest had created. It was my calculated risk that a person as attune to the paranormal as your wife would be an easier target for the High Priestess."

"You set us up even more than I realized. But then you actually needed my help to find that bell."

"I'll admit that was the most challenging part of the endeavor. I had others working on it, but you have proven to be the most successful I've ever hired at finding these items."

"With Sandra possessed, that was all that remained. That's why you gave a final deadline." Max made a show of nodding to Modesto's sage wisdom but a thought suddenly caused an authentic frown.

"Something troubling you?" Modesto asked.

"Dr. Connor. There was no way a ghost killed her — not when she put a ward around her office. I saw firsthand how Drummond struggled to get in there and couldn't. Which means that it was another staged event. So, why did you kill her? It couldn't have been because she told us your plan. She warned me of this back when I dealt with the whole Blackbeard thing. There was no point in killing her now."

"For one, she betrayed me. She showed that she could not be trusted, and just because I didn't dispose of her immediately, hardly meant that I forgave her transgression. For another, there was the matter of the bell."

"That's the real answer. If she got hold of that bell, she gained control of this entire situation, and you did not want her to have that kind of control. That's what you feared."

Modesto bristled. "Fear? Me? Do you have any idea what I have endured to reach this point? Can you comprehend the sacrifices I have made for this?"

"I'm sure you have had —"

"You know nothing." Modesto spit the words hard enough to dislodge a lock of his hair. It spilled over his forehead, yet he never fixed it. "A spell as complex as this one, as important as this one, requires more than mere skillful planning. It rests on the sheer will and courage to see it through. That was where Dr. Connor proved lacking. I killed her like I did Dr. Ernest, and you know what I discovered? They both were surprised I could do such a thing. I saw it on their faces. How could that be? I realize I may appear outwardly like a stuffy butler, but surely Dr. Connor knew the ruthless man I am underneath. You're not surprised. Why were they?"

"They've never been on the receiving end before."

"Perhaps."

"And now you will be, too." Max unbuttoned the top three buttons on his shirt. Unable to hold back a little gloating grin of his own, Max revealed a thin, white wire taped to his chest. "The FBI have been listening all along. You've admitted to two homicides, though I'm pretty sure that all your talk of witches, possession, and magic spells will set you up nicely for an insanity defense. And don't try running. They've got us surrounded."

Modesto's reaction troubled Max more than anything so far. There was no fear. No shock. Not even a hesitation. Just a simple raising of the corner of his lips. "If you're relying on the FBI, you have a problem."

Max's throat tightened. "Oh?"

"Kalon finished the prep work on the spell a while ago. I've merely been waiting for the last crucial ingredient."

"There's another object?"

"The journal is an item closest to the soul we wish to bring back. The hair from Blackbeard is filled with the magic's foundation. When a source of extreme power is applied, Tucker Hull's soul will burst into this room. But if he cannot find a body to occupy, then the whole point is moot. Thus, the bell. We force Patricia out of Sandra's body, and before either woman has the chance to regain control, Tucker Hull enters. But we needed that catalyst, and once again you provided."

"I did?"

"Only one thing is powerful enough to jolt a lost soul back to the living — the rage of another lost soul."

Max's eyes shot to Drummond. The ghost was furious.

Modesto's smarmy, sarcastic tone thickened as he spoke. "And here you thought you had goaded me into revealing everything, when what I needed was time to let Drummond realize how trapped he is, to hear how I slaughtered his friend, to let him understand how you've all been my pawns and how worthless he truly is. Now, he's too far gone. There's no returning him. He is the catalyst, and as I believe I hear the stomping of feet downstairs, I know that I've timed this perfectly. Your FBI friends cannot get up here before we cast the spell because, you see, it's already been cast. All that remains is for Kalon to release it all and bring back Tucker Hull!"

Swiping her hand in a wide arc, Kalon broke lines in all five circles. Drummond shot out lightning fast, straight for Modesto, and straight over the journal, the bowl, and the bell.

Chapter 26

HEAT BLASTED FROM THE BOWL, knocking Max and Modesto back several steps. A deep red light strobed and Drummond screamed out. Whatever the spell had done to him, it wasn't enough to contain him. Drummond darted toward Kalon, backhanded her into the bookcase, and turned his dark eyes upon Max. Thick, dark smoke poured off Drummond — some of it flickering like flames, some of it dribbling like fog.

"Marshall, calm down," Max said, trying to coax the ghost back like he had done before. But Drummond huffed like a wild bull, lowered his head, staring straight at Max, waiting to attack.

"Why should you be calm?" Modesto said, and Drummond's head snapped toward the man. "You've been set up, used, and made a fool of. You have every right to be angry, furious, a raging madman, if you so choose." Drummond inched closer to Modesto. "That's right, you annoying piece of garbage. I dare you to strike me."

Max understood that Modesto provoked Drummond to keep him angry, keep him turning, but why was he trying to get Drummond to hit him? Max moved toward the bowl. Drummond hissed at him and pulled back a fist. "I'm not going to hurt you. I want to help you."

"He lies!" Modesto bellowed. "He is the one that brought these objects to me. Without him, I could never have cast this spell that hurts you now. And I am the one to have done it all. You are my puppet. You are weak and worthless. For decades, you've been nothing but a pawn. Even your greatest love was nothing but a witch's whim."

Modesto's words fired Drummond until the ghost opened his mouth and screamed. The air surrounding Modesto turned white with frost, but Modesto only smiled. His words had done more than enrage Drummond, though. They sparked Max's thoughts.

He noticed that Patricia had yet to move, even though her circle had also been broken. She remained seated and serene. Why? Max recalled how he had heard her muffled voice through the walls while he looked for the bell. She had pleaded with Drummond, offered to give up things for him, wanted to be with him. If her pleas had been authentic, if she truly cared about Drummond, what was the point of sitting there doing nothing?

From Max's previous encounters with the High Priestess, he knew she did not handle things calmly. Which meant that this behavior had to be strategic, and since Modesto did all he could to enrage Drummond, Max figured he needed more of that vicious energy than was present. Patricia stayed calm in order to deny Modesto her energy.

She doesn't want Tucker Hull back any more than I do.

Why would she? If Tucker Hull returned, she would have to struggle against his power both financial and magical or become his witch. So, remove the rage and she removes the catalyst.

But she failed to understand how mad Drummond had become. She didn't know him as well as Max — how could she after being stuck in a wall for decades? Max saw that hulking beast that had been his friend and knew Drummond had more than enough energy to fuel Modesto's spell.

An idea popped into Max's head — intuitive, risky, and possibly foolish. Perfect.

With a warrior cry, he dived for the handbell. His eagerness overtook his agility causing his fingers to snap closed too early. Instead of clasping the handle, he bumped it with his knuckles. It slid away from him. Its lip caught on the uneven floorboards, and the bell tipped over, rolling under Max's desk.

Even as he heard Modesto's shout, Max scrabbled across the floor. Like a mouse desperate to find a safe escape, he pressed up against his desk. Unlike a mouse, he could not slip underneath. No time to pull the desk away from the wall and get in the open side. Instead, he stretched his arm under the back lip, feeling around, trying to snatch that bell.

A memory flash in his head from elementary school — standing in front of a wall of boxes with holes cut out, being told to stick his hand inside and identify what he felt, not wanting to but reaching in because teacher demanded it, feeling little bugs crawling over his hands, kids laughing, teacher opening the box. "See that? It's just string hanging from the top," she said, but he dreamed of crawling bugs for weeks.

Max swallowed down the lump climbing up his throat as his hand probed the unseen beneath the desk. The tip of his finger brushed against something. He felt for it again, hoping it wasn't wet, hoping it didn't bite him. Metal. He touched metal. The bell! He tried to get it to roll closer toward him, but his finger seemed to only rub the edge.

He pushed away images of cockroaches discovering his hand. That's when an icy grip wrapped around his ankle and yanked him back. Max screeched both from surprise and from the cold pain numbing his foot.

Floating over him, Drummond gazed down. The ghost's eyes held only madness. Despite the pain Drummond often complained of when touching the corporeal world, he took hold of Max's neck and lifted the man up against the back wall.

Max tried to protest but his freezing throat could not form words. His hearing dropped and returned in waves. When he could hear, everything echoed as if they stood in a massive cavern.

"FBI," a voice called from miles away.

"No, Drummond!" Modesto yelled. "You want me!"

As the sound faded, Max's vision darkened. He had been close to dying before, and that time, a deep sadness overcame his body. This felt similar. He saw the ghost blob that was Leed glowing like a fluorescent rock as he hid amongst the books on the shelf. He saw the spirits of Sandra and Patricia both overlaying Sandra's body like some bad effect from an old 70s horror flick.

With a high-pitched whine, his hearing returned and so did Modesto's incessant yelling. "You idiot! You can't even become a dark spirit correctly! No wonder your mother hated you."

Drummond whirled around, dropping Max onto the desk. As Max struggled for air, he heard Modesto laugh.

"That's right. Your crazy mother wasn't so crazy after all. She locked herself up in that madhouse for one reason only. To get away from you!"

Banging on the door. "FBI! Open the door or we'll —"

The next seconds happened faster than normal yet moved slowly in Max's eye. Drummond launched toward Modesto, snarling as he bared his teeth. Max rolled off the table and wrenched it away from the wall. As Max reached for the bell, he saw Drummond reach for Modesto.

The FBI smashed open the door. Max raised the bell above his head and winced at what might come. Two men wearing bullet-proof vests and carrying assault rifles stormed the office. Modesto, smiling ecstatically, reached into his coat and pulled out a human skull. "Meet Tucker Hull!" he said as Drummond slammed into him. Max rang the bell.

All the sound stilled for an instant.

The explosion that came ripped apart the office. The FBI men were thrust straight out of the room and down the hall. A shockwave pressed Drummond flat against the ceiling and Patricia flew out of Sandra as if punched in the jaw. Modesto fell onto his back, laughing like a drunkard. A hurricane of magic swirled around them all, tearing the desks and books to pieces.

"Sandra!" Max shouted, trying to be heard above the howling winds. He crawled toward her, each inch a struggle. She remained seated in the chalk circle. The gale winds pressing against him never touched her — bright colors of magic shot around the room yet always avoided her. Max called out for her again but she made no response.

Despite the intense winds, Max neared his wife. He tried to call her once more but a cold hand grabbed his head and slammed it into the floor. Blood gushed out of his nose. He rolled on his back, dazed, and the cold force pressed on his chest. But when he opened his eyes, he saw Drummond still stuck on the ceiling.

"Patricia!" Drummond screamed.

The cold lifted and Drummond's head rocked to the side as if slapped hard. Max didn't waste time worrying. He rolled back to his stomach and crawled the final two feet to his wife. He clambered to his knees and held Sandra's shoulders.

"Honey? Look at me. Are you there?" Her eyes looked dead like a coma patient — unresponsive and unaware. "Please, be in there." Tears streamed down Max's face. "Please. You're everything to me. I know life has been rough for us these last few years, but I couldn't do any of it alone. I've always needed you. I know you think you don't give me enough, but you do. If anything, I don't show you enough. Without you, I'm lost. Don't leave me. Please."

The outer wall of the office shattered — brick and glass blasting outward into the street. Max clasped Sandra's hand, but her eyes closed and she slumped forward. The weight on his shoulder grew heavier. Dead weight.

He arched his head back and wailed. Through his teary eyes, he saw the blurred image of Drummond. The ghost's arms surrounded the air in front of him, and his mouth lay open as if pressed in a kiss.

A cold hand touched Max's chin. He braced himself to be struck by Patricia once again. But Patricia was above him kissing Drummond. And the hand, though cold, brought no pain. He looked down and saw Sandra, his Sandra, gazing up at him.

A new pain burst in his chest. One filled with joy. He lowered his mouth and gently touched her lips with his. She grabbed the back of his head and pulled him in tight and hard. The kiss intensified as if they could press into one another and make the world around them disappear. But after a moment, she weakened. He pulled back to make sure she was okay — only exhausted.

"I love you," he said and heard Drummond echo the sentiment above.

The magic storm subsided. Wood and glass clattered as it found new resting places. Bits of paper drifted to the floor like autumn leaves. Time returned to normal.

The FBI rushed in, waving guns and barking commands. Max tried to raise his arms but the pain in his abused body refused to yield. He settled for collapsing on the floor with Sandra falling on top of him.

An FBI agent grabbed Max and Sandra, sat them up, and yelled words in their faces. A calmer voice said something in the distance, and through bleary eyes, Max saw Agent Stevenson approach.

"It's okay. Just arrest that one," he said. The other agents converged on Modesto.

As they escorted Modesto away in handcuffs, Stevenson turned to Max. "We've got a lot of questions for you."

Max's entire body numbed. "You recorded it all, didn't you?"

"That doesn't mean I understand it."

"Can it wait until tomorrow? We'd really like to rest for a bit."

"Medics are on the way to check you out. Frankly, you both look like you need some time in the hospital."

Max squeezed Sandra's shoulder. "Maybe so. But then we can answer questions at the hospital. Okay? Please? We ain't going anywhere, and you caught the guy who killed everyone. You even have his admission on record — even if the rest of it sounds crazy."

"As long as you go to the hospital, I'm okay with that. Besides," Stevenson said, gesturing to the office, "you got a hell of a cleanup to deal with still."

Max forced a grin which came off more like a pained wince. The EMTs arrived and immediately started to check out Max and Sandra. They flashed a light in his eye and asked him basic questions.

He listened as best he could, answered what he could, but his eyes focused beyond them, to a pile of rubble near the bookcase. It shifted. First a little. Then the debris tumbled away, and Kolan rose up, brushing off the dirt from her black dress.

She stepped away from the pile, graceful and surefooted, and moved to the exit. None of the FBI, none of the EMTs, nobody appeared to notice her. At the doorway, she turned to Max and offered the most malicious grin he had ever witnessed.

"I've got a lot to learn about the world," she said — but her voice was a man's voice. And though he had never heard it before, Max had no doubt in his mind — the voice belonged to Tucker Hull.

Hull walked away, unnoticed by all.

Drummond floated down to the floor, no smoke burning off him, and he watched Hull leave. Then he turned to Max. "Well, that's not good."

Max smiled for real now. Only the Drummond he knew would say that. His friend would be fine.

He heard Stevenson ask a question, but it was too late. He couldn't stay conscious any longer, and with all those important to him safe, he had no reason. Max passed out.

Chapter 27

THE WEEK THAT FOLLOWED dogged Max at every turn. That first night spent in the hospital had been met with police and FBI questions. The drive home involved some reporters following him. And days that were meant to be restful and recuperative filled up with more police on the telephone, visits from the FBI, and ambushes with reporters. Despite it all, Max and Sandra managed to hole up in their house and heal.

One afternoon, Max hopped onto the living room couch, propped his feet on the coffee table, and flicked on the television. Sandra curled her feet under Max's legs and rested her head on a throw pillow. Some mindless reality show blared away with a contestant claiming that she had signed up to win this thing, not to make friends. Max looked to Sandra with a knowing grin, but she barely registered any of it.

She had been quiet since their return. At first, he thought she suffered from amnesia. Not full-blown *I don't know who I am* amnesia, but a localized situation in which she could not recall what had happened to her while Patricia had taken over. But as the week progressed and he mentioned the events that had transpired, he saw it in her eyes — the poor gal knew everything. She had been cognizant of it all, even as she was powerless to do anything about it.

Drummond dropped in from the ceiling. "What's on?" he asked, floating next to the couch.

"Just junk."

"We don't have a case, so might as well watch it."

Drummond had not left them alone since they got home. He meant well, but between his constant chatter to them and his constant chatter to the ghost-blob Leed — which he still kept in his pocket — Drummond made Max consider running back to the hospital. Or perhaps just a library. Anywhere that he knew Drummond would avoid.

Max chided himself for such selfish thoughts. Drummond had been through a lot, too, and in some ways more. After all, Max got his

Sandra back. But Patricia — after their kiss and with no vessel to park her cursed spirit, she dissipated like a fog blown away by the hot sun. Max tried to comfort Drummond, assured him that with all the spells cast and completed, her soul must finally have been allowed to rest, but he still caught Drummond with a long, dark gaze and a mournful frown.

One night, Drummond said, "You know, I even feel guilty about my new freedom." The destruction of the office had somehow untethered Drummond — or, at least, widened his range. Max couldn't be sure and Sandra wasn't ready to explain any of it to them. Drummond went on, "At the end, I knew she wanted nothing more than to be with me, and instead, she's been cast away, lost in an eternity of darkness."

"You don't know that. None of us know what happens when we move on."

"That's nice of you to say, but think about it — she was a witch, a High Priestess, and possessing Sandra was the least of her crimes. I love her, but I'm not delusional about her."

Max wondered if he could say the same for himself. He loved Sandra so deeply that he suspected he overlooked and excused her flaws. Isn't that part of being a husband? Accepting the whole person for better or worse?

"I take it back," Drummond said, pointing to the remote control. "This reality crap is really crappy. What else is on?"

Max leaned forward for the remote when a knock came to the front door. He waited. The knock came again.

"Reporters?" Drummond asked.

"Why don't you go peek and find out?" Max snapped and immediately regretted his tone.

"Okay, okay. No need to get snippy." Drummond stuck the top half of his body through the front door, then pulled back in. "It's your FBI pal, Stevenson."

"I thought we were done with all this nonsense." Max yanked open the door. "What do you want?"

Stevenson's initial smile faltered but he recovered fast. "It's good to see you, too. I'm heading out soon. Everything's wrapping up here, and I wanted to come say good-bye. May I come in?"

They walked into the kitchen. With robotic coldness, Sandra rose from the couch and followed.

Stevenson shifted from foot to foot. "I wanted to thank you both for taking the great risk you did. Most people don't have that kind of bravery, and I don't think we could ever have solved this case without it. In fact, I think Max knows that we probably would have arrested the wrong man."

"You mean me," Max said.

"But, thankfully, that didn't happen. Unfortunately, I have to apologize to you both as well for the failures of our justice system."

Max didn't like the sound of that. "You're not going to arrest me, are you?"

"I don't understand why, especially with a clear admission of guilt on the recording you got for us, but the DA won't prosecute Mr. Modesto. He said that all the witch talk and raising the dead talk and such gives Modesto a valid insanity defense. I said that was fine with me. Insanity requires an admission of guilt, and I'd rather that nutjob spend a sentence in a mental institution than no punishment at all. But the DA wouldn't budge."

"Modesto's free," Max said matter-of-fact. After all, the Hull family always had excellent political connections.

"I'm afraid so. If you want, I can arrange for a patrol car to watch your house for a few nights, just to make sure there's no retaliation."

"Thank you for the offer but no. We know Modesto well. He got what he wanted from all this. He won't bother us now." Max doubted that was all true. In fact, the moment all the attention died down, he expected Modesto to visit with a tasteful gift in hand, an apology for the unpleasantness that had occurred, and a hope that they could focus on the new case his employer wanted to present. All said through gritted teeth that wanted nothing more than to bite Max's heart out. Max looked forward to that day because he wanted to tell off Modesto. Besides, until Sandra said otherwise, they were done — as she had pointed out before, without her, Max only had access to one ghost.

Stevenson awkwardly worked his way back to the door. "Anyway, thank you again. If you change your mind about the patrol car, you have my card. Call me anytime."

Max held the door for the agent. "I'm sure you've heard this before, but I hope I never have to see you again."

Stevenson laughed. "At least, not in this way." He put out his hand. "On behalf of the FBI, thank you."

They shook hands, and Stevenson walked off to his car. He turned back once yet never said anything more. He simply chuckled to himself and returned to his car.

"Never felt too kindly to spooks," Drummond said, "but I'll make an exception for that guy. He could have made things very difficult for you both, but he seems to know when to let it all rest."

Max smiled at Sandra and hugged her. He had done that a lot more lately — every chance he could. "I doubt he would get very far in his career if he started insisting that all of this had actually happened. Better to focus on the concrete things — murder, corruption."

"The return of a centuries dead leader."

"That one he'll probably forget to mention."

Drummond laughed. "It's good for us to be joking around again. Especially at this stuff."

As Sandra nestled against Max's chest, Max said, "If we didn't, I think I'd be the one turning into an evil spirit."

The day dragged on. They watched television for a few hours, nibbled on take-out leftovers from the night before, and slept. Though nobody had mentioned it, Max knew they all were aware that this could not continue for much longer. Soon, they would have to figure out their next steps.

Right before they slogged upstairs for bed, an answer arrived in the form of another knock at their door. Max did not have to say a word. Drummond checked it out.

"It's a young guy. Oh, crap."

"What is it?" Max asked, pulling Sandra closer to his side.

"He's got a manila envelope in his hand, and I can see the name Hull on it."

All the sore muscles and half-healed wounds flared across Max's body as if to warn him away in case his brain failed to do the trick. He wondered if he should have taken Stevenson up on the offer for a security patrol. But if this man was indeed a messenger for the Hull family, he wouldn't leave their doorstep until he delivered that envelope, and any security the police provided would be easily controlled by the Hulls. To underscore Max's thought, the young man knocked harder on the door.

Max walked to the door like a condemned prisoner — slow and unsure. He opened it a crack. "What do you want?"

The young man looked as nervous as Max felt. "Sorry to bother you so late. I've got an envelope to deliver to Maxwell Porter. Is that you?"

Max put out his hand. "You know it's me." He whipped the envelope out of the man's hand. "Get out of here before I call the cops." A worthless threat.

"Sorry, again, sir, but I'm under strict orders to wait for a reply."

Max closed the door. He walked over to the kitchen and dropped the envelope onto the table. Sandra and Drummond joined him.

Drummond whispered to his pocket, agreed, and gestured to the envelope. "We think it's safe to open. So, don't just stare at it. You know that kid won't leave until you answer whatever Hull's asking."

"I wasn't worried it was a bomb or anything," Max said. "But I know that we won't like anything written in there."

Sandra sighed and ripped open the envelope. She pulled out the single sheet of paper and handed it to Max. He hugged her again and kissed her forehead. Then, holding the paper in his right hand and keeping his left wrapped around Sandra's shoulder, Max read to the group:

Dear Mr. and Mrs. Porter and Mr. Drummond,

I trust you are recovering well from your recent troubles and wish you nothing but good health in the future. My own recovery has been strong and rapid, and I assure you that though I've only just returned, I am in full control of all Hull business matters.

After extensive consultation with my most trusted advisor, Mr. Modesto, as well as other knowledgeable individuals, I believe I have a clear understanding of how your small group has fit in with our larger organization. Sadly, I must inform you that the friction of this relationship has become unhealthy for us and, I suspect, for you as well. We can no longer continue along this path with you.

Therefore, I want to thank you for your service and inform you that all ties to the Hull family and the Hull business must be immediately severed. Obviously, this means the office you have ruined and the house we provided are no longer at your disposal. Furthermore, to insure that no false accusations or assumptions are made regarding our relationship by outside sources, all access to Hull-related endeavors will no longer be granted to you. Please understand that the Hull family owns, donates to, or touches upon a considerable number of businesses in North Carolina. Most, actually. We realize this may cause you difficulties in the surrounding area and will require you to move out of state. We apologize for the inconvenience.

Finally, as the returning head of the Hull family, I want you to understand beyond any doubt that you hold no leverage against this family. What you once considered your main threat, the family journal, is no longer an issue. An unfortunate and bizarre fire broke out in the jail cell of the young man in possession of the only copy of the journal. Both he and his copy are nothing more than ash.

A reply to our messenger that you understand and will comply would be greatly appreciated.

Sincerely,

Tucker Hull

Max read over the letter a second time before he could think. He knew a lot of Tucker Hull's history, but to be the recipient of, what amounted to, a threat to get out of town or face the consequences left him with a chill. One had to be fearful of a man like Hull — a man who had no problem putting a threat down on paper, a man who knew more about darkness and its magic than any other Max had come into contact with, a man who had been dead until a week ago.

"I guess this is over," Max said, his shoulders drooping. He put out his hand to Drummond. "I know you can't really shake my hand, but I wish you could. You've been a great and loyal friend. Sandra and I will miss you."

"First of all," Drummond said, folding his arms across his chest, "we don't know how far I can go before I get snapped back. It's very possible that I have no limits to my range now. So, maybe this doesn't have to be good-bye. And second of all, are you really going to pack up and get out just because the Hull family doesn't want you around?"

"I almost lost Sandra to that monstrous family. I'm not going to —"

"By now, you ought to know that if they're pushing you hard to leave, there's a good chance it means you should stay. That they're afraid of you."

"Let them be afraid. I don't care. I'm not —"

The front door swung open. Max and Drummond turned to see Sandra standing in the doorway. She had Tucker Hull's letter in her hand, and in front of the messenger, she crumpled it into a ball. With a flick of her wrist, she tossed the paper ball at the young man.

"Tell Mr. Hull to watch out." Her hard tone sounded even stronger with the scratchiness her unused vocal chords produced. "Tell him that we are not leaving this town."

As she closed the door, Max saw the messenger's cheeks pale. That poor man did not want to face any Hull, let alone Tucker, with that message. More importantly, though, Sandra had spoken.

Max rushed over to her with his arms spread wide. He scooped her up, spun her around, and kissed her hard. "Are you okay? Are you back?"

She playfully smacked Max's chest. "I never left, you fool." Though still cold in her delivery, every new word seemed to replenish Sandra's old self a little more.

Drummond clapped his hands. "There's my sweetheart!"

Before Max could get too excited, Sandra put her hands on her hips and said, "Looks like we don't have a home anymore."

"I'll go get some moving boxes, and we'll start packing up," Max said.

Drummond popped up between them. "Hold on, there. You told that kid to tell Hull that you weren't leaving."

"We're not. But this isn't our house anymore."

Sandra said, "We've got to find someplace new to live in."

"And a new place to run our business."

"And we barely have any money."

Max chuckled. "Sounds like old times."

Sandra giggled. "At least, it's not boring."

"You two are ridiculous." Drummond put out his arms and pointed at himself. "Did you forget who you're friends with? You need a cheap house to live in? I can get that for you. Pick out the house you want and I'll get some of my ghost friends together. We'll haunt that place until they'll give it to you for practically nothing. And don't forget, my friends have plenty of jobs for you guys. We'll be fine. Don't you worry."

Drummond rambled on for a while, but this time Max truly did not mind. In fact, he kind of liked the reassuring sound of his friend's voice. But he would never admit it.

Afterword

Every town on Earth has a fascinating history of murders and mysteries. The older the place, the more bizarre the tales become. Just ask anyone living near a castle in Great Britain. Thankfully, for both of us, Winston-Salem has been around for a long time (at least, long by American standards) and has a rich history of strange happenings.

The Zinzendorf Hotel fire, the DeGraff murder case, the Frank and Lucy Hine case, and the Sarah Tilkey tragedy, are among many of the true stories found in this book. Well, true at their core. I have, of course, embellished upon them by adding in the entirely fictitious cursed Bells of the Damned and their ramifications.

The photo of Patricia Welling in Tanglewood Park is a fiction, though the location is real. The photo of the Zinzendorf Hotel fire is real and can easily be found on the internet. Take a look at it. It's amazing.

Thank you for once more taking the time to join Max, Sandra, Drummond, and myself. I promise, if you keep reading their stories, I'll keep writing them.

About the Author

Stuart Jaffe is the madman behind the *Nathan K* thrillers, *The Max Porter Paranormal Mysteries*, the *Parallel Society* novels, *The Malja Chronicles*, *The Bluesman*, *Founders*, *Real Magic*, and much more. He trained in martial arts for over a decade until a knee injury ended that practice. Now, he plays lead guitar in a local blues band, *The Bootleggers*, and enjoys life on a small farm in rural North Carolina. For those who continue to keep count, the animal list is as follows: one dog, two cats, three aquatic turtles, nine chickens, and a horse. As best as he's been able to manage, Stuart has made sure that the chickens and the horse do not live in the house.

For more information about Stuart and his books, please visit *www.stuartjaffe.com*

Made in the USA
Monee, IL
14 November 2020